"Go ahead, struggle, I like it that way."

He kissed her hard, hurting her mouth.

"Roger, don't!" she cried, pushing at him fiercely.

"If he can sleep with you, I can. Don't you know that twins, in one way or other, share everything?"

He pinioned her arms with one of his and tore at her clothing.

"You're mine. You're going to know that before you go out for your summer's romp. I've dreamed so often of this, but of course I thought you'd be a virgin. I should have known there's not a woman in the world worth that kind of trust. You're all sluts, like my mother, like— that's it, struggle. It'll be all the sweeter this way, and, in the morning, I *will* have something to tell Chappie, won't I?"

"I'm going to scream," Kiersten said shakily as his hand closed painfully hard on her bared breast. "I don't want to, but if you don't get out of here, right now, I'm going to scream this place down."

"Did you scream with Nolan?" he asked.

Books by Frances Casey Kerns

Cana and Wine
The Edges of Love
The Errand
Savage
This Land is Mine

Published by
WARNER BOOKS

SAVAGE

Frances Casey Kerns

WARNER BOOKS

A Warner Communications Company

Grateful acknowledgment is made for permission to quote "If You Will
Weave Me" as published in THE COFFEEHOUSE SONGBOOK, by
Charles Sens © 1966 by Oak Publications, A Division of Embassy Music
Corp. Used by permission. All Rights Reserved.

WARNER BOOKS EDITION

Cover art by Mara Macaffe

Warner Books, Inc , 75 Rockefeller Plaza, New York, N.Y 10019

 A Warner Communications Company

Printed in the United States of America

First Printing: May, 1981

10 9 8 7 6 5 4 3 2 1

For Jack Because It's Special

SAVAGE

1

"I'll be in the toilet a few minutes," announced Burt Cunningham, opening the door to the garage's grubby little office.

"All right," said Anne Owen absently, arranging papers on the gritty desk.

It was Andy Harrison's garage. Burt pumped gas and did minor things like tire repairs. Andy had gone home for his lunch and while Burt was in the toilet, where he spent a good deal of time reading comic books, Anne would be responsible for any customers who might come in.

"Leave the door open so I'll be sure to hear," she said to Burt. The office's one small window was cobwebby and so smeared with grease residue and dust that she couldn't be sure of seeing a car at the gas pumps.

Anne worked at the garage a few days each month, keeping Andy's books up to date. She did the same for several other businesses in Spring Hill, managing to make a decent living for herself and Kiersten. If Mama hadn't left the house free and clear though, Anne couldn't have managed. Anne had never much liked Spring Hill. It was a very small town, only about a thousand people; everybody kept well up with everyone else's business, particularly so did her brother George and his wife Amy keep track of Anne. But when Tim had gone to Korea, Mama had been ill and had needed her. Then Kiersten was born, Tim was killed, and Mama died. Anne had the house, a young child, and she was stuck with Spring Hill. It was not the size of the town, really; she detested cities. It was George's being here and the fact that Spring Hill was so southern and the people so *interested*—caring, they would call it.

Anne had been brought up as the daughter of a construction worker, always moving, always, more or less, a stranger, and anonymous. George had happened to finish high school while they were living near Spring Hill, had met Amy and decided to stay on. When Anne's father was killed in a construction accident while Anne herself was a high school senior, Mama had decided to use part of the insurance money to buy a house in Spring Hill. Mama had always thought George was perfection personified, so the place he had chosen to make his home must surely be perfect.

George's father-in-law owned Spring Hill's only grocery store of any size, and George had been the store's manager for several years now. They were always trying to make a match for her, George and Amy. Every time they asked her and Kiersten for Sunday dinner, Anne knew it was for the purpose of presenting yet another prospect. The most recent time, it had been Frank Petty, a widowed farmer with four teenage children. Anne thought she might have liked the farm, possibly the children, but she couldn't stand Frank Petty, sly and appraising in a bumbling sort of way. George and Amy, and other well-meaners in Spring Hill, wanted to tell her how to dress, keep house, bring up her daughter.

And it was for Kiersten, too, that she really wanted to be away from here. The four-year-old talked with a slow drawl and was beginning, in spite of Anne, to think in the circumscribed ways of the North Carolina mountains. How could she not? Anne wanted to take her to live in another, perhaps larger town, in the North, the Midwest, the West, where there might be more variety, more tolerance. But, with the job she had, she could scarcely manage to save anything. If she sold the house, George would have a fit. Well, maybe he would just have to have one. Next year Kiersten would be ready for kindergarten, and maybe, this summer, they'd just put the house up for sale and go.

Anne shivered. It wasn't the idea of leaving Spring Hill. She was used to moving, meeting new people, coping. It was, rather, a slight shiver of excitement and also of cold; it was chilly in the office with the door open. She usually kept it closed, to muffle the sounds of work from the garage and to keep out more dust. There wasn't a sound just now, but the outer doors were open and the March day was chilly and raw.

She got up to turn up the small space heater and started violently when a voice called from outside, "Anybody here?" It wasn't a loud voice, but it projected through the place, through Anne. She straightened up quickly and stepped down into the garage.

"I'm sorry, I didn't hear you drive in," she said, then saw beyond him that there was no car at the pumps.

"I didn't," he said. "My car's about two miles out of town and it's going to have to be towed in."

He was a stranger, and, in retrospect, Anne knew that was when she had started to love him, as he stood there with his hands in his pockets, looking impatient and a little grim. He was a big man, tall, broad-shouldered, muscular, with dark hair. He turned half to the light coming in through the big doors and she saw that his face was rather long and angular, with blue eyes that looked used to seeing far distances.

"You've got a tow truck, haven't you?"

"Yes," she said. "I'll get Burt."

She went out, around the side of the building, and knocked on the Men's door.

"Burt, somebody needs the tow truck."

Price Savage stood there, just inside the garage, out of the chilly breeze, and waited. He thought about the girl—the woman, more like—she must be in her late twenties, sandy hair, dark brown eyes, a roundish open face, what he supposed might be called wholesome. She was tall, five-eight or -nine, giving him five or six inches to stand above her. She moved with grace, a kind of unconscious dignity, unhurried but efficient. Later, he would say in his reticent way, that he had loved her when she stepped down out of the garage office. And that would be a gift to Anne, his saying it, a gift of himself, his inward privacy. Price rarely said he loved anyone and neither of them had ever really believed in love at first sight.

Anne came back quickly, hugging herself for warmth. Burt followed almost immediately. He put his comic book on a shelf and shrugged into an ancient leather jacket.

"Accident?" asked Burt salaciously.

Irked as he was by the breakdown, Price almost grinned. The man made the word twice as long as normal with his drawl, and he looked so hopeful.

"No," he said. "I've got a front wheel bearing that's frozen up. I thought I could get to the next sizeable town. What is it? Royal?"

"Well," said Burt, deflated, "le's go on an' git 'er, though I don't think Andy'll git to 'er today." He gestured at the pickup and tractor already hulking in the dimness of the garage.

When they came back with the car, its front raised onto the tow truck, Andy was back from his lunch. Anne was at work again in the office, but with the door still left open.

"Froze plum up, is she?" asked Andy pleasantly, looking out at the car.

"Yes," Price answered, a little embarrassed at the impatience that had kept him driving.

"Didn' give you no warnin'? Growly noises, somethin' like that?"

"Well, yes, but I thought I'd get to a bigger town. I mean . . ."

"Sho'," said Andy easily, "I know what you mean. But I run a

11

good business here. You can ask anybody. I gar'ntee my work. But I can't git to 'er, maybe, till tomorrer.''

"Is there anywhere else . . . ?''

"Not 'less you want 'er towed into Royal. Cost you a good hunk a money. I'll have to order the bearin's outa Royal. I reckon you'll want 'em both replaced while we're at it, bearin's an' seals. I ain't got any'll fit.''

"And how long will that take? To order?''

"Well, you see, my orders come in on the bus, an' we don't git the bus but twict a week. Yesterdy was Tuesdy an' the bus come. Won't be back till Fridy.''

"I don't suppose there's any place I could rent a car? Go and get the parts myself?''

"This here's no big city,'' said Andy, smile broadening. "We ain't got no Avis or like that. We may can find somethin' you can use. I'd let you have my car if it was runnin'. I got a fuel pump to replace. My wife's havin' kittens about that, but you know what they say about the shoemaker's children. Listen, I tell you what you do. Go over to Mae's place an' git yourself some dinner. I've got a hurry-up job on this tractor of Jess Malone's. I'm about done with the pickup. After that, we'll pull your car in, see how bad it is. If she's plum froze, it's liable to be a right smart of a job to git the wheel off. I'll call Dick Harvey in Royal an' see has *he* got your parts. We'll think about it an' ask around. It may be that somebody's goin' to Royal tomorrer or next day an' would pick up the parts for me. This here's a farmin' community, you understand, an' ever'body's right busy this time of year. Never mind this weather today, it's plowin' an' plantin' time an' there ain't many spare vehicles. Then, too, some is apt to be a little bit leery about lendin' to a complete stranger. No offense, you understand. I see you're from Coloraydo. That's a long way from home.''

Then Andy called into the office, "Annie, you had yore dinner yet?''

"No,'' she called back, putting a weight on her papers.

"Did you call Ed Barkley?''

"He wasn't home. I talked to his wife. She said they'd pay on Friday.''

"Always says that,'' said Andy resignedly and looked at Price as if for confirmation. "They've got the money, just stingy about payin'. I'll see ole Ed at the American Legion dance on Saturdy night an' I'll collect then. Now, Annie, you go along with Mr.—uh . . .''

"Savage,'' Price supplied.

"—Savage, show 'im where Mae's is at, see they treat him right.'' He wrung Price's hand and switched on the garage lights

Price didn't need a guide to Mae's; it was practically right across Main Street from the garage, but they went over together. Most of the lunch crowd had gone, but all the eyes that were left in the cafe were on them as, glancing a question at one another, they sat down to share a table.

"You *are* a long way from home," said Anne solicitously.

"Yes, I am," he said shortly, "and I can't afford to waste days and days here. Calving will have started at home as it is."

His voice, even in irritation, thrilled her, so deep and soft. He had taken off his hat and she could see now how tanned he was. The skin of his forehead was very fair. He might have been thirty or fifty. It was that kind of face, already weathered and not destined to change much with the years.

"You live on a ranch then."

"Yes, Secesh."

"Where is it? My dad was in construction work, highlines, so was my husband. I've lived in Grand Junction, Colorado Springs and—let's see—Durango."

"Well, you missed us. Almost everyone does. Our market town is Hurleigh. It has three or four thousand people."

"Yes, I know where that is," she said with more excitement than it would seem to merit. "It's in the northwestern part of the state, isn't it? I think we passed through there at least once, going to Ogden, Utah."

"No, but wait," he said, smiling a little. "Our place, Secesh, is about seventy miles from Hurleigh, from any main highway. It's in a place called Dunraven Park. A park in the mountains, you know, is just a good-sized valley with a small outlet. They used to call it Dunraven's Hole. This Dunraven and his partner Kilrayne used to spend winters in there with a band of Utes. They were trappers, the whites, back in the eighteen-twenties and -thirties."

Abruptly, he felt abashed at having talked so much. Ordinarily, he was a very reticent man, and particularly so for the past two years.

Alma, the waitress, brought them menus and glasses of water.

"Hello, Alma," said Anne, trying to be nonchalant under the stares and glances. "This is Mr. Savage. Andy has his car over at the garage."

"Pleased to meet you, Mr. Savage. I hear you're from Coloraydo. How's Kiersten, Anne? That is the *sweetest* little girl."

"She's fine, thank you."

"Is she with Elsie Bennett today?"

"Yes," said Anne. It seemed Alma was determined about letting this man know that there was a child involved.

Alma wanted to talk more, find out some things about the strang-

13

er, but she couldn't think just what to say at the moment so she walked slowly away, smiling back at them over her shoulder. "You just let me know when you're ready to order."

"Why do they say Coloraydo?" Price asked irritably. "You don't. In fact, you don't sound like them at all."

"A lot of people in Spring Hill have never been any farther than Royal, Mr. Savage, and it sometimes seems as if they actually enjoy mispronouncing things."

"Call me Price if you like," he said shyly.

"Oh, but I thought you said—"

"Price is my first name, Price Savage."

"I don't think I ever heard Price as a first name."

"It was my grandad's, and his mother's maiden name."

"Well, anyway, I can pronounce Colorado because I've lived there and a lot of other places. I went to fourteen different schools, growing up, and that's not counting business school. I remember the first time we went to Colorado. We came in from Kansas, from the east, you know, and I was disappointed. I thought there'd be mountains the minute we crossed the border."

He nodded. "There's a lot of the high plains before the mountains begin."

"But you're *in* the mountains, your ranch?"

"A high valley, about seven thousand feet, with mountains all around."

"Were you born there?"

"On the ranch? Yes."

"I always loved the mountains, but, you know, if I were just guessing, I might have guessed you were from New England, down east, as they say."

He smiled a little in surprise. Smiling softened his face, made it look vulnerable, but it didn't look to Anne as if he smiled often.

"My grandad was from Maine. My grandmother was born in Australia, went to school in England, then lived for several years in New England before they married. We've always been pretty isolated so the—what do you call it?—idiom got passed on, I guess. I've just been back to Maine, not visiting relatives, only to see what it was like. Grandad's people were ship builders, or rather boats, fishing boats mostly."

"You mean your ranch—Secesh, is it?—is the only one in this Dunraven Park?"

"No, there are about twenty families, I should think, besides the ones who work at the sawmill at Mills Crossing, but we were rather like outcasts for a long time. Most of the other families were Mormon in the early days, but that's changed, to a degree."

14

Alma was standing by the table again. "Ready to order?" she asked brightly.

Neither of them had looked at the menu, but both ordered cheeseburgers and french fries. Almost everyone else had gone now and Anne caught a glimpse of the cook, peeking out of the kitchen to get a look at the stranger.

She laughed when Alma had gone reluctantly away again. "You should have come into town riding a white horse and wearing two guns, strapped down and low. Then it would be just about like the movies."

"They do look a lot, don't they," he said uneasily. "But it would be the same in any town this size, I guess."

"Tell me about Secesh," she said with too much eagerness, then tried to keep her face more indifferent.

"Well, Grandad found it, homesteaded it, bought all the rest of the land he could get. We run eight hundred to a thousand cows, which is a lot for that part of the country. My grandad was something of a genius, I've always thought. He graduated from Harvard at nineteen, then went looking around the West until the time of the Civil War. He had a hard time deciding to go back and fight, but he finally did go. He was wounded in his first battle, always walked with a limp. He'd been in Dunraven before he went east and he came back again and founded Secesh, made it one of the best ranches around. He said he called it Secesh because *he* had decided to secede from the Union. He wanted the Stars and Bars—the Confederate flag—for his brand. He'd fought on the Union side, of course, but he wanted that flag just for cantankerousness. That turned out to be too difficult, so he made the brand a bar sinister—"

"What's that? It has to do with heraldry, doesn't it? I always have wondered."

"If you have a square, then you put a bar, beginning in the upper left-hand corner and running diagonally to the lower right corner. In heraldry, it means there's been a bastard somewhere in the family. On one side of the bar, we have a star—he said that was for neither flag—and on the other side, an S, which stands for both Savage and Secesh."

There were a few moments' silence and he said diffidently, "I don't usually talk so much."

"But I like hearing," she said warmly. "He must have been a very interesting man, your grandad."

"Yes. He lived to be ninety-seven and up to his last few years he was actively running the ranch, but he also found time to read and think a lot. And my grandmother was quite a person in her own right. She had been a school teacher for years before they married. Her name was Mercy Clinton. She always worked the ranch, too, just like any hand. She still used a lot of Australian phrases, like we didn't round up a herd of cattle, we mustered a mob. She lived to be eighty-eight and I'm lucky to have known them both.''

"Were there a lot of children?"

"No, just my dad and one other baby who died. You see, Grandad built up the ranch and he built this big house. Then it came to him that the house ought to be full of kids so he'd need a wife. He went back to Maine, thinking he'd more likely find a woman there who'd suit him, and because he hadn't been back since he'd taken his shares of the boatyard in cash from his brothers while the Civil War was still going on. He was over fifty then and Grandmother—she never let us call her Granny or anything else—Grandmother was almost forty. But they suited each other so well that they didn't seem to think much about how many childbearing years might be left.''

Alma plunked their lunches down before them. "Are you here to stay with us a while, Mr. Savage?"

"It begins to look that way," he said laconically.

Waiting a moment for more, she moved away finally, to start clearing tables.

"How did she know where I was from?" asked Price, a little startled by the realization that she had known.

Anne smiled. "Probably a lot of people saw the license plate on your car while it was being towed, or they've gone over to look since."

"Oh," he said. "Yes, I suppose so."

She said, "I might be able to borrow my brother's car tomorrow to go to Royal. I can't even try today because I know his wife's gone out to her folks' farm."

"That would be good," he said, but he didn't feel all that certain any more that it would be. He liked being with her. He hadn't talked this much in so short a time since—since Darlene, and that had been only in the beginning.

"I guess there's a hotel where I can stay?"

"A block down that way and on the other side of the street."

Anne was thinking what George and Amy would say about her borrowing the car. The idea of wanting to drive off with a total stranger! Well, she could go alone, she and Kiersten. Only she wanted to be with him, have him with her.

They were mostly silent as they ate the food which neither particularly wanted. It was a comfortable, companionable silence. They both felt that.

Finally, Anne said shyly, "Come to supper with us this evening?"

"I think I'd better not do that."

"Why not?"

"Well . . . people would talk. You see, I *do* know about small towns."

"Of course they'd talk," she said defiantly. "But they always talk. Talking's about all there is for entertainment."

Again, there was silence while they finished their meal. Alma offered dessert, both refused. She brought the check.

"You will come, won't you?" Anne asked as they stood up.

"All right, Anne," he said softly. "I have the notion you don't much like being called Annie."

"Just sometimes," she said, trying not to let him see the shudder of pleasure that his voice and his nearness produced. "Go to the next street past the hotel, then two blocks south. Our house is small and white, with a swing set in the front yard. By the way, you don't mind children too much, do you? Kiersten is four, never stops talking and loves having company."

"I've got twin boys myself," he said, not meeting her eyes, turning away to pay the check.

Anne felt cold all over except for her burning face. She went out of Mae's, though common courtesy made her wait for him on the sidewalk. How could he be married? Somehow—stupid woman!— she had thought she knew him, knew so many things about him, one of them being that he was definitely single. The idea that he was, could be, married had somehow just never entered her head. Well, she wouldn't try to uninvite him to supper, but that would have to be the end of it. These other things, the stirrings and excitements of the past hour or so, would just have to be put down with a tight lid. She felt ineffably sad; she was suffering a great loss. Even Tim, to whom she had been married for two years, had never made her feel as she had for this past brief time.

Price came out, looked at her now rather pale face, her sad eyes and did not dare ask questions. They crossed to the garage, both of them looking bleak. Anne went directly into the office where Andy was just hanging up the phone.

He said to Price, "My supplier in Royal's fresh outa Plymouth wheel bearin's. He's sendin' to Raleigh right away, but it'll take a few days. By then we can find a car you can use, or it'll be time for the bus again."

Anne was miserable all the afternoon, finishing up her work in the garage office—the door kept tightly closed again—walking to the grocery store, then to Mrs. Bennett's house to pick up Kiersten just as the little girl was waking from her nap, starting the first preparations of supper amid the little girl's chatter.

17

"Mommy, just look at poor Pussycat. She gets so lonely when everyone's away. You should let me take her to Miss Elsie's, too."

A light cold rain had begun to fall. She'd be the scandal of Spring Hill when they knew she'd entertained this man, this stranger, this married man in her home after dark. But it wasn't Spring Hill she gave a damn about, she thought, viciously banging pans. It was *him*, Price Savage. His name wouldn't stop repeating itself in her mind. She had never in her life felt this way about anyone, not ever, not to mention at a first meeting. And now . . . "I have twin boys myself."

A little friend of Kiersten's came over to play. "I can stay a hour, Miss Anne. Mama said would you watch the clock?"

"Play in your room, Kiersten," said Anne, too shortly, "and only there. We've just finished cleaning the living room."

"Come on, Judy," said Kiersten. "We can pretend cook supper. After a while we're going to have real company for our real supper."

Anne was relieved that Judy's hour was up before he came. Had she told him a time? She couldn't remember. Anyway, maybe he had decided not to come at all. That would be best, of course, only . . .

She was cooking a lamb roast and trying to think of all the movies about trouble between cattlemen and sheepmen. Probably he hated lamb and maybe that's why she had chosen it. It would serve him right for not having told her right in the beginning: "Howdy, ma'am. My car's broke down an' I'm married." He didn't wear a ring, or she had failed to notice if he did. She had been so avidly looking at his face. It wasn't a handsome face, in the generally accepted sense, but so intent, or seemingly so, upon her face and whatever she had said.

2

He came shortly after six, carrying a bottle of white wine and a potted red geranium, wearing different clothes from the afternoon and, obviously, with a fresh haircut. He looked almost as shy as Kiersten did at first sight of him, boyish and awkward as he held out his offerings.

"How nice of you," said Anne, taking the things and faking a smile. "You didn't have to bring anything. Nothing at all."

Price hadn't known if he should bring anything, but there was a tiny florist's shop across from the hotel and a liquor store around the corner. He had not known if she drank wine or gave a damn about plants, or if he should go to supper with her at all. Almost, he had decided not to come, but there was a kind of magnetism about her. He found he badly wanted to see her again, not to spend this dreary evening alone. Besides, he hadn't caught her last name if it had ever been given, so there was no way he could call and make an excuse for not being there.

Anne, feeling angry and awkward, put the plant in the center of the table—the truth was geraniums made her sneeze—and the wine on the counter. As she turned, he was standing there and, for just a moment, he took both her hands in his. This, she would learn, was a gesture of intimacy, of deep friendship or love. Her hands felt small, lost, but in safety and warmth. She turned away, busying herself at the stove as an excuse. No, he had no ring, but many men didn't wear wedding bands.

"Kiersten," she called nervously, "come say hello to Mr. Savage. Now where has she gone?"

Kiersten had had a good look at the man when Mommy let him in, then she had diffidently withdrawn to the hall to peek around its corner. Her shyness would wear off quickly enough and she would be as loquacious as a magpie. Anne was counting heavily on the little

19

girl's chatter to get her through whatever there was to be of this evening.

With her blue eyes cast down, Kiersten advanced a small step into the kitchen. She said to the floor, "You're a *big* man. Mommy said we'd have company, but she didn't say you'd be so big."

Price, smiling more than Anne had seen before, said, "You look like your mommy. I bet you know that, don't you?"

" 'Cept for freckles," she said, still not quite looking at him. "Lloyd Gould says I got more freckles 'n anybody in the world, but he's not polite."

"I like freckles," answered Price soberly. She'd be just about the age the boys were when Darlene had taken them away to live in Denver. She was like Anne, sandy hair, roundish face, with blue eyes rather than Anne's brown ones, deep clear blue, and guileless like her mother's. He had heard at the barber shop, getting the haircut to kill time, that Anne's husband had been killed in Korea. It made him happy to be with the child, a painful, wistful kind of happiness, but he felt convinced that the mother had decided the whole thing had been a mistake.

He said to Kiersten, still very serious, "Tell me your name again, will you?"

"Kiersten Owen. Kiersten starts with a K and Owen with an O. I know lots of my letters."

"You like books then?"

"Yes. I guess I have about a million," she said matter-of-factly, finally looking directly at his face.

"Well, I hope you don't already have the one I've brought you." He went to where Anne had hung his damp jacket and took a small book from its pocket.

Kiersten grinned all over her freckled face. "No, I don't have this one. Will you read it to me?"

"Kierstie," prompted Anne, "what do you say?"

"Thank you. Will you read it to me?"

"A little later, maybe."

"Anyway," she said importantly, "I have to go and see about my pretend supper that's cooking in my room. Do you want to come?"

"Not just now."

She went off, carrying the book and chattering to herself, but then she was back. "I have a cat."

"Do you?"

"She's in my room. Her name is Pussycat. I don't know your name."

"It's Mr. Savage," said Anne from the stove.

"It's Price, too," he said.

"What does that begin with? What letter?"

"A P."

"Okay," she said and ran off to her room.

He turned back to Anne, but she was very much occupied with the supper. He was convinced she had changed her mind about inviting him here. What should he do? The thought of going away from them, back into the chilling rain, back to the dusty, ill-furnished hotel room, alone, made him shiver.

Anne said, hearing the acerbity in her voice, "You've been keeping yourself busy, a haircut and buying all those things."

"I don't like doing nothing," he said uneasily and went to stand by the steamy window. "I'd offer to help you now, if you'd tell me exactly what to do. I'm not much good in a kitchen."

There was a little silence before he said, "Kiersten has a cute little voice. I've never heard one quite like it."

"Yes," she said. "It's as if she had a slight case of laryngitis all the time. When she first began talking, I took her to a specialist, just to make sure. He assured me it's only her normal voice. She certainly uses it enough."

There was another, longer silence. It was raining harder. You could hear it on the roof, and dripping down, above the small noises she was making.

He said uncomfortably, just to break the silence, "It may be as much as a week before my car is ready and Raleigh is certainly too far for borrowing someone else's car. I ought to be home right now. It's time for the calving to begin. We only have three hands and it's about all they can do to keep up with the feeding. There's still plenty of snow at Secesh. We take the hay out to the cattle on sleds, with draft horses, a lot easier than trying to use tractors. Rain in March is a strange thing to me. Back home, it would just be more snow."

He stopped, made himself stop. He was going on more than the little girl. He wanted to talk to Anne, but not like this, not just going on to fill time and to try to get around whatever was the tension in the kitchen.

"It is spring though, here," she said absently. She was feeling miserable, with a strange forlorn loneliness while he stood here in the kitchen not ten feet away and Kiersten banged things in her room.

"Yes," he said, "I've seen the flowers and the trees leafing out It's a little hard to believe. We never have spring before the end of May. Then it lasts about two days and it's summer."

"I was thinking this afternoon," she said carefully. "You said you've been to Maine. Isn't this a strange way back to Colorado?"

"I'm not much for traveling," he said, seeming a little embarrassed "I wanted to see some of the country while I was out It won't likely

21

happen again. I've been away from Secesh nearly three weeks and I've only been in one other house besides this one, my aunt's, my mother's sister in Vermont.''

"Your mother came from New England, too?"

"Oh yes, we're pretty solid stock. My aunt is the only other one of Mother's family left and she's getting ready to move into a retirement community in California. Mother ought to go with her. She's not well at all, and she's never liked Secesh. But she's a dutiful woman, my mother, and she isn't likely to leave until Penny and Hugh are grown. They're my brother's children. Both their parents are dead.'' Why in *hell* did he just go on gibbering?

With her back to him, Anne said cautiously, "Your wife . . . doesn't she like to travel, or . . . ?"

He was silent so long that she had to turn and look. His expression was surprised, concerned.

"My wife? We've been divorced for a couple of years. I didn't tell you that?"

She laughed a little, but tears prickled at her eyes, tears of relief and—joy? He crossed the few feet between them and took her lowered chin in his hand gently. "Did you think I'd completely scandalize you like that? Did you?"

"I—I didn't know." And now the rain outside curtained with its sound a warm safe place. The best place in the world. "You mentioned that you had twin boys and I . . .''

"I have,'' he said and she saw the quick pain as he tried to hide it. "They're six. They live with their mother and her dad in Denver.''

"Oh,'' she said meekly.

His hand was still holding her firm chin and he bent and kissed her forehead. They were still standing there, close together, when a sound from the hall made him draw away. Kiersten was standing there, wide-eyed.

"Is he going to be my daddy?'' she asked and, thankfully, without waiting for an answer, "Mommy can we have candles on the table?''

Price let Kiersten strike the matches, then steadied her tiny hand with his big one as she touched match to wick.

"You'd never, never light matches, would you?'' he said in that deep gentle voice, "unless some grownup is there to help you. They can be very dangerous.''

"No, I wouldn't,'' breathed Kiersten soberly.

Anne caught the look of pain again, in the depths of his eyes as he bent to steady a candle. How he loved little children, she thought. Almost, she found herself wishing his wife had not left him. She said, wanting to make up to all of them now for her earlier misery and curtness, "I have some wine chilled. We'll save yours for later, all right?"

The rain enclosed them in a warm, dim cocoon through supper. They could be the only three people in the world. Kiersten chattered, Anne sneezed from time to time because of the geranium, and Price ate heartily of the lamb for which he normally did not care.

While Anne cleared up in the kitchen, Price read the new book to Kiersten in the living room. He had offered to do the dishes, but Anne said she'd stack them. Plenty of time for washing up in the morning. Kiersten, in pajamas, sat snuggled on his lap as if this reading were a natural nightly occurrence. Pussycat lay sprawled on the arm of their chair. When Anne was putting her in bed, Kiersten said, "Let's do have him for a new daddy. Just everybody has daddies at their house, not just pictures, so why can't we? Miss Elsie said you're too young not to marry again and that I ought to have a daddy. She said it to Mrs Kale and they didn't know I was hearing. What does it mean to get married?"

"We'll talk about that another day," said Anne. "It's already past your bed time."

"If you don't want to get married with him, maybe I will. I'm going to sleep with this new book. Could I read you the story in it?"

"Not tonight, Kierstie."

"It's about a little girl and her puppy that she has. I wish I could have a puppy."

"We can talk about that another time, too."

"Price says they have dogs and puppies where he lives. Can I keep the light on so I can read this story again?"

"No."

"Well, could you leave my door open, in case if I want something? Or I might be afraid of the dark or some lightning might come."

"We'll close your door and you won't be afraid of anything. If you'll only lie still and be quiet, you'll be asleep in two minutes."

"I forgot to kiss Price goodnight."

"Well, can't you just—"

But she was out of bed, running in the plastic-footed pajamas so that she skidded, laughing, into his arms. "I love you," she said very naturally, and Anne saw again, over Kiersten's snuggling head, the wash of pain over his face and through his eyes.

"Come on now, Kierstie," she said rather sharply, "get back into bed."

"I need a drink of water," announced the little girl. "And I think I forgot to pee."

"All right," said Anne, the necessities accomplished, "no more talking, no more running around. Just bed."

"Mommy, I can't stop my mouth. It's awful hard to do that. Will he be here in the morning when I wake up?"

"No, Kiersten."

"I'm going to tell the other kids and Miss Elsie that I might get a daddy after all. Mommy, don't you love him?"

Anne kissed her, hugged the warm sturdy little body close. "Goodnight, Kierstie."

"When will I be five?"

"Not until next October. It's a long time away."

Anne sighed, picking up a pile of toys that blocked the door open.

"For my birthday wish, I want a puppy and Price to be my daddy. Is that okay? Could I have that?"

"Sometimes wishes come true," said Anne very softly. "Now *go to sleep.*"

In the living room, after asking her permission to smoke, Price had filled and lighted his pipe. When she came from Kiersten's room, he was looking through the current issue of Spring Hill's weekly paper. With Kiersten silenced or at least behind closed doors, Anne was aware again of the softly falling rain. It felt so right, all of this.

"Can I get you something to drink?" she asked as he looked up. "We could try your wine now."

"All right," he said comfortably.

"How are you with a corkscrew?" she asked. "I'm lousy."

He followed her into the kitchen. The cork came out in several pieces, but finally the bottle was open.

They returned to the living room, glasses in hand. Anne sat down on the shabby little sofa and he sat beside her, though with some space between them.

"To," he began, holding up his glass, "to Spring Hill."

She smiled a little ironically as they touched glasses and drank.

"Now," he said after he had drawn his pipe back to life. "I talked all through lunch, so tell me about you."

He watched her face with that intent, waiting expression that convinced her he really wanted to hear.

"Well, my dad was in construction work, highlines. We moved around a lot. My brother George, who's ten years older than I am, was born in California and I was born in Indiana. I went to fourteen different schools. Have I said that? I was thinking about it today and it seems you already know. I can't remember what I *have* said. My dad was an Irishman—second-generation American—but still very much an Irishman. My mother would have called him a no-good if she hadn't liked the role of martyr so much. He drank a lot, spent some money on other women and gambling, but he never missed a day's work. I always knew he liked me a lot and he was always singing. I was his child; George was Mama's boy. Mama hated all the moving around and just about everything about our life.

"We came here once when George was a high school senior, not to Spring Hill, actually, but to Royal. George met Amy Hendrix and stayed on when we went somewhere else—Florida, I think it was. Ten years later, when I was a high school senior, Dad was killed in an on-the-job accident in Michigan. Mama stayed on there so I could graduate with my class. Then she couldn't get to Spring Hill fast enough. She said I'd marry some rover like Dad and leave her all alone, but that George was a settler and she could always depend on him to be around if she lived near him. By that time, George and Amy had the three children and George was running Amy's dad's grocery store, the only real one in town. Poor Mama, she kept saying things like how she wanted to plant flowers and be there to see them bloom, really get to know her neighbors. I think she was finally happy here, doing those things, and with George and his family close by.

"I stayed one summer, then I started business school in Raleigh. I'd wanted to go to college but couldn't seem to manage it. There was quite a lot of insurance money left after Mama bought the house, but she wanted it, needed it, for her old age. She never wanted to be a burden to her children or anyone.

"I went to work in Cleveland, in one of the offices Dad's company had worked out of. Mama and George were horrified that I, a young girl alone, should want to go so far from home. There was quite a row about it, where they accused me of being like Daddy, but I went. I never had liked the South. . . . More wine?"

"I'll get it," he said and returned from the kitchen with the bottle.

"Go on," he said, sitting down and filling their glasses. He really did mean it.

"Well, I didn't much like Cleveland either, or my job there, but I went on with it; I had to, or come dragging back here like a whipped puppy. After about a year I met Tim Owen, and a few months after that we were married. Tim did do the same kind of work Daddy had done and we were—compatible in some ways. Like I could be all ready to move on in about two hours.

"Tim was drafted and ultimately sent to Korea. I meant to stay on in New Mexico, near the last place where he had been stationed before going overseas. I liked Albuquerque. Secretaries, bookkeepers, file clerks can usually find a decent enough job. But then, just a few days after Tim had gone, Mama had her first stroke. She really needed someone with her all the time, so I packed up again. It was only after I got back here that I realized I must be pregnant.

"So here I've been for almost five years and that's my life story. Mama wanted me settled so she left me this house. As things turned out, she did need Daddy's insurance money. She had to spend a lot of time in the hospital before she died, something over two years ago. She took in sewing as long as she was able. She had always wanted to have her own custom dress shop. She was a wonderful seamstress. Anyway, she had enough money to pay her bills, and for the kind of funeral she'd have wanted. Tim was killed exactly a month after Kiersten was born."

She sighed. "So here we are in Spring Hill, sort of—trapped."

"And is it more of the roving life you'd like?"

His voice, so near, so deep and soft, made her shiver.

"No. I like to see my flowers bloom, too, but not in Spring Hill. George and Amy are right here—across town, but that's only a few blocks. They think it's their duty to look after us. So does almost everyone else. The work I have is not enough for me to be able to save much. I'll have to sell the house. George will have fits, and it's even a little scary to me, but I want to be away from here before Kiersten starts school. I want to take her some place where she'll lose the God-awful drawl. She'll be in kindergarten in the fall, so there really isn't much time. I've been thinking of upstate New York. I remember liking it very much when we lived there once, the mountains and lakes. . . ."

She picked up her glass and emptied it. When she set it down, Price refilled it. "Now it's your turn," she said, leaning back comfortably.

"Why did you name the baby Kiersten?"

"It was Tim's mother's name. In his letters, he'd asked me to use the name if the baby was a girl. If she'd been a boy, we'd agreed to name him Jamie, for my dad."

"Kiersten is a name that would fit right in in Dunraven Park. When the Mormons started coming west, quite a few settled in the Park and most were Scandinavian. Right now, I can think of a Kristen and a Kirsteen."

They were silent while he filled his pipe again. It was something of a ritual and he concentrated all his attention on it as he seemed to concentrate on anything he was doing or listening to. When it was drawing well, she prompted, "And your life story?"

"I think I talked enough at lunch today."

"You talked about your grandparents and the ranch—Secesh—but you said very little about yourself."

The pipe still did not suit him, and he was silent, working at it.

"Are you from a big family?" she persisted.

"As a matter-of-fact, I had one brother, ten years older than me."

They smiled into each other's eyes at the coincidence of it.

"My mother is pretty straitlaced, too, and my dad was a—well, a heller. They stopped sharing a room long before I can remember. There are lovable things about mother, but she's so damned dutiful. Her father was a Methodist minister, some very distant relation of my grandmother's. When his wife died, he brought himself and his two grown daughters for a rest cure at Secesh. Dad, Clint, married one of them, Emily. I don't think there was ever any—deep feeling between them. Dad wanted sons to carry on with the name and with Secesh. Mother wanted—well, to do her duty. She never liked the ranch. In fact, deep down, I think she hates it."

He drew on his pipe and leaned forward to sip at his wine.

"It was as if they divided us up. When Stanley was born, she said, without words I'm sure, 'This one's mine. Hands off.' Stanley was Mother's maiden name, just as Clinton had been Grandmother's. Anyway, he looked like the Stanleys and behaved like them—so mother says—which means perfection. When I came along ten years later, I think she washed her hands of me about the first time she set eyes on me. I was a Savage. Stanley never worked on the ranch, but God, I did, from the time I could walk, it seems. That's not a complaint. I've always felt that Secesh and I are part and parcel of each other. I couldn't live any other way.

"Stan went to college and then he decided to become a career army man, in the quartermaster corps. He was killed in an accident in nineteen-forty-two, before he ever left the States, but he's a war hero to mother. That's twelve years ago now, that he died, and he'd left home a good fourteen years before that, but we still have 'Stanley's room.' She always calls it that, though it's Hugh's now and has been for five years. Stan married a local girl, from the Park, Mary Ellenbogen. They own half of Dunraven, Mary's brothers do. Mary died of cancer in forty-seven and the kids, Penny and Hugh, came to live at Secesh. Any of the Ellenbogens would have been glad to take them, but I think Mother would have lost her mind with someone else bringing up Stanley's children. They're fifteen and thirteen now, and she cries sometimes because they'll be grown and leave her so soon."

He paused for long moments. "You don't really want to hear all this."

"I do, Price," she said fervently.

He filled their glasses, sipped at his, then drew on the pipe again.

"There were a lot of deaths in our family in a relatively short time. Grandmother died in thirty-two, then Grandad three years later.

27

My dad had never been able to do as he liked with Secesh while Grandad was alive. When the old man was gone, Clint decided to raise rodeo stock, along with the beef cattle. He'd been working at the breeding for five years, and there were beginning to be some pretty good young steers and horses. In nineteen-forty, he bought a new bull and brought it home in a horse trailer. He tried to unload it on his own—it was the middle of the night when he got home—and it killed him. I found him in the morning, gored and trampled." He closed his eyes for a moment, still seeing the ruined body.

"How awful for you," she breathed, feeling the sting of tears behind her lids.

"So Secesh was, in effect, mine. Stan didn't want any part of it, except for a yearly check when we sold off the cattle. Those three deaths were, I think, a relief to Mother, though she did all the proper things about mourning the grandparents and Dad. All three of them had always—intimidated her more than a little. A decent interval after Grandad died, she'd spent a lot of money redecorating and refurnishing the house, while Dad was spending more on the rodeo stock. When Grandad was alive, Secesh had always had a respectable bank balance. He'd had a good bit of money to start with, from his share of the boatyards and fishing interests. The land cost him practically nothing and he'd bought his stud herd while cattle were cheap. Between them, Mother and Dad ran the bank balance down to practically nothing, so now we live like most ranchers, from one year to the next. I've had to take out a couple of mortgages, though for now everything's paid up.

"I couldn't go to war or to college—not that I really wanted to do either—but somebody had to run the ranch and those were hard times, though beef prices were good. Sometimes it would be just Reuben and me. Reuben Scales was born at Secesh in nineteen hundred. I remember Grandad saying once, 'If you ever decide to sell Secesh, remember Reuben goes with the place. Get a good price for him, over and above the stock and equipment.' Reuben's—let's see—fifty-four. He's a little banty rooster of a man who can outwork, outtalk, and generally outdo anybody he comes up against. Nobody likes him—except me, I guess—he's such a cantankerous old goat.

"So, back to Mother and the general story. Those first three deaths didn't really bother her, but when Stan was killed I thought she'd lose her mind. I got my aunt, Mother's only sister, to persuade her to go away for a while, and she was only at the ranch off and on until Penny and Hugh came to live with us. She's—vague sometimes—dreamy—half as if she weren't there at all. . . . I don't know what any of us would do without Fern—Fern Marvle. She was born at Secesh, too, five years before I was. She was married there, raised her two daughters there, her husband Arthur died there just a few years ago. Arthur was a fine mechanic and a good horse handler. Fern just goes on looking after us. She's the closest I'll ever come to a sister. She'd have you believe she's hard as nails, but I doubt there's a bigger, more generous heart in the world.''

He scraped the dottle from his pipe into an ashtray.

"I'd better be going, Anne. It's almost ten and I don't hear any more rain.'' He took her hand and held it gently.

"Price,'' she said gently, ''aren't you going to tell me about— your little boys?''

He was utterly still for a moment, staring at nothing, that shadow of pain crossing his face. Then he let go her hand and took out his wallet.

"The picture's almost two years old,'' he said dully.

"But they're so *different*,'' she said. "I mean, you said twins. They're both fine-looking boys, but I guess I expected . . .''

"The dark-haired one looks and is very much like his mother. The fair one looks like Grandad, with Grandmother's eyes.''

"He also looks very much like you,'' she said gently.

He returned the wallet to his pocket and began to talk, almost tonelessly now, turning the wine glass in his big hands and looking into it.

"Liam Nolan came to Hurleigh during the war, as a section foreman for the railroad. His wife Molly died not long after that. They'd had only the one child, Darlene, and I think Mrs. Nolan was into her forties when Darlene was born. They spoiled her. She had everything she ever even thought of wanting, while they went around in patched and darned clothes and couldn't keep their house in proper repair. Other people spoiled Darlene, too, because she was, is, so— beautiful. And she can be so what my mother calls 'fetching' when she wants to be. She got wild in her teens. Her dad couldn't see it. I—I loved her, or thought I did. I—deliberately tried to make her pregnant so she'd have to marry me and stop fooling around with all those other guys. It worked, but she hated me for it when she realized, and I guess I can't blame her. Then, as she thought about it, she decided somebody who owned a place like Secesh ought to have a lot of money for travel and such, and maybe it wouldn't be so bad after all once she'd had the baby.

"Liam, her dad, was pleased about the marriage. He'd been worried about her, though he could almost convince himself she'd never take a step outside propriety. I still consider Liam Nolan a friend of mine, though he has this big blind spot. Mother was happy. I was twenty-seven and she'd been wanting me to marry for years. She thought Darlene was such a beauty and that we ought to lease the ranch or something and all go live in a city somewhere.

29

"When we knew the baby was going to be two, Darlene had one tantrum after another. She was absolutely furious and her fury hasn't dwindled much in six years. One was bad enough, but who, at her age, could possibly *want* to be saddled with twins? And, as far as she's concerned, there really *is* only one, Roger. Nolan is her cross to bear. He was a sickly baby, two pounds smaller than Roger when they were born. Roger has always been perfect for Darlene. She wouldn't even consider a name for Nolan, wouldn't take care of him when he was a baby. Mother looked after him, or I did or, mostly, Fern did. I guess it was this same old situation of dividing up the kids. Roger was her darling and anyone could have Nolan.

"When the boys were two, Darlene's dad was sent to work in Denver. He rented his little place in Hurleigh because he means to have something to leave to Darlene. She'd waited around all that time for something like a very expensive wardrobe and a trip to Europe, and was finally just about convinced that, though we did have some money, it was tied up in the land and stock and always would be. She went to Denver to live with her dad and get a job. She took some business courses before she could get anything besides waitress or clerk's jobs. She got work in a hospital admissions office, but then she threw that up to work as a cocktail waitress in one of the fanciest clubs in Denver. The money was better, considering tips, and I'm sure she gets plenty of those. There's also more interest in her there, personally.

"All this took a couple of years, during which she'd left the boys at Secesh. Her dad got his leg badly injured in a railroad accident and was retired with a pension. Darlene decided she wanted a divorce, and the boys—her dad could look after them while she was working. Actually, she only wanted Roger, but she said he was so used to being with Nolan that it would upset him too much to be separated. I was more than willing to go along with the divorce, but I brought a custody suit for the boys. That made her more determined to have them and she won. Mothers generally do. So . . . I haven't seen them for almost two years."

"Don't you have visiting rights or . . . ?"

"I don't get to Denver often, once or twice a year, maybe. When I've been there, I've called about taking them out for the day. She's always had excuses; they had colds or something. She doesn't want me visiting with them at their house. I did go there once, about a year ago, at night when I knew she'd be working. I knew Liam would let me in, but they were sleeping. I don't really know them any more. I guess I never will."

"Oh, Price, I'm so sorry." And she turned impulsively and put

30

her arms around him. For a moment he was rigid in her embrace, then he turned to her, pushing his face into her hair.

Anne had only a three-quarter bed in her room to give more space. Both of them laughed in slightly hushed, desperate voices as they tore at their clothes, speculating about whether there would be room for two. But it was all right. They forgot about the bed's size in a moment or two.

Anne had not had intercourse since Tim went overseas all those years ago, but it was Price who trembled most violently and the lovemaking was over very quickly. They lay holding each other, and he said into the silence, "I'm sorry. That couldn't have been very good for you."

"Oh, but it was," she breathed, "and there can be—another time, can't there?"

"Yes," he said, "I'd like many more times." He sat up on the side of the bed. "I didn't notice any crowding, did you?" And they both laughed.

He was looking at a small bookcase for which there was no space in the living room. "You like reading."

"Love it," she said happily.

"I don't read as much as I should any more. There never seems to be the time. When my grandparents were alive, everybody in the house found time for reading. They saw to it. Grandmother taught Stanley the basics before there was even a school at Mills Crossing, which is our community, about in the middle of the Park and seven miles from our place. She taught Fern, too, and did her damndest to teach Reuben. We've got a library at Secesh. It's in the L of the living room, but hundreds of books and—"

Both of them started violently at a peremptory knocking at the front door. They stared at each other for a moment, then began giggling like sneaky children as Anne scrambled into robe and slippers.

"Annie, honey," said Laura Lee Johnson solicitously, "I'm sorry if I got you up or somethin'."

"No, Laura Lee, I was just—doing some ironing." She tried to block Laura Lee's view of the living room with her body, not opening the door very wide.

"Oh . . . well, I just thought sure somebody must be sick, all the lights on an' it after eleven o'clock. I had to go to the bathroom an' I saw the lights. I said to Cy that, since it'd stopped rainin', I'd just run over an' make sure you was all right. He called me an ole busybody, but I was *worried*. I just had the feelin' I was *needed*."

"Everything's fine, Laura Lee, really. I guess I just forgot to turn off some of the lights. Thank you for coming."

"Well, I'm right relieved. All right. Goodnight, honey."

"My God," said Price as she sprang into his arms again on the bed. "Do you think she saw me come here?"

"I don't know and I don't care," said Anne, almost making a song of the words. She had already flung off the robe and now kicked off the slippers.

"I'm thinking of your reputation, not mine, you know," he said, laughing and holding her close. "You won't seem to think of it."

"I don't want to think, not of anything."

This time their lovemaking was much slower, more lingering and tender. When they were replete, they lay very close for a long silent time, working their way indolently back from wherever they had been in that wonderful togetherness. Anne wondered if she could ever bear to live outside the muscular warmth of his body again. Price wondered if he wasn't getting himself into something too quickly, too deeply. He was not ordinarily a man of impulses and, the few times he had been, they had always turned out wrong. Neither did he give his love, his trust, or even his friendship without consideration. There had been a time, only this morning, when he had thought he never wanted to fall in love with a woman again.

Almost as if she were reading his mind, Anne said softly, "I want to tell you something, two things. First, I have to say 'I'm not that kind of girl.' There hasn't been anyone since Tim. Oh, Price, I hadn't realized how starved I've been. Second, and most important, in case we never—see each other again, I want to thank you for trusting me. I have a feeling you don't do that easily, but I could feel your trust when you talked to me about your wife and little boys and, even more, while we made love. Thank you."

He burrowed his face into her hair, a little embarrassed and a little frightened. She had made herself so vulnerable, so fragile to him. Could he handle that? Then, again on impulse, he spoke, half-whispering against her neck so that she shivered in delighted pleasure, "Then I'll tell you something. I haven't had intercourse since Darlene. It isn't that I haven't tried, but I couldn't—keep an erection, when it came to that."

"Do you still love her?" she asked quietly, lying very still, tensing a little to stop a threatened trembling.

"No. Maybe I never did. But she could—cut me down to size so easily in the beginning. Before the end she hated me, and when she got the boys . . . she's a what do they call it? an emasculator. I guess she did a reasonable job. I—I thank you for setting things right again."

She held him very gently, knowing instinctively that he would never tell this to anyone else, afraid to move, almost to breathe, to do anything which might shake his trust.

They were both growing drowsy when he laughed softly and stretched, yawning. "I can't stay here all night. Is there an alley or something in back? Laura Lee may be going to the bathroom again as I leave."

3

It was a long time before Anne slept. Her feelings were fear and joy, anticipation and the near certainty of disappointment. How could she go on now, alone? How could she not?

She woke early, after mixed troubling dreams. Daylight was just beginning to seep in around the window shades. She lay there for a few moments, orienting herself in time and space. Thursday, one of her two days a month at Hess's Drygoods Store. But last night . . . she shivered deliciously, then lay tense. She would never see him again, not like that. He was not an impulsive man. His wife, the loss of his sons, had been a terrible wounding. If he ever cared again, it would happen slowly and with great caution. And yet . . . only a few hours ago . . . well, one thing was sure. She wou'ln't put off leaving Spring Hill any longer. This very day, she would see Ed Wheeler, the realtor, and turn the house over to him for sale. It wouldn't bring much; property wasn't all that much in demand in Spring Hill, but they were increasing the size of the sawmill and that might bring in a few more people by midsummer. She'd have to take a full-time job wherever they went. The money from the house wouldn't last long, but Kiersten would be in kindergarten in the fall—surely there would be a day nursery or somewhere where she could feel safe about leaving the child, then first grade . . . But suppose he asked her . . . no, she was being sillier than a daydreaming teenager.

Still, she sprang out of bed, had a quick shower, and cleaned up the kitchen after last night's supper, and all the while she sang softly, the old folksongs her father had sung. Sometimes, her heart seemed to give an actual leap, but she tried to tell herself just to go on with business as usual. Even so, the idea of really leaving Spring Hill, finally doing it, was excitement enough, wasn't it? Ah, my girl, that's not what's upsetting the rhythm, not the half of it anyway. But he had been here, had told her things he would never confide to anyone else, hadn't he? And their lovemaking—again that shiver that was almost pain because it was such beautiful joy.

She was putting away the last of the dishes when Kiersten came in, still drowsy, sweet-faced, and not so talkative, for a few minutes at least. They had their breakfast, and Kiersten began to ask questions again: Would Price come again? Would he bring another present? When would he live at their house if he was going to be her daddy? If his house was far away, how far was that? Had she, Kiersten, maybe been there when she was "a tiny baby, first borened?"

Anne kept trying to hedge and change the subject. She knew all too well that if she said, "Kiersten, we're not to talk about him, not to anyone else," it would take a ten thousand word dissertation on why, and still Kiersten might "forget." Her version of last night would be all over town today, via Elsie Bennett the baby-sitter. Then, when Laura Lee Johnson heard it, she'd remember coming over last night at eleven o'clock, finding Anne in robe and slippers, with "the house lit up like a Christmas tree."

Anne smiled grimly as she helped Kiersten get dressed. George and Amy were pillars of the Baptist church. It might develop that they would actually be glad to have her out of town, by whatever method.

Price hardly slept at all. What was he going to do? If only the damned car could be fixed today. He'd see her for a few moments, just to say goodbye. After last night, he couldn't just run. But the car wouldn't be fixed and God knew how long he'd be here. Besides, the truth was he wanted to see her again, and not to say goodbye. There was some magnetism between them, something he'd felt immediately when he stepped out of the garage office yesterday. It wasn't just sexual attraction, though that had been a beautiful experience for which he would always be grateful and would always yearn for again. She wasn't a widow on the make as some dumpy little balding man had hinted in the barber shop with a "hee hee," when the talk had somehow got round to "Annie, George Cavanaugh's sister." She wasn't that at all, and there was so much more to this than sex. If sex were all that was involved, he'd never have talked so much, certainly never told her those things about the boys, Darlene, his recent impotence. Remembering embarrassed him. He wasn't sure he could look her in the eye again, having said all that on the first day. But he *would* see her again. Even if he tried not to, it could hardly be avoided in a town like this. But was this just to be written off as "Interlude in Spring Hill?" "Thank you, I'll never forget . . . ?" He knew he couldn't forget, but what was to be done about it? Spring Hill and Secesh were so far apart, no chance for a proper courtship, and she might hate the ranch as Darlene had, as he had always believed his mother did. He couldn't ask her, not by any means, just to . . . They didn't know each

36

other, not at all. Yet . . . and there was the little girl. "I want to marry you, have your daughter, adopt her so that someone who's almost mine will be at Secesh, maybe care about it as I do. I want to have other children, yours and mine, try to forget the boys. . . ."

Finally, he got out of the rumpled, lumpy, squeaky bed in a kind of disgust of indecision. He could see that the lights were on in Mae's Place down the street. It was six-thirty. The thought of food made him feel a little sick, but he needed coffee, a lot of coffee.

Stolidly, he endured the stares of sawmill workers having their breakfasts, the mild flirtations of the waitress—not the one who had been here yesterday. He bought a pack of cigarettes from a machine. The pipe was too much trouble and he felt too itchy and irritable to bother with it. "Sometimes the best thing a man can do is follow his hunches," his grandad had said more than once. "I saw this place, Dunraven Park, before ever the war started and knew I'd have to come back here if I lived. Sometimes a man just *knows* and when that happens, he's got to have sense enough to go ahead with a thing or be eternally sorry." But *did* he know? One moment he did and the next . . . One thing was certain. If he had to stay here, if he meant to go on seeing her, he'd have to do it in ways that the town could accept. He knew small towns and communities. He didn't want to ruin her reputation. A scandal could be made of nothing, and there was already more than nothing here.

He finished the last of several cups of coffee, half the pack of cigarettes, and went out to the street. What now? He couldn't bear idleness. The drugstore, maybe? Buy some books to take back to his room?

It was a fair day, all signs of clouds gone, and to Price it seemed unreasonably warm. He had brought a jacket, but only carried it over his arm.

The drugstore was not yet open. He saw Andy Harrison opening up the big garage doors at his place and walked slowly over because he could think of nothing else to do.

"Mornin'," said Andy heartily. He shook hands. This was a hand-shaking place and Price wasn't much of a shaker, but he liked Andy's firm friendly grip. "What I done after you left yesterday was I called Raleigh and told them to send the parts for your car straight here instead of to my supplier in Royal. Be in on Saturdy's bus. We'll have your wheel off of there by the time they git here. Not to hold you up any more, you know. You ought to be able to be on your way some time that day."

"Saturday," Price said glumly.

"Well, I guess that'll seem like a long time to you but, you see, that's another bus we only git twict a week."

"I know," he said and grinned rather sourly. "You had it yesterday."

"That's it," said Andy, grinning back. "You got to git used to the rhythm of a place like Spring Hill. Ever'thing always happened yesterdy, or it may happen tomorrer or the next day. I was raised in Atlanta an' it took me a while to git used to a small place but I kind of like it now. You know, I'd let you have the tow truck to go down to Raleigh yourself, but the whole damn front end's in bad shape. Ever'thing that's mine is in bad shape, just waitin' while I work on other people's vehicles. My wife may leave me over that fuel pump for our car. Today, you see here, I got a ring job to do an' that's a bitch. An' I got Arch Goss's stock truck, needs a radiator. An' then . . . well, you see how I stand here talkin' an' not gittin' on with any of it. See how used to Spring Hill I've got? Besides, today I'm in a special bind. Burt, my gas pumper, called in sick. What it is is he tied one on at the Outlaw last night. Does that onct or twict a month an' then he's hung over for a day or two. He ain't lyin' when he says he's sick. I never saw a man suffer so much the mornin' after. So what I'll have to do today, if I ever start work, is keep droppin' ever'thing to come out an'—"

"I'll work for you."

"Huh?"

"I said I'll work for you. I can pump gas and maybe help in the garage. The truth is, I'm not a bad mechanic."

Andy looked at him with a speculative grin. "Then how come you to let that wheel git plum froze up?"

"Stubbornness," said Price ruefully. "I'm a long way from home and I need to be there. I kept hoping it might just—go away."

"A dreamin' man," said Andy, nodding. "Well, I'd be glad of the help. I can't pay you much but—"

"You don't have to pay me anything. I'll be glad of something to do. I'll be back as soon as I've changed my clothes."

He worked through the morning. Gas business was slow and he spent a good deal of time working in the garage. Andy went home for lunch; came back.

"Better go git yourself some dinner. Uh—I hear you had supper last night with Annie an' her little one. She's a fine girl, Annie."

Andy's eyes looked as if he were leaving a lot unsaid. Price didn't want to know what.

Once again, he crossed to Mae's. Anne was there, sitting at a table with two other women. She gave him a nod and a small smile that seemed uncertain. He returned the gesture and took a counter stool. He was hungry now and ordered a steak. Everyone still stared at him, but now there was something more in the looks. He was not just a stranger any more, but someone they knew something about, or thought they knew.

The lunch crowd began to thin. The two women left Anne, seemingly with regret. She sat there with a cup of coffee. Price took his dishes and joined her. For a moment their eyes caught and held The look was one of unadulterated love. It shook them both

He sat down and said casually, "I have a job."

"Yes, I heard."

"I heard that I had supper with you last night. Andy just told me."

"Oh, Price, I know," she said, flushing. "I'm sorry. It's Kiersten She was talking about it before I got out of the baby-sitter's house I tried to think of a way to explain to her not to say anything, but there would have been all sorts of complications and she probably couldn't have kept her mouth shut anyway. She really does like you, an awful lot, and . . ." Her voice trailed off and she could feel more heat in her face.

"I'm not sorry," he said softly. "And I hope you're not, not really."

"Well, no. Of course I'm not. It's just that I . . ."

"Will it ruin things for you? Laura Lee's going to get around to putting things together for everyone else."

"I don't really care about that. I don't really like coming to be the town's current subject for gossip, but it will pass."

"Will I see you again? Is there some place besides this where we could have supper tonight, the three of us?"

"Not really," she said, some of the tension going out of her "There's the Pine Cone House, but it's three miles outside of town "

"I'll see what I can do. Would you mind very much going there in Andy's tow truck?"

She smiled. "No, but I could just as well cook something. There's plenty of lamb left over for a casserole, or I could—"

"No more lamb, all right?" he said fervently and they both laughed softly.

"Then you really did hate it," she said with a hint of malice "I think I bought it because I thought, at that time, you were married "

"And geraniums make you sneeze," he said. "There's a lot to learn."

"Price, is there?" She was almost whispering, her now sober brown eyes cast down to a wet ring on the table.

"I don't know what's happening here," he said. "I'm completely confused until I see you. Then I—"

He broke off and followed her eyes to a man who was coming to the table, a dark-haired, balding man with a face like a ferret.

"Hello, George," she said, seemingly imperturbable. "Price Savage, my brother, George Cavanaugh."

Price stood up and George automatically offered a handshake, though neither of them wanted it. George's face looked as if it would break if he smiled. He sat down, ordered coffee, and began asking Price questions in a clumsily casual way. After a short time of very brief answers, Price stood again.

"I have to get back to Andy's," he said curtly, then to Anne, "What time will you be home? I'll call you."

"Certainly by five."

"Nice to meet you," muttered George. He obviously didn't mean it and Price pretended not to have heard.

"Now, Annie," George began sternly after lighting a cigar and clearing his throat several times.

"George, don't start. Just don't start. I'm a big girl now and I'm going to live my own life."

"All I was going to say," he said reproachfully, "is that Amy would like for you and Kiersten to come for supper tonight."

"Do you have another Frank Petty in the wings who can't wait for Sunday dinner? Oh, never mind. I know what it means: the third degree after supper. I really don't have anything to tell you, George. Besides, we're having supper with Price again. Oh yes, I do have one thing to report. I've put the house up for sale. That'll be all over town by now."

"You've *what?* Because of this—this man? Somebody you met yesterday?"

"George, be calm. You'll get an ulcer. I've told you all along that I didn't intend to stay on here forever. I don't want Kiersten to go to school in the South. Well, she starts kindergarten in just a few months, so don't you think it's time I made some move?"

"To where?" he demanded.

"I'm not sure. The house isn't going to sell tomorrow or next week. I'll have plenty of time to decide."

"It looks right strange—bad," said George portentously, "that you'd—take up with this complete stranger one day and put your house on the market the next. What *do* you think you're doing?"

"I think I'm going back to work at Hess's," she said sweetly and dropped a hand lightly on his head in passing.

Price called shortly after five. At six-thirty, he came to the house in Andy's tow truck. Anne was retying the sash of Kiersten's pink and white ruffled dress, so she simply called "Come in" when he knocked.

"Hello," he said with a tentative smile. "Your coach awaits."

"I heard it," she said, smiling back. "That will attract everyone's attention nicely."

"What's a coach?" asked Kiersten and, without waiting for answer, "Price, will you swing me up so my head bonks on the ceiling? Judy's daddy does that."

The Pine Cone House was a nice restaurant with a good menu. People came there all the way from Royal, so that not nearly all the customers knew who they were. Most of the men were dressed in suits and ties.

"I haven't got a suit," Price said, a little abashed. "I've had them over the years, but I gave the last one—the one I was married in—to the Salvation Army. My mother keeps giving me ties for Christmas. I must have fifteen ties that have never been worn. You look fine though."

She was wearing a burgundy-colored dress that set off the fairness of her skin and brought out the red in her sandy hair.

"I don't have many dress-up clothes either," she said, looking at him in the well-fitting brown slacks, quietly checked sports jacket, and, of course, a western-style shirt. "You mustn't let it go to your head, but I find you very handsome."

"And I look nice, too," put in Kiersten. "Mommy, where did I get this dress? Did we buy it? How much did it cost?"

And so the evening went. They tried to have a leisurely dinner and conversation, but it wasn't easy, with Kiersten wiggling and talking almost constantly.

On Friday and Saturday nights, the Pine Cone House had live music, but this was Thursday, so there was only the jukebox. It was a quiet one, with big band music from a few years back. Price put in some nickels and they persuaded, cajoled, and ordered Kiersten to stay at the table while they danced for a few minutes. Anne found Price a good dancer for such a big man and he found her intoxicating.

"I shouldn't have walked out of Mae's and left you alone with your brother," he said apologetically. "Was it bad?"

"No, it was just George. I shocked him some more though, told him I've put the house up for sale."

"You have? Why?"

"Well, didn't I tell you I want to get out of here before Kiersten starts school? I've got to get moving on it. It—it's nothing to do with—you. Please understand that. It's likely to be months before the place sells, but it got George's mind, a little, off whatever stories are going around town."

"How old are you?" he asked after a little silence.

"Twenty-nine," she said. "That sounds so fakey, I'll almost be glad to be thirty."

"I'm thirty-four," he said. "Would that be too old?"

"For what?" And they both laughed.

"My birthday's in January," she said.

"And mine's in November," he said.

"Do you think the astrologists would say we're compatible?"

"That's more up to us, isn't it? Look, I can't dance with you much longer. It's too—enticing. I haven't danced much for a long time, and I guess I don't have the—physical discipline I once had. That's what you do to me."

Kiersten had slipped from her chair and come to the edge of the floor. Her lower lip stuck out and there were bright tears in her blue eyes. Price scooped her up and, until the number finished, they tried to dance, holding her between them.

In town again, Price returned the tow truck to Andy's and came back on foot. Kiersten, having struggled all the way, was in bed and asleep. This time, they were careful about which lights they did or did not turn on. The bedroom was dark and cozy while they made love. Afterward, they talked, about everything, politics, wars, their childhoods, their ideas on bringing up children. . . . Finally, hearing the courthouse clock striking, Price peered at the luminous dial of her alarm clock.

"It's midnight, Anne. I'd really better go."

"I've thought you looked tired today." But he wouldn't tell her he had hardly slept last night.

"What are you doing tomorrow?"

"Well, I owe Mr. Hess one more day, but I could do it—later."

"Is there some place we could have a picnic? Out of town, but without using a car? Burt came to the garage about four. He seems to think he's going to go on living after all. Andy won't need me, nor will anyone. I get a little desperate, thinking about all that time on my hands."

"That's a great idea," she said, "and I know a place on Cedar Creek, not much more than a mile from here. Shall I leave Kiersten with Elsie?"

"Let's take her. Maybe there'll be less speculation that way. Besides, I kind of like her."

Anne was angry with herself for the prickle of tears behind her lids and she said, sounding more forlorn than she meant to, "Sometimes it seems you're only seeing me to see my daughter."

"You know that's not true," he said softly and put his arms around her with gentle warmth. "But I do like kids. Please don't mind. Have you ever thought . . . when you marry again, would you want more children?"

"Yes," she said. "I'd like two or three more some day. Kiersten can be a trial, but she's also been my salvation these past four-and-a-half years."

Price got up, opened the hall door a little so he could see, and began dressing. Anne pulled the covers around her and lay still in the warmth his body had left.

They had their picnic the next day. Kiersten had brought a tennis ball which she insisted was her football. She ran around, playing with the ball, finding wild flowers, getting too near the creek, and generally keeping them busy. Price came back, breathing hard after a game of "football."

"She runs around twice as much as I do, and talks into the bargain. Where does all the energy come from? Do you think she'd like horses, calves . . . ?"

"She loves animals," Anne said. "Poor Pussycat takes a lot of rough treatment, but she is most certainly loved. I would have liked to let her have a puppy for her next birthday, but I guess we'll be living in a furnished apartment somewhere. I don't know, maybe that will have to wait a while."

After a time, Anne made the little girl lie down on the picnic blanket for a nap. Price covered her with his jacket, promising another football game when she woke, and he and Anne walked a short distance into the woods, holding hands.

"It seems strange that most of the people here are still wearing coats and scarves and the like," he said. "If it was this warm at home, we'd think it was summer. God, I've got so much work waiting for me. I hope Reuben's found another hand or two. We have to go on taking hay to the cattle until the new grass comes. There's the calving, fence work, moving the stock off the hay fields, fertilizing, clearing the irrigation ditches . . ."

"Are you ever *not* busy?"

"Well, no. There's a time in late fall, if the snows don't come too early. . . . Winter's not so bad, if we've got enough hands. There's just the feeding to do most of the time. That only takes seven or eight hours a day."

They were silent for a time, until he said, almost defiantly, "Ranching isn't easy for a woman. There's all the housework and a good many wives help almost every day with the outside work."

Anne took this as a warning. "Doing what?"

"Oh, well, whatever the men are doing. We usually keep enough hands at Secesh so that that's not necessary. Mother never learned to do any of the things, like riding or driving a tractor, but at haying time, which is the busiest long stretch of all, Fern can drive hell out of any of the machinery."

She thought of saying, "I suppose I could learn," or, acidly, "Why haven't you married Fern?" but decided keeping quiet was her best course.

43

"And it's lonely," he said slowly. "For women. Not much time for socializing, not many people to socialize with."

"Is there a school?"

"Yes, seven miles from Secesh, at Mills Crossing. There's a church there, an LDS church, a general store and post office, a bar and cafe called the Reserve, a service station, and a small sawmill operation. I don't think the school has a kindergarten. What kind of tree is this?"

"A black walnut. Haven't you seen one before?"

"No, not that I know of, just some of the wood."

She began to name plants and trees for him. All too soon, they heard Kiersten calling.

They walked slowly back to the house in the late afternoon, with a very tired little girl. Anne opened cans of chili for supper, letting it heat slowly while she put away the picnic things. Kiersten had cried when Anne refused to let Price bathe her, so, at his pleading look, Anne had given in. Tomorrow he would be gone. He had skirted an idea so many times, but had always drawn back, like a kid, touching a hot stove on a dare. She would *not* ask him. She knew it would be a thing she'd never get over, wondering if he'd taken them, in great part, simply because he didn't know how to say no gracefully.

With supper over and Kiersten in bed, they sat for a long quiet time on the sofa, his arm about her, his free hand holding one of hers.

Finally, she said, trying to be matter-of-fact, "Your parts are coming on the Raleigh bus in the morning?"

He nodded. "Andy said he'll have the wheel off when they get here, about ten-thirty."

"Then you'll be leaving."

"I have to, Anne. I'm almost a week behind as it is."

"Yes, I know."

"Will you—can we—go to bed again?"

She cried silently while they made love. The bedroom was dark. Afterward he got up reluctantly and began to dress. She got into her robe and slippers.

"Is there some wine left?"

"Yes," she said and went into the bathroom to wash her face.

When she came out, he had the wine bottle and two filled glasses on the coffee table. She would have taken her glass and sat in the old rocker, but he said pleadingly,

"Don't do that. Sit here. I want to make a toast."

She sat down, waiting miserably. Why couldn't he just go now? Now that it was over.

There was no toast to make. Words came from him without his

half considering them now. "Anne, I can't leave you. I love you. Would you—could you possibly come away with me? I'll promise to try never to let you cry again."

"Oh, Price, I love you!" she whispered, almost, but not quite numbed by relief and gratitude. She was crying again.

He put both their glasses on the table and held her against him. She could feel his heart pounding.

"I should have asked you that first night, but I haven't been able really to—believe in this. It's like living a dream."

"I can be ready," she sobbed, trying to get control of herself, clinging to him, truly believing it was real now herself. "I've already told Ed Wheeler, the real estate man, that most of the furniture will go with the house, but there are a lot of things . . . Kiersten's toys and . . . could we have them shipped later, do you think?"

"Why don't I go to Royal as soon as the car's fixed and get one of those rental trailers. They surely have them, don't they? And I can also make a cage for Pussycat while you're packing."

"You'd even take Pussycat?"

"I don't see how we could *not* take Pussycat, do you?"

She held up her wet face and they shared a long ecstatic kiss. When they drew apart, Price was smiling, as broadly as she had ever seen him; the smile had spread to his eyes, which sparkled dimly with wetness.

"All right," Anne said eagerly. "I'm probably not the fast packer I used to be, and there is more accumulation since we've been here five years, but we can probably start in the late afternoon tomorrow. Will that be all right?"

"It will be an honor," he said very softly, then sternly, "but let's make sure we have things straight. I'm not asking you to marry me—not now. I want you and Kiersten to come to Secesh and stay a while, see how it suits you. It will be a different kind of life from what you've had before and I don't want you to walk into it blind. A lot of people would hate it. Mother talks a lot about the wind. She's said, hundreds of times, that it wouldn't be so bad if the wind didn't blow all the time. Well, it doesn't always blow, but mostly. I want you to get to know Secesh because it's a lot of what I am. I could never live anywhere else or any other way. Then, in a month, or two or three, we can both decide about whether we ought to get married."

"I thought you weren't going to ask—anything. Sometimes you'd come so close to it, and then you wouldn't."

He laughed a little and held her close again. "Sometimes, I thought I wouldn't either."

She drew back to look at him.

45

"That's not to say I don't mean it," he said quickly. "I love you. I loved you when you came out of that gritty little office. But it's—put me in shock."

"I know," she said meekly. "Oh, Price, I've never felt this way about anyone. I think it's a good idea, waiting to see and really getting to know one another. We both ought to be old enough and have enough sense to be able to do that. And there ought to be plenty of chaperoning material at Secesh besides Kiersten, two women and two teenage children. Even George . . ."

"What *about* George? Shall I go and see him, first thing in the morning?"

"No, I'd better do that."

"I won't have you do that. We'll both go. Here, sit up and drink your wine. To us," and he touched her glass and they drank. Then Anne, a smile suffusing her wet face, touched glasses again and said ebulliently, "To Spring Hill and your wonderful broken car. To the bus system, to Andy and—to George."

They were up most of the night, discussing plans, or simply sitting silently, together. This time Kiersten got one of her wishes. Price was there for breakfast.

George and Amy were implacably immovable, without understanding, as Anne had known they would be.

"Going off with a man you've known three days," George spluttered. "Why you can't even get yourself any money or close out your checking account. Bank's not open today. Suppose you want to come back home?"

"I can close the account by mail," Anne said calmly, though she wanted to cry, wanted him at least to wish her well.

"And suppose you find out how foolish you're being, after there's time for that? I'll tell you one thing, young lady, don't call on me."

"She won't," Price said. He spoke quietly, but there was something ominous in his tone. "I can promise, she won't ever have to call on you."

Amy, a short plump woman with graying hair, looked up for a moment at this big man who was "ruining" her sister-in-law. He was intimidating, so she turned to Anne and, crying, said shakily, "For the Lord's sake, honey! Think of your child if you won't think of the rest of us—I mean—of yourself."

Impulsively, Anne put an arm about the plump shoulders. "Kiersten's very happy, Amy. We'll be fine, and the scandal in Spring Hill will die down faster than you think. What about when Helen Sankey, a married woman, ran away with the Watkins man last year? There'll be something new by next week or, certainly, by the week after that. For instance, I understand that Mr. Hess is going to ask his wife for a divorce to marry Betty Simmons. She's only seventeen and he's at least fifty. I've talked to Mr. Hess this morning, by the way, apologized for not being able to finish my work for him this month. I'll write you, if you want me to.'' She glanced at George.

"You do as you please about that," snapped her brother, "but I wash my hands of you. What would Mama say if she was here to see this?''

Anne bit her lip to stop its trembling. "She'd say I'm like Daddy," she said softly. "It's what you've both always said when I wasn't pleasing you." Then she threw up her head defiantly. "But I'm not so sure that's all bad.''

"We'll go now," Price said quietly, taking her arm.

He took Kiersten with him to get the rental trailer from Royal, so that Anne could work faster. When you'd been used to moving all your life, it was surprising to other people how many things turned out to be superfluous. The smallish trailer was not quite full. There were Anne's books, her limited wardrobe, her mother's sewing rocker; all the other things were Kiersten's, books, toys, clothes. Price made the wood and screen-wire cage for Pussycat, and they left Spring Hill at shortly after four that Saturday afternoon, stopping last to say goodbye to Andy, who did wish them well.

Kiersten fell asleep almost immediately on the back seat. This had surely been the most exciting day of her life and she would always remember it. They were going far, far away, to a place where there were lots of cows, where she could learn to ride a horse, where she might have a puppy; Price had said so.

Both Anne and Price felt exhausted, once they were on the road, but there was the exhilaration as well. Neither of them had had much sleep this past week, and they were more than a little giddy in the beginning. Still, except for necessary stops, they drove all through that night and the next day, taking turns at the wheel. Some time during the night, Kiersten released the hook on Pussycat's cage. The cat, who had been meowing rather desperately all through the ride, now prowled silently about the strange station wagon. She would not stay placidly on the little girl's lap as Kiersten had meant her to do. Kiersten whimpered a little and fell asleep again. Anne was dozing in her seat when the car swerved violently. Price muttered, "Goddamn it to hell," then sighed in relief and exasperation. Pussycat had draped herself around his neck and there she stayed for several hours, purring intermittently into his left ear, until his shoulders ached and he pushed her roughly into the back several times. Finally, she gave up and lay on his jacket behind the back seat.

On Sunday night, they stopped at a motel, not the "rustic" tourist cabins where most travelers still stayed in the 1950's, but a large comfortable place with a restaurant attached and room service. They took two rooms, as Price said to Kiersten, "One for the girls and one for me." But they were adjoining rooms.

They ordered supper from room service, feeling that Kiersten might eat better if they were alone, rather than in the restaurant. Besides, they were all totally exhausted.

Anne said, stretching gratefully, "I like cowboys. They're free with their money and some of them aren't half bad people."

Price had brought in a handful of road maps to show them all where they had been and where they were going. Kiersten thought they should surely be in Dunraven Park very early in the morning. It looked so very close on the maps.

Price then took a piece of motel stationery and drew on the back of it a more detailed map of home.

"The Shadow River," he pointed out, "starts up in Wyoming. Some Spanish priest named it the River of the Valley of the Shadow of Death. That was when he and some other explorers tried to get up it through Spanish Canyon, here at the southwest end of Dunraven Park. Spanish Canyon is just about impossible to get up on the river, but they're building a dam now, just below where the Ute runs into the Shadow, that will fill up half of Spanish Canyon, and back up the Ute almost to Hurleigh. Here, to the southeast of Dunraven, between us and Hurleigh, is the Fairweather Plateau. There's a little town in the middle of it called Fairweather, maybe two hundred people, and ranch land all around. The town of Fairweather is maybe thirty miles from Secesh.

"Now, this big ridge of mountains, running west from the Continental Divide Range, is the Shadow River Mountains. The river cuts through it with Kilrayne Canyon. It's even more of a ba—a difficult canyon than Spanish. Some of our land lies up in the mouth of it.

"And here's Dunraven Park. It's like an arc of a big circle, about fifteen miles long and six or seven wide. The more-or-less flat side of the arc is the Fairweather Plateau, the arcing side is the Shadow River Range, as it swings from running west to running south. The mountains are sort of—nailed down where they run around the Park, by three peaks, all of them over thirteen thousand feet. This one here, at the end of Kilrayne Canyon, is called Kilrayne Mountain. About in the middle is Warrior Peak, and here, at the Spanish Canyon, is Dunraven Mountain. Down here, across Fairweather and in the Ute River Valley, is Hurleigh, seventy miles from Secesh. The Ute runs into the Shadow, here would be the new dam, which I don't like, then they run into the Colorado down in Utah.

"About in the center of Dunraven, we have Mills Crossing,

which I think I've told you about. Secesh is at the extreme north end of the Park, and west, or northwest of the river. Our land runs up into the mountains, into the valleys, small ones, of Cranky Creek and Picketpin Creek, where we pasture in summer, and where we get the water for the irrigation of the lower part of the ranch, for the hay meadows. Above our land, to the west and north, is the Baxter National Forest. The house is about here. It's—''

The room service waiter was knocking at the door.

They ate mostly in silence, with some whining from Kiersten. She had scarcely eaten since they had left Spring Hill. She was so tired of the car and they didn't give her much to look forward to, saying it would take some more days to get there.

Anne looked away from coaxing Kiersten to find Price's eyes on her.

"You haven't said anything," he said rather wistfully. "Do maps bore you?''

"No," she said, meaning it. "When you draw it like that, I can see just how it is, just how the land lies, but it's all so—so big, Price. I've passed through country like that, lived in some small towns in that sort of country. It—it awes me, especially now, after five years in Spring Hill. It's so relatively empty and it looks as if Secesh is simply huge. I just hadn't realized . . .''

"Well, maybe I overdid the boundaries a bit," he said, smiling shyly. "But it is the biggest ranch in the area still, for all practical purposes, under one-man ownership. The Ellenbogens, across the river from us, have a good deal more land, but it's divided now between three brothers. The Bergens, down at the south end of the Park, have as much land, but they lease a good bit of it to relatives up on Fairweather. There's talk they'll sell out when the old man dies, maybe try to sell the place as a dude ranch. I don't like that either, though it's none of my affair.''

"You said you'd show us the house," whined Kiersten. "I want to be there. I don't like to drive and drive and drive and go far away.''

"Eat some more of your supper, Kierstie," persisted Anne.

And Price said, "If you eat half of what you've got there, I'll make you a drawing of the house.''

She took a bite. "Is this half?''

"Not yet. Keep going.''

"You draw so well," said Anne.

"I can draw, too," insisted Kiersten. "I can't make a picture of your house because I don't know what it looks like, but I can draw other things, can't I, Mommy? A long time ago, when I used to be big, before I got little and borened again, I used to be a lady that made pictures for books.''

"You did?" said Price.

She nodded vigorously. "That was my job. I worked there —somewhere—drawing pictures."

"How much money did you earn?"

"Oh, about six hundred dollars, or maybe four dollars. I don't 'member, but one time—"

"Eat," said the relentless mother.

Price drew the house for them when they had cleared the dishes off the small round table. It was a large T-shaped log structure, built against the side of a small hill and overlooking Cranky Creek. The crossbar of the T was flanked on three sides by a screened porch and it was very large, containing, on one side of a hall that ran the entire length of the house, what looked to be a huge L-shaped living room and a dining room. Opposite these were the kitchen, office, and what they called the bootroom, complete with bathroom where the men could clean up when they came in from work.

"The grandparents were fanatics about trees, so we have a lot around the house, some of them about eighty years old. They don't normally grow out in the valley like that. And by the way," he said hopefully, "maybe you'll help me with the bookkeeping. I'm a total loss with it. Besides, I haven't got the time. I've been taking the information to someone in Hurleigh to put together for me."

"Fine," she said, smiling into his eyes. "Now I know why you picked on me to drag off into the wilderness."

There was an attic under the peaked roof of the crossbar and a cellar beneath the kitchen. The cellar was not always dry, he said, but was usable for storage, with shelves. Laundry was done in the bootroom.

The long part of the T contained six bedrooms, climbing up the hillside, with a few stairs in the hall between each pair. Two of the bedrooms had their own baths and there was another, opening off the hall, to serve the other four. At the top of the house and the end of the hall, there was another door, opening onto the top of the small hill.

"Dad and Mother had all the bathrooms put in when she redid the house. Before, there'd only been the one in the bootroom and that's not heated in winter. When Grandmother came out, Grandad made a log springhouse for a big spring that's nearly a half mile up from the house. He buried the pipe deep enough so it wouldn't freeze and the water flows down by gravity, so we've almost always had running water, though we didn't get electricity until about six years ago. In the winter, even though we had a bathroom, which most people didn't, we still took our baths in a tub in the kitchen because the bootroom wasn't heated until we put in the big forced-air furnace after the electricity came."

"But, Price, it's a huge house. I love it already."

He grinned, shyly pleased. "Grandad said they called it the Secesh Hotel and Savage's Folly when he was building it. Most ranchers give more attention to their outbuildings than to their houses, but we've got good ones of those, too.

"Right about here is the old homestead place, three rooms, still in good condition. That was Fern's and Arthur's house while their girls were growing up. Since Arthur's dead and the kids have moved away, Fern stays in the big house. We've got a couple now, Joe and Hannah Fergusson, who live in the homestead place, and Hannah cooks for the hands."

He took the last piece of stationery. "So, here's the house, roughly. And here's the creek. Across it, the homestead, bunkhouse, and a lot of barns and sheds."

"Mommy," whined Kiersten, "I want to let out poor Pussycat."

"Well, I suppose you can," said Anne. "I think we're all through with opening the outside doors for the night." She looked to Price who nodded. "Come on and let her out, then we'll find your pajamas. You've got to get to bed."

"I slept all day in the car."

"No, not nearly all day."

"I want to sleep with Price, not you."

"No," he said, tickling her as she came to lean against his side. "Your snoring would keep me awake all night. Your poor mommy's used to it."

A face that had been about to become suffused with tears again turned to giggles. "I don't snore, do I, Mommy?" she said, following Anne into the next room.

"Push the top of Pussycat's cage way back, Kiersten, so she can get at her litter box."

The cat moved out gingerly and went sniffing daintily and dubiously about the strange room.

Price stood in the doorway. "I'm going to call Secesh. You two shouldn't be a complete surprise to them. Besides, they'll be expecting me there by this time."

It was his mother's faint, slightly shaky voice which answered the phone.

"Hello, Mother, it's Price."

"What? Who do you say?"

They had had telephone service for only a few years, three party lines to serve the whole of Dunraven Park. Emily Savage had always had difficulties talking on the telephone, and this sounded to be one of her vague periods.

"It's Price, Mother," he said more loudly.

"Son, where *are* you? What on earth has happened? We thought you'd be here at least two days ago. Reuben's driving me mad with his constant nattering and—"

"My car broke down," he said, enunciating clearly.

"You've had an accident!" she cried shrilly. "Oh dear God, I knew it! I was saying to Fern just this morning—or maybe it was yesterday—"

"Not an accident, Mother," he said patiently. "Just something went wrong with the car and I had to wait for parts in a little town in North Carolina. Now, listen carefully, please. In that little town, I met a girl, a wonderful girl. Her name is Anne. She has a four-year-old daughter named Kiersten. We're on our way back now. They're coming back with me, Anne and Kiersten. We may be there late on Tuesday. Can you hear me, Mother?"

"Oh, Price, you've married again!" She was crying. "And the last time was so hard on us all—"

"We're not married, Mother. Anne is going to have a look at Secesh first."

"What? You're *not* married? And you're traveling together? That's awfully—risqué, isn't it, son? What will people think?"

"It's really all right, Mother. We have a four-year-old chaperone, and a cat."

"What's that, dear? Oh, *I* just don't know what to think or say "

"Mother, is Fern there?"

"No, she went to help Hannah with something. I *do* need a cup of tea and I can't find where she's put it. I was just looking when the phone rang. I wasn't even really sure it was our ring. You know, Price, Fern hides things from me. Penny and Hugh are out, too. I just can hardly bear this house empty."

"Are you all right, Mother? Is everyone else well?"

"Oh, I suppose so. We've had snow and more snow, and the wind—"

"Do you know if Reuben has found any more hands?"

"Price, you know I keep my distance from that man whenever I can, his dirty mouth, his smell, and complaining . . .''

"Have the calves started coming?"

"I just don't remember, dear. Hugh mentioned something recently, but I don't know if he said they had or they hadn't." Her voice brightened. "Have you seen your aunt Ruth?"

"Yes, she sends her love. She's going to be moving to California next month, you remember."

"She's what, dear?"

"I'll tell you all about it when we get home. Mother, you will remember, won't you, to ask Fern to get a room ready for Anne and Kiersten?"

"Well, all right, dear, but I still can't think it's right, your traveling with a woman this way. Is she divorced? That's bad enough, but if you're breaking up someone else's home—"

"Anne's husband was killed in Korea over four years ago."

"Oh, she's a widow? Well, so am I. I wonder if her husband was anything like my Stanley. Well, perhaps we'll have *something* in common, after all. Oh, Price, I do hope this one's not a beautiful little tramp like—"

"Mother, I have to hang up now. We'll try to be home by Tuesday night. If we're later than that, don't worry. Remember how the snow is on the passes at this time of year. All right?"

"Yes, dear, all right. I'll be glad to have you home again, even if you are always out working. Everything just seems to go more smoothly when you're here. Price, Fern is *so* bossy to me. The children are better behaved when you're here. You know—"

"We'll see you very soon. Don't forget about the room. Good-bye now. Take care."

Kiersten was almost asleep as he came silently into the darkened room, but she opened her eyes a little and asked for a kiss and a hug.

"I love you, Daddy Price."

"I love you, little Kierstie."

He whispered to Anne, "Would you be good enough, ma'am, to oblige me for just a little while?"

"I'd be most happy to," she whispered back, then yawned. "That is, if I can outlast—" she gestured in the dimness at the restless little girl.

He was sitting, smoking his pipe in his underwear when she tiptoed through the door and closed it.

"I *hope* she's really asleep. The conversation with your mother sounded difficult."

"Yes, well, I've told you she has vague times."

"You haven't said how old she is."

He frowned, trying to recall. "Seventy-two, I think. Anne, you're getting into a lot, going to Secesh. Fern's been actually running the house for years now. Before she was old enough, her mother, someone Grandmother brought out because she, Grandmother, was being a ranch hand, ran it. Mother doesn't do much besides her fancy work and wandering around in her dreams. Fern is bossy and outspoken as hell. If she likes you, you're really in. If she doesn't, she can make life pretty miserable, and her likes and dislikes tend to be unpredictable."

"Will she be scandalized because we're traveling together?"

He grinned wryly. "Better ask the opinion of Dunraven Park. Never say anything on the phone there that you don't want known by the community. If you think Spring Hill was bad, you have a surprise coming."

"Then why did you fret so much over my reputation in Spring Hill?"

"Because I was a stranger there. We're thick-skinned at Secesh, so far as gossip is concerned. Maybe Fern will be scandalized a little, on the surface but, deep down, it takes quite a lot to scandalize, or even surprise her."

"You love her very much, don't you?"

"I've told you, she's a sister. She's five years older than I am, so she's just—always been there. I got along far better with her than with Stanley. Fern's mother was a mulatto woman who came up from the South to work in a New England cotton mill. She married a man who was half Mohawk and half white, but he was killed in some sort of work accident. Grandmother found Rachel pregnant and widowed, with no one to turn to, so she brought her to Secesh to keep house. Rachel died when Fern was fifteen years old. She died two years before Grandmother did. But what I was going to say about Secesh, there'll be Hugh and Penny, too. I'm afraid they may not take too kindly to a stranger, just at first, and—"

"Price, are you trying to talk me out of something?"

"I just want you to know everything that may possibly be, to be prepared and not—surprised or . . . ."

"All right, I think I know. We'll just have to wait and see how it works out, all of it. Now, are you going to make love to me, or have I kept awake for nothing?"

"It's been my intention," he said in his slightly New England imitation of a western drawl. He stood up and lifted the nightgown over her head gently, his big rough fingers snagging in the soft fabric.

It was a delirious long time that they lay there, teasing each other, whispering, moving their bodies in ways to tantalize. After a long time, when both were gasping, unable to wait another moment, he entered her almost violently and they clung together like two drowning people.

Neither of them was aware of a slight pressure on the empty part of the bed. Just as they had reached satiation, beautifully, together, a rough little tongue began to work industriously on Price's bare hip. He jumped away, cursing.

"That *cat!*" he was almost yelling.

"Shh!" said Anne, bursting into a fit of uncontrollable laughter. "I thought you'd been stung by something," she gasped, "or that Kiersten had come in." She wiped tears from her eyes on the sheet, still convulsed. "Pussycat," she got out merrily, "Pussycat really likes you very much."

"I ought to kill the damned thing," he said through his teeth, but then her laughter became contagious, and he had to stifle his own in a pillow, once he had kicked Pussycat none too gently off the bed.

Anne had never seen or heard him laugh like this, had wondered if he could. The fact that he was doing so was just one more beautiful part in the weaving of the pattern of their love.

Briefly, Price lifted his watery-eyed face from the stifling pillow to gasp, *"Catus interruptus,"* and they were off again.

Accidentally, blissfully, she fell asleep, curled against him as they finally stopped laughing. He slept immediately and she, too, only a few moments later, knowing she should have gone into the next room, but unable to bear leaving him for just a little longer. To her great relief, she roused before dawn and so was in the proper bed when Kiersten awoke.

4

They came to Secesh near midnight and it was snowing. Kiersten had been delighted with all the snow as they crossed the mountains west of Denver, but she had long since become bored with it and fallen asleep again on the back seat. Price was driving; Anne would never have dared it, particularly after they had passed through Hurleigh. The road there was not paved and had not been plowed for some time. After they got through the little town of Fairweather, it was even worse. She couldn't see much beyond the falling snow, but the winding road down off Fairweather Plateau scared her. It was all steep grades and switchbacks and rough; the trailer bucked and jerked at the car.

"You're going to have to order warmer clothes for yourself and Kiersten," he said into her silence as he casually negotiated a particularly sharp curve.

They had seen no traffic since meeting one other car just this side of Fairweather, or had it been a pickup?

"I've lived in snow country," she said tensely, a little defensively, "but I wonder if I can ever learn to drive in it again."

"Sure you can," he said easily. "The important thing is just to go easy with your feet. Never tramp on the brake or accelerator. You'd be surprised how many people, born in this country, have never learned that."

At the bottom of the grade, he had to get out to clear the windshield. With the drop in altitude from the plateau, the snow had become wetter, great plopping flakes that the wipers were not handling. Sitting encased in warmth, Anne noticed that a hefty wind gently rocked the car. It moved the snow so that it was impossible to tell what came from ground and what from sky.

"Here's Mills Crossing," Price said a little later. It was all dark. "There are two roads from here, running along either side of the river. The county isn't responsible for them. Ranchers have to keep them open. I sort of hope everybody on our side has found the time to do some plowing."

This was even worse. Though the road had been plowed earlier in the day, the wind and new-falling snow had made drifts so deep that they scraped ominously along the bottom of the laboring car. The trailer hung back, bouncing and grinding.

"Here's our road," he said at last. "Just about a mile up Cranky Creek and we're home."

Here the drifts were not quite as deep because of wind direction, but he had to get out again to clean the windshield. A west wind, thought Anne, and it seemed to be getting stronger.

"There's a light in the heifers' barn," Price pointed out after a time. "Reuben or somebody must be working on a calf. I hope they don't see our lights. I'd just as lief they not know I'm back till the morning."

They crossed the creek on a little bridge, climbed a small grade with some difficulty, and stopped before the front steps, which someone had obviously swept clear of snow a short time ago. The porch light was on. Price had maneuvered the car so that Anne could get out onto the steps, but she did not move until he waded around and opened her door. Suddenly, she was very apprehensive. It was the weariness, she told herself, and the frightening roads. She stood up stiffly, trembling a little, and his arm was around her for a moment, warm, reassuring. He lifted Kiersten, wrapped in a blanket, from the back seat.

Lights were coming on in the house and the front door was opened before they reached it.

"Well, finally!" said Fern Marvle and gave Price a hug.

He gave Anne a gentle push into the hall and closed the door before introducing them.

Fern was a tall woman, almost six feet, with black hair, drawn back severely, and quick perceptive black eyes. Her *café au lait* skin stretched tightly over high Indian cheekbones. Everything about her seemed to radiate health and energy.

"Come in the kitchen," she ordered brusquely after the introductions. "I've kept it good and warm."

"You haven't waited up?" asked Price with concern.

"Well, I have and I haven't. I've been to bed two or three times, even got a little sleep, but things are going on. Three heifers calved this evening and two of them won't have a thing to do with the calves. We've got one here and Hannah's got one at her house."

The kitchen was a big room, with an oil-cloth covered table in its

58

center. A combination propane and wood range hulked large at one side, with a coffee pot always kept ready on the warmer. There was a fireplace as well. Anne went to it instinctively and there, in a large carton, was the newborn calf, moving feebly, making little-calf sounds. She dropped to her knees and stroked it. It wasn't even completely dry yet.

"I think I forgot to tell you about the fireplaces," Price said to her. "We've got the furnace now, but there's a fireplace in every room, except for the bootroom. Mother and Dad talked about bricking them up when they had all that work done on the house, getting wood stoves to put in them, things like that. But somehow they didn't. I'm glad."

"It was the spirits of old Mr. Price and Miss Mercy," said Fern firmly. "They'd never have stood for it."

Anne was fascinated with Fern's speech. It was partly southern, a heritage from her mother, and partly New England, or English. After all she had been here with Mr. Price and Miss Mercy talking to her through all her young life. She said "Cahlf" and that sort of thing. Price didn't broaden his a's quite like that. His speech was more definitely New England. He did a strange thing with A's, particularly when they were in contact with R's. For instance, "hard" became, almost, "had."

Kiersten, disturbed by light and movement, stirred in Price's arms. "I want Mommy."

"My word," said Fern, smiling delightedly, "this child *is* from the South."

Anne got up to take the little girl, both she and Price working to disentangle the blanket.

"We're here, Kierstie," said Anne softly, "at Secesh. This is Mrs. Marvle and—"

"Hon, let her call me Fern. I'd feel odd with anything else."

"Can't you say hello to Fern, Kiersten?"

"No."

"I'm sorry," said Anne over the child's head. "She's sleepy and she—"

"I've raised enough kids to know not to expect much in the way of politeness," said Fern calmly, still smiling at Kiersten. "I used to put diapers on Price and—"

"You did not," he said, outraged.

"Well, I did," she said firmly. "They fell off because I was so little myself, but I tried. I remember." Fern's smile was large and white-toothed. She said to the child, "We'll get to know each other when it's daylight, won't we, hon?"

"Look at the baby calf," said Anne, taking Kiersten to stand beside the carton. "Isn't it the dearest thing?"

"You wouldn't think that so much if you had to get up in the night and bottle feed the thing," said Fern, rattling cups out of a cupboard.

"I'll do it," Anne said stoutly.

"I want Pussycat," wailed Kiersten.

"I'll get her," said Price, "and some of the luggage."

The two women in the kitchen appraised each other when he had gone. Fern said brusquely, "That's a fine man. I feel like his sister. When that little snippet he married took away his boys . . . well, he won't be over that for a long time, if ever.

"It happened two years ago, but he's pining. You'll see him just stare off into space when he thinks no one's looking. He can be a hard man, too, quiet most of the time, gruff and rough-spoken sometimes, but he's the finest there is. I just want to be sure you know that."

"I do know how fine he is, Fern," said Anne fervently, "so we already agree about that."

Price came back, leaving the suitcases in the hall, but bringing Pussycat in by the fire. The cat saw the calf trying to raise its head, and spat in fear.

"That's just what we need around here, one more cat," said Fern, but she was smiling again at Kiersten. "They all stay out around the barns, but we must have a dozen. I'll bet Pussycat is a house cat."

"Can I let her out?" asked the little girl.

"Not now," replied her mother.

"I'm making you some hot chocolate," Fern told her. "I had two little girls and they always liked hot chocolate better than almost anything."

"Where are they?" asked Kiersten, looking round.

"Oh, hon, they grew, faster than I was nearly ready for. One of them's married and living in Portland; the other's in Chicago. Those places are both a long way off."

"We came from far, far, far away."

Fern set cups of coffee, the cream, and sugar on the big table and went back to stirring the chocolate.

"What can I fix you to eat? There's some steak left over from supper or sausage and eggs would be quick and easy."

"I'm not hungry, thank you," said Anne. She was still feeling hollow, a little sick and shaky, but good.

Price said, "How about the steak and eggs? Reuben is going to know I'm back any minute."

"I've *told* Reuben," said Fern portentously, "that if you did get home tonight, he's to leave you strictly alone. Price, your mother said to wake her if you came, but I don't think we ought to. She's not been herself at all, the past week or so.''

"No, let's let her sleep.''

"It's the winter. She's had about all she can stand.''

"Where have you put Anne and Kiersten? I'll take their things up.''

"Why, in the room across from your mother's.''

"But that's your room.''

"It's been my room for a little while. It was yours for a little while, too.''

He went out, saying nothing.

"It was his and Darlene's room,'' said Fern grimly, "only he hardly ever slept there. After the first few months, he moved back to his own old room at the top of the house. I hope you won't mind too much. It's one of the two best rooms in the house, with its own bath.''

In fact, Anne did mind a little. She said, "If it's been your room, I don't like to put you out.''

"Oh, I've just moved up to the middle room across the hall. I can probably hear Emily better from there if she wants anything in the night.''

Anne slept quickly. This had been Darlene's bed and the wind was making a low shriek outside, but nothing could bother her much in her exhaustion. She woke early, not knowing why at first. She still felt very tired. She could see a new-risen sun, a terrific brightness through the heavy drapes. She looked around the large room, old oak furniture rubbed to a dull sheen. The fireplace had been lit last night, though she had scarcely noticed. Now she couldn't see an ember, but it still made cricking noises, cooling off. There were large bright hooked rugs on the floor beside the bed and in front of the fireplace. The floor itself was polished hardwood. She and Kiersten were ensconced in a big brass bed, with so many covers she could scarcely manage to turn over. This had been his bed and . . . No, she wasn't going to think and brood about that.

The sounds that had wakened her came again, definitely the noises of breakfast preparation. She would learn quickly that Fern, efficient and unflagging, always seemed to make as much noise as possible with whatever job she was doing. Anne's room was next to the kitchen, though a few steps above it.

She got out of bed cautiously, not to waken Kiersten, dressed hurriedly in the cold, looking in her suitcase for a cardigan to put on over the too thin blouse, then she looked out of the window. Everything was waves of glaring whiteness. From here she could see what

Price had called the homestead cabin, smoke coming from its chimney and being bent sharply away to the eastward by the wind. She heard the wind, pushing fitfully against the house. She could also see a great many outbuildings, their roofs mostly cleared of snow because it had blown away. She saw a person moving swiftly around among the buildings, but could not guess who it might be. Then she sought a wider view. She could see what must be the mountain Price had called Warrior Peak, and a good part, to the south of the ranch, of the great uplift of the ridge, the Shadow River Mountains, snow being pulled off the peaks in bright streamers. Now she took note of the trees around the house and buildings, evergreens and bare-branched cottonwoods and willows. She heard a horse whinny and the bawling of several cattle. This was the first day of April, her first day at Secesh. It was still very definitely winter, but who cared about that?

Again, the clash of pots and pans. Anne went out, closing the door carefully. Fern was in the kitchen and Penny with her.

Penny was a tall girl for her age, with dark hair and eyes, despite which people said she had the Ellenbogen look of her mother's people, fair skin and Scandinavian features. She also had a bright, ready smile.

"Well!" said Fern, catching sight of Anne. "No need for you to be up so early, not this morning, anyway. You could be company for one day."

"I don't really want to be company," said Anne soberly. "What can I do to help?"

"Well, you can feed that bloody calf, if you really want to. I'll heat the milk a little. Wouldn't you like to walk around some? Look at the house while the milk's warming?"

Anne crossed to the dining room, a large table, many chairs, a sideboard, and china cabinet, all beautiful in oak and cherry. She went through the connecting door to the living room. The ell of the room was, as Price had said, a library. Bookshelves lined the walls, floor to ceiling and, in the middle, there were two sets of double shelves, so that one had a choice of three aisles by which to reach the hall door. The rest of the large room was something of a surprise. The floor was entirely covered by a lush-piled baby blue carpet. The furniture was delicate and what she thought of as spindly. Knickknacks occupied every flat surface, carefully placed on lacey doilies. The sofas and chairs had more doilies on their arms and backs. The walls were covered in a flowery blue and white patterned paper. She touched one, felt the good sturdy paneling underneath. This must be a part of the redecorating job Price's mother had done. No wonder they had to have a bootroom, if anyone wanted to come from working outdoors into this delicate unrealistic room.

There was a piano, an old upright, which looked as if it had been here before the redecoration. Its top was covered with photographs. She found one of Price which must be several years old. He was looking straight into the camera, dutifully, not smiling. She saw one of Penny and her brother Hugh together, then one of people she was sure must be Stanley and Mary, then, yes, two more of Stanley. She found an old faded one that must be Emily and Clint's wedding picture. There were no pictures of the twins or of Darlene. She thought Price must have removed them, or perhaps Fern, to save him the hurt of it.

At last, her eye was caught by the portrait above the mantle. The man was the elder Price Savage; no one could doubt it, having seen the younger. So the woman must certainly be Mercy Clinton Savage. Later, Price would tell her the portrait had been done in 1905, when a hungry artist happened on Secesh, and how both his grandparents had grown impatient to the ends of their lives whenever they noticed the portrait and recalled how much of their time had been taken up sitting for it.

The old Price was very tanned, but his forehead showed an extremely fair skin. His hair was so light that the real white in it was almost indistinguishable. The young Price had the same features, flat planes, good regular features, a face that might have been there to see or dare the Vikings in their first landings on the isles of Britain. Both Prices had the same far-seeing blue eyes, but the grandson had inherited his grandmother's and his father's hair, a rich, dark brown. Mercy was rather dwarfed by the size of her husband, she must have been a very small woman, but there was a look of tenacity in her small squarish face, an expression that looked as if she ought to be able to handle anything, including her big husband.

Anne turned to the windows. From the front she could see down to the lines of willows along the Shadow, then across over small rolling hills to the looming escarpment of Fairweather Plateau. From the side she could see what must be Kilrayne Mountain and the small dark slit of the opening of Kilrayne Canyon. From the back there was a view of the little hill up which the bedrooms climbed in their tiers and, if one looked high enough, the towering ridge of the mountains.

While she was still looking there came a polite, stifled cough behind her. So this was Emily Stanley Savage: thin mousy brown hair, mostly gone white now, small rather prominent brown eyes, with glasses and looking uneasy, a heart-shaped face which must once have been very pretty before it became lined, confused-looking, and disconsolate; a small woman, frail.

"You must be Nan," she said in a weak, rather shaky voice and smiled wanly.

"Anne," she said and took the small delicate cold hand.

"Oh yes, of course, Anne. I don't know why no one has lighted the fire in here." Very New England. "I understood there was a child . . . ?"

"Yes, Kiersten. She's still sleeping, Mrs. Savage."

"Oh, do call me Emily if you're going to be here a while. I do appreciate politeness, but I have never cared much for the name Savage. There's a lot in a name, you know, and Savage sounds so—well, savage."

Emily nodded brightly, after a little silence. "Yes, Price has told me a good deal about you this morning."

"He has? I didn't think he'd be up."

"Oh yes. I would hazard that boy doesn't average six hours of sleep in twenty-four. I don't sleep well or soundly myself. This morning I wakened well before daylight and couldn't get back to sleep, so I heard him moving around. I had some tea while he drank a cup of coffee. He's certainly become more talkative since his trip. He always was a quiet boy, but lately—well, he has had some very sad troubles. So have we all. He'll be in soon to have his breakfast I expect. It was his father and grandfather," she said conspiratorially.

"I beg pardon." Anne found herself doing those things to A's.

"They brought Price up. I was scarcely given the right to one word about his upbringing. They taught him to believe this ranch is the whole world. He could leave it now, might have left years ago when his wife . . . He could lease it and we could live rather nicely from the income, or perhaps he could just spend part of each year here. I will admit it was good therapy when he lost his children, always to have so much pressing work to do, but I hope you haven't come here expecting to *see* much of him. You won't, unless you learn all about calving, riding, irrigation, tractors, and all the rest of it. I'm not saying there's anything bad or wrong about Price. He's a fine boy, you do understand that. He's always been very considerate and kind to me, though that—thing with . . . Well, it almost worried me out of my mind, but it wasn't his fault, not for the most part at any rate. I know you must be very fond of him or you wouldn't have given up everything back at your own home. Tell me, do you have brothers and sisters? Are your parents still alive?"

"My parents are both dead. I have only one brother."

"Price had only one brother, my first son Stanley. My dear, they were as different as day and night. Stanley wanted to learn something more than ranching, to better himself. He went to college. I never was able to persuade Price to do that, even with his grandparents and his father gone. He always said he didn't have the time. He is well read and well spoken, that I certainly grant, but my Stanley—"

"Excuse me Mrs.—Emily. I told Fern I'd feed the calf. Could we go into the kitchen and talk? You're shivering."

"I'm never warm in this house." She sniffed, looking as if she might cry. "Calves in the kitchen! Sometimes I think the humans here would do just as well to move right into the barns."

She's not going to like Pussycat, thought Anne as they crossed the hall.

Price was in the kitchen with Hugh and Reuben. Hugh had black hair and slightly prominent brown eyes. At fifteen, he was about Anne's height and he would never grow taller. His roundish face was usually sober, and rather pompous. Emily repeated often that he was the very image of her Stanley and of his Stanley grandfather.

When Anne saw Reuben Scales, the memory of a song her father used to sing flashed immediately into her mind: "I am the wee fellory man, A rattlin' rollin' Irishman, And I can do all that ever you can, For I am the wee fellory man." She had never quite known what a fellory man was, but Reuben must surely be one. Reuben was no more than five-feet-four, a scrawny, steel-wire sort of man, with a long, usually glum face, nearsighted little blue eyes, and only a fringe of light reddish hair, grizzled with gray, left about his wrinkled bald scalp. The scalp and whiskered face showed olive skin; the rest of him, what there was to see, was bronzed.

All of them, Price, Hugh, and Reuben, were in socks and slippers, but Reuben kept on a heavy sheepskin coat. Anne caught the smell of him when they were being introduced; it was strong. He gave her, for an instant, a small hard hand that could almost be called desiccated. There was dirt under his nails and in the cracks of his hands that must have been there, as Reuben himself would have said, "Since who laid the chunk."

He was about to say something to Price when Fern said crossly,

"I guess you've come to eat here, Reuben?"

"Well, yes, *ma' am*," he said sourly. "*Miz* Marvle, if that meets with yore approval. I got a lot to say to Price an' not much time to say it. Besides, Hannah's stingy with her food."

Anne was a little disappointed to see that Penny was feeding the calf. Price had come to her, kissed her briefly on the cheek, and was holding her two hands as he had done that first night in her Spring Hill kitchen. His hands were still cold from the outside work.

"What do you think so far?" he asked softly.

"Price, it's strange. I feel—at home."

He smiled and let her go.

Fern was saying disgustedly, "When was the last time you washed?"

"Just right out yonder in the bootroom," snapped Reuben. "Price seen me."

"I did," Price confirmed. "After a while certain things just become part of a man. Have a heart, Fern."

"For lunch and dinner," Emily confided aside to Anne, "we eat in the dining room. Then *he* eats with the rest of the workers."

They sat down around the table, Emily as far from Reuben as possible. The men eagerly consumed bacon and eggs, pancakes, biscuits, and oatmeal.

"Well, now there's four of us besides you," said Reuben. "That'll give us two teams of feeders and one man to stay and watch the heifers."

"Yes, I'm glad you found Slim."

Reuben turned to Anne to give her the information that Slim was "a great big fat son—feller." He said to Price, "But you couldn' have gone off at a worst time. I tried my damndest to git two more besides Slim. Slim's never had no part of calvin' an' don't know how to drive work horses, much less harness 'em up. Leon ain't much better. I don't expect neither of 'em to stay long."

Hugh said, "They might stay longer if it was summer. With the bunkhouse shut up tight and you there, they can hardly stand to stay in the place."

Penny and Fern grinned, Reuben looked threatening, maybe even a little hurt.

Emily said mildly, "Hugh, dear, you might have said something more polite," which made Anne smile, too, behind her hand. Reuben had removed his coat, the better to eat, and the smell *was* stronger.

Reuben reached across the table for pepper for his eggs. "Well," he said to Price, "we ain't lost but the one calf so far, out of, I'd say, twenty-five."

"When are you getting this one out of here?" asked Fern.

"I'll take it when I go back," Price said. "Maybe one of the old cows will have it." He turned to Reuben. "Why don't you stay in today? Watch the heifers. Maybe it'll help your arthritis."

"Arthritis, hell," snapped Reuben while Emily pursed her lips. "I'll go out. Them horses knows me. You stay with the calvin'. You don't look good rested. We're in for it with them heifers for at least the next month. I don't trust none of them others, 'cept maybe Joe, with it. Got no real reason to trust you. Them heifers you bought last spring is still awful small. Mistake to git 'em, I still say. You'll have a peck a trouble with ever'one, so you just take care of it." He reached for a biscuit. "Your dad wasn' never much of a hand with calvin'. Your grandad was all right, but I tell you who could bring 'em was that little bitty Grandma. Miss Mercy could turn a good hand to nearly anything. When we used to hay with horses, before all this new-fangled stuff come along, she—''

Fern broke in. "Reuben, you want the butter, don't you? Well, for the Lord's sake, don't stand up to reach. Penny, pass Mr. Scales the butter.''

It seemed to Anne that they put away a great amount of food in an amazingly short time. Hugh and Penny excused themselves to go and gather their school things. Fern had their lunchboxes ready. When they came back, Hugh said to Price, "The battery keeps going down on the green pickup. It was cold last night. I doubt I can start it.''

"An' that's another thing," blustered Reuben around a mouthful. "We've *got* to find us a good mechanic. Now that we got all this machinery, half the goddamn stuff ain't workin' most of the time. We ain't had a decent machinery hand since Arthur died.''

Fern stared at him. "Is that a compliment? Just an out-and-out compliment to Arthur?''

"I think I may faint," said Penny.

"Arthur could be a handy man to have around, was all I was sayin'," said Reuben, looking a little sulky.

"You've got me," Price ventured.

"Oh yeah, shore 'nough! Let yore wheel bearin' freeze up. Whenever you work on somethin', what you mostly do is spend your time goin' to Hurleigh or sendin' to Hurleigh after new parts, till hell wouldn' have it.''

Price was lighting a cigarette. "How am I supposed to fix something that's broken if I—''

Fern said drily, "Arthur could just materialize parts, out of thin air.''

"Well, he *could*," averred Reuben. "He could just go in that shop an' make up what he needed, not be always—''

Price said to Hugh, "You can take the damned station wagon today. Give me a couple of minutes and I'll help you take off the trailer. Someone has to take that trailer back to Hurleigh as soon as the roads are a little better. Anne, I'll bring in your things as soon as I can get to it.''

"One of the womenfolks'll have to take the trailer back," said Reuben. "We can't spare a hand for that.''

"I'd do it if my license wasn't restricted," said Hugh, seeming to pout a little.

"You're not one of the womenfolks," said Reuben shortly. "I'm tryin' to make a hand out of you. It's slow an' it ain't easy, but I mean to keep at it. You—''

Price, who was facing the hall door, smiled and said warmly, "Well, good morning, Miss Kiersten. Come in and have some breakfast."

She moved very slowly, shy in the presence of all these strangers, sidling toward her mother's lap.

"Now who's this here?" asked Reuben almost gayly.

"Kiersten," said Anne, picking her up, "do you remember meeting Fern last night? This is Mrs. Savage, Price's mother, and Mr. Scales, who works on the ranch, and these are Hugh and Penny. Price is their uncle."

Kiersten hid her face against her mother's shoulder.

Fern, pouring coffee, said, "I'll get you some breakfast, hon. What would you like to have?"

No answer.

Emily was peering at the child curiously. She seemed to have forgot there was a child.

"I always did favor little girls with freckles," Reuben said with unusual gentleness.

Penny had knelt down beside Anne's chair and, still shy herself, was talking softly to the little girl. "What's your name again? Please tell me."

"Kiersten," she almost whispered. "It starts with a K and Owen starts with an O."

"I love your cute little voice and southern drawl. My name's Penny. Do you know what that starts with? A P."

"Like his," murmured Kiersten with a quick adoring look at Price.

Hugh and Price went to unhook the trailer, Reuben calling after them, "Don't waste no time. We ain't got it."

But Reuben himself stayed on in the kitchen for a little longer, looking with a kind of fond wistfulness at the little girl, while Penny stayed by the chair.

"Can we be friends, do you think?" Penny asked.

Kiersten slowly nodded. "Do you want to see Pussycat?"

"You've got a *kitty*? A real one? I don't have time now. I have to be ready to go to school when my mean old brother is or he'll leave me."

Kiersten's face fell. "You can't be my friend if you go away."

"But I'll be back this afternoon and we can look at your kitty. I bet she's pretty. Then, if it's all right with your mother, I'll take you out to the barns and show you baby calves and at least one new foal Do you know what a foal is?"

"*That*'s a baby calf," said Kiersten, pointing to it.

"But there are lots more, and a foal is—"

There was a peremptory honking from the front of the house. Penny picked up her things. "Don't forget my name, okay? I'll see you later, little lambkin." And she ran out.

"Can I go with her tomorrow?" asked Kiersten, still very softly and shyly. "I like her. What's a lambkin?"

Price came through the kitchen as they heard Reuben slam out of the bootroom door. "I promise to bring in your things before noon."

Anne said, "I can get them, and I will."

Kiersten put up her arms to him. "Could you put me up to the ceiling?"

He obliged, several times, and she was convulsed with laughter. Emily still looked at the child with questioning vague eyes.

She said, "Price, dear, I do hate to start, practically the minute you get home, but do look at all the snow you've tracked in."

Price glanced down at his wet slippers and gave her an apologetic look. "Yes, Mother, I'm just going." Then he said to Anne, "When you can have the time, come out to the barns. It looks as if I'm going to be there all day. We'll have to get you some boots, and riding boots as well. Meantime, borrow someone's, Fern's or Penny's. I want to show you the place."

Anne scrambled an egg and made toast for Kiersten. Emily wandered out of the kitchen and Anne went to the sink.

"Let me do the dishes," she said to Fern. "I really don't want to be company."

"All right," said Fern readily. "I need to get some cornbread made for the stuffing we're going to have with the chicken for dinner. You know, don't you, that that meal at noon is dinner, even if Emily does keep trying to have it be lunch. At night, we have supper."

Anne said carefully, "She can't—help with the housework?"

"Oh, sometimes, but it's better if she keeps out of the way. Poor thing, she's got so absentminded lately. She does usually clean the living room and her bedroom. They're her pride and joy. She got to choose all the furniture and carpets and such. Bless her heart, she hasn't had much in the way of choices around here. Old Mr. Price and Miss Mercy, Clint, too, were all strong stubborn people. They made up their minds without ever saying a word to her. She wasn't the right sort to bring to a place like Secesh."

Fern smiled. "I still have to laugh whenever I think of Miss Mercy—her name, I mean. That little woman didn't have a merciful bone in her body. She always said she wouldn't ask anybody else to do a thing she wouldn't or couldn't do herself. The trouble was, she did everything. Mr. Price, he took things a little easier, wasn't quite so demanding of other people, but that little woman was always pushing, pulling, driving. She was a fine woman. So is poor Emily in her way."

Anne looked out the window. She could see the poorly plowed Secesh drive where it met the river road, and the station wagon, slithering around the curve there.

"Isn't Hugh just fifteen? I didn't know anyone that age could get a driver's license."

"Rural boys can, for getting to school and the like. Hugh wasn't but eight when he and Penny came to live here and they had him driving tractors that first year. I've got a notion Price wouldn't mind if he wrecked that station wagon."

"Oh? Why?"

"Darlene made him buy it. He must have told you some about her? She wanted one of those silly looking, little, no-account sports cars. When the twins were born, Price went as far from a pickup as to get a station wagon for her, but no farther. He never has kept the car up in shape. I think it's going to stop on him one of these days and he'll just let it sit where he leaves it and rust away. When the divorce came, she was determined to have that car, but he wouldn't give it up. He hates it, but I guess he had to draw a line somewhere. She got the boys, and all that alimony and child support.

"That was a bad job of a marriage right from the start, or maybe from before that, even. He was glad enough to see her go, you can believe that, but when she came back and took the boys . . . well, he still grieves. He just seemed to get worse instead of better as time passed. About six months after they left, we had him in the hospital for a good long time, with a raging fever, and the doctors never did know what caused it, but I do. It took him a long time to get his strength back after that, and still he grieved so bad, not showing it, you know, or trying not to. He's a changed man, I can tell you that. He's talked more this morning than he used to do in two days, and I don't think it was the trip, but what he's found. Anyway, when he just couldn't seem to get over the boys, Reuben and I were finally able to persuade him to take a trip somewhere."

"Reuben?"

"Yes, believe it or not, he cares for Price, loves him like a daddy would—Reuben's kind of daddy. I've missed the boys a lot myself. I did a lot of taking care of them, especially Nolan, and I'll always love them. Did Price tell you they have separate birthdays?"

"No."

"Roger was born just before midnight and Nolan just after. Nolan was a lot smaller and he was sickly for the first year or so.

Darlene would hardly touch him except—well, I know she mistreated him at times, though she always managed to cover it up pretty well. Price had moved back to his old room a long time before the boys were born and he was up with Nolan many's the night, while *she* slept in peace.''

"Fern, when I was looking around the living room, I didn't see any pictures of the twins or . . . all those other pictures . . . ?''

"The day Price lost the court case he came in and took them away. I don't know what he did with them. They're not in his room, not visible anyway. You know Darlene was gone from here two years before she came back and said she was ready to take the boys? Price had Nolan on horses by that time. Roger was afraid of riding. Price wants so much for this place to go to a son of his. Hugh's interested, works right hard, but I think it's partly because he feels he has to. Price wants somebody that Secesh is part of, like it's part of him. A son is awfully important to him.''

"Yes, I know.''

"But why he picked *her!* Silly little flibbertyjibbet, eighteen years old when her sons were born. . . .''

"Is she very beautiful?''

"Hon, she's the prettiest thing ever come down the pike. Anybody would have to say that, but that's *all* there is to her. She's about as deep as that plate you're drying, but she hasn't got half a brain and that's always tied up with being selfish, spiteful . . . but, oh my word, *yes*, she's beautiful. Price was twenty-seven when they married. He's always been a considerer, even when he was little. But this was just one of those things. I think he just saw her at a dance one night in Hurleigh and decided on the spot he had to have her. It was all unusual, especially when we all had to get to know her so well.''

"And now,'' said Anne wryly, "he's brought me home after we've known each other less than a week . . .''

"Well, you're not of Darlene's stripe at all. I could see that first thing, right when I set eyes on you last night and if I didn't believe it, I wouldn't be talking to you this way. As I understand it, you're going to stay here some time, look us and the ranch over. I tell you, if Price was a singing man, he'd have been singing this morning. I'm *so* relieved.''

Fern herself usually sang or at least hummed at her work. Anne liked her for that, among many other things, because she, too, did the same thing.

Fern said, "I'm afraid you won't see much of Price. Ranch life's hard on a woman that way. But he's smitten, that's clear. It's in his eyes, and it's a good steady look, not the half-wild one he had for a few months with that—with Darlene."

"Mommy, I want Pussycat. Can't I let her out of our room now?"

"You'd better keep her there, Kierstie. I'll find something for her to eat. We gave her water last night. Do you remember?"

"I think it would be fine if the cat had the run of the house," said Fern. "Except we might try to keep her out of Emily's living room and bedroom. Kiersten will get cold if she stays in her bedroom with it, and we wouldn't want that, would we, baby?"

"I'm not really a baby," said Kiersten shyly. "Some day, I'll be five."

"What should I call you then? Lady?"

She considered it. "Yes, that might be better."

Anne helped with some other household chores. Once she went into the living room and found Emily there, sitting before a crackling fire, working on a very delicate crochet pattern.

"That's beautiful," said Anne.

"Do you really think so? I like pretty work. I like reading, too. *Nice* books, you know, the older novels we have. You see that Price did remember to bring in wood and light the fire here for me. He really *is* very thoughtful, when he has the time. His grandfather was like that. I wasn't so much—afraid of his grandfather. Price's own father . . . well, he was always busy somewhere else."

Anne's eyes had gone back to the portrait. She had not noticed before that Miss Mercy had gray eyes. She hadn't seen those in any of the descended family. They were interesting eyes, once she'd noticed them, far-seeing like the men's, but they also looked as if they'd be incisive and deep-seeing, close up. Price's eyes did have that quality.

Emily did not look up at the picture, but she said, "They were fine people, Clint's parents, but . . ."

When it became obvious that she was not going to continue, or had lost the thread of her thought, Anne said, "I'll come back in a while. There are some other things I have to do."

Emily didn't seem to have heard.

In borrowed boots—Penny's were too small, Fern's too large—Anne swept the steps and carried the things from the trailer into her and Kiersten's room. The little girl was in the kitchen with Pussycat drinking milk. Kiersten was chattering happily with Fern, so Anne, wrapped in an old duffle coat of someone's, went down among the buildings.

There were so many buildings: sheds full of machinery the like of which she had never seen, or at least had never noticed; a large shop with so many tools she couldn't possibly have identified; horse barn; hay barn—almost no ranches in this part of the country had hay barns she would learn later.

She had felt eyes on her since she crossed the bridge and, finally, turning away from yet another shed, she saw a plump, friendly-looking, middle-aged woman, standing in the door of the homestead place.

"Can you tell me where the calving barn is?" Anne called.

Probably she should go over and introduce herself. This must be Hannah. But it was all too true, what they kept telling her, she wasn't going to be seeing nearly enough of Price and she felt she just must see him now, at least for a few minutes.

The woman put a hand to her ear against the wind.

"The calving barn," Anne mouthed carefully.

Hannah nodded, pointing.

Almost the first thing she saw was an old rump-sprung armchair with a small space heater beside it, an open book lying face down on its seat. Then she saw Price by a stall in a far corner. He had a rope in his hands and perspiration sheened his face. His shirt sleeves were rolled high, his muscular arms flecked with blood. The rope led to the small hoofs of a calf, the feet barely protruding from the heifer's birth canal. Each time the heifer strained in contraction, he strained at the rope and a little more of the calf's legs appeared.

"Hello," he said in a pause, breathing rather hard. "We're going to have to get you all sorts of outdoor clothes. Kiersten, too. How are things going?"

Then they were straining again, he and the heifer.

Anne said, "Everything seems to be fine, but isn't what you're doing hard on the calf?"

"It's harder on the heifer," he panted, "if she doesn't get help. This one had a foot turned back. It's taken us some time and she's tired. Also, it's a little hard on me. You might just have a thought for that."

"I *am* sorry," she said tenderly and he gave her a glance that made her shiver with pleasure.

Another period of strain, the heifer groaning and swaying on her feet, then relaxation again.

Price said, "I think the head will come with the next one, then it'll all be downhill and shady."

"I've never seen anything born," she said softly, moving a little closer. She saw now that there was fresh cow dung on his pants and boots.

"Well, you're about to see something born, and I've got two

other heifers in here with their labor begun. I think the one behind you there is carrying twins."

The small head came. Gently he manipulated the shoulders between contractions and in a few minutes the calf was delivered. The mother looked round with dazed eyes. Price unhooked the chain which had held her in the stall. The heifer turned shakily, sniffed curiously at the slick, wet calf and then began vigorously to lick it, while Price was still untying the rope from its front legs. The calf struggled and made small noises that sounded like protest.

"Good," Price said, "a natural mother. A lot of first-calf heifers aren't. If they don't take to a second calf, we get rid of them. Not good breeding stock. I gave the one from the kitchen to an older cow and she took it right on with her own, thank God. That usually doesn't happen."

"What if someone else didn't take it on?"

"Well, then we'd bottle feed it, teach it to drink from a bucket as soon as possible and feed it with milk from the milk cows."

He had gone to scrub his arms in a bucket of water he had left on the space heater. "This calf is a heifer, in case you hadn't noticed."

"How can you tell?" she asked innocently.

He turned to her, staring, saw she was teasing and smiled.

"This is a mucky job. Do you want to take it over?"

"It's not mucky. It's beautiful to see birth like that, but I don't think I'm quite ready to take it on."

"Then don't come down here being facetious. Reuben would have kicked you out before you'd even finished asking that fool question. We have little time for jocosity here. This is a working ranch."

He had straightened and she smiled up into his smiling eyes. He put his arms around her, smelling of soap and antiseptic, being automatically careful that the lower parts of his clothes did not touch hers.

"I love you, Annie. I know you don't much like being called that, but let it be something special now. Or have you got a middle name?"

"No, I haven't got a middle name," she answered after a kiss. "You can call me almost anything you like. It's special. Oh, I love you so! My dad thought everyone should have only one name."

"Mine was the same. Are you going to marry me?"

"You don't have the time now. We're both supposed to think this over very carefully. Is there some great hurry, all of a sudden?"

"It's a pretty good way of getting to know a lot about a person, taking a long trip as we have together. Yes, there's a hurry. I want to sleep with you."

"Well, we certainly can't do any more of *that* until we're married. I couldn't, not here at—at home with . . ."

"So that's the hurry."

"All right," she said, holding him fiercely, "when the work lets up, *if* it does, and when Kiersten's a little more used to everyone. We will leave her for a *short* honeymoon, won't we? Is there ever time for such things? Or have you already made up your mind to have her along, so you can play 'football' when you're not—"

He silenced her with a long deep kiss which left them both a little shaken and silent for the moment.

5

They were not married until almost the middle of June. The calving was long since done, the cattle had been mustered for vaccinating and branding the calves, and then, because it was an early spring, most of them had been moved to the higher pastures. The hayfields had been fertilized, most of the irrigation work was done, the ditches running with water. Hugh was out of school for the summer. They still had Joe, Slim, and Leon, but Reuben was glum.

"Couldn'a picked a worst time than this for goin' off," he worried to Price. "What am I supposed to do about—"

"Whatever you think best, Reuben," Price cut in with a teasing grin. "We'll only be away a week or so. You've been here longer than I have. God knows you tell me that often enough."

"Well, what *about* Hugh? The little brat's gittin' to act like he owns this place."

"Do what you think best," Price repeated calmly. "I don't doubt you could beat him in a fair fight, come to that. You've had more years of experience, though he is a lot bigger than you."

That hurt and Reuben walked away, sulkily. He hadn't had to say "a *lot* bigger than you" like that, had he?

They went to Hurleigh for a marriage license and Price traded the red station wagon for a sleek brown Buick sedan which they chose together. They went back to Secesh. Fern helped Anne with some sewing. When the waiting period was up, they were packed and ready. Price and Anne in the Buick, followed by Fern, Emily, Penny, and Kiersten in a pickup, went to a justice of the peace at Fairweather and the ceremony was over quickly.

Emily cried. She said to Anne, "You know it's not because I'm not happy. This is probably the best-matched wedding Secesh has ever known. I just couldn't help thinking of how beautiful Price and

Darlene's wedding was. They had the biggest church in Hurleigh and—"

Fern hustled her into the pickup and drove away, Kiersten looking rather forlorn on Penny's lap, but all of them waving back.

As the two of them drove along, Price finally broke the silence. "You know, don't you, that Mother isn't really—aware of what she's saying a good deal of the time?"

"Yes, of course, it's all right," she said, laying a hand on his. "I had a big wedding, too, the first time. My mother insisted on it."

He nodded. "It was Mother and Darlene and her dad. Liam Nolan wanted to put on the biggest show of a wedding and reception Hurleigh had ever known. Darlene expected it. I paid most of the bills. Liam wanted to handle it all, but it would have been hard for him. He'd still have been in debt and it would be even harder, retired as he is, on a pension."

A silence and he changed the subject. "You think Kiersten will be all right, don't you?"

"Oh, yes. Fern and Penny are just about her two most favorite people in the world, and she's had our trip explained to her often enough."

"Then she'll be in better shape than Reuben," he said a little grimly and they both laughed.

They spent four days at the Grand Canyon. In the midst of all the other tourists, and in their hotel room overlooking the great gorge, they were, at last, blissfully alone, anonymous to others, aware of little but each other.

In their absence, Kiersten had been moved into the room next door. Now all the rooms in the house had occupants. This seemed to please Fern inordinately.

On that first night back, in her light nightgown, Anne stood, unconsciously staring at their bed.

"Does it bother you?" Price asked softly, putting his arms around her from behind.

"What?"

"That this was Darlene's room, that we . . ."

"No," she said, more firmly than she felt. Now she was really being silly.

"Because if it does, we could probably put together another bed from the attic. There are lots of things up there. This bed has seen a lot. The furniture in here came from across the hall when Mother redecorated and rearranged. It was once Grandmother and Grandad's furniture." He laid a hand on the bed's burnished foot. "They both died in this bed, my grandparents. I hope that doesn't bother you either. My dad was born in it. It could tell a lot of tales, except maybe the new mattress that came while we were away has dimmed some of the memories."

"Kiersten and I slept here almost three months," she said, "with Pussycat. That ought to put a damper on some of the other things. Oh, Price, let's have a lot of kids! Let's make Secesh full of children."

He tightened his arms and smiled down on her. "Let's start now."

They were at dinner on a Sunday a few weeks later. Emily was lamenting how she wished they could all take the Sabbath off.

"We used to do that," she said, "or as nearly so as possible, until Miss Mercy died. She saw to it."

"Well, Mother, I'm not the manager Grandad was, or Dad. We seem to have to work every day. God knows, I'd like to look forward to one day off in seven, but it just doesn't happen that way. We used to have more hands and seemed to be able to keep them longer. Most of the ones these days think they're fools to stay with ranch work any longer than they have to, and they're right. Now we've got to start trying to get a hay crew."

Hugh was not at dinner. He and Leon had taken packed lunches and gone up to work on the new fence they were building in the high pastures. Anne was still waiting to see that part of the ranch. Price had told her how beautiful it was.

"The house should have been built up there," he had said, "except that there's so much more snow. There'd be that much more road to plow."

Joe and Reuben were away, working on a weir gate, and Slim was supposed to be moving some yearlings. After dinner Price had six saddle horses to shoe and the ditcher needed work.

Emily said with revulsion, almost fear, "Just listen to that wind!"

Mornings were often relatively still at this season, but almost every day around noon the wind would begin to gust up and not be completely calm again until after sundown, if then. It whined and buffeted now around the big dining room window.

Emily said, to the table in general, "There was a letter from my sister Ruth in that mail Hugh brought up from the store this morning. She's all settled in that retirement place in California and all she can write about is how nice it is. She took a two-bedroom apartment, she says, just so there'd be a place for me. She writes about the flowers and how there's no wintertime, never snow."

"Why don't you go out for a visit?" Price suggested offhandedly.

"Well, dear, I'd like to, I really would, but I feel I'm needed here. For one thing, I wouldn't desert my Stanley's children. They'll be grown and gone away soon enough as it is."

"You are needed," said Fern firmly, "but it wouldn't hurt for you to take a little vacation. You've hardly seen your sister in all these years and I think we would manage for a while."

"Well, I suppose I might give it some more thought. Ruth says it's hardly ever windy and—"

The phone rang in the hall. Penny sprang to answer it. It was still something of a new toy.

"It's for you, Uncle Price," she said, coming back after a moment. "Some female."

It was Darlene. The sound of her voice ran through him like a shock, an unpleasant shock.

"Hello, Price, it's Darlene." She waited.

"Yes?"

Had something happened to one of the boys? More likely, she wanted extra money.

"We're in Hurleigh," she said in that faint, slightly lisping voice. "Daddy's house here is vacant so we came out to see about more renters, Daddy and the twins and I and—the man I'm about to marry. . . . Price, are you there?"

"I am," he said coldly.

"It's Clarence Tate, the man. I think you know him. His folks had a big peach orchard south of Hurleigh, but Clarence's daddy died a while back and Clarence has sold the orchard. That's another reason we're here."

"All right. What is it you want?"

"Well," she said gaily, "I thought you might like to have the twins for the summer."

His heart pounded, choking him. He stopped breathing.

"Dad can't handle them all summer alone. Clarence and I plan to have a *real* honeymoon. We'll be leaving Denver in a few days for New York. Then, when we come back, we'll still want some time alone, more or less. You understand how it is. . . . Dad takes the Hurleigh paper still and we read you married again not long ago When you married *me* it was haying time and *we* went nowhere. Of course, I'm not so bitter about that any more, after all these years. We *had* to get married when we did, though I thought haying season *could* have been over. That was the latest you'd ever had, I remember you said. Is it like that for your second time, *having* to? It isn't for me."

He covered the mouthpiece and drew a long, shuddering breath, then said huskily, "When do you want to bring the boys?"

"Why, this afternoon, silly. That's why I'm calling. We've had a little fix-up work done on the house here and found new renters. They'll be moving in tomorrow so we have to get out. But, Price, I want it understood that it's *just* for the summer. And your payments aren't to be stopped. The alimony will end, of course, when Clarence and I marry, but just because you may have the twins there doesn't mean—"

"Yes. All right." Sweat on his palm almost made him drop the phone.

"Well, we'd be back to get them before school starts, probably the Labor Day weekend. They hardly seem to remember you, you know. Children forget fast. I've told them to call you Price now. Clarence will be their daddy. Is that agreed?"

"Yes."

"I'm sure Rogie won't give you a minute's trouble or worry, but Nolan isn't turning out good at all. I suppose being on the ranch could be good for him. I hope they won't be too much for your new wife to take on. Didn't the paper say she was a widow with a little girl? Of course there's old bossy Fern and—how's your mother?"

"She's well enough."

"My goodness, Price, you're as tight-mouthed as ever, aren't you? Though I do remember you talked a lot to me, once upon a time I'll let you go now. We should be leaving in about an hour. I thought we might all have supper out there, just for old times' sake, no hard feelings and all that. Daddy can hardly wait to see you. He always was a fool about that place."

Price had put another piece of chicken on his plate just when the phone rang. Now, back in the dining room, he pushed it absently around his plate and stared at nothing. They all looked at him expectantly, but he met no one's eyes, said nothing for a while, trying to control his breathing, his voice.

Finally Fern said, "I'll make your cup of tea, Emily You'll be wanting to get your nap."

"I don't know if I can sleep," said Emily morosely, "with this everlasting wind."

Price raised his head as Fern went to the kitchen. "Kiersten, have you finished your lunch?"

"I did, Daddy. I ate my plate all clean. See."

"Then go and take your nap, please."

"Mommy made apple dumplings," said Kiersten, her face beginning to pucker. "She said if I ate my plate all gone, I could—"

"I'd like you to go," he said, with the first harshness they had heard him use toward the child. "You can have your apple dumpling later. Penny, will you go with her and help her?"

Kiersten was crying as she left the room. Anne looked at him askance.

Fern came in with a big tray, coffee pot, cups, Emily's cup of tea, a big pitcher of cream, and a platter with the apple dumplings. She looked around the table, then settled on Price's face.

"Emily, hon, would you like to take your tea in your room? You don't usually eat dessert so maybe—"

"I'd like mother to stay," said Price. "Everyone will have to know right away, but, Anne, I thought you might want to explain this to Kiersten on your own, since she hasn't known up to now that the boys exist."

"The boys!" said Anne, and Fern asked, "Was that Darlene calling?"

"Yes," he said, and for a moment his blue eyes were pure elation. "She wants to leave them here for the summer."

"The twins?" quavered Emily. "Coming home?"

Price's expression darkened again. "They're all coming out here, Liam and—the man she's marrying."

"Who?" demanded Fern.

"Clarence Tate. Do you remember him?"

"My word!" said Fern, shocked. "He must be nearly old enough to be her father, and about the ugliest man I've ever seen."

"Who is it?" asked Emily confusedly.

"His family had an orchard, Mother, near Hurleigh. I doubt you know him. He's sold the orchard now and—"

"Oh, well," said Fern, "that explains a lot. Wasn't he wounded in the war?"

"Yes, I think he got a medical discharge and some sort of disability pension. She—she said they'd like to have supper here."

"No," said Fern, bristling. "I won't do for her, Price. Not one thing. Mr. Nolan's a nice, good old man, but *she* expects to be waited on hand and foot, and I don't doubt her new to-be'll be the same. I won't play servant—or slave—to her again."

He said miserably, "Fern, you know how she is. If we don't, she might not . . ."

"She might not leave the boys," Anne finished gently. "We can manage one meal, can't we, Fern? Or if you won't, then I'll—"

"Then you won't mind having them? The boys, I mean?" He was looking at her with gratitude, and there was a sheen of water in his eyes.

"Oh, all right," Fern conceded ungraciously. "This one time."

"Will they all be staying the night?" asked Emily fecklessly.

"They will not," said Anne firmly.

"Where will we put the boys?" wondered Fern, beginning to plan.

At this point, Penny returned. "She cried and cried," she said reproachfully to Price. Then, puzzled, "What's going on?"

Fern told her quickly. "I was just wondering where we'll put Nolan and Roger."

"Make Hugh go to the bunkhouse," said Penny maliciously "He thinks he's such a fine ranch hand. No, I know what. Let Kiersten and me move in together. I'd love it. I really would."

"But, Penny, you've just given up your room to her in the past month," protested Anne. "There are all the toys, and Pussycat and—"

"It's okay. All these bedrooms are big enough for several people. I can move my things back fast enough. We could bring that cute little spool bed down from the attic for Kierstie. It won't take much space. She can have her side of the room and I'll have mine."

"Yes," said Fern nodding thoughtfully. "Let's try that, if you really don't mind, Penny. Then we can put the boys in Price's old room. If they're rowdy, they won't be so likely to bother . . ." she said with a significant glance at Emily, "the rest of us."

Emily said dolefully, "There have been so many room changes in this house lately, I can scarcely keep up with them."

"Well, don't you worry about it, hon. We'll keep them straight Wouldn't you like to go and have your rest now? I should think you'd need it, after this surprise."

"I do feel a little tired, but I don't want to be lying down when they come. That's no proper way to receive guests."

"Guests, my foot!" began Fern, unable to stop herself, but Price said, "I don't think they can be here before four, Mother."

She stood up slowly and Anne said, "Shall I carry your tea for you?"

"Oh no, thank you, dear, I can manage. I'm really quite all right. You know, Anne, I don't believe you've even seen a picture of Darlene and the twins. I just don't know where those nice pictures went, but, if you'll take my word for it—and no offense to you, dear—Darlene must be the most beautiful girl in the world. How old would she be now, Price?"

"I don't know, Mother," he said, flushing. "Twenty-four, I suppose."

"She's scatterbrained," said Emily, "careless about her vows, careless enough to get a divorce. To be completely honest, Secesh has never been my favorite place in the world either, but *she* wouldn't stay. *I*'ve been here since nineteen eight, but she gave no credence to her vows. She was a very—disturbing girl, but some of the things she asked for weren't completely unreasonable. If she could only keep her mouth shut and behave like a lady, one would be treated to one of the most wonderful persons in the world. Oh Anne, I don't mean . . ."

The flush had drained from Price's face, and he was quite pale.

Anne said quickly, "I understand, Emily. Let me—"

"The first time Price brought her out here, I simply couldn't believe my eyes. I saw soon enough what she was, but I still kept thinking maybe she'll settle down, or maybe Price will . . . And I thought what beautiful children she and Price should have, and they did. Little Roger is the image of his mother. Nolan looks like the Savages and isn't nearly so handsome but—"

"Come on, Emily, have your rest," said Fern, stern with anger. "We have to get dinner cleared away."

Price came and put his arms around Anne uncertainly. The hurt was in his face. "I'm sorry."

"And *I'm* sorry," she said fiercely. "How could she go on talking like that? Well, it'll be all right. Once the others are gone, we'll have a fine summer."

"Darlene said until just before school starts," he said, the joy in his voice again.

Fern snorted dubiously as she stacked dishes.

Price brought some things down from the attic. Anne and Penny went to help and for the first time Anne saw the old furniture, fine leather and wood, the things Emily had put up here when she had made her changes in the house.

"Well," Price said nervously when they had finished, "I'll see how many of those horses I can get shod."

Fern turned on him. "You *be* here, at this house, when they come. I don't want anything to do with that little bitch and I can't see any reason why Anne should either."

"Yes," he agreed meekly. "I can see the river road from the corrals."

Penny said, "I'll help with the cleaning up, then I'm going to spend the afternoon with my colt. The boys are okay, but I don't want to spend any time with *her*."

Fern said, "You go ahead now, hon, if you want to. You've done a gracious plenty of work in this house since school was out."

With the dishes carried into the kitchen, there was silence for a while, except for Fern's clattering and banging.

Finally, she said hotly, "You understood, didn't you, right off, that if we don't do everything to suit her, she'll likely not leave the boys? She tortured him like that for four years. I just could turn Emily over my knee and spank her. I don't know it for a fact, but I believe Darlene was seeing other men while she still lived here, going out in that red station wagon he bought her. With *all* of it, Emily would still talk to Price at times about giving in to her, moving off the place, leasing it or something. It was what Emily wanted so much. She's so hard on him, cruel and unseeing. It's never even seemed to occur to her what he's done for all of us, working his butt off on this place. Do you realize he was twenty when Clint died? *Twenty*, and he took over Secesh. Oh, Reuben's been a lot of help in his way, but Reuben's no business man. Price couldn't *live* away from here. I suppose I ought not say it, but I'd hoped it was over. After this, if she *does* leave them, the Lord only knows when she'll let him see those boys again.''

"Oh, Fern, he's so happy."

"Yes, I know that, but she might not even let it last through the day. She's like that. What he tried, finally, two years ago, was to get her to leave one of the boys here, Nolan, if she wouldn't leave them both. As far as Darlene's concerned, she's never had but the one child, Roger. I expect you know she was pregnant when they married. She was madder than hell about a baby. I don't know, maybe I'm talking out of turn. Maybe he's told you all about it."

"Not so very much," said Anne, looking away out the window as she scrubbed at a pot.

"Yes, that's our Price, down to the ground. He came out of it angry as could be, embarrassed, hurt, mostly hurt. Feelings like that will shut him up tighter than a jug."

"I want to hear, Fern. Well, it's not so much that I want to; I think I ought to."

Fern was making ready a huge roast of beef to put in the oven. It would need the rest of the afternoon to cook. "Penny," she called just as the girl was going out. "Stop at Hannah's and tell her we'll send down enough meat for the men's supper." Having slammed the oven door, she began, clatteringly, to dry the dishes.

"Well, Darlene was mad enough about having one baby, but when she found out it was going to be twins, there wasn't any peace in this house. That was when Price moved back to his old room at the top of the house. At any little upset, or at nothing at all, all that time, she'd cry, scream, throw things. All of us were ready to go crazy and poor Emily kept telling her how pretty she was, what beautiful children they ought to be and that surely didn't help Darlene's moods any. Mostly, she took it all out on Price. She hadn't even known how *not* to have babies, running around Hurleigh, waving her cute little fanny at everything in pants.

"Well, her time finally came and I went with them to the hospital in Hurleigh. It was the early part of April and we had a snow storm, of course. The roads were bad, but Price has always been a good driver. She screamed and yelled with every move he made, about how he was going to kill us all. And when her pains came, she was a wildcat. She used language Reuben may not even know, screaming it at Price because it was all his fault. You do know the boys have separate birthdays?"

"Yes," said Anne.

"Roger was born on the third of April, a little before midnight, and Nolan was born on the fourth, a few minutes after twelve. They gave Darlene ether or whatever, and she didn't really wake up until some little time after the delivery. They brought the babies to her, and she saw Roger, with that dark red hair, looking like her, and she just told them to take 'the other one' away, that she'd never wanted twins. She named the baby Roger Paul, saying those were the two prettiest names she knew for a boy. When they asked her about naming the other baby, she just simply didn't care. Price suggested Nolan, her daddy's last name, and that pleased Liam a lot. He'd been at the hospital all this time. He said the baby's second name, at least, ought to be Price. I was standing right in the room when Darlene asked the doctor if it would ruin her figure to breast-feed *one* of them. And that's what she did.

"Arthur was sickly then, and Ivy, our youngest, was still at home, so I was still living in the homestead. Price and Emily and I raised Nolan. Price took him into his own room at nights and took care of him. He wasn't a strong baby, though he grew out of it. Darlene would get fighting mad if she had to listen to him cry. I *know* she spanked him and knocked him around, just a little tiny baby.

"She stayed on those two more years, though she was actually gone a good bit of the time. Her friends from town would come out for a visit, to get a free meal or two. I've heard her tell them, many's the time, that Roger would inherit 'all of this' one day. He was the oldest son, she'd point out. It never seemed to occur to her that Hugh and Penny would have a share, and Nolan didn't count for anything.

"Then her dad was sent to work in Denver and that was all she needed. She couldn't bear Secesh any longer. She'd go stay with Daddy and get a job. The boys could stay on here till she was settled. Even Roger didn't count for much, just at that time.

"Arthur had died and Ivy was gone away to business school. Emily was getting more—vague like she is, and Price couldn't handle two-year-old twins and do any of his ranch work. Darlene already had Roger spoiled rotten, and Nolan afraid of his shadow, but we brought them along, and they were fine little boys.

"Then, just after the boys were four, Darlene's daddy was hurt, one of his legs nearly ruined. When he got home from the hospital, Darlene had a free baby-sitter, so she came and took them. She'd been threatening that all the time they were here. Price sent her more money than he had to, more fool he, and sometimes she'd write a line or two, saying she needed more money, and that she'd be coming to take the twins soon.

"When she did come, she had presents, three or four things for Roger and a little rubber ball for Nolan. I should be ashamed of eavesdropping, I guess, but this is family. Price asked her to leave Nolan with us. As usual, she had eyes and attention only for Roger. She hedged around about it for a while, just to hurt Price more I know, then she said Rogie was used to having Nolan with him, that he'd be lonely, shocked, left with his grandpa alone and Nolan had to go, too. Besides, she said, brothers belonged together, especially twins. We've always tried not to call them twins, Price and I. It was his idea. He said each of them ought to have his individuality.

"He went to see a lawyer in Hurleigh the day after she took them. He didn't sleep, didn't eat right, and, of course, it took the thing so long to go through the courts, and still he lost. Finally, it all caught up with Price, chills, that high fever, talking out of his head We made a bed in the station wagon and took him in to the hospital, him fighting it all the way when he was conscious. The doctors never could find what was really wrong, except, they said, total exhaustion, nervous and physical. They thought he'd die. One of them, Dr. Coolidge, that I'd known from when Arthur was sick, told me that first night he didn't think he would live till the morning. It took a long time for him to get his strength back, and him going to work like a dog as soon as he got back here. This place saved him, though he nearly killed himself with the work. And still Emily can talk to him like . . . Well, do you see why I feel that maybe it would be better if it was all over, final? If he could just try to forget the boys. . . ."

"Yes, I see," said Anne, her eyes blurred with tears. "But I don't think he's the kind of person who *can* forget. I want to have a baby as soon as we can. Maybe that will help. . . ."

"That could be the best thing that ever happened for him, besides you," agreed Fern gently. "It could—"

"Mommy?" said Kiersten from where she hovered in the doorway. "I want my apple dumpling. Why wasn't Daddy nice to me?" She looked ready to cry again.

6

Nolan, Roger, and Grandpa sat in the back seat of the new Oldsmobile that Clarence and Mama had bought. Roger sat by his window with his hands folded in his lap, looking out only now and then. Nolan looked out all the time, tending to turn sideways and draw up his feet, which got him in trouble with Mama, but he kept forgetting. Roger said he didn't remember much about Secesh, just, a little, the people who lived there. Nolan remembered a lot. He remembered Fern, how she cooked good things and sang all the time, and hugged them a lot. He remembered Grandmother, but not so well; she could play the piano and smelled nice. Penny and Hugh were blurrier. Penny had been nice, but Hugh was never willing to be bothered with little kids. He remembered Reuben, calling him "Cottontop" and "Towhead," and teasing him about learning to chew tobacco. He remembered just how the house was, and the sheds, and the upper pastures where Daddy had taken him once, riding on the saddle in front of him, when they were just looking over the cattle. Most of all, he remembered Daddy. Mama said they were not to call him Daddy now, but Price; Clarence was supposed to be their real daddy after this. Nolan remembered Daddy making him eat trout, which he didn't like, but he had enjoyed the fishing for it. He remembered Daddy teaching him to tie his shoes before Roger had learned. He remembered being in the calving barn; maybe he had even helped a little. He remembered that Daddy didn't talk as much as most people, but he had nice eyes, when he looked at you, that made you feel nice and warm. And, maybe best of all, he remembered the time Daddy had put him on a horse all alone, holding his own reins, and they had gone—not so very far, though it had seemed a wonderfully long way then—to doctor a sick calf.

Nolan wanted to go back so much it hurt him. He thought he might have dreamed something about Secesh every night since they'd been away. He couldn't seem to help squirming with excitement and eagerness, but that was the wrong thing to do—he was always doing wrong things—but if he wasn't *very* good, Mama had said he'd have to go back to Denver and spend the summer with Grandpa. Mama meant it when she said things like that. He was always being punished, having to stay in the house, having things taken away from him, getting slaps or spankings or—other things.

Nolan loved his grandpa, but Liam had a leg that gave him bad trouble and there were a lot of things in which he couldn't share. They were good friends and did share many things, especially the music. Nolan guessed the two of them could have a good time, talking, playing, and singing all they wanted to while Mama was away, but a whole summer at Secesh stretched before him like a tantalizing mirage. It seemed almost forever, if only he could do the right things and Roger didn't make a fuss. If Roger really said he didn't want to stay, cried, then they wouldn't stay. He would have to go back with Roger, and Roger would be always interrupting whatever he and Grandpa did together. Roger really didn't want to stay. He had said to Nolan privately that if Nolan wanted to so much they would do it, but he changed his mind about things like that. Mama said that—bad as Nolan was—Roger needed him, and maybe that was true. Roger was always wanting to play games in the house, do things Nolan didn't care about, not wanting them to be separated. Nolan had learned not to show more of his feelings about something he wanted than he could help, especially about something he wanted very badly. If Mama thought he was getting "wild," it wouldn't happen.

Just now, Grandpa was shifting his bad leg around against the back of the front seat and Mama turned half round and caught Nolan.

"For God's sake, turn around and sit *right*. You're six years old and can't even sit in a seat. Get your feet down. If you touch that upholstery with your shoes, I'll knock your teeth down your throat."

"Darlene, mavourneen," said her father mildly, "it was me, pushing against your seat. I'm sorry. Chappie wasn't shifting."

"Oh, Daddy, don't always jump in front of him when I'm *trying* to make him fit for civilization. You spoil the brat rotten." Then back to Nolan, "Just look at your brother! Look at him, I said. Rogie's always such a little gentleman. If you were only half . . ." she turned away in disgust.

Liam patted Nolan's hand, a quick surreptitious pat, and Roger looked out the window.

Liam looked with consternation at the back of his beautiful daughter's head, but then he was wondering again at how he and his plain, dear Molly had come to produce such a beautiful child. Liam himself had been something of a dandy in his day, though nothing like good-looking. His hair had once been black, and he had blue eyes in a round Irish face. He had never been a big man, but could hold his own in any fair fight. He had had to leave Ireland in a hurry because he was involved in the 'Sixteen, the Easter Rising. He had landed in New York and stayed there a few years, working with a cousin. He met Molly O'Reilly there and, after a rather long courtship, married her. Molly was such a sweet lass, small, with light reddish hair. From their union, long after they had moved west, after they had given up hope of children, had come Darlene, and what a lovely reward she had been! She was small and dainty as could be, with dark chestnut hair that gleamed and fell to her shoulders in deep waves. Her brown eyes, when she was in a happy frame of mind, were enough to melt the heart, big and soft, sometimes sparkling. She had grown up to have a luscious little woman figure—bless Molly who was flat-chested and nearly straight up and down. Liam had used to tease Molly, in private, of course, about another man having been somewhere in the woodpile and she'd slap at him and turn red as a beet.

But Molly had died when Darlene was in her teens, just when a girl needed her mother most, and Liam had been at a loss as to what to do with her. She began to stay out late, and the boys she occasionally brought home were not much to his liking. Then, at a dance or somewhere, she had met Price Savage. He was no boy, but a man well into his twenties, and Liam had liked him. He seemed to have something of a steadying effect on Darlene and you could see his adoration for her in his eyes. Liam knew of the ranch in Dunraven Park, of the family's fine name, and that they were well-fixed, though he had not, like poor Darlene, expected much in the way of high living for the young couple. He had known the money was mostly tied up in Secesh.

Well, so the two of them had had to get married. That happened to a lot of young people. Liam had been pleased as punch about the twins, though they made quite a responsibility for poor Darlene, and she only eighteen at the time. "She'll settle in," he had assured Price. "She'll make a fine little mother."

Then Liam had been transferred to Denver and he had been lonely. He had always driven out to Secesh every few weeks, in his old Ford sedan, in the good weather. He never wrote that he was lonely or meant to imply it. He didn't want Darlene fretting about that, but one day, there she was. She couldn't stand it at the ranch any more, she had said. She never saw anything of Price, and wouldn't, unless she took on man's work. Price beat her sometimes, she had said and cried.

Liam knew his daughter, to an extent. Loving didn't make a man completely blind. He didn't believe Price had ever laid a hand on her in anger, but he did know how ranch life was, how some wives worked and slaved alongside their husbands and became old and raddled long before their time. He didn't want that for his girl either.

Darlene had worked as a waitress and gone to business school in the mornings. He had hated to see her having to do both, but there was no money to have it any other way. She had got a secretarial job, but had given it up after a short time and taken the cocktail waitress job in that fancy place where someone had helped her get work. She made more, with the tips, and she said she liked working around happy people, not in the hospital, where people were so often sad and even crying.

Liam had the accident and when he was finally out of the hospital, Darlene brought the boys to live with them. Liam was happy. He felt deep sorrow and empathy for Price, but that couldn't stop his own joy. He had been fifty-seven then, two years ago, a broken man, some might think, but the twins gave him a new lease on life. Roger was a beautiful child, the image of his mother, though in a masculine way, and he was going to be a big fellow like the Savages. He was two inches taller than his brother; Nolan was still a bit small for his age. Roger didn't have much to do with his grandpa. He was always looking at books, putting together puzzles or models and the like. But Nolan was Liam's happiness in his old age and infirmity. The boy would listen by the hour to the stories and music of Liam's youth, and already he was learning the banjo and fiddle with a speed that delighted Liam and took his breath away. Chappie's hands were too small yet for the guitar. Right now, Liam would bet, if they were alone, Chappie would be humming "Riley's Handy" or "The Wake of Tom Murphy" or some such. He had confided to his grandfather that, almost every morning, he woke with some tune already going through his head.

Liam didn't like his Darlene's marrying Clarence Tate. Clarence wasn't much to look at, a smallish, scrawny man with light-blue, shallow eyes and brown hair which he was losing fast, but all that was really nothing against him. One thing Liam didn't like was the gloating look that came into the man's eyes when he was around Darlene, like a miser, counting his gold. Also, Clarence obviously had no feeling for the boys. He was soft and respectful with Roger, but you could tell that was only because Darlene expected it, not for any friendliness he felt toward the child. And already he had struck Nolan several times, not a decent spanking on the bottom, but a heavy swing or two with his hard little fists. Liam couldn't take that, but Darlene always said the boy deserved it.

They had started planning to marry months ago, when Clarence's father had died and the orchard had gone up for sale, planning a honeymoon in New York for two or three weeks and all the rest of it. The money wouldn't last long, Liam knew. In a year or so, they would have run through it and Darlene would be back at that cocktail place, for he knew Clarence Tate not to be a working man. He had done as little as possible as a youngster, then had got that back injury in the war, which made an excellent excuse. Furthermore, Clarence was thirteen years older than Darlene. Price had been nearly ten years older and Liam had thought that a good thing, but not this. This marriage wouldn't last, maybe not even as long as the last one had, and what would that do to his Darlene? To the boys? Already, she was making them call Clarence Daddy.

Another thing which bothered Liam, possibly even more than Clarence, was the vast difference Darlene had always made between the boys. He understood that some people, even one's own child, could simply rub one the wrong way, be an aggravation, but she was too extreme. Roger was spoiled and Nolan, when his mother was around, was cowed. He was a good boy, Chappie. He tried so hard. Liam said little to the mother, feeling they were, after all, her children and that, since she was working and receiving the money from Price, he was, essentially, in *her* house. Anyway, if he so much as hinted at the problem, it made her angry and Nolan got the worst of it. But it was a constant worry and sorrow.

Liam had assumed, as Darlene and Clarence had seemed to do, that if and when the plans worked out, the boys would simply stay on with him through the grand honeymoon. Then, two weeks ago, had come the Hurleigh paper, with the announcement that Price Savage had remarried, a girl from away somewhere, named Anne something. The next morning, Darlene had got up smiling. "Those two pieces of news we got yesterday go together, Daddy," she had said, looking pleased with herself.

"How's that, my girl?"

"Clarence got word there's a definite buyer for the orchard. We'll have some of the money in two weeks or so. And then we read Price got married. Daddy, old sweetie, you're going to have a vacation."

Liam hadn't understood.

"Why, we have to go to Hurleigh, anyway," she had purred, "so we'll just take the boys to Secesh, maybe for the whole summer."

Liam hadn't liked the look in those lovely brown eyes; it was too much like the way Clarence Tate so often looked at her.

"Here comes the hill," Nolan said softly, meaning the grade down from Fairweather, which he couldn't quite see yet.

"I don't remember any of it," said Roger, looking ahead.

"Neither does he," said Darlene shortly. "He's just saying he does. You were only babies when you left here."

Everything about Nolan irritated her, his very existence. There was the way he talked. Both the boys had learned to talk at Secesh, where they were all so proper and better than anyone else, with that show-off accent. Both of the twins picked up some of Daddy's brogue, but she couldn't see any way of avoiding that. Roger had dropped most of the Secesh ways, except his gentlemanliness, which hadn't really come from Secesh, but which he had been born with. Nolan, on the other hand, still pronounced a word now and then the way Price did, or Price's crazy mother, or that hag Fern. Darlene always corrected him, sometimes physically, but he kept on with it, just to aggravate her. Sometimes she wished she'd let Price have him, but Roger did need some company, though he certainly wasn't getting the best. Roger liked to keep to himself essentially, knowing his intelligence and manners were far above those of other boys, but he did seem to have a need for Nolan, always trying to get Nolan interested in something better, to spend more time together. Roger would be brokenhearted without his bratty brother. Besides, it would be giving in too much to Price, who deserved exactly what he was getting.

But Nolan did remember about the hill. He looked to his grandpa, who nodded, almost imperceptibly.

Chappie was growing now, out of the smallness and sickliness of his babyhood. He was thin and small, but he was growing, might catch up with Boy-o yet. Roger didn't like being called Boy-o, but Liam had heard Nolan tell his friends they could call him Chappie if they liked. Nolan had fair hair, so fair it looked like straw that had weathered a winter. His face was like the Savages'—perhaps that was part of Darlene's problem—a face of planes and angles, a good face, a fine one when he grew into it, like Price's. But the face was too old for a scrawny little six-year-old. His eyes were too old, too, a man's eyes almost, that looked as though they had been accustomed for a long time to seeing far and deep. They were gray eyes, with no trace of brown, blue, or green, but with the ability to shift the shades of gray with the boy's feelings. Ordinarily, they were expressive eyes, but the boy had a way of closing them, not with his lids, but blanking them out when he needed to. No six-year-old should have to do that. When they were open and frank, Liam liked to watch those eyes while he told the boy stories or taught him songs. He'd seen the eyes once before, in the portrait over the Savage mantel, the eyes of Chappie's great-grandmother, Miss Mercy as they called her.

"Bitch of a road," grumbled Clarence Tate, gesturing for Darlene to light him another cigarette. "This sure is the hindside of nowhere."

She lit two cigarettes. She had taken up smoking before she left the ranch, simply to irritate and outrage Emily and the others. She was thinking, I can still make him miserable. There's no reason why he should be *too* happy, *if* he's happy.

Nolan eased forward. There was the Shadow, Mills Crossing, the bridge.

"Turn right after you cross here," Darlene said.

"How the hell much farther is it?" growled Clarence. "This kind of road's sure not good for the car, rough as it can be nearly all the way from Hurleigh."

Emily opened the door as they drew up in front of the house. She still looked the same, thought Darlene, maybe a little older and crazier. That just went to prove what a place like this could do to a woman. Then that damned Fern was behind her.

Price was walking quickly up from the corrals, restraining himself from running. Surely a man's children, when they were no longer his, shouldn't have such a hold over him. Nobody should. Well, Anne. But that was wholly different. Every day, he felt safer with Annie.

Darlene was out of the car. She came hurrying toward him, pulled his head down, and kissed him on the cheek. "What's a little kiss between old marrieds?" she said shrilly so the others would be sure to hear.

Clarence, looking very sour, had followed her. He held out his hand to Price, looking as if he wanted to strike. Price took the hand for an instant; it was soft, like a woman's, and damp.

But Price had eyes only for the boys. Nolan had virtually tumbled out of the car into Fern's warm arms. Roger got out more sedately on the other side, walked around, and dutifully kissed his grandmother. Now both boys stood on the steps, looking down at their father. Price went up two steps and, only for a moment, put a hand on each boy's head. The hands removed, Roger gravely shook one of them. Nolan looked down at his feet. Impulsively, Price took the child's hands in both of his. Nolan looked up at him very solemnly, with those probing gray eyes. For a moment Price could hear his own grandmother saying sternly, "Price Savage, that will *not* happen again. Are we agreed?"

Anne was standing in the doorway now, with Kiersten peeking round her. Price took the boys to her, Darlene and Clarence following closely.

At the car, Liam was still edging his way out. His leg had got very stiff with the ride. Fern reached in and all but hauled him out bodily.

"How are you, Mr. Nolan? You old Irishman, you. It's good to see you again."

95

She helped him get steady on the cane.

He said, grinning, "You wouldn't be interested in a second marriage now, would you, lass?"

Nolan was wishing his dad hugged like Fern, but he remembered that that sort of thing didn't happen often. Neither he nor Roger was much interested in their dad's new wife nor her daughter, though Anne had kind eyes. Roger didn't want to be here at all and Nolan was so afraid he, or someone else, was going to do something to make their mother change her mind. He only wanted her and Clarence and, yes, even Grandpa, to be away, so that he could *know* he was really here.

Darlene looked speculatively at Anne, tall—statuesque, graceful, some might say—but she was certainly no beauty. She didn't appear to be pregnant. Price must have found a new way of getting himself a wife this time. The child was a scraggly-looking little thing.

Anne gave her back stare for stare. She would *not* be intimidated, jealous of the past or any of it, but God! The girl was beautiful. Of the boys, Anne had immediately chosen Nolan. Roger was too like his mother, too perfectly beautiful in his boyish way, with a smug, complacent expression on his flawless face, though there did seem to be shadows of something more in the depths of his brown eyes. Nolan was a Savage, but with Miss Mercy's eyes, and curlier hair. His skin was extremely fair and there was a delicate look about him, almost frail. His very light hair was thick and curly. It had been carefully parted on the right side, but kept falling from the left, down across his broad forehead, not just a lock, but a veritable swath of curls. She pushed the hair back, gently, compulsively, and he gave her a small tentative smile. That was like Price, too, the rare smile, and even less rarely did it spread to his gray eyes.

"Well!" said Emily with false uneasy eagerness, "come in, all of you. We thought you'd be here just about now, so we have a little tea party almost ready. I expect the twins, at least, will be hungry. Boys usually are."

They filed into the living room, except for Fern who went back to the kitchen, where Penny had come back to help her.

Darlene and Clarence sat on a loveseat, their arms conspicuously around each other.

Also conspicuously, Roger tried to help his grandpa ease into a chair, then said to Emily, "Could I bring you that stool for your feet?"

"Why, yes, Roger, that's very thoughtful of you."

"He's always like that," said Darlene proudly, smugly

Roger often wished he were not so "good." He thought some of Nolan's misbehaviors rather enviable, like the time a year ago when he had stuffed Roger's teddy bear down the toilet and caused an awful mess, but Roger could never seem to think up things like that. Since his very earliest memories, his mother and almost everyone else had told him how good he was, how thoughtful he was, what a little gentleman. Sometimes he almost believed it himself, but it wasn't really true. He had plenty of bad thoughts, like wishing his grandpa would die so Nolan would spend more time with him, like wishing it was him not Nolan the other boys came outside and yelled at, like . . . He sat down primly on the raised hearth. They didn't see his goodness so much here, Price and Fern didn't at least. He did remember that and it scared him. If he let himself go, if he did mean things, would he still be Roger?

"I believe the wind's dropped off a bit," chattered Emily. "You must remember, Darlene, how it blows out here."

Anne and Price were sitting at opposite sides of the fireplace, exchanging quick glances now and then. Nolan stood, fidgeting uneasily, behind Grandpa's chair. Kiersten hovered by the doorway into the dining room, trying to look but not be seen by these boys who were to be her brothers for the summer. She wasn't at all sure she wanted brothers, not when they were bigger than she was and had come so suddenly.

Darlene said to Anne, "Haven't they got you in pants yet, out riding the range or crawling under some greasy tractor?"

"Not yet," said Anne coolly. She did have pants. A large order had been made for her a month after she and Kiersten came to the ranch. Now she was learning to ride. She turned to Mr. Nolan.

"My father's people were from County Mayo."

"Were they now? Were they?"

And that started them off, seeking names and places in common. "I don't think I knew any Cavanaughs, not well, that is to say, but . . ."

As the tea things were brought in, he was asking, "And what might your first husband's name have been? The father of this wee lassie who looks Irish enough."

"His last name was Owen," said Anne.

"Oh, aye, a Scot," he said, not able to keep the disdain out of his voice. And that was an end of that subject.

Looking at Anne, but making a gesture toward the skulking Kiersten, Darlene said, "It's a shame she has all those freckles. Isn't there a cream that would take at least some of them off?"

Anne felt mildly rueful about Kiersten. She had wanted to get

97

"all dressed up" when she was told about the boys' coming. By now, she looked worn and tattered, pinafore wrinkled, blouse askew, hair looking as if it had never seen a comb.

She said coolly, "We like freckles," and caught an approving wink from Price.

Emily shakily poured tea and Penny handed round the cups, then made a brusque excuse to leave the room again. Anne got up and passed the plates of sandwiches and little cakes. Fern plumped herself down in a chair and threw a look at Darlene, who had always maintained that Fern should eat in the kitchen and keep her mouth out of family business.

Emily said to Clarence, "We always had tea when my husband's parents were alive. Someone would take it out to the working men, even. I do think it makes a nice touch, especially in the summer, when the light lasts so long and dinner is so late."

Darlene said shrilly, *"Nolan! Now* look what you've done! Dropped cake on the rug. Can't you *ever* behave?" She had also seen him watching Price, with that hungry look she hated.

Price picked up the cake with a napkin. It didn't leave a mark.

"Is your little girl clumsy and awkward and careless?" Darlene asked Anne.

Anne said, "Kiersten, do come in now. Sit here on the hearth rug and share a sandwich with Nolan. Here, I'll cut it for you."

"Rogie never makes a mess," Darlene began, but her father broke in to say, "How many calves do you have this spring, Price?"

So the talk turned to the ranch, and then to Clarence's boasting about what a good price he had got for his dad's place.

"I was wounded in the war, you know," he said with some pride. "Shrapnel in my back. They couldn't get it all out. It gives me a lot of trouble. I can't work long at anything, so we need the money. I don't want *my* Darlene to have to work all her life, and that place they live in isn't fit for her. It won't be easy to make the money last, not with two growing boys, but I guess we have to do what we can."

Tea was finally over. Anne and Fern gathered plates, cups, napkins and went into the kitchen.

"You know, Price," said Liam wistfully, "it could be that I won't be here again. I'd admire to have a look around your buildings again."

"All right," said Price, relieved. He got up and unobtrusively offered the old man his arm as an adjunct to the cane. "Do you want to come, Clarence?"

"May as well," said Clarence, sounding bored. He stood up and, sure everyone was watching, gave Darlene a long possessive kiss on the mouth.

"Can I go?" asked Nolan, tensely and very softly. He wanted to look at Price, but his mother wouldn't like that, so he looked at no one.

"Aye, come along, Chappie," said Liam without waiting for anyone else to answer.

Roger said sensibly, "I guess I won't go this time. I might get my good clothes messed up."

"That's my good boy," purred Darlene as the others went out.

The truth was Roger didn't want to go He was afraid of being left here, didn't want his mother to leave, yet, sometimes he hated his mother. She never tried to see who he really was, didn't even imagine him as a real person, completely separate from herself. Nolan *would* go, of course. Nolan knew him, far better than anyone else in the world, but Nolan loved this place and he wasn't afraid of anything. Nolan rarely ever had best clothes, just Roger's hand-me-downs, because he was always tearing something or getting dirty. Roger wished *he*'d get dirty. He had tried it but it went against his own grain.

"I've brought some pictures," Darlene was saying. "They're of the twins, made over the last two years. I thought you might like to see them, Mother Savage."

Emily was taken aback. Darlene had never called her that before.

"Why, yes, I'd love to," she said, "but I must find my glasses."

Roger sprang up. "Let me get them for you, Grandmother."

"Why, all right, dear. That's very courteous of you. I believe I left them on the dining room sideboard."

As Anne came in from the kitchen, Darlene was handing the grandmother a fat packet of pictures and saying, "Excuse me a minute. I have to go to the bathroom. Oh, don't worry, I know where it is."

As Roger walked past Kiersten, she said shyly, "I've got a cat."

He seemed to ignore her

"Isn't he just the dearest child?" whispered Emily to Anne. "You rarely see children, particularly boys, with such beautiful manners."

"I think he's scary," said Anne grimly, then softening, "and sad."

They looked at the pictures and Anne was bored. Fully two-thirds of them were of Roger and none of Nolan alone.

Emily said, "I have always thought twins ought to have rhyming names, or at least names that begin with the same letter. Their middle names are Paul and Price, but Darlene would never have them called that."

While the women were occupied, Roger went near Kiersten again.

"Where is your cat? In the barn?"

"No, she's a house cat. Do you want to see her? When Daddy's very best cattle dog has puppies, I get to keep one."

They went through the dining room and into the hall.

"We just moved my room today," said Kiersten proudly. "I get to be with Penny while you're here. You're not really my brother, are you?"

"No," said Roger. "I'm your stepbrother."

"What does that mean?"

"I don't know for sure," Roger had to admit. "I think it means something about we don't have the same blood. That's what Mother said, something like that."

"Good," she said matter-of-factly. "I don't want any brothers, 'specially *your* brother."

"Why not? He's okay."

"He likes my daddy too much. I was watching him, and he's with my Daddy now."

Penny was not in their room. Pussycat lay sedately on Kiersten's bed.

"Is it a girl cat?"

"Yes, but she can't have any kittens. She had a operation."

"It's harder with cats, but do you know how to tell the difference between girl and boy things?"

"Yes, you know what they wear and what their names are and—"

"No, but I mean the *real* way?"

"Well . . ."

"Do you know how babies get made?"

"They grow inside their Mommy's tummies and then they come out."

"I saw my mother and—our new daddy one night when they thought everyone was asleep. I mean how babies get started. If you take down your panties, I'll take down my clothes. Boys and girls have different things that fit together. It's the same with dogs, and even cats, I guess. Want to see?"

She nodded dubiously.

"Go ahead."

"Let me see you first."

At the barns, Liam had a hundred questions and comments. Clarence trailed along, uninterested and disdainful.

Finally, Nolan was able to get in a word. "Is that Dearie?" he asked, indicating an old mare with her foal in one of the corrals.

"It is," Price said, surprised that the boy should remember the gentle mare. "How do you like her new foal? Do you want to get in with them? Here, I'll just lift you over "

Liam hobbled around the corner of the corral to see better. Clarence dropped a cigarette stub in the strawy dirt and, irritably, Price ground it out with his heel.

"Well," Clarence said to him softly, leering a little, "what would you say? After a chance at both of them, wouldn' you say I'm gettin' a better deal with my first time than you've got your second time around?"

Price, eyes sparking with anger, said, "I'd say, I wish you well. She'll stay with you, maybe, until the money runs out, and by then you'll be goddamn glad to be done with her. And I'd say you look like a fool with her lipstick all over your mouth."

Clarence glared at him, mouth working, then turned sharply back toward the house. When he was out of their sight, he scrubbed at his mouth with a handkerchief.

When Darlene finally returned to the living room, Anne stood up.

"I want to see where the kids have gone," she said.

"Oh, I'm sure they're playing somewhere nicely," said Darlene complacently and sat down to burble over the pictures again with Emily.

"Have Roger and Kiersten been in here?" Anne asked Fern in the kitchen.

"How would I know, honey chile? I'se jes' the ole maid-of-all-work, slavin' over a hot dishpan." But Fern was smiling. Anne had tried to make her go back to the living room while *she* slaved over a hot dishpan. "No, no kids have been in here."

Anne walked up the first four steps in the hall. Their door was open, hers and Price's, and she had made certain of closing it before these people came. So this was why Darlene had taken so long. Of course she knew where things were. This had been *her* room first. Anne took a cursory but furious glance around. She had been in here, snooping, for maybe fifteen minutes. I ought to go down and slap her face, she thought, grinding her teeth.

Instead, she went on to the next room, Penny and Kiersten's, and there they were, Roger and Kiersten, with the bottom parts of their clothes off, exploring eagerly.

Anne tried to be calm. "All right," she said with only a little sharpness. "Both of you get dressed. This is not a thing to be done."

Kiersten looked frightened. "He told me to and I—"

"I didn't," said Roger defiantly. *"She* wanted me to."

They were both scrambling back into their clothes. She'll tell my mother, thought Roger with a surge of hope, then I won't have to stay here. But *they* were doing it—Mother and Clarence, or something. Still, it must be pretty bad the way *she's* looking.

But, no, his mother would never believe that he had been bad. It was the little girl's fault. But these people here at Secesh didn't seem as easily fooled as his mother. When he tried his hardest at home to be bad, it just always ended up with Nolan getting the blame. The truth was, his mother was stupid. This was a word recently added to Roger's vocabulary, and it fit her so well. Maybe all women were stupid. His grandmother seemed to be. And now this Anne was not bawling them out, or spanking or slapping them around. She just stood there, waiting, until they were both dressed, then straightened their clothes a little, though Roger knew his didn't need it. Then she said warningly, "Nothing like this is to happen again. Do you both understand? Only certain people undress together, and you are not two of them. Kiersten, go into the kitchen and help Fern with something."

Kiersten ran off, but Roger walked demurely down the hall ahead of Anne.

In a corner of the living room, Clarence was saying to Darlene, "I've put the kids' stuff on the porch. We're going, as soon as your dad gets back up here."

"But I told them we'd stay for supper—"

"No, I don't want to drive that road after dark. It ain't fit for a new car, even when you can see good. Now come on, get ready."

"I want to," she began, and he said warningly, "Do you want to be in New York by next week or not?"

Darlene flounced a little, going over to pick up her purse. Oh well, let him be masterful for now. She'd take him down a notch or two soon enough. She smiled to herself at what a foolish man he was.

Emily, compelled to be polite, said uncertainly, "We had planned that you'd be here for dinner. I think Anne and Fern have—"

Darlene cut in, speaking to Clarence. "I'm not doing anything to upset *those* plans, sugar. If we just—"

"All you want to do," he said vehemently, "is wave us two men under each other's noses."

Emily withdrew discreetly.

"I don't give a good goddamn about her, but I've had enough of your showin' yourself off to what used to be your husband and in-laws. Now, are you comin', or do you want to live here again? I guess your daddy does."

They were on the porch when the three came slowly up from the buildings.

"Rogie," Darlene was calling back into the house, already feeling alone without the child to exhibit. She held Roger close for long moments and whispered to him. For Nolan, there was only a perfunctory glance and, irritably, "Try not to make trouble."

Clarence said, with so much defiance his voice cracked, "I *guess* we'll be back around Labor Day. We'll let you know."

Nolan went down onto the drive and hugged Grandpa. "I'll miss you," he said, and it was very true.

"Aye, Chappie, it won't be the same around home," said Liam, his eyes misting.

Roger came and shook hands with him manfully.

And then the car was gone in a cloud of dust.

They all breathed sighs and relaxed consciously, all except Roger.

"Well," Price said, "I've got one horse half shod. I'd better go and finish with him."

"Can I go with you?" asked Nolan immediately.

"Me, too," said Kiersten.

"Go and change your clothes, Kierstie," said Anne. "And close the door when you're dressing."

"I won't go," said Roger pompously, though he was inwardly terrified. She *had* left him, here among these strangers. Anne was going to tell his father what he had done. . . . But he said determinedly, "I can take our things to our room if you tell me which one. I've brought some coloring books and some books to read."

Alone on the porch, Anne told Price about the incident in Kiersten's room. They frowned together, silent for several moments, then he said, "Well, it's a thing that happens. Let's just pretend it didn't, unless it comes up again."

"That's what I thought," she said, feeling better. She wanted to tell him about Darlene's intrusion into their bedroom, but he looked too tired, too strained.

He said, "I appreciate you're being willing to have them here. You do know that, don't you? You're an exceptional person."

"They really are as different as they look," she said thoughtfully. "Just from this little time, I'd say Nolan needs love and Roger needs help. Maybe we can do something for both of them through the summer."

Nolan and Kiersten were outside the corral where Price was working. Nolan didn't feel safe yet. Maybe tomorrow, when his mother and Clarence should be on their way back to Denver, he could really relax. He said to the little girl, "Can you ride horses?"

"No, but I'm going to learn."

"I rode horses when I was littler than you."

"You didn't."

"Yes, I did, and some day I'm going to have a ranch just—just like this one."

"So am I, but we won't have it together because I don't like you and you're not my really brother."

"I don't like you either. I bet you can't climb this tree."

"I could but I don't want to."

"You're just saying that because you can't really do it."

"I can but I won't. I won't do anything you say. You can't have *my* daddy. I won't ever, ever have a ranch with you or be your sister or climb a tree or do anything that *you* tell me."

"Who cares?" said Nolan.

7

It was the end of Christmas vacation. Roger and Nolan were more than eight and a half. Nolan was in the kitchen, peeling potatoes for his mother.

The money from Clarence's father's orchard had run out and for several weeks now Darlene had been working as waitress in the restaurant of a big downtown department store. She was angry that the money didn't last, but glad enough to go back to work. She had hated staying home. Clarence had a job, too, driving a garbage truck. He had held this one all of two weeks. With the money they earned, plus Clarence's and Liam's pensions, plus the child support from Price, they were able to live very comfortably. For more than two years they had lived in a very nice neighborhood, but six weeks ago had moved back to this one, where most of the houses were small and drab. Here, there was room for a garden, which Liam and the boys would tend. Darlene preferred to spend money on clothes for herself and Roger, on going out at night, rather than on the higher rent. She liked having the newest, best car in the neighborhood, showing herself off to the neighbors in better clothes, being what Clarence inelegantly called "a big frog in a little pond."

People had said she'd never stay married to Clarence, but there were some advantages to it. She could see other men for instance, and if there were any slip-ups, which she never intended should happen again, *if* she got pregnant, Clarence would be handy. Also, he helped with the boys, taking pride in Roger's achievements, trying to knock some sense and manners into Nolan. Most important, Clarence adored Darlene. She needed that, someone's adulation in which to bask and preen. Clarence was certainly not much, but he would do, remain faithful to her beauty and cleverness all his life. She should have married a younger, handsomer man, but it was hard to find one, with the prospect of some money, who would take on twins, along with an infirm father, as well as a new wife. Clarence had followed her around like a wistful, hungry puppy for years, every time he was in Denver.

The house where they now lived was similar to that which Liam had rented when he first came to work here. It stood on a two-acre plot, room for the garden whose produce Liam would can, with the boys' help. Many of the neighbors kept pigs, chickens, a milk cow It was a neighborhood near tank farms, railroad sidings, actually outside the city. Darlene was ashamed of living there, but the low rent afforded her many other things. There were two bedrooms downstairs, along with the living room and kitchen. One bedroom was for her and Clarence, the other for Liam and Nolan. Roger had the upstairs room, large, with two dormer windows. Darlene had enjoyed fixing the place up with new furniture, especially Roger's room. Liam and Nolan had some of the old things they had moved from house to house. And there was an old, falling-down barn in back, where Liam and Nolan played their infernal, everlasting music when the weather was warm enough.

Darlene was irked now, frustrated and sullen, because she had to prepare supper. She shouldn't have to do that after working all day. Usually Liam had the meal ready when she and Clarence came home, but he had been in too much pain for the past two days to get out of bed for more than a few minutes, or so he claimed

"Nolan, you're wasting those potatoes," she snapped "Don't take off so much."

There was no reason why the kid couldn't have got supper, she was thinking. God knew, he didn't study or do anything else worthwhile.

Nolan was thinking of the past three summers, which the boys had spent at Secesh. Last year during haying he had driven the tractor with the scatter rake a good deal of the time, and he could ride well now. Once, when they were moving cattle, his horse had shied at something and done some bucking, but he had managed to stay on. If he was riding a good horse, he could be a real help with the stock. He wanted to stay there forever. It was perfect except for Hugh, who didn't like him. There was little snot-nosed Kiersten, who constantly followed him, trying to do everything he did, and sometimes succeeding. But Roger didn't like it at the ranch, though he liked Fern and Anne a lot, especially Anne. Still, he wouldn't have been going, and that meant neither would Nolan, except that Clarence insisted on "getting them out of our hair for a while."

And Roger needed to be with Nolan in a way that both of them recognized but neither understood. Nolan thought often of running away to Secesh, feeling sure that Price would find some way to keep him. There was a forlornness in his love for Price. At this age, he could not recognize that the love was returned, though he did feel that Price wanted him at the ranch. But there was this need of Roger's, and he had been convinced over the years that Roger should have what he wanted. There was also Grandpa's and Nolan's love for one another. This was the only love of which Nolan was certain. Just now Nolan's hands were finally getting big enough to play the guitar, the instrument he wanted most in the world to play. He tried to stretch his hands every day, fretting the guitar, and he feared his grandpa might die, with no one with whom to share his music and stories.

Sometimes last summer, when Nolan had happened to be in the house and there seemed to be no one else around, he would slip into the living room and try to play the piano. He played very softly, some things he had heard Grandmother Emily play, and some other tunes that came into his head. Grandmother had gone to live with her sister in California and now came to visit for only a few weeks in the summer. She was giving Kiersten piano lessons and sometimes played other things afterward.

Anne had caught him playing once. "Nolan, that's wonderful!" she had cried, startling him painfully. "Do you have a piano at home? Where did you learn to play?"

She had even brought it up at the supper table. "He ought to have lessons, too."

Price had frowned, saying with something of scorn in his voice, "Piano lessons are fine for a girl, but a boy, getting ready to be a man, maybe a ranch hand some day, has more other things than he can possibly learn in the course of a summer."

Nolan had been embarrassed, ashamed, but he was learning to read music this year, in a choral group at school. After watching and listening for a while to Grandpa's music, other things he heard or made up came so easily that note reading was, maybe, a waste of time. He had flushed and lowered his head at Price's obvious disapproval that day last summer, but the music was there, always there, and it had to come out somehow. Just now he was humming in his mind an old Irish lullaby. He did not hum aloud. Mama didn't like him to do that.

Taking up another potato, he thought of what Christmas must be like at Secesh. If there was snow enough, they went to get the trees with horses and the old sleigh. They made a party of it, Kiersten had gone into a long explanation of that. If there was not enough snow, they took one of the four-wheel-drive vehicles and it was still a party. There would have been a big tree in the living room, touching the ceiling, and so many gifts piled around its base. Fern would have cooked so many good things to eat. . . .

Nolan didn't have to think much about the potatoes. He had helped Grandpa enough with getting suppers ready. Roger had helped, too, when Nolan had first begun to try, but then he had stopped, just as he had lost interest in the garden. They had had a small garden at the other house, and much more room inside the house. Next spring, Grandpa was already planning, they would have a huge garden. Roger had tried to learn to play Grandpa's banjo, too, but he had tried only once. When he found he could make no progress in his first attempt, the thing was finished for him.

Like the bicycle.

Roger had told Nolan he prayed every night for a month for a bicycle for Christmas, and he had got it. Nolan had been given a set of six small cars.

"Maybe you'll have a bicycle," Clarence had told Nolan scathingly, "when you're old enough and not so clumsy."

And, "Yes," put in his mother, "when you *deserve* one. Look at Rogie's report cards, straight A's, and what do you do? Just barely squeak through is what."

"You're old enough and you deserve a bicycle," Grandpa had said that night, seeming to talk to the darkness, seeming to have the words wrung from him. "If I'd known they were going to do it this way, I'd have kept back more of my own money."

Grandpa always cashed his pension checks, keeping a little pocket money for himself and turning the rest over to Darlene. Price sent extra money at Christmas and birthdays, but Darlene was the only one who knew this, since she was the one who always opened the mail and looked it over first.

Roger had learned quickly to ride the bike in a wobbly fashion. It was a mild, open winter and they could spend a lot of time outside. He was the envy of the neighborhood, but refused to let anyone, including Nolan, touch the bicycle. There came a day when he fell on the graveled street. It happened that no one saw him and he wasn't hurt, but sorely, angrily embarrassed. The bicycle's red paint was badly scratched on one side by the gravel.

Roger had gone to where Nolan and Jeff Bixby were playing marbles on a spot of dry ground. He said, very soberly, "Nolan, I want to talk to you."

When Nolan came away with him, Roger said, "You can have the bicycle."

"What? Why?"

"I don't care about it any more. It was fun for a few days, but now I'm just—not interested. I want you to have it."

This sort of thing was always happening, Roger's wanting something so badly, and then, once he had it, having it pall on him in a short time. Just a few months ago, he had thrown a coveted spelling trophy into the trash. Their mother was still wondering where that was and accusing Nolan of having stolen it out of spite and jealousy.

Nolan wanted desperately to try to ride the bicycle. He went to where Roger had left it, by the back steps, hearing Roger say to Jeff, "I'm pretty good at marbles."

But Jeff had said, "Naw, I want to watch Chappie. Maybe *he*'ll share the bike."

Nolan walked the bicycle over to the next street, in case his mother or Clarence looked outside. He was elated at how well he could balance, better than Roger had done on his first day, or his second. He was rolling right along, up by the highway, the neighborhood kids watching in admiration and envy, when he hit a large rock and fell to the side, bringing the bicycle down on top of him. The left side of his face was badly scratched and bleeding. His left arm ached, bone deep, but he got up quickly and looked at the bike. It had fallen on him. It was all right, but only then did he see the scratches along its right side.

Roger was in the little crowd of kids. He said sympathetically, "Here, let me walk it back home. You're bleeding on your shirt and something will have to be done to get the dirt out of those scratches on your face."

"You wanted me to get blamed for that," said Nolan bitterly, trying not to cry and gesturing at the marred side of the bicycle.

"I didn't, Chappie. Honest I didn't."

Clarence was in the kitchen, looking through the newspaper, a can of beer beside him on the table. Grandpa had hobbled down to the bar, a block away, as he often did when there wasn't snow. Mama wasn't home yet, but there was no way of slipping past Clarence to get to the bathroom.

"What's happened *now?*" he snarled at sight of Nolan's scratched and bleeding face. "Well, answer me! Are you deaf?"

"I was riding the bike and—"

"You was what!" a great yell of anger.

"I let him," said Roger quickly, in mollifying tones. "I wanted to share it. I even want to give—"

Clarence got up and walked past them to the back door. There was no escape. He peered at the bicycle in the early dusk.

"Scratched the bejesus out of it, didn't you? And it not a week out of the store!" He was taking off his belt. "Ripped a hole in your shirt for your poor Mama to have to fix after she's been working all day! Blood on it, too!"

"He didn't do the scratches," Roger said earnestly. "I did, and then I . . ."

"Roger, you're supposed to be such a God-awful smart kid. Why are you always takin' up for this little bastard? Go on about your business, before I lay a couple on you."

When Clarence whipped, you had to take off your shirt, undershirt, too, if you had one, and let down your pants, shorts included. He struck with the belt, from shoulders to thighs. After he had hit Nolan several times, he yelled, "You're the one scratched up that bike, ain't you?"

"No," gasped Nolan. They had talked about how much he cried as a baby, but he had stopped crying after that first time they were taken away from Secesh.

"No, *what!*" shrieked Clarence, with a particularly fierce lash.

"No, sir," whispered Nolan between clenched teeth. Nothing they could do would make him call this man "Daddy."

The beating went on, as usual, until welts, oozing blood, covered his back, buttocks, and thighs.

"Now," said Clarence, triumphant, panting, "take that shirt an' wash the blood out of it. Then go to your room. Don't give no thought to supper. You ain't havin' it. Don't let me see your ugly mug again tonight."

Nolan used the shirt to bathe the dirt from his face, then, reaching round as best he could, to wash off his back. He then washed out the shirt itself and hung it on the shower rod. He crept to the room he shared with Grandpa. His face had almost stopped bleeding. Blood from his back might get on the sheets, but he couldn't help that now. He was shaking with cold, weakness, and anger, and felt sure he would throw up. He could hear them in the kitchen. Mama and Grandpa were both home. If Grandpa had been here earlier, all this wouldn't have happened to him. Mama and Clarence saved the really bad things until Grandpa wasn't around the house.

When the nausea had passed and the burning pain was a little less, he lay there and thought about Roger. Why did Roger need him? For blaming things on? But Roger had tried to stop Clarence, hadn't he? Once, last summer, Nolan had speculated aloud that it might be arranged so that he, Nolan, could stay on at Secesh forever, and Roger had said, "Don't, Chappie. We *need* to be together. Brothers need that, especially twins."

Nolan had heard somewhere that identical twins, separated at birth, could find each other just by instinct, when they were grown. He and Roger were far from identical, and their twinness meant little to Nolan. It was no special tie. He wondered if he loved Roger, or if Roger loved him. He hadn't meant him to take the blame for the bicycle, or had he? Roger was constantly at him to spend his time only with Roger. "Don't play with those other kids. They don't deserve it.

Let's put a puzzle together or something." When Roger was sad, which was rather often, he wanted Nolan with him, though Nolan rarely understood the reasons for the sadness. And Roger wanted to share his triumphs, even if Nolan's only part in them came from looking on. More than anything, Roger wanted his brother's overt respect and approval, though neither of them could realize or understand this at the age of eight, and it would be more than twenty years before the full realization, still without full understanding, would come to Nolan.

Mama and Clarence had gone out that night. Before Grandpa did the dishes, he came to Nolan with warm water, soft cloths, and a cream for the cuts and bruises.

"It'll get on the sheets," said Nolan, meaning the cream. He spoke dazedly, between chattering teeth.

"Devil take the sheets," snapped Grandpa with tears in his eyes. "I'll wash 'em myself tomorrow."

And Roger kept saying brokenly, "Chappie, I'm sorry. The bike's still yours. I'm so sorry. Could you say it's all right?"

"Of course it's not all right," Liam told him curtly.

Roger began to cry. "But I didn't mean this to happen. I only want to be sure he knows that. I only want to know he understands . . ."

"It's all right," Nolan said fuzzily, "but I don't want the bike."

"But I want—"

"Leave him be, Roger," Liam said unsteadily. "Can't you just leave the boy be?"

Now, two days later, peeling potatoes, Nolan dreamed of Secesh. He dreamed of it without Hugh, who was high-handed and bossy, refusing to think of him as anything but a little kid, when Nolan should be next to his father or at least to Reuben in the chain of command some day. He loved the land, liked almost any task they set for him. Roger said they would share the ranch four ways, Hugh, Penny, and the twins. He ignored Kiersten's rights, cute, freckle-faced little Kiersten, whom Price had adopted. She was only a stepchild, Roger had pointed out once, as he and Nolan were stepchildren of Clarence's, but it wasn't like that at all for Kierstie. Price loved her, wanted her to be a part of things. Each time the boys came back after a summer at the ranch, their mother would ask something like, "Haven't Price and Anne got a baby yet? You just wait. They'll have a houseful. You twins will be done out of your inheritance."

Nolan didn't believe that. They might have the babies, but Price, his real dad, wanted him at Secesh—didn't he? Price was cautious, reluctant to give praise or indications of love, but Nolan believed in him. Nolan was certain that he loved Price; next to Grandpa, he loved him more than anyone in the whole world. Price was just careful not to show much because he knew Nolan always had to go away at the end of summer. Price was only demonstrative toward Anne, and sometimes toward Kiersten. Sometimes this made Nolan jealous and wistful, but it didn't mean that he, Nolan, didn't love everyone at the ranch. There were Fern and Anne, even Penny, who mothered him, Reuben, who cursed and yelled at him for wrong moves at work, even Hugh, a little, because he had learned a lot just by watching Hugh closely, but most of all, he loved Price—and Kiersten.

He smiled, remembering how he and Kiersten argued and quarreled about almost everything. She was tough. She didn't cry or pout when her points were proved absolutely groundless, but stuck to them like a fierce little bulldog, and he did the same. At first, they hadn't liked each other at all. Most of the time they pretended they still felt that way. But they were learning together, and now and then one would give the other a grudging look or word of admiration. Kiersten got to stay at Secesh the year round and—

Nolan's thoughts were broken abruptly because he had sliced his thumb badly with the potato-peeling knife. He sat staring at the thumb for a few moments. It didn't hurt, but blood was running down, all over the potatoes. He moved to the sink to wash them and to let the cold water run over the cut.

Darlene screamed. She couldn't bear the sight of blood, even someone else's. The boy just kept standing there, dripping blood into the sink. Desperately, she shoved him away from her. Nolan stumbled backward and fell, striking his head a vicious blow on the corner of the table. He lay still then, and there was more blood. Darlene screamed again.

Liam struggled up from his bed and, fumbling with his cane, managed to totter into the kitchen, his leg aching so badly that it made him sick and dizzy. Roger ran down from his room, hearing his grandpa say, more harshly than he had ever spoken to his mother, "What have you done to him, lass?"

"Blood!" she cried hysterically. "His hand was bleeding all over . . ."

Liam managed to sit down on the floor. He couldn't kneel.

"Get clean wet cloths," he said curtly to Roger.

Chappie's head was cut to the bone just behind and above his left ear. He was breathing, but there scarcely seemed to be a pulse.

Liam said sharply, "Stop blithering, lass, and call an ambulance."

"An ambulance! Oh, Daddy, I didn't mean—"

"What the hell is all this?" demanded Clarence, who had come in with none of them hearing him.

Darlene flew into his arms and tried to explain amid wild sobs. "He was bleeding . . . cut himself . . . potatoes . . . oh, Clarence, you know I can't stand the sight of blood. . . ." And she drew back and vomited on the kitchen floor.

"We don't need any ambulance," Clarence snapped at Liam, stepping away from his wife a little. "The brat's probably faking. Nolan! Get up from there and—"

"Just stop that!" ordered Liam. "Roger, you call the ambulance. I can't do everything." He was holding cloths against Nolan's head, blood soaking them.

"He's dying!" cried Roger. "Look at—"

"*Call!*" cried Liam.

"I didn't mean it to happen!" wailed Darlene. "He's so clumsy. You know how clumsy he is. He just fell back . . ."

"No ambulance," snapped Clarence as Roger moved, trembling, toward the telephone. And, to Liam, "Do you have any idea what that would cost me, old man?"

"Maybe we'd better," sniffled Darlene. "We can't just let him . . . I wouldn't want him to . . ."

Ultimately, Clarence carried Nolan to the car, making sure, at Darlene's direction, that an old blanket was wadded under the bleeding head. Liam told them to wait until he dressed, but they drove off without him.

The old man sighed as he hobbled back into the kitchen, and there were tears in his eyes.

"Roger, Boy-o, you'll have to clean up all this mess, where your mother vomited, and the blood . . ."

"Grandpa, is he going to . . . ? Will Nolan be all right?"

"I don't know," said the old man shakily. "This is some Christmas holiday he's had."

Things had started going wrong with the bicycle thing, thought Roger, mopping with distaste at the floor. Was all of it his fault? If Nolan died . . . He *needed* Nolan. It wasn't fair for him to get hurt like this when Roger depended on him so much. Sometimes, Roger hated Nolan for that dependency. Nolan knew it was there, but was usually so closed to his brother. He seemed to be able to go away from Roger, even when they were in the same room together. He hurt Roger and Roger sometimes despised him, but he couldn't—die. There was no such thing as *one* twin, was there?

Nolan came back to consciousness slowly. There was a song in his mind, "Sammy's Bar." How could that be, with the pain? He couldn't bear it. The song had to stop or . . . a new wave of oblivion was sweeping toward him, and he pressed into it gratefully.

113

The next time he came near the surface he knew he was in a hospital. He had never been in a hospital, but he had been in doctors' offices, and the sounds, the smells . . .

It was like the time when he had been four, shortly after they had left Secesh. He had had to go to the doctor then. He had been hungry. His mother was fixing lunch, having just got up after her night job. Grandpa was gone out somewhere, Roger was in his room. He supposed he had been whining. They said he had used to whine a lot. Suddenly, his mother had grabbed him, dragged him to the sink, and poured boiling water from the teakettle over his arm. He remembered screaming and screaming, even when they got him to the doctor's office. His mother had told everyone that he had spilled the water on himself, that he was such a clumsy, awkward child, always getting into things where he had no business, that sometimes she had doubts about his sanity. Somehow Nolan had known he mustn't contradict her. When they had come home, Grandpa had taken Nolan in his arms and rocked him. Then his mother had cried.

"Don't look at me that way, Daddy. The way you're looking, anybody would think it was my fault. I believe you care more about him than you do about me, about my feelings. Don't you know what *I've* been through?"

Finally, Nolan had fallen asleep in Grandpa's arms. But there had been other such times in doctors' offices. Never the same doctor. But this was not Grandpa's arms. He was too big for that sort of thing now anyway.

He opened his eyes for a moment. The pain in his head blurred everything, but he saw that he lay on a table in a small cubicle with a curtain drawn across its open side. There were many things in cabinets, bigger things on the floor. A bottle of something hung above him and what looked like blood dripped rapidly through a tube and into his arm through a needle at the end of the tube. He closed his eyes, fighting nausea. "As I went down to Sammy's bar . . ." He could feel that someone had come into the room and was looking down at him, but he kept very still and didn't open his eyes. "Hey, the last boat's a-leavin' . . ." How *could* there be music when he hurt like this?

The person went away and in a few moments, there were voices outside the curtain.

A stranger said, "His skull isn't fractured and that's a wonder."

"Oh, I'm *so* relieved!" cried Mama softly.

And Clarence said jovially, "He's a tough little—kid."

"We've noticed," said the other carefully, "that his face has been badly scratched recently. There's quite a bad bruise on his left arm and there are recent—stripes on his back . . . ?"

"Wrecked his brother's bicycle," said Clarence rather sullenly after a moment. "Both got bikes for Christmas. They're twins. Nolan took the other bike and really messed it up. He's a bad actor at times. Needs a firm hand to keep any control at all."

Darlene hurried into the conversation. "Sometimes," she said pathetically, "we can't help having doubts about his being—you know, completely—right in the head."

"Tell me about this head injury," said the doctor coldly.

"He was trying to peel potatoes," she said. "Sometimes, he tries to help. He cut his thumb—I knew he'd do something like that. He held it and ran around the kitchen, screaming. Then he slipped or tripped or something—he's always been a clumsy, awkward child—and he fell against the corner of the table. Doctor, when he comes to, we can take him home, can't we? We really can't afford a hospital and I swear he'll have care as good as—"

"If you'll just sit in the waiting room," said the doctor crisply.

Nolan wished he was asleep again. His head hurt so badly, and now his thumb ached and throbbed as well. He stole a look at the thumb. It was encased in a great, fat, pressure bandage.

"So you're awake," said the doctor, coming in through the curtain and smiling at him. He didn't look very old and his eyes, when he smiled, were merry blue, something like Grandpa's. "My name's Dr. Lewis. What's yours?"

"Nolan."

"Nolan what?"

"Savage." Clarence didn't want to adopt them and Darlene had agreed. It might stop the child support payments. Anyway, Nolan would never have said his name was Tate, even if it legally had been.

"Well, you look like something of a savage right now, all scratched and bandaged. Tell me, how did you come to get this knock on the head?"

Nolan longed to say that his mother had pushed him, that Clarence beat him with a belt at least once a week, to tell all of it to this very clean young man, but that would only make everything worse at home and he was going to have to go back there.

"I fell," he said tiredly. "I cut my thumb and then I—fell."

"I see. How about these scratches on the side of your face and the bruise on your arm?"

"I wrecked my brother's bicycle."

"And the welts on your back?"

"I—my—Clarence punished me. About the bicycle."

"And do these things happen often?"

"No." It was not quite a lie. There had been only the one incident about the bicycle.

115

"I understand you have a twin brother."

"Yes."

A nurse came in with a syringe and some other things

"We're going to give you a shot for the pain in your head It's pretty bad, huh?"

As he checked the boy's eyes and other reflexes, Dr. Lewis went on talking. "How old are you?"

"I'll be nine in April."

Why couldn't he stop talking? Just leave him alone? The shot hurt, too, and there was a lot of it. He wished they'd just let him lie here, on this padded table, and fall asleep. Almost, he wished he'd be sick enough never to go home again. Then they'd have to call Price, wouldn't he? . . . But there was Grandpa at home, who must be very worried. And there was Roger . . .

"Does your brother get punished with a belt or strap?"

"He doesn't do things that get him into trouble."

"And is he awkward and clumsy?"

"No."

"How did you get these scars on your arm?"

"I don't remember."

In the waiting room, Dr. Lewis said, "We're giving him a unit of blood. His reflexes are all right and his mind seems clear enough, considering. I suppose when he's finished with the blood, you can take him home, if you feel you absolutely have to. It seems to me he ought to stay here for at least a couple of days, under observation. You must watch him carefully, for vomiting, dizziness, blurring vision, or anything unusual. He certainly has a concussion. I'll have to ask you to sign a paper that says he was released against medical advice. He—"

"What do you mean?" demanded Clarence belligerently "He's our kid. We do what we damn well please."

"That's what bothers me," said the doctor grimly. "It looks to me as if this boy is being mistreated. I could call in other authorities Not nearly enough is being done yet about battered children. If you treated your dog as it looks as if you treat this boy, anyone could turn you in and have it taken away from you. If you want to sign the paper, I have to let you take him. We've got him sedated. He's not likely to wake up until some time tomorrow morning. I understand you both work—"

"His grandpa will be at home with him," Darlene said quickly "He fairly dotes on the boy."

"I sincerely hope someone does," said the doctor tersely "If he shows any of the signs I've mentioned, vomiting, dizziness, blurred vision, high fever, he should be brought back here immediately

116

Now, if you want him to leave, this is the paper. He should come back in a week to have the stitches out."

Darlene said a little frantically, "Did he talk to you, doctor? Did he . ."

"I won't sign another paper," blustered Clarence. "We've already wrote an' signed enough to cost a mint."

"Are you his legal guardian? I understood you were a stepfather."

"Huh?"

"I'm his guardian," said Darlene. "Clarence, I'm going to sign it so we can all get out of this horrible place."

Clarence carried Nolan to the bed in the room he shared with Liam. He all but dropped him onto it as Liam held back the covers and Roger hovered near. Darlene brought a bucket. "In case he vomits," she said with revulsion.

"What did the doctors say?" demanded Liam.

"Said his head wasn' cracked," grunted Clarence. "But I'll tell you one thing: this has just about ruint my back. I'll have to call in sick tomorrow for sure."

He hobbled away into the kitchen as Liam and Roger began gently to get Nolan into his worn pajamas. At the hospital, they had taken off the bloodied clothes and put him into a gown, but he needed the flannel pajamas here. The bedroom was unheated, the night cold.

Briefly, Darlene told her father what they had said at the hospital, but not about the doctor's suspicions, nor that last paper she had signed. Then she said, "Rogie, did you have any supper? Did you, Daddy?"

"I don't want supper," said Roger. "I'm going to stay here by Nolan, all night."

"Oh now, honey, that's just a little silly, isn't it? School begins tomorrow. You'll want to be ready for that. It's already after midnight. Besides, Grandpa'll be here, right in the other bed."

"I want to stay," said Roger, thrusting out his lip.

"Well, all right, for a little while, but get a blanket to wrap around you." She wandered into the kitchen, where Clarence immediately demanded food.

Later, she tried to make Roger go to bed again, but he refused. She dragged a big soft rocker in from the living room.

"At least sit in this," she wheedled. "You can't stay in that old straight chair forever. And wrap up good. When you get tired, you go on up to your nice bed. I'll leave the kitchen light on so you can see how to get there." She kept fussing with the blanket, trying to make sure it was tucked around him warmly. Roger pushed her hands away in exasperation. She went on, "And we won't wake you for school.

117

It's so late and with your grades it won't hurt for you to miss a day "

When he knew his mother and Clarence were asleep, Roger slipped quietly up to his room to put on pajamas and robe, both of which he had received for Christmas. He hated this room because he was so often alone in it. Nolan ought to be sharing it. It was bigger than the one he and Grandpa had. Then they could do everything together. Nolan was always playing music, or running around with the rough, stupid neighborhood kids if he didn't have chores to do. Roger didn't like music. Actually, he was tone deaf, and this made for very strong feelings of resentment and jealousy over this thing he could not begin to conquer. He wasn't supposed to play with the neighborhood kids and he rarely had chores, unless he simply wanted to do them. Clarence wanted him out of the way, no matter how falsely nice he might seem, and Mama said he should just stay up here in the nice room, on which she had lavished so much time and money, and study or do "worthwhile things." Roger didn't need to do much studying to keep up his high average at school. Nolan was the one who needed to study, but he wouldn't unless punishment or dire threats made him get down to it, and he hardly had time for it anyway. Roger could have helped him so much, if he weren't so stubborn about coming up here and letting Roger help. Nolan liked to read. Maybe he just read more than Roger did, but not school books. They could read together up here, study, play games, put together puzzles and models, talk and talk. Roger got everything he wanted, too easily, so that he felt none of it was really worth having, but he couldn't get what he wanted most, a real share in his brother's life. Nolan shut him out of that. So far as material things were concerned, Nolan seemed to want nothing—except the music on Grandpa's old instruments—so that there was no apparent disappointment when he got nothing. Roger wanted to help Nolan, to make up to him somehow for the differentness with which they were treated, for the fact that things came so easily to him, but Nolan wouldn't let him. Nolan had that way of closing up, hiding within himself. Grandpa was Nolan's real friend, Grandpa and the people at Secesh. Roger liked them at Secesh, too, Anne, Fern, Penny and even Kiersten, but he knew Price had no liking for him. It seemed Price had just looked at him, that first summer they had gone to stay there, and dismissed him. He didn't expect anything of Roger, while Nolan went everywhere with him and learned what he liked. Roger didn't really want anything to do with the ranch, but he wished his real father wouldn't just push him aside in his mind. That seemed to make Nolan do the same thing even more. Sometimes it seemed Nolan resented the fact that they were even brothers, but they were, they were twins. Nolan didn't like them to be called "the twins." It seemed to mean to him an added tie, to which he was not willing to admit. Well, they were twins, and Roger went on, desperately wanting this one thing it seemed he could never have, his brother's respect, friendship, love.

He went silently downstairs and crept into the back bedroom. Grandpa had finally fallen asleep and was snoring rather loudly, the lamp still burning on the dresser. Nolan had turned on his side while Roger was out of the room. He lay with his back against the wall, knees drawn up, and he breathed through his mouth, shallowly and quickly. He might be awake.

"Nolan?"

No answer.

"Chappie?"

Still nothing.

Roger touched his face. It felt too warm. He squeezed himself into the narrow bed, lying precariously on its edge, until Nolan, moaning faintly, stretched out his drawn-up legs. Roger was suddenly angry. It seemed as if, even in sleep, Nolan tried to move away from him.

"I'm going to stay here tonight," Roger whispered fiercely. "No one can stop me, not even you, and you won't die. You won't *dare* die."

8

The rain began early that August day, around three or four in the morning. It came on a real storm, with high wind, lightning and thunder, but after an hour or so it settled into a gentle, straight-down rainfall. The storm wakened most of them in the house at Secesh, but when it calmed and rain went on falling, they sighed with pleasure, snuggled back into their covers and slept.

Price never needed an alarm clock. He woke with the first grayness of dawn. Anne was not so timed to the ranch, and doubted that she ever would be. He woke her, getting out of bed, muttering imprecations at the rain.

"Why not just relax?" she murmured sleepily. "It's past time you had a day off."

"We've got all that hay ready to be stacked or baled," he muttered crossly. "Four hands besides Reuben and Joe and us here at the house. There's plenty to do. I won't have them just sitting around, eating up profits. Besides, do you know what happens to hay crews if they get loose in the middle of the work? They don't come back, that's what."

"Yes, love, I've seen it happen," she reminded him. "Think how long I've been here. I'm not much of a greenhorn any more."

"Well, I don't want them to start thinking about going to Hurleigh, or even Mills Crossing. There's plenty to be done, work on the calving barn, that new corral we've got the poles for. I ought to go and check the upper ditches. Want to come with me? We can take the pickup. This is just a gentle rain."

"Price," she said slowly, "Dr. Swenson said he'd give us whatever tests he can, whenever we had the time. Could we go to Hurleigh today and get that taken care of?"

"But there's work on the machinery and—"

"We've been waiting over three years and I just don't get preg-

121

nant. Don't you want to try to find out why? If there's anything we could do . . .''

Already dressed in his working clothes, he came and sat on the bed and kissed her.

"Let me go and see how it feels around the bunkhouse. *You* relax for a while. I'll tell Fern you won't be in for breakfast yet. Probably all the kids will still be sleeping."

"No," she said, yawning, getting slowly out from under the covers. "I'm awake now, I may as well be doing something."

It was chilly and she hurried into her clothes. She had taken to wearing pants and work shirts during her first summer at Secesh and they were now her standard apparel. She could handle a horse reasonably well now, drive a tractor, milk the cows, fork hay, do many things whose existence she had not even thought of until three years ago

"After you've checked," she persisted, "can't we still go to town if things seem all right?"

"I suppose so," he said without enthusiasm, then smiled at her "Yes, I'll take you to lunch at the Ute Valley Inn. You do still have a dress somewhere?"

"And let's invite Klaus and Virginia and the kids for supper if the rain keeps up," she said. "Ginia and I have been promising all summer how we'd all get together if it ever rained."

Fern was already in the kitchen, banging pots and pans. She was another who never needed an alarm clock. And Nolan was there with her. With Emily gone, the family always ate in the kitchen now, unless there was company or some other special occasion. Emily had decided not to pay a visit to the ranch this summer. She had written them apologetically, reminding them that she was seventy-five years old and her nerves couldn't seem to stand what they had used to. The bustle and pressures of Secesh in summer were so wearing. Perhaps she'd come at Christmas time this year, when Hugh would be home from his first term at college. Couldn't Price see about having the twins then, too, so she could still see all the family?

In a way, Anne thought, it was a pity Emily had chosen not to come this year. This season had gone more smoothly than most. Spring had come early. The weather had been generally good. Price had got together a better hay crew than he was normally able to do. The children, growing up all too fast, were less noisy about the house than they had been in former years.

There had been changes throughout the house. In the kitchen, a new and better propane range and a bigger refrigerator. In the bootroom, an automatic washing machine and a huge deep freeze.

"I always did hate canning," Fern had admitted, once they had the freezer.

They made a large vegetable garden each year, though many plants were frost-bitten in their prime.

"I know what I want somebody to do today," said Fern now, breaking eggs. "Pick my green beans. There ought to be a bushel or more ready, and I can have them in the deep freeze by dinnertime."

Hugh came in to say, with yawning scorn, "That's no job for a ranch hand."

"A real ranch hand," Fern told him patiently, "runs cattle. How many cows have you set your eyes on since haying started?"

"It'll be muddy," he pointed out, certain that he, at least, was not going to pick beans.

"It'll be muddy working on a corral," she said with the comfortable knowledge that she was in the right.

The other children straggled in. Nolan was already dressed in his working clothes. Roger, when he came, had on a pair of neatly fitting slacks and a short-sleeved plaid shirt. He had shown signs, last summer, of an allergy to the sun, not that anyone had expected him to work outside anyway. Penny and Kiersten had got out fleecy winter bathrobes and slippers against the chill. They were followed by Rookie, the puppy Price had let Kiersten keep two years ago. The dog, a fine-looking specimen of his breed, slept in the girls' room. Kiersten had agreed to let him be trained as a cattle dog. He showed promise, but she would have him sleep nowhere but beside her bed.

Emily had been shocked last summer by a dog in the house, reminded unpleasantly of how, when Miss Mercy and Price the elder were alive, animals had gone in and out of the house at will. It had been Miss Mercy who had introduced the use of cattle dogs into this part of the country, and Secesh still used them, more than any ranch in the region. Price was an excellent trainer and handler.

The summer before that, Emily had been even more shocked and saddened by the metamorphosis of her beautiful living room. Anne had had the shabby but quite serviceable couches and chairs made of very good leather, and the scarred but handsome tables brought down from the attic, and Emily's delicate, impractical pieces put up there. She had found a way to take off the paper, so that the beautiful old dark wood paneling made up the walls. She had put away most of the photographs and what Price called "namby-pamby pictures." On a trip to Denver, she had bought a few large and appropriate paintings. She had taken up the light blue carpet, made the hardwood floor beneath it shine again, then had placed several hooked rugs of varying sizes about the room, their colors bright and pleasing against the dark wood. Fern turned out these rugs in winter rather like a machine, when she wasn't busy knitting socks for everyone. Anne had made and lined bright draperies for the big windows. It was no longer a "company room," but a family place, where they gathered in the long winter evenings, bright fire snapping, for homework, reading, sewing, music, talk. Poor Emily had asked timidly if she might have a few of her "best pieces" sent to the California apartment.

Reuben and Price came into the kitchen now, Reuben rather disdainfully carrying their share of the milk Hannah had already taken from the cows.

"Goddamn weather!" he said bitterly. "We had us a good start made for onct, an' now, look at this." He had forgot to get rid of his tobacco outside and went to do so. Then he sat at the table and heaped his plate eagerly, despite a scowl.

"Well, do you think you can keep them busy?" Price asked.

"Dam' right I can," said Reuben determinedly. "This ain't no big pourin' rain, just enough to keep the hay wet. They can git that new corral up. Did you want Dave to work on the baler, or do you aim to take care of that yourself?"

"Let him have a go. Anne and I are going to town."

"Humph! You're worse'n any kid, high-tailin' it for town at ary little sprinkle. What kinda example does that set for your crew? That Frank's got a car, you know. How am I supposed to manage if they all decide to pile in an'—"

"Remind them that if they work, they get paid," said Price tersely.

"I want to go with you," said Kiersten. "I haven't been anywhere since haying started."

No one had noticed, until now, how she had come to the table. Along with her heavy robe and slippers, she was wearing her new cowboy hat and large sunglasses.

"Well, if you ain't Miss Josephine Cool!" said Reuben, laughing heartily.

Nolan said seriously, rather smugly, "Ranch people are *supposed* to be at home during haying."

"At least take off the hat, Kiersten," Anne said, more severely than she felt.

"I want my beans picked," reminded Fern.

"Hugh," said Price, "why don't you go up in the pickup and have a look at those upper ditches? From the way the water's running, I know the beavers are at work again. As soon as the ground's dried out, we'll have some beaver dam blasting to do. You can check some on the cattle, too, though that really needs a horse."

"I don't think you ought to tear up their dams," said Roger solicitously.

"Well," said Hugh, hesitating, then, "oh, all right."

Penny said, "Couldn't we all take the day off? Hugh could drive us into Hurleigh in his car, some of us, at least."

"I've got books I should return to the library," said Roger.

"There's a whole library here," said Hugh curtly. "What do you need with books from town? Anyway," turning to his sister, "*if* I went anywhere, except for work, it wouldn't be to take along a carful of kids. You *can* go along with me to check the ditches. Maybe be of some help."

"I don't care to check ditches, thank you," she said primly. "I'm going to spend the entire day taking care of my hands. Just look what a mess they are."

Kiersten said, "I'd go with you, Hugh, if you asked."

Silence.

"Well, then, I wish I could make my new shirt today. It's been a long time since we got the material."

"You can't sew," Nolan teased her scornfully, then, "I'll go up with you, Hugh."

"You're not big enough to be any help," said Hugh disdainfully. "You always try to get into everything and all you are is in the way."

"I *can* sew," flashed Kiersten. "Didn't I make that dress last winter? You saw it."

"She did," affirmed Roger.

"It looks like a sack," said Nolan offhandedly.

"That's what it's *supposed* to look like," she snapped. "It's a sack dress. You wouldn't know anything *right* if it hit you in the eye."

"You'd do better to work with Handsome," said Nolan calmly. Handsome was Kiersten's own horse. "He's out of hand. Anybody can see that. You've made too much of a pet of him. Want me to handle him some for you?"

"He is not and I do not. You stay away from Handsome. You've got Gretchen, or most of the others, if you want a horse to handle."

Hugh said, "He can train a horse just about like you can sew."

Both of the younger ones were firing up to make a come back at Hugh together when Price said, "All right. That's enough from all of you."

Fern had been scribbling busily on a pad, a list of things they needed from town. Reuben had got a page of it and was writing laboriously.

Penny said to Kiersten, "I'd help you with the shirt but I know *I* can't sew."

Fern said, "I'll see if I can find a little time to help you, Kierstie, when I'm done with the beans."

Reuben said sourly, "I never in my life heard so much talk about beans."

"I'll pick them," said Nolan resignedly.

"Why don't I do that?" said Roger brightly. "And you can work with your horse or whatever."

"Because you don't have any boots," said Nolan curtly "It's muddy."

"Well, but couldn't I borrow yours?"

"He's only trying to be helpful," said Kiersten sweetly, "let you play cowboy."

"I don't," began Nolan, flushing, but Price said shortly, "Don't start again, you two."

Anne said, "We'll return your books, Roger," and to the table generally, "We thought of asking Klaus and Ginia and the kids for supper." This brought smiles all round. "Will that be all right, Fern? If your list gets much longer, I won't get back in time to be of any help."

"That'll be just fine. Why don't we barbecue hamburgers? And I can make baked beans and potato salad and such."

"I thought sure you'd be havin' the damn green beans," said Reuben.

"No, she's going to freeze those," said Price "Save them."

Anne said, "I'll call them before we leave."

Later in the car she said to Price, "How long since we've been in a car alone?"

He smiled. "I don't know. I feel like a kid on a high school date Let's just run away."

She moved close to him. "A date with a girl who'll give out?"

He laughed. "It's *put out*, you crazy little wench."

"Oh well, yes," she said, flushing and laughing. "But you *do* take my meaning?"

"I do," he said, and still laughing, took one of her hands. "I'd like that very much, but where can we go that we won't be known? We wouldn't want such word getting back to Secesh, with all those young, unmolded minds."

There were several cars around The Reserve, the small bar and cafe at Mills Crossing.

"Looks like some have started early," said Price.

"I'm always surprised at how much business the bar does," she said. "I mean, so many of the people I've met here are fine upstanding Mormons and they don't drink, do they?"

"You've mostly met the old settlers. It's the mill hands and loggers at The Reserve, hay crews, a few ranchers like us, still outsid-

126

ers as far as the old LDS are concerned, and some jack Mormons like Klaus Ellenbogen and his family.''

"Will Hugh inherit anything from the Ellenbogens?''

"No. He thinks he will, but I don't see how. There are his mother's three brothers, Klaus, Anders, and Jergen, and they each have several kids. I don't know how the land's going to go round as it is.''

"And what about Secesh?''

He frowned. "They'll have to fight that out when I'm dead, I guess. Hugh wants the place, but it's not because it's part of him. He's a manager, all right, and he might do a fine job, but he doesn't *feel* the place. Maybe that sounds crazy to you, but . . .''

"No, I think I understand,'' she said, wishing so hard for a child of theirs, together, that her eyes prickled with unshed tears.

After a little, he said, "I've heard that old man Lars Bergen is very sick in the hospital. I ought to stop and see him for a few minutes today. His children have all moved to Hurleigh or farther and some are saying they've already got a buyer for his ranch, somebody from back east who plans to make a guest ranch of it, trail rides, fishing, river trips down to the new lake. I don't like to see that kind of thing begin in the Park.''

He was carefully negotiating the muddy curves up on to Fairweather.

"They've started paving this road from the other end,'' Anne mused. "They did about five miles last summer and are going to get another good bit done this year. Still, I can't imagine there would be many guests who'd come this far into the back country. Look! There's another herd of deer. There must be thirty of them.''

She never failed to be delighted at these frequent sightings. The deer were particularly in evidence in the early mornings, at dusk, and on cloudy days like this. People frequently struck them on the road. It was sometimes completely unavoidable. They were at the ranch, coming down to browse by the river, with their own trail past the house and buildings. There were elk, too. They kept to the high country except in winter, when they were pests at the stack yards, trying to get at the hay, tearing down the fences they couldn't jump. In early spring, they came down to feed on the new-greening grass, and got quite near the house when the light was poor. What a wonderful country, Anne thought, for perhaps the thousandth time.

Price was saying, "You'd be surprised at how many would come if enough advertising was done, virgin fishing streams and all that. I don't doubt they'd keep open for hunting season, too, with guides, guaranteed kills and the like. Thank God, Secesh is as far away from the Bergen place as it can be.''

There was another silence and he said hesitantly, "Annie, are you—all right at Secesh? I mean, is it—enough for you?"

She laughed. "Enough? It's about twice what I can handle."

"But you know what I'm saying."

"Yes, and it's fine, Price. It's lovely, most of it. I thank God every day for Fern. I couldn't handle it at all if I had the housework to do, too."

"Honestly, I never meant you to get so involved in the outside work."

"I know," she said, smiling, laying her hand on his. "We're always shorthanded; well, almost always. Price, I love it. Sometimes I hate it, too, but I'm under the place's spell or whatever. I could never be happy anywhere else. . . . If only we could have a kid or two, ours, together. Dr. Swenson says if nothing shows up in the tests he can do, there's a specialist in Denver . . . Darling, do you think Darlene could possibly be persuaded to let the boys come to us for Christmas? It would be lovely to have them."

"No," he said resignedly. "About the only way I can see her doing that is if I offered her more money and I won't do that. The money she already gets isn't going for the boys—well, not for Nolan. He's getting too big now for Roger's hand-me-downs. You saw how he came here this year, his arms and legs sticking out of everything. We get him a new wardrobe every summer, and she won't spend a cent on him. I've tried to get him to talk about how it is for him at home, but he always asks some question about the work, changes the subject. I'm afraid things are pretty bad."

"Do you think we could take him away from her altogether?"

"I've tried that once, Annie."

"But the boys are old enough to speak for themselves now."

"The courts say they're not old enough to *choose* for themselves until they're fourteen. Besides, I don't know that Nolan would speak for himself in that case. Old Liam depends on him. They love each other. You should have seen the old man's face when I went to bring the boys away this summer. Darlene would use the argument again, that brothers, especially twins, shouldn't be separated, and I don't doubt that Roger could put on a good show, helping to prove it. I think Nolan would be afraid to say much on either side, knowing he'd likely have to go back there and live with them."

"You think it's that bad?"

"I do, yes."

He lit a cigarette. They were at the top of the grade.

"But we ought to be able to *do* something," she said, angry with the feeling of helplessness.

"If Nolan won't talk, and he won't . . . if Roger won't back him up if he *did* talk, and he won't. Roger is very well occupied looking after Roger's interests."

"You know," she said gently, "Roger loves you, too."

He shook his head immediately.

"He does, Price, and he's not a half-bad kid if you spend a little time with him, let him know that he doesn't have to be perfect all the time."

"There is nothing that Roger and I could ever share."

"He looks too much like Darlene," she said empathetically "That stops you before you can even start."

He made no answer and after a while she said, "Well, at least they're getting away from Darlene and Clarence summers. Remember how Kiersten resented them that first year they came? Now she can hardly wait for the time when they come back."

"I don't quite see why. She and Roger seem to get along all right, but she and Nolan do nothing but quarrel and argue."

"That's just how they are with each other," Anne said, smiling. "Kierstie told me this spring that she loves both her brothers, but Nolan best, 'Even if he is a snot,' she said."

Then, "You know, I worry about Roger. When Nolan's with us, he has the ranch and you. But I feel there's a little old cynical man inside Roger, keeping counsel, keeping accounts, scorning everyone and everything. He certainly has nothing but negative feelings for women."

"Is he misbehaving? Has he said things to you . . . ?"

"No, it's just the feeling I have."

"I don't see why he has any reason to feel negatively toward women, after the way his mother's—"

"But that's just it," she broke in earnestly. "Darlene shows him off for *herself*, for getting people to notice *her*. He senses that, young as he is. I think he already knew it that first year they came here. He thinks women are put on earth for his benefit—through their own selfishness—to be twisted round his little finger. Price, couldn't you try to spend a little more time with him, get to know him, to love him a little?"

"No. Sometimes it's all I can do to stand him in the same house. It must be wonderful to be just nine years old and to know absolutely everything. I know it's not his fault he's so haughty and conceited, and in some ways he's not that different from Hugh, but . . ."

"But you *do* love Nolan?"

After a moment, he said quietly, "I can't afford to, not too much, at any rate. Less than three months out of the year and she might change her mind about that at any time. . . . He has the feel for the land. I can feel that, but God only knows what he'll grow up to be. I have no real say in that."

"Well, I don't suppose a parent ought to have the final say about what any child is going to be or do but . . . oh, if we could only keep them! Roger could still change to some degree, I think, and Nolan loves Secesh—and you, so much."

He sighed, then tried to smile. "Well, what we need to do is get a family of our very own going, and not spend too much time and energy worrying about the others. It doesn't do us any good and it really can't help them, not the boys at any rate. You know, it's not so long till I'll be having another birthday. Maybe I'm just getting too elderly to start a new family."

"It certainly doesn't seem that way in bed," she said and moved even closer to him.

Dr. Swenson's nurse said she could better fit them in in the early afternoon, so they did their shopping, Anne at grocery and drugstores, Price at hardware, feed and ranch supply businesses.

"I knew we should have brought a pickup," he muttered, trying to fit everything into the trunk and back seat of the Buick.

They walked back to the doctor's office after lunch, both of them a little tense, chatting to cover it.

When Dr. Swenson, a gentle, balding man in his fifties, had finished examining Anne, he said, "Get dressed now and come into my office. I'll only need a few minutes with your husband."

She thought Price looked a little pale under his constant tan. The doctor sat down at his desk, across from them, looking sober.

"This is something I think you should hear together so that, some time, when you're ready, you can talk about it together. Mr. Savage, you tell me you fathered twins, something over nine years ago. Since that time, have you had a serious illness? Prolonged high fever?"

Price shifted uneasily in his chair. "I don't—yes, about five years ago."

"Were you hospitalized?"

"Here, in Hurleigh."

"And what was the diagnosis?"

"They didn't seem to decide on that. I was tired; they . . ."

"It's all right. I can check the hospital records, but I'm afraid it won't make any difference in what I have to tell you. You're sterile, unable to fertilize the ova. A prolonged high fever *can* do that. I can explain the mechanics, but I think you both understand . . ."

Price was flushing violently.

"Can anything be done?" asked Anne, almost whispering. She reached out for his hand, but Price drew away from her.

The doctor was shaking his head sadly. "Nothing. I'm very sorry."

Price, standing, pale again, said, "What do we owe you?"

"Pay at the desk, please," the doctor said gently.

They were silent walking back to the car, silent for a long time after that. Price looked fixedly at the road ahead. Anne fought tears. She had so desperately wanted their child, at least one, but it was for Price that her throat ached and her eyes hurt with tears she swore she would not shed. Men were such captives in this society's mores, particularly here, in the West. If it had been her, some lack in her that prevented their having a baby, she could have cried all the way home and then some, but he could only sit there, clenching the wheel with whitened knuckles and stare at the road, his face devastated though his mouth was steady, hard, with white around the lips.

"I can call Ginia," she said and cleared her throat. They were just coming into Fairweather. "From here."

"Why?" His deep voice sounded ragged.

"I thought maybe you'd—rather not have company tonight."

"I'm not any less than I have been," he said fiercely.

"Oh, Price, you know I didn't mean—"

"Then why shouldn't we have friends over?"

"It's just that you look so—unhappy, and I thought maybe—"

"Aren't *you* unhappy? Doesn't it bother you that I'm—not really a man?"

Even in his misery, he realized how much he had come to trust her—to be able to say that to anyone . . .

"That's not true and you know it," she flashed angrily. "If there was something about me that wouldn't let us have a baby, would you want me to feel less a woman, less female, particularly with *you?* I will *not* let you do this to yourself, to us. If you were impotent, that would be another matter, but you're certainly not that."

Another long silence and she said, "We could see about adoption."

"No."

"If we got a tiny baby, it would be just like our own before we'd know it."

"We have enough problems with kids, adopted or not."

"But you adopted Kiersten. You said—"

"For Chrissake, will you stop picking to pieces everything I've ever said?"

Then another lengthy pause before he said unsteadily, "Don't

131

you think I've wondered often enough if the twins are really mine? Darlene was—free with herself. Maybe this happened to me years ago. Maybe I've never—"

She said shakily, "Roger could have any father. He looks so much like Darlene that the father wouldn't have mattered much. I've heard of twins having different fathers, but, Price, you know very well that Nolan is a perfect composite of your grandparents, and so, of you. You can't doubt who his father is."

They were starting down the Fairweather Grade now. The light rain had stopped, but the road was still muddy and treacherous. He was driving too fast, the first time she had known him to let his emotions get the upper hand of his physical mechanisms.

"And Nolan's all I'll have," he said so quietly she could hardly hear. "Hugh's going to study ranch management and that's what he wants to do, manage, not work. I've put everything I have, almost everything I am into Secesh, and there has to be someone to carry it on."

Anne said, "I think that may be exactly what Nolan wants, but please, Price, sweetheart, remember he's only nine years old. Love him, let him love you, even if he's here only for summers. His feelings for Secesh will grow from that."

Price was glum and short-tempered when they got back home He barked at Joe, who came to ask a question, cursed Hugh's report of the condition of the upper ditches and Dave's slow progress on the baler, snapped at the younger children indiscriminately.

"I'm going to change clothes," he said to Anne as she was putting away groceries, "see if I can get anywhere with that baler."

"You've got less than two hours," Fern reminded him. "Ellenbogens are coming at six."

"They can damn well wait if I'm not finished. We've got to be in the fields tomorrow. Where's Nolan?"

"Following Reuben around, I expect," said Fern tersely

"He may as well start learning something about machinery," said Price, stalking toward the bedroom.

"My word! What's the matter with him?" asked Fern mystified and irritated. "I know he didn't want to go to town, but was it that bad?"

"It was that bad," Anne nodded and indicated that no more should be said. When they were finally alone in the kitchen, she told Fern, letting the tears come at last. Perhaps she should have said nothing to anyone, but she needed it, and Fern was a sister to them both. She needed to know, to understand Price's devastation. Poor Price! Who could he tell?

"It's the way he was raised," said Fern, wiping roughly at her own eyes, "by his daddy and grandad, even Miss Mercy. A *man* doesn't have such a thing wrong with him. A *man* can't cry and talk it over. A *man* never gets hurt inside, or, at least, no one ever knows about it."

"What I'm afraid of," said Anne, then amended, "well, I'm afraid of a lot of things, like that he'll never let himself forget about this—this problem that really doesn't matter worth a damn to me—to us—to what we have together. But what I'm also afraid of is that so much responsibility is going to fall on Nolan. Price has already said that Nolan is all he'll ever have now, to carry on with Secesh. I'm afraid he's going to make it a real load, a burden, more than a little child can handle."

"Oh-*oh*," said Fern intently. "That baby can't handle much more responsibility than he's already got. He's a strong boy and, unlike some people, knows just how much he can handle. If Price makes the place a burden to him, pushes him too hard, he could lose him, and I don't see how they, or any of us, could get through that. That Nolan is already his own person. He loves Price and this ranch, but he'll back off if he thinks he's just being used. He already has enough of that, I know it. We'll just have to see, hon, try to ease things when we can."

Roger, Nolan, and Kiersten, with Rookie and Pussycat, were on the porch, waiting for the Ellenbogens, playing around. Klaus Ellenbogen was the brother of Hugh's and Penny's dead mother, so all the children called them Uncle Klaus and Aunt Ginia. Virginia was the music teacher at both Fairweather and Mills Crossing schools. In summer, she left her house entirely to the hired woman and worked in fields and pastures. They had five children, ranging in age from sixteen to seven.

Kiersten said to Nolan, "I thought you were going to help Dad with the baler. Now, you've got your work clothes all changed."

"I was, but I—couldn't do anything right, so he told me to milk the cows and feed the calves. Hannah had already started that, so it didn't take long."

Kiersten lay sprawled on the floor, fondling the dog's ears.

"Ow!" she cried. "Take your dirty old foot off my hand, Nolan Savage."

He wasn't hurting her, but he grinned wickedly. "I'm your stepbrother, so I can *step* on you."

The rain was done. Blades of sunlight touched the western mountains. The air was fresh and chilly, bearing the first omen of autumn. Hugh was lighting up the barbecue grill down in the side yard.

"Did you make your shirt today?" Nolan asked Kiersten, lazily shifting his foot away.

"Part of it. Fern helped me with the cutting and the sewing machine. I still have some to do."

"When you've practiced a lot more, you can make one for me."

"Thanks," Kiersten said wryly. "You're so generous. Come on, Pussycat. What's the matter, girl?"

Roger sat swinging gently on the battered old glider, his face smooth, a little smug. He hated seeing them together, Kiersten and Nolan, knowing their banter and quarreling meant the opposite of what it seemed. That was the only really bad thing now about spending the summers at the ranch. Maybe next year he'd refuse to come. Then Nolan couldn't come either. They could start some real project together, maybe a tree house, just the two of them, with no neighborhood kids allowed.

"Next spring," Kiersten was saying, "I get to raise a calf for 4-H."

"You'll let it get scours and die. You always think the poor little things ought to have more milk, when their bellies are already swelled up to bursting."

"I will not. I bet you couldn't raise half as good a calf as I'm going to."

"All you'll raise it for is to be butchered and eaten," reminded Roger grimly. "In Denver, there's this summer day camp, where you can go and swim, learn to make all sorts of things. I think I'd rather go there than come back here again, wouldn't you, Nolan?"

Nolan's eyes flicked up at him and away.

Roger said with scorn, "What's the good of all this work, just to do more work, and the same old things over and over again? If you make a painting or something at this summer day camp, it's done. It's not like just raising one crummy generation of calves after another. And they have a reading program—"

Anne came onto the porch. "It's going to be chilly tonight. I thought a fire in the living room would be nice."

"Here," said Roger, getting up quickly. "Let me bring the wood in."

"You wouldn't really go to that thing he's talking about?" Kiersten asked softly.

"Not unless I have to," said Nolan. For an instant, she caught a stricken look in his eyes.

"You just *have* to come back here because . . . Chappie, look at Pussycat, how she's scratching at her neck. Do you think she's choking or something?"

They both ran to the little cat, crouched in a corner.

"Try to hold her," said Nolan. "Be careful. She is hurt some-

134

how and she may try to bite and scratch, but maybe you can . . . talk to her, while I try to see what's wrong.''

What was wrong was that a very small rubber band had been put about the cat's neck. It was deeply embedded now, in fur and skin. Finally, Nolan was able to cut it with the knife he had been given that summer. The cat sprang away yowling, leaving long scratches on Kiersten's arms.

The two children looked at each other.

"Who's been around the house this afternoon," Kiersten whispered, horrified, "besides Fern and me?"

They both knew.

Anne came back for kindling, Roger following closely, insisting he would get it.

"Kiersten, what's happened to your arms?" asked the mother. "You're bleeding."

"Mommy, somebody put a really little rubber band around Pussycat's neck. She was choking to death. See, here it is. Chappie cut it with his knife."

Anne stared at the short piece of rubber, appalled. "Who would *do* a thing like that?"

"It was Roger!" cried Kiersten. "I know it was. It had to be."

Roger was meticulously stacking kindling on his arm, his face bland.

"I was reading all afternoon," he said coolly. "I didn't even see the cat till I came out here. Nolan likes to play tricks on you. You two are always—"

Nolan stood there, looking her candidly in the eye. Anne said, "We'll talk about this later. The Ellenbogens are coming."

Roger said softly to Nolan, "You do get bored here, don't you? Especially when Price is away?"

Nolan looked down at the uneven porch floor. He was so accustomed to taking the blame for everything, but he wasn't going to do it about this thing with Pussycat. So why did he feel so ashamed?

There were fifteen people at supper. It was a noisy, hungry, congenial group. Klaus Ellenbogen got talking about county politics and Anne, who was the only one besides Fern to recognize it, saw some of the pain and confusion leave Price's eyes, at least for the time being.

The children scattered after supper. The women went to the kitchen. Kiersten and the two younger Ellenbogen children, Terry, who was ten, and Kara, who was seven, spread a Monopoly game on the big dining room table. Nolan meant to play with them, but Roger

135

said in a soft peremptory voice, "Let's go to our room and play checkers. We haven't had a good game all summer."

"No, I'd rather—"

"Do you want to stay in Denver next summer?"

When the dishes were finished and the women had sat talking in the living room for a while, Ginia's eldest daughter Jo, said,

"Let's have a sing-along, Mom. That'll bring kids out of every corner and get Dad off the subject of the Hurleigh paper. He's beginning to look—what do you call it?—apoplectic?"

Ginia went readily to the piano and gradually everyone gathered round her. Nolan got up to leave the boys' room. He usually lost badly in games with Roger and didn't quite understand why Roger even wanted to play him.

"I'm going to ask for a chess set for Christmas," said Roger, putting the checkers away neatly. "A really good one. You'll have to practice a lot to keep up with me."

They sang standard old songs: "I've Been Working on the Railroad," "You Are My Sunshine," "Oh, Suzannah!" Every Ellenbogen had a strong voice and could harmonize. The Savages were not so lusty, but they sang along happily enough, except for Price, who sat in a corner and reminded himself to smile now and then, though the light was dim there.

"I wish you'd brought your fiddle, Terry," said Ginia, and Jo added for the Savages's benefit, "Yeah, he's getting so good we can almost live with it. I wish I had my clarinet."

"If they all turn out to be musical," said Klaus, "Lord save us, we're going to need an instrument truck to follow along behind the station wagon."

"Nolan has a guitar," said Fern matter-of-factly. "Brought it with him for the first time this summer. Go get it, hon."

He was all but petrified with shyness. "It's—it's my grandpa's."

Anne smiled at him encouragingly.

Kiersten said, "You and Mama sing some of those old Irish songs you know."

"Sure," encouraged Ginia. "You people aren't the only ones in the Park that came from an Irish background."

It was a battered little instrument and Nolan had been playing for only a year. His left hand still ached with the stretching to fret if he played for long at a time. Grandpa had said he was to have all four of the instruments, guitar, fiddle, banjo, and what Liam called the Irish whistle, something he had made himself. He had encouraged Nolan to bring the guitar away this summer, so that his hand wouldn't forget how to stretch. Nolan carried it into the living room diffidently, glancing first and very quickly at his father, who was frowning.

136

He tuned very quickly to the piano.

"The piano needs tuning," he murmured softly to himself, but Ginia heard.

"It does. Do you have perfect pitch?"

"I don't know. I don't think so. No one's ever told me—"

Anne eagerly requested a few of the Irish ballads. Nolan played but she was left to lead them alone, in a good soprano voice. The rest joined in, or hummed in harmony, Ginia catching them up easily with the piano.

"How long have you been playing?" she asked Nolan.

"Just since last fall."

Roger said importantly, "He plays Grandpa's fiddle and banjo, too, and that thing Grandpa made, his Irish whistle."

"I'm not very good," said Nolan, just above a whisper, his fair face flushed darkly.

"My boy, you are excellent," stated Ginia. "Who's been teaching you?"

"My grandpa. He taught me about making chords with the guitar. I picked up some things from the radio and . . ."

"I should say you did! Play something for us. Just you."

The whole upper part of Nolan's body felt flushed. He was so fair that, even tanned, he knew his face was flaming. His gray eyes flashed round the living room, seeking something. What? Release? Encouragement? The family all smiled at him, except Hugh, and he couldn't see Price's face now.

Roger sat on the floor with Kiersten, leaning against the arm of one of the big old sofas. He said cajolingly, "Go on, Chappie. You're always playing to yourself. Sometimes I can't even get to sleep."

Nolan looked desperately back to Anne. "Please," she said. "We're all just family."

Nolan tried to swallow whatever was choking him and to breathe naturally. He sat on the floor, leaning against the piano. He was aware of the guitar, the warm curved shape of it in his arms. He touched a few chords gently, tentatively, then bits of music began to flit through his mind. It was as if he went away, left the room and his shyness, very nearly left himself. He was alone with the music. He leaned his head more relaxedly against the piano and closed his eyes.

The others stared. Ginia, smiling, made the sign of the cross. Even Price leaned forward and watched the seemingly delicate fingers, moving with such surety over the strings.

Roger said, just barely aloud, "Chappie has everything."

Kiersten heard and tore her eyes away from Nolan to look at him. He was not aware of his own expression, but she thought he was going to cry.

Nolan finished. The bits and pieces of music in his mind had been melded together. He was not aware that he had played for more than five minutes.

There was a moment of silence, then hearty applause. His awareness was back, the burning embarrassment.

"Why, Nolan, I never knew," said Anne, awed.

Fern said, "Hon, that was the nicest thing I've heard in a long time. There's nothing as good on the radio."

Ginia said, "What was it? What is it called?"

Nolan gulped. "Just some old reels and jigs and handies Grandpa knows, all sort of—put together."

He hated the attention, though they were being very kind. He stumbled to his feet and went to put the guitar away, feeling that their eyes burned holes in his back.

"The child's a musical genius," stated Ginia. "Perfect pitch, a photographic ear, and did you see his face while he was playing? He forgot where he was, everything." She turned to Roger. "You say he plays other instruments?"

"Grandpa's old things that are all cracked and chipped." Roger smiled his brilliant smile, but there was something of sulkiness in his voice, for those who knew him.

"All that well?" Ginia persisted.

"I really don't know," he said, looking modestly down at the floor. "Twins aren't alike in everything, you know. I'm afraid I'm tone deaf."

Later, alone in their room, Anne said exuberantly to Price, "Wasn't Nolan just wonderful? Did you ever *dream* he could do anything like that? You know, Ginia asked him later if he could play that piece again and he said he didn't know. Sometimes he remembers and sometimes he doesn't. She told him he ought to write them all down. He said he doesn't have time and hasn't had nearly enough practicing of reading music, not to mention writing it. She asked him if he wants to be a musician when he grows up and he said, 'No, probably a rancher.' But, Price, did you see his face while he was playing? He was in a dream, he just . . ."

Price was putting the things from his pockets on the dresser. His stony lack of response had run down her enthusiasm. He said sternly, "Ranchers don't have much time for dreams."

They said little more and Price fell asleep quickly. Between them, he and Klaus had drunk a good deal of bourbon. Anne was glad he slept almost immediately, would not brood, for now, over what Dr. Swenson had had to tell them, but she wanted to plead with him to leave Nolan free to be his own person, have whatever he could. She lay listening to the wind, fingering softly around the house, then she remembered Pussycat and the rubber band. That couldn't just be dropped. It had been a cruel, sick, sadistic thing to do and there were no longer any children in the house too young to know better. An inquiry must be made in the morning. She *knew* Roger had done it and wondered, feeling a little nauseated, what course he would find for explaining it away or for making it look as if the blame lay elsewhere. Each summer she was coming to see more clearly that, somehow, Roger needed help, and to know that she was not nearly qualified to give it. He was pathetic and she rather loved him, in a pitying way. Probably, he deserved more of her concern and protection than Nolan. She was convinced that Nolan was made of tougher stuff, like his father, and would be a coper, a survivor, landing on his feet often simply by his own determined momentum.

9

That fall Nolan got a paper route in the afternoons. He had to turn over half his earnings to Clarence, buy school lunches and other necessities with what was left. He took the route because he knew they would not be going to Secesh that next summer. Roger had talked and talked to their mother about the summer day camp for next year, and he had also joined the Boy Scouts, of which Darlene approved heartily, because he might meet some "halfway decent boys" in the association. Nolan could not join; it was too expensive, with the uniforms and all, unless he wanted to save up from his paper route. Nolan was gradually saving—Grandpa kept the money for him—but not for a Scout uniform. He wanted a twelve-string guitar. He had seen and heard one played on the television that was new in their house.

The route manager of the newspaper had been hesitant about taking him on, even when he stretched his age a bit, but he was conscientious about the job, all through the hard cold winter, using, at Roger's prompting, the hated discarded red bicycle.

On *his* birthday—Nolan had always been glad they had separate ones, though all the celebrating was always done on Roger's—he took a bus downtown and looked at guitars. Only through store windows; he hadn't nearly enough money saved even to go inside. It was a Saturday and when he went back and finished his paper route, no one was home. His mother worked on Saturday, had Sunday and Monday off. Clarence had not been working at all for some time now, but he wasn't very often home when their mother was out.

There was a note on the table in Grandpa's hand: "Supper in oven. Take out at six o'clock." And underneath that, in Clarence's scrawl, "Put cole in heeter."

Nolan went into the bedroom, feeling heavy and sad. It had been a mistake to look at the guitars. He pulled Grandpa's old battered one out from under his bed and began, almost unconsciously, playing out his feelings. The blues, "When them blues gits low an' sad, lord, lord, lord . . . ?"

Roger had had a birthday party. It was supposed to have been for both of them, of course. Roger had invited four boys from his Scout troop. Nolan wasn't allowed to ask any of the neighborhood kids. There had been a cake, Roger's favorite, made by a bakery, with "Happy Birthday Twins," and ten candles on each side. Mama had given Roger a lot of official Scout things, canteen, pack, dishes, sleeping bag, and the fine chess set he had somehow failed to get for Christmas. Nolan had received two sets of school clothes and a new cheap jacket. But at least they *were* new, something not handed down from Roger. Nolan had grown almost as tall as his brother, though he was still of slighter build. He thought his shoulders were broadening. He wanted to look like his father, six-feet-two, with wide shoulders and strong as a bull.

And that, of course, made him think more of not being at Secesh for the summer. The boys were not supposed to write Price, ever. Darlene had said she would let him know that they would be involved in town this summer, not coming to the ranch. Nolan knew she would wait until the last possible minute, perhaps not write at all, but let him come here, expecting to pick them up. He wasn't sure he wanted to write Price either. Price had been strange to him in the final weeks of last summer after he had played the old guitar while the Ellenbogens were at the house. He had let Nolan know, without saying it, that music wasn't for a *man*, not total immersion in it at any rate. And Nolan couldn't *not* have music. It wasn't that he loved it more than he loved Price or Secesh, but music was a part of him, so much a part that no doctor could ever cut it out, no person or place, no matter how important, could ever excise it from his life. It was himself, and he cradled the old guitar and tied together a bunch of sobby, masochistic country-western songs he had heard on the radio, with some improvisations and bridges of his own.

He thought he might write Kiersten, but suppose she wrote back? Darlene insisted on being always the one who took mail from the mailbox and looked it over. He'd tell Kiersten not to write back. He just wanted to let them know they wouldn't be coming. He put the guitar on his bed and went to look for paper. His mother had some fancy stationery, a gift from him at Christmas time, which she never used, but he didn't want that. Finally, he tore a page from a spiral notebook he used for school.

"Dear Kierstie" no, "Dear Kiersten, We will not be coming to Secesh this summer. Roger is in Scouts and is going to a summer day camp. I have a paper route. I told my boss I was twelve and he believed it. Today, I am only ten. Tell the others we are not coming and that I miss them all very much. This was the year Price said I could start handling the work horse colts." No, he erased that last sentence, "Next year in school, I can take a course in basic mechanics so maybe I will be more help."

He stopped, thinking about the incident of Roger and Pussycat. They had talked about it the next morning at breakfast, who had put the rubber band on Pussycat's neck, and Roger had maintained he knew nothing. Later he went to Anne and confessed, saying he had been afraid to admit it before Price. He said he had put the band on the cat, not realizing it would get so tight, meaning to leave it on only long enough to put a ribbon bow on it to surprise Kiersten. Then Fern had asked him to do something and he had forgot about the cat. He had made this confession in the kitchen while Nolan was in the bootroom, waterproofing boots. Roger cried and said how sorry he was, begging Anne not to tell Price. But she had not been taken in. She agreed that she would not tell Price, but said that Roger would have to do it. Price had whipped Roger, hard, with a strap, but not in the naked, humiliating way Clarence would have done it, if Clarence had ever dared lay hands on Roger.

Nolan was trying to think what else he might add to the letter without being maudlin, without letting the loneliness and disappointment show too much. He did not hear the car in the driveway, but he heard Clarence slam in at the front door, remembered the note on the table, and glanced guiltily at Grandpa's alarm clock. It was a quarter to six, so he hadn't let the supper be ruined, but what about the coal? This room was always cold in winter, so he couldn't tell about the rest of the house. He slid the guitar under Grandpa's bed, the letter with it, and met Clarence in the kitchen.

Clarence had brought home groceries and a case of beer. He told Nolan to bring in the beer. It was a raw bitter day for April. You could smell the feedlots because the wind was northeasterly. When he came back into the house, Nolan knew the fire in the heater must be nearly out; it was damp and chilly.

"Didn' you put coal in that heater?" demanded Clarence. "Your mama purely hates to come home to a cold house, an' you've let it git colder'n a bitch in here. Where's the old man? Out to Danny's, I suppose. Think I'll go down there a few minutes myself. Why ain't you got that coal up here?"

"I just—got home." Nolan knew he was really no good at lying.

"You lyin' little bastard!" Clarence grabbed him by the arm. "Now you git this place decent before your mama comes home an' I git back or, so help me God, I'll kill you. I've had just about all I can stomach of both of you little sonsabitches."

143

Nolan dared to say, "All right, I'll do it. I'm sorry—"

Clarence let go of him with one hand and wrenched open the warped old cellar door. "An' none a your sass!" he yelled, giving the boy a kick which flung him headlong down the worn splintery old stairs.

Nolan did not lose consciousness. He only wished he would. He felt the snap in his arm as he tumbled, felt the dirt cellar floor under his face, felt cold and sick and frightened. Vaguely, he heard Clarence slam out of the house.

After what seemed a very long while, he dragged himself slowly to his knees, and stood up. It was dark here, and cold, so cold that he thought that was what must be causing the numbness, the strange unreality, and at the same time, the feeling that all this had happened somewhere, sometime before. Gradually, he climbed up the unlighted stairs. Near the top, he realized he had forgot the coal, but then, in the kitchen light, he saw his arm, and at the same instant it began to hurt, unbearably. It was his left arm, and about half way between wrist and elbow, he could see a bone end through frayed skin. Other parts of him hurt as well; there was blood coming from his nose and out at the tattered knee of one of his new pairs of pants, but he scarcely knew that. Swallowing fiercely, struggling, he got the little way to the bathroom before he threw up. Then there were a few moments of blessed oblivion.

Rousing, he heard someone come into the house, Roger and their mother. They were talking happily about what a nice coincidence it was that they had met on the bus coming home.

"It's so cold in here," Darlene said irritably. "I do so hate to come home to a cold house, and they all know it. Daddy? Nolan?" she called.

He lay on the bathroom floor and made no sound.

"Roger, honey, could you go down and fill the coal scuttle? Be real careful now, sweetie, not to get any of that filthy dust on your nice uniform. You look so nice and I'm *so* glad you had a good meeting this afternoon. What's this note? Oh dear, it's after six. Supper is probably all dried out. Clarence and I will be going out this evening, dancing and all that, but I guess I forgot to tell Daddy. He's made enough for all of us. I guess it isn't too dry and I'm hungry."

He heard her opening the oven, heard Roger in the cellar, then at the stove in the living room.

"I hate, too," Darlene was going on, "to come home to an *empty* house. I'm the only one that works. Wouldn't you think they'd have *some* consideration. Well, no, the supper's not ruined. We'll just sit down in a minute and eat, Rogie, if they don't show up, otherwise, the food will be cold, too. Oh, there's the car now, I think. I had

144

hoped Clarence would meet me at the bus stop, since he has nothing else to do and it's so raw today, but . . . I suppose he and Daddy have been down at Danny's Place, and would you look at all this beer!''

They came in, Clarence apologizing. ''I left a note, an' then I *told* that damned Nolan to git this house warmed up for you, honey.''

''Maybe he hasn't come in from his paper route yet,'' said Liam.

''Yes, he has,'' snapped Clarence. ''Didn't I just say I *told* him—''

''Grandpa!'' a weak, shaky wail.

The old man, gripped by a fright that was almost terror, hurried as fast as he could toward the sound of the voice.

''Oh my God!'' gasped Darlene and staggered back against Clarence, half-fainting. ''Blood,'' she moaned weakly.

Nolan had a place within himself where he could go—it had always been there—away from Mama's whinings and yammerings and accusations, from Roger's demands and bullyings, even from Clarence's belt. Usually there was music in this secret solitary place. Tonight there was no music and the place itself was trying to elude him as Grandpa said, shocked, ''For God's sake, Chappie, what's happened?''

''The stairs,'' he muttered, struggling as the old man bent painfully toward him. ''I can stand up. It's all right.''

He knew he was crying and he hated himself for that, but the pain . . . Still, he wouldn't let Roger help him and Grandpa was too unsteady and feeble to be of much support.

''Stairs?'' said Roger. ''You mean the cellar stairs? How did you—''

''Get some clean cloths,'' Liam was ordering, ''and I think there ought to be a tourniquet above his elbow.''

Darlene said shakily aside to Clarence, ''You're going to have to take him to the hospital again. I'll have to call Roy and Judy, tell them we can't be there, I *had* counted on this evening, after working my tail off all week. Clarence, don't take him to the same one where we—you know.''

''I'm going along to the hospital this time,'' said Liam firmly ''You stay here, my girl. You're as white as a sheet.''

Nolan walked to the car on his own, gritting his teeth, and into the emergency door at the hospital.

They X-rayed his arm almost immediately, then gave him a shot for the pain and worked on his other wounds, trying to staunch the bleeding of his arm, waiting for the orthopedist.

Again, outside a curtain, he heard people talking.

Clarence said, ''This will cost an arm and a leg. Me an' Darlene had a heavy date planned for tonight.''

And Liam coldly, "You worry over odd things at strange times. Darlene's got the insurance where she works now. What I want to know is what happened to that boy? He said the stairs."

"I reckon he fell down the cellar steps, goin' to git coal. I left a note, tellin' him to fuel the heater. It was right on the bottom a that one you'd wrote about supper."

"And that's all you know," said Liam wearily.

"Didn' I come into Danny's, have one or two drinks an' then bring you home? How do I know what the little bastard's up to?"

A young resident named Andrews stayed with Nolan most of the time. He gave him a local anesthetic and sewed up the torn knee. There were six stitches. Nolan watched dispassionately, but then the nurse turned to grab a basin and he was sick again.

After the shot began to have some effect on his arm, Nolan discovered that other parts of him hurt, almost everything. Dr. Andrews helped him gently to turn, then said, "You're a pretty banged-up kid. Feeling a little easier now? Dr. Blakeley ought to be here any time. Want to tell me what happened? It looks like you may be with us quite a while."

The music was coming now, a lusty sailor's song, "I remember one day we was out on the line; When I think on it now, boys, we had a good time . . ."

He did want to tell the doctor, all of it. But when a thing like this was found out, social workers or somebody came into it, didn't they? Maybe even the police? Maybe you got sent to a foster home, and there was Grandpa and Roger . . . If he could just tell this scrubbed, sympathetic young man, maybe go home with *him* for a few days . . . And then the social worker or whoever would send word to Price, wouldn't they? But did Price want him as he was? He had been harsher, less patient those last few weeks of last summer, as if he wanted Nolan to be someone else. My name is Nolan Price Savage, he thought fiercely, and I am me. We're all stuck with that.

The song went on, "She was drivin' bows under, the sailors all wet, Makin' ten knots wi' her main sky s'l set." Then he noticed the young doctor, watching him, waiting.

"I was going to our cellar to get coal," he said groggily. "There's not much light. I fell down the stairs."

"Wow!" said Dr. Andrews. "All the way from the top?"

"Yes."

"But someone—is that your grandpa out there?—I thought he said they found you in the bathroom. Was that downstairs?"

"No," Nolan said. "I had to throw up."

The doctor couldn't repress a wider smile. "Someone ought to give you a medal for cleanliness." Then, more soberly, "Well, cellar stairs explain the dirt and bruises, and the arm, I guess. You're even going to have a shiner of an eye. We thought your nose was broken, but it seems to be okay. Nolan, look, I'm going to be a pediatrician. You know, that's a doctor who takes care of kids. I see a lot of kids. I saw you, at the emergency entrance, walking in here from your dad's car. You just don't look to me like an awkward clumsy kid, like I've heard."

"He—Clarence—has a bad back, and Grandpa can't walk without his cane."

"So you just had to do it on your own," said Dr. Andrews gently, his eyes probing Nolan's. But one of Nolan's eyes was half-closed from bruising, the other from the sedation.

There was another sailor's song, "So I spent all me tin on the lassies drinkin' gin, And across the western ocean I must wander."

The doctor pressed on kindly. "But tell me something, old buddy, Scout's honor, were you home all by yourself?"

"I'm not a Scout."

"You're a tricky one, is what you are."

Then Dr. Blakeley came in. They explained it all to Nolan: there were two bones in the forearm, the radius and the ulna—he could never remember which one was broken, but they said it was a miracle both had not been. They took him upstairs to put him to sleep.

"You know those old nails you see scattered around building sites?" asked Dr. Andrews. "That's what Doctor Blakeley gathers up to pin people's bones together." Then, "Hey, you know I'm kidding, don't you?" The boy didn't seem capable of a real smile, even sedated.

"We'll wait for a few days," said the more sober Dr. Blakeley, "to make sure there's going to be no infection, then we'll put a cast on, from above your elbow to below your wrist. You'll probably have to bear with that for about two months." Nolan didn't care. He clutched at sleep. "I've spent all me tin . . ."

Clarence had tried to baulk at any stay. "Just fix him up and we'll take him home."

Dr. Blakeley spoke curtly. "He'll have to be here for at least a few days. This is a compound fracture, man. There's always the danger of infection, and he's lost some blood. Maybe you hadn't noticed."

Clarence paced and muttered when they had taken Nolan to surgery. A few days! Suppose the brat talked? He hadn't meant to hurt him—not this much—just to get him started on his way to the damned cellar. Darlene wouldn't care if Nolan was taken away from them, though she felt he was in some way necessary for dear little Roger. And that old man, sitting over there with his hands on his lousy cane, would raise all kinds of hell, have Price Savage into it . . . the courts . . . If *both* kids got taken away, given to Price, Clarence would be as happy as a lark, but Darlene, well, she just couldn't live without her darling little Rogie, and she'd blame him, Clarence, though he'd seen *her* slap Nolan around pretty good, especially when he was littler and the old man wasn't around to see.

As he passed near, Liam said, "Don't you think you ought to call Darlene? She'll be worried sick. Does she even know which hospital we came to?"

"Tell you what, old Gramps. I think I'll just run home and tell her. Why don't you come, too. They said the kid would be out for hours." Maybe it wasn't too late for them to have some dancing at that new place Judy and Roy had talked about.

No, he couldn't manage if Darlene were to leave him over the brats. She was his status symbol. Every man that set eyes on her wanted her. He could put up with her whining, badgering him to get work, even with the damn twins and the damn old man, as long as she was *his*. He liked to watch other men looking at her. He didn't have much, but there was this, a woman all other men coveted.

Liam said stubbornly, "I'll stay till Chappie's awake."

Well, that was the end of any plans for going out. Darlene would never leave Rogie home alone. He thought, you old fool, but said tersely, "That could be all night."

"Yes, but it's no matter. He needs family here."

"Well, I better go take care of Darlene. She's likely to be into hysterics by this time."

They let Liam into the recovery room. Nolan drifted in and out of consciousness.

"Grandpa?"

"It's me, Chappie. How are you now, lad?"

"I'm all right. Nothing hurts."

And later, "Did you stay here by yourself? I mean, is Clarence gone?"

"He went home some time ago."

"How will you get back?"

"I'll take a cab later. I've got money for that. You're not to worry now, over that or anything else."

After a long pause, "I'll have to give up the newspaper job."

"Aye, well, you'll be fit soon enough, and you can get it back, or something else."

"What's that?"

"That's a bit of blood they're giving you to make up for what you lost."

"Oh yes, I remember from the other time . . ." He slept again.

The next day Darlene came to the hospital. That was the day Nolan stopped thinking of her as Mama or Mother, or anything besides Darlene or something worse. He saw her at the door to the ward, with a man, simpering as the man indicated he would wait in the corridor. She was all dressed up and smelled nice. She brought him a small box of candy and two brand new books. She leaned over the bed and hugged and kissed him. He rubbed hard at his cheek because he knew her lipstick always came off on people, but she didn't seem to notice.

She said, "Oh, Chappie, we've been *so* worried!"

He wanted to scream, "Don't call me that. It's not a name you're allowed to use."

She smiled at a passing nurse and said for her benefit, "I took some time off work, just to visit you. Mr. Marsh, from the store, drove me over. Your daddy's gone out to see about a new job. We saw your doctor. He says you're doing fine. How do you feel? You're all right, aren't you?"

Nolan nodded briefly. He had heard her talk about Mr. Marsh from the store, but she didn't work today. The store wasn't even open today. Where was Clarence? Probably at Danny's or some place like it. Nolan didn't know precisely what was wrong, but he knew now that his mother always lied and that she must do other things as well.

"I explained to Dr. Blakeley—and Clarence and Daddy explained it to them last night—how you were home alone and going to the cellar for coal. How you fell down the stairs, old rickety things. What I can't understand, honey, is why you didn't turn on the light down there. Rogie and I noticed how the light wasn't on after they'd brought you to the hospital. Oh, Nolan, Rogie is *so* lonely. He's just lost all by himself. But you know, sweetie, how apt you are to be awkward and clumsy, and to try those old stairs in the dark. . . . Well, you *do* just worry me to death. You told the doctor how it happened, didn't you? That you were home alone and—"

"You don't have to worry about anything," he said curtly and bit his lip.

"Well, I certainly *do* worry," she said, looking sorrowfully at another passing nurse. "I thought this would be something you'd outgrow, this what Daddy calls fumblefootedness, but, I swear, sometimes I think you're not going to *live* to outgrow it."

She looked, as deeply as he would let her, into his gray eyes with her big soulful brown ones, trying to convey her message, but she was the first to look away.

When she left, after a lot more gushing and another kiss, one of the nurses came to him.

"Well! What nice presents! Do you feel like a piece of candy?

149

It's all right if you have some." She had noticed he was very white.

He shook his head. "Let the other kids share it."

"That's awfully nice of you, but I'll bet you'll change your mind later on. What about these books? We have a reading stand so you'll only need one hand. Want to have a look?"

"No. . . . Thank you."

She went out and came back with the thermometer and blood pressure cuff. It wasn't time to take vitals yet, but the boy didn't look right at all.

When Nolan came home again, everything was normal. Clarence complained about having to pick him up. Darlene said nothing when he came into the house. Grandpa hugged him in the kitchen, Roger followed to his bedroom.

"Gosh, I wish I looked like that," he said enthusiastically. "Do you know you're all green and blue and purple all over? Can I be the first to sign your cast? Oh, I see other people have already done it. People from the hospital? Well, shall I sign it next?"

"Go away," said Nolan and dropped exhaustedly into his bed.

He lost the paper route, of course, and he had to stay out of school for two weeks, which almost lost him the school year. But Liam went to every one of his teachers and explained, then Roger brought home books and assignments so that he was able to keep up, but only just.

Toward the end of the two weeks, when he was up all day and feeling well, Nolan knew the worst part of this broken arm. He could not play any music and there seemed little else to do. Bits of melodies, harmonies, arpeggios, runs, and progressions tumbled through his mind and there was no outlet. Liam played for him, but he couldn't *tell* Grandpa what to play, how he was hearing it. Then they remembered the Irish whistle and that was some surcease, though, even two-handed, it could carry only one voice at a time.

When Nolan went to put it away under the bed with the other instruments, he found a piece of paper, dusty and worn-looking. It was the letter he had begun to Kiersten. He brought it into the kitchen where Grandpa was looking through the newspaper.

"Grandpa, if I write a letter, will you mail it for me, in that box down by Danny's?"

"Be glad to, Chappie."

He wrote: "This letter was interrupted about two weeks ago when I got a broken arm. It was a compound fracture, my left arm. I have a cast and a sling now and am doing fine. I go back to school next week. I will find another job next summer. I would like to hear from you, but please don't write back here. Send the letter to my friend Ed Johnson (he filled in the address) and Ed will give it to me."

Then he couldn't think how to stop and, finally, simply signed his name.

By mid-June the cast was off, though Nolan was still supposed to go easy on his arm. He was playing sandlot baseball though, so he thought it would be all right to look for other work. Using the bicycle again, he rode almost two miles, into a much better neighborhood than theirs and managed to secure six lawns to care for through the rest of the summer.

Roger went to the day camp by bus five days a week. They were swimming, going on field trips, seeing movies and doing their choices of crafts. There was, of course, not money enough for both the twins to go and Nolan didn't care much.

Clarence had got a job as flagman for a construction crew. When he came home in the evenings, one would have thought he was the first man ever to hold a job. He demanded constant attention: bring him this, adjust the TV, get him that. Even Darlene catered to him—a little.

Liam was not well. He hadn't felt right since the beginning of May, dull and listless, tired all the time, with a persistent cough, and his leg was paining him more than it ever had, except right in the beginning. Darlene had said once, only once, and that in a dutiful, absent way, that he ought to go and have it checked. But he complained so rarely that she quickly forgot it in the press of her own concerns.

When Nolan was home, he and Liam were usually there alone together. He tried to talk to the boy, tried to tell him what little he'd learned from life, tried to explain, make allowances for, Darlene.

"And you be your own man," he said once sternly, more life than usual coming into his voice. "A man lets another man take himself away from him, he's no' but a shell."

Was he talking about Liam, Nolan wondered, about the way Liam had given himself to Darlene and to the rest of them?

"And then there's your brother," Liam said awkwardly, another time. "He's had so much, but he needs so much more, of different things. It may be you'll need to keep an eye out for him as long as you both live. Roger's smart; he can do anything he may want, but he needs somebody to cheer him on, not for *their* glory, but for his own. He doesn't think much of people in general, but he respects you. Another man's respect is a gift, though it can be a burden, too. You can look out for him, a little, can't you, Chappie? You're far the stronger."

When he was on the couch at home alone, Liam lay there, paying little heed to the quietly babbling television, or more usually, he lay in his bed. It was a particularly hot summer and the house was stifling most of the time, but the pain in his leg was too constant and enervating to let him move around much. Sometimes Nolan would persuade him to be helped into the back yard where there was a peeling old lounge chair and a bit of a breeze. He could overlook railroad cars, being shunted around in a small yard at the bottom of the hill. The boy would bring pillows and Liam said yes, he was fine and comfortable, but nothing really eased the pain, or the malaise.

Nolan read him two letters from Kiersten, the little girl at Secesh, Price's adopted daughter. Chappie, smiling, said she wrote just like she talked, which must be a blue streak. But they were good little letters, breezy, full of news about the ranch, and Liam was gratified that the boy would share them with him. He wondered why Price and his second wife had no children, but that would be none of the boy's knowledge.

After the second letter, he said gently, "Your dad's important to you, eh, Chappie?"

Nolan, looking at the letter he was folding, said, "Yes, I guess so."

"Would you like to go and live there, at Secesh, for always?"

"I—don't know."

"I always had the notion you would."

"Well, there are things—I just don't know any more."

"Wait and see what life brings, is it? Aye, and that's a good way to live, for it's all we *can* do, really, in the end, isn't it?"

Nolan had now been assigned the preparation of breakfast and supper, as well as whatever he and Grandpa had for lunch. Except for Roger, nobody ate much breakfast. Clarence and Darlene wanted only coffee and toast, but Roger wanted the whole meal, and complained every morning about how his eggs were cooked. Nolan had to use Grandpa's alarm clock to be sure of getting up on time, so both of them were wakened. Liam almost always said he wanted nothing, but Chappie would bring him tea and toast. He'd developed a yearning for good, strong, hot tea of late and it embarrassed him a little, like some shortcoming. He'd let the boy help him prop up in bed with their combined pillows, and take the old battered tray on his lap with a slightly abashed smile of thanks.

Nolan didn't mind being up early, though he resented the breakfasts, except for Grandpa's. The days were very hot and he liked to try to get his lawn work done before noon.

On this particular August morning he had two lawns to water and two to mow. Yesterday he had been promised his paper route back in September and that pleased him. He helped Grandpa to the toilet.

"Do you want to watch TV?"

"No, I'll just go back to bed for a bit, I think."

Liam lay there in the stifling little room. He heard the boy leave, wheeling the damned bicycle around the house. He lay there and thought about the 'Sixteen, the almost glorious Easter Rising, when he had been young and full of sap and daring.

Nolan rode along, pretending the bicycle was a horse and he was at Secesh. Other vehicles, moving about the streets, were stock he'd have to round up later.

One of the ladies whose lawn he cut asked him to do some errands for her, pick up some things her husband had ordered from a hardware store, and then to go a long way out of his way to get a piece of dress goods from a friend of hers. She gave him five dollars in addition to his lawn work earnings.

It was mid-afternoon, past three. Sweat poured from him and his arm hurt, but he was feeling pretty good. All during those errands, a melody had been forming in his mind, with improvisations. When he got home he'd play it straight away for Grandpa. This one sounded like Grandpa, the way he was once. Nolan could never remember having heard it, but he had seen it in the depths of the blue eyes when they sparkled. Well, maybe he wouldn't do it straight away. He'd find them something cold to drink first, and maybe Grandpa would be a little hungry for a change.

He called to Liam when he came into the house. There was no answer. The living room was empty. He must be napping, though how anybody could sleep in this heat . . . and the bedroom door was closed besides.

He pushed it open quietly. At first, he thought Liam *was* napping, lying on his back with one of his hands doubled up against his cheek and his mouth open, the way you saw pictures of babies. Then he saw the eyes were open.

"Grandpa?" he whispered.

After a moment he went in, tiptoeing as if Liam might wake. There was a pleasant expression on the old face, as if he were thinking of something happy. Tentatively, Nolan touched the hand that lay across the thin old rib cage. It was cool and dry in the summer heat.

His first feelings were misery, loss, anger. "Why didn't you tell me?" he cried within himself. "I should have been here. How could you leave me like this?"

Slowly the bitterness ebbed and he stood there, thinking little, not knowing what to think. Finally, he said very softly, "I'll be back."

He went into the kitchen and drank a glass of water, then another. He wanted ice water, but it didn't seem that he should have that.

He returned to the stifling bedroom and sat on his own bed,

keeping very still and silent for a long while. The new melody was tormenting him. This wasn't a time for music, or was it? Slowly, he drew the old guitar out from under Liam's bed—any other summer, they'd have kept the instruments out in the falling-down barn—and he said softly, "There's something I want you to hear. But first, I remember this song you used to sing when I was little: 'O storms of the night, let your fury be crossed; Let no one who's dear to old Ireland be lost; Blow the winds gently, soft o'er the foam; Shine the lights brightly and bring them back home.' " He gulped, glad there were no words to his new melody. He had managed pretty well to sing the old lullaby in a soft, clear, almost steady voice.

"I wanted to play this for you when I got home today," he went on, almost whispering. "It's got a lot of Irish in it." And he played it quietly. It would be one of his songs he would always remember and in later years he called it "Liam's Song."

Then, putting the guitar away, he started to cry. "I'm sorry I wasn't here," he said brokenly. "Maybe you needed something, or I could have . . ."

He ran into the bathroom and threw up the water. It seemed a long time before he could stop crying and retching.

When that finally happened, he washed his burning face and went back into the bedroom. Far back, under Liam's bed, behind the instruments, was a little trunk that had come all the way from Ireland. It had some papers in it, letters, and his Grandma's faded worn wedding dress. Under these things, in an old sock, was the money Grandpa had been keeping for him.

"They'll be looking at everything now," he told the old man. "You'll understand if I just take this somewhere else."

He ran out to the old barn. There was a loose board on one of the inside walls and he stuffed the sock quickly behind it. The money couldn't be left there. The mice would get at it, for one thing, but he'd have to think about that later. He didn't want to think of anything now.

Back in the house he washed his dusty hands, arms, and face at the kitchen sink, then turned and looked dazedly around the room. Darlene had said something cool tonight, did he think he could make a fruit salad? God knew she had showed him how enough times, she had said, and the things he'd need were all right there in the refrigerator. Nolan put them together. Hot rolls, she had said, the brown-and-serve kind.

He stopped in mid-movement. Would Grandpa have wanted a priest? They had used to go to church, before Grandma died. No, more likely, Grandpa would want some of the boys from Danny's to come and hold a wake, a real old-fashioned wake, like he'd talked about, back in Ireland. Could that be done? He'd try to do it, in spite of Darlene and Clarence and Roger, but then there were those things about coroners and such that he'd seen on television. Probably, he should have called someone a long time ago. No, but let them do it. He wanted this last little time alone in the house with Grandpa. They'd done little enough for him while he was alive.

Usually the three of them got home at almost the same time, Clarence meeting Darlene with the car at the bus stop, and Roger, arriving on the camp bus just a little later.

Supper was ready, the rolls in the oven, the fruit salad arranged in a large bowl on the table with a pitcher of iced tea. Places were set for three. He went back into the bedroom, closing the door. He tried to pry the old window a little more open, but it wouldn't move, so he sat on his bed and was still.

Darlene called out as the three of them came into the house, "Dad? Nolan? The bedroom door is closed; Daddy must be napping, though how he can stand it in this heat. . . . Do you *realize* how hard it is to come out of that air-conditioned store into *this* oven?"

"I told you," said Clarence sharply, "that if you didn't spend so much on clothes and fancy hairdos and such, we might have a better house, *with* air-conditionin'."

"Oh, Clarence, I don't see why you have to be *at* me all the time. *I*'m the one brings the most money into this house. I don't know why you have to be so grouchy when I'm so dead tired."

"At least supper's ready," said Roger. "I'm hungry. I wonder where Chappie is."

"There's no tellin'," sighed Darlene. "We may as well eat."

"He didn't set a place for himself," Roger pointed out.

"Oh, he may be eating with some of those scruffy kids he plays with," she said wearily. "He needs a lot more supervision than Dad can give him."

"I told you we ought to have sent them both to their daddy, like always," Clarence said maliciously. "That kid's got altogether out of hand this summer. Needs a good lesson to git him back on the track."

Through the closed door, Nolan could hear their voices droning on, mostly Clarence's, about what a hard day he'd had, inconsiderate, disobedient drivers, and the broiling heat.

When he thought they must be almost finished, Nolan said softly to the figure on the bed, "I have to tell them. You know that, don't you? I want it to be something that will really get their attention. I hope they'll lose their suppers. I want them to remember something at least about you."

He touched the hand, now very cool, and fought the tears out of

155

his eyes. "I love you, Grandpa. I don't think there'll be a chance to talk to you again. There couldn't be a better Grandpa in the whole world."

Then he went and opened the door. They all stared at him. He came and leaned his hands on the vacant side of the table so that they should not see he had begun to tremble all over. They had emptied the bowl, the pitcher, and the pan the rolls were cooked on. They kept staring at him and he wondered fleetingly what he looked like that would keep all of them silent this long.

"Grandpa's dead," he said quietly, steadily.

10

For their eleventh summer as well as their tenth, Roger and Nolan did not go to Secesh. Roger attended the summer day camp and had two weeks of Boy Scout camp. Nolan worked his paper route and got a job a few hours each evening working at a service station near the house.

On his twelfth birthday, as on his tenth, Nolan went to look at guitars again. This time he had money, almost two hundred dollars, and he had chosen what he wanted. His heart banged with excitement, but he shortly left the store desolate. There was a little park where three streets formed a triangle. He sat on a bench there, trying to pull himself together.

With Liam gone he was seldom home now. He worked, after his paper route and on weekends, at the service station across from Danny's Place. He had told Roger, "You'll have to fix the meals now," and Roger had said craftily, "Will you pay me?" "I will not," Nolan had answered definitely, "but Darlene probably will."

There was little time for schoolwork, but he managed to keep up. There was little time for music, but he had chosen his twelve-string, skipping school lunches, wearing clothes until they virtually fell apart, using stubs of pencils, writing on both sides of papers, which threw his teachers into despair. He had saved a hundred and ninety dollars and they would not let him take the guitar.

A man sat down on the bench. Nolan scarcely noticed.

After a while, the stranger said, above the noise of traffic, "You look to me like a kid with troubles."

Nolan looked at him. He was a small man with a round open face, shabbily dressed but clean, with quick piercing eyes.

"I wanted to buy a guitar over there," he said without hesitation. He needed to tell someone and felt, rather oddly, that this stranger might understand. "I've got a hundred and ninety dollars, but they won't let me take it. I was going to pay fifteen a month but they say that's not enough, and I guess they're right. It costs six hundred and fifty before tax and it would take a long time to pay for, but I'm getting older. I can get jobs that pay more. They say I'm too young to sign a note anyway.''

"This must be some nice guitar.''

"It is. It's a Martin twelve-string. I was in around Christmas and they let me play it a little.''

"You're good with a guitar, huh?''

"Well, with a six-string I am. I really haven't had any practice with a twelve.''

"Play anything else?''

"Fiddle and banjo, and a sort of flute.''

"I was a musical kid,'' said the man musingly. "Played bass in a band for a lot of years and you see where it got me, just an ordinary bum. Maybe you ought to keep clear of this musical stuff.''

"I can't,'' Nolan said quietly.

The man was thinking. Nolan watched his face avidly.

"Suppose your father signed the note? You got a father, ain't you?''

"A stepfather, but he'd never . . .''

"I had one of them, too. Treated me like shit. I'm not talking about your real stepfather. Suppose I signed the note, promised more money, like, say, fifty a month?''

"But you can't. I don't—''

"We're supposin' now. Where do you live?''

Nolan told him.

"All right, you don't live there no more. Think up an address about as far away from there as you can get. I'm new in this town, so I don't know the streets and all. And a different name.''

"I could never pay fifty dollars a month. It's taken me two years to save what I've got.''

"You send 'em somethin' ever' month, from the fake name and address, and they'll be more or less satisfied. Business people expect to take some losses. It's built into their prices. They get somethin' from you, it's better than nothin', right? Or, if you can't pay, don't worry too much about it. I don't think they could find you. I know they won't find me, because I'm leavin' this burg quick as I can. It's damn cold. Look around. It's April an' still winter. Maybe you'd want to come along. I ain't had a partner in a long time.''

"I can't leave.''

"Well, no, I can see you wouldn' be much good at jumpin' freights if you got to haul along two guitars and the rest of that stuff.

158

Tell me, you said you played this guitar around Christmas time. This the same one?''

"Yes."

"Well, maybe we could get the price down some."

"They say I could buy it if I paid more a month and if some adult signed the note. But they also said they'd do a credit check."

"With me, kid, you can walk out of that store carryin' the guitar in ten minutes. Want to try or not? What's to lose?"

"Well, suppose they find out later and—"

"They repossess their property. Not much else they can do. You're a minor, and you'll have had the use of it for that long, *if* they find you. You had any raps before?"

"What?"

"Trouble with the cops. Arrests."

"No."

"Well, repossession is all they'd do, and that costs them money. If you really mean to send 'em somethin' ever' month, it's my opinion they wouldn' bother. Here, you write down names and addresses, where I work, so I can memorize—"

"But I don't—"

"You scared?"

"Yes."

"You got any money, besides what you was goin' to pay down?"

"About five dollars."

"You give that to me, after we've made the deal in the store. We'll call it a finder's fee. I can get quite a lot of pretty good wine for that and then, when I'm warmed up a little, I'll get out of this damned place."

He was shoving a ragged piece of paper and a pencil stub at Nolan.

"Better yet, go to that phone booth over there an' pick a name, with an address a long way from where you live. Then they can look it up in the book, too."

"No, I won't do that."

"Why the hell not?"

"Because it would get those people in trouble."

"Oh, all right, make it all up then. Where do I work?"

"I really mean to pay for the guitar." He was trembling a little, with fear, excitement, and daring. "Today's my birthday and I thought—"

"Yeah, yeah, you pay for it. Happy birthday. You keep honest if that's the way you have to do it. Where do I work?"

"You're a—a garbage collector."

"Well, that's the God's truth, but why?"

"Because I know about how much they make a month. That has to be on the note. They showed it to me."

"What else? How many kids I got?"

"Two, besides me."

"My wife work?"

"Yes. She's a—a waitress."

"Sounds about par for the course. I suppose she'd run around with customers and such. They'll want to know about other payments, on the house, like that, you figure it out."

"They'll want to see some identification, too."

"Say, that's right, good thinkin'. I got a driver's license, but it's from Illinois. All right, we'll have to use my real name. It's Harry Blevins. Say we moved here two years ago. That's how old the license is."

"Do you have any union card or—"

"Nah, I forgot to bring that down today. What else?"

"Well, I think they want references, besides where you work, I mean. And you've been a garbage man ever since we came here. They don't like people changing jobs."

"Okay. We rent our house. Make up a name for the landlord. All our relatives live back in Illinois. Let's say I'm buyin' a car, a used one. Put down a car dealer for good credit."

"This isn't going to work."

"Sure it is. You never take a risk, you never get nothin'. Besides, if it fouls up, I'm the one'll be in trouble. You're a minor, right?"

They were in the store for twenty minutes, Nolan going hot and cold by turns.

"Phone number?"

"We got no phone," said Harry Blevins smoothly. "The things are a damn nuisance especially with a gabby wife and three kids in the house."

"Is there a number where you can be reached?"

Harry gave Nolan a surreptitious nudge and he came up with one that sounded right for the neighborhood they were listing.

"That's our landlord's and he don't want to be bothered except for an emergency."

"You mean you haven't had your driver's license changed to Colorado in all this time?"

"Look, I work hard every day. Those license places aren't open when I'm not workin'. It'll expire before long. Then I got to take time off to get it fixed up, right? The car dealer we bought from here didn't make any fuss about the license."

"Put down the license number of your car, please."

"What is it, son, do you remember? The kid's a whiz with rememberin' numbers, just like he's a whiz with music. We come down here on the bus today. The wife, Betty's, got the car today. Boy, were we suckered on that lemon! Can't keep the heap runnin' half the time. This guitar better be worth the money. The boy here, it's his birthday present. Plans on bein' a musician, you know, one earns his bread 'n butter with it. Think of me, a garbage collector, with a kid's maybe gonna play in Carnegie Hall one day! You ought to hear what his teachers say! . . . Now, on this price. I personally know you've had this instrument around a long time. You want to move your stock, I know, so how about givin' us a break? Say six hundred even, includin' tax?"

"I couldn't do anything like that without the manager's approval."

"So ask him. And throw in a case. A fine instrument like this has got to have a case."

Somehow, the price, case included, came down to six hundred and twenty dollars.

"All right," said the clerk, looking slightly dazed. "This is Saturday. We should have the credit check run by Monday afternoon. You can pick up the guitar any time after that."

"Listen," said Harry cajolingly, "*today*'s the kid's birthday. He works after school on Monday. So do I work; so does his mother. How we supposed to pick it up then? You got this money down. This kid's been workin' his butt off to save it up. He's been countin' on havin' the guitar *on* his birthday. Have a heart. I'd hate to go through all this here preliminary business again, but you got competition that's maybe a little more flexible, little more human."

They walked out of the store, with Nolan carrying the fine, new, beautiful instrument in its case, which was also so obviously new that he felt everyone on the sidewalk was staring with envy or suspicion, or both. He was shaking and had to struggle not to turn back, look guiltily at the store.

"Where's your bus stop?" asked Harry jauntily.

"Around the corner and two blocks down."

His lips felt numb, frozen. His trembling and apprehension lessened a little when they had turned the corner. He put the guitar down carefully, resting against him, and emptied his pockets except for bus fare.

"Thanks, *son*," said Harry, chuckling. "It's been fun knowin' you. You might work up to bein' a real con artist. Enjoy the guitar, and happy birthday."

"Thanks, I—I think. I really will pay for it."

"Sure you will. You ain't got to convince me. It was that honest,

161

earnest look on your face that got to them back there in the store. If you ever want to pull off somethin' like this again, remember it was Harry Blevins showed you the ropes. So long now. Take it easy."

They shook hands and Harry was gone, whistling on his way.

Nolan went through the long wait and the long bus ride in a daze. On the bus he held the guitar standing upright, his arm around the case. What if somebody tried to steal it, or it got banged up somehow? What if the people at the music store . . . ? But he had it, he was holding it close to him. If only Grandpa could know! Maybe he did. He might not approve of how it had been acquired, but he, Nolan, *would* pay for it, every penny and with interest.

They were supposed to go to Secesh this summer. Darlene said she didn't want them left on their own again. Clarence agreed heartily. Nolan wanted to go, more than almost anything, but he also had to earn money. He set his jaw, never giving a thought to how much he looked like Price, except for the eyes, which were now steady and defiant with decision. He would write to Price, tell him he thought his work should be worth half wages at least this year. After all, he was twelve and strong for his age, though looking deceptively slight. There would be no overhead for him at the ranch, no turning over a share of his earnings to Clarence. He might not get the guitar paid off during the summer, but he could make a good dent in what was owing. If only the store didn't trace him somehow before June, when he would be away! He hugged the guitar. There were already songs in him, waiting for it.

One night in the following week Roger came into Nolan's room uninvited. Nolan, sitting on the old straight chair, was softly, lovingly playing the new guitar. What a beautiful thing it was, fast becoming a part of him.

"You weren't here at supper," said Roger, sitting on the bed.

Nolan had told them at the beginning of the week, that he would not be home for supper any more. He had persuaded the service station owner to let him work, while he, Mr. Bates, went home for his own supper. Nolan ate what he could find when he came in, after nine, closing time. He made no answer to Roger, just laid his cheek against the guitar and went on playing.

"There's some pretty serious talk going on. I don't know when I've seen Mother and Clarence talk together so much. They're watching TV now, but they didn't turn it on until just a few minutes ago. You're hardly ever around, so I thought you'd want to hear what's going on, or what may be."

"What?" asked Nolan absently, still playing.

"We may be moving to Hurleigh soon."

He stopped and stared at Roger. "Why?"

"I don't want to, do you?"

"I don't know. Tell me why."

"Because there's a lot more to do here. I'd have to change Scout troops—"

"I don't mean that. Tell me why they're talking about it."

All of them had been shocked by the new guitar. Nolan had lied, saying he had saved enough to pay for it outright. Neither Clarence nor Darlene had any concept of the cost or value of such an instrument, but Clarence had said that if he could save like that, he ought to be turning over more money for the family good, and Darlene had demanded to know why he hadn't bought some decent clothes instead. If they moved to Hurleigh, maybe the music store people could never trace him, if they decided to try. He had written to Price, asking for a paying job, asking him to reply to Ed Johnson's address, as Kiersten had been doing all this time, but there hadn't been time enough yet for an answer. If—

Roger was saying, "The renters are moving out of Grandpa's house again. Mother owns it now and we pay more rent here than she gets for that house. She says she could go to work in the railroad office, that some people there would remember Grandpa, and her, from when she was a girl. She had those courses, when we were little, in typing and filing and all that. She says she's tired of being on her feet all day, having to handle food all the time, even if the tips are good and she probably wouldn't make as much in Hurleigh. She says she loathes Hurleigh, but they're never going to get anywhere here, if Clarence won't keep a job, and you know he's hardly worked a day in the past year. They think living will be cheaper in Hurleigh. I've told her I don't want to go and she says she really doesn't want to either, but sometimes things are just that way. Sometimes you have to do what you don't want to and maybe it will turn out better than you think."

"What does Clarence say?"

"He likes the idea. He says he might get a job in a store his cousin or someone owns, that sales work might not be hard on his back."

Nolan thought about it and began to smile faintly.

"But, Chappie, think about it. There's only one movie theater There's a bowling alley and a pool hall and that's about all, for so-called fun. They don't even have a swimming pool, maybe not even television yet. And the school! It's a little dinky place and they wouldn't have half the equipment we have here. If you want to work all the time, the way you seem to, there wouldn't be nearly as many jobs to find. It's just an old cow town, less than four thousand people. It's nothing."

Jobs would be a problem. On the other hand, Hurleigh was only seventy miles from Secesh. Maybe Darlene would let him go there to stay. He and Roger could get together sometimes.

Roger said urgently, "Chappie, they're talking about it for right *now*. Not even for when school is out or anything like that. Clarence says he knows a guy with a big truck who'd do the moving for less than a company would charge. Aren't you concerned? Don't you care?"

"Yes," said Nolan. "I hope we do it."

Roger said angrily, "I should have known. Why *wouldn't* you hope that? You're never going to grow up to be anything but a guitar-playing ranch hand anyway."

"What are you going to be?" asked Nolan, stretching, yawning.

"I don't know for sure yet, but *something*. I'm going to college, I know that."

"Well, then, I guess I'll be working to pay your tuition."

"Oh, don't be such a martyr!" He grew thoughtful and said, smiling a little, "There is *one* thing about the house in Hurleigh. It only has two bedrooms."

"So?"

"So we'd be sharing one. I always have wanted to do that but Mother keeps saying I ought to have my own room. I'd just—like to have you around, even if you don't like me."

"We share a room when we're at Secesh."

"But you're never around."

"I won't be around in Hurleigh either."

"You're acting as if you think you're just about grown up and can do as you please."

"I just about am, and do. Give me one good reason why I should want to stay in any house where Clarence or Darlene is."

"Well, you're not grown up. Neither am I. I wish we were. Clarence still knocks you around. You're not too big yet, even for his weak back."

"He may have done his last of that."

There was a silence and Roger said intently, "Tell me the truth about when you got the broken arm."

"All right. He kicked me down the stairs."

"Gosh! He really did. I always thought so. Then how did you get back up?"

"I climbed, Roger. How else?"

"Well, he's never dared lay a hand on me."

"Nor a foot," Nolan agreed easily.

"Why is there such a difference? Haven't you ever wondered about that?"

"No, because it's clear as day. Darlene really hates all kids, but she thinks she loves you, because you're like her—beautiful, and because you're always so damned good where it shows."

Roger lowered his head, flushing. "I'm not good, Chappie. I don't even want to be."

"I know that."

"I get so tired of it, of hearing about it. She's just stupid, plain stupid."

"Well, you keep putting it over with her, and some other people."

"I can't seem to help it. It's a—a pattern, a rut I've been in since I can remember. They don't like me at Secesh, at least Price and the men don't. If I let myself be normal, nobody does much."

"What's normal?"

"Well, you know, some—some mischief now and then."

"You mean like that time with Pussycat? That wasn't mischief, it was sick."

"Well, what *can* I do?"

"I don't know, Rogie," he said mockingly.

"Don't call me that," said Roger fiercely. "You know I hate it. Why can't we ever *talk?* You always end up being nasty, or just plain not hearing me. Can't you just answer a civil question?"

"I really don't know what you can do to be not good. Smash windows. Steal a car."

"Have you done those things? Would you do them?"

"No, but I'd get blamed somehow if you did. You can count on that."

"I don't, Chappie. Scout's honor, I don't *try* to get you in trouble. I never have. I *want* to do bad things, something so bad that even *she* will have to see it and admit I did it. I'm so sick of being a pet poodle. I want to have friends like you do. I know that doesn't have to involve doing bad things, but I feel I *have* to, just to prove something to other people, and to myself. How do you manage just to—pick up friends, just any old where?"

"I don't know."

"Well, how can *I* do it?"

"For one thing, don't be so snooty, so pee-puddle perfect."

"I am smarter than most people. Those tests we've had in school prove it. They prove it about you, too, and always surprise hell out of everybody. I can't help being smart, and I won't play dumb."

"I don't play dumb. I just—be."

"Being smart is a thing to be proud of."

"Well, what do you want me to do, Roger? Make you over in your own image?"

"You're misquoting the Bible or something. You shouldn't . . ."

"Look, I know you, like a twin brother. Don't start coming all over righteous with me. I know you go to Sunday school and the rest of it, but what's it get you? It just makes some people think how good you are. I also know a lot of other things about you."

"I don't even know why I try to talk to you. Can't you see I'm asking your advice? And all you do is put me down."

Nolan had gone back to playing softly. He said absently, "You're your own person. If you want to change what that is, then do it. I can't do it for you, nor can anybody else. Talking won't make any difference."

There was a lengthy silence, except for the soft music being worked out, until Roger said soberly,

"Let's plan to go to college together. We could both work and pay our way or, probably, Price would pay. We could be roommates, take the same classes, and I'd help you if you got behind. I could—"

"Doing things with me won't make you different. It just points up the differences between us. You have to be yourself and live with that. It's the same for everybody. Anyway, I don't think I want to go to college."

"Hey, Chappie," he was suddenly smiling broadly. "If we do have to go to school in Hurleigh, they probably don't have more than one class per grade. I've always wanted us to have classes together, but the schools here wouldn't let us."

"God!" groaned Nolan softly. "What difference is that going to make, except to point up how much better your grades are? You see? *That*'s the sort of thing you really want from me. Go away. Go to bed. You need your beauty sleep."

Roger was deeply hurt. His hazel eyes were vulnerable, glistening with moisture.

"What I wonder most about," he said unsteadily, "is why you simply can't like me, not ever."

"Oh, I like you well enough, Boy-o. Now get out. There's something I have to work on."

"With the guitar?"

"No, I want to practice cracking my knuckles."

"There! You—you condescend to me. Don't you know how I hate that? You have no respect, no friendship for me. You treat me as if—"

"All right. Okay. Yes, with the guitar. Now, please, goodnight."

They were moved to Hurleigh by the first of May. Nolan had managed to send twenty dollars to the music store just before leaving, but he could not find work immediately in Hurleigh. However, also just before they moved, he had received a formal note from Price, saying that he would be hired for the summer, at half wages, if he earned them. Nolan liked the business-like tone of the note. He smiled about it proudly to himself and kept it, along with Kiersten's letters, hidden fairly securely with what little money he had left.

One warm day in May, he was kept after school to complete some English work. Roger offered to wait, but Nolan told him to go home. There was a roast that had to be cooked for supper, and no one there to put it in, because Clarence actually was working as a salesman in his cousin's dry goods store. The teacher excused Nolan, with warnings, after three-quarters of an hour.

He walked slowly out of the junior high building and around the high school. This was fine weather. He felt good, and indolent. Spring fever, he supposed. In less than a month, they'd be at Secesh. Darlene had said that maybe it wouldn't be necessary for them to spend the summer there after all, that because Hurleigh was so much smaller, there would be less trouble to tempt them. But Clarence said they should go, and he gave her that look that said his back might go out if she didn't agree. Darlene seemed strangely happy to be back here. She had got a job in the railroad offices almost before they were moved into Grandpa's old house, and she was more likely to be agreeable these days, more likely to go along with Clarence—on some things.

Clarence had decided to want a baby. The boys could hear their talk, if it was loud enough, through the bedroom wall. Clarence said petulantly that she had produced twins for Price Savage; why wasn't she willing to bear his child? She flashed back that Price had "done her dirty," got her pregnant when she was a kid and didn't know anything, ruined her young life. Besides, for Chrissake, she was thirty years old now, not about to start another family, and he'd better keep using rubbers or forget it.

Nolan stopped abruptly outside a basement window of the high school building. He looked in, though he didn't need to. There was a bass player, a pianist, a guitar player, and someone with a cornet. They were playing jazz. After a few moments, he ran to a door, found the stairs, then the room. The door was open. He stood there and they all stared at him as they finished the number.

"What do you want?" asked the pianist in a surly tone.

"I was just—listening. Is this a regular group? I mean do you practice often and play places?"

"It's none of your business," said the bass player, "but we practice every day. The band teacher lets us use this room. We're called The Jives and we play places, all right. Now, what's it to you?"

"I wondered if I could—play along."

167

"On what, junior?"

"Well, could I just—borrow the guitar? Just for one number?"

"You've got a nerve, ain't you?" said the boy with the guitar, menacingly. "Who are you, anyhow? How old are you, ten?"

"I'm fourteen," he lied casually. "I'd go get my own instruments, but we live clear across town and you might be through before I—"

"Come on!" they hooted at him. "You're not fourteen. None of us has seen you around school."

"We just moved here."

"Well, nobody touches my guitar."

"I'd feel the same way," Nolan said earnestly, "but just for—"

"Ah, let him have it, Larry. We got to get rid of him somehow an' get on with business."

Nolan took the guitar with great care and sat down.

"Now," said the pianist patronizingly, "we were about to play 'Lady Be Good.' Do you know it?"

"I've heard it."

"He's heard it," announced the cornet player and they began.

After they had gone through the number twice, the pianist said, looking a little stunned, "Play a break this next time around."

Nolan did so and they finished with the cornetist leading again.

"Who the hell are you?" demanded Larry, retrieving his guitar. "You must have practiced that song a lot. We're all juniors in high school, been playing together for two years."

"My name's Nolan Savage. We just moved here."

"You already said that," noted the bass player dubiously. "What else can you play?"

"I've got a twelve-string guitar, and a six, a fiddle, banjo, and a kind of flute."

"I meant what *songs*, little boy." They were all staring at him again.

"Well, I guess—just about anything."

"Sure!" scoffing, "How long does it take you to learn a song?"

"One time through," he said quietly. They were embarrassing him and he'd had enough.

They guffawed, in the way of young boys, like cockerels just learning to crow, and punched each other in shared derision.

"Give him back the guitar," instructed the pianist, feigning weary boredom, and to Nolan, "We like to play jazz, but most of the places we play, they want cow music or rock. Do you know 'San Antonio Rose?'"

"Yes."

"Play it."

After a moment they all joined him, and the bass player sang the song.

"Now," said the cornetist, still sounding scornful, but unable to keep the amazement from showing. "Play 'Rock Around the Clock.' "

When they had gone through that once, Nolan said mildly, "I could do it better with the twelve-string."

They were staring at each other now. "You really play all those other instruments?" asked the pianist, without scorn now. Then he had to try to redeem himself a bit. "When do you plan on having a voice change?"

"Ever play bass?" demanded the bass player.

"No, but I think I could. It's like the low strings on the guitar, but like a fiddle, too, no frets."

"Try it, squirt, see if it's so damn easy. You got to get in the runs and everything or it don't count. Play 'Rock' again, you guys."

Nolan felt he played very badly, but the owner of the instrument said, "Tell the truth now. When did you learn to play bass?"

"Just now," he said soberly.

"Piano?" asked the pianist, obviously impressed.

"I've only ever played a little, but I think I could pick it up if I had some practice."

"Cornet?" asked the boy holding that instrument and looking uneasy.

Nolan shook his head.

"Tell you what," said the bass player magnanimously. "You bring all that stuff you say you've got. Bring it tomorrow. You can lock it up in here with our things. Then, after school, we'll see if you really can do it."

"And," said Larry, "you got to let me have some time with your twelve-string. You played my guitar."

The following day, after they had played for more than two hours, the pianist, whose name was Homer, said, "Want to join us? We agreed to ask you if you wasn't lying. Mr. Alden, the band teacher, wants to talk to you, too. He's got a cello he'd like for somebody to play in the high school orchestra. The orchestra ain't much but . . ."

Nolan was flushing scarlet. "I'd like to join you," he said. "I'd like it a lot, but I haven't told you the whole truth. I'm not in senior high, only junior and—"

"Jesus God!" muttered the bass player, Butch. "We figured that out, but you play like . . ." He broke off, staring again.

"And I'll be going away for the summer. To work on a ranch."

There were a few moments of silence, more stares, and then Jim, the cornetist, said, "We've got two gigs before school's out. One's an

American Legion dance. They like cow music. The fiddle and banjo would go good there. The other's the junior-senior prom, a lot of rock and some jazz. Want to play for those?''

"Yes," said Nolan, deeply happy.

"But," said Butch quickly, "we don't split the pay with you. Not until next fall, when you've been around a while, really proved yourself ''

Nolan almost said "Pay?" in a pleasant state of shock, but he managed to keep quiet, only smiling. Then soberly, "All right That sounds reasonable."

Anne and Kiersten came for the boys, to take them to Secesh. Roger took a good many clothes and books. Nolan had only one small, battered suitcase, but he also had all the instruments. He wanted to practice, any time he had a few minutes, all summer. He willingly sat, squeezed into the back seat among them, while the others rode in front.

Darlene watched the car drive away with distaste. They—Price—had another new car, while she, Darlene, was making do with one that was more than two years old. This was the last summer the boys were going to Secesh, no matter what they or Clarence thought. She couldn't stand that Anne, with her cool, matter-of-fact ways, or that chattering, freckle-faced little girl. The kid was growing leggy now, like an awkward colt, but she wasn't developing any figure. If _I_ had a daughter, Darlene thought petulantly, everything in pants would be after her. Sometimes she wished most fervently that Roger was a girl, so that she, the mother, could teach her things. But then reconsidering, she knew she would be violently jealous of so beautiful a girl child, that it would remind her of her age and make life generally miserable.

Now that they were back in Hurleigh, she ought to arrange to have a talk with Price some time soon. There was the question of the twins' inheritance. She ought to be able to feel sure they'd be properly provided for. He'd adopted Anne's kid, and there were blessed Stanley's two brats, but he'd have to provide for his own. She had every right to know what arrangements he'd made about a will. And it was none too soon to begin planning about things like college. It would be wasted money on Nolan, but couldn't she still draw the child support until both were twenty-one? She'd have to look up the court papers on that.

Then, still standing there at the window, staring unseeingly into the empty street, she thought about Davis King and felt better about everything. Davis had been a clerk in the railroad office when Daddy had used to be a section foreman here. He was already married then, with a couple of little kids, but he had taken Darlene Nolan's virginity when she was sixteen, shortly after her mother had died.

Davis King was now division superintendent, he and his wife pillars of the community. He had been in the outer office the day she went to apply for a job, and he had remembered. She could see it clearly in his eyes. He had asked her to come out for coffee when she'd finished filling out the application, saying easily to the staff in general that her father had been a good friend of his.

Over coffee, they had teased each other tantalizing with hints of memories. He had said she hardly looked a day older, and that was almost true. Darlene took very conscientious care of her face and figure. There was no gray in her waving chestnut hair. Her hazel eyes were the same, wide and feckless.

Davis had changed. He had a good-sized paunch and was going gray, but then he must be at least forty now and he was certainly more to look at than stodgy old horny Clarence, who was always preening himself in her shadow. She was still attracted to Davis and he to her. They got together before the Tates had been in Hurleigh a week, one night when she had "worked late" to try to bring up her typing speed. You had to be careful in Hurleigh. It wasn't Denver, where anonymity was so easily found. They had just stayed in his office, with a big comfortable sofa. Afterward, with the door still safely locked, he had taken a package from his desk drawer.

"I couldn't give you much, all those years ago," he had said tenderly. "I want to see you have nice things, like this necklace, and I know you don't get much from Clarence Tate. Why you ever married him, honey . . . well, anyway, can't you just say you found the necklace or something? When can we get together again?"

Darlene started now at the voice in the room behind her.

"When are we havin' supper, sugar? I thought I might go down to the pool room a while. I didn't imagine, when we decided to move, that they wouldn't have any TV in here yet. This always has been a backward place but, all in all, I think we were right to make the move, don't you?"

Darlene didn't want to turn and see Clarence there. He was fat as a barrel and soft as dough. His hands were always busy when she was close to him, even in public. It was nice that he kind of showed her off the way he did, but she liked him less with every passing year. With the twins away . . . and Davis's wife was taking their kids to visit her folks in July. They ought to be able to—

"Darlene, sugar?"

"Oh, what?" she snapped, turning.

"Want to go to bed?" he asked with a leer which he probably thought was romantic. "Now that the brats are out of the way?"

"No," she said petulantly. "Not now."

She thought rather wistfully of the times Clarence had beaten Nolan. Right after that he was always at his sexiest, which wasn't

171

saying a lot, but she couldn't help wishing; those times were getting fewer with the years.

Clarence looked irritated, disappointed, but he said only, "I was just sayin', don't you think it's best all around that we decided to come back here? My commissions at the store git better nearly ever' week."

"Yes, Clarence, I think it was right to come here. I really do. I'll be glad when we've saved up enough for a good down payment on a new car. That old wreck we've got is getting me down. And, about supper, let's go out. Let's eat out a lot this summer, since we don't have to pay for the twins, since there's just the two of us."

11

Nolan earned his wages that summer. Then, every night, though supper might not be finished before nine o'clock, he practiced. His hands were scratched, blistered, then the blisters broke and finally callouses formed, but still he played music.

The music irritated Price. He had liked Nolan's note, asking to be paid, the first correspondence he had had with either of his boys. The note had been a simple, straightforward, business-like proposition. He could not fault the boy's work, it was more like a man's and he worked well, so long as he and Hugh were kept apart.

Hugh had one more year to go in his courses of ranch management. Each summer he came home full of ideas for changes, a few of them good, most untenable. He threw Anne's bookkeeping system into limbo. He walked, rode, and drove the ranch like a boss. He was more than ready to take over Secesh, but only because he felt it his duty in life. Hugh was a very dutiful sort, but he lacked the *feel* for the land. Reuben tried to stay clear of Hugh and, when he could not, there were flaming arguments which Price had to try to pacify. Hugh badgered Nolan unmercifully, jealously, and more than once, fists came into play. Hugh was beginning to ask, subtly and otherwise, just what the disposition of Secesh was going to be. Price was not ready for that.

"I'm not forty years old," Price grumbled to Anne.

He sensed the love of the place in Nolan. He watched the boy gulp breaths of the new-cut hay when the machinery was past with its smells, saw him, when they were in the upper pastures, touch a magnificent ponderosa pine, his lips moving, speaking to it, saw him gently persuading a shying horse, doctoring sick cattle.

They were the biggest one-owner ranch in the area, but Hugh talked expansion, buying more land, more cattle. He talked of their being able to live in Hurleigh, or even Denver, turning things over to one or more managers. Nolan frowned at such talk. He obviously could hardly bear the thought of the place not in Savage hands, but, with Nolan, there was the music . . . always the music.

Penny had had two years of college now, training to be an elementary school teacher. She was also seeing a lot of one of the Bergen boys from Hurleigh, who had attended the same university and was ready to begin law school.

The old Bergen home place, down in the southeast end of the Park, was indeed being turned into a dude ranch, with rustic little cottages, a string of trail horses, and the rest of it, strangers from the East, from outside, coming in to own and run the place. They were even putting in a heated pool and an airstrip. The Park was changing; even Secesh was changing. Sometimes Price felt older than forty. He didn't want to live to see the day when Secesh might be a tax write-off for some corporation, which was certainly what Hugh seemed to be working toward.

The Forest Service was putting more restrictions on grazing, charging more per unit of stock. There had been a mild but galling disagreement this spring with old man Gunnar Nelson, on the next ranch south, over water rights. There had not been the usual amount of snowfall over the winter, and Gunnar needed more water than he was entitled to, out of the ditches south of Cranky Creek. Secesh had the oldest water rights in the Park. Old Price Savage had been a canny man about such things. The younger Price let Gunnar have most of the water he wanted. He was an old man, over seventy, and the best grudge-holder in Dunraven. If he didn't get the water, he'd be constantly at them for the rest of his days, about cross-fences, mixed-up cattle, plowing the river road, anything he could think of. Besides, Price wanted to see the Nelson place go on as long as possible, prospering, until old Gunnar was dead and his damned kids sold out to some land and cattle company, or worse.

Hugh was furious when he found out about the water having been diverted to Nelson's ditches, so irate and loquacious about it that Price finally said, "You don't own Secesh yet, Hugh. Now lay off I won't discuss it any more. Even you can hardly bring the water back." Hugh scarcely spoke to anyone for several days, which was something of a relief for all of them.

Some time during every winter, Fern paid visits to her daughters, Rachel and Ivy, and their families. There would be days when Price got done with the feeding early, before Kiersten returned home from school, that there would be only Anne and himself, alone in the big house, with the wind whining or moaning or whooping around it. Those were strange, uneasy times that made them both sad, and reminded Price inexorably of his sterility.

They had gone out this past winter when Fern was back, to visit with his mother and Aunt Ruth in California. Emily was frail and in very fragile health. She had suffered a light stroke a few days before their arrival.

She said, pathetically clinging to Price's hand, "I may never see Secesh again."

He had been a little surprised, touched, by the tears in her eyes, but she quickly let him know they were for Stanley and Stanley's children.

"You do always see to the wreaths for Stanley's grave—and Mary's?" she asked him querulously, and, "Who have you got using my Stanley's room now?"

Yes, Nolan was the one for Secesh, but Nolan lacked the concentration. Nolan had two loves and a good rancher couldn't afford that.

When the boys went back to Hurleigh in the fall, Nolan sent another two hundred dollars to the music store in Denver and bought himself a respectable wardrobe for school and for playing with The Jives. Then he found himself a job as stocker in a feed store, afternoons and Saturdays. At first the manager had said he wouldn't be strong enough, and it was very heavy, hard work, but he did have the strength, whether he looked it or not.

The Jives had a new piano player. Homer had moved away. This one was named Scott King, and they could practice at his house whenever they liked. He was the second child and only son of Davis King, the railroad division superintendent, and his mother doted on him, encouraging almost anything he wanted to do.

The bass player, Butch Moreno, also said they could practice at his house any time. Butch's mother was dead, his father an alcoholic who was rarely around and didn't care what went on when he was.

Usually though, all of them preferred the King house. Mrs. King made plentiful snacks available and had cleared out a large basement closet for the holding of their instruments.

Since all the others, except Scott, had part-time jobs, they usually practiced in the evenings, often for three or four hours. All the other boys were now high school seniors. Nolan never actually admitted his own age, though, of course, they found out. They called him "kid," and teased him a great deal, but all were a little in awe of his playing, and he began to do arrangements for the band, so that their numbers didn't just sound like carbon copies of some record or other.

The band was more and more in demand. The most they were ever paid for a gig was fifty dollars, which divided into only ten dollars each, but it was enough for them.

After three hours at the feed store and four hours of practice, often with no substantial supper, Nolan would sit in the old garage of Grandpa's house and work on arrangements by its single dim light.

175

He could write them out now, sometimes without playing a note. Some of his weekly earnings always went for staff paper, which the only local music store had to special order for him.

Through the fall weather he kept Liam's old instruments in the garage. There was a slinky new car there now, sometimes, but still plenty of room for the instruments wrapped in straw, and for the rickety old straight chair, which he used for composition and playing. Darlene complained if he kept the instruments under his bed, said they collected dust. God knew why she worried. She certainly never cleaned the room, though Nolan knew she often went through it very thoroughly. He had a special hiding place for his money, an old hollow tree down along the river. He would put in the money, then stuff the hole with leaves and hope no one went exploring. At any rate, neither Darlene nor the others wanted him playing in the house at midnight, or at any other time. Nolan was locked out almost every night, but Roger would leave a window screen in their room unlatched, so that Nolan came and went almost as he pleased. So long as he turned over some of his earnings to what Clarence called "the family good," Clarence was pleased never to see him at all. Darlene railed about the life he led, slapped him if he tried to say anything in return, but really, Roger was the only one who missed his presence. With Nolan unavailable and virtually inaccessible, Darlene hired a woman to come in two days a week to clean and cook. This woman, an elderly Swedish lady, had little but contempt for working in such a small house, and for the "goings on" there.

The weather was growing cold now, and the large temperature variations were hard on the old instruments. In fact, the head of the banjo was in bad shape and Nolan was not at all sure it would last till spring. He couldn't very well go into debt for a new banjo while he was still paying for the guitar, not even had there been a Harry Blevins to help him.

He never left the twelve-string in the garage. Sometimes it was in his and Roger's bedroom, but more often, he left it at Scott's because somehow he felt safer doing that. Mrs. King had bought a lock for the instrument closet and had keys made for each of The Jives, promising that the closet would be off limits to anyone but the five of them.

One night when they couldn't practice, Nolan got home in time for supper, the first time in a long while. Darlene and Clarence had scathing remarks to make, but he was ravenous and paid them little attention. When the meal was finished, Nolan was told to clean up the kitchen, company was coming. Roger helped him with the dishes, then wanted to play chess or, better, just talk.

"I've got to study," Nolan said, yawning tiredly, "for that history test tomorrow. I haven't read any of it."

"I'll quiz you and give you the answers. It's not hard to guess most of what old Quimby is going to ask. You can memorize the answers. You've got a good memory. Sometimes I think that's all that keeps you in school."

"No, I'd better do it myself this time."

A couple arrived to visit with Darlene and Clarence. They were drinking and dancing to phonograph music, getting louder and louder as the evening progressed.

Clarence and Darlene went out often. Occasionally, they were at dances where The Jives played. Sometimes they just spent the evening at the Stockman's Bar. Rather often Darlene had to work late and Clarence spent those evenings at the Stockman's or the pool room next door to the bar. But not tonight. The noise, even with the bedroom door closed, got to be distracting. And Roger wouldn't stop talking.

Finally, Nolan took his history book into the bathroom. He sat on the toilet lid, holding the open book, but he wasn't thinking much about it. He was thinking of Secesh, and particularly of one rainy morning when Ginia Ellenbogen had called him.

"I thought we might spend a day with music," she had said pleasantly, hopefully. "I'll pick you up. Bring all the instruments, but I want to show you some things about the piano, and I also have some records I want you to hear."

There was a pounding on the bathroom door, Clarence demanding loudly, "Who the hell's in there?"

"It's me," Nolan answered resignedly. "I'll be out in just a minute."

The records had been classical guitar, and they had opened a whole new world for Nolan. He couldn't come close to mastering them, but therein lay some of the fascination.

"I want to play like that," he had said, smiling shyly at Aunt Ginia.

"You will," she had said stoutly. "I'd bet anything on it. If you can—"

"Goddamn it, Nolan, there are other people in this house," bawled Clarence.

"Yes, I'm just coming."

"You're what?"

"I said I'm just coming."

"Is that some fancy talk from your hoity-toity relatives, or are you in there jerkin' off?"

There were hoots of laughter from the adults in the living room and Nolan felt his face flame. If he could concentrate for just a few minutes more on the War of 1812 . . .

177

Suddenly there was a smashing at the door. The hook's eye pulled out of its socket and the door slammed back against the wall

"I won't have no kid in my house playin' with himself!" shouted Clarence, his face red and bloated with anger.

Nolan hadn't even had his pants open, but he knew nothing would make any difference. He tried to edge past, but Clarence's heavy fist caught him in the mouth, loosening two teeth and starting a stream of blood.

"Look at this little bastard of yours!" Clarence yelled at Darlene "Lockin' himself up in the bathroom to jerk off, with comp'ny in the house."

The visitors were staring at Nolan; Darlene had turned her eyes away at the sight of blood. The woman said thickly, "His mouth's hurt."

"You damn right," bellowed Clarence. "An' it'll be more'n his mouth."

Nolan bent down to pick up the history book he had dropped Clarence drew back a little and kicked him viciously in the ribs. The place was painful for weeks; a rib had been broken, or surely cracked, but Nolan mentioned that to no one.

"You gonna take the belt to him?" asked Darlene fuzzily.

"Ah, hell, there ain't no hope for the little sonabitch," said Clarence disgustedly and went back to dancing. He pinched Darlene's breast painfully and she snuggled against him.

In the boys' room, Roger had heard it all. His own face was pale He got cold wet cloths for Nolan's mouth, and, "Were you?" he finally could not restrain the question.

"No."

After a while, his mouth still bleeding, Nolan said resignedly through a cloth, "You may as well tell me the questions and answers I can't get them from the book now."

The following Sunday, all The Jives were invited to Scott's house for lunch. Mr. King was catching up on some office work, they said, and Scott's two sisters were occupied elsewhere. Following the meal, they practiced through most of the afternoon. There was a country-western dance to be played on the following Friday night. Scott had resurrected some old western swing records so that they could learn to play more than the currently popular cowboy music. They kidded Nolan about his swollen mouth, saying some boy must have caught him with the wrong girl, but they also called him, unabashedly, "boy genius."

He felt good, walking home. His rib hurt some with every breath and almost every movement, but he could almost ignore it. He had caught up, to a degree, with some of his studies that morning. He was managing to handle everything reasonably well.

Aunt Ginia had told him about a scholarship, available from a small school of music in New England. It could be won for excellence with one instrument, for composition or arrangement. . . . No doubt, they wouldn't recognize violin as fiddle, or banjo, or Irish whistle, but if he could learn more about classical guitar, arrange some pieces for the twelve-string, rather than six, find the time to practice   . But that was a long way off, for after high school graduation.

The band teacher had arranged for him to be able to play cello in the high school orchestra. Small schools could better afford to be flexible. Nolan wasn't much good at the cello yet, but neither were any of the other kids in the little orchestra much good. Sometimes, in odd hours or half hours he could find, he practiced at the band teacher's house on the teacher's own cello, a fine instrument. He was teaching Nolan a lot about music theory and classical application. Darlene and Clarence had railed and sneered at his taking up school time being in the orchestra, when they had finally found out about it, but he got academic credit for it, so for the time being they were more or less letting it pass.

It was getting very cold now, the beginning of November. Possible snow was forecast for tomorrow. The sun was setting, shooting bright lances through a bank of dreary-looking clouds.

The car was gone; it almost always was. Maybe they were all out. Nolan decided not to leave Grandpa's old instruments in the garage any longer. He hadn't brought the twelve-string home. He couldn't carry everything. Besides, it was kept at such a nice even temperature at Scott's house. What if he had a mother like that? One who would provide special closets without even a key for herself? . . . Well, for a part of the year he had Anne and Fern.

He hadn't started any fuss about moving to Secesh for good as he'd thought he might do this year. He'd like to live up there, be a real year-round part of the ranch, especially with Hugh away at college. But there was the band he could have here   and there was the way Price felt about his music. He said little because Nolan never stinted himself at work, but Price's hostility and opinions could be very clearly sensed.

Nolan went into the garage and dug the six-string guitar out of the straw They must all come in today, go under his bed.

He entered the house by the back door. It was very quiet and he felt something strange about the door's not being locked. Both Darlene and Clarence were very big on locks, so if everyone was gone, why was the door open? He stowed the instruments, thinking he would

179

scramble himself four eggs for supper, if there were four eggs in the house.

When he was in the kitchen, he heard a faint sound, almost like a groan. He called out, "Anybody home?" No answer. The sound must have been his imagination, maybe the wind picking up. Still, it bothered him. He put down the skillet and went into the living room, switching on a lamp. Empty. Then he noticed that the door to the front bedroom was ajar. He called out again, then went hesitantly over to the door, pushed it a little more open.

Nolan could not move for what seemed like forever. Clarence was sitting on the edge of the bed, bare from the waist down, his thighs spread. Roger was kneeling between his knees. . . . "Cocksucker!" Nolan had heard the word often enough at school. He didn't say it, but it smashed through him, seeming to rob him of breath.

They were all frozen for that moment that seemed like eternity, then Roger scrambled away, hiding his face from his brother. Clarence, grappling with his clothes, began to curse Nolan.

"I'll kill you, you sneakin' little sonabitch!" He had got his undershorts on and was whipping his belt from its loops on his pants

Nolan took one step backward before the first onslaught, aimed at his face with the buckle end. Then he grabbed the belt in both his hands. He said, unsteadily, but very quietly, "If you ever think of touching me again, I'll beat hell out of you. I think I could do that now, fat and soft as you are. And besides that, I'll tell Darlene about—about . . ."

"Nolan!" Roger's voice was a whine, a plea.

Nolan turned and left the house. He stayed out until he felt sure all of them had been long asleep.

The next evening there was no band practice. Nolan went home with Butch Moreno when Butch showed up at the feed store at closing time. Mr. Moreno, as usual, wasn't at home. They made themselves some supper and then just fooled around for a while, listening to old records, talking, mostly about things that didn't matter much.

It was past nine when Nolan went home. The house was dark except for a small light in the hall. The car was not in the garage and he remembered this was also the night of Roger's Scout meeting Maybe it would be really blessedly empty this time. The doors were locked and he made his entrance through the bedroom window. He ought to be studying.

Roger . . . was his uppermost feeling pure loathing, or a deep, hurting pity? He didn't know yet. Maybe he never would. Maybe the best thing was to try never to think of it at all. He would try to get some work done on an English paper.

He flipped the light switch beside the window and there they were, all of Grandpa's instruments, lying between the two beds, smashed to pieces. Someone had stamped on them. Even the Irish whistle that Liam had carved with his own hands was broken into four pieces. Nolan's first feeling was numbness, disbelief, then came the fiercest anger he had ever known, then it was as if something that had been a part of himself, alive, trusting to him for care and safety, lay there smashed and broken.

Eventually he got a flashlight and shovel. He dug a deep hole in the weedy back yard, hurrying. A few heavy flakes of snow drifted down on a chill north breeze. He didn't notice, not that or anything. He got a sheet, an almost new one, and tenderly wrapped all the pieces of all the instruments in it, fighting the burning in his throat and behind his eyes. He put the sheet in and filled the hole with desperate haste.

Replacing the shovel and flashlight, he went back to the terrible bedroom. With the light out, he undressed with shaking hands and burrowed under his covers, making himself as small as he possibly could, crying now, in great, hoarse, rending sobs that made the bed heave. It seemed he might never be able to stop the tears, but they had passed when he heard the car, then Darlene and Clarence's voices in the front of the house.

Darlene called out, "Rogie?" She came to the bedroom, turned on the light. Nolan lay still, feigning sleep, his head still covered. She went away.

A little later, he heard Roger come in. Voices went on in the living room for a short while, then Roger came into the bedroom. The light again. Roger would be folding and putting away his Scout uniform. Finally, the light was out again and Roger got into his bed. After a long while, he said pleadingly, "Nolan . . . ? Chappie?"

No reply.

"I know you're not asleep. Don't you know I've got to talk to you? . . . Listen, it's not such a very *bad* thing. I mean, a lot of boys—and men—you know—*do* it. I like girls, too. That is, I think I will, when I'm a little older. Chappie, please talk to me. You haven't said anything since—since yesterday."

"Just shut up," said Nolan, his voice muffled by the covers, hoarse from the crying.

"But I want you to understand. You've *got* to."

"Well, I can't and I'm not likely to, so leave me alone."

"It hasn't been happening very long. I think maybe it never would have started if I'd had more friends to . . . if you'd been around more so we—"

Nolan flung back his covers. "You're not going to blame me for *that*. I won't take it, Roger, and you'd better understand that straight-away."

"But you—you looked like I was—filth."

"Yes, I suppose I did."

"What's wrong with it? Tell me that!"

"It's not—natural." And then Nolan, sickly fascinated, asked, "Does he—do that—to you?"

"Yes," said Roger defiantly, "and it feels good. It feels great! A lot better than jerking off."

"My God!" groaned Nolan. "Are there other people who—that you . . . ?"

"No."

A long tense silence.

Roger said, "I'll stop if you think it's so—filthy and—abnormal."

"It's no decision of mine. I tell you, stop trying to give me your responsibilities!"

"Clarence says he's done it a lot—with other guys—and it doesn't make any difference about how he feels about Mother—how they—"

"If you don't shut up, I'm going to be sick. Clarence is crazy."

"Perverted, you mean. And I am, too?"

"Draw your own conclusions."

"You mean more to me than anybody in the world. We're twins, Chappie. I can't stand it if you hate me and think I'm sick in the head. Honest, it's *not* bad. It's—normal, for some guys."

"Clarence says that, I suppose."

"Yes, but so do some other people. I've been getting books . . anyway, I don't *need* anyone to tell me if I'm bad or good. I've got a conscience and I know in my own mind whether I'm—"

"That's what you should have said years ago. Now you don't need me, do you?"

"If something feels good—is enjoyable—that doesn't mean it's a sin or—"

"Oh Christ, let's not get into sin and salvation."

"But you're so—disappointed or upset or righteous or . . . I just don't want you to hate me."

"You're a smart kid, Roger. I've heard a lot about that. How could you let a dirty pervert like Clarence . . . ?"

"I told you, *I* feel all right about it."

"Well, then fine. Live your life."

"But I want you to *understand*! Do you?"

"No."

"Do you hate me?"

"I don't know. I think I feel sorry for you."

"I don't want your goddamn *pity!*" They had been keeping their voices down, but this last was a desperate, wrung cry. "Oh, hell," Roger said more quietly, sinking back on his pillow, tears coming into his eyes. "There's *nothing* I can ever do that would get your respect anyway."

"So you're going to go on with it?" Nolan said coldly.

"I guess that's none of your business, since you won't—"

"Well, *that* sure as hell won't win anybody's respect, except maybe Clarence's. Suppose Darlene finds out?" Nolan couldn't stop this last question. He had been the underdog too many times.

"You wouldn't really tell her, would you? You know how she is." The whine had come back to Roger's voice and the words were shaky. "She'd be moving us back to Denver so I'd have to see a shrink or something. She's already said, more than once, that she thinks I ought to have psychological help. She can hardly say the word. But she says adolescence is a bad time for boys and their mothers don't always know what to do, how things ought to be handled, that because I'm so much smarter than most other kids, she thinks some professional guidance . . . But you know what she doesn't know? She doesn't know that what they call aberrations, especially in boys, always turn out to be their mothers' fault. You won't tell her, though, will you?"

"I want to know who smashed up my things."

"Things? What things?"

"All of Grandpa's instruments were broken to pieces some time today."

Nolan wished, for this moment, that the light was on. He thought he could know the truth if he could see Roger's face. Maybe not though, Roger was getting craftier every year, showing less in his face, telling lies with an almost amazing glibness.

Finally, Roger said, with a deep concern that would sound convincing enough for anyone else, "Oh, Chappie!"

Nolan said relentlessly, "It was you or Clarence."

"Or maybe Mother," said Roger, sounding stunned, horrified. "She'd do a thing like that. You know how she hates all the time you spend with the band and your music. She's always saying how you could be working that time, or studying or—"

"Roger, stop speculating," he said fiercely. "I asked you a question."

"I didn't do it," Roger said hotly, "and I don't see how you could think for a minute that I would."

"It's easy to think so. Because of yesterday."

"Oh Jesus, you'll try to make me pay for that for the rest of my life!" Then, with what seemed real sympathy and concern, "Your new guitar, too?"

"No."

"Where is it?"

"It's safe, I think, and it's going to stay that way "

"I always have thought we could trust each other," said Roger with heavy sadness. "I trust you, but you never have . . . I always felt that if there weren't two other people in the world who could trust each other, there ought to be us. You think I'm lying right now, don't you, about the instruments?"

Nolan said wearily, "It really doesn't matter a whole hell of a lot now, does it? They're gone."

A silence. They could hear Darlene and Clarence, moving around in the other bedroom.

Roger said softly, solicitously, "What about the band?"

"It's not the band," Nolan said, his voice breaking "It's that those things were Grandpa's and—oh shit! Don't talk any more "

He thought Roger was sleeping. It seemed a very long time since the sound of the last words had died in the room. He lay there with the ache of the smashed pieces in his chest and throat, not really caring any more if Roger was a pervert, not giving a damn about anything except the mutilated wood and metal. Tears were squeezing between his eyelids again, hot, scalding tears of helpless hurt and anger.

Then there was movement from Roger's bed, a squeaking of springs and he was sitting on Nolan's bed beside him.

"I really do know how awful you must feel," he whispered gently, softly, his hands fumbling for Nolan's face, pushing back the swath of curls from his forehead. "I'm awfully sorry if you can't believe I didn't do it, because that's the truth. Let me try to make you forget for a little while. Let me show you—"

Nolan was on him with a cry. Roger screamed as his brother's fist smashed into his nose.

12

Strangely, the boys' relationship became closer for a time after that weekend. They talked more, about the school, the town, even very occasionally about more serious things such as philosophies of life, possible plans for the future. They never discussed the Monday night and the Sunday preceding it.

Nolan had broken Roger's nose. It was a clean break and healed of itself. The nose became fine and straight again. Darlene had come rushing into their room, screaming, at the sound of the fight, and had fainted at sight of the stream of blood covering Roger's lower face. When she was somewhat revived by Clarence's none too gentle methods, and with Roger's face covered, Darlene and Clarence had taken him to the hospital. After X-raying the break and giving Roger something for pain, the doctor had sedated the wailing Darlene and recommended that she be taken home and put to bed at once.

She had screamed at Clarence to "teach Nolan a lesson he'll never forget. Beat him bloody," but Clarence was strangely passive and did nothing, in the direct gaze of Nolan's steady gray eyes. Nolan had hurt his own right hand so badly that he could play nothing for two weeks, but they never discussed the night. Only Roger said, when the swelling and bruising was leaving his nose and he stood staring at a mirror, "I wish it had been a bad break. If my nose were flat or crooked, I'd be better off."

"Why?" asked Nolan, staring at the wavy chestnut back of his brother's head.

"I'm tired of being called pretty boy and of having kids make jokes about how I look."

In the fall when they were fourteen, Nolan got a job at an all-night service station out on the highway. He worked there, Mondays through Thursdays, from four until midnight, and all day Sundays. This left time to play with the band, but scarcely any time for practice.

185

He studied and wrote arrangements between customers. He had paid off the twelve-string and now, with the cooperation of the band teacher, was buying a fiddle. They needed it for the Jives, and the small school orchestra needed it. It was almost like learning to play all over again when the fiddle became a violin and he enjoyed it. He practiced between customers, too.

Larry, the Jives original guitar player, had gone off to college and the boys decided that the remaining four of them were enough. Scott King would go to college one day, but, while making up his mind which major to choose, he was working for the railroad. Butch Moreno, the bass player, worked at a garage; Jim Pitman, the cornetist, at the lumber yard.

One Saturday night they had a date to play in Kendall, a coal-mining town some forty miles from Hurleigh. Roger asked to come along.

"Maybe I'll have nerve enough to dance with somebody," he said dubiously. "Anyway, I'd like to see and hear what you do."

Darlene and Clarence were both out, so there were no objections. Roger dutifully left a note on the kitchen table.

Jim had an old station wagon and they piled the instruments in the back of it. The boys were quieter than usual, feeling slightly uncomfortable in Roger's, a stranger's, presence. Finally, Butch, who still did most of their vocal work, started going over a new song. Jim and Scott joined him. Nolan would not sing. His voice was in process of changing and he never knew what it might do. The singing eased things in the car, that and the fact that Jim had brought along a couple of six-packs of beer.

"When we're through tonight," Butch suggested comfortably, "let's all go back to my house. The old man will be asleep, or maybe in jail. He worked most of this month and he's laid in a good supply of liquor. He can't have drunk it all by the time we get back. Besides," he looked round uneasily at Roger, "I saw my cousin from Denver over the weekend, got some other stuff we might want to try—that is, after we take pretty boy home."

They were coming into the outskirts of Kendall. Jim said, "Anybody know where this place is, the American Legion post?"

None of them did. He said, "I'll stop at that motel over there. You go in, Chappie, you're by the door, and ask them, or look in the phone book or something, if they've *got* a phone book."

Jim parked at the side of the building, and Nolan went through a small corridor to the office. There, standing at the desk, were his mother and Davis King, Mr. King writing on the registration form. Darlene looked directly at Nolan for an instant, not even long enough for anything to show in her lovely, long-lashed hazel eyes, before he ducked back into the hall.

He went out again, feeling his face hot, glad of the darkness at the side of the building. "They said to keep on Main Street; we couldn't miss it."

This proved to be true, but as they pulled around to the front of the motel to leave, there, unmistakably, parked at the office door, was Davis King's Lincoln. In quick glances under the lights, Nolan searched Roger and Scott's faces. They hadn't noticed, or it hadn't registered.

Scott said, "What are you looking at me for?"

Nolan said readily, stammering only slightly, "I was just wondering what kind of shape their piano's going to be in."

He was completely free at home now. No accounting was due anyone. He would still turn over some money toward the family good, but they had no right to ask his exact wages. Darlene had been the only one left who still nagged and yelled at him, slapped him sometimes for "being smart-mouthed." Now that was going to stop, too. He was free, but he could feel no exuberance about it. What a mess people were! And Mrs. King was such a nice, quiet, generous person.

The music went well, the audience was appreciative. It was three o'clock by the time they returned to Hurleigh.

"First we take baby brother home, right?" said Jim.

"I'd like to come with you," Roger said wistfully. "I'm hardly a baby brother. We're twins and I happen to be the elder."

"Well, you don't look it. Nolan's been passing for two or three years older than he is ever since we've known him. You couldn't do that."

"What does it matter, if you're just going to someone's house?"

"Is he safe, Chappie?"

"Yes."

Butch's father had a bottle of bourbon left and was nowhere about. They each took a glass of the liquor, with water. Butch put on records, rather loud, then, from a very secret hiding place in his bedroom, brought out what he had got from his cousin, cigarette papers and marijuana.

The Savage boys exchanged quick looks. Neither of them had tried it before.

"Don't drink too much or too fast," cautioned Butch, rather ineptly rolling a small joint. "It can ruin the effect."

They smoked four joints among them, forgetting the bourbon. Nolan felt dreamy and bits of beautiful music circled in his head. Roger got sick, probably from the bourbon, they thought, and he was mortally embarrassed.

187

While Butch, with a broad smile, was lethargically making another joint, Nolan and Scott went out and got the instruments. They turned off the record player. There was no piano here so Scott tried the fiddle. It was very bad, and hilarious.

Nolan played his guitar, sitting on the floor, leaning back against the arm of a chair, oblivious of what the others might be doing. He played what he was seeing, hearing, the light, drifting, indolent half-thoughts.

"Hey, man, that's really great," said Jim, holding the joint for him so Nolan wouldn't have to stop playing.

"You know what you need though?" said Butch. "An amplifier. The twelve-string can be plenty loud, but when you're on your own, you usually play so quiet."

Nolan shook his head, slowly but emphatically. "No way. I'll never use one." His voice was slow and dreamy, like the music, but his face was very serious. "I hate them." He didn't break the thread of the slow strange music.

Jim said fuzzily, "If you had just six strings, you'd have to have an amplifier."

"But I don't," replied Nolan. Then he stopped playing for a few moments and told them how he had come to acquire the twelve-string. They all laughed hugely and slapped him lightly on the shoulders.

He held the guitar again, saying, "But some day I'm going to have a really fine classical guitar."

"That'll put you way beyond us," said Scott, suddenly looking as if he might cry.

Roger said, "Can I try the cornet?"

"Sure can," said Jim, handing it over.

Roger could make the instrument sound and all of them except Nolan began dreamily trying to show him how to form notes. It was pretty loud and pretty terrible, and they all got to laughing. Nolan, smiling dazedly, eyes unfocused, went on with his own music.

None of them knew just how long after that it was that the loud knocking came at Butch's front door.

Chief of Police Briggs took his duties very seriously. He had no intention of letting drugs get a foothold among the kids of his town. This was a clear case. The house was rank with the smell of the stuff.

A neighbor had called about the noise next door at after four in the morning. The whole town knew Antonio Moreno and his drunkenness. They waited, hopefully it seemed, to make such calls. Chief Briggs always told his men he was on call, no matter what the hour, so the night officer had called him. So there they were, the two of them, loading dazed but happy boys into the two police cars. They

188

had even caught Butch Moreno holding; that is, he had enough marijuana in his shirt pocket for about two more joints.

At the small police station the boys were still happy, stupefied, Chief Briggs called it, under the influence. Their parents were called.

"Look," said Scott reasonably, "three of us are over eighteen, but those other two are minors."

"Is that true?" snapped the chief at the twins.

"Yes," said Roger, beginning to be a little afraid now.

"No," said Nolan, now hearing blues music in his head, low-down wailing blues, the kind you could really dig into. Then he remembered they had left their instruments scattered around Butch's living room. Suppose Butch's father came home and . . . ?

"Look," he said very soberly to the night officer, "I have to go back and get my guitar and fiddle because—"

"You just shut up, you little hophead. You ain't goin' nowhere Speak when you're spoken to."

Chief Briggs knew all of them. He didn't even bother asking their names before calling the parents. He made it his business to keep a careful account of the teenagers in his town.

He said maliciously to Butch, "Your dad's here already. In a cell. Drunk and disorderly again, and you're going to turn out even worse. I've always known that."

What Antonio Moreno did when he was drunk and disorderly was sing louder than the jukebox in the Stockman's Bar, loud and offkey, and another song, until the other patrons couldn't stand it any longer. No one could stop him until he passed out.

Now Butch started humming something, his face flushed; the other boys went along and then they got to laughing again. Chief Briggs looked at them with extreme distaste and bawled for quiet. They couldn't stop, but managed to stifle their mirth to a degree.

Scott's parents were the first to arrive, Mr. King, Nolan thought hazily, looking as if he hadn't had any sleep. Then Jim's father came Clarence and Darlene were there a few minutes later, Darlene having had to take time to make up her face. But she was sobbing, the makeup running in ugly streaks. Clarence cursed and kept tucking in his shirt.

Scott's father, after Chief Briggs had explained the situation in his most scandalized, censorious way, asked if the boys might not be released to their parents on personal recognizance until they should have to make an appearance in court.

Briggs said angrily, "I suppose so. We don't have any previous offenses against any of them, though that one's daddy is here in this jail right now "

"Release Butch to us," said Mrs. King without hesitation. "We'll vouch for him."

Darlene was sobbing, "Oh, Rogie, how could you let him get you into a mess like this? I know you'd never have done anything of the kind on your own. *He* can stay here. He deserves it, out of control at home and—"

Roger moved away none too gently from her embrace, his face flaming.

Darlene turned fiercely on Nolan. "You! You've never been anything in your life but trouble. You—"

Nolan broke in very softly as Jim's father was talking to Chief Briggs, "Well, it's nice that we all had such a good time in Kendall, isn't it?"

Her face went scarlet, then pale as death. She moved away from him, as far as she could get.

The final upshot of it all was that Butch got thirty days in jail and six months' probation. He had been caught holding; the "orgy" had been at his house. Scott and Jim got suspended sentences, and the twins, after Darlene had cried for an unnecessary and very humiliating half-hour to the judge, about how they'd never been in any such trouble before, were sent home as minors, told, in effect, in a long harangue, to go and sin no more.

"It was all kind of—interesting," mused Roger on the night after the court hearing.

"I'm glad you think so," Nolan said wryly, then with concern, "I doubt it's all that interesting for Butch."

"Well, people ought to have—you know—experiences. Would you smoke again if you got the chance?"

"If I was locked up in a bank vault, maybe."

"It didn't really have the effect on me it seemed to have on you guys. I suppose that was because I was sick after the first cigarette. Do you smoke now? Tobacco, I mean."

"Sometimes, but it's not a habit I can afford."

"Would you smoke at home if you felt like it?"

"Why not?"

"It's like you're really—grown up. You just do as you please."

"No, what I'd please to do is go and live at Secesh all the time."

"Give up the band?"

"I wouldn't like doing that, but it's time I really began working on the classical stuff if I'm going to apply for a scholarship. It's only a few years now."

"I wish we could go to college together and you know I can't go to a music school. Tell me something. Why did Mother defend you, too, today? I've never seen her do that. I was afraid she'd be—you

190

know—like she always is about you, and that you might have to go to jail."

"I don't know," said Nolan blithely. "Maybe she's mellowing with the years."

Nolan was in trouble again in the spring when he was fifteen, and this time it was more serious. On a Saturday afternoon, the boys had been practicing, fooling around, then they went downtown in the evening. Scott had finally gone off to college, and they had a new piano player named Jerry Houston. Jim was talking of enlisting in the army before he should be drafted, so they decided, having no dance to play that night, that Jim should be given a possible pre-enlistment party. They went to the B. and L. Cafe for Mexican food. After that, they saw a western movie.

Jerry was the only one of them with a car now. It was a beat-up old Chevy that he and Butch worked on almost constantly to keep it viable for band trips. They hadn't brought it downtown tonight. In Hurleigh you could easily walk to just about any place you wanted to go. As they roamed the streets, talking and laughing about the possibilities of army life, they came upon a beautiful cream-colored Cadillac, parked on a dimly lit sidestreet.

"Say, man, just look at this!" breathed Jerry, awed.

"Wonder who it belongs to?" speculated Jim.

"Probably somebody staying at the hotel," Butch said uneasily. "Come on, we don't want to be found loitering around a thing like that."

"Bet it ain't got ten thousand miles on it," dreamed Jim.

Jerry opened the front passenger door and slid in with a luxurious sigh. "Man, this is somethin' else! Just to—hey, looky here! The keys!"

"Come on, man," said Butch urgently. "I already got one rap. Old Briggs and his boys would pick us up for looking at a car like this."

"I *got* to have me a ride," said Jim. "Just a little teensy ride. They won't have anything like this in no army motor pool."

"I'm drivin'," said Jerry challengingly. "I'm the one found the keys."

"That's all right with me. I just want a *ride*."

Jerry got out and went round to the driver's side. "You two comin' or not?"

"What do you think?" Butch asked Nolan, frowning deeply.

"I think it's crazy, but it would be fun."

He slid into the back seat and, after a moment, Butch followed, grumbling worriedly.

Jerry eased the car through the sidestreets of town and out onto the Fairweather road. It was a very minor state highway, but was paved now, all the way to the community of Fairweather.

They all sighed in relief at being out of town, and with the luxury of the car. Jim and Jerry examined the dash and instrument panel minutely.

When they were about five miles out of town, Jerry decided firmly, "I'm gonna open her up."

"No, don't," said Butch and Nolan together, and Butch said pleadingly, "Let's just turn around when we can, put it back before it's missed."

"Naw," said Jerry, "I got to do it, got to see what she feels like. I may never get a chance like this again."

"Don't," said Nolan again, and his voice, which had been showing signs of settling to a soft bass like Price's, cracked a little.

Nothing they could say mattered. Jerry was gently, inexorably pressing down on the accelerator.

"Just like ridin' on cream," breathed Jim.

And suddenly there was a deer, leaping into the headlights. There was no time for Jerry to touch the brakes or swerve. The big car struck the animal head-on, then it lurched and careened around the road until it finally came to rest, tilted at a steep angle in a very deep ditch, the entire left side smashed in. Then the silence seemed interminable.

"Anybody hurt bad?" asked Jim, almost whispering as he pulled himself up off Jerry.

"No," said Jerry and Butch, Butch dragging himself away from Nolan's side of the car.

Nolan had struck his head hard, just above the back window, but he sat up and mumbled something dazedly.

Another long pause.

"All right, *now* what the hell do we do?" demanded Butch angrily. "You two just *had* to do this. Jerry, you *had* to open her up. Now what do you say?"

"Well," hazarded Jim, "what about trying to hitch back to town?"

They climbed with some difficulty out of the steeply tilted vehicle.

"We go to the cops when we get back," Butch said firmly, then, "you all right, Chappie?"

"No cops," cried Jim. "We don't know anything about this."

"Yeah," agreed Jerry fervently. "Come on, let's make some distance away from here."

Nolan couldn't seem to walk straight, trying to keep up with them. Butch gave him a cigarette. It made him feel queasy, but seemed to clear his head a little. His head hurt. There was blood running down the side of his face.

After what seemed a long time, a pickup came up, going toward town. Jim waved a thumb frantically in the lights. The driver stopped, gesturing them into the back, not really able to see them.

"You were kidding about the cops, weren't you?" Jerry asked Butch, slightly more relaxed. "My old man would throw me out of the house."

"It's the only way I can see, man," said Butch earnestly. "There'll be some way they can tie us in with this anyway."

"No, there won't," said Jerry fiercely.

"What about fingerprints?" said Butch adamantly.

"Would they do somethin' like that, just on a—a stolen car?"

"With my luck they would. Briggs is out to get my ass, any way he can."

Jim said shakily, "What do you think, Nolan?"

"I'll go with Butch," he said, surprised at the steadiness of his voice.

"Well, what if we don't all go," said Jerry, sounding very scared. "Would you two rat on us?"

"No," said Butch scornfully. "If you haven't got the guts to—"

"Hold it a minute," snapped Jerry. "I turned eighteen last week, but Nolan's still a minor. Suppose you said you were driving, kid, and—"

"It's no use," broke in Jim dully. "Here comes the only state cop ever patrols this road."

The lights had begun flashing at the truck.

"There's a dead deer back there," said the patrolman, "and a smashed Cadillac in the ditch."

"I saw the deer," said the driver, "but I didn't see no car."

"I was wondering about these fellows you got in the back of your truck. Looks like one's kinda bloody."

Jerry jumped from the other side of the pickup and started running. The patrolman did not follow or draw his gun.

"Pick him up later," he said coolly. "You wrecked the Caddy, right, boys?"

So they were in the sheriff's office this time. Jim gave them Jerry's name. The deputy on duty badgered Butch about his former arrest and his father's record.

Nolan sat on a hard bench, holding his aching head, yearning to go to bed, in a cell or anywhere, it didn't matter. Butch kept giving him cigarettes.

"You okay? You need a doctor?"

"No."

"No to which one?"

"To everything."

They let him go and wash his face. The cut was high up on his left temple and a great bruise was forming under it. His hair was matted with blood, the left side of his face covered with it. He cleaned the cut as best he could with paper towels, gritting his teeth and holding onto a basin with one hand. It looked like he needed stitches.

Parents came again, Butch's father among them this time. The officers would not believe that one of the three boys present had not been driving the car. They woke up the magistrate to set bond.

Darlene was wild with fury. Clarence seethed, but there was something resigned about it.

"You'll go to jail this time," cried Darlene in something that sounded like victory. "Just where you've been heading all your life."

"Makin' me put up *our* car as surety," mourned Clarence bitterly. "You'll git no help from us when you go to court this time."

The highway patrolman put a hand on Clarence's shoulder as they were about to leave. "I think you ought to run your boy by the hospital. That's a deep cut and it's bled a lot."

This time there were no simperings about clumsiness and awkwardness. They told the emergency room nurse he had been in an accident and sat glaring, waiting for the doctor.

When the doctor arrived, called from his bed, he asked Nolan what had happened and Nolan said simply, wearily, that he had been stealing a car.

The hearing was set for ten days later, in county court. Again, Butch was held in jail. His father had nothing with which to secure his bond.

Nolan went uncertainly to his service station job next day. The owner had heard about the incident, as had the whole town, but he said, "You've always been honest with me, so far as I know. I'll wait to hear what the judge has to say. Keep workin'."

Jerry's parents had brought him to the sheriff's office that morning and he had admitted to driving the car, to having been the prime mover in its theft. There was talk that Jerry and Nolan would be expelled from school.

"I don't think they'll send you to jail or anything like that," said Roger sanguinely. "After all, you *are* just fifteen. Maybe we ought to call Price."

"God, no," said Nolan vehemently.

On Friday afternoon, when he didn't work, Nolan walked slowly home from school. Roger was at some school club meeting. Nolan was thinking wearily of the studies he had to get caught up in. It wasn't that long till finals week for the year. The Jives had been supposed to play dances, both tonight and tomorrow night, but they, the band, had been cancelled. Nolan was more concerned about Butch than himself. The whole town seemed determined that Butch would turn out worse than his father, and he wasn't like that at all.

Almost without being aware of it, Nolan saw that Clarence's, or rather Darlene's car was in the driveway. Then he saw that two other cars were parked in front of the house, and that the front door was open. He stood by the door for a moment, looking in without being seen. Clarence was huddled up, small and tense on the couch, his face in his hands, crying. His cousin, Will Hodges, was on one side of him, and the cousin's wife Dorothy on the other. Dorothy was patting one of Clarence's hands, just patting and patting. Will had a hand awkwardly on Clarence's shoulder.

A neighbor, Mrs. Oliver, was there, looking uncomfortable, as if she needed something to do. A man who, Nolan thought, was the pastor of the church Roger sometimes attended, sat uneasily on the edge of a chair.

Nolan knew before they told him, before they even saw him, that Darlene was dead.

Will Hodges got up and came toward him. "Son, there's been a tragedy."

"How did it happen?" asked Nolan without expression.

"But you don't even know—"

"I know it's Darlene. What happened?"

"She's been shot!" cried Clarence lugubriously. "An accidental shooting, *they* say."

Will said, "The police came to the store to tell your dad not much over an hour ago. We picked up her car at the railroad office and—"

"Accidental?!" Clarence was almost shrieking, fresh tears spurting from his small eyes, his face suddenly looking very flaccid and old. "It couldn' of been accidental. That bastard killed her an' this whole town is goin' to try to cover up for him. I'll kill him, I tell you, I'll—"

"Let us get you some coffee, Clarence," broke in Dorothy placatingly.

"They were out on a sideroad," Will began telling Nolan again softly, "about ten miles east of town—"

"Is it really necessary to burden the boy with all of it just now?" asked the pastor kindly.

"It is," said Mrs. Oliver with firm conviction, "because he's the one can break it best to his poor brother. Roger and their mother were so close. This is just going to kill Roger. The whole thing will be all over town in another hour. They'll both have to know."

"Davis King was with your mother, in his car," Will told Nolan and waited, for a look, a cry, but Nolan's face remained almost expressionless. "He reported the business to the sheriff's office himself, drove the car in with the body in it. He said—well . ."

"He said they'd been seein' each other for years," cut in Clarence's agonized voice. "He shot her because she was goin' to break it up."

"Davis's story," said Will relentlessly, "is that she *did* say she wanted to break it up, unless they both got divorces and got married. He had a new rifle in his car and *said* she wanted to look at it, and it went off, accidental."

"How could a body, settin' in a car, shoot herself in the head with a rifle?" cried Clarence and broke into hoarse sobbing again.

"I went with your daddy to identify the body," said Will, very low. "She was shot through the temple, not even much blood. Just looked like she was asleep."

"Did they arrest Mr. King?"

"I think it's just a formality, till bond is set. They seem to believe him, that it *was* an accident."

Nolan walked through the room, and to the back of the house, to put away his books and jacket. She would never scream or whine or simper here again. He felt nothing. Just—nothing.

He heard Mrs. Oliver say harshly, "That's a *hard* boy, hard as nails. Did you see, he didn't even have a word or touch of comfort for his daddy, never hardly batted an eye himself."

When Roger came in a half hour later, Nolan was back in the living room. The others were still there, Mrs. Oliver busying herself over supper in the kitchen. No one would eat, she supposed, but a body had to do something neighborly, at a time like this. She never had cared much for the Tates, that woman, dressed fit to kill and all made up before she poked her head out the door. Mrs. Oliver wasn't at all surprised that she'd been having an affair, probably more than one, if the truth be known. She didn't think much of Clarence either, or the other boy, but Roger—the boys' last name was something else, *hers* by another marriage—Roger was such an almost unbelievably handsome young man, and so polite and helpful.

Clarence, his face puffy almost beyond recognition, looked up at Roger, who was staring around him in bewilderment, and said pathetically, "Your mother's been—killed."

Roger stared for a moment longer, then, dropping the books he carried, gave one wild cry and ran from the house.

"For the Lord's sake, go after him, Nolan!" cried Dorothy.

"Yes!" shrieked Mrs. Oliver. "There's no telling what the poor child might do."

Nolan caught up with him in less than two blocks. He took Roger's arm firmly.

"Stop running."

Roger slowed to a fast walk and they went on that way together until long after the street had become a country road. Roger kept scrubbing at tears with his hands.

"You don't—even seem surprised, or—how did it happen?"

Nolan told him, quickly and simply.

"*Did* he shoot her?" asked Roger, his large hazel eyes magnified by tears.

"I don't know."

"*Were* they having an affair?"

"Yes."

"How do you know that?"

"I just do."

"You know too many things, or at least you always *seem* to know."

"Do you want to go back now?"

Roger stopped beside a pasture fence. Nolan let go his arm. Roger cried for a time like a small child. Nolan stood waiting quietly. The grass was greening up well. A few Angus cattle moved about the far side of the enclosure. Nolan found himself wanting to go to kind, indulgent Mrs. King. It would take a while for Scott to get home from school in the East. Why did he want to go there? To apologize. For what?

When Roger had regained some control, he said shakily, "Do you know what's wrong with me?"

"I think so."

"It's not so much that she's—dead . . ."

"No."

"I don't know when I started to hate her, a long time ago, so long I can't remember, and now I feel so—I feel so—guilty."

"Well, I guess I don't understand that."

Roger's mouth quivered. "You don't—I mean one doesn't— *hate* one's mother."

"That depends on the one and the mother, doesn't it?"

"You haven't even cried, have you?" Roger asked tremulously.

"I don't feel like crying."

"Well, what do you feel like then, laughing?"

"I don't feel like—anything."

They turned together and started back toward the house. When they had covered half the distance in silence, Roger said forlornly, "Chappie?"

"What?"

"We should call Price now, shouldn't we?"

"Yes. Maybe Clarence has already thought of it, or some of those other people." Nolan himself had been thinking of it. He wanted it more than anything in the world at this moment, but drew back from it in uncertainty.

"I wish—I wish Price cared something for me. He likes you, a lot, maybe he loves you, because you share things about the ranch, but . . . he never talks to me more than he has to, or looks at me either. It's like he'd rather think I'm not there. . . . If those others haven't called, will you talk to him? I don't want to make a fool of myself or . . ."

"I will," Nolan said and suddenly he felt near the verge of tears. To have Price come, and Anne, to have someone else share the responsibility . . .

They arrived from Secesh shortly before nine. Clarence had his cousin there to keep him company through the dreary miserable night. He had had a good deal to drink by now.

"We've arranged for two rooms at the Valley Motel," Price said. "We'll take the boys there, unless you've some real objection."

"Objection!" said Clarence scathingly. "Roger might be a little comfort here, but you take that other one where you please. *He*'s in trouble with the law again himself."

"Do you want to come, Roger?"

"I—yes, sir."

"Get some things together then, both of you."

From their bedroom, the boys could hear Clarence going on in his hoarsened pathetic voice.

"*That* one, the Savage of the two, has been nothin' but trouble since the day he was born. He worried and grieved his poor mother nearly to . . . The latest thing is that he stole and wrecked a car. He's got to be in court Monday mornin'. There's a hearin' comin' up then on King, too. I've heard they've let the motherfucker go, just on his own say-so. You're goin' to have to handle this about Nolan. I won't never say another good word for him.

"It's hard for me to think right now, to try to plan on anything. I think Dar—Darlene's—funeral will be on Sunday, an' I expect both them boys to be there. That ain't nothin' but decent. I don't want you comin' nor your wife. She was—*mine*. You got no call to be there.

"I think I'm goin' to sell this place, git the hell away from here, but I'd take Roger with me. He's a good boy, an' he'd be comp'ny. I wouldn't have to try to git through this completely alone. That is, I'd take him if you kep' up the child support payments on him. There's no tellin' how long it'll take me to pull myself back together an' git work—unless I'm in prison myself. If they let that bastard King go

198

free, I'll have to kill him myself. There just won't be no other way. But, about Roger's support, you can see—"

"I'm going to talk with a lawyer tomorrow, Clarence," Price said dispassionately. "I'll see about taking guardianship for both boys."

"An' you mean to stand by Nolan," surmised Clarence mournfully, "after all he's put us—his mother—through. A good spell in reform school might be the best thing could happen to him."

"I think I should have been told about this when it happened," Price said coldly. "We'll see about Nolan."

"An' your wife's willin' to take this on?"

"Of course I'm willing," said Anne, trying to keep anger from her voice. "These are Price's boys. I happen to love them."

No one was hungry, but the four of them went into the small restaurant next door to the motel and ordered a bit of supper.

In their rooms, Roger, looking white and thoroughly exhausted, went to bed. In the next room, Price and Nolan sat on two plastic-covered chairs, a small table between them. Anne sat on the bed, vowing to keep silent.

Price said coolly, "Do you feel like telling me about the car?"

Nolan looked at him squarely. Anne suppressed a gasp. Except for the color of their eyes, their faces were like mirror images, even the same intent, slightly defiant expressions. Nolan's swath of straw-colored curls fell down across his forehead, erasing some of the striking similarity. He was only a child still after all, and a confused and despairing one at that, it seemed to her.

She said gently, "I could take a little walk."

"No, stay," Price said, without turning.

They kept looking at each other in that deep searching way for another moment. Do you recognize each other, Anne wanted desperately to ask. Please do!

Then Nolan, swiping back his hair, told his father quickly and simply about the Cadillac. He told him, too, about the marijuana arrest last fall. And all the while they kept watching each other's faces, eyes, in that direct, concentrating way, almost as if they dared each other to be the first to look away.

He's too young, Price, Anne wanted to shout, too young and too vulnerable to you to be stared down like that.

Finally, Nolan looked away, and they were silent. He wanted to tell his father about the thing with Clarence and Roger. He wanted to tell him about seeing his mother with Davis King in Kendall months ago. He wanted to tell about being kicked down those cellar stairs, about being shoved back so that his head was almost broken against the kitchen table, about the boiling water being poured over his arm, almost too long ago for memory, about the slaps, fists, belts, and curses. He wanted not to carry around any more, alone, all those things he knew. And there was finding Grandpa and . . .

Those things were there, in his eyes, somehow, eyes he had practiced blanking out for so long. Anne sensed them; she thought Price did, too.

Tell him you love him, she willed. Put your arms around him and hold him, a long, long time.

But Price said, "Dallas Bixby has been our lawyer for years. I can see him tomorrow, even though it is Saturday. I think we can manage some arrangement about this car thing, but—"

Nolan broke in, gulping, "Butch Moreno, he's—my friend, and he's in worse trouble. Do you think . . . ?"

He was even growing to sound like Price, Anne thought, the sadness rising higher within her, when he could keep his voice where it belonged.

"I can talk to Dallas about the other boy, but, Nolan, you'll be coming to Secesh to live now. We'll have no more trouble, of this or any other kind."

"Yes, sir." The words were almost inaudible, but they were holding each other's eyes again.

Finally, both turned away at the same instant and sat staring down at the worn spotted carpet. There was a long silence until Anne said unsteadily, "Why don't we try to get some rest now? We're all worn out."

Nolan said painfully, "Do I have to go to her funeral?"

Price said, "I suppose everyone would think it looked better if you did."

"I don't care what it looks like."

"All right, then, no."

The boy stood up, looking haggard and ineffably weary. When Nolan had reached the connecting door and put his hand on the knob, Anne stood up quickly and went to him. She put her arms around him. He was rigid in her embrace except for a moment when she felt him begin to tremble, then he gently disengaged himself, holding onto one of her hands for the briefest moment.

"Nolan," she said softly, tears in her eyes, "we love you, both of you. It will be good to have you home."

For just an instant, he turned back again, and she was struck afresh by the likeness to Price's face.

"Good night," he said in that soft deep voice, giving her just the flicker of a smile which didn't come near to touching the bleak, tired gray eyes.

13

The matter of the stolen car was settled with the judge when he found that Price would be taking Nolan to Dunraven Park and assuming full responsibility. The Savage family was known to him. Through Price's lawyer's efforts, Butch Moreno was released on probation and, that summer, came to work at Secesh. Butch was becoming a good mechanic and they needed him.

Dallas Bixby, the attorney, said to Price, "I'm afraid you're going to find yourself paying for a good part of that Cadillac. The insurance company is sure to sue. The boy who was driving is most liable, but . . ."

"When we sell the cattle in the fall," Price said grimly, "we'll do what we have to."

He kept Nolan and Butch on half-wages that summer as partial recompense, though both were doing men's work.

Davis King was put on trial for involuntary manslaughter, but not found guilty. He was the only witness, and so convincing that the jury chose to take his word. Scott was at home, missing his spring quarter at college. After the trial, Mrs. King took all the children and moved back east. Davis, it was said, could have kept his job with the railroad, but he was too humiliated, too shamed, too stunned to stay in Hurleigh. They said he went to plead with his wife to take him back, but that she refused. No one in Hurleigh heard of him again.

Following the jury's verdict, Clarence Tate made dire threats on King's life, but then he got very drunk and ended by spending the night at his cousin Will's house, sobbing hoarsely until he fell into a stuporous sleep. The house that Liam had made so sure of leaving to his daughter was sold, and Clarence left town; Will said, "to visit family back in Nebraska." He, too, was not heard of for a long while.

Before Christmas, that year when the boys were fifteen, Anne and Kiersten made a long shopping trip to Denver. They stayed with

Penny, who was now teaching third grade in a city school, while her new husband Chris Bergen finished law school. Anne bought Nolan the classical guitar, some sheet music, and records recommended by Ginia Ellenbogen. She wanted the boy to have these things come easily, knowing what short shrift he had been given by way of presents all his life. Besides, it had been a good year for Secesh. Price was, naturally, not pleased.

Nolan and Roger now had separate rooms, the two at the top of the house which had once been Stanley's and Price's. With his door closed, Nolan could practice as long into the night as he chose without disturbing anyone. He was often red-eyed and rather haggard looking in the morning, but gave no one, except Hugh, reason to complain of his work.

Nolan and Terry Ellenbogen with Terry's fiddle, and Butch Moreno with his bass, often played for square dances and other such entertainments, both at Mills Crossing and up on Fairweather. Terry had a car. He was good with his instrument, but had no desire to try to make a career of music. Terry wanted to be a doctor. Ginia, Terry's mother, had a proprietary air toward Nolan.

"He's a professional," she told Anne with great confidence, "and I feel as if I discovered him. We've got to give him every chance to go on with it, unless Price gets absolutely out of hand."

Joe and Hannah left Secesh and in their place came a young couple named Columbo and Juanita Garcia. Juanita cooked for the hands. All too often Butch and Reuben were the only ones in the bunkhouse. Reuben was becoming so stiff and tormented with arthritis that everything possible was done to keep him off the winter feeding crews, which made him more difficult to live with than ever. He spent a lot of time in the kitchen, arguing and talking with Fern. Before school in the mornings, and afterward in the late, all too short, afternoons, the work around the buildings waited for Nolan and Kiersten.

There was talk of bussing high school students from the tiny school at Mills Crossing to the slightly larger one at Fairweather, more than twenty miles away, but this had not been implemented yet. Roger so obviously excelled at everything in the Mills Crossing classes that he was slightly embarrassed and the few teachers were delighted and a little awed. Both he and Nolan were beseiged to play football and basketball; they were big strong candidates. Roger would not even consider a contact sport, and Nolan had too much work to do.

Hugh's demands were multitudinous and unrelenting. Nolan wished fervently that they might have had one winter here without Hugh. Sometimes Price privately told Hugh to "give over a little." He knew there was jealousy of Nolan and Kiersten. Hugh feared what part of the ranch they might inherit, and that made Price resentful and a little more tolerant toward the younger ones. Nolan was his own child, Kiersten his by adoption; killing the two with work wasn't going to change that for Hugh.

No one seemed to expect anything at all of Roger on the ranch and that hurt him, made him defensive and jealous. He tried his hand at a number of things, but always failed, had to be bailed out by someone else.

"Don't even go down about the buildings any more," Hugh finally ordered him. "You make more work than you do."

Roger was, at least, able to take on most of Anne's bookkeeping chores, which relieved her for other things, outside and in. And Fern and Anne were proud of his excellence in school, his wide reading, his not-quite-named ambitions, and his good looks.

In the summer when the twins were seventeen, when they had been living at Secesh for more than two years, things got very bad so far as the work was concerned. There was a good crop of hay, but extra hands to help with bringing it in were scarcely to be found. They all worked like slaves, Anne and Kiersten included.

Hugh had Nolan working on the stacks, the hardest job of all. The dried hay was gathered and brought to the bottom of a slide. It was then pushed up the slide and into a stack pen, where it had to be spread evenly with pitchforks so that, when the pen was taken away, the stack would stand and would hold together for later moving to the stackyard. At first, Nolan had had a young kid named Billy working with him, but Billy was so awkward with the pitchfork and stopped so often to contemplate his blistered hands, that he was more in the way than a help, so Nolan did the work alone. It was a grueling job, trying to keep up with the pusher alone, and one day when they came in for dinner, Nolan was pale and exhausted, wondering how he could possibly go back to it again.

When they were half finished with the meal, eating mostly in silence because of tiredness and the need to get back to work, Fern remembered something. "That old man Gunnar Nelson called this morning. He said there's a break in the fence up on the ridge between Cranky Creek and Elk Creek, and that some of our old cows and calves are mixed in with his yearlings."

Hugh sighed gustily, dropping his shoulders with weariness.

Price said, "Somebody'll have to go up there."

Hugh said irritably, "Yes, the old man would die before he'd pull anyone off his hay crew to take care of it. Let's send the two weak cogs. Nolan, you and Kiersten take a pickup and a couple of horses—"

"Weak cogs, my granny!" flashed Kiersten. She had been driving a tractor with one of the rakes and had got it stuck in a boggy place that morning. Hugh wasn't going to let this be forgotten and it rankled. "You were stuck there yourself two days ago with the mower. Hugh, sometimes I think you're the devil himself. You are *so* nasty!''

"Take some posts and wire, the fence stretchers, and—"

"We know about fixing fences,'' said Nolan curtly. "Should we get the cows back before or after we've fixed the fence?''

Price came to them as they were putting the two saddled horses into the trailer.

"If anybody asked me, I'd say that you two have all but got the afternoon off. If you have the time, cross over to Picketpin and see how the stock looks up there. Take some salt blocks. Check the upper ditches; I'd bet there are at least six new beaver dams. God, we're so far behind here I don't see how we'll ever catch up. Take Rookie and Matey. They'll sort the stock from Nelson's, if you two don't get into an argument over what signals to give them.''

Ever since there had been a Secesh, there had been a dog named Matey on the ranch. Old Price had used stock dogs, and Miss Mercy, having grown up on a huge Australian station, had, perhaps, been better at handling them than he was. The Secesh dogs had no pedigree, but were of a border collie type, though a good deal larger, black, with white and sable markings. Price bred them very selectively and their offspring brought a good price, though this not being basically a region for stock dogs, the new purchasers, untrained at handling them, were often disgruntled and disappointed. Price could take three or four stock dogs and handle as many cattle as would normally require four men. He trained his dogs with care and patience, and they meshed with him in work, almost like a part of himself. Kiersten's dog Rookie was fair at working, but this current Matey was the best. He was Price's almost exclusively, and Kiersten and Nolan felt honored at being allowed to use him. They grinned at each other with the shared recollection that Hugh could not handle the dogs at all. They simply would not work for him.

"Wow!'' murmured Kiersten when they had jounced out of sight of the ranch buildings. "Maybe it's okay to be a weak cog after all.''

She would be sixteen in October, was growing tall like her mother. Her sandy hair was bleached even lighter by the sun. The freckles weren't so noticeable on a tanned face. Her blue eyes seemed to take in everything. She had an interesting voice, always as if she had a slight case of laryngitis, lively with its slight break and very expressive. Sometimes they sang on winter evenings, when the darkness came blessedly early. Kiersten's was a hauntingly good voice for singing, with those little breaks in it, a strong contralto and clear. She loved singing and could carry a melody or do simple or complicated harmonies almost without thinking about them. She was humming something now, as she usually was, though Nolan couldn't distinguish what it was because of the rattling and banging of the pickup and horse trailer.

He kept trying to ease his shoulders and back, which were sore and aching.

"Want me to drive?" she asked.

"No, it's okay."

Nolan had grown to almost six feet tall. His build was still rather slight, though his shoulders were broadening nicely. He would grow little more, and Roger was still the taller by two inches. His very fair hair was almost no color at all in summer. He didn't like to wear hats, but tied a bandana around his head to catch some of the sweat and keep it from rolling into his eyes. There was a very white strip around his forehead, though the rest of his skin never tanned very darkly. The gray eyes were still too old for him.

They rode through the few rough miles mostly in silence. It was too hard to talk above the noise and both of them were trying to rest. When they had gone as far as they could with the truck, taken the horses from the trailer and mounted, then they could talk. It was very still up here in the woods, the wind a mere breeze flowing through the treetops, some birdsong, the sound of the creek following them for a long way up the ridge.

Kiersten said, "Have you told Dad for sure you're going to music school?"

"I've told him that if I can win the scholarship I mean to go."

His voice had settled into a deep quiet baritone, like Price's, Kiersten thought, only better. Sometimes it sounded as though Price were speaking through layers of cotton, muffled. Nolan's voice was clear and he could, unconsciously, use a fine projection so that, though he spoke in normal quiet tones, he could be easily heard and understood across a large room. His singing range was marvelous, from a deep bass to a low tenor, always clear and strong.

"And what did he say?" Kiersten asked as they rode toward the fence line, the dogs following.

"He said he won't pay for any of it. The scholarships don't include room and board."

"But that's shitty and I'm going to tell him so. Roger wants to go to college. So do I, when the time comes. He seems willing enough to pay for that."

"Well, music isn't what men do. He doesn't expect much in the way of manliness from Roger, and you're only a girl. He said I might change my mind, with another year of high school yet to go."

There was the faintest of accents in his wonderful voice, the Irish from Liam, the New England pronunciation or turn of phrase they had all picked up from Price and Fern. Kiersten loved to hear him talk and sing. His voice sent shivers up and down her spine.

"Roger wants to be a professor of something," she said, "and I want to study art. That's not exactly your run-of-the-mill, straight-off-the-ranch stuff."

"I told you, he doesn't expect the same things. He's counting on my not winning the scholarship."

There was a little silence before she said, "He loves you too much."

"He what?"

"Mother and Fern and I know that. He doesn't want you going away for any reason."

"I want the music," he said slowly, "and I want Secesh. I can never have the ranch as long as Hugh's around."

"That's something I'll never understand," she said angrily. "Why Daddy lets Hugh treat you the way he does."

"Hugh treats everyone like that."

"But not so *much!*"

Nolan thought that he was well-accustomed to having fault found with everything he did, but he didn't say that.

"Maybe it's my trial by fire," he said absently, then with an enthusiasm he couldn't hide, "anyway, if I do win, I plan to start in summer school, so I'd be leaving pretty soon after high school graduation next spring."

"Oh, Chappie, that's a lot less than a year away," she said, suddenly swept by sadness at how much faster time passed as one grew up.

They found the break, dropped the fencing materials they had tied to their saddles, got the cattle sorted and returned, the fence mended.

"We make good partners," Kiersten said. "There's time to go over to the Picketpin side."

"All right. Let's just ride across, straight from here."

"No, let's go back and move the truck. It'll be faster that way and we have the salt blocks."

"There have been no salt blocks needed over here."

An argument ensued, which Nolan finally won. They rode over the high ridge between the watersheds of Cranky and Picketpin creeks, looking over what cattle they could find.

"This is the best part of ranching," said Kiersten happily, recovering from her loss of the argument.

"The grass looks good," he said.

This was not so true when they got down to the Picketpin ditches.

The beaver had indeed been busy. They stopped by the little irrigation lake to give the horses water and rest.

The dogs quested casually, and Nolan and Kiersten lay back on the mossy bank, silent for a long time. The sun told them it was nearing five o'clock. A ground squirrel chattered at them incessantly.

"What are you thinking?" Kiersten finally asked softly.

"Besides almost falling asleep, I was thinking how glad I am of the winters I've spent at Secesh. It's pretty special to see the deer and elk coming down to feed along the river when the snow gets too deep up here, to hear a mountain lion scream, to watch eagles every day."

"And in summer there are the nighthawks," she said dreamily, "and always the coyotes."

"And Hugh," he said, grinning rather grimly.

"You don't really want to leave, do you?"

"Only for a while, to try with the music, then I think I'd want to come back."

"Have you said that to Dad?"

"No. There'd be no point in it. He'd probably think I was just trying to con him out of some money."

After a while, she said, "Is Roger really sad? Sometimes he seems so morose and . . ."

"Roger needs to go away from here. He's been used all his life to being very important. He gets—overlooked at the ranch in the busy times."

"And what times aren't busy? Have you always looked after him? Known his needs?"

"I guess so. In a way."

"Tell me about when you were boys growing up, all that time you weren't here."

But he didn't want to talk about that. He said instead, "So you're going to be an art major. Then what?"

"Well, maybe commercial art. I'd rather just try to do my own thing, but that would mean a lot more money and a lot more time. I don't want to take money from anyone else, once I'm through with school. Maybe I'll go to New York. I'll hate it, I know I will. And I'll live for vacations when I can come back here. It seems we both have to—prove ourselves at something else before we can feel free to come home again. When we're elderly, and rich, let's come back and buy out Hugh's share."

He said, "I've always wondered why they didn't have some kids of their own, Anne and Price."

"Mother told me there was some physical problem, that they couldn't. That's why it's so important to him to have you want Secesh,

207

so that he can turn the major interest over to you, his own flesh and blood."

"I don't think he wants that at all. I always seem to disappoint him."

"Oh, you're both so stubborn and—and private. You don't know a lot of things that are staring you right in the face . . . . . Chappie, which girl do you like best in the Park?"

"I've never really had a date."

"I know that, because you're always playing when there's a dance or anything. Kara Ellenbogen and Inge Pedersen, for two, are crazy about you. But I asked a question."

"I like you best," he said softly.

She shivered and looked away. "Do you? Truly? Or am I just a habit?"

She pushed the hair back off his forehead.

"Truly," he said, taking her hand. "There are a lot of years, a lot of things to be taken care of first, but I think, some day, I'll want to ask you to marry me."

"You will?" Her face was shining. "How long have you thought that?"

"Since I was about six."

"You haven't. We hated each other on sight."

"I didn't hate you. I was jealous because you had come to live here and I couldn't."

"And I thought you were trying to take Price away from me, just when I'd got a daddy."

"But I thought, even then, that you were about the prettiest little girl I'd ever seen."

She laughed in sheer surprise. "Well, you certainly can't still think *that,* not with all my freckles and—"

"You're pretty," he said firmly. "You're wholesome and what Grandpa would call bonnie. When I think of you, it's as bonnie."

"I like that," she said shyly. "Will you write me, while you're away, and call me bonnie?"

"Yes."

They were both looking at their joined hands, rough and scratched and calloused.

She said, "I'd like to marry you some day. I accept."

"No, don't do that," he said soberly. "You need to meet a lot of people, all kinds. You've hardly been out of the Park since you were four years old."

"Well, but could we make love?"

He stared at her, smiling faintly, finally saying, "Kierstie, bonnie little Kierstie, I don't think we should do that."

"You don't want to?"

"Yes, but—"

"I've always wanted you to be the very first, maybe the only one, ever. I've thought a lot about it."

"You have?"

"I'm hardly a child any more. I think sex ought to mean something. I want to—have the experience—with you. I could never just hop from one guy to another, just for—the physical part of it. It's got to be more than that, and it is, right now, so will you?"

He flushed. "I haven't—got a condom."

She grinned. "Aren't you one of those guys who always carries one, just in case? Anyway, it's safe. I just finished my period."

"How do you know about all these things, safe and unsafe, carrying condoms?"

"Nolan," she flashed impatiently, "you've got to stop thinking of me as a little kid. And I'm not going to beg you. If you won't, then—"

He turned and took her in his arms. "I will," he whispered against her neck. "I just hadn't dreamed I'd be so lucky."

She shivered at his touch, the sound of his voice, the feelings that were taking place in her body, but she said, almost matter-of-factly, "I want to take off all our clothes."

He was trembling. It was over too quickly. She gasped once, with pain, then clung to him fiercely.

After a little time, he asked fearfully, "Was it bad? I hate hurting you."

"It wasn't bad at all," she said with a small, secret, reassuring smile, then soberly, "Have you ever done it before?"

"No. I wish I could have known how to make it better for you."

"I'm glad you never did. I wish you never would, with anyone else. You don't have any idea how insanely jealous I am of you with other girls. Want to have a wash in the lake?"

"All right, but it's going to be cold."

They both felt rested after that, refreshed and eagerly excited They lay in a sunny spot and gently, lingeringly, began to explore each other.

"Do you think it was like this for Adam and Eve?" she whispered

He shook his head. "It couldn't have been nearly so good."

"Oh, Chappie, don't ever go away. I mean so far that I can't touch you with words or a letter or phone call. You do that sometimes, you know, right in the middle of a bunch of people. Your eyes just—show nothing. It's as if you're not behind them any more. Don't ever do that with me. I love you so much."

"I won't ever mean to do that with you I love you so, but

remember, bonnie Kierstie, there are a lot of years and a lot of people. Maybe you'll come to love someone else."

"I don't think so, but maybe you will?"

"No," he said softly.

"Chappie, I really hate Inge and Kara when they talk about you. And they're two of my best friends. I'm ashamed, but I'm always going to be so jealous."

They made love again, slowly and with the deepest and tenderest of feelings.

"It was so good for me this time," she murmured drowsily. "It couldn't possibly be so good for you."

"Yes," he answered, still holding her with infinite tenderness.

Finally, they dressed and remounted their horses, calling the dogs. The sun had slipped down not much more than an hour farther, but it seemed they had been here a very long time, opening their deepest selves to one another.

"You see," Kiersten couldn't resist saying, "we'd only have a couple of miles to ride now if we'd brought the truck around."

"Riding is supposed to be what ranching is all about," he pointed out. "That's all there is to it in the movies. We're going to miss the evening chores. You ought to be glad of that. I am, and of other things that have happened today."

"Will you be ready and eager to start stacking tomorrow?"

His shoulders sagged at the recollection of that.

They rode mostly in silence, holding hands when there was room for the horses to move side by side, looking deeply into each other's eyes.

It was almost sundown when they reached the truck, and they had a rousing argument about who was going to drive back.

"You'll never get turned around with the trailer in this space," he pointed out, but gestured to the keys in the ignition. "Look how late it is. I'm starving."

"Yes," she said, getting triumphantly behind the wheel. "There's a possibility we could get into trouble for getting back so late. It wouldn't be nearly so late if you didn't argue so much."

She backed and filled delicately, but the trailer wouldn't follow properly.

"Don't say a word, Nolan Savage," she said threateningly. "I'm going to learn."

"Can't I even say anything that might be helpful?"

"No," she snapped, then had to laugh. "Take your damned hands away from your eyes, and, yes, tell me how to make the trailer go where I want it to."

Ginia Ellenbogen went with Nolan to Denver for the scholarship tryouts in February. Anne, Kiersten, and Roger had wanted to go badly, but, testing Price's feelings, Anne had said to the others and to Nolan that he might do better, feel less shy without a lot of family there.

"I am his music teacher," Ginia had pointed out exuberantly to Anne. "Though, God knows, there's not been much I could teach him."

Ginia called Secesh near ten in the evening. Anne came back from the telephone beaming.

"Ginia says he's won. It's not really official yet, but one of the judge's wives is a friend of hers."

"Bless his heart," said Fern, eyes shining with wetness. "Well, now we know, I think I'll get to bed. He's been so worried and scared about this. He must be just sick with the excitement and having it all over, finally."

"And so happy," said Kiersten, a little wistful, but smiling broadly.

Roger said, with a smile that didn't feel or look real, "It's what he's been after for years."

Roger and Kiersten were playing chess. She was getting quite good at it and had persuaded him to stop work on an English paper to play tonight because she was so tense and nervous with the waiting.

Price got up, knocking out his pipe in the fireplace and said curtly, "Don't stay up too long, you two."

In their bedroom, Anne said pleadingly, "Oh, Price, as you'd say yourself, give over. Be happy for Nolan. Tell him when he comes home you'll pay his expenses. Give him a chance to feel perfectly happy, and safe."

"I've had such hopes for him," he said stonily, his back turned. "Even when he was little, and especially since they came here for good."

"But you've only been thinking about what *you*'ve wanted. There really are other ways to success. You love him. Let him know he's not such a disappointment to you. Don't his hopes and wishes count for anything?"

"Will I turn off the lamp now?" he asked tersely.

In the living room, Kiersten was saying, "It's men who need liberating, not women, especially in this part of the country. Daddy just has this idea that a *real* son of his can't possibly be, or want to be, a musician."

"But Chappie's won," said Roger. "I knew he would. He always has, even when everything has been stacked against him."

"How do you mean?"

They left the chess game and he told her a good deal about their boyhood. Kiersten shuddered at the vicious cruelties that had been heaped on Nolan. Roger's own childhood had been just as sad in its way, but she could still feel Nolan's body, water-chilled and sun-warmed against her own. There were tears in her eyes. In just a few more months he'd be going to Vermont, and that was so very far away. She knew he'd never tell her how badly he'd been treated in years past. She longed to be holding him now, to have his trust in her grow. She wondered if he'd ever feel safe trusting anyone, after these things Roger was telling her.

"And yet," Roger was finishing, "it's a strange thing. I'm the one who's always had everything, figuratively speaking, but it's Chappie who's really had everything."

"I don't understand," she said rather absently.

"Well, like friends. Don't you remember when we first started to school here how the kids flocked around him? I don't know why that is. I mean, he's certainly a fine person, a worthy friend, but . . ."

"But you're better looking, to most people," Kiersten said thoughtfully, honestly, "more extroverted. Maybe you're too good-looking, Roger. It's kind of scary, and you're obviously so much smarter than the rest of us."

"Nolan has said something like that, and I suppose it could be true, but what I'm trying to say is that he has—triumphs. You might say he won, over Clarence and our mother. He could triumph over Hugh if he wanted to stay here and really try. When I win, get what I think I've wanted, it's—it's nothing, not worth having."

"Maybe most things come too easy for you."

"Yes, that could well be true. It's a lonely, a disheartening kind of life. Nothing seems worth trying for after a while, yet I don't have what I really want. I'm not even sure what those things are."

Kiersten put up a hand and touched his sleek chestnut hair.

"You know," he said, taking her hand, "my mother taught me a fine contempt for women, just by being what she was, shallow and—and stupid, showing me off all the time to show off herself. The women here at Secesh, you and Fern and your mother, have shown me that maybe I was drawing too big a generalization. All women aren't Darlene. Still, I haven't yet had a date. I can't get up the nerve to ask anyone because I'm afraid if I get to know her better she'll turn out to be a chattering nincompoop like my mother . . . . Well, I'm going to ask for one now. Will you be my date for the junior-senior prom?"

Tears pricked Kiersten's lids again. "Oh, Roger, I can't."

She had decided, last summer, not to accept any dates while Nolan was still at home. He would be playing for the prom, couldn't dance at all, but she certainly would not go as his brother's date.

She said, "We sophomores have to do all the work, you know,

the decorating and serving and the like. Thank you for asking, but I can't go, not as a date. I know some girls who'd be delighted though. Vera Christiansen for one. What it is is that you make most girls a little—afraid. I guess they're in awe of you."

"I don't like that," he said irritably. "I can't respect people who feel, or seem to feel that way. I guess that's why Chappie and I have stayed friends, at least *I* think we have, because he doesn't feel in awe of anything."

Kiersten was busily banking the fire, thinking how Nolan had seemed awed by their shared experience up on Picketpin. When she turned, Roger was standing very close to her.

"Would you kiss me goodnight, just for—friendship's sake?"

She offered her cheek, smiling, but he put his arms around her, his mouth on hers for a long moment.

"In two years," he said with a strange note in his voice, "you'll be at the university with me. Nolan won't be there."

She drew away from him firmly. She felt sorry for him, and a little afraid, not for the reasons they had been discussing, but because . . . Because what? Did he know about her and Nolan? It almost seemed he did. Certainly neither of them would ever tell, though she had felt, that night when they got home from the high pastures, that everyone could read it in their faces, or, certainly, in hers.

"Why do you say that?" she asked a little unsteadily.

"Because you're his girl, aren't you? You have been for years and years, though—I don't know—maybe neither of you knows it yet. But it's a thing called puppy love, Kiersten. I think, with a clear track, I could get you to change your mind. But don't you see, this is what I've kept saying this evening, Chappie has everything. Sometimes, I get his leftover friends. Sometimes, people are aware of me, here on the ranch, though never Price, he's too busy noticing Nolan. I'd like very much for you to be *my* girl, and I think you might come round to being that, if he's out of sight and out of mind for a while. You've drifted into this pattern, whether you're aware of it or not, but Vermont's very far away."

Kiersten cried in her bed, some of the reasons not altogether clear. She was deeply happy for Nolan, that he had won the scholarship, but their physical distance would be so far and there were less than four months left before he would be going away. She thought of what Roger had told her of the horrors of his brother's childhood, and wished that, just for a few moments, she could hold Nolan as a little boy in her arms, make him feel loved and safe, freed of violence forever.

And she cried for Roger. Why, she could not say, and she didn't want to try to search out the meaning. She thought again of the two of them, Nolan and herself, way up there on Picketpin, mentioning Adam and Eve, and it was, somehow, as if Roger, even thoughts of him, were the serpent. She wanted no tempting snakes in her Eden.

14

Nolan had some savings. He sent money to reserve himself a dormitory room at Albion, and there was the bus fare to Vermont Each time he changed busses he got down and carefully watched the transfer of his instruments, the twelve-string, the classical six-string, and the violin. At the bus station in the little town near the school he found a cab, one of the two the town possessed

"No need to ask where you want to go," said the driver as Nolan carefully placed the instruments, the suitcases being of no moment.

His heart filled with joy, excitement, anticipation at the man's words.

Most of his registration had been completed by mail. It would be the following day before it could all be finalized. He moved into the dormitory quickly. The room was small, cell-like, very ascetic. They had written him that it was very hard to find rooms off campus because householders objected to students' practicing at all hours.

He went to the admissions office to make his presence known, and, because he was early, was able to acquire a job as janitorial assistant for four hours a day. This would cover his room and board for the summer semester, with a little left over.

It was a beautiful campus, small, with no building more than three stories high, set in rough rolling land, among giant maples, oaks, and elms.

Going back toward his room, he stopped and sat on a bench. On the warm early summer air, he heard the sounds of piano, French horn, violin, clarinet, and oboe, each playing its own piece, mixed and beautiful, something he seemed to take in through his very pores as he took the warm hazy sunshine. To *live* music!

When he had dreamed there a while, he had to rouse himself to the recollection that it would not be all music. Half his credits had to

215

come from regular, basic college classes, and there would be the janitorial work. Then he noticed, looking around with more attention, more consciousness, that he missed the horizons of Dunraven Park, the escarpment of the Fairweather Plateau along one side, the arc of the Shadow River Mountains closing in the rest. He had not realized until now how he had come to watch the peaks, Kilrayne, Warrior, and Dunraven, for everything from the time of day to the buildup of storms. He felt afraid and lonely. Maybe he wouldn't really be good enough for Albion. There would be students here who had practiced their instruments daily from the age of three or four. Perhaps he couldn't keep up his scholarship. To his surprise he already missed Secesh sorely, Reuben, Butch, Anne, and Fern. He wished he and Price might have parted on better terms. If Price had said, "Stay. I need you here. I want you here," would he have given up all this? Most of all, he missed Kierstie, was eager for her letters which brought bits of Secesh, wherever they came. They had agreed not to write "love letters," not yet, but he did love her, and his loneliness increased.

He missed Roger, too, but this was not loneliness. It was, rather, like having a weight lifted so that he seemed able to breathe more easily. He even missed Hugh, in something of the same way.

But there was the muted sound of the various instruments and compositions, coming through open windows on the gentle air, making him sit lethargically, listening, smiling, wanting to lay hands on an instrument of his own, but still sitting. Yes, it had been right to come. This was something he had to do in his lifetime, if only for a year, a term. He meant to take it for all its worth to him, and to win merit.

He kept the scholarship with no problem, but his music instructors found him both fascinating and infuriating. He had won entrance to the school with the classical guitar, but he wanted to play everything, to compose, transpose, arrange, and vary. He was like a starving man, gobbling music. He had a violin, which he played passably well, but he wanted to play cello, at which he was not so good in the beginning. He had a fine classical guitar, but kept arranging music for it to his twelve-string. He played a practice piano far into the night, going over sheet music two or three times, then, with what Aunt Ginia called his "photographic ear," striking out on his own with the shorter compositions.

"You think you can improve upon Beethoven?" demanded one disgruntled instructor.

"No," said Nolan shyly, "but I think when music is written and published, it belongs to the players. It's as if you heard or read a story. The story is yours then, and if you tell it, it comes out a little differently.''

At the end of his first year he accompanied two people in the spring recital and played two pieces of his own, one with the classical guitar, another which he had arranged for the twelve-string.

At the beginning of his second summer, one instructor asked him harriedly how he expected ever truly to excel at anything when he insisted on such diversification. Nolan said simply that he wanted to learn all he could.

He passed the required college subjects, but only just. He never had time for that sort of study and grade point averages mattered to him not at all.

Anne called him one evening at the beginning of that second summer to say that Grandmother Emily had died. She, Price, Kiersten, Roger, Hugh, and Penny would fly to California for the funeral. Would he come, too? Nolan said he couldn't. It was true; classes had begun. Besides, hearing her voice, he was afraid that if he went home, he might not come back, happy though he was here.

Kiersten wrote him almost every week. He answered with hurried but loving notes. Anne wrote often. Sometimes she included a check for fifty or a hundred dollars. Nolan returned the checks, saying it was Price's money and he had to do this on his own, though he appreciated her thoughtfulness. At Christmas she sent a check for two hundred dollars, writing, "It's not *just* Price's money. This is a Christmas present. If you return it, you'll break my heart.''

Roger wrote long involved letters for which he wanted Nolan's questions and comments, mostly about his own studies at the University of Colorado. Nolan could only manage to send him three or four notes per semester.

They all begged him to come home for Christmas or for breaks between semesters, but he couldn't. The necessity for him to keep whatever job he had made a good excuse, and these breaks, with no irksome compulsory studies, were the times when he could move more freely in his own diverse realm.

He lost the janitorial job in his second fall semester, simply because he forgot to sign up for it. He found work as a night watchman at one of the town's two cotton mills. He played and arranged and composed and studied during working hours, and did not have a coat suitable for the frigid winter weather. Rarely did he sleep more than four hours in twenty-four.

During his third summer, he began teaching young students from the town. This was an interesting task in the beginning, and it was a necessary class, with credit, but his pupils were mediocre and unenthusiastic and he had to keep a tight rein on his temper. The foremost thing he learned was that he would not become a music teacher.

In the fall semester of that third year at Albion, Nolan met Michael Lyman. Michael was there as a piano student, but he also had a banjo. They coerced a violinist into trying to fiddle for them, and had a good trio for folk music, all of them with good voices. After research in the library, Nolan came up with some very old Christmas songs, which he blended into a medley for the three of them to play at the Christmas recital. The instructors were mildly shocked, but the music was baroque, in spite of the banjo, and they were also titillated. However, the fiddler went back to being a violinist.

Michael and Nolan were asked to play three-night weekends at a ski lodge some fifty miles from Albion. Michael had a car and Nolan found another scholarship student who was delighted to share the night watchman's job with him.

"We need another player," said Michael urgently, "and some more instruments, since you can switch around the way you do. Look, there's this girl I know, Carol Pinelli, plays flute. She'd come with us. Could you make some arrangements using a flute? She plays really well, but needs music to read."

In the beginning, Nolan wrote everything out for Carol, but she caught on faster than Michael had given her credit for and she liked playing folk music. Chiefly, Nolan suspected, she liked it because it meant being with Michael. Carol was a day student at Albion, living in the town with her husband and two tiny boys. But she was out to "find herself," she insisted, and that, evidently, included finding Michael Lyman.

One night after their second set at the ski lodge, Nolan was brought a note. "Have a drink with me," read the spidery handwriting. "The waiter will show you the table."

They often had such requests and usually tried to fulfill them, for the sake of business, theirs and the lodge's.

This customer was a small dainty woman with big brown eyes and a look about her of getting what she wanted. Her dark hair was fashionably long. Nolan guessed that, under the makeup and hair tint, she was probably forty.

"My name is Deedee Gorman," she said, holding on to his hand too long. "And I know you are Nolan Savage. I do love that name. It sounds so—pagan. Sit down, please. What will you have to drink?"

"Nothing. Thank you."

"Oh, come, dear! You must have something with me. It isn't good for the house if you don't keep the customers busy drinking, now, is it?"

"All right, a marguerita then. Thank you."

With the drinks before them, she said, "I have a house near Albion, within easy walking distance, in fact. My late husband left it to me. It's been used mostly as a summer place. He had some interests in one of the mills, so there were affairs to be settled and I thought it would be interesting to stay on and have out-of-town guests to celebrate Christmas up here. Well, now we're well into January, and I'm still here, as you can see."

She offered him a cigarette. He declined, but took the gold lighter and struck flame to hers.

"Mr. Satterthwaite, at the school, was an old friend of my husband's. Some of us were at the Christmas recital, or parts of it, and Satty's told me a great deal about you. . . . Wouldn't you like to hear what he's said?"

Nolan looked at her, smiling slightly. "I'm not sure," he said candidly.

She laughed. "I do love honesty. Do you know you have a very interesting face? It's like a Viking or—or maybe something even earlier, and with those dark eyes that are nothing but gray. . . . Well, Satty tells me you're a maverick, but a terribly bright and talented one. He says you simply devour music, and won't be classified or categorized. Some of the instructors are a little afraid of you because you're so quick, so good with whatever you do. Others find you a very stimulating challenge. There now, that wasn't so bad, was it? He also tells me you're a scholarship student, and must work for your room and board. You must hate losing time in work that you could be putting into music."

"It's not so bad," he said, a little overwhelmed by her tone, which was very definite and aggressive.

"Well, I've had this idea." She spoke without smiling and her face seemed hard and determined under the makeup. "Ordinarily at this time of year I would be in the south of France, Italy, Spain, but I just seem to keep lingering on here. For this semester that's about to begin, I should like to do something for Albion, make my own contribution. Ben, my husband, would have liked that. Tell me, what do you intend to do with your life after Albion? Go on the concert stage? Alone or with an orchestra? Which instrument will be your stock in trade? Satty tells me they haven't figured that one out at the school yet."

These were questions Nolan had been considering in brief moments when he found the time. He should have two more years at Albion to complete its college and music courses, but of late, he had felt a restlessness from time to time. It had begun with his and Michael's going out to play, and it was growing worse.

Not particularly wanting to discuss his plans, or non-plans with this woman, he said vaguely, "I'm not sure yet. I like doing arrangements."

"And you do them beautifully," she said without hesitation, but with, he felt sure, little knowledge. "I know you did several for the recital and that you do them for this little group you have here. Of course, I'm no authority on music but, as they say, I know what I like. You also have an excellent voice. I don't know if you realize the projecting quality and depth of it. Even when you're singing in the background, very quietly, while one of the others leads, your voice simply sends shivers. At any rate, doing arrangements is very worthy, but it does seem to me it would be putting you, your talent, too much in the background."

He shifted uneasily and drank, but she seemed to expect, demand an answer. "I'm just not sure . . ."

"Very well, that's really none of my business, is it? Let me tell you the contribution I'd like to make. You can come and stay at my house, forget about having to have a job for this semester at least. There's a large den downstairs that's practically soundproof. It has a piano. You could practice there as much as you like, even with friends."

In exchange for what? Nolan almost said with a guileless gaucherie, but stopped himself. It was in her face. Already, she looked as if she owned him, as if some price had been paid, some deal consummated.

"That would be very kind of you," he said, stammering only a little. "But I think I have things pretty well under control for now. I have a night watchman's job four nights a week at the Darby Mill, and we're working hard to make something out of this group."

"Don't close the door on it," she said, sounding ominous. "No doubt we'll be seeing each other again, since I live so near the school and take an interest in it."

Going back that night, Michael asked Nolan to drive, saying he was too tired. Nolan could not remember when he himself had not been tired. Weariness had become a part of him, bone and fiber. Michael was not too tired to fool around with Carol in the back seat or, later, to bring up again the subject of his uncle Alfie, who was a booking agent for musicians.

"If only we could find another person," he lamented. "Folk music's really in now and we'd have it made. Would you skip summer school, Chappie, to go on the road?"

"Yes," said Nolan, smoking Michael's cigarettes to keep awake. "If we had the right people."

Carol said in her small breathy voice, "I think Nolan thinks I'm not the right people."

"No, it's not that. I like arranging with the flute. It makes our group different from others."

He could have said that her soprano voice was too weak to carry a song, and too cultured for good folk music, but there was no need for that. He could also have said he didn't think she should leave her husband and two babies for Michael Lyman, who was always going to be a drifter, in all ways.

"I'm good with the banjo," Michael was saying, "and Carol with flute, especially with you to arrange for us and play your twelve-string. What we need is someone who's more diversified, like you, who can do well on more than one instrument. I'll tell you what I'm going to do while we look for that person. My birthday's in May. I'm going to tell my folks that what I want is a modified, medium-sized bus. I've already got the plans drawn up for the changes. They've got the money."

Nolan laughed softly and lit another cigarette. Even the snowstorm outside was lulling rather than alerting.

He said, "That would be quite a birthday present."

"It doesn't have to be new," said Michael deprecatingly, "just modified."

"They won't like your going off, roaming around the country, will they?" asked Carol, "when you're supposed to be in music school?"

Michael said rather grimly, "They don't much care what I do, so long as I don't live at home—a bearded, banjo-playing hippie. I don't belong at Albion either. I never even wanted to study piano. You should have seen old Harriman's face when I told him I'd like to do my spring recital thing on banjo. He said it's scarcely even a recognized instrument, but I think I want to try it. Could you arrange something that's sort of pseudo-classical, and accompany me, Chappie? We're supposed to solo on our own particular instruments and the piano just isn't mine."

"All right," Nolan said. "Sounds like fun."

"Uncle Alfie wants to hear us when we've got it all together. There's a chance we could do something like cut a record before this year is over. Think about that, gang, while you're looking for that other person. And, of course, we have to have a name. Have you been thinking about that? Say, Chappie, was that dame who called you over to her table a Mrs. Gorman?"

"I think that was her name."

"There's a cool guy," said Michael mockingly, "he thinks that was her name."

"Wow!" said Carol. "There are a lot of stories going around town about her. They say she threw a Christmas house party that lasted about a month and used up about fifty cases of booze. This husband Gorman was about her fifth or sixth. Fortunately for her, all the others didn't die. Don't let her get her hooks in you. I've heard she collects talented people like some others collect paintings, just to fasten them in place and show herself off through ownership."

Less than two weeks later, Nolan lost his night watchman's job because he was found by the mill manager, sleeping very soundly on the job. They gave him two weeks at the dorm to come up with the next payment for room and board. No jobs were to be had, with so many students looking, and the town in something of a depression.

He had offers. Michael said his father would be glad to pay his fees for the whole semester. Nolan, refusing with thanks, thought bitterly of Price. Carol said there was a spare room in her mother's house she felt sure he could use. Nolan declined; he would be unable to pay, for a time at least, and there would still be the matter of food. Furthermore, he wanted no more of the possibility of somehow being involved in the triangle that was Michael, Carol, and Carol's husband.

The money they made weekends at the ski lodge kept him eating, but the two weeks for dorm fees passed and he had no job. He moved his instruments and clothes into Michael's room, even tried sleeping there, in the small floor space.

One snowy evening as he was returning from checking on a hotel night clerk's job, already taken, he was thinking of Kiersten's last letter. She was now in her second semester as an art major at Boulder. Her letters were chatty and flip. She said she had more guys lined up for dates than she knew what to do with. Didn't he date? He never wrote about it, or much of anything else. She wrote that, occasionally, she dated Roger. There was a lot of status in dating upperclassmen, Roger now a junior. She said Roger was, of course, absolutely brilliant in his studies, but still seemed a little lost without his twin. She said *she* was lost without Roger's twin, then she wrote some things about Secesh.

Walking wearily through the early dusk, Nolan yearned for Kierstie, for Secesh. He thought of feeding on a day like this, the big work horses steaming in the cold still air. He even thought wistfully of lifting and breaking apart the big hay bales for the hungry, following cattle, until every muscle in his body was exhausted, his breath a fog in the cold, sweat running down inside his heavy winter gear, throat and chest aching from gulping the icy air. And then it would be done, the sled empty except for the hay that had spilled down from the broken bales and he could lie back in it and go home. The bootroom, stripping wet cold clothing, a hot shower, with smells of supper from the kitchen, and, afterward, homework, reading, or playing and singing around the big fireplace. It had been all folk music that they sang; Anne's, like Liam's from Irish or Scots backgrounds; Fern's from her southern mother, freedom songs, spirituals, the Saxon masters' songs, and a few songs of the sea and of Australia which Fern remembered from Miss Mercy and Mr. Price.

Folk music was, in fact, very popular now, at the beginning of 1969. Michael or Carol would dash to him with a "new" folk song they had just heard or read, and it would turn out to be something he had known all his life, but hadn't thought of for a long time. Therein might lie his future, he thought. They had formed the nucleus of a group; hopefully, it would grow. Perhaps he could find work as an arranger for some of the people who had already made names in folk music, David Harris, Susan Lister . . . He grinned wearily. There was nothing like starting at the top. . . . The thing right now was to finish out this semester. He would not be denied that. Since he had attended summers he would have, at the end of the semester, four full years of credit. A year short of graduation, but he didn't care much about ceremony or a degree. He was restlessly ready to go on now to something else, but he would have this semester.

Michael sometimes thought of staying on in school because of the draft. The lottery system was being used and, so far, Nolan's birthday had been well down the list. He would not serve in Vietnam. He had taken no part in the demonstrations, but if he were drafted, he would go away. This was the worst, the most stupid of unholy wars. He would hate leaving the United States. He had hated leaving Secesh, but then there had been so much to look forward to. Now, if he could be transported, see the big house, with smoke coming from its chimneys, hear Fern's no-nonsense banging around in the kitchen . . .

A car drew up beside him on the icy road, a long white car, he could see in the near darkness.

"Mr. Savage, I believe," said a woman's voice in tones of what seemed to be satisfaction. She reached across and opened the passenger door wider.

"Now don't tell me you've forgotten. That's not the least bit flattering. Quick, my dear boy! Get in before I freeze to death."

When he had complied rather numbly, she said, "My dear, you're looking very worn and weary. How old are you?"

"I'll be twenty-one in April."

"No twenty-year-old should look so tried and tribulated. I guessed you were twenty at the Christmas recital, but then, the other night at the ski lodge, I thought I might have been wrong. You have old eyes. That's not a derogatory statement. They are very interesting eyes, particularly in a face like yours. They look as if they've seen a great deal, up close and at far distances. But, you know, you also have a way of making them—go blank, and that isn't complimentary.''

She was driving past the entrance gate to the school.

He said, ''I have to get out—''

''No such thing. You're coming home with me to dinner.''

Then she put on the brakes and the car slewed round on the icy asphalt.

''Oh, dear, I ought to have a chauffeur, but I hate having them around all the time. You get out and come round and drive, please. I'm sure you're a far better driver. You *are* coming home with me. First, though, I'd like you to get one or two of your instruments. You may play for your supper.''

He had a lot to drink that evening, thinking to hell with his money problems for this one evening, thinking to hell with Secesh, the draft, all of it. . . . All except Kierstie, bonnie Kierstie, but, eventually, though briefly, he forgot Kiersten as well.

The dinner was a sumptuous affair. He had to watch her to be sure he was eating properly, using the correct implements. He was not even really hungry. The warmth and liquor were making him desperately sleepy. There was wine with the meal and his glass seemed always to be full.

''I have three servants who go with me everywhere if I'm to stay more than a few weeks,'' she said at some point, ''my personal maid, Annette, my chef, and butler.''

Nolan thought the staid, stuffy-seeming butler winked at him then, but he was never sure.

After dinner, when Mrs. Gorman asked if he would like a drink, bourbon and water was the first thing that came to mind, so there was a glass of that always at hand.

''Don't play me your school music,'' she said, smiling rather gloatingly, ''play me what's really you.'' She watched his face hungrily as he tuned the twelve-string, hardly aware of her.

The deep-cushioned couch was not comfortable for playing. He moved to a straight chair upholstered in puce velvet. She moved with him, across the room, and sat on a hassock, continuing to watch greedily.

Nolan didn't like her expression when he finally noticed it. He had a good idea of how this evening was supposed to end, but he sipped his drink, closed his eyes and thought of Liam's old stories. He settled on the story of Tom O'Mara, with themes of the little fishing village, of Tom and his boat, of Tom and his large and growing family, of the seal who spoke to Tom from Scarra Rock, and of the sea, always the sea, in all her moods.

"Very nice," said Deedee Gorman, but, just when he opened his eyes, he thought her face looked bored, a little petulant. "I do wish you wouldn't play with your eyes closed. I'd like to see what's going on in them."

"It's the way the music comes," he said simply. "I have to think about that, not what's going on around me. Mrs. Gorman, thank you for dinner. It's started to snow again and I—"

"Precisely, you must spend the night, mustn't you? And please, don't ever call me Mrs. Gorman. My name is Deedee. I've told Stephens to make up one of the guest rooms for you. There are plenty in this house. Come along and I'll show you. You do look very tired and sleepy."

It was a luxurious room with an opulent bath.

"Satisfactory?" she enquired with a coquettish smile.

"It's very nice but—"

"Oh, stop that, my Savage, Of course you're staying. I know you've lost your room at the dorm."

"But I can't pay—"

"Oh, don't be as naive as a kindergarten child," she said impatiently. "You'll pay, starting now. Undress."

"What?"

"Undress. Fully."

And when he had, staggering only a little, she put an arm about him and brought him to stand under a bright light, turning him this way and that, stroking him. Nolan's whole body seemed to be burning.

She laughed possessively. "Beautiful male body. Beautiful erection. You are so fair and unblemished. And, do you know, you blush all over? Charming."

She pointed to the turned-down bed. "Wait for me there."

Now all the lights were out. He could hear her undressing. Evidently, her body was not for scrutinizing. She pulled back the drapes and came to the bed.

"All the world's a stage," she said, running her hands over him gloatingly. "Pretend we are players to a *huge* audience. Give your very best performance."

"Sex should mean something," Kiersten had said. He wanted to stop this because of what Kiersten had said, because of Kiersten, but his body had the upper hand, his body and Deedee Gorman.

Later they slept. Nolan awoke less than two hours later, immediately trying to orient himself. His head ached horribly. He got up gingerly and silently turned on a small lamp to go into the bathroom and look for aspirin. When he came back, having found none, he noticed that Deedee's makeup didn't come off all over everything as

225

his mother's had always done. Something new? Or just something Darlene hadn't known about? And, strangely, her hair was hardly mussed.

Then he remembered he had left his guitar downstairs, leaning between wall and chair. He put on his pants, went down, put it in its case and stood it in a corner, out of harm's way. Then he went up again, carefully turning out all the lights he had used.

What did this woman mean to him? Nothing. But what they had had together, two hours ago . . . ? Still nothing. He felt almost neutral toward her, with dislike having the slight upper hand. It shouldn't count for anything, this night. And if he stayed, in all this luxury . . . ? All he knew just now was exhaustion. It looked extremely cold and grim outside.

Deedee was awake, wanting to know where he had been. When he explained about the guitar, she didn't look pleased.

"I—uh—also thought I might find some aspirin," he said awkwardly.

"Hangover already?" she cooed. "Get back into bed. Deedee will fix."

She brought him two aspirin and a glass of bourbon and water.

"This sort of thing happens only once with Deedee," she warned coquettishly, "waiting on her men. From now on, *you* bring me things."

He swallowed the aspirin with only a small sip of the drink and set the glass on the night table. She slid sensuously under the covers beside him.

"Now," she purred, "before those take effect, Deedee has some things for show and tell. You're very handsome and pleasing, my Savage, but, you see, sex isn't just a matter of in and out. Women want their share of the fun, too. Deedee is going to teach you. Not all in one night, of course, how to drive women mad and how to satiate them so completely that they swoon at your feet. I have been called a nymphomaniac, but that simply isn't so. I've heard that nymphomaniacs are actually frigid and that certainly isn't true of me. One simply needs the right set of circumstances, the right mood, created by the right man. Are you ready for your first lesson in the course of life called pleasing Deedee?"

After half an hour, she left him.

"You did very well," she said with that gloating, possessive little laugh. "I'm always in my own bed for morning coffee. We won't disturb you in the morning."

He did not think of her or of what they had done again that night. He thought of nothing, but fell into a deep dreamless sleep which did not end until near noon.

226

He got his clothes and other things and moved into Deedee's house that evening. He knew it was a mistake, but he was drawn to her, in spite of the feeling of dislike, which never changed, and he was drawn to the luxury of the place, after weeks, months, years of tiredness. There would be no material bills for food and lodging.

"It's a mistake," Michael told him worriedly as Nolan gathered his things. "Women like that eat young kids alive. Devour them You'll never get any work done. You'll be giving up the group, next thing, and—"

"I won't be devoured," Nolan answered soberly.

15

But he very nearly was consumed, or felt so. Deedee wanted to be with him every minute he was in the house. She followed him to the promised den and talked, or read aloud from the harshly explicit novels she so treasured, while he studied, worked out arrangements, played out difficult passages. Often she turned on the big television console there, though there were three other sets in the house. All these things were not so much bother when he could encapsulate himself in music, but when he was trying to work on studies of compulsory subjects, they were maddening.

"Well, you're *in* the house," she pointed out petulantly. "Why shouldn't we be together? You're a kind of companion, aren't you? Oh, hell, I don't know why I stay here. I ought to put this mausoleum on the market and go where there's some life. You could come with me, to New York or—"

"No. I'm going to finish the semester."

"Don't you realize you're a kept boy?" she said viciously, "a gigolo?"

"I realize that very well," he said quietly, hating her, hating himself. "I don't want to change anything about what you might want to do with your life. I'll move out whenever you say."

"And go where?" she challenged.

"I don't know, but I'll find something." He was still looking desperately for a job in the few odd moments that came to him.

She gave huge house parties for people up from New York or from Boston. Fortunately, these took place mostly on weekends when he was away at night, playing at the ski lodge. He spent the days at the school, practicing, working with other people, using the small escape of Michael's room. On school days he never came back to Deedee's house until very late. When he was there and there were other people present, she exhibited him like a trained monkey.

"Play something. People want to dance. Make up another round of drinks, Stephens is busy."

And she talked about him as if he weren't there. "If it weren't for the eyes, he'd look washed out, don't you think? With all the fair hair and skin. Do you know he blushes all over? Isn't that darling? I'd love to take him to Europe, but I don't know if I could keep the men away from him, not to mention the women, do you? And isn't it a marvelous face? His voice! I can never stop shivering when he talks, which isn't nearly often enough."

She would sweep back the hair, exposing his entire flushed face and he would stand there, like some product she was trying to promote, longing to bite viciously the hand that held back his hair. He was constantly humiliated, deeply ashamed, but he stayed, because every night she came to his room. Even when he was away, playing with the group, or finding other excuses to stay away, she would wait up. The next day, she would, as she said, "Sleep the day away so I can be fresh for you." She showed him delights he could never have imagined, both for himself and for her. He would do as she directed and, even while his face flamed in the darkness with embarrassment and self-loathing, he would know he was not going to move out tomorrow. When she was wholly satiated, she would take apart the intercourse, moment by moment, action by action, chiding, praising, correcting. It was by far his most difficult, enjoyable, and exciting class.

The band could not practice in her den as she had suggested. She was too ubiquitous, making ridiculous suggestions, trying to attract Michael, while making snide remarks to or about Carol. She wanted Nolan to be jealous of her with other men and, when it seemed he cared not at all, she would fly into a fury, or, far more to his liking, a sulk.

He knew he was weak, perhaps depraved for staying with her, but there were those few weeks when he didn't have to struggle in the regular ways, about where his next meal was coming from or where he might spend the night.

One night after a long practice session, Nolan, Michael, and Carol went for a ride. It was well into March, the ski season ending, and they were out of a job. They stopped at a large place outside of town called the B&K Roadhouse. It was a busy place, and very noisy, with loud jukebox and talk.

Michael found one of the proprietors, Kate, and she came and sat with them at a small table for a few minutes.

"Folk music?" she said, thoughtfully blowing a large smoke ring. "No, kids, I don't think it would work in here. We get a rowdy crowd in here. They want hard rock. We got a band comes in on weekends, amplifiers, and lots of noise. The only work we got open right now is bartending. Any of you can tend bar, I'll hire you on the spot."

Nolan said immediately, "I can."

He took his hand down from covering his right eye. In these past weeks, he had developed an occasional tic in his lower right eyelid, which he felt everyone must notice. It was embarrassing, infuriating, and he felt that somehow everyone must know it was a result of his time with Deedee, a kind of badge or branding.

"You're from the music school?" Kate said, somewhat accusingly

"I need work," he answered.

"From six at night till two in the morning?" she challenged

"All right. Is there a place where I can sleep?"

"We got rooms upstairs, but they're all full right now. I guess we could put a cot in the stockroom for you until something opens up. I suppose you'd want to eat, too. We serve sandwiches as you can see. That's going to pretty well use up your starting salary, room and board. You get Monday and Tuesday nights off. By the way, you are twenty-one, aren't you?"

"Yes," he said. It was only a lie by three weeks.

"How are you going to manage it all?" asked Michael worriedly when they were back in the car.

"You're biting off more than you can chew," said Carol rather smugly, "but then, maybe you've already done that with darling Deedee."

"Michael, if you can take most of my things again, and pick me up in time for morning classes, I can manage."

"I'll bring you back out here, evenings, too," said Michael, "but what about all the people who've asked you to do arrangements and accompaniments for the spring recital?"

"I've made a good start on those. I'll have daytimes Saturday and Sunday and nights on Mondays and Tuesdays."

"Well, I'll be glad to see you get away from La Gorman. What's happened to your eye, anyway?"

"Nothing. The lower lid just twitches sometimes. It must look stupid as hell."

They let Carol out at her house.

Nolan said hesitantly, "Will she really go with us if we go on the road? It's none of my business, but I can't help wondering . . ."

"Carol's looking for fulfillment," said Michael comfortably "She figures if her husband wanted to do something like this, he would, so why shouldn't she? Both sets of grandparents are around to help look after the kids. She and Max—that's the husband—lived together for almost three years before they were married, and when they did get married, they agreed to the same no-strings attachment they'd had before. That's what Carol and I would have if we went on the road. Look, we all know her voice isn't strong enough to carry songs and she's had too much formal training of what there is. She's trying, but she can't seem to get rid of all that vibrato stuff they teach in singing lessons. I think we need another guy *and* another girl. It would mean splitting the money more ways, but a quintet would be something a little different from all the trios and duos running around all over the place. Can you think of anybody?''

Immediately Nolan had thought of Kiersten. Her voice was different, interesting, strong enough, and very expressive. In her last letter, she had written that she was taking guitar lessons just for fun. She also asked why he had not written. It had been a very long time. Nolan could not bring himself to write Kierstie when he was going, every night, to Deedee. Perhaps he could never face her again. Still, the idea of her joining the group was exciting. There were almost three months left before the end of the spring semester and he was not going to be with Deedee again.

"I might know someone," he said, trying not to let the pleasure sound too much in his voice. "Somebody from back home. It would depend on a lot of things. Her parents would have fits, for one."

"Do you mean the girl you get letters from? Isn't she your sister? I mean, it's the same last name, so I always thought   ''

"She's my stepsister.''

"You hayseeeds, fresh in off the ranch, don't seem to understand arrangements like Carol and I have, and I don't suppose there's a prayer your parents, or step-parents, whatever they are, would understand. Wouldn't you rather look for someone who's not from the same family? Maybe she just wouldn't go for an arrangement.''

"I thought we were talking about another girl for the band, not an arrangement.''

"Yeah, okay, sorry. Arrangements cut expenses, for one thing. But, speaking of such matters, here we are at La Gorman's little summer house.''

"If you'll wait, I'll get my things. It shouldn't take long.''

"Sure, I'll wait, but what do you want to bet it takes quite a while?''

"I haven't had a paycheck yet.''

Across his bed was spread a new array of slacks and shirts, plus a sports jacket. This was the second time Deedee had ordered clothes for him, without even a consultation. He pushed them aside, got his suitcases and began packing his old clothes. Then he stopped, went downstairs, got his instruments, and stowed them safely in Michael's car.

"Want me to come in and help you finish?"

"No, it shouldn't take ten minutes."

"I wish you had had a paycheck. I'd like to lay some money on this "

"Maybe she's asleep."

Michael grabbed his arm. "Hey, I was about to forget to tell you, my dad's had somebody find us a bus. It's six years old and has had a lot of use, but they're working on it and modifying it according to the plan I showed you."

"That's great," said Nolan, but he couldn't really drum up much enthusiasm. Probably there would never be a viable group. Maybe he wouldn't even get through this semester, maybe not even this night. If he did finish the year, then what?

Go home, cried a voice within him. You'll have proved something by finishing four years in three. You've had what you wanted—mostly. Now go back to Secesh and be Price Savage's son. I'm not the son he wants. Why in hell didn't they have other sons? This is something like being Roger's twin. It was a responsibility I couldn't handle, had to get away from. So why go back? We already know it doesn't work.

The current problem is what do I do right this minute. How do I get out of this house without some damned kind of trouble? Should I leave her a note?—thanks for the hospitality . . . ?

There was no need for a note. She was standing in the middle of his room.

"And may I ask what the hell you think you're doing?"

"I'm leaving," he said, going back to the suitcases. He would take nothing she had given him, so the packing would be quickly over

"Nobody," she said icily, "leaves Deedee. *I* do the leaving, when *I'm* ready."

"Look, I appreciate—all you've done for me. As soon as I can, I'll try to pay you for—for the board and lodging, but I've found a job and I have to take it. You've been wanting to leave here for weeks. I hope—"

"You hope, my ass. Put those suitcases away. It's time you stopped playing your little music game. You'll stay with me until *I'm* through, maybe until I find another husband, some nice agreeable old man with money. Even then I might want to keep you around for, shall we say, further entertainment?"

She was blocking the doorway as he came very near with the two light suitcases.

"I'm sorry," he said coldly. "Get yourself another boy. That seems to be no problem for you."

233

She shrieked, raking the long nails of both hands down his cheeks.

Nolan dropped the suitcases, set her aside, picked them up, went along the hall and down the stairs with epithets ringing in his ears. Darlene used to scream something like that.

Stephens appeared from wherever he slept, his bathrobe rumpled, along with the rest of him.

"You're leaving us," he said mildly.

"Yes, Stephens. Thank you."

Deedee was still shrieking, now from the top of the stairs.

"Madam may want Annette," said Stephens calmly, turning toward the maid's room. "Goodnight, Mr. Savage."

"Wow!" said Michael as Nolan set the suitcases in the back of his car and got in. "You can still hear her, all the way out here. Man, did she do a job on your face! You ought to see it."

Nolan said coolly, though he was shaking, "Can I sleep on your floor tonight?"

B&K was a popular place, always busy. The B stood for Bill, and he was the other bartender. He was kind about explaining, on the run, how to make the drinks Nolan had never heard of Two girls served the tables—and, Nolan suspected, performed other services—so their orders were added to those of the bar itself. He was given a half hour's break at ten to eat whatever he liked from the kitchen's limited choice. If business slacked a little from time to time Bill took short breaks, going into the dingy little office to read the sports page Kate worked the cash register and was general overseer

The loud talk and jukebox music were unrelenting. Nolan went to bed with his head pounding every night, when they had finished cleanup at nearly three o'clock. He slept poorly, on the World War II vintage army cot, with not enough blankets. He lay there, when he had creaked the cot into a semi-comfortable position, feeling the darkness, the poor ventilation, hearing rats scrabble among the tall stacks of cases.

His alarm woke him at seven. He washed up in the men's room—showers were taken at the dorm—ate whatever was left in the empty kitchen, met Michael outside, and was present for his first class at eight. His formal classes were finished by two-thirty, so he had three hours in which to work with the people whom he was to accompany in the spring recital, and to do his own arrangements and practicing.

He had Saturdays and Sundays, Monday and Tuesday nights, when he didn't work at the bar, and he often used the whole nights for his own work.

Sometime around his birthday he caught a heavy cold and was constantly miserable, but he was grateful for two things: he was now actually twenty-one; and the facial scratches Deedee had given him were almost faded out, so that people stopped grinning at him and making "cute" remarks and speculations.

On a weekend in April a new band came to play at B&K. It was another head-splitting rock band made up of four men. Nolan immediately noticed—as did everyone in the house—the bass player. He was a black man, a huge one, standing at least six-feet-five, rangy, big-boned, and heavily muscled.

"Bet they don't have trouble with *nobody*," mused Bill, drawing beers.

"Don't you know him?" asked Kate, overhearing. "He's got a room right upstairs here, foreman or something over at the Darby Mill. That shows how much attention you pay to anything."

The bass player changed instruments during the night, playing piano, guitar, or drums. Nolan noticed him when he could. The man was good, tremendously good, with what he was doing.

When they had a break, Nolan took one, too, saying he had to go to the men's room. He went back to the tiny windowless place called a dressing room and found the four band members being served sandwiches and drinks by one of the table girls.

"My name's Nolan Savage," he croaked hoarsely to the big man, offering his hand.

"And mine's Rex McIver," said Rex, engulfing Nolan's hand. "You always talk like that? Got some vocal chord problem?"

"No, a cold. I'd like to talk to you."

It was very noisy still. The jukebox had been started up again. Rex took his drink and sandwich, saying calmly, "Let's step out in the alley."

"I go to Albion," Nolan began to tell him, stopped by a seizure of coughing.

"Man, you look like somebody's been beating you around the eyes, you're that tired. You work here every night?"

"Just five nights a week."

"Well, you're not going on to Albion or any place else, you don't take care of yourself." The voice was a rich deep baritone, compassionate-sounding.

"We've got a group—folk music. There're just three of us now and we're looking for one, maybe two more people. Would you be interested?"

"Nice soft quiet music? Not plugged in?"

"Yes. The other guy, Michael Lyman, has an uncle who's a booking agent for musicians. If we can get together the right people, and if we're good enough, he might—"

"You mean to travel around the country?"

"Yes. We're getting a bus."

"You finishing up at Albion?"

"No, not really, but I'm quitting when this semester is over. I'll still lack a year."

"You're a scholarship student, I take it, from the looks of you."

"Yes."

Rex was obviously southern, but he had, just as obviously, worked hard at getting rid of most of his accent. He said kindly, "I always have thought their scholarship setup was a little cruel for folks haven't got the money to go all the way. Has it been this tough for you all the time? Working like this, I mean."

"No, I've had easier jobs."

"You sure God must have wanted to go to Albion. I did, too, once, or to some place like it. But I won me a basketball scholarship to Princeton, prelaw. Great big Alabama-dirt-farmer-buck-nigger in prelaw at Princeton! But I quit. Couldn't hack it any more, once it got through my thick head that there's not much justice in the law, only precedents. God only knows who's got the guts to set those precedents. I'd thought I'd go back home to Alabama and work civil rights cases. Well, here I am in Vermont, a foreman over at Darby's, twenty-eight years old, and still not quite knowing how it all happened."

"Would you come and hear us some time? Play with us?"

"Well, I reckon so. What instruments you got?"

"I've got two guitars, and a vi—a fiddle. Michael's got a mandolin and banjo, and Carol has a flute."

"Flute? That ought to add some nice sound. Well, I've got a string bass. I can plunk it, or play it arco. I'm just renting this electric dude. I've got a mandolin, too, but it's got no place that I can find in hard rock. Sometimes I just get so hungry for music I'll do anything. I'd like to get my hands on a fiddle again, or a guitar or banjo for that matter. Have you got a room upstairs here?"

"No, I'm sleeping in the stock room."

"Well, I got a room. You keep any of your instruments here?"

"I've got my twelve-string here tonight."

"A twelve-string. I've never laid hands on one of those. Feel like coming up for a little while after closing?"

Nolan didn't, but he agreed.

"Mine's the door on the left at the top of the stairs. Don't take the one on the right, now. That one's Elfie's and she might be entertaining. I'm afraid I didn't really get your name."

"It's Nolan Savage, but friends sometimes call me Chappie."

"Well, I don't know how I'd stand up with you Albion people, but I believe I'd like to try."

The guitar had never seemed so heavy as it did when he dragged himself up the stairs at three in the morning, not even when he and Harry Blevins had taken it from the store.

"Say, now, that is some nice instrument," said Rex as they opened the case on his bed.

"I stole it," Nolan said and grinned.

"You did?"

"Oh, it eventually got paid for. It's a long story. I'll tell you sometime, it's not something I tell just anybody. Do you want to try the guitar?"

The huge hands made the instrument look almost small. Tentatively, Rex strummed a few chords, then he began to play quietly, an old Scots ballad Nolan had known most of his life. Rex gestured with his head, to the huddle of the bass fiddle, enclosed in its canvas bag in a corner.

Nolan sneezed several times, taking it out, then he stood up to it and began an accompaniment, with bow.

"Well, now," murmured Rex when they finally stopped, "that was just downright good. Want to start a mutual admiration society? Here, you play your own a while."

Nolan's mind was blank of music to play. He was so feverish, he felt he was hallucinating. Finally, he struck into an old bluegrass number, "You Could Hear the Whistle Blow a Hundred Miles." Rex, grinning, was with him immediately, without bow, doing runs and licks on the bass that left Nolan a little breathless.

"What about," began Rex and stopped, looking at him. "Boy, you are one sick kid. Here, give me that."

He replaced the guitar in its case and stood it in the corner with the bass.

"Your face is as red as a beet. I got some aspirin here. Let me get you some water."

Rex went out, came back, while Nolan felt he was wavering on the chair. He took the aspirin and drank the water greedily.

"I'll get you more water in a minute. First, get into bed. You have to go? Well, I'll come along, at least part way, because it looks to me like you're going to fall down, just any time."

"My cot's downstairs," Nolan mumbled.

"Never mind that. I'll get it. Now you get your clothes off before you pass out."

So Nolan lay in Rex's bed. There were springs poking up, near to the surface of the thin mattress, but it felt like heaven, partly because he seemed to be floating a little above it.

Rex came back and set up the cot.

"I can't let you," murmured Nolan.

"Let's see you get up from there and stop me," said the big man, grinning. "Kate sure took you, making you sleep down there in that hole. There have been two rooms that I know of empty up here just this month. This is not exactly the Ritz and most people can't stand to stay long, with all the noise downstairs at night. Kate's a tough lady. I'll bet she took out of your wages just as much as if you'd had one of these fine rooms. Some people are just born babes in the woods. If you haven't got galloping pneumonia, it'll be the God's wonder."

He took a gallon jug and went away. Nolan vaguely noticed the books on a homemade shelf along one wall. He tried to read some titles, but his eyes wouldn't seem to focus. Rex came back with a jugful of water and poured a glass.

"This is a clean jug," he said, grinning. "Had cherry cider in it once, but that was all."

Nolan didn't care what might have been in the jug. He drank the water gratefully.

"Now, try to sleep," ordered Rex, preparing himself for the cot.

Sleep came quickly, but was short-lived as he kept turning restlessly, moving listlessly, waking himself again and again.

Rex said, from the cot into darkness, "Tell me about stealing the guitar, if it doesn't hurt you too much to talk. Maybe a little talk and the aspirins will make you easier."

So he told him, amid coughing paroxysms, about Harry Blevins and the guitar.

He slept and dreamed of Darlene, Roger, and Clarence, woke with a start.

Now Rex was talking easily about his Alabama boyhood. It did not occur to Nolan that night that the other man must never have slept.

Nolan slept again, dreamed he had done an arrangement for a string quartet, handed round the scores. It was the final practice before spring recital, and all was going well until they turned a final page and came upon notations he had never seen. It was a horrible cacaphony of dissonance and everyone—now they were in the auditorium with an audience—and everyone was staring at him with cold accusation. There was something threatening, fearsome in their faces.

Again he woke with a start, shivering and sweating, and Rex was there, going on with his stories of boyhood, almost as if they hadn't been interrupted by a few minutes' sleep.

Nolan slept again. This time, he dreamed of Kiersten, white-faced, looking at the moving red lips of Deedee Gorman. He woke himself with hoarse sobs, his face suffused in tears and sweat.

Now Rex came and sat on the edge of the bed, wiping gently at

238

Nolan's face with a big, clean-smelling handkerchief. Nolan moved reflexively away.

Rex said quietly, "I'm not queer. You got nothing to be afraid of from me. You need some help is all."

He lifted the drenched shock of hair off Nolan's forehead. "My mama always said it was a good thing if a person with a fever started to sweat, so I reckon this is good. Here, better drink some more water. Want to talk about the dream?"

Nolan went into a fit of coughing. "I—I don't—remember it," he was finally able to lie.

"Somebody come to pick you up mornings?"

"Yes, what time is it?"

"Just after six, but lie easy. You're not going anywhere today, unless maybe I decide to the hospital. I'm bigger than most anybody, and people usually do what I say when I decide something."

"But today's Saturday, I need to—"

"You need to shut up. I'll go down and tell your friend you're not available when the time comes. What kind of car's he drive?"

"A red Dodge but—"

"And his name?"

Nolan was seized by another spasm of coughing. "Michael Lyman," he finally gasped.

"Well, now, Chappie, I'm going to give you a couple of other pills. I was afraid for you to take them with your fever so high, but that's better now. They're sleeping pills. I got them when I first moved up here, above the bar. Now I can sleep through anything. These are pretty strong, and I don't know how they'll go with what you've got, but you sure as hell have got to have some rest."

Nolan swallowed the pills and drank two glasses of water.

"You haven't had any sleep at all, have you?" he asked rather dazedly.

"Lord, I couldn't sleep on that pissant of a cot. There's too much of me. What I'm going to do now is have a shower. Then I'll look back in to see how you're doing. Then I'll have me some breakfast at that place down the block, be back in time to catch your buddy Michael. After that I got to go and work half a day. Then I'll catch up some on sleep before it's time for us to play again tonight. I'll tell Kate or Bill you won't be working."

"They're going to have a fit. It's Saturday night and—"

"You want to make a bet with me, Chap? I'm betting on the side of your not being indispensable "

Nolan smiled weakly and made a conscious effort to relax. It felt damned good to be taken care of. He had rarely been sick within the

239

time of his memory, though he must have been reminded a million times that he had been a sickly baby. When he *was* sick, there had been Grandpa, then for a long time no one, until Anne, and Fern, and Kiersten. Kierstie, bonnie Kierstie . . . He was growing drowsy now, but couldn't seem to stop the restless, listless movements.

Rex, returning from his shower, said, "What had you figured to call this folk group?"

"We were trying to decide between The Gaels and The Druids."

"Oh-oh," said the big man and laughed. "You haven't got it painted on the side of that bus or anything yet? My name may be right, McIver, but the color definitely wouldn't fit."

"Rex, you know there won't be much money in it, not at first. Everything we make will have to go for traveling expenses and—"

"Chappie, I've been a music bum all my life. I ought to have begun to settle now, but I've not somehow. I'd like a wife and some kids some time, but I'm not sure this is a world to lay on kids, or maybe even on a wife in a wife's role."

Nolan told him then about Carol's arrangements with her husband and with Michael.

"Well, maybe that's all right for them, but Carol and her husband had no business bringing two little kids into it. Suppose the grandparents don't want any part of it. Then you've got two more little unwanted young'uns, in a world too full of them already. Now, like I've been telling you, I come from a family of eight kids myself, but we were all loved—not too well fed sometimes, but loved. What about you?" he asked, lighting a cigarette, "you come from a big family?"

Nolan told him then, drowsily, a little of some of the things he had never told anyone. As he was drifting at last into sleep, he said, the words slurring together, "I've written Kiersten. Maybe there'll be a letter today."

"Kiersten's your girl?"

"Yes. I wish she'd come with the band. You'd like her, Rex."

"I don't have much doubt I would. Here, you want one more glass of water?"

Nolan slept until the nightly noise started up in the bar downstairs. He was weak, but no longer feverish, only lethargic, relaxed for the first time in a very long while. Rex brought him food and instructed him to go no farther than the toilet.

"B&K don't know you're up here. Just don't show your face."

Nolan picked a novel from among Rex's books and tried to read it, but even with the noise downstairs he fell asleep again shortly.

16

Nolan was practicing with a graduate violinist, accompanying her on cello. The spring recital, the end of his time at Albion, was to be the next day.

"Listen, Laurie, you're digressing from the score just here. If you do what you're doing, then I have to change the cello part as well."

"But it sounds so much better," she said earnestly, "don't you think so? I thought of it last night."

"I do, but they've got it on the program as a piece by Schumann. If we don't play the score, then they're going to say we did a variation without listing it."

"And you'll get blamed," she said, smiling. "Okay, can we do it again, starting from there?"

The playing was going well, but something made Nolan glance up to the small window in the practice room door. He almost overturned the school's cello in his haste to rise. He flung open the door.

"Kierstie, bonnie little Kierstie!" She was in his arms, snuggling her head under his chin, crying a little as she laughed.

"Oh, Chappie, *three* years! You are such a *deplorable* correspondent."

"But what are you doing here? How did you—"

"I told Mother and Dad at spring break that you were probably going to leave after this semester. They wanted—we all wanted—some of us to be here for at least one of your recitals. They bought us plane tickets, Roger and me, so we could come. Roger's up on the next floor, peeking in windows, looking for you."

She stood back a little, devouring him with her eyes, unable to resist pushing back the hair from his forehead.

"You look so tired."

The violinist gave a discreet little cough. They both started and flushed.

Nolan said, "Laurie Levinson, this is Kiersten, my girl from back home."

The two girls spoke, then Nolan and Kiersten stepped farther into the hall with a quick excuse.

"You are still my girl?" he asked, looking searchingly into her blue eyes.

"I wasn't sure until now, but it feels that way."

He said, through the open doorway, "Laurie, could I have a half hour? My brother's here somewhere." And to Kiersten, "I don't know where we'll find for you to stay. The town is always jammed with parents and other people at this time."

"We have reservations," she said smugly. "Made them two months ago, just in case, also a rental car."

"Tell me about—"

At that moment, Roger appeared on the stairs. "So *there* you are!"

He rushed up to Nolan, meaning to embrace him, but Nolan took both his hands in that way Price had and they looked at each other. Roger felt hurt, disappointed. Here was what he considered a part of himself, the complement that had been missing for three years, now holding him at a distance, keeping himself most definitely separate.

"Well, if you've got rooms and a car, there's not much I can do for you, is there?" said Nolan, smiling, still not quite believing this. "Let's go across to the next building and get a cup of coffee at least."

"We know you're terrifically busy right now," said Kiersten "Don't let us take too much of your time. I was wondering, while you're practicing with other people, could we sit, very quietly, and listen? We found programs at the hotel and I see that you're doing arrangements and accompaniments for three people, besides your own things."

They sat at a little table and practically everyone who passed by knew Nolan. He introduced them, "my brother and my girl." Roger seethed inwardly with hurt and anger. Just who did he think he was, introducing Kiersten like that, "my girl," after three years of only the briefest of occasional notes and no more—or had there been more? Things she hadn't told him? Kiersten had certainly never mentioned to him that she was Nolan's girl, but she sat smiling broadly at the introductions, leaving her hand still on the table while Nolan covered it with his.

"So what's happened about your folk group?" she asked gaily, both of them seemingly oblivious of Roger's disapproval.

"We've got a blue bus, modified for carrying lots of instruments and suitcases, and with a bunk, so at least one person at a time can rest while we're traveling. Michael's uncle, the agent, came up to hear us a few weeks ago. He's got us some bookings in small, ill-paying places around New England, then as far south as Baltimore, almost two months' worth of bookings."

"Already?" she said a little breathlessly. "The last time you wrote you were still looking for another person and you didn't even have a name for the group."

"We're calling ourselves The Stewards. That's painted in red on both sides of the bus. And we still are looking for another person, you. Have you thought it over? Will you—"

Roger cut in smoothly. "Our return tickets are for the fifth, three days from now. Anne sent a check for you so you can fly back with us and stay a while at Secesh."

Nolan frowned. "I can't do that. Just when we're getting this thing set up . . ."

Kiersten said, "Mother said to say they'd like you to come home, but that you don't *have* to use the check for that."

A tall willowy girl with long black hair walked past, then turned, openly to stare at Roger for a moment. He was used to having that happen and smiled modestly.

"Hello, Muriel," said Nolan. "This is my brother Roger, and my girl Kiersten from back home in Colorado. Muriel is a second-year piano student. I'm sorry, I've forgot your last name."

"Simpson," she said, lingering.

"Would you care to join us?" asked Roger. "I'll get you some coffee."

"I'll go with you," she said, and, as they went to the counter, "I don't know Nolan very well except that he's fantastic at everything he does. I've never heard anything about his family. I didn't know he had a girl, though I know he never dates—too busy. I certainly didn't know he had—a brother."

She yearned to touch the sleek chestnut waves of his hair.

"We're twins," said Roger rather sourly, paying for the coffee. So Nolan hadn't even found his existence worthwhile enough to mention. He, Roger, always told people about his twin brother.

"You're kidding," said Muriel, looking him over again unabashedly. "You look *nothing* alike. Listen, I know Nolan is involved in about fifty things today. Maybe I could show you around the school or something. There's a dance tonight and I don't have a really firm date . . ."

Back at the table Nolan was saying, his hand still covering

243

Kiersten's, "There are so many things, people I want you to meet, things I want to show you, but today and tomorrow are total losses I've got practices scheduled—"

"I knew it would be like that," she said, only a little wistfully "I understand. You're not still working, are you, at that bar?"

"No. I quit a week ago, when I'd saved money enough for a few clothes and new strings. I am still staying with Rex McIver, in his room, to cut costs for both of us. He's still working at the mill, but finishes up there tomorrow. We have our first booking on the eighth."

"I guess I hadn't dreamed it would all be happening so quickly with the group," she said uncertainly.

"Rex is the person I want most to have you meet. Michael and Carol are okay, but Rex is somebody special."

Roger and Muriel had gone to stand by a large window and she was pointing out things to him.

"There's a dance tonight," Nolan said.

"And you're playing," Kiersten answered sadly.

"No, I'm not. I was, but I never dreamed . . . I'll find somebody else."

"*Could* I sit in for the practice sessions? It looks as if Roger may not want to now. Maybe he never did, with his tin ear."

She could not help scrutinizing carefully the faces of the girls who knew him. She was ashamed of her jealousy, but it was most definitely there. After all, he had been with some of these people for three years, while she . . .

He said, "We'll have to ask the people I'm accompanying."

"I'll be very good, and quiet as a mouse. Chappie, I just want to be with you, whatever you're doing. It's only three days and I—"

"Come with us, Kierstie. There won't be a chance for you to hear the group until the day after tomorrow, but . . ."

"I don't know," she said harriedly, suddenly near tears. "I just don't know. Mother and Dad would have such a fit. They'd say we were living together and—"

"Wouldn't we be?" He could not quite catch her eye. "Well, there's Carol. You could say you were rooming with her."

"First we'd have to get round Roger. He seems so suspicious and—jealous."

"Of what?"

"Oh, nothing, really, not yet, at any rate, but haven't you seen his face when you've introduced me as your girl?"

"I guess I wasn't watching," he said rather coldly. Here it was again, Roger's intrusion into his life, pacify Roger, make it all right, acceptable to Roger. "Is there anything in particular for him to be jealous about?"

He took his hand from hers and covered his right eye, which had begun to twitch.

"We've had some dates, but I've written you that. I never thought they were anything serious and, I thought, neither did he. I think it's me he resents. He always has wanted you all to himself when you're together. What's wrong with your eye?"

"Nothing. The lid twitches sometimes. Probably, no one else would even notice, but it seems to me it must look crazy. Roger always wants what he doesn't have. He—"

"Chappie, be nice to him. If he loves anyone in the world, it's you. He was absolutely lost without you at first and even after three years I think he still misses you, almost as much as I do, in his own way."

He said relentlessly, holding her eyes now, "Will you come with us if you like the group? You could think of it as just for a little while—the summer maybe—and then if you don't like it, you could go back to school. We need a girl with a good strong voice."

"But my voice is—weird."

"It's not. It's interesting and expressive. Carol can't handle a lead and she can't sing harmony at all. That's strange because she can play harmonies with her flute. She is good with that."

"I don't play anything."

"You wrote about guitar lessons."

"Well, just some chords," she said deprecatingly.

"You'd pick up more."

"I just don't know what to say right now. I've been thinking, all right, thinking and thinking. It would hurt Mother and Dad terribly."

"Let's be married then."

She gave a little gasp, hesitated for a long moment, looking away from him. "I—I don't know what to say about that either. I think I'd love going with the group for a while, but I have a feeling this is going to be a long-term thing for you. I don't know if I'd want to do it for years and years. I want to finish art school one day. There's all this talk about fulfillment, especially for women, so that seems to be mine. Maybe I'd get a job and work only a few years, then go back home to Secesh. That's where I really want to be, in the final analysis, don't you?"

"Not with Hugh there. Not with Price feeling the way he does."

"You don't know how he feels. You're his son who loves the ranch. He'd like you to carry it on. We don't live under primogeniture any more. There's nothing that says he has to leave the lion's share to Hugh. If you went home—"

He cut in, "—and was exactly what he wants, expects me to be . . . He had me riding and working summers from when I was six years old. I do love Secesh, yes, and I'd like to go back one day, but I can never come up to his expectations, his demands, verbal or otherwise. I'd have to be another person to do that.''

"I don't believe that," she said vehemently. "If the two of you would only talk—"

"I don't have any more time," he said curtly. "I have to get back to practice. The last thing I remember was a question of marriage."

"Give me time to think," she pleaded, tears filming her blue eyes.

"But you're only supposed to be here three days. I thought it was understood that some day we'd marry. That would solve your worries about hurting other people—"

"It was *not* understood," she flared. "It hasn't been mentioned since that time up on Picketpin, and that's almost four years ago. You take a hell of a lot for granted. I told you, I don't think I'm ready for marriage, that *we*'re ready. Obviously, neither of us knows what we're going to settle down to. It's liable to be two completely different things and—"

Nolan had looked away. "Yes, Laurie, we were just coming. Would you mind if Kiersten sits in on the session? And my brother, too, if he wants to come?"

Roger said smugly that Muriel wanted him to come for a walk around the campus, that he couldn't really appreciate the music. Actually, he didn't want to go with Muriel. There was a lot more between Nolan and Kiersten than he had imagined. But, of course, it wasn't as if they were going to be alone together. He'd try to see that that didn't happen.

The spring recital was a day-long, evening-long affair, three hours each in morning and afternoon, four in the evening. No one attended all of it, except students, for whom it was a learning process, and instructors who were grading on composition, arrangement, or proficiency with a particular instrument. Detailed programs were printed, with the approximate time of each performance. Friends and families slipped in and out of the large auditorium between pieces.

Nolan had at least one thing to do in each session and Kiersten stayed for it all. She got there early, sitting near the front with her light spring jacket on the seat next to her, saving it for Nolan when he was not working. Roger preferred to sit at the back so he could come and go easily. He seemed always surrounded by girls, but this was a normal situation for him, until he had put them off with his cool pedagogy.

They went out to dinner, a very late dinner, to celebrate. Kiersten had given Nolan the check, the gift from Anne, and he picked up the bill for dinner, feeling strange at being so affluent, even briefly. Michael and Carol were there, Rex, and Roger's most current follower, Joyce Gilmore, a voice student.

When they had finished eating and dancing the place was closing. Nolan and Rex went back to the room above B&K, Nolan holding Kiersten close first, saying softly, "I love you. I want you so much." Both of them were trembling.

"Your brother doesn't like your having his girl," Rex said mildly when they were alone.

"She's never been his girl. He always wants what he doesn't have, and then, *when* he gets it—because he almost always does get it—he doesn't want it any more."

"That is one handsome dude. Don't let him get her. She's a winner, freckles and all."

Rex lay down across the bed, diagonally, so there'd be room for his length. "You must be tired of music, surely. Ten hours of it in one day "

"I would be, I guess," said Nolan, trying to adjust himself on the old army cot, "if I hadn't had a part in some of it."

"What I heard was good, really fine stuff. Made me wish all over again that I could have studied at Albion. Are they coming to our group practice tomorrow? Roger and Kiersten?"

"Yes. Their reservations for going back to Colorado are for the next day. She can't make up her mind about joining us. Every time we try to talk about it, we seem to end with an argument."

"Then just wait, give her a chance. That's a born music girl, maybe not for the classical stuff, but for singing, being part of a group. Don't fuss at her or put on pressure. When she hits her stride, starts jiving with the rest of us, she'll go along."

They had been able to arrange to use one of the school's small auditoriums for practice until the time they would be leaving. Rex and Nolan picked Kiersten up at the hotel early, Roger saying he would come along later in the rented car. He did not say that Joyce Gilmore would be spending a part of the morning in his room, before catching her noon train to Boston.

The Stewards began work at nine. In order to pronounce each word, play each note precisely together, they needed conducting. Michael did this, with Nolan's arrangements, grabbing his banjo from time to time to play breaks between verses.

They were going to be playing small clubs and coffee houses so they had worked out four forty-five minute sets. Michael was their spokesman. He told funny stories, introduced group members, and did a lead-in story on each other. Folk music varied with the performer, so even for the songs he knew she knew Nolan had scrawled their exact words for Kiersten. Most of the things they did were up-tempo, entertaining, because that's what the crowds liked, but into every set they slipped at least one ballad and some blues. When they came to a blues song called "He's Solid Gone," Nolan said, "Take this one, Kierstie. Lead it. Fern sings it in the kitchen at home."

She flushed. Up to now, she had been only softly harmonizing, watching them all very closely.

There was a brief lead-in and, at Michael's signal, she began tentatively, "Sometimes I am happy, sometimes I'm blue . . ."

It got easier then. As Rex said, she hit her stride. When they had finished, the others applauded spontaneously. She blushed more deeply, tears of joy and embarrassment filming her eyes.

"You were born to sing the blues, babe," Rex said softly. "When Chap tried to tell me about your voice, all I could imagine was a whisky voice, but it's not that at all, not deep and furry, just a little husky and very nice. We'll have to beat off record scouts with a stick Now, just for the hell of it, let's take a break from the formal stuff Let's do something we can really dig into, with harmony and all the rest of it."

They sang "Going Down the Road Feeling Bad," with an instrumental break between each verse, switching the lead from singer to singer. Carol always sang melody because she couldn't do otherwise, but her small light voice was an adjunct to whoever might be leading a particular verse. Michael held to his banjo, but Nolan and Rex switched instruments madly between them, twelve-string, bass, mandolin, and fiddle, falling over each other in the process so that all of them were laughing. Kiersten marveled at how small the instruments looked in Rex's big hands, particularly the little mandolin. Carol's flute leads or harmonies were delightful. They had given Kiersten a six-string guitar, but she chorded so softly that even she could scarcely hear.

Their voices were wonderful together, particularly Kiersten's, Rex's, and Nolan's. Rex had a husky rich baritone, and Nolan did bass parts with the projection that came so naturally to him, and Kiersten sang her strong, slightly breaking alto. Michael's voice was a clear tenor, but no better or different from many others, though it blended well.

Michael was taping everything and when he played this song back they all kept looking at one another and smiling, slightly embarrassed at hearing themselves, but tremendously pleased with what they could do. In every verse Kiersten listened carefully to the way Nolan's voice bound them all together, not too noticeable, but there, like the foundation of a house, holding up the structure and causing all the other components to merge beautifully.

248

"I've got an idea," said Michael delightedly as he shut off the tape machine. "Before we get back to the nitty-gritty of the formal thing, you two know that song 'Henry Marlowe,' where one verse is the guy and the other the girl? You and Kiersten sing it, Chappie. Whichever one of you whose verse it isn't, harmonize, okay? Go through a couple of verses before we record."

When the song was recorded and played back, Nolan and Kiersten smiled into each other's eyes, and there was more than pleasure and satisfaction in the music.

When the tape had been turned off, Kiersten broke into a delighted laugh. "My God, we're beautiful, all of us."

Then you will come with us, his eyes said, though he spoke nothing, only moved a step to his left and kissed her on the forehead.

For most of the rest of the day, they went over and over the set pieces, over bits of them, beginnings of verses, ends of songs.

"I hate some of this stuff already," said Carol. "I wish it could all be fun and games, like it was there for a little while this morning."

"Ah, but we're being professional," said Michael. "You don't make a record out of pick-up songs."

"We're not making records yet," said Nolan, "and we're going to do as many different things as we can work up. We're not going to be making any money for a while so we may as well do what we like and enjoy ourselves."

"We'll put in 'Henry Marlowe' and 'Goin' Down the Road' and 'Solid Gone'," said Michael. "That's for sure. Now, do you guys want to work on the instrumentals—again?"

Carol and Kiersten went to the back of the auditorium to listen. Michael was playing banjo, Nolan his twelve-string, and Rex fiddle.

Roger had arrived long since, had been in and out of the auditorium a number of times, pacing restlessly. It didn't matter to any of them worth a damn if he was here or not, he thought sourly.

"How does that sound?" Michael called back to them once.

"Super," said Roger, in as bored a tone as possible.

Damn it, he didn't know how it sounded, and they all must *know* he didn't know. If his brother was going to ignore him, take away Kiersten, why should he feel anything less than bitterness and sarcasm for the bloody band?

When they had finished with one of the instrumentals, Nolan and Rex switching deftly from instrument to instrument, a voice behind Carol and Kiersten startled them.

"I say," said a young professor in his first year at Albion and very proud of his carefully acquired British accent, "that was quite good—for folk music. What do you call it?"

249

"We call it 'Old Dan Tucker,' " called Michael. "So did somebody else a long time ago. Thanks for the good word."

"When in hell are they going to stop?" Roger demanded of Kiersten as the afternoon waned.

"I don't know," she said happily. "Maybe never."

"Hey, Kierstie," said Michael, "we're going to do 'Amazing Grace' again. You girls come back. Your harmony on that, and Nolan's, puts me right back down home in the good old fundamentalist church."

"Where you've never been," said Rex.

"Why do we have to do a crappy hymn?" demanded Carol, climbing wearily back on to the stage.

" 'Cause it sounds purty, sugar gal," drawled Michael. "And it makes a nice sing-along for the audience. Got to have some audience participation or we'll lose the bastards."

By seven o'clock they were all exhausted, not really willing to stop, not wholly pleased with what they had accomplished, but Rex said if they got too "sassy and satisfied," they'd all fall flat on their faces, or maybe fall the other way. They had taken a lunch break, but it now seemed days ago. They happily agreed to go to dinner in the new bus, which Michael handled proudly, like a hot rod. They were all so tired, they were coming near the edges of hysteria. Everything was funny and every comment on it funnier. Rex and Kiersten got into a drawling duel, each of them laying on the southern accents that both had worked hard to rectify.

All laughed hilariously, except Roger. He sat behind the others on the bus, rarely smiling, and then only with his mouth, lonely, bored, even looking slightly pale.

After dinner Nolan and Kiersten, Michael and Carol got up to dance. They were too tired for it really, but all of them were so high on music they might never come down.

"Just you an' me, babe," said Rex, grinning, alone at the table with Roger.

With a glum nod, Roger barely acknowledged having heard.

"I take it you don't care much for music "

"I'll be goddamn glad when Kiersten and I are on that plane tomorrow."

"Didn't you hear her say she's going with us, at least for the summer?"

"She'll change her mind before tomorrow It's a—an influence Nolan has over her. She'll think about it tonight and change her mind."

"Those two belong together," Rex said softly, "and not just for singing." Then he made a try at diplomacy. "Chappie tells me you're a sociology major, want to be a professor."

"When did he tell you that?" snapped Roger.

"Well, last night," Rex began defensively.

"Before that, had he ever told you or anybody else he had a twin brother?"

"As a matter of fact, he talked quite a lot about you, the first night we met."

"Are you two—I mean, do you . . . ?" he was flushing hotly.

"That ought to make me mad, pretty boy, real mad," said Rex easily. "No, there's nothing between us but handshakes, maybe a borrowed pair of stretch socks now and then. I think all this bunch is relatively normal in those ways."

Which made Roger flush even more deeply.

Rex, who took some pride in his ability to read character, was embarrassed as well. What was there he could safely say to this sulky kid?

"Where would you like to teach?" he asked rather gingerly, "when you're ready for that?"

"I don't know. In the East somewhere. I think I'd be going to Columbia now, but my dad refuses to pay out-of-state tuition. Maybe I can switch as a graduate student, pick up some money as a teaching assistant."

Well, this seemed like more solid ground. "Going to summer school?"

"No, I'm going back to the ranch and rest up for a while. I suppose Nolan has told you about Secesh, the big place our family owns."

"Yes. Among other things, he's told me it's a lot of work. Doesn't sound like a very restful place to me."

"Well, the family doesn't *have* to work so much now. Mostly, it's just habit. Hugh, our cousin, is managing the place, though I guess our dad doesn't think so, and he usually has a good big crew of hands. I can't do much outside work, hay fever, sun allergy. Sometimes I help with the bookkeeping, that sort of thing, but mostly I study and rest."

"Is it because Albion is out-of-state that your dad wouldn't help Chap with his fees? He's near killed himself these past three years."

"Dad doesn't approve of music as a vocation, not even much as an avocation. He doesn't care what I do, or Kiersten, but he expected Nolan would give Hugh a run for his money about managing the ranch. But Chappie isn't going to kill himself. Nobody need worry about that. He's strong and strong-minded. Whatever happens, he always manages to come out on top."

"Mmm," said Rex. "You working while you're in school?"

"No, it's important to me to keep up a four-point grade average,

251

which I've done. It'll look great on my transcripts when I start applying for jobs. Nolan has told me his average is no better than a low C, on regular college credits, I mean."

"Have you always felt this need to be in competition with your brother?" Rex put up a hand to hide a grimace. Who the hell did he think he was, some headshrinker, and why couldn't he keep his mouth shut?

"There's no competition," said Roger, his eyes turned to the dance floor, but evidently not minding the question. "It's never in doubt. Chappie always wins."

"It doesn't sound like that to me," Rex couldn't stop himself from saying, as he saw, thankfully, that the others were coming back to the table.

"Kierstie," he said brightly, "have you ever heard a song called 'Sportin' Life'?"

She shook her head, smiling, more at Nolan than at Rex.

Rex said, "We're going to have to do a number on that one, Chap. You don't know it either? Okay, it's southern blues, and you're not the only one in this bunch can work up arrangements. Her voice would be the absolute greatest for it."

"Michael's got a really good introduction for you," said Carol to Rex. "He's going to call you our token basketball player."

Rex grinned absently. "I ain't studyin' no basketball player," he drawled. "I'm thinkin' about the blues."

"I think we need a dobro," said Michael.

"Whatever the hell that is," said Carol.

"It's a metal guitar," Rex told her. "Or I could bottleneck."

"Whatever the hell that is," repeated Carol, and they all laughed, except Roger.

"You run an old broken bottle neck or a knife blade or something along the strings while you're playing. It makes a hell of a neat whangy blues sound."

Roger signaled the waiter for another drink. He had had quite a few.

"Anyone else?" They declined. They wouldn't even drink with him.

"Can you bottleneck, young Savage?" Rex was asking.

"No, but I don't think I've ever seen it done."

"Don't let him see you," said Michael conspiratorially, "or he'll excel no later than the next day."

"I refuse to be intimidated by mere musical genius," stated Rex unequivocally. "My stuff, that I just funk around with, sounds just as good to the average public ear as his learned grace notes and obligatos

Furthermore, I have a good five or six inches on him in height, and God knows how much in pounds."

"I'm impressed," said Nolan, straight-faced. "I really am terrifically impressed. You can sleep on the cot tonight."

Carol said, out of giggles, "I guess we're all a little drunk."

"You are right, my dear," said Michael judiciously, pronouncing carefully, "and, as chief member of this auspicious and serendipitous aggregation, I suggest—"

"Wait a minute," they were clamoring, "what chief member?"

"I got the bus, didn't I?" he cried. "And it's my uncle Alfie."

"Let's go," sputtered Rex, convulsed with laughter. "Maybe not as chief, but definitely oldest member of this aggregation, I really have to insist we go. People are starting to look at us funny, and who can blame them if we're going to argue over Uncle Alfie?"

They went out, holding each other up. Roger drained his glass and followed, furious, hating them all. Why had he come? Well, he could see to it, at least, that it wasn't going to start off all sunshine and roses.

Back at the hotel, Kiersten had a long hot shower and got into her nightgown. She couldn't seem to stop smiling. Who knew? Maybe she never would. A knock at the door startled her.

"Who is it?" she called, reaching for her robe.

"It's Roger," he replied rather thickly.

He, too, was in robe and slippers, his room being only a few doors down the hall.

"Kiersten, we've got to talk."

"All right, Roger, but not for long, okay? I'm really tired and sleepy."

They sat down in facing chairs and he looked at her for a long moment. She would hardly meet his eyes.

"Have you really decided to *go* with these people?"

"Yes, I have, for the summer at least. I thought you understood that. It's fun and they actually do need me."

"You come here and think about it for two days and—"

"No, Chappie wrote me about it sometime ago."

A silence. Now, though her face was flushing, she would look at him. He said cruelly, "What do you think that's going to do to them at Secesh?"

"I know," she said sadly. "But I am past the age of consent. I have to live my own life."

"You're going to live with Nolan, you mean?"

"Roger, be a pal. Tell them Carol and I are roommates. I'm not exactly going to say that on the phone, but I'd like it to be—sort of understood. I think they'll believe that because they'll want to."

"But that won't be the case?"

"It's really not your business," she said defiantly, looking away

"Ah, but it is, Kierstie, because I—care about you very much Some people just have to have flings, sow wild oats, whatever they call it, but I can hardly go away leaving you mixed up with these people."

"What do you mean? You keep calling them 'these people'."

"Carol and Michael, for one example. She's a married woman with two small children, and they've been sleeping together for over a year. Are you just going to fling all you've been taught to the winds? Don't you care about morality, right and wrong, any more?"

"Roger, you're the sociologist. I had one soc class. Don't you know that mores and folkways are changing? You should be able to accept that. Michael and Carol are not my affair."

"Very aptly put. Your affair is Nolan. Have you already slept with him?"

"That's none of your business."

"Which means yes. How much of that time before he left home did you spend—"

"Roger, go to bed. I'm not discussing it any more."

"Yes, you are, or I am. Because I want you to know some things. I feel you *have* to. I've heard nothing but Nolan for these past days. I've heard from every quarter. I'm just about choking on my brother's name. My brother," he said scathingly, "who never even admitted to many people that *he* had a brother. Beings twins is supposed to mean two people being rather special to each other, but he forgets I exist, and no wonder, I suppose, with all these people acting as if he's the world's eighth wonder. I've felt sometimes, though he seldom wrote me, that we had a—a special communications link over the miles. Now, I find he's all but forgot that I'm alive."

Kiersten was touched. She reached out for his hand. "I know he didn't mean it to be like that. It's just that people go different ways as they grow up. He's been so involved with the music ever since we got here and he knows you're not interested—"

"I might have tried to be if he'd been able to spare a few minutes. He's everybody's flaxen-haired darling, even the professors', even when he's dropping out. I suppose we never had much in common, really, but there were things I wanted to talk with him about, coming all this way . . ."

"The plane doesn't leave until after noon tomorrow. You could have the morning together. I know, if he only realized—"

"Oh, stop it, Kierstie. I'm not here for your pity. He does

realize. He knows very well what our relationship has always meant to me. For him it's just been something to get off his back, like he finally got Clarence off his back by growing up, and by . . . Like he got our mother off his back. Do you know he always hated her? He laughed when we heard she was dead. . . . But that's not why I came in here. In all my unmusicalness, I've done a lot of walking around these past days, talking to people, mostly other students. There are some things I've found out that I feel you have to know, so you can make a sane judgment about this thing that you say you're ready to chuck everything for and do."

"I don't think I need to know."

"You certainly do. For a period, quite a long period, last winter, when Nolan couldn't come up with his dormitory fees, he lived with a woman in one of those large houses up on the hill above the school. She was twice his age, a very notorious woman in this little backwater. She *kept* him, do you understand that? Bought the clothes on his back, the food he ate. He was her gigolo. Do you know that word?"

Kiersten had withdrawn her hand from his. She was stabbed by the sharp bitterness of jealousy, but surely Nolan . . .

"I don't believe that," she said coldly.

"Well, of course I'm told he was in dire straits, no money at all. I suppose you could find a way of condoning it that way, through your rose-colored glasses.

"But I also assume that *you* have remained faithful to *him*, no matter what. I've certainly never heard any talk about you at the university and you've certainly been cool enough toward me."

"I've never been in dire straits," she said stiffly, "and neither have you."

"All right. Then what about this affair with McIver? You must know that Nolan is bisexual, if not homo. Clarence perverted him at puberty."

She sprang up. "That, I know, is a bold-faced lie. There's no—*affair* with Rex. Roger, I want you out of here. *Now!*"

"Dire straits again?" he said, smiling, not moving.

"No!" she cried. "You go too far. You might have had a case of doubt with that first thing, but you have to overdo it, belabor your point. Nolan has asked me to marry him. I feel fairly sure I will some day. You can tell that to the folks and to yourself if you think it might make things look a little better for old sticks-in-the-mud. I will not listen—"

He laughed harshly. "Nolan? Marry you? Or anyone? Oh no, sweetie, that's just smooth talk to soothe a little country girl's conscience. He'll never be willing to take on the responsibility of marriage. Look how he's run from every big responsibility, refusing to do his part when we were kids at home and Darlene and Clarence were so hard on us, refusing to do his share at Secesh, dropping out of school here."

He stood up and, before she could move, was holding her tightly against him. "And he'll never marry *you*, because I mean to."

He kissed her hard, hurting her mouth. "Go ahead, struggle. I like it that way."

"Roger, don't!" she cried, pushing at him fiercely.

"If he can sleep with you, I can. Don't you know that twins, in one way or other, share everything?"

He pinioned her arms with one of his and tore at her clothing.

"You're mine. You're going to know that before you go out for your summer's romp. I've dreamed so often of this, but of course I thought you'd be a virgin. I should have known there's not a woman in the world worth that kind of trust. You're all sluts, like my mother, like—that's it, struggle. It'll be all the sweeter this way, and in the morning I *will* have something to tell Chappie, won't I?"

"I'm going to scream," she said shakily as his hand closed painfully hard on her bared breast. "I don't want to, but if you don't get out of here, right now, I'm going to scream this place down."

"Did you scream with Nolan?"

"What you've been doing," she gasped, fighting him desperately, "the things you've been telling me about him are—are projections. I've had a psych class, too. They're things you've done, or wish you'd done, like sleeping with that big beautiful black man, like—"

For an instant, his hold on her loosened slightly. She jerked herself back enough to knee him violently in the groin.

He doubled up on the carpet, sobbing in pain and humiliation.

Kiersten moved to the small desk and, having rearranged her clothes as best she could, took hold of the chair there.

"I didn't want to hurt you," she said, crying now, "not in any way, but if you don't get up and get out of here as soon as you feel you can, the next time I'll use this chair."

Roger finally left, his face burning furiously. He got dressed, moving gingerly, still a little stooped, and went downstairs. He bribed the bartender, who was just closing, to sell him a bottle of bourbon. In his room again he drank so fast and desperately that he was sick, barely getting to the bathroom in time, and hurting his injured parts terribly with the heaving. Even with the drink he did not sleep until after he had heard the town hall clock strike four.

Kiersten, too, was a long time getting to sleep. She had ripped off the torn nightgown and robe—she would never wear them again—and gone back into the shower. After that, she lay crying and trembling for a time, wide awake and frightened, staring at the closed door in the light of the lamp she could not bring herself to turn off.

Roger's crazy, she thought incredulously and recalled her simile of him, long ago, as the snake of their—her and Nolan's—garden of Eden. But he's *crazy*. He's actually *dangerous*. He needs help. Nothing he says can be believed. Nothing . . .

For a little time she considered getting dressed, going to Nolan, to tell him about his brother's condition, and for security. But, no, Rex would be there, and there'd be all the explaining, some of it she never wanted Nolan to know. If only there was a phone in their room, she'd call and ask him to come here, say she'd been frightened by something, desperately needed the safety of his presence.

And suppose Roger did lie to him in the morning, said that she, they . . . ?

The words "sibling rivalry" came back from her psych class. But, God, this was carrying it a bit far. How could Roger be so insanely jealous, when he was the one who had always had everything —especially when they were kids—almost before he'd thought about wanting it? He had told her himself, but what could she believe?

He wants to *be* Nolan, she thought, and lay there holding her breath a moment with the revelation. Well, she couldn't blame him for some jealousy, some envy. Certainly, if she had the choice, she'd be Chappie instead of Roger. But it was as if he wanted to absorb Nolan, have him at his every command as he had, more or less, done when they were young children. He wasn't interested in twinness at all. He wanted them to be one person.

She did not hear the town hall clock strike. Her mind was too involved in its frightening circling. Maybe she should try to explain to Dad and Mother, get them to try to see that Roger had psychiatric help. But how could she tell them? What could she tell them? "Roger tried to rape me because I'm going away to live with Nolan now?"

Nolan . . . Chappie . . . Oh, please! Make it be daylight soon!

17

In the morning Kiersten and Roger met in the dining room. It was accidental, a meeting neither of them wanted. Roger looked ill, Kiersten tired and hollow-eyed. He stopped at the table where she sat drinking coffee.

"Kiersten, I—"

"Go away, Roger. Don't say anything."

"But I have this terrible feeling that things happened last night, that I made a fool of myself. Only I can't remember—"

"All right," she said angrily, "we'll say you were drunk, don't remember, and didn't know what you were doing. Now will you just drop it and keep away from me?"

"You're really going through with this group thing?"

She maintained a hostile silence.

"What do you want me to tell the folks?"

"Nothing," she said curtly. "Nothing at all. I'm calling Mother this morning, before you even leave, to try to counteract the lies and insinuations—whatever you're going to have for them."

"But it won't be lies that you and Nolan . . ."

She stood up, searching in her purse for change.

"You can have this vacant table if you'll please pass on the money for my coffee."

When Nolan called from the B&K Roadhouse, she said she hadn't slept well. Could she beg off for the morning? He was concerned. She tried to reassure him, but he was all too aware of the tension in her voice.

"Kierstie, are you thinking of changing your mind? Because if you are, I'll understand. I won't like it but—"

"I swear to you it's not that. Pick me up about one, okay?"

When it was eleven o'clock in Vermont, it was nine in Colorado.

Kiersten placed her call and knew a little relief when it was her mother who answered.

When Nolan came for her in Rex's car, which had been sold and would go to its new owner the following day, he found her pale, with only the hint of a wan smile around her mouth at seeing him. Gently, he touched her shoulder, turning her back into the hotel room, and closed the door.

"Tell me what's wrong. Tell me everything."

"Has Roger gone?"

"He left for the airport about a half hour ago."

"Did he—say anything?"

"About us? Yes, quite a lot. So are other people going to, bonnie Kierstie."

"I know that. . . . Did he talk—about last night?"

"He said I ought to know he'd done everything he could to persuade you to go home with him. Does that mean something I ought to know about?" he demanded as a flush crept through her pallor.

"No, I just thought he might have . . . I called Mother a couple of hours ago."

"You did? I wish you'd waited until I was around."

"Why?"

"To help take—whatever there was to take."

"No. I had to do it. It's my responsibility."

"*How* is it yours?" he asked a little angrily.

"Because I'm a girl and girls always get the final decision in—something like this. I'm responsible—"

"For God's sake, Kiersten, I didn't know you were that old-fashioned. Nobody's pushing decision, responsibility onto just you. You're a free agent—"

"So that's why," she snapped. "Don't badger me, Nolan. I can't stand it."

"Was it bad? With Anne?"

"Not so very. That made it worse, if you can understand that. She tries to be very realistic and understanding, says we're old enough to make our own decisions . . . I told her about Carol. I mean I didn't exactly insinuate that Carol and I are going to be roommates, but it's something they can tell the neighbors, if they like. I waited to call until I thought Dad would be out of the house. That's a sort of cop-out, I suppose, making her be the one to tell him, but I just couldn't have talked to him. He's going to have a conniption."

"Yes. Like with shotguns," he said grimly.

"But Mother can usually sort of get him calmed down, given time."

"Kierstie, I'm sorry. This is how I want it to be, but it's hard and—"

"Let's go and have lunch some place quiet," she said, trying to look brighter. "Is there rehearsal?"

"There's always rehearsal, though I spent part of the morning with Roger. He'd been saying he wanted to talk, but it didn't turn out to be much. He wouldn't keep off the subject of us and there wasn't much I could say to him about that. Rex has already got an arrangement fixed up for you of that blues song he was talking about last night."

As they sat over lunch, he took her hand.

"Will you reconsider and marry me?"

"No, Chappie. Not now."

"Did you mention that to Anne?"

"I—I'm not sure. We talked for quite a long time, or I did, mostly. I couldn't seem to not chatter, trying to compensate a little. It may have come up. It's not, you know, that I don't think it's important. It's just that I can't remember . . ."

He nodded gravely. "Can I stay with you tonight? Please."

"Not—not in the hotel, and I don't have much money . . ."

"Then we'll go back and get your things, check you out. There's a nice motel on the other side of town, if you . . ."

"Wouldn't it be—easier, if we wait until we're—on the road?"

"Well, maybe, in a way, but I'm not sure you understand all about that. Uncle Alfie's making reservations for only two rooms per night, and they won't be of the best. Michael called him to say there'd have to be two beds in one room and one in the other. The idea being three men and two women. Rex will have to—rotate."

"Oh God!" she said miserably.

He grinned a little, flushing. "He doesn't like it any better than the rest of us, but it's the money, you know. We're all putting in whatever we have to start with, Rex his savings and the money he's getting for his car, Michael money from home. The rest of us don't have much to contribute, but we'll need every penny. These first bookings aren't even going to cover expenses. I promise you Rex won't make things embarrassing. He's talking a lot about getting a girl of his own, if that's the way to have a separate room. He wouldn't say or do anything to make you uncomfortable for the world. On the nights when he's with us, we just won't . . ."

She tried to smile. "You'd better make a reservation at that motel then, if you have the money, until we're ready to leave here."

Anne waited until they were alone in their bedroom that night. Price and Hugh had been having another argument. Hugh wanted to

261

mortgage Secesh to buy up the Sandersen place, a smallish ranch up on Fairweather. Price refused. Hugh had talked again, sullenly, of enlisting in the army, saying that perhaps his place was fighting for his country, as his father had done, not the ranch at all.

Price had said coldly, "Secesh will go on, Hugh. You'll have to do as you think best."

This was not a good time to talk, Anne knew, but when *would* be a good time? The work was going fairly well, at least there was that. They had moved the cattle, fertilized the fields and had the irrigation water going.

"Price, Kiersten called this morning."

"She did? Why? Aren't she and Roger back in Denver now? Won't they be home tomorrow?"

"Roger will. Kiersten has decided to go on the road with the folk group Nolan and those others are forming. She's been rehearsing with them and she says it's great fun. She wants to try it for the summer, at least."

"Fun, my ass!" He had begun to breathe harder and his face looked like thunder. "One of these commune things. Who does she propose to live with? Or are they going to switch around?"

"Price, don't. You know Kierstie's not like that. She says there's another girl and—"

"It's Nolan, of course. Well, isn't it? How long have they been planning this? Or was it going on before they left?" His eyes sparked furiously.

"When they were children," Anne said quietly, trying hard to keep her tone neutral, "Fern was predicting that Nolan and Kiersten would marry. Kiersten did mention marriage, for some time in the future, when they've got their long-range plans straightened out. She says they're very happy."

"Happy, hell!"

"Price, young people do this sort of thing these days."

"You—we ought to go back there and bring her home. We ought to start packing and call for—"

"She's too old for that. They both are. Kierstie will be nineteen in October. Parents just don't have those kinds of rights any more Besides, my darling, if you'll recall, we had some hanky-panky before we were married. If we did it, it must be *done*."

"That was a whole different thing, Anne."

"Ah, yes," she dared to smile faintly. "It always is, isn't it?"

"He'll never marry her," Price said viciously "Can you imagine him taking on the responsibility for a wife and family when he walked out on what he could have had here?"

"Price, he didn't really *have* anything here. Hugh was always riding him unmercifully. So were you and Reuben and—"

"People have to learn to crawl before they can walk," he said unyieldingly. "What do you think it was like for me when my dad was alive, and the grandparents? He wasn't but eighteen when he left here."

"But he always thought you meant to leave the major share of Secesh to Hugh. They start quarreling on sight and you never backed Nolan."

"I never backed Hugh either."

"You just let Hugh badger and bully—"

"I tell you it was good for him, made him be sure of his stand and strength. I tell you it was nothing compared to what I had when I was growing up. If Nolan *or* Roger showed a damn's worth of interest in this place, it would be theirs, with the rest getting a share at stock-selling time, the way Stanley did."

"You never even hinted that to Nolan, did you?"

"There was no reason I should have. He always had a guitar or something in his hand, or his nose stuck in a book, and you and Fern and Ginia Ellenbogen and the whole damned Park telling him what a genius he was."

"I remember a lot of times when he had a pitchfork or a hay hook or some such thing in his hand, and his nose, half his body, in a broken-down baler or a—"

"And now he's going to be a music bum, long hair, beard, dope, the whole worthless affair. He's taking *your* daughter with him, and you don't really seem to care."

"I do," she said quietly. "I don't think it's going to be half what you're making out, but I do care—very much."

"And Roger will be here," he went on fuming, "analyzing the hell out of every word, every *thing*, badgering me about going to Columbia, and with hands that never touch anything dirtier than a dusty book. I tell you, Anne, neither of those kids is worth a damn. Not to me, nor to Secesh. Sometimes, I wish to God they'd never been—"

"Don't say it, Price," she said quickly, putting her fingers to his lips. "Please, don't ever say a thing like that."

There was a long silence and he turned out the light, then tossed around angrily, trying to find a comfortable position in the bed.

"So we're just going to let this thing ride," he said sullenly. "That's what you've decided."

"It's what *they*'ve decided, and I don't see that there's a thing we can do but make the best of it."

"Roger will have a good deal to say about it when he gets here. Roger is never at a loss for words, but I don't want to hear it."

"Neither do I. Talking with Kierstie is enough for me. But, Price, they really are trying to be honest and fair with us. She could have just not called to tell me, just not come back with Roger."

"*She* may be trying, but what has Nolan ever done? Was he with her when she called? I thought not. How many times has he even sent a bloody letter these past three years? And now, besides everything else, he's dropping out of the damned school he was so determined to get to, before he's even finished. Don't you see what I mean about responsibility? And, by the way, I saw the check you made out for him when you wrote the one for the others' plane fare and such. I may not keep the books, but I do, sometimes, have occasion to use the checkbook. How much money have you sent him?"

"Not very much. I tried at first, but he always returned everything except for what I insisted were Christmas or birthday presents."

"I said he wasn't to have a penny."

"I know that, but I consider that half of this whole proposition is mine until we're dead, and I'll do as I please sometimes with some of the money. I work for it, too. This last was a—a graduation present and I hoped he might use it for plane fare home—just for a short visit if nothing more."

"He's not even graduating. He's probably spent the money on marijuana and—"

"Oh, stop it! Just stop it." She was crying. "You're not fifty years old and you're acting as if you're a hundred, behind the times, refusing to give an inch and—"

"I want to be behind the times when they're what they are these days."

"You don't even *know* what they are. You're as set in your ways as Reuben Scales, and he's twenty years older than you and never got past the second grade. What the hell difference does long hair make? Or beards? Or traveling around the country, doing something you like to do?"

"Don't cry," he snapped.

"I *will* cry, Price," she sobbed angrily. "I'll cry all and when I damn well please."

After a time, he turned over and gently, tentatively, put his arms around her.

"I'm sorry, Annie. I know you're worried and hurt and—and the things I am. I've no call to make it harder for you."

"I'm worried about Roger, too," she said, sniffling.

Awkwardly, he wiped at her face with a corner of the sheet.

"I gave up on Roger about twenty years ago. He's just sort

of—something you have to live with sometimes, tolerate, like the mosquitoes when we're irrigating. What is it you're worried about?"

"Well, it came out, I guess, in something Kiersten said, though I can't remember her exact words. She talked a good deal, just chattering, some of it, to relieve her feelings. She mentioned something about Roger's lying, that we should pay no attention to most of what he has to say. He does lie, Price."

"He always has done," he said shortly. "He not only looks like his mother, he took in a good many of her habits as well."

"But I think it's getting worse and, evidently, so does Kierstie. She's been with him a great deal more than we have, especially this past year. You never can be sure of the things he says and, even worse, I'm not sure he knows the difference. Kierstie said something like that. I really think he should—see a psychiatrist."

"Oh, for Chrissake, Annie! Do you know what those people charge? And there's nothing *in* all that. He's just a born liar."

"You're sounding like Reuben," she said with a resigned sigh. "Tonight wasn't the time to bring up everything, I suppose, but this has been bothering me for years. I noticed Roger's—deviousness got worse when Nolan left. Chappie has been, to Roger, an alter ego all their lives. Roger depended on him, as—some other people did, and when he was gone, Roger seemed to feel he had to be *more* somehow, take over some of Nolan's personality . . ."

"I don't understand talk like that."

"Oh, of course you do."

"It's the kind of thing a psychiatrist would say, I don't doubt."

She sighed again, then tried to brighten her tone. "Well, it's going to be a good summer here. I'm determined about that. Penny and Chris and the two little girls will be here in a few weeks to spend their vacation. That should get this big old house hopping again."

"It's too bad Penny and Hugh aren't reversed," Price said wearily. "I could get along a lot better with her running the place than him, not that he's taken over—not by a long shot."

"Do you think he really might be serious about joining the army?"

"Not really. Not unless, some day, I really call his bluff."

"It would be so terrible to have any of them over there fighting. It's such a wrong war, and not worth the loss of any lives."

"Well, we're in it," he said, obviously thinking of something else.

After a silence, he said rather sullenly, "I still don't know what you mean by a graduation present. He's dropping out. You reward that?"

"Have you ever thought that maybe Nolan's learned all they have to teach him? Ginia and I were talking about that the other day She says it still takes her breath away, remembering how fast he could absorb things."

"Humph. I'm responsible for the existence of two bloody geniuses, and neither of them worth a damn. Between you and Ginia, everything about Nolan gets squared away, doesn't it? Even when you have to do a lot of—what do they call it—rationalizing."

"See, you know psychiatrists' words, too," she said, hugging him.

"Let's see if we can get some sleep," he said curtly. "I've got to be working on the Cranky Creek ditches early in the morning."

They turned away from each other, their bodies touching lightly, a sleeping habit of years' standing.

Anne had thought she might not be able to sleep, but she was drifting toward drowsiness when Price said, wide awake, "Annie, it's our fifteenth anniversary next week."

"I know, darling."

"That's a kind of landmark. We ought to do something special Want to go to Denver and shop, do some things?"

"All right, yes. That sounds like fun, just the two of us. Let's don't stay at Penny's. Let's get a room somewhere."

"I guess I could be away for a few days. We've got a fair crew this summer, and Hugh can't mortgage the place out from under us without my signature. Besides, I think that just about that time there's a sale of what would seem to be very good Hereford bulls, just out east of Denver a way."

"Oh," she sighed and laughed a little.

Again, she was drifting toward sleep, when he said, his voice breaking slightly, "Oh, goddamn it to hell!"

"What?" she asked gently, immediately concerned by the emotion his tone conveyed.

"I can't get it off my mind, the mess these kids are making. First the boys and now Kierstie. . . . If we could have had kids of our own . . ."

She turned and lay against his back, her arms around him.

"Oh, Price, why *will* you keep torturing yourself with that? If it were something about me, would you want me always dwelling on it, tearing myself apart with blame and guilt? The kids we do have are going to turn out fine. Maybe it won't be in the ways you or I would have it, but they'll be all right, do well."

"Will they?" he said bitterly.

"Children we might have had would be every bit as strong-minded, determined on their own courses, their independence, and,

266

no doubt, they'd have disappointed us from time to time. Would you want soft mushy kids you could mold like wet clay?"

"I don't know," he said restlessly, "but you should have made Kiersten come home. . . . Nolan as well."

The Stewards rehearsed through the afternoon. The song Rex had thought of for Kiersten, "This ole night life, this ole sportin' life, it's killin' me," was perfect for her and they decided to add it to their repertoire, after she had taken a good deal of kidding and innuendo.

She and Nolan had said they wanted to leave the rehearsal by seven. They had meant to borrow Rex's car again, but Michael insisted they be driven to the motel in the bus. It attracted a good deal of attention, with all of them sitting there while Nolan was inside registering, particularly from some young children playing about the area.

"What about eating?" asked Michael solicitously as Nolan returned.

"There's a restaurant here," he said, going to the rear of the bus to pick up their suitcases.

"Well, which room? This is a chauffeur service, right to your very door."

Nolan looked resignedly at the key tab. "One-thirty-two."

"That's not upstairs, is it?"

"No, I'm told it's around that way somewhere. I wish to God it was upstairs and you'd have to live up to your word."

Michael whistled softly through his teeth as he maneuvered the bus. In the little silence while he was finding the room, Nolan couldn't stop a memory of Deedee Gorman. He could feel himself flushing. He never wanted to think of her again, never wanted Kiersten to suspect his shameful behavior. Kiersten was thinking of the lies Roger had told her last night, determining to put them out of her mind forever.

They got down at their very door, Nolan carrying the bags, the key sticking out between his fingers. He put the suitcases down. The children had followed the bus.

"Goodbye," Nolan said, enunciating very clearly, waving toward the bus, which still sat there, motor running, door open.

"Can I play your twelve-string tonight?" called Rex.

"Yes," he hissed, nodding vigorously and making go-away gestures.

"Gee, you got your very own bus," breathed a little boy.

Kiersten began to laugh.

"Can we make some surprise changes in a few arrangements?" called Michael.

"You can go to—"

"The Stewards," said a little girl, spelling out the words. "What does that mean?"

"We're stewards of music," said Kiersten, and the children looked impressed.

"Now you're sure you've got everything you need?" called Carol.

Both Nolan and Kiersten were now laughing, and waving vigorously.

"Better see if the key works," counseled Michael.

"Yeah," said Carol. "You look a little silly, just standing there and waiting with the children. They probably have to go to the bathroom or something."

And finally they whirled away in a cloud of dust and scraps of paper.

"*Can* we use your bathroom?" asked one of the little boys soberly. "Our mom told us to stay outside thirty minutes and I don't think it's been that long yet."

"Yes, it has," said Nolan. "It's been at least that long. You're getting tired of playing and your mom is probably worried about you Run away and find her."

"You don't run away and find your mom. You run away *from* your mom."

"Where did those other people go with the bus? Golly, I'd like to ride in that bus."

Kiersten, trying to stifle giggles, said, "They went to jail They spend every night in jail. You wouldn't want to ride with them "

"Gee! Why?"

"Can't we just go in?" she whispered to Nolan.

"No."

"Why?"

"Because that isn't the way it works."

"What works?"

"All right, kids, goodnight. Unless you want us to call the bus back so you can go with them."

The children moved away warily, but not very far. The entire area was well lighted.

Nolan fumbled nervously with the key, had trouble getting it into the lock and the lock turned. Finally, the door was open and Kiersten started to step inside, but he put a gently detaining hand on her arm

"This," he said, dropping the key into his pocket, "is how it works."

He put his arms around her, kissed her softly on the mouth, and carried her into the room.

"Oh, Chappie, how sweet. I was forgetting that kind of thing "

"What's wrong with her?" asked one of the children, all of them straggling back toward the open door.

"Did she break her leg or something?" asked another avidly

"I bet she did, getting off that big bus."

Nolan none too gently pushed them aside to pick up the suitcases.

"Our uncle broke his leg once, and they put him in an ambulance—"

He closed the door on them, double-locking it, and he and Kiersten fell into each other's arms, laughing.

A few minutes later, as they lay on the bed tensely molded against each other, she said breathlessly, "Chappie, it's just like before, only better. I've remembered all this time how it felt to be with you like this. I used to think about it, dream about it at night, and I never masturbated, like so many of the girls do. I didn't need to."

"My bonnie, bonnie girl."

His warm sure hands caressed her and she shivered, pressing even more closely against him. After a few moments she gasped, "That's so wonderful, but I can't wait any longer. Please . . . ?"

There came a loud knocking at the door.

"Jesus Christ of the Latter Day Saints!" burst out Nolan, then, in a more controlled voice, "Yes?"

"It's the manager, sir. I'd like to speak with you for a moment, if I may."

He got up quickly, pulling on shirt and pants. Kiersten, quickly pulling up the disarranged covers, watched him wide-eyed.

Nolan left the chain on the door, opening it only as widely as that would allow

"I heard there's been an accident," said the harried-looking little man.

"An accident?" said Nolan blankly "You did?"

"Yes," said the manager "Something about your wife having hurt her leg."

"Oh . . . oh—well, no. She was just feeling a little—faint "

"There was mention, too, about someone's going to jail."

"To jail?" said Nolan soberly. "I wouldn't know anything about that."

The manager hesitated, then said, "I do hope your wife is feeling better."

"Yes. She's lying down now, and feeling better. You see, she's years older than I am, and very fragile."

"Oh, well, yes—uh—I see. I do have to look into these things, you understand. Insurance . . . I do hope you'll both enjoy your stay with us. I think you'll find the restaurant quite good."

"Thank you, I'm sure we will. But do you know what makes my poor wife madder than hell?"

"Well, I—uh . . ."

"If someone comes knocking at the door when she's just getting settled into bed. Now I'll be the whole night trying to talk her out of a lawsuit or something. But I do understand your concern. Goodnight "

They were both convulsed with laughter, his face buried in her long thick hair.

"Years older and fragile," she said, spluttering. "How dare you? I'll see you pay for that one."

Again he removed his clothes, and this time he had entered her, slowly, lingeringly, while she clung, arching her body to his, when a knock came on the door at the other side of the room which led into an inner corridor.

Nolan flung up his head, very angry now. "What—is—it?" he called, spacing the words with fury.

"It's the maid, sir," came a small intimidated voice. "I think we forgot to leave ashtrays in your room."

Silence.

"Sir? The ashtrays? What will I do with them?"

"That's the day's most perfect opening," he muttered. "I'm going to tell her what she can do with the ashtrays."

"Don't, Nolan," gasped Kiersten, heaving beneath him with fresh laughter. Then she called out, "Just leave them out there, please."

There was no more sound.

"Do you think she's gone?" he demanded.

Still stifling giggles, she said, "Yes. Do go on."

"It's enough to bring on impotence," he said petulantly.

But impotence was quickly forgotten. They were gloriously, miraculously together. When they lay spent in each other's arms, Kiersten said tenderly,

"A honeymoon couldn't be any better." Then she was seized with another fit of giggles.

"Or worse," he said grimly, but, after a moment, he began to laugh with her.

"Do you know," Kiersten said, very serious now, "I was afraid I might cry tonight."

"Why, bonnie Kierstie?" He lifted himself on an elbow to look down into her face.

"Only because it's—been so long, and I wasn't really sure how you felt about me, about us—some of the time."

"I'm sorry about the letters. . . . I've always loved you. Please know that now, if you didn't all along."

She drew a tremulous sigh, but smiled into his eyes. "Then there was making this decision . . . Mother and Dad . . . and last night . . ."

270

"What, last night?"

"Well, it's just that—it seemed I had so much to think about and . . . and I guess I was a little embarrassed with the others, just for today, and I was just—afraid I might cry."

"I hope you never feel there's reason to cry again. Let's always have smiles, if not hysteria."

And they were laughing again.

He said, "Hungry?"

"Starved."

"Me, too. Shall we have room service, madam?"

"Oh, definitely. You could at least take into account my age and fragility. Anyway, I couldn't face that manager or the maid or those little kids."

"Okay. Never mind. We are recluses."

He got up, found a menu and brought it back to the bed so they could read it together. His right hand was covering his eye.

"Let me see, Chappie," she said, gently pulling away the hand. "Really, it hardly shows. Does it affect your vision or—maybe you ought to see a doctor."

"No, it has nothing to do with my vision. I don't need a doctor. It's only a nervous tic, irritable."

"Do I make you nervous and irritable?"

"You scare hell out of me. I'm afraid I'm dreaming, that I'll do something wrong, wake up and you'll just be—gone."

"I won't, you know. Right now, I can't think of any possible way you could get rid of me."

"Well, the tic will go away with some of the pressure off. What do you want to eat?"

When he had placed their orders, he began pulling on his clothes again.

"I'd better pick up the damned ashtrays before somebody falls over them and finds a way to sue us. Besides, I want a cigarette."

As he drew deeply, she said, "You never used to smoke much."

"I don't smoke much now. I can't afford it. Does it bother you?"

"Only because I know what it could do to you."

"Well, I'll go easy with it again, now that some things are settled."

"What particular things?"

"School. Finding you again, for the group, but mostly for us. I really didn't believe The Stewards could ever be until you and Rex joined us."

"But you're still going to have to carry the group. Michael and

Carol are all right. I mean they're okay people, good at what they do, but you can't have much of a folk group with just a banjo and a flute and no one to do arrangements.''

"Rex can play anything. Some of us can sing anything. You really have got the most marvelous voice.''

"Yours is better. I get the shivers, just listening to you talk, and the way you sing . . . You speak so softly, sing so softly, yet you can direct it to one person or a whole roomful of people. No, don't laugh it off. I'm just telling you what's true. I noticed that violinist you were accompanying, Laurie, at your practice, every time you said anything, very softly, just to her, about the music, she'd sort of shiver. At least you'd better have been talking about the music. It's the same with your singing. You can hold people spellbound with your voice Oh, darling, I hope I never ruin anything with my—jealous feelings I love you so much and I resent other people even being close to you I know that's ridiculous and I'm going to work hard to get rid of such feelings, but you are so handsome, so—''

He touched her lips gently. "I think the tic is disappearing already.''

Kiersten got up and dressed in the nightgown and robe she had bought for this night. She brushed her long, straight, thick hair, tying it back with a green ribbon which matched the robe.

Nolan watched her avidly, in silence. She was a little uncomfortable under his gray gaze, but also very pleased, very important and wanted.

"This should have come first,'' she said, "while you went out and smoked a cigar or something.''

"No,'' he said, grinning. "First came the bus, then the kids, then the manager, then the maid. Have we made love yet?''

"I hardly see how you could be unsure of that, but, just in case, maybe there'll be time for it again later.''

They were laughing again when the bus boy brought their tray

They ate mostly in silence, often looking deeply into each other's eyes. Then with the tray outside and both doors securely locked, they showered together.

"You are so beautiful,'' he said, his soft deep voice making her tremble, all those wonderful, excited, hungry feelings flooding her body again.

"I'm not, Chappie.''

"Let me pay you compliments when they're true. I love you so, my bonnie little Kierstie.''

They dried one another with great and prolonged tenderness and were gasping with desire long before they reached the bed. This time there were no interruptions.

18

In retrospect, that first summer was a hellish time. They played many small clubs and coffeehouses in the East and Northeast, ill-ventilated, ill-equipped, and ill-paying. They barely earned enough to keep the bus running, buy poor food and lodging, and, of course, pay Uncle Alfie's commissions. During the warm weather Rex insisted on sleeping on the bunk in the bus. It was far too short for him, but he arranged a bridge of instrument cases and baggage so that his feet rested on an opposite seat.

Sometimes they were booked for as much as a week in one place, sometimes for three or four nights, but most often for only one night. They spent more than half their time in the tired, unair-conditioned bus. Occasionally they all slept there, when there was not enough money for lodgings. They worked up new arrangements, practiced them and old ones, while one or another drove the bus from engagement to engagement. All took a turn at driving except for Carol, who was afraid of trying to handle the big vehicle. They would sit at the front, in as small a cluster as instruments would allow and Michael, braced by the back of the driver's seat, would conduct them in endless repetition and correction. Then they would switch drivers and conductors so that those two people could rehearse. It was funny to see Rex or Nolan bracing themselves in the narrow aisle with the big bass fiddle.

A great deal was going on in the country, the world then, the continued escalation of the war in Vietnam, demonstrations, riots. Nolan was irritated, a little dismayed that he could not seem to keep in touch with current affairs. Even through the busy years at Albion, he had managed to read newspapers in quick, random moments. Now, when he was not eating, sleeping, driving, or actually playing, there were always arrangements to work on, often not even time for sleep. Kiersten and Rex tried to keep him apprised. They often discussed

273

their views of world affairs on the bus or over meals. Michael and Carol were usually noncommittal, bored, impatient. Michael called himself a "peacenik," but he was far too wrapped up in what he considered The Stewards' progress or lack of it to have more than token opinions, gleaned from things he had read or heard from others in past years. Carol simply did not care.

Oftentimes the management or an interested group gave a party for them after a performance; no one cared that they might not have slept for twenty-four hours. They wanted a bright, lively group of Stewards, who could begin playing all over, accompanied by amateurs and, freshly, last until the small hours of the morning.

They were always tired, in need of sleep, occasionally without sufficient food, but they went on with it, because it was for the most part fun, because they were young and strong, committed to what they were doing. It was almost enough, for all of them, when the small audiences laughed at Michael's jokes, applauded the numbers and, best of all, when there was the occasional awed silence at the finish of a number, before applause burst forth, or when it came, spontaneously, in the middle of a number. Kiersten stayed on when the summer was over.

By that time word was getting round about The Stewards. Uncle Alfie booked them into several small universities, which held their best audiences, first in the Northeast, then in the South. By Christmas time he had brought a record scout to hear them and a date had been set for the cutting of an album.

They were still almost constantly moving, staying in rundown motels, sometimes having to choose between a meal and new strings for their instruments. They had to find a time and place each week to do their laundry. They were exhausted, their clothes getting old and worn, but they were beginning to be popular in the relatively small, esoteric circles of this new generation which had "discovered" folk music and loved it.

They had, in the beginning, named the rattling old bus Security, because, aside from instruments, it was really all they had, their place to sleep and eat and rehearse when necessary, their means of getting from one booking to the next.

One day Michael said a little dreamily, "When we can afford it, we ought to all get clothes alike. That would look neat. What do you think would be the best colors, for all of us I mean?"

"When we can afford it," said Carol rather bitterly, "we just all ought to get *clothes*, never mind alike."

"Well, I don't mean like a uniform, you know, but you girls could maybe have long dresses alike and we guys could have matching shirts and trousers."

"Let us dream of reality," advised Rex, rubbing his eyes. "I'd just like to be able to buy a whole carton of cigarettes at one whack."

Michael, hardly deterred, said, "Well, at least both girls have long hair."

"So do you," said Kiersten, yawning, "plus a beard."

"All of us ought to," said Michael, touching his shoulder-length dark brown hair.

"Not me," said Rex. "No way. I guess I belong to the hooked generation, but I'm going to carry a razor, go to a barber when I can afford it, even if we go to the very top."

"Right now," called Nolan who was driving, "I'm dreaming of a barber shop." He flung back, again, the swath of curls which covered his forehead and was beginning to obscure his vision.

"Let it grow," said Carol. "I wish I had curls like that. You've got more hair than your head can accommodate. It would be beautiful long."

Kiersten gave her a sharp look, then felt ashamed of herself.

Nolan said, "It's helpful sometimes to be able to see."

"You mostly play with your eyes closed," Carol pointed out. "Even sometimes when we're being conducted."

"But it's really not a good idea to drive that way."

It was growing dark. They were on a rather busy highway in Georgia, with a concert scheduled in three hours at a small university still some sixty miles away. The winter dusk looked cold, with threatening rain clouds. Michael's father, in having the bus revamped, had neglected the heating system, which hardly produced any warmth at all and brought a strong smell of diesel fuel into Security.

"Stop the bus!" yelled Rex suddenly, startling them all. "I mean right now, Chap. Pull over. The shoulder's wide enough, and back up till I tell you."

Nolan obeyed, causing disgruntled honks from other traffic.

"What the hell is it?" asked Michael, trying to see something worthwhile.

"If you need to stretch your legs," said Nolan, maneuvering, "this is not really the best place."

"It's money," surmised Carol. "Some armored car lost a bag of money. Small bills."

"It better be something at least that good," muttered Michael. "We haven't got time to spare for whims."

"Or even rest stops," said Kiersten.

"Okay," said Rex. "Stop right here. Open the door." He got out.

"It's a dog," said Kiersten, peering through her smeary window. "A little dog, lying in the ditch."

"Oh God," breathed Michael, "just exactly what we've always needed."

Rex climbed in and sat down, holding the small animal in his arms. It looked around with slightly glazed eyes, throwing its long-eared head in fear and pain.

"Can I go now?" asked Nolan dryly

"This," said Rex as the bus pulled back into traffic, "is a genuine redbone hound pup."

He was sitting beside Kiersten, feeling the dog over with huge gentle hands. Kiersten stroked the little animal with compassion. It gave her hand a few tentative licks, almost as if it were apologizing for being.

"His back leg's broken," said Rex

"No!" cried Michael, "we are *not* paying vet bills."

"I wanted a dog like this, when I was a kid," said Rex, "so bad I could taste it. They're wonderful hunters."

"Well, we *really* need that," said Carol. "There's not going to be time to eat before this gig, I just know that, but maybe afterward, he can rustle us up some coon or possum."

"Would you guess he's about two months old?" said Kiersten.

"About that," agreed Rex. "I don't find any other injuries, except he's scratched up some and covered with dirt."

"And you're getting all that stuff on your best, almost your only, clothes," pointed out Carol.

"No vet bills," repeated Michael a little desperately.

"It's not a bad break," said Rex reasonably. "I think I can take care of it myself, with some splints and rags."

"And where will those come from?" demanded Michael.

"He can shave splints off the sounding-board of his bass," said Nolan, "and tear up that deplorably loud plaid shirt for rags."

"Tearing up that shirt would be worth a lot," said Carol. "I'm sick of it. The colors are just never going to fade."

"We *will* take care of this puppy," said Kiersten with firm compassion. "He can be our mascot."

"Another mouth to feed," groaned Nolan, "and injured into the bargain."

"I've been telling you all I was going to get somebody to sleep with," said Rex defiantly.

"Let's name him Lord Randal," said Kiersten eagerly. "You know: 'Where've you been all the day, Randal my son? Where've you been, my pretty one . . . .' "

"Do you have to encourage him?" demanded Michael wearily.

But they patched Lord Randal up and he became a part of The Stewards. One night while they were doing a concert, leaving him on

276

the bus alone, he frustratedly chewed a hole in Carol's suitcase, the best piece of luggage among them. After that Rex blithely took him on leash to the concert stage. After a while, the leash was not needed. He was introduced along with the rest of the group and lay placidly at Rex's feet through the program, occasionally giving his tail a thump when one of them looked down at him, watching the goings-on with his big sad hound's eyes, but most often sleeping contentedly with now and then a snore, or a soundless but most distinctive bit of flatulence, which came near to breaking them up in the midst of more than one song.

Lord Randal never ate dog food. They begged scraps for doggy bags in the places where they ate, made special rest stops just for him, when he began to pace the aisle with a particularly pensive look. He was, most definitely, Rex's dog, but he loved the rest of them, too, even Carol, who vowed her hatred of him daily.

"Somebody might as well have had a kid," grumbled Michael, but he gave the dog surreptitious pats and was often the one to ask, with his ingenuous young-looking smile, for scraps from restaurant kitchens.

When their record album was released, during their second summer together, it pictured the group, in new clothes, with Lord Randal standing, proud though forlorn, in their midst.

Kiersten kept up a more or less regular correspondence with her mother, Anne's letters being delayed in the forwarding through the agency. She also answered Roger's letters, which were addressed to both Nolan and herself.

During that second summer, when they were in California, Anne wrote that Hugh had enlisted in the Air Force and would be going into pilot training.

"Oh, poor Daddy," said Kiersten when she had finished reading that letter to Nolan. "He and Hugh never got along that well, but at least Daddy could be away now and then with someone to trust as foreman. Now what will he do, I wonder? Reuben's too old really to be able to manage things."

"Maybe Butch," said Nolan absently.

Butch Moreno had married a local girl named Yola Swenson. They now lived in the old homestead place with Yola cooking for the ranch hands.

"What's your letter?" Kiersten asked with interest, seeing that he was rereading it. It had come directly from the agency.

He looked up, his face glowing. "David Harris is asking that I arrange some things and accompany him on an album. He's heard our record and was at that concert in Phoenix."

"That's wonderful!" she cried, jumping up to hug him.

David Harris was currently the top name among male folk singers.

"How will you manage it? I mean, what will we do?"

"The two agents are going to get together on a time with the record company. They say I can fly to New York when both Harris and I have a little time off. He'd like to send me the songs he wants to do and I could work some things up for them in the meantime I feel—honored, that he'd trust me like that. Of course, he may not like the arrangements."

"He will. You deserve some honors. I'm so happy, so proud of you."

In late summer, while Rex, Michael, and Carol played at one of the less expensive beach resorts, Nolan flew east to work on the record. Kiersten went home for a brief visit. She had to ask her parents to lend her money for the flight though The Stewards were now in far better financial condition than they had ever been

It was toward the end of haying season at Secesh and they were, as usual, shorthanded. Kiersten spent her days on a tractor

"It feels good," she said at the end of her first day home

She was in the kitchen helping Fern and her mother with supper. Roger was at the ranch, too, but contributing nothing to the work.

"It's so good to have you," said Anne tenderly, "even for a little while."

"Mother, I—I didn't know if you'd want me   "

"Why, Kiersten!"

"Well, with the things we're doing, the way Nolan and I   '

"Honey, we miss you, both of you so much. Your dad, even I, can't really approve some of what you're doing, but that doesn't make you any the less our children. It doesn't mean we don't love you or want to see you."

"When's Nolan coming home?" asked Fern, loudly replacing a pot lid. "Why couldn't you and your whole bunch stop some time, if you pass through Hurleigh?"

Kiersten looked to her mother.

Anne said, "Uh—arrangements would have to be a little different here, but we'd love to meet them all. You could stay over one night surely, if you ever come that near home. Kierstie, the record album is just wonderful. You're real professionals. You should hear Fern and Ginia and me—all the people who know you here—boast and brag "

"Dad, too?" asked Kiersten, looking away.

"Well, he's proud of you, but you know how little he says sometimes."

"Too stubborn," stated Fern, "to admit anything not his idea is worth much."

"Kierstie," said Anne, looking sad and wistful, "isn't Nolan ever coming home again? It's more than four years now. Won't he ever forgive Price? How did he seem when I wrote you Hugh was enlisting?"

"Well, your letter about Hugh came on the same day he got the one about working with David Harris. He was excited about that, we all were, so not much was said about Hugh. Oh, Mother, Chappie's going to be really famous one day. Not just with folk music. It seems very possible to me that he'll be asked to do a movie score or something like that, and not in the very distant future. There's nothing showy or gimmicky about his arrangements. They're just so *right*, so perfect, for whatever they are."

"Then you don't think he'll ever really come home? Back to the ranch work, I mean?"

"He loves what he's doing. We all do. If we didn't we couldn't have gone through what we have. I don't see The Stewards lasting forever. Groups break up. That's just a fact of life. But Chappie will have so many other things offered him. Hugh won't be away forever and—"

Fern said with her customary firmness, "I give him two more years, three at the outside, before he's back here to stay. Oh, maybe he'll be flying off to help with a movie or something now and then, but I've watched him, along with the rest of you, growing up here. This place is in his blood, just the same way it's in Price's. He can't stay away forever. That is, if he and his daddy, both of them stubborn as mules, ever get to where they can talk it out."

"But he's worked so hard for what he's getting now," Kiersten said. "You should have seen him last year at the end of school. He was so exhausted. I don't think he'd had more than five hours of sleep at a stretch in all those three years. This past year hasn't been that much better, for all of us, but we're getting there. I wish you could have heard Nolan doing those classical accompaniments for other people, and his own things. Even the instructors who hadn't liked his innovations and independence about music had to give him the highest marks."

Anne said, "Ginia was concerned that too much instruction might be bad for him, make him lose his own style."

"Well, I don't think it did, not one bit, though that may have been one of the reasons he didn't care to finish at Albion. Now he's beginning to get the recognition he deserves, from other people who know a lot about what they want in music. I know you're right, Fern, when you say Secesh is in his blood. I can see it in his eyes, feel it in him, because it's in my blood, too. But he's going to have more musical-type offers than he can handle before long. That's one reason

279

why the group can't last forever. It wouldn't be much without him. Coming back here would be a hard choice to make even if Dad were to ask him, and then there'd be Hugh, when his enlistment period's up."

"Hugh may decide to stay in the Air Force," Anne said worriedly. "There at the last, before he left, he was talking so much about his father's having been a career service man. He was so angry with Price for refusing to set the business up as a corporation, mortgage Secesh to buy up a lot more land and cattle. Then, too, I'm afraid he's going to be sent to Vietnam and . . . Well, Nolan will always be needed here. I don't think he knows how very much Price wants someone of his own blood to carry on with Secesh."

"He ought to realize it," Fern said curtly. "Price had the boy working here, summers, from the time he was six years old. If the place wasn't in Nolan's blood, he'd have been sick to death of it before he was half grown."

The only thing Price said to Kiersten which remotely resembled an interest in Nolan's future came when they were briefly alone in the bootroom one evening.

"Do you think Nolan will ever be ready to give up this foolishness and get on with some kind of a man's life?"

"Daddy, he's as much of a man as anybody," she said angrily. "It seemed to be perfectly all right for me to go to art school, and that I want to finish some day, but you never gave Nolan a cent for the schooling he wanted. Roger's going to be a perennial student it seems and you accept that, but being the best musician in the world isn't manly of Nolan. You ought to be proud, happy for him at any rate. He's—"

"There was a time when I thought I might expect more of him than literally playing around all his life," he snapped and ended the conversation by going to take a shower.

Roger drove Kiersten down to Hurleigh's tiny airport. She had studiedly avoided him, but he was really the only one with time for providing transportation. She thought she could detect changes in him, that he was more at peace with himself.

He said, "We haven't had much chance to talk. I've felt you were avoiding me. . . . I've written you about the full scholarship I've won for my master's work in New York."

"Yes, and I've sent congratulations. Then what? Your doctorate and teaching?"

"I think so, yes. There's something I haven't written, or told anyone. All through this past school year, I've been tutoring the son of a psychiatrist. He has a learning disability problem. In return for my tutoring three evenings a week, I've been having a weekly hour of therapy. I realized I needed it after we were at Albion. There was that night when I got so drunk I couldn't remember things. I don't like to think of being out of control that way. And there was the way I've felt about Nolan, then and always. I think I've begun to get some insight into a lot of things now."

"I'm glad, Roger," she said soberly. "I hope you'll be very happy with all your future."

"Does Chappie read my letters?"

"Yes, usually."

"But he never writes."

"He's never been much good at that. He's really very busy, doing our arrangements, and now beginning to work with other people. I'm the one who has some time to keep up correspondence with other people."

"Are you going to marry him?"

"Yes, I think so. Some day. I'd still like to get my degree in art, just because I like finishing what I start, if for no other reason. There's plenty of time."

You won't marry him, thought Roger, you never will. But now he knew enough restraint not to say it.

"I still think about him a lot," he said instead, "miss him, even after all this time. I felt so close to him when we were kids. I really needed him, and he was there, but he never reciprocated with those feelings. I realize that, but I still wish we were closer. I still feel very close to him and, yes, I suppose I still need him, in some rather unhealthy ways. He's always been most of the things I've wanted to be."

"Roger, you're a champion in your own right, straight A's all the way through school, succeeding at everything you put your hand to, the handsomest person anyone's ever seen. You can't mean about the music. I mean you—"

"No, not the music. Nolan's always been—free. Even when we were kids and Mother and Clarence bashed him around all the time, he was free. He's got something inside him, a place, a resource, that makes him—invulnerable."

Kiersten thought about that on the plane. It was true, in a way Nolan had that way of blanking out his eyes, withdrawing, refusing to admit involvement but, she thought tenderly, so often those are the times when he's most vulnerable of all.

In their second winter of existence, The Stewards cut a second album. They were in demand now, as Rex said, "different and very truly run after." They were making money, not a great deal, but there was something left over after Uncle Alfie had taken his cut, after expenses had been met. They were staying in better motels, not having to watch the right sides of menus so carefully. Rex and Lord Randal could consistently expect to have a room of their own, to which, for a night or a week, Rex often brought an admirer to stay. They discussed buying a new bus, but kept having Security overhauled as needed, this bus having become so much a part of all their lives.

One cold February night they were playing a large university in Illinois. They had arrived the preceding day, had had a chance to try out the auditorium, things they never used to be able to do. There had been an anti-war demonstration on the day of the concert, plus a sit-in and lie-in in the school's main offices, protesting some policies. The atmosphere was fraught with tension. There was talk by school officials of cancelling the concert, but they decided that would only compound their difficulties. Let The Stewards, who were receiving a good fee, either relax some of the students' tension or take some of the flak of it.

Michael peeked through the curtains while they were setting up and there was some hissing from the body of the auditorium.

"The place is full," he reported, "but the looks on their faces say 'we dare you to make us enjoy ourselves.' "

They were introduced by the president of the student council, who received boos. They went immediately into their first number, a snappy showy bluegrass tune, which the audience applauded only phlegmatically.

" 'Sally Goodin',' " yelled someone. This was another bluegrass number from their first record. This belligerent request received more applause than their first playing had done. They looked at each other and agreed to go on with the program as planned.

The hostile audience laughed only perfunctorily at Michael's best jokes. When the group had played and sung a very fine version of "We Shall Overcome," in which the audience refused to join, there was no applause at all, but bitter catcalls and, most venomously, "No, man, we got to work through the system."

Rex stepped forward and sang a beautiful rendition of Woody Guthrie's song "Pastures of Plenty," after which there was a yell, "Let the dog sing!"

Michael, retuning his banjo, said out of the side of his mouth, "They're going to kill us. They're going to come right up here and eat us alive."

Rex said coldly, "Out of every cloud some shit must fall."

"We've had tough ones, but it's never been like this," murmured Carol, looking scared.

"How can we get hold of them?" said Kiersten rhetorically.

"Let's give them 'Sally Goodin',' " said Michael, "instead of the ballad. We'd never live through the ballad."

So they went through the old play-party song at their very best, voices exuberant, instrumentation snappy, coordination perfect.

"Sing along with us," urged Michael encouragingly. " 'I had a piece of pie an' I had a piece of puddin', an' I give it all away to see Sally Goodin'.' "

Again, only scattered cooperation and applause.

Someone yelled, "How much do you guys get paid?"

Someone else, "Yeah, we could stay in our rooms and listen to the record if we wanted to hear that one."

And another, "Don't you know there's a bloody shitty war going on? What do *you* do about it?"

Then they all began chanting, "Hell, no, we won't go!" stamping feet, filling the auditorium with fury.

"Well, we almost made it to intermission," said Michael wryly.

"Do you want to quit?" called the student council president from the wings, above the rising din.

"Do we have a choice?" muttered Michael.

"One more try," said Nolan dubiously. What he had in mind had never been done publicly. He had scarcely even practiced it while actually telling the story.

He took his twelve-string and sat near the footlights, struggling to put down his innate shyness, knowing he would be all right if he could forget himself and the audience with the music. His eyelid was twitching but that couldn't be considered now. The guitar could be played quite loudly, but he touched it softly and looked over the audience. With the lighting as it was, it was hard really to see them, make eye contact, but he waited, looking, his face and eyes deceptively serene as he began to play his own theme from one of Grandpa's old stories.

The theme ran, "Tom O'Mara, on the Rock of Scarra lies your future, what you will. Haul your gear, have no fear, It's all your wish, the good or ill." There was the theme, and there was the sound of the sea, rolling and booming in storm, dancing lightly in calm.

The students began to quiet, staring, still hostilely, at this one group member alone before them. Some of them, the true folk buffs, knew Nolan's reputation, that he did most of The Stewards' arrangements, that he had made the record with David Harris, that his talents were being sought by others. They began to shush others who, reluctantly, looked at the calm, chiseled, rather craggy features, the straw-colored hair falling over the wide brow, the calm gray eyes searching among them gravely. The hall began to quiet to the full compelling sound of the guitar.

Nolan played and sang the theme again, played the sea. Then, very quietly, with that wonderful projection of his full deep voice, he began, still playing the sea, the sun, the wind, to tell the story of Tom O'Mara.

"In County Clare, on the western shores of Ireland, there lies a little fishing village called Kashel. Kashel lies at the head of a little bay, Scarra Bay. It's not a good bay, Scarra, not a good harbor. It's not well protected from the great Atlantic Ocean and there are shoals and ledges in the bay. At its mouth, in the middle of its best channel, lies the Rock of Scarra, a great boulder, almost an islet, that goes under when the tide is high and has a buoy to mark her."

The auditorium had gone very still now, as the students watched him, listening. Nolan had closed his eyes, leaning his head back a little, remembering, lost in the music, scarcely aware of where he was. His fingers brought them the tiny fishing village with its boats tied up, rocking gently in the swell. Some of Liam's brogue crept back to him, only a trace, but it made his voice the more compelling.

"A long time ago, in the village of Kashel, there lived a fisherman, Tom O'Mara. Tom fished winter and he fished summer; he fished calm and he fished storm, for he had a wife and young ones and his old mother to feed and shelter.

"One early morning in the month of February, Tom went out. It was a raw day and a bitter wind blew from the east. Tom had a dory, with sail and oars. There was a rime of ice along the shore and about the anchored dory. He wore his oilskins against the stinging spray. It was not a stormy day, just a rotten one, and Tom rowed out through the bay, meaning, when he'd passed Scarra Rock, to put up his sail and make for McCann's Bank.

"When he came to Scarra Rock, there was a rime of ice about that, too. The whole great boulder was covered with a misting of ice from the spray, and there was a seal, trying to climb onto the rock. The skim ice kept breaking under him.

"O'Mara said, 'Here, I'll help you,' and he broke a path through the rime ice with his oar.

"The seal climbed up and he said, 'Thank you. Betimes it might be I can help you. This is my rock. I lie here for the sun when the tide's out, and, when there's no sun, I lie here for the resting.'

" 'Yes, I know you,' said O'Mara. He did. All the

fishermen knew the seal. All the village of Kashel knew the seal -to be one of the magic people who could walk, a man, on the land if he chose.''

Nolan played and sang the theme again, very softly. The members of the group behind him looked at one another in questioning, suppressed awe. The audience was utterly still.

"The seal said to Tom O'Mara, as he was rigging his sail beyond the Rock, 'What would you be wishing for on a day like this? That you were home by your peat fire?' Tom said, not paying much heed, 'I'd wish for a catch big enough so that I could *afford* to be at home by the hearthside.'

"He went out onto the banks. Not many other fishermen were abroad in that biting cold. Tom caught fish. He couldn't stop. His dory was near to foundering and, if the sea had come on rough, she would have done, surely. The tide was rising full when he had to go in or sink. Scarra was covered; the seal was gone.

"Some time later, O'Mara was caught out in the devil of a spring storm. He should have known better, should have made in sooner, he had been raised on the sea and the weather. It was a black storm. He couldn't see for the snow and the salt spray on a driving west wind that tried to drive him in too fast, faster than he could get his bearings. As he passed the Scarra buoy, he thought to himself, 'Well, I'm this far. I pray God I can miss the shoals and ledges in the bay. If I lose this old boat, we can all give ourselves up for dead or the poorhouse.'

"Then a great wave came ramping in from the west" (and Nolan played the crying wind and the looming wave) "and it carried Tom O'Mara's dory over the little bay and all its dangers in blackness, up onto the shore in a place of soft deep sand, where it let the dory down like a mother laying her babe in its cradle.''

The theme again, the entranced, waiting faces of the audience leaning forward as one, while Nolan was actually lost to them; he was with Tom O'Mara.

"Some years later, on a dappled summer day, O'Mara was passing the rock, bound homeward with a good catch. The seal was there, sunning himself, and they greeted one

285

another as friends. The seal said, 'Would there be aught I can do? Something's troubling you, I know.' Tom said that he had six young ones at home and it was almost his wife's time to bear a seventh. 'She's been poorly. I am that worried. She's a good woman. I love her, and what would the weans do without their mam?'

"When Tom came to his house, he found the midwife had come and gone. His old mother's eyes were running with tears of joy. His wife had borne twins and all was well with the lot of them. Tom, looking down at his wife and the wee ones, thought with a smile that was just the least bit wry, 'It could have been just the one. I don't recall that I mentioned any such as two at a time.' "

The theme again, singing softly with a little smile on his face. Michael began to sing it softly too, but the other three shook their heads at him.

"The years passed and passed and Tom O'Mara was an old man. His mother was long dead. His wife was gone. He had seen daughters married, held grandchildren on his knee, and two of his sons had been lost in the sea. Tom had seen the seal many and many the time and they always greeted each other, but Tom asked for little. His way was his own to make. He knew that. He was a proud man, and strong. But there came a time, in a winter gale, when he had to say to himself that his strength was not as it had been. It was a poor day for the fishing and the wind had come on to blow out of the northeast, chilling him to his bones.

"As he passed the Scarra buoy, he could not see the rock for the day was growing black and the waves were high and choppy. As Tom edged the dory into the little bay, he thought, 'This could make a man wish he'd been born something else, an inlander, a crofter, a peat cutter, shepherd. I wish to God I'd never go to sea again.'

"And," Nolan said very softly, the guitar just audible and all of them, in front of him and behind, leaning forward, caught on the soft resonance of his words, "and they found Tom O'Mara the next day, when the wind and the sea were down. His little dory was drifting about in the bay, with not a mark on her, oars shipped, sail furled. And Tom had no mark on him, but he had been dead the night and he never had to go for the fish again."

Once more the theme, very very softly. He stopped in utter silence, opened his eyes reluctantly, stood up, moved his chair soundlessly back to the group, a high flush rising in his fair face.

Suddenly the auditorium erupted in applause that seemed to shake the building. The students were on their feet, tension gone out of them, but stamping, pounding, yelling for more. Rex and Michael were slapping Nolan's back with such fervor that he almost dropped the guitar. Kiersten, her eyes filled with tears of pride, took the instrument and held it close to her. Nolan was trembling slightly

Carol cried above the noise, "Beautiful! That was absolutely beautiful!"

The student council president yelled, "They want you to do it again. Would you?"

Nolan shook his head. "I couldn't," he almost whispered. Kiersten was the only one who heard. She thought he looked tired, drained, but there was joy in the depths of his eyes.

"Well, they're not going to let you take an intermission without at least one more number," shouted the president. "They'd tear the place apart if you completely stopped right now."

"Let's give them the ballad," shouted Michael. "Come on, Kierstie. Ready?"

Nolan sat a little behind the others, leaning his cheek down on the big guitar, his right hand unconsciously covering his eye. He did not play, only sang softly the bass harmony part in the refrain. He was thinking, Grandpa, you gave me more, much more than either of us dreamed.

The second half of the program was a total success and they did three encores. They were mobbed backstage. There was going to be a party; they must come. The Stewards agreed, but explained that they would have to go and eat first.

When, finally, they were out in the frosty air, gulping it gratefully, packing away their instruments in Security, a tall, lovely-faced woman with long black hair which blew about her face like a curtain, came and touched Nolan's arm tentatively.

"I'm Susan Lister," she said in a warm vibrant voice

"Yes," he said and put down the instrument case to shake her long beautiful hand.

David Harris was the top male singer in folk music, but Susan Lister was so far above him or anyone else that she seemed almost from another world. It was she whom Nolan had dreamed most wistfully of arranging for and accompanying. His face was still but he felt an inner tremor.

"I'm here because this is my home town," she was saying.

"I've listened very carefully to the records you've worked on and I've never in my life been so glad of coming to a concert. I almost decided not to come with things so agitated, but God, I'm glad I didn't miss this."

He introduced her to the others, all of them a bit star-struck, but she gave them only perfunctory notice.

Rex picked up the instrument Nolan had been carrying and took it into the bus. There were still many students about them, talking, laughing, asking questions of various members of the group, but they, too, knew Susan Lister and were in awe of her. It was as if she had drawn a magic circle around Nolan and herself. No one dared venture to ask for her autograph, nor his either, now that he was with her.

"How long will you be here?" she asked.

"We leave for Fort Wayne in the morning."

She looked sorry, irritated. "I *have* to talk to you."

"We're going for something to eat, then there's a party . . ."

"No, not that. Not tonight. I want to talk with you about cutting a record, maybe using your whole group but . . ."

"That has to be arranged through the agents and——"

"I'm very well aware of that," she said, smiling. "But we can *talk* about it, can't we? Look, I know you're tired. I know how it is after a performance and I know you should be at the party, but I've got my car over there, the blue one. Would you come out to my house for a while? It's my folks' house, actually, but they'll be asleep. I'll give you something to eat. Would you bring the twelve-string? I swear I'll try not to impose on you too much. There are a few songs I'd like to try out, get your ideas on. Tell me, how old are you?"

"Almost twenty-three."

"My God!" she groaned with a small, rather bitter laugh. "And I'll never see thirty-five again. If I'd started performing for real at your age . . . What do you want to be when you grow up? How about a legend in your own time?"

He smiled, blushing.

"I won't keep you long," she persisted without need. "I'll drive you back to wherever you're staying."

"I'll get the guitar," said Nolan.

"I'll be in the car."

The others had clustered near the door of the bus. He walked around them, and they followed him. Rex sat in the driver's seat and started the engine.

"Just a minute," called Nolan from the back. "I'm going with her, just for a little while. She wants to talk about some songs and she's mentioned all of us doing a record with her."

Michael said, "Christ, if you don't come back with us to that party, they'll be ready to eat us alive again, Chappie."

"First things first," Rex said soberly.

Nolan came back, edging the guitar case carefully along the narrow aisle. He put a hand on Kiersten's shoulder, then bent and kissed her cheek. "I won't be too late. I promise." And he was gone.

Kiersten knew a physically sickening stab of jealousy. Lister had looked at him so possessively and, clearly, he was at her beck and call. Of course he is, she thought, angry with herself. People who have never even dreamed of folk music know who Susan Lister is.

The others were speculating, in delight that at least one of them had found an in with Susan Lister, in apprehension about the students' party without Nolan.

Into Kiersten's mind flashed one of the lies Roger had told her that night at Albion: a woman twice his age . . . Oh, you are so ridiculous! she flared at herself.

They were out on a less lighted street now, looking for the restaurant which had been so highly recommended. She fondled Lord Randal's ears, keeping her head down so the stupid tears couldn't show. After that wonderful story, the fantastic music, the tremendous reception, she had wanted so to be alone with him tonight after the party, to hold him, make love with him, try to tell him how marvelous he was, how proud she was of all his achievements, how lucky she was to be . . .

Don't you dare start with the apron strings, Kiersten Savage, she told herself fiercely. But he's going to slip away, said the voice of the hot tears. He's too good for The Stewards, for me. Tonight we've all started to lose him.

19

Susan Lister was with The Stewards after that night. Not physically, but her influence was definitely felt and it was mostly for the good.

Nolan found her delightful to work with. Her voice was strong and rangy, from a deep clear contralto to a limpid middle soprano. She had had no formal vocal training—which could be deadly to folk singers—except for choral groups in high school and college. For the ten years that she had been singing publicly, she had made a careful study of her genre. She could adopt the proper twang to make old mountain ballads sound credible and realistic, could give credit to a Negro spiritual, or lilt through an Italian dancing song with perfection. Her mother was Italian. Susan also did songs in French, German, and Spanish. Languages had been her college major.

They had literally played through that night. It was after five A.M. when she returned Nolan to the motel. There had been talk, too. She was, by nature, a shy, introverted person, and lonely.

"You're a good listener," she said at one point, a little embarrassed by her freedom of speech with him. "You watch me so carefully with those nice calm gray eyes. I feel you're taking in what I don't say as well as what I do say, really absorbing it."

She had left a husband and small daughter to have her career. "Jim was a junior executive in an aircraft company in California. He couldn't very well give that up to come traipsing around the country with me on the off chance that I might have some success. . . . It was Chia, our little girl, who made the decision almost impossible. I love her so."

Her big dark Italian eyes suddenly filled with tears. So this was what gave her the sad, lost look which audiences found so appealing.

"She was a baby, two years old, when I first went to New York. I used to see her, send her letters and pictures and presents, hoping

291

she wouldn't forget. But, not so long after I left, Jim asked for a divorce and married again, so I thought I would be an interloper between Chia and her new mother. I stopped seeing her openly, and sending things. Now, I just try to get glimpses of her, when I'm out there, going to school or something. Here's the latest picture I have of her.''

A young girl with olive skin, dark hair and limpid eyes, already giving indication of Susan's full bosom and ample body.

''She's very like you,'' Nolan said.

''Yes. Her stepmother resents that, thinks she may remind Jim too much of me, but that really isn't something she has to be concerned about. Jim and I never got on that well. There were problems from the first, mine not his. You see . . . It's past three in the morning and I've had quite a lot of wine. I'm going to tell you something almost no one knows. I feel I can count on you to keep it that way. I've always been a—a closet lesbian.'' She turned her eyes away from him and went on in an almost inaudible voice. ''It's—something I can't seem to conquer, therapy and all. I like men, love some of them. They've always been far better friends to me than most women. In fact, I think I love you. It began when you came down by the footlights and started shutting those brats up. You have magnificent talents; you're good to look at. I very badly want you as a friend, but I don't have—designs on you. Some women, I know, are saying 'Come out of the closet, let it all hang out,' but I just can't do that. I've been too inhibited by parents who think, or make me feel they think, I'm not a very worthwhile person, by a husband, by old-fashioned standards. I've had very few—incidents. It's pretty well under control and I mean it to stay that way.

''The coltish little girl with the freckles is yours, isn't she? It's written all over her face for anyone to see. She's darling, and talented, and she adores you. If a time should ever come when she's—jealous—and I hope we may have enough association for that to become a possibility—you have my permission to tell her, but, please, not unless you absolutely have to.''

They went back to music then. It wasn't a couple of songs on which she wanted his ideas, it turned out to be a large number. Some of them, she had already recorded and, having studied them previously, Nolan showed her what he would have done with them, had he been arranger and accompanist. Susan seemed saddened and delighted at the same time.

''Why didn't I, or someone, think of that?'' she said at one point. ''Well, we'll just have to record it again, won't we?''

When they were finally in her car, driving across town, she said, ''Would you consider touring with me? There's no accompanist I've

292

ever wanted so much. You could see back there at the house that I don't play all that much or well myself. You—perfect everything. I simply love what you do, all of it."

Then she named a figure which stunned him a little, considering what The Stewards had earned in the past year.

"Thank you," he said. "I really mean it. It would be an honor for me, but I can't. I have commitments. . . ."

"Yes, I suppose I understand. You do all the arranging for your group, don't you?"

"No, Rex does some of it. He's very good, and versatile. Everyone in the group contributes ideas."

"Your girl—what's her name?—yes, Kiersten, has a most interesting voice. And Rex, that's the black man, isn't it? is very good. But the other two are just window dressing. It's my suspicion that young Michael somehow provided the money to get the group started, and the other girl is *his* girl, so, of course, she came along. The flute is beautiful in the arrangements where it's used, and he's a fair, showy banjo player. Tell me this: would you and Rex and Kiersten come with me? You'd get good billing, plenty of chance to do your own things. I'd love to have the three of you working with me."

"I don't think we could do that. We owe—"

"Nolan, when you're set on a career, as you surely must be, you can't be too concerned about owing people. That sounds hard to you. You're very young and idealistic, but there is a certain amount of *using* people in a business like this, in any business, I suppose. You're wasting some of your talent by staying with the whole group. You're worlds above Michael and his girl. Think about it. Meantime, if you have no objection, I'm going to see about a recording contract for The Stewards with the company I record for. It's a much bigger operation, with a bigger ad budget and better distribution. I take it you're not too bound to your company, since you did those records with David Harris."

"No, they've just been taking us an album at a time. They don't really have much faith or interest in folk music."

"You will cut an album with me, won't you, soon?"

"If we can arrange schedules, it would be a privilege."

"Stop being so modest. Your talent is greater and far more diversified than mine. Believe me. I've had years to learn my limitations. Where did you get that story you told tonight?"

"From my grandfather. He was Irish."

She laughed. "I gathered that. You hadn't practiced it much, had you? It seemed to take a great deal out of you, though you lost yourself in it."

"I hadn't practiced it at all, really," he admitted diffidently.

"He died when I was ten, Grandpa. That was before I could do much with music. After that I used to think his stories and make up accompaniments, but I never—performed one before."

"How many do you have?"

"How many what?"

"How many stories?"

"Oh, a lot, if I can remember them."

He was thinking that he had reached a high point in his life this night, and that, strangely, he still felt not so very different from that little boy who had listened to Grandpa. Weren't high points, great steps upward, as he felt this meeting to be, supposed to change people? Perhaps nothing could really change one. At times tonight, Susan had seemed very much the girl who had always received too much "constructive criticism" from her parents, particularly her father.

She was saying, "Would you do one of the stories on my album?"

"I—don't know. It's hard."

"Because you're not used to performing alone?"

"Yes, partly that at any rate."

"Will you try to get used to it? You've committed yourself, you know. You're going to have to include one of those stories in every program now, or answer to a very disappointed audience. You don't mind playing alone, do you?"

"No."

"You have such magnetism in your voice, as well as in your playing—such power to hold people. Who's your agent?"

He told her.

"What sort of contract do you have with him? He's very small potatoes, you know."

"A yearly contract."

"Would you like to come with my agency?"

"Well, you see, Alf Bamberger is Michael's uncle. He did a lot to help us get started—"

"There you go with being obliged again. He's had his commissions, hasn't he? Before the group has ever seen a dime? Think it over. Talk to the others."

"A part of the problem," he said with difficulty, "a part of *my* problem, is that I don't really know how far I want to go with this, how long I want to go with it."

"With music, you mean?" she sounded and was surprised.

"Yes."

"You'd consider quitting?"

She tried to see his face in the instrument panel lighting and swerved the car dangerously.

"I don't seem to stay with anything very long," he said apologetically. "I fought like hell to get into school at Albion; I did four years in three there, and I worked all that time because my scholarship only covered tuition, but I quit a year before finishing. Now, with the group, especially since we've made records and audiences insist on hearing the same songs over and over, I . . ."

"You're bored," she said, "not willing to rest on your laurels?"

"Something like that, I guess, and there's . . ."

"You can tell me," she said gently. "It's five o'clock in the morning. Anything can be said."

"My family, my—dad—has a ranch in Colorado. Some day he may—need me."

"A ranch! My God, Nolan, you wouldn't give up all you have and can have to be a—a cowboy?"

"I think I—might. I've always wanted the music—and Secesh, the ranch. I'm beginning to feel that I've—proved my point in music, and I think, if ever there was the chance . . ."

"The chance?" she said, still incredulous. "You can't go home and put on your spurs or whatever and—"

"No, it's an involved story. I don't think I understand the whole of it myself."

"Well, if you want my personal opinion which, no doubt, you don't, I say it's a bunch of nonsense. What a loss to have someone of your abilities—punching cows, or whatever it is you'd do."

"Interest in folk music won't last. It's already dying down and it won't come back until the next generation discovers it for themselves."

"But there'll always be some loyalists," she said earnestly, "and some performers, like me, who can't do anything else. That's not your problem, though, because you can do anything you want to. You've told me you play classical guitar and cello and God knows what else."

"I'm getting a little tired of the road. We all are. I guess I'd like to be settled somewhere."

They had reached the motel. She drew the car up beside Security and sat there with the motor running, a gently detaining hand on his arm. The night had turned bitterly cold; a few flakes of snow randomly starred the windshield.

"Join a studio orchestra," she suggested, "or a symphony."

"I don't like cities."

She increased the gentle pressure slightly. "You are indeed complex and very difficult. Is the ranch what Kiersten wants, too? Are you two going to get married some day and raise little singing cowboys?"

"I want us to marry. So does she—I think she still does, but she

295

wants to finish her degree in art. She's only had one year. Neither of us, I think, knows yet just what we're going to do with the rest of our lives."

"Suppose she got her degree. Wouldn't she feel compelled to *do* something with it, as you're doing with your music?"

"I—think so. We haven't really talked about it for a long while. There hardly seems to be the time, or energy. But she—loves the ranch. As much as I do."

"I've had a lot of time," Susan said thoughtfully, "to study people. "I've been so often among crowds of strangers for the past ten years that that's about all I *can* do, besides just stop thinking. I think I observe very closely, especially other music people. I would guess that Kiersten would go along with you, whatever you decide. If you settled in a city she could finish her degree, work afterward, or not. For God's sake, Nolan, don't bury yourself, and her, with all your talent, on some *ranch!* Do you know the Bible? Well, there are things about hiding one's light under a bushel, burying one's talents, refusing to use them and let them grow. Even the Good Book advises strongly against such behavior."

There was a little silence before he said, "I'd better go in. I—thanks for the music—and the talk. I've never talked this thing over with anyone except Kierstie and that was a long time ago, and not very thoroughly. What she'd like most, I think, is a—reconciliation with Price, my dad, and I can't see how that's ever going to come about, so this kind of talk is pretty pointless."

"Oh, so it's like that. He doesn't approve of music as a career?"

"No. Not for a man."

"Well, to hell with him," she said strongly. "Let it *be* your career, as it should be. Go to the ranch when he's left it to you, may he live forever."

"It's not that simple," he said, sighing, and with a small diffident smile, "and I do have to go in."

She took her hand from his arm, but said shyly, "Nolan, can we be friends? I want to know Kiersten, too, and Rex. What a magnificent specimen *he* is. I don't have many real friends and I'm—lonely."

"I think we'd all like that very much."

"When are you due to cut your next record?"

"In April."

"I'm to be in New York for most of that month and part of May I keep an apartment there. It's a grungy place, but pretty big. Come stay with me, all of you."

Nolan actually wrote to Susan Lister, or at least he sent arrangements of songs she asked for, along with suggestions. The Stewards

296

subscribed to several folk music magazines from the United States and other English-speaking countries. They found old songs and gleaned new material. He was always on the lookout now for songs that would suit Susan.

When they went to New York, they did stay with Susan. Kiersten wanted to refuse. She loathed her jealousy, which only seemed to compound it. He had been out almost until dawn that night in Illinois. She had made herself not question him, which only served to add fuel to her imagination. Michael and Carol were delighted with the idea of being invited to the home of *the* star. Rex, as usual, was not particularly impressed, wanting to know only if Lord Randal would be allowed in the place.

The apartment was large. There were several bedrooms. Susan explained that she was sub-letting it very cheaply, as New York rentals went, from a classical musician who was, with his large family, indefinitely in Europe.

On the nights when none of them worked, they had long sessions of music in the apartment. Kiersten was able to lose some of her animosity toward this other woman. She treated all of them as if she were a big sister, almost a mother, and she was so obviously not "after" Nolan, except for his talents.

Susan decided that on the new album on which she and Nolan were working she wanted Rex to play bass on several numbers and she asked Kiersten to do harmony on two songs with her. Nolan accompanied her in everything. Susan begged him to do one of his stories on the album, but he refused, with a reticence that even he did not quite understand. He was putting "Tom O'Mara" on The Stewards new album. Susan's new recording was labeled THE LUSTER OF SUSAN LISTER by Susan Lister and Friends. Nolan, Rex, and Kiersten were pictured on the jacket, in the background. Michael and Carol were bitter, though they said little to the others. Kiersten felt The Stewards slip another notch. It would be all right with her, she thought, if they broke up. She was very tired of the road, but she wished the breakup need not come with hard feelings.

One day Carol said to her derisively, "Don't you know when your guy's being taken away from you?"

Kiersten's concern about that came at longer and longer intervals. She liked Susan, almost in spite of herself, found her warm and generous, sensed her loneliness.

"Don't you think we should let Roger know we're here?" Kiersten asked Nolan when they had been in New York for several days and he had not seemed to think of his brother. She had no desire to see Roger, but felt enough family obligation for both of them.

297

"Call him," answered Nolan, preoccupied.

"Chappie, please, you do it. That would mean so much more to him. I think I understand some of what you feel about him, but you—we—have so much now. Can't you share a little? I don't mean let him have the stranglehold he used to have over you and may still want. I told you he had therapy all through his last year at Boulder. I suppose he's trying. You're strong. You needn't let things go back to where they used to be. Just—care about him a little, let him know. You don't realize how important that is to him. He's your brother."

"My twin," he said, but without much bitterness.

He asked Susan, then called to invite Roger to a spaghetti supper the girls had planned.

Even Roger, with no interest whatever in music of any kind, knew the name Susan Lister and was secretly impressed that Nolan and the others were making a record with her, not to mention staying with her while in the city. When he saw her he thought her the most beautiful woman in the world, and Susan was, quite frankly, a little shaken by his looks.

"I thought Chappie was handsome," she said candidly, in front of all the others, "but, my God, this one is beautiful!"

Roger was able to restrain himself from preening visibly. He had cultivated a fine chestnut moustache, which added virility to his handsome face. He still looked younger than Nolan, though there was nothing of innocence in his large hazel eyes.

Susan had instructed that Roger be told to bring a friend if he chose. There was a girl, Alicia, a rising model, with whom he had been having a mild affair, but he did not ask her, was tired of her already, bored and derisive. On sight of Susan, he was doubly glad he had not asked Alicia.

"What a lush hunk of woman that is!" he said privately to Nolan, who frowned. "Getting on, but still *very* attractive."

Nolan turned to look at Michael, who was talking to him. Chappie had nothing to say to him any more, thought Roger angrily, nothing.

Susan had invited a young black jazz singer she knew as a date for Rex. She was a small, petite, and very pretty girl named Ellen.

"Uh-*huh*," said Rex as they were introduced. "Almost better'n a redbone hound dog any day."

Ellen laughed and shot back, "What do I do if I want to kiss him? Stand on a chair?"

Roger did a good deal of the talking during supper. It should do them all good, he thought, to get their minds off music for a while. His master's work was going well. He had the promise of a teaching assistant's job next year. Meanwhile, he was doing some volunteer work at a ghetto storefront counseling office. His master's thesis was going to come from that. He had done a crash course in Spanish because practically all the office's clients were Puerto Rican. He loved New York; didn't they all? He meant, eventually, to have a professorship in a school at least near the city.

After supper, while the girls cleared up, Roger tried again to talk directly with Nolan.

"You know Hugh's being sent to Vietnam?"

"Yes, Anne wrote us."

"What happens if you're drafted? *I* won't be, so long as I'm a student."

"I leave the country," said Nolan without hesitation.

"You'd do that?"

"I would. Look, Roger, you're the sociologist, you must see what this war is all about. I'm not going to be shot at for an imperialist capitalist cause that's none of mine."

Roger grinned. "I suppose you just made that up this minute, 'imperialist capitalist cause.' "

"No, that's not mine either, as you know very well, but it fits my ideas. Couldn't it be that those people don't give a damn for democracy? Would just like to be left alone to harvest one rice crop they plant, in peace? Any kind of government could do that for them."

"That sounds a bit pink-o. Haven't you been on too many college campuses lately?"

"You've been on campuses for years. No, I'm not a Communist or a socialist, maybe not even a very good conforming liberal. I love this country, but not right or wrong. This is a sick war, reflecting a sick society."

"That sounds like it ought to be my line."

"Yes, it does."

"Well, this war will pass. They always have. I'm more concerned with my own individual future. I think it shows promise, don't you?"

"It seems to."

Why couldn't Nolan show him the least bit of admiration, respect? It had to be there, as it was in everyone else he met, even in a musical genius, all wrapped up in himself. Fear, even outright hatred would be better than this careless indifference. Everyone else Roger knew showed their respect and admiration and, sooner or later, he lost any slight interest in them. He hated admitting to himself how important Nolan's view of him had always been. He hadn't even quite admitted that to the psychiatrist he had seen in Boulder. But he *would* have his due. One day, even Nolan was going to . . .

He stopped the thoughts by saying casually, "Aren't you and

Kiersten ever going to get married? I thought that was supposed to be in the cards.''

"I hope it's somewhere on the agenda.'' Nolan had been feeling Kiersten's—what? Disapproval? Disenchantedness? He was becoming deeply concerned, but his words were light and nothing of his worries showed in his face.

Roger had had a good deal of wine to drink with supper and was now on his second scotch and soda. He was not drunk. It was just that he was determined to break through to Nolan, make him show something, even hurt or anger.

"Kierstie's okay,'' he said expansively, "the salt of the earth, as Fern would say, but don't you get a little bored with her? I did, that year we were at the university together. Someone in your position must get all kinds of chances to ball really beautiful broads. What goes on here in this apartment? Do you play switch and fuck? After all, a bunch of hippies together . . . Even the black number's not bad. This Lister must be sensational.''

Nolan looked at him for a long time, in that cool direct way that had always made Roger uneasy and angry. Roger remembered that it used to infuriate their mother and Clarence, too. They'd slap him around for that look. Roger wanted to do that now, but instead determined to outstare his brother. In the end, though, he had to blink his long-lashed hazel eyes.

"Well, isn't she?'' he demanded belligerently.

"Yes, she is,'' said Nolan coolly. "But not in the way you mean. I wouldn't know about that. There's something more, you know, to broads besides balling them.''

"Is there?'' said Roger with a little scornful laugh. "I'd like to know what, then, because I sure as hell haven't seen it. Don't tell me you're a feminist, too? Or maybe it's the basketball player who's more your dish of tea? Oh, never mind answering that.''

"I hadn't meant to.''

"But *what* is there, tell me, to a female, besides her female parts?''

"That's not worth trying to answer either.''

"How long has your group been together? Two years?''

"Yes, about that.''

"And you think Kiersten's been faithful all that time, with the other musicians around, and all those admiring fans? Surely you've found plenty of material to work on besides her.''

"Roger, I don't really think we have anything at all to say to each other.''

"Well,'' persisted Roger, "maybe she *has* been faithful. Poor little Kierstie really doesn't have much in the way of looks. She's

300

built more like a boy, and she has some very hard to break through old-fashioned scruples, but you . . . Look, twin brother, could you do anything toward fixing me up with La Lister? No? All right. I've always been able to handle things quite nicely on my own. Did you see the way she looked at me? Hear what she said? How do you like the moustache?"

"I think it's gorgeous, Roger, utter perfection," Nolan said coldly and walked away.

"We're not playing a note of music tonight," announced Susan as the women came in from the kitchen. "We all know that if we start, we wouldn't be able to stop. We will put on records and dance and party. This is one evening that's not going to deteriorate into a jam session."

She went to the stereo and loaded the spindle.

"Furthermore, I am not even playing any recording that any of us has had anything to do with. These are old, big band records that I happen to love. Maybe you kids don't even know how to dance to them. It's not that standing apart and wiggling kind of stuff."

"I know, babe," said Rex. "It's what they call down home 'hug dancin',' and I've always been given to understand that it's very wicked."

"Oh, good," said Ellen. "You bend way down and I'll stand on my tippy-toes and we'll see."

They were all laughing as they began to dance. Roger took Kiersten in his arms.

"Not *that* close," she said, sounding very irritable, though she still smiled.

"Aren't you tired of being a gypsy?" he asked softly.

"We're all a little road weary," she admitted. "But The Stewards are doing so well now."

"It doesn't hurt one bit to have Lister's patronage, I suppose How did that start anyway?"

"She was at a concert we did a few months ago."

"And fell for Chappie, isn't that it? Look at them. She doesn't mind how close he holds her. They make a handsome couple, don't they? The dark and the fair. Wouldn't you like to do a painting of them? They really are striking. Look at the facial lines, his so rugged, hers so soft?"

"Oh, stop it."

"I'm only trying to appeal to the artist in you. What *about* art, Kiersten? Have you given up on it?"

"No, I don't think so. Susan says we're all young enough to try a little of everything."

"Oh, it's Susan says now, is it? And how old is Susan?"

"Around forty I think."

"A little old for Nolan, isn't she? But then I guess he's always had a preference for—"

"Roger, if you don't stop, *I* will. I won't come near you or say another word to you all evening."

"All right, little Kierstie, I'm sorry," he said earnestly. "This is another subject entirely. Why don't you just stay here in New York? Marry me? You know I've always wanted you, loved you. We could have a good stable life together. You could go back to school if that's what you want. Someday we'd have a kid or two. Wouldn't you like to be the wife of a promising prestigious professor? You say you're tired of the road, seem to be wanting to settle down. How long since Nolan's mentioned marriage? Isn't he just taking you for granted these days? You'd never be happy with him anyway. He's too conceited, too self-serving, too—"

"Roger," she said wearily, "if that's really a proposal, I have to say thank you, but this is not really a new subject, it's the same old thing. I'm convinced that if you're capable of loving anyone else in the world besides yourself, that one is Nolan. Why can't you try to be lovable? Then maybe he'd reciprocate."

"The hell with that," he said bitterly. "Did you see him at supper when I tried to talk a little about my plans, my future? He just kept staring off into space, or eating. I'd bet he didn't hear a word."

"If you want his admiration, his respect, then be—"

"I will not change myself to fit some mold of his. I used to try to do that when we were kids. There's no touching him. He's always been too wrapped up in himself."

"Remember I had that class, Psych 101? I still remember what projection means."

He stiffened. "A little knowledge is a dangerous thing. I guess you'll just have to learn about him for yourself, but you're a hell of a slow learner. Just remember, *I* love you. Even I won't wait around forever, but some day you may come to see—"

The tune had ended. Kiersten walked away from him without another word or look, went straight to Nolan. Roger's face burned with fury. At his elbow, Carol said, "Do you want another drink, or will you dance with me?"

Roger got himself under control. She wasn't a bad piece, though far from Lister, and the admiration in her face was quite plain.

When they had danced for a brief time, he said, "I understand that you and your guy—what's his name?—Michael, weren't included on the recording with Miss Lister. That must be a little hard to take."

302

"Damn right," she said with acerbity, "especially for Michael. He's the one who got this group together, got his folks to put up money to give us a start, but Lister doesn't care for banjos. Michael could have been making a lot of money by now, in his dad's business . . ."

"It hardly seems fair."

"Yes, he's given up everything."

"And you gave up a family."

"Yes, I did, and this is what comes of it all. *We*'re literally kicked into the background, while Nolan and Rex and Kiersten run circles around *her*."

"Why don't you quit, leave them flat? Aren't there a lot of twosomes in folk music?"

"Oh no!" she laughed a little bitter laugh. "We've talked about it. That's exactly what they're after and we're not going to make things that easy."

There was a little silence and she looked up at him with a different kind of smile.

"I'm sure you're already egotistic as hell, but I have to tell you you're the absolutely best-looking thing I've seen in pants. No wonder Nolan never mentions you."

"Well, now," he said, smiling into her eyes, "I don't mind hearing that at all. You're not half bad yourself. Do you think—uh—Michael would mind very much if you and I took a little walk to my place? It's only a few blocks from here."

"Michael and I have always had a no-strings relationship. It's the only kind either of us could tolerate. Do you have some etchings you could show me?"

"Something like that," he said, laughing.

They got their coats, Carol explaining blandly that they were going for a little walk. Roger thanked Susan for her hospitality, in case, he said, he didn't come back up with Carol. He had a good deal of reading matter to get through before tomorrow, he said. He did not bother saying goodbye to his brother or Kiersten.

A little later, as he lay in bed with Carol, both of them fondling eagerly, he said, "Tell me, do Nolan and Kiersten have a no-strings relationship?"

She made a little derisive sound. "So far as I can tell, they're both *straight* as old strings."

"What about the black guy?"

"Him, too," she said scornfully. "Sometimes he has a girl, but if it came to messing around with someone else's, knowingly, that is, I don't think he'd consider it. You'd think all three of them came right

303

out of the Victorian Age. But do we have to keep talking about them?"

"Sweet cunt, we don't have to talk about anything."

The Stewards went on together for another year, with steadily increasing popularity, but things were never the same within the group. They bought a new bus and Rex allowed with no little irony that losing Security had made the difference.

Nolan was often away for brief periods, accompanying and arranging for other people. Rex was asked to join a recording studio orchestra in Nashville. Each of them wondered, from time to time, why they didn't just split up, end it, but the money was better than ever. They were coming to be the best-known folk group in the country and what they made in that third year was a fortune compared to the first. It was a meteoric rise and all of them knew it was chiefly due to Nolan's talents, but by spring Michael had begun putting him down onstage as well as off. In that spring they returned to New York to make another album, their last.

Susan Lister was in town again and invited them to stay with her, but Michael and Carol refused.

"I've wanted to write you," Susan bubbled eagerly to the other three, "but I decided to wait and see your faces. Guess who's playing Carnegie Hall in June?"

"We know," said Kiersten as they all congratulated her. "Word gets around. Folk musicians are really a small, close-knit, gossipy group."

"Oh, all right, so you knew," said Susan, laughing. "It will be my second time there, but it always seems like such an achievement. What you don't know is who my three accompanists are to be."

They all stared at her. Kiersten finally said,

"Rex and Nolan are very understandable, but not me. That makes no sense at all."

"Yes, it does. I want you and Nolan to do that 'web of birdsong' thing you do so well together. I want you to sing harmony with me on at least two songs. I want Rex to sing 'Pastures of Plenty,' I want the guys to do at least two instrumentals where they do all that trading around. I want—"

"Wait a minute," said Rex, raising a hand. "This is supposed to be Susan Lister at Carnegie Hall."

"Yes," she said with a little smug delight. "I may just retire after this one, make a record now and then, but it makes me a prima donna, doesn't it? It means I can have anything I want, doesn't it? Well, *doesn't* it?"

"Yes, *ma'am*," said Rex, grinning broadly. "Will you be wanting Lord Randal, too?"

They finished cutting The Stewards' album. Michael and Carol announced they would be leaving soon for Boston, where Michael's father had been waiting for Michael to join him in his brokerage firm. They were extremely vituperative about the Carnegie Hall concert. They demanded that the bus and a few instruments which had belonged communally to the group be turned over to them; also that they be allotted a larger share of the royalties from this last album, since the others would be going on in the music business, in which they had all been given a start by the largesse of Michael's father and Michael's uncle Alfie. Rex, Kiersten, and Nolan went along with their demands, then they left Uncle Alfie's agency for the one which handled Susan Lister and some other important people.

Within a few weeks, the new agent, Donatelli, asked Nolan if he would be willing, later in the summer, to go to Hollywood and work on the sound track for a movie, composing, arranging, and playing.

"Wow!" said Kiersten breathlessly.

Nolan had rushed to tell her so that, maybe, she would be the first to know. She held him close and pushed the hair off his forehead.

"Things are just about going too fast for me. You're going to do it, aren't you?"

"I'd like to try," he said a little dubiously. "You know what I keep thinking? That nothing that happens makes me any different. It seems it ought to, but I'm still the person that left Secesh, or maybe my personality dates back even farther than that."

She looked at him probingly. "Your modesty is real. You *are* still the same shy kid who played for Aunt Ginia that first time at Secesh so long ago."

"But don't you feel the same way about yourself? Don't you realize it sometimes, on stage, or when you see your picture on an album?"

"Of course I do, but *you*'re the big personality. Maybe all 'personalities' are just literally that, to themselves, the same people they've always been. I just don't see how you stay so—self-effacing. You're a beautiful person."

He kissed her. "You'll come with me, won't you?"

She looked away. "I—I don't know, Chappie. I've been talking with a friend of Susan's who teaches art here. I've been thinking that maybe I'll spend a part of the summer at Secesh, then come back here and go on with school. It—it seems to be time. I don't like New York, but this is a really fine school, there's so much more exposure to art here. There would be so many more job opportunities . . ."

His eyes had grown bleak. She went on chattering, feeling miserable, and very self-conscious.

"I've always told you I'd want to do something about art some day, just to prove I can. Surely you, of all people, should be able to understand that.''

"Yes, I do, but can't we . . . We haven't talked about marriage for a long time. Let's talk about it.''

"Let's not," she said gently. "What's the point, if I'm here and you're in California?'' She bit the inside of her lip, determined to show nothing of tears.

"Then I won't go.''

"Of course you'll go," she said, her eyelids pricking, a lump rising in her throat.

"And you'll stay here, or come back here.''

"Yes, but you won't be in California for so very long. Mr. Donatelli has already said he can get you all the work you can do, arranging and accompanying. Maybe then we could—''

"I don't want to stay here. I'm going to have to turn down most of that work. We could go on as a trio, you and Rex and I.''

"Chappie, we've all agreed we're sick to death of the road.''

He put his hand up to cover his eye, not aware of the movement.

She said gently, "Come to Secesh with me, for whatever part of the summer you can. It wouldn't be a rest, but it would be a change.''

"Does that have something to do with us, with our future together?''

"I—I think maybe it does.''

"Why?''

"Because, some day—I'd like us to have it. More than that, I want you and Dad to make up, the best you can.''

"Our marriage, sooner or later, is conditional on that?''

"I'd just like to see it happen, in case anything else should happen and it would be too late. Nolan, you're somebody in your own right now. Not that you haven't always been, but so many other people know it now. Can't you afford to forgive him?''

"I have forgiven him. I don't know when it happened, but that's all right now, for my part. If I went back, though, it would be like deliberately walking back into adolescence. I'll never be anything but a kid to him, a not-very-masculine, not-very-bright kid.''

"I don't mean you should go back to try to run the ranch now, not unless you want that. *Do* you want to go home, see them all—''

"Yes.''

"Then . . .''

"Kierstie, people talk a lot these days about identity. In spite of not feeling much different, I think I'm finding mine, but it's still shaky, still dependent on other people. I don't want to go back there, even for a little while, to be treated like—''

"If you feel your identity is shaky, it's because of things that happened to you as a kid, but it seems to me you've always had a very definite identity. Maybe it's stronger than you know. Roger told me, a long time ago, about some of the things that were done to you when you were a little boy."

"Roger lies a lot."

"Yes, but was he lying about your being knocked around all the time, about your mother pouring boiling water on you, about Clarence kicking you down the cellar stairs, about Darlene knocking you down so that you hit your head against a table and almost—?"

"I don't want to talk about those things. I stopped thinking of them a long time ago."

"They are true, aren't they? I've seen some of the scars. . . . How Clarence used to beat you with a belt and—"

"I don't want to talk about it."

"But, Chappie, why didn't you tell Mother and Dad? They'd have taken you away from them, seen to it—"

He said resignedly, "At first I thought a lot of kids must live that way. It seemed to be natural for some people. Then I didn't want to leave Grandpa. After he died there was still Roger, and there were the chances I had to play with bands, things I couldn't have done at Secesh. By that time I wasn't afraid of them any more, they were afraid of me. I was bigger and I—knew some things about them."

"Back in the beginning, when you realized it wasn't a natural way to live, did you blame Daddy for not just knowing? Kids so often think grownups are omniscient, that they should just *know*, without having to be told."

"Maybe I did feel that, a little, in the beginning. And . . . Price has always wanted a son. He had two, but neither of them worked out. I thought then, and I still believe, that I can't live up to what he wants, expects."

"Do you know what those things are?"

"Not exactly. Maybe he doesn't either—to be just like him, to behave—"

"Nolan, he's a very strong-minded, strong-willed man. He respects only people who are like him in that way, and you are. I don't think he'd respect you at all if he felt you were weakly trying to mold yourself in his image, not that you've ever done that, certainly. He may *think* that's what he wants, but he'd hate it. You can keep your identity very nicely, at the same time you two admit, tacitly or otherwise, that you love each other. It's there. Neither of you can hide it from me. Mother knows, and Fern. Be friends."

"I'd always disappoint him. I always have."

"Well, he's not one to shovel on praise, but *you* know if you're doing a job well, even a job of friendship. Don't tell me you're that dependent that you *don't* know. You've never been dependent in your life. That's why Roger is always at you. He's jealous; he wants you dependent, on him."

"Thank God, you haven't been nattering for Roger to be called here again."

"I'm sorry for him. I'd like to see you two . . . oh, I don't know what, but I think I've had enough of trying for that. Maybe he's getting—sicker, I don't know They've said that you weighed two pounds less, a third less than he did when you were born. I can almost see him, pushing you into a tiny corner of the womb, trying to absorb all the nourishment and you as well "

"Wombs don't have corners," he said rather absently.

She smiled. "Well, at any rate, there's nothing dependent about you, though he's always trying to force it."

"Price would like dependence, too "

"No, he wouldn't. If you saw him, he'd be bitter about these six years, but I think if you looked for them, you'd see glimmerings of his pride in you."

He smiled sardonically and there was a little silence before he said urgently, "Kierstie, bonnie Kierstie, I am dependent on you. I love you. I'll never love anyone else. It's a long time since we've talked about marriage. When I bring it up, you talk about Roger's id or something. Can't we talk about it? Have I done something? Is there—"

"It's nothing like that. I just don't think this is the time "

"You're talking about our breaking up, separating, whatever it's called, after all this time and I know I don't know all the reasons why Have I ignored you, things, been too busy to see . . . Look, I want you with me all the rest of my life. I had sort of believed you wanted that, too, that that was the way it was going to be."

She shivered at the words, the deep vibrant softness of his voice, but she could not yield, not with wanting to go on with school as she did, not with her distrustfulness, which she was certain at times, was completely unfounded. Things had to be worked out in her own mind and she would not trouble him with what was surely nothing at all.

She said, very softly, around the renewed lump in her throat, "I do feel the same, but not marriage yet, okay? People who are married should be together, sharing everything, making babies. We're just not ready for that, are we?"

He sighed, looking away from her, the clock on Susan's sideboard blurring a little. "Maybe not."

"I love you, Chappie, and I'll never stop either, but aren't you going to be late for rehearsal?"

20

On the morning before the concert at Carnegie Hall, Carol Pinelli called Kiersten at Susan's apartment. For just a moment Kiersten was hesitant, not recognizing the name or the voice, then she was ashamed. It had been only a few months since The Stewards had broken up, how could she *not* know?

"I'm back in New York," Carol was saying. "This is the big day, right? I've got a ticket. Listen, Kierstie, would you have lunch with me? I know you're busy, but a just-for-old-times'-sake, no-hard-feelings lunch? I'd like to see you again, talk to you."

Again Kiersten hesitated. They had rehearsed long and strenuously yesterday, vowing it would be their last rehearsal. Nolan was with the agent, Donatelli, about the movie thing. Susan had said she was going to stay in bed and read a gripping mystery novel to keep her mind occupied all day. Rex had gone out somewhere, even Lord Randal was out. Kiersten was nervous, and the empty-seeming apartment was bothering her.

"All right, Carol. Where and when?"

It was a small restaurant, inconspicuous and not so expensive. Carol was there before her.

"Want a drink? I'm having several."

"Thank you, no. Maybe some tomato juice."

"I guess you shouldn't drink on the big day, right?"

"Carol, you don't look well. Is something wrong?"

"You bet your biffie something's wrong. For starters, Michael's been drafted."

"Oh? I didn't know. He hasn't left already?"

"He left yesterday. We came down to New York for one last fling before he went to some hellhole down south for basic training. His old man's got a lot of clout. He did everything he could and still Michael had to go. He said to say he's sorry he had to miss the concert. I don't know what I'm going to do now. Max doesn't want me back, my husband, and I don't want him. I had some savings from that last year with the group and there'll be the record royalties, but that's sure as hell not enough to live on. Let me know if you know any rich old lechers. I will *not* clerk in a department store or wait tables. As a matter of fact, I thought your friend Susan might know of something I could get. You know, receptionist or something. She knows so many people."

"I can ask her."

Their food was put down before them. Each had ordered only a sandwich, but Carol kept signaling for fresh drinks for herself.

"I've thought of applying as flutist with some small symphony, but I really have had it up to here with music for the time being. I didn't ask you out for your pity or anything. I asked you, to see you again, and because of—a couple of things I thought you ought to know.

"We figured, Michael and me, that you and Nolan might be talking pretty seriously about marriage along about now, and there are these things . . . . Well, living together is one thing, but marriage is something else. At least it would be, for a good, clean-cut, wholesome girl like you. You'd only do it for keeps, wouldn't you? You know what they say: the wife is always the last to know, so I thought you ought to know *before* you're a wife."

Kiersten turned her water glass on the table, feeling herself flush. "Carol, I don't really want—"

"Honey, it started a long time ago, before the group really started; that is, the part we know about did. We came to know, in all that time on the road together, that you and Nolan had had some sort of understanding before you ever came east to Albion and, you being the person you are, we figured you were faithful to him through all that three years or whatever it was before you got back together.

"Well, faithful he was not. For instance, after the three of us, me and Michael and Nolan got together, there was this rich old dame with a place up on the hill above the school. Nolan was having it rough, I admit that, no money, couldn't find a job. I offered him a room at my folks' place. They'd have let him owe for a few weeks until he found something. But this old dame picked him up and kept him for quite a while. I mean *kept* him. He was on exhibit, probably at stud, for all her friends that came up from the city. She bought him clothes, led him around like a pet poodle on a leash, and you've always been so proud of his pride!"

Carol's voice was rising a little, derisive and scathing. "And there were other people he went with up there, girl students and, I've heard, boys. And then there was Rex."

"Carol, I want you to stop. I won't listen to any more . . ." But she was hearing Roger say, "Dire straits . . . I've heard it from the students . . ."

"Well, maybe those things shouldn't be counted against him. I mean you were very far away and everything. But it's just to set the scene. All those times he went away to work with other people, he never slept alone. Kiersten, you know what a grapevine this business has. *Everything* gets around. All of us have tried to protect you, but I think the time has come when you *have* to know. How do you think we, or he, got in so fast and so solid with Susan?"

"Stop it!"

"I can give you proof about those two. You remember when we all stayed at her place last year? Rex and Michael and I went out one night to fool around some bars. Susan didn't go. You didn't either You had a headache, remember? You looked absolutely lousy. Susan, good sweet Auntie Susan, said she was going to give you some strong medicine that would knock both you and the headache out. Well, when we came back, just as we got the door unlocked, we saw Nolan duck out of *her* room. You may think I'm making this up, may not want to believe it because of the way things got tense in the group there at the last, but you can ask Rex about this one. And then—"

Kiersten stood up shakily, her face feeling cold, drained of color. She opened her purse, put money on the table and walked out, with Carol calling after her.

She walked almost obliviously around the fume-filled streets for a long time. It wasn't true. None of it was true. Roger made up lies as facilely as another person would tell truth. Carol was violently jealous of their separate success. At last she remembered the night of the spaghetti supper at Susan's, when Roger and Carol had gone off together. Carol hadn't returned for a very long time. She was flooded with such vast relief that sudden tears filled her eyes. Of course, they were telling the same lies.

She realized then that she was lost and asked a policeman the fastest way to get back to the street where Susan's apartment was. "The best way would be to take a taxi," he said, looking at her rather strangely. "You're a long way from home."

She did find a cab. It was after four o'clock. None of them knew about her going out. They would be worried.

Nolan met her at the door, his face very sober. "We couldn't imagine what had happened to you."

"I—I decided to go out for some lunch, and then I got walking around until I got lost. Isn't that crazy? Today of all days . . . Chappie, what is it? Something has happened   ?"

313

He put an arm about her, led her into the living room, and drew her down on a sofa.

"Anne called about two hours ago. Hugh's been killed."

"Oh no!" she said, her hand going to her mouth. She was conscious, as if she were two people, that that was what people in books and movies always said and did at such a time, but it was such a natural reflex. "What happened?"

"He was in a helicopter that took off from the base on Guam. Something went wrong. It caught fire, exploded in the air, and fell into the sea. There were no—no bodies to be recovered. They're holding a memorial service on Tuesday. I said we'd be there."

Kiersten was sobbing now, holding onto him almost violently. It wasn't just Hugh; it was all of today, all of a lot of things from the past.

Nolan let her cry, vaguely surprised that Hugh had meant this much to her.

"Kierstie," he said at last, very gently, "we've got the show tonight . . ."

"Oh God, I can't."

"Please?"

"Oh, Chappie, just today I've come to hate this crappy business more than I can tell you. I hate 'the show must go on.' I can't live like that any longer."

"Just one more time. I swear no one will ask it of you again if you don't—"

"Don't swear!" she said, pulling away from him, suddenly more than a little hysterical. "I never know when I can believe you anyway."

"Kierstie, I don't—"

Susan had come in. She stroked Kiersten's hair gently with one hand, holding a glass and something else in the other.

"Here are a couple of tranquilizers, love. They may make you drowsy, but they'll help you get through—"

"No!" Kiersten almost screamed. "I don't want your damned pills. I'll do it. I'll do the goddamn show, just leave me alone. All of you, leave me alone!"

She locked herself in the bedroom she and Nolan shared and finally stopped crying. Poor Hugh. Poor Penny, who had always loved and looked up to her smug badgering older brother. But these tears were sham tears, not really for Hugh at all, or only a little perhaps. Strangely, when she had seen Nolan, touched and been touched by him, she had gone back to believing every lie anyone had ever told about him. But they weren't true, they couldn't be true!

She stared at herself in the mirror: red swollen eyes, drained white face. Could all this be covered with makeup? More important, could she trust herself to give her best tonight? Most important, could she trust Nolan? About anything? She knew only one way to try to handle the problem: directly. Some time, some time soon, when there was privacy, she would have to ask him. She had no choice. Surely those things were all filthy, slimy lies, but they would slither around in the bottom of her mind until she *knew*. But *would* she know when he told her?

Finally, she came timidly out of the bedroom, apologized to Nolan and Susan, tried to eat some of the light supper Susan's maid had prepared for them. Then she was standing with the three of them offstage, Nolan holding her hand, looking at her with concern, and she heard David Harris make the announcement which ended: "This performance is being recorded so that you may, in a few months, purchase it for a lifetime of memories, with you, as audience, playing a part. And now, we proudly present, in concert at Carnegie Hall, Susan Lister and Friends."

Kiersten was not nervous. It was as if she had in fact taken some drug which dulled the senses and at the same time brought a strong false sense of euphoria. She heard every note, watched and listened to the others with great pride. When it was time for her to sing with Susan, she went through words and harmonies flawlessly. They had rehearsed the songs so many times, partly because of her own nervousness, that she could have done them in her sleep. The song with Nolan was not quite so easy, the love song, which meant a great deal to them. Didn't it have special meaning for him, too? The thing to do was not think, to sing the words as words only. They got through it, to enthusiastic applause.

Kiersten saw, heard, and felt the audience participate with a rather boisterous joy when they were invited to do so. She saw them mesmerized by Nolan's telling of the story of Brigid Flynn. She saw them listen to Susan's singing, carried from emotion to emotion by the wonderful power and versatility of her voice. She saw them lean forward, amazed and delighted by the numbers wherein Nolan and Rex exchanged instruments or picked up others from the floor, virtually without missing a beat. She heard the final applause, joined in the two encores in which the audience was also asked to take part.

Again, there was mobbing backstage. Roger and Carol were among the many friends, acquaintances, and strangers. Susan Lister and her friends did not notice that they had come back together.

David Harris was giving them what he called a monstrous party, to wait for the reviews in the morning papers.

Nolan said quietly aside to Susan, "I'm taking Kiersten back to the apartment, all right?"

"Of course. I'll come with you if you think I could be of any help."

"No, I hope she can just get to sleep soon. That seems like the best thing."

"Yes, it does. There are pills in my night table, if you can get her to take one or two. You were both absolutely fantastic."

Kiersten clung to him, shivering, as they lay in bed together. It was a very warm night, but Nolan got up and turned off the room's air-conditioning.

"Do you think we did well?" she asked, holding him again.

"Yes. Will you take a sleeping pill? You look so tired."

"No, I just want to be—with you. Thank you for coming away with me. You should be at the party."

"You know I've never cared about that kind of thing."

Well, here they were, in privacy, but she couldn't ask him now. Oh God, not now.

"I don't think I ever got round to telling you, Anne wished us well and she said they wished they could be here."

"I sang in Carnegie Hall," said Kiersten dully, but marveling a little. "I wonder if it will ever seem like more than a dream?"

"Well," he said uncertainly, "it's a pretty special thing, but I guess, underneath, it's not that different from any other concert. We've had plenty of those. You're still shivering. Will you drink something, some liquor, or something hot? I could—"

"Chappie, make love to me."

"Oh, my bonnie girl, you're so tired. Something's bothering you, and I don't think it's just Hugh. Won't you tell me?"

"No, just please . . ."

"You ought to be trying to get some sleep."

"You don't want to make love?" Her voice was small and tight.

"Of course I want to. Can't you feel that I've been wanting it all this while? I only thought—"

"Please. Let's not think. Do everything to me. Make me your slave. Make me forget . . ."

"About Hugh?"

"Yes. About the whole world."

Much later, she said a little dazedly, "It's silly I know, but I'm so afraid of flying in those little planes between Denver and Hurleigh."

"This is what I'll do in the morning. I'll see if we can get reservations on the night flight tomorrow. For myself, I don't seem to mind flying so much when it's dark. I'll see if I can get us into first class. There's more room there and less people. You don't feel quite so hemmed in. If we go on that flight, we'll only fly as far as Denver, then we'll get a rental car for the rest of the trip. How does that seem?''

"Yes," she said, "it would be wonderful to be driving in the mountains again. It must be beautiful at Secesh right now, with the spring just really coming."

"Are you going to take all your things and just stay a while?"

"I hadn't thought so much about it, but I guess that's what I'll do. Tomorrow they're having pre-registration for the art school. I think I'll sign up for that."

"All right. Now will you let me find a sleeping pill for you?" She nodded meekly.

When he had brought it, he said gently, "Kierstie, please tell me what's wrong, besides about Hugh. Did something happen to you today, or . . ."

"I don't want to talk about it yet," she said, looking away across the dimly lighted room. "I'll tell you some time."

"I love you."

"Oh, Chappie, and I love you."

After a time, she said drowsily, "Will you try to talk with Daddy now? Now that Hugh won't be coming back?"

"I don't know. Maybe."

She slept finally, and Nolan slept for a time. The small noises of Susan and Rex returning to the apartment woke him. He slipped carefully from the bed and put on a robe.

"Sorry if we woke you," said Susan with consternation when he appeared. "Is Kiersten all right?"

"She's sleeping now."

Rex was holding newspapers in front of Nolan's face. He had to push the sheets away a little to focus on the print. He began to smile.

"Not bad, huh?" said Rex.

"Not bad by half," Nolan answered.

"I'm so proud of all of us," said Susan enthusiastically, but Nolan thought she didn't look so very happy.

Rex said, "I've got to take his lordship out for a walk, and then I'm going to sleep for about a solid week. You know, Chap, that studio orchestra offer I got here? I think I may just take it. I don't care much for New York, but it might be interesting for a while. It seems to be time I grew up and settled down."

Susan smiled at him. "Could it be that Ellen Wilsmore is helping you decide about that? You seemed to have quite a lot to talk with her about, tonight and on several other occasions I've noticed."

"Oh, you never know what may influence fate," Rex said breezily and went out with the dog.

Susan said, "I've had too much to drink and I want coffee. Have some? First, let me get out of these clothes."

He stood looking through the papers until she came from her bedroom, a little of the bosom of a frilly mauve night gown showing at the opening of her belted silk robe, then he followed her into the kitchen.

They talked about the concert and the reviews until the coffee was poured and they sat down across from each other.

"Is something wrong?" he asked.

Susan rubbed at scratchy eyes.

"Something over a year ago, at about this time in the morning, I told you something I know you've never breathed to anyone, but tonight at David's party someone called me a queen in a very nasty way and I heard the words 'bull dyke' from two other people's conversations. Maybe I'm just being paranoid, but it's upset me—a lot. I haven't had an—affair for more than two years now. Despite all this 'come out of the closet' stuff, I know it would affect my career—and me. I don't think I could stand it, knowing everyone knew. I think I will give no more concerts for a while, except for a few that have been firmed up. Maybe I'll do another album in the winter. I want to stay here and try therapy again. If you could know what it did to me, to see Kierstie hurt and crumpled and crying this afternoon . . . Please don't be concerned. I'd never . . . never . . ."

"I know that," he said gravely.

Her hands trembled as she held the coffee cup between them.

He said, "What makes you think people are talking about you? It could be anybody."

"The girl—the last girl—was there tonight, at the concert and at the party. She was very bitter when we—broke up. I think she got the idea that because Kiersten and I sang together we were . . . You see, she and I used to sing together sometimes, though not on recordings and onstage. She called me 'queen.' I know it's usually a term used for male homosexuals, but the way she said it, 'You're truly the *queen* of folk music now.' "

"I'm sorry."

She tried to smile. "On that same night over a year ago, I told you you were a good listener. You still are, and I know you have troubles of your own, besides your cousin's death. What will you do after the memorial service?"

"Come back here for a while, to work on that album with good old John Sage—"

"Isn't he a fun old sweetie," she said, smiling now.

"Yes, but it's hard enough to keep him sober and remembering what we've done the day before. After that, I guess I'll go on out to the coast.''

"And Kiersten?''

"She says she's going to pre-register for art school today, then spend the summer at the ranch.''

"I rather thought you two would be marrying when the road work was over.''

"Well, it seems we're not going to be,'' he said with a hint of anger. "I guess I'll go and try to get a little more sleep now.''

He stood. "Thanks, Susan, for everything you've done for us.''

"It was your own merit,'' she said warmly, also standing. "And why does this sound like goodbye?''

Nolan thought bleakly that his and Kiersten's lovemaking had also felt like goodbye. What had he done?

He said, trying for lightness, "We're going to get a flight for Denver tonight. I'll see you when I come back to work with Mr. Sage. Kierstie's going to be here for school and if she won't marry me I think I'll be trying to find places other than New York to work.''

Susan put her arms around him. "I'm so sorry. You two were meant for each other. Surely it will work out eventually.''

Abruptly, Susan began to cry. Her arms tightened about him, her beautiful head lay against his shoulder. She was sobbing loudly, speaking unevenly, like a little girl.

"Chappie, you're not going there—back home—to stay? I mean, with your cousin dead, does it mean . . . ?''

"I don't know what it means, Susan,'' he said, somewhat taken aback, stroking her back awkwardly.

"But you've said ranch life may be what you want,'' she said accusingly. "How can I bear to lose you forever? You're so good for me, and it would be such a God-awful waste. I'd hoped we might stay together, now that the group's broken up.''

"We've just been talking about the other commitments I have. I couldn't stay at Secesh now, even if I wanted to. I—''

"But it *is* what's in your mind, isn't it?''

"I don't know what I've got in mind,'' he said, confused and, it seemed, unjustly angry with her.

"I've come to need you, to count on you so,'' she cried miserably, still accusing.

Neither of them heard the soft closing of a door. Gradually, Susan quieted. She drew back a little and looked up at him shyly through long wet lashes.

"I'm sorry,'' she said sadly. "I haven't behaved so childishly in years. I'm just overwrought by tonight, by . . . please understand.

You've been such a good friend to me and you're so damned talented. I really wanted you to work with me and it would be such a waste, besides my own selfish reasons.''

"I—appreciate your concern," he said rather stiffly.

"But not my outbursts," she said, trying to smile. "I am sorry."

She took a step forward and they were in each other's arms again. She kissed him lightly on the mouth.

"Of course you must do what seems best, best for you and for Kiersten. It's just that I've come to think of you as—as a brother. I always wanted a brother. I think of you, depend on you, whether you're right here or not. I wish you nothing but good things, whatever they may be. Goodnight, love, but not goodbye."

In their bedroom, Nolan saw by the hall light that Kiersten was huddled small on her side of the bed, her back to his. He closed the door without sound, got cautiously into bed. Tentatively and very gently, he put out a hand to touch her shoulder. She scarcely seemed to breathe and felt tense under his touch. Softly, he spoke her name. No response. She must be sleeping, but it seemed a strange taut sleep and it worried him. What was it that troubled her so deeply? He must know before they got back to Secesh. After that there would not likely be much opportunity for any private discussion. He withdrew his hand from her shoulder, suddenly overcome by exhaustion and a depression so deep that he hardly seemed capable of movement. All right. So much for Carnegie Hall, maybe for all of the past three years that truly mattered. He turned heavily onto his other side and fell, finally, into a dull unrestful sleep.

Kiersten was still awake, her breathing made ragged by hopeless tears as Nolan's breathing grew slow and deep. "How can I bear to lose you? . . . I'd hoped we might stay together . . ." She had seen them in the bright kitchen light, standing there in each other's arms, dressed in their robes. She hadn't been able to see Nolan's face, but she could see Susan's profile, suffused in tears, could clearly hear her sobs and her words.

So it was true, all of it was true. How could she bear to face him, talk to him again? But it must be faced, he must tell her, honest at last, all of it. That seemed only fair to both of them, to have it all in the open, to leave no doubt in his mind as to why she was deciding . . . Susan's damned sleeping pill had not, evidently, been as strong as the two of them were counting on, but *he* was certainly sleeping now, seemingly untroubled by remorse, guilt, or any such feelings. The sleep of the just, she thought with a fury so sudden that she almost struck out at his back. She wanted to hate him. She *would!* She clung to that. It stopped her tears, made her cold and stiff and silent, anger overlaying the ineffable pain. Finally, after daylight had come, her swollen eyes closed and she slept again, heavily, borne down by weariness and the unbearable weight of her anguish.

They had a drink at the airport bar and Kiersten had another, a double, as soon as the stewardesses started to serve things. Neither of them wanted the snacks that were offered. The drinks relaxed Kiersten so that she stopped clenching her hands on the arms of her seat and being startled by every small bump of turbulence and every footstep. They were silent for a long while. Nolan had a briefcase with him and might have worked on some of the Sage arrangements, but he felt this was not the time. He sat in the window seat and occasionally looked down at the lights which seemed to fly past on the ground. Kiersten sat with her clammy hands twisting together in her lap. The first-class cabin was less than half full, and they were well away from other passengers.

Finally, she said tautly, "Nolan, there are some things I've heard and others that I've . . . I have to ask you some questions."

"All right," he said, with a tensing feeling of fear.

"In your last year at Albion, did you—live with someone?"

He put his hands over his face and, after a time said huskily, "Yes. Kierstie, I'm so ashamed about that—that episode. I hoped you'd never have to know. I was so tired. I don't mean to make excuses. There are none. It was the most humiliating, degrading time of my life."

"Did you have affairs with students or other people?" She was working to make her voice neutral. It was very small and he leaned closer to hear. She drew away.

"No."

"Men?"

"God no! Except for—that woman, there's never been anyone but you."

"What about Susan?"

"Where have you come up with all this?"

"For one thing, I had lunch with Carol on the day of the concert, yesterday, though it seems a much longer time ago. What about—other people when you went away from us to work?"

"No, Kierstie, I swear—"

"I told you before, don't swear to me unless it's the real truth."

"But I'm not. I wouldn't—"

"What about Susan? You didn't answer that."

"No."

"That first time we stayed at her apartment, Carol said that she

321

and Michael and Rex had been out late. I had a headache and didn't want to go. You stayed, too. Susan gave me a pill that she said would knock me out and it did. Do you remember that?''

''Only vaguely.''

''They were coming in late, and just as they got in, they saw you duck out of Susan's room and back into ours.''

His face had flushed and then paled. His hand was covering his right eye, but he looked at her very steadily with the left one

''Yes, I do remember that. I got up to go to the bathroom I'd been looking through those folk magazines, and I'd come across a song I thought Susan might like to do. I saw under her door that her light was still on, and I went in to show it to her. It was 'Hills of the Border,' and she decided we ought to work it up.''

Kiersten was silent, but finally said bitterly, ''I always thought I'd know if you were lying to me.''

''What the hell makes you think I'm lying now?'' he demanded angrily.

''Because last night, or rather this morning, *I* had to go to the bathroom, and I saw you and Susan with your arms around each other in the kitchen, kissing.''

''Oh, Kierstie, that was . . . Susan's not even   ''

But then he closed his mouth in a hard, grim, straight line He would *not* tell her. If she wouldn't trust him, believe his word   He hadn't felt so near tears in years. What could he do to make her believe, *know*, that there had never been anyone else? Deedee didn't count. She had been a folly of his youth that made him want to crawl under the seat now. But he had answered her honestly about Deedee. Even if he told her Susan's secret, he knew, somehow, that she wouldn't believe him.

Kiersten reached up and snapped off her reading light. There was now no illumination near them. Silent tears were spilling down her cheeks. Nolan's face was turned toward the window He had admitted the one thing. How could she be sure at least some of the others were not true, when she had seen him herself, with Susan? After a long time, when she could make her voice approximate calm, she said, ''I don't want to rent a car in Denver. I'd rather take one of the small planes and have this trip over as quickly as possible ''

He made no response.

She got up and moved to another aisle seat, asking a passing stewardess for another drink.

21

They did not speak again. The family and friends seemed not to notice. After the memorial service in the packed little church at Fairweather, where Anne sometimes went, a crowd of people came back to Secesh to prepare and eat a funeral meal. Penny and Chris and the little girls were there. Chris would have to return to his law office soon, but Penny planned to stay on for a while with the children.

Kiersten would not look at Nolan. She was afraid of his eyes. After her tears, after the liquor had worn off following the flight, a great and fierce anger had begun to burn in her. It was better than the scalding hurt, and she nurtured it.

Before the large meal had really ended, Nolan took the little girls, Mary and Emmy, outside. They did not understand grief and sorrow and had remained hushed and bewildered. He took them down among the buildings, where they made the acquaintance of Butch and Yola's two small sons.

Butch was working in the large shop, welding some part of the ditcher. He came out, removing his goggles, delighted to see Nolan. They sat on an old worn log, smoking, talking quietly, watching the children.

"The spring was late coming this year," Butch said worriedly. "We're behind with everything, but I guess that's nothing new. There's just one hand in the bunkhouse now besides Reuben. We're really going to be hurting if we don't get some more help soon."

He lit another cigarette. "So you're going to Hollywood?"

"Yes, in a couple of weeks."

"We've got all your records. I don't mean just The Stewards', but all the ones where you play for other people. I can't wait until the Carnegie Hall one is released. Yola and I enjoy the records a lot. Even Aaron knows the words to some of the songs. I think he's going to be a musical kid. Too early to tell about Billy yet. I play sometimes still

323

around the house, or for a square dance or something, when there's somebody to play with me. Terry Ellenbogen's been here a lot to play summers. He's doing his internship now, and won't be around this year, I guess.''

"What kind of doctor's he going to be?"

"Last I heard, a woman's doctor. What do you call 'em? Some string of letters.''

"Is he married?"

"No, sometimes he brings a girl when he comes home for a short visit, but I don't think it's ever been the same one. The Park's changed quite a lot, you know, road paved almost as far as the top of Fairweather Hill, high school kids getting bussed to Fairweather. We get a lot more hunters and fishermen in than we used to. Good for business down at Mills Crossing, but not much else. Damn nuisance for us, to say the least. Old man Gunnar Nelson, down the road, has got his place leased to some sportsmen's association. Secesh is posted all over the place, but we can't keep 'em out. They say we have to give access to the national forest land. Price don't go along with that, but we put up more signs. They go right through, leave gates open, let the stock get mixed up, cut fences when they take the notion. We put locks on the gates, they shoot 'em up. Somebody shot two heifers last fall, just wounded one of 'em, but she couldn't get up. It must have been a week before anybody came on her. Pitiful.

"I worked a couple of weeks last fall for Shadow River, the dude ranch. Elmer Strathensberg, remember him? He and his wife are running the place, though it's owned by somebody back east. We'd sorted and vaccinated here, were waiting to ship. It was one of our easy times. Elmer asked me to guide some hunting parties. Eastern flatlanders, Jesus! You do everything from wiping their noses to pointing their guns. It was good money, the best I've ever made. They tip like money was going out of style, but Christ! . . . Strathensbergs run boat trips, too, summers. They go down through Spanish Canyon, which the dudes think is real white-water tripping, and down into the lake where they fish.

"Has anybody told you the government wants to turn Kilrayne Canyon and everything west of it across the range into a wilderness area? I think it's a good idea. Before that, four or five years ago, they were talking about trying to build a four-wheel-drive road up the Shadow through there. As it is now, we can't keep people off that land that belongs to Secesh, right at the mouth of the Canyon. A wilderness area might not change that much, but it sure as hell would be better for us than the four-wheel-drive idea.

"Roger and Kiersten back here for the summer, are they?"

"Kiersten is. I suppose Roger is, too."

Nolan had deliberately not let Roger know that he and Kiersten were taking the night flight out of New York. Roger had come on the next day, making two trips to the Hurleigh airport necessary for the people at Secesh. Had Roger been talking to Kiersten? Is that where she . . . ?

"What?" he said, having missed Butch's last question.

"I say is Roger going to school the rest of his life?"

"I think he's got a year or two more for his doctorate, but then he plans to teach, so it sort of amounts to the same thing, I guess."

"Well, he's been here just about every summer. People are impressed with what he's doing, whatever it is, but he sure as hell don't do much about Secesh. Anne and Fern treat him like a guest, while Anne goes to the hay fields and he sits on his butt, studying."

The children came up to them then. Billy, just toddling, and with a dirt-smeared face from falling down, clung to Nolan's knee and gave him a wide, wet, gap-toothed smile. Nolan picked him up and Aaron, just four, squeezed onto his lap as well.

"You can't!" cried Mary indignantly at the boys. "He's *our* uncle Nolan, aren't you?"

"No, ours," said Aaron, ensconcing himself more firmly. And Billy said, "Unca Nowan," looking up into his face.

"I'll be everybody's Uncle Nolan," he offered with a smile that Butch found sad somehow.

Nolan reached out, the boys on his lap, and tickled the two little girls.

"Billy walks in cow poo," announced Emmy, giggling.

"You boys go on and play," Butch said firmly. "Show the girls the baby chicks. And, Aaron, if Billy crawls through any more corral bars, you're both going to be in trouble. You're supposed to watch out for him."

They went away, all talking at once, trying to impress one another.

"Kids like you," Butch said. "You ought to marry and settle down. I guess about the luckiest day of my life—or night—was when we stole that cream-colored Cadillac."

Reuben came along, looking smaller and ornerier than ever, his body twisted slightly with arthritis.

"Well, towhead, I've not had much of a chance to say nothin' to you. No, don't stand up, for Chrissake. When people sets, I look bigger. Ever' damn kid on this place outgrows me, even some a the girls. What are you aimin' to do with yourself now? Ready to come back here an' try to make a hand? I expect we could git you in shape in, say, five, ten years."

The hand he rested briefly on Nolan's shoulder was small, hard, and dry, gnarled like a piece of leather left a long time out in the weather.

"I'm under contract now," Nolan said, "some records and a movie—"

Reuben stopped him with a gesture, unimpressed. "Ought to be under contract to your own home place, to your daddy. Kids these days got no sense a responsibility, no roots. Truth is, they just plain got no sense. You see that blue roan mare yonder in the corral? You used to be about half good with a rope. She's got a wire cut on her off hind leg an' I know I can't corner the ole whore to doctor her. See can you rope her for me."

Chris Bergen came down from the house at this point.

He said, "Penny and I were wondering where the girls got to." He shook hands with Butch and Reuben.

"We're looking out for them," said Nolan, pointing out the children as they came around the corner of the chicken house.

"I appreciate it," said Chris warmly. "This is hard for Penny. Kids this age don't understand and shouldn't have to try to. Listen, I'm driving back to Denver tomorrow. I really have to go, though I'd give a lot to spend a few more days here with Penny. You're welcome to a ride. Roger will be coming along, too."

"You mean he ain't gonna set here on his asshole all summer?" demanded Reuben.

"He's going to work at a camp for disadvantaged children, he says," answered Chris.

"I guess I'd better go while there's an offer," said Nolan. "Thank you."

Chris said, "I'll go back to the house now. Thanks again for looking after the girls."

"I'll get the mare for you, Reuben," offered Butch, moving toward the corral.

"Won't neither," snapped the old man, thrusting the rope at Nolan and spitting tobacco juice. "I want to see if this here famous musician even remembers how to make a loop."

Nolan took the rope and Reuben went on, "I recollect when you was a little bitty kid, no bigger'n that oldest gal yonder, you used to tell me how you was goin' to be a famous rodeo roper, nothin' but a champion. You remember that? Now look at them hands. You couldn' hold a sick cat on a rope, less'n you took sixteen dallies an' had a strong horse."

Nolan shook the rope out and made his loop. Butch thought his eyes looked sad, until he made them go flat and empty in that way he had.

He missed with two throws, Reuben smirking, grunting derisively. Then he caught the mare, and the children, attracted by the action, gave a cheer.

"She's ringy," Reuben warned him, getting on with it. "Come in here an' help me while I git some medicine on that cut."

"Let me do that," said Butch. "He hasn't changed his clothes."

"You watch the young 'uns," snapped Reuben. "He ain't goin' to come all over a damned dude on me."

They went into the corral and tied the mare to the fence, leaving her left side exposed. She kicked out with the sore leg.

"Watch 'er now," cautioned Reuben. "Keep 'er still. Damned bitch!"

"I don't remember this one," said Nolan.

"Course you don't. When have you been around? This here is the last foal ole Dearie dropped. She ain't got the manners her mother had, but she's right young yet. Price bred Dearie to that roan stud Anders Ellenbogen has got that last time. I told him not to. Still think it's a mistake. That stud's too mettlesome by half. He calls this one Lass, says she's makin' up to be a fine cow horse, says she'll drop fine foals. Stand still, you no-account . . . I recollect your great-grandma, Miss Mercy, was doctorin' a horse one time, a brown geldin', they called him Fox, kind of a red brown. He kicked her halfway acrost a corral, little bitty woman, but she was a good animal doctor, an' seen they behaved, too. Soon as she got her breath back, she come at him with a piece of corral pole, 'bout two feet long. She got the doctorin' done. Didn't have no rope neither. That was some kinda lady. Always called the corrals an' pastures paddocks. She was raised up with five brothers on her pa's place off yonder in Australia . . . . Let 'er loose now; I reckon that'll do."

When Nolan turned, Price was standing outside the fence. He could see Butch and the four children down by Butch's house, where Yola had come out and was changing Billy's droopy diaper.

Reuben said to Price, "Looks some better. Scabbed over too quick to begin with was the main trouble."

He limped off to return the medicine to the tackroom.

A lengthy silence fell. Price and Anne had talked last night, or Anne had. One thing she had said was, "Ask him, Price, it won't kill you to let him know he's needed—wanted here. You do want him here, don't you? Well, *don't* you?"

"He knows where home is," Price had said curtly.

"He does *not!*" she cried. "He knows you've been disappointed in him, thinks he can never come up to your expectations."

"You and Kiersten have been having a talk, I'd guess."

"Yes, we have."

"I'd not have them living together under this roof without—"

"He's got contracts to fulfill until some time in the fall. He'll be leaving again right away. Kierstie seems to have her heart set on that art school in New York. They wouldn't be together. Besides, I think there's . . . something wrong between them. They've broken up or—don't you notice how they avoid each other?"

"Is she pregnant?"

"Oh, Price, of course not. Girls don't have to have that happen to them these days."

"Well, she ought to be. They ought to be married and—right about this thing, after all this time."

"Maybe they should, but it doesn't look to me as if they have any intention of it and you're just avoiding the subject. *Ask* Nolan—"

"And have him say no—again?"

"He never has really said no. There were things he wanted to do first. You two are so much alike I don't think I can stand it. Suppose you'd felt *your* father, or grandfather, didn't want to set eyes on you again?"

"They had no cause . . . . No, he wants to be renowned, play at Carnegie Hall." The tone was bitter.

"Can't you even give him his due in that?"

"Why would somebody who plays at Carnegie Hall want to bury himself in a God forsaken—"

"Price," she said intently, her eyes filling with tears, "it's six years since he's been home. If you don't talk to him like another human being, like somebody you care about, he may never come again. Maybe he doesn't want the ranch, but the finding out won't kill you. It would be better than not knowing at all, wouldn't it? If you won't talk to him and we never see him again, we'll both know whose head that will be on."

"He's—what?—twenty-four? He can make up his own mind without any special talk. That's what you've always told me, isn't it? About the lot of them? Let them make up their own minds."

"But he can't—he shouldn't have to try—without having all the real facts. If he thinks you don't want him back, that you have nothing but scorn for what he's done, what he is . . ."

"Did you see his hands? Soft as a woman's except where he's got callouses from those instruments. Nearly as bad as Roger's have always been."

"Oh, for God's sake!" she had cried and turned her back on him.

After a little he had tried to question her about some of the arrangements for Hugh's memorial, but she would make no answer,

328

the first time in their life together that she had put them beyond speaking.

Price was filling his pipe now, by the corral, giving careful attention to it. Nolan slid the extra bar, lit a cigarette.

"Those things cause cancer. It's proved."

"So do a lot of other things."

"I see you can still throw a rope."

"If I have enough tries. In a closed place."

He got the pipe going, sucked at it energetically. The boy would not look him straight in the eye. He saw him raise his right hand toward his face, not the hand that was holding the cigarette, then let it drop.

"It's bad with Hugh gone," Price said and cleared his throat. "My grandparents, nor Dad either, ever dreamed there might be a chance of Secesh going out of the family."

His father was what? Nolan calculated, fifty-two? He had aged. Six years had made a difference. He was gray at the temples, with streaks of it running all through his dark brown hair. When he's all gray, Nolan thought, he's going to be the exact image of Great-grandpa Price in the portrait, except for his eyes. Lines were etched more deeply than he remembered around this Price's mouth and eyes, his craggy face seemed more weathered. Nolan had noticed him wearing glasses for reading. They stuck out of his jacket pocket now, in their case. He, too, had not yet changed clothes after coming home from church.

Price said tonelessly, "I won't live forever."

No answer. The boy looked older, more than twenty-four. There were deep shadows under his eyes which looked like permanent fixtures. As their glances met and passed on, Price saw the nervous twitching of the lower right eyelid. Those gray eyes, just like Grandmother's, Price couldn't recall that hers had ever tried to avoid issues, nor had he ever seen them blank out in that way Nolan had, as if he had gone away from behind his eyes.

"There's Kiersten," Price said almost carelessly, but with a faint note of sadness. "She's got no Savage blood, but she loves the place as if she had. In her time she may be almost as strong as my grandmother, in her way, but I can't see her handling things alone. Anyway, she's got her heart set on this art business. Who's to know what may come of that? Roger sure as hell doesn't give a damn about the place, except as somewhere to rest up after his labors at learning. Penny loves Secesh, but they'd never live here."

Still no answer. Nolan looked at the flame of his cigarette, saw that his hand was trembling a little and bent down to stub out the fire carefully.

Price was getting angry, but he said, almost levelly, "Maybe it'll turn out in the end, the way Hugh always wanted. A family corporation, with never a Savage on the place."

Nolan straightened up and they looked at each other searchingly Now it was Price who finally turned his eyes away under the intense scrutiny.

Nolan said very softly, the faintest smile barely curving his lips, "You're planning to die? At fifty-two?"

"No," said Price, feeling defensive and hating it. "I've got a good many years left, but arrangements have to be made."

"Because I could never come back here and learn everything all over again on my own."

"Reuben's free with advice."

The smile gone, he said almost inaudibly, "I don't want to learn from Reuben."

A silence, in which they both looked up at the close ridge of the western mountains. The stiff breeze seemed a little lost, uncertain, gusting from first one direction then another.

Price cleared his throat. "By the looks of those clouds around old Warrior, we might get a shower later on. We could use a good rain right now."

Nolan nodded soberly.

"What do you think of my Lass?"

Nolan turned to find he meant the mare.

"Well, I always favored geldings for working, but . . ."

"Ranger's still around. He's not down here, but up with the other horses, you know. He'd be about ten now, wouldn't he?"

"More like twelve."

"We've not used him much these years. There's a good crop of young ones, especially a strawberry four-year-old that I mean to work with this summer. He's got no name yet, though I expect Penny and Kiersten will come up with names for everything while they're here "

After another silence, Price said, tightly again, "They tell me you're under contract."

"Yes."

"Binding?"

"A contract is always binding to me—my word is."

"Till when?"

"What?"

They were looking at each other again, and Price was sure the boy was being deliberately difficult now.

"How long do the contracts last?"

"Till October, then I've got a record to do in February or March."

Price grunted. "Right at mustering time, then again, maybe when the calving's begun."

"There's the haying and the winter feeding."

"Well, yes, there's always that. And other years to come."

"I might want to go away sometimes, in those years, to cut an album with someone."

"I'd hope it wouldn't be at the height of—anything."

"We'd try to work it out."

"We've got no spotlights here, no applause, not many females to keep your damned hair pushed out of your eyes."

"No."

"You'd settle for that, after all the fame and fortune and—"

"There's not been much fortune, and fame can burn out overnight. Secesh will always be here."

"You'd settle for Secesh?"

"I would, Price."

He added quickly, "With shares for the others, I mean and—"

"Yes."

"And I make the decisions, until *I* know I'm too old for it."

"I thought that."

They reached out suddenly, taking each other's hands spontaneously, holding very hard and still.

"You'll marry one day and have lots of sons." It was a kind of command. "The place needs a lot to choose from for going on in the family. Young ones have a way of being strong-willed, going off on their own. You'll know how that is for yourself one day. You'd best bring those little girls along now. Penny wants them to have a nap, with some of the extra people out of the house."

Nolan collected Mary and Emmy and brought them, very unwilling, to their mother. He left then, by the door at the top of the house, and walked far up Cranky Creek. So you could go home again. Sometimes his eyes blurred. Secesh. A little music now and then. If only Kierstie, Kierstie . . .

When he finally came back, an early dusk was falling, spreading out from the clouds that roiled around the western mountains. He came in the same way he had left. Bedroom doors were closed, the house quiet except for a faint rattling from the kitchen. He walked down the short flights of steps and the noise grew louder. It was Fern in there, of course.

"Just warming up a few things for supper," she told him busily. "You, for one, ate almost nothing at dinnertime. Has your daddy talked to you?"

"Yes."

"I thought he had by the look of his face. Couldn't get a word out of him. He's gone down to the buildings now, about the evening chores."

"I'd better change and go down, too."

"No, hon, they ought to be done soon. It's going to rain I hope it's a soaker. What did you say?"

"About what?"

"Oh, you're as hateful as he is. About staying, or coming back?"

"I said I will."

She grinned hugely. "And he was on you like a duck on a June bug, wasn't he, to start building fences or clearing ditches or the like?"

"Well, I have contracts to honor until October."

"But after that you'll be home."

Her very dark eyes filled with tears and she rattled pans ferociously She had grown even gaunter, Nolan thought, was becoming a little stooped. There was a lot of white in her hair. She was five years older than Price.

"I see you've got a dishwasher," he observed.

She sniffed and gave a quick swipe at her eyes. "I didn't want it at first. It was Anne's idea. I thought it was more trouble to rinse the dishes and put them in there than to just go ahead and wash them. Now, though, I don't know how we'd do without it. Oh, yes, we've got a lot of improvements. There's the bigger washer and the clothes dryer, bigger freezer. And there's the TV. We don't get good reception, and only two channels, but we're living just like downtown now, compared to what I can remember. But I tell you one thing, especially winters, this old house has seemed awfully big and empty with just the three of us in it. There have even been mornings—just a few, you know—when I've been actually glad to see Reuben come twisting himself up here to have breakfast and start in with his complaints and cussedness. A lot of evenings, we've spent listening to your records. It made us lonely for you and Kiersten, but awfully proud, too."

"You listened to the records after Price had gone to bed," he said, smiling a little.

Fern thought that she would give a lot to see the smile spread to his eyes, hear him laugh, even in this time of mourning. She said firmly, "No, Nolan, it wasn't. You know he always did like to stay up and read by the fire, winter evenings. He's proud of you, whatever he may say or act like. Now, this winter, we'll have you here to play for us yourself. You'll want to keep in practice, won't you? Those stories you tell, with the music, they just make me goosefleshy all over. They're the most wonderful things I've ever heard. Beat hell out of television."

She was walking past him on her way to the big refrigerator. She paused, lifted his hair, and kissed him on the forehead.

"Now," she moved on, "about all it would take to make me about the happiest old granny in the world, would be for you and Kiersten to make it up."

He moved a few restless steps, touching a copper pot hanging on the wall. "Make what up?"

"I don't know, hon. Just—whatever it is. I've always had the two of you matched up in my mind, since she came here with her mama all those years ago and you boys came back to spend that first summer. You've been—well, you've been in love with each other for all this time now, haven't you? Why should you end things, just when you're ready to come home and—you know what old lady Nelson said once? That if you married it would be incest, but there's not a drop of blood kin between you. Some people just can't live without—sensationalizing. Why don't you marry now, after . . . You two young ones ought to have this place, together. And your children."

"Kiersten wants to go on with her art. I've about had my fling with music."

"That's not what's wrong," Fern said with conviction. "Is it?"

"Fern, are you making potato cakes?"

"I am and you need a lot of them. You always were skinny, nice broad shoulders, but skinny. You remember Reuben and the hands used to go around calling you N. B., for No Butt? Well, we've got to get some meat on you, and the sooner the better. Some say musicians have an easy life, but it doesn't look to me like that. You and Kiersten both look absolutely worn out. You know, now that I think of it, you've looked older than your years since I can remember. That's not meant to be uncomplimentary. You're a fine-looking young man, but you look tired, too, like you don't sleep enough. Working out in the fresh air ought to help with that, I expect, when you come home. You just look to me like you need looking after. I mean to see to it they don't put too much on you in the beginning, so you can settle in easy. Anne will help with that, and we'll get you fed up good and in fine shape. But about Kierstie—"

"What about Kierstie?" asked Kiersten, coming into the kitchen.

"I've just been trying to ask Chappie what's come up. Between you two, I mean. There's nothing that can't be settled with a little—"

Nolan escaped into the bootroom, and so outside. Lightning lanced down onto Warrior Peak. Thunder rumbled with a ponderous hugeness, reverberating round and round the Park and among the mountains. The first drops of rain began to fall, the hard-wrung mountain rain, and there was the smell peculiar to the dust of this place as it was first wetted down. Nolan held his face up to the chill water droplets. "There's nothing that can't be settled . . ." He couldn't try to talk to her any more, not when her face went hard and angry at sight of him, and she was already determined upon what she was going to believe. Maybe he could put it in a letter. Would she resent the fact, now, that he was coming back to Secesh? Or would she—magical thought—change her mind about going east in the fall? "To every thing there is a season, and a time to every purpose under heaven." Did he believe that, with Kiersten feeling as she obviously did? Was there that much of idealism, of blind hope left in him? Yes, by God! He'd write her from California, get his thoughts and feelings together and separated properly and try to put them into words. They *should* have Secesh together, and their children.

22

My dearest bonnie Kierstie,

I wanted to begin writing this letter on the last night I was at Secesh, but we were both angry then, and hurt.

I did the recording with John Sage and it was some of the most fun I've ever had. At one session he was so drunk he couldn't stand up, and that's when he did his best work. At others, he was just mildly sloshed and was only grand. He's a fantastic old man, though I'm afraid he won't keep going much longer at the rate he puts away the liquor. We had supper together after almost every session. He told one wonderful story after another, but ate almost nothing.

I am not happy with the Hollywood scene. For one thing, I just don't like it here. I think you would feel the same. Also, there are too many people looking over my shoulder as I try to work up the music, telling what I can and can't do. When I get it all put together, however, I think they will buy it, for the most part. This is a movie about Benito Juarez. I have been listening to a lot of Sabicas, Montoya, Romero, etc., and, I fear, using bits and pieces here and there, it's what crazy Peter Shickele calls "not plagiarism, but recycling." Some of the work, I think, is really fine.

I have bought a car. It's almost a necessity out here. It's a silver station wagon, and foreign, so when I go back to Dunraven, everyone in the Park, on Fairweather, and at Hurleigh can recognize me for the flaming liberal that I am. I am getting together a good stock of records, classical, jazz, and folk, and I'm choosing stereo components to take back with me. With these, the store of books already in the house which Anne has kept up to date, and occasional prac-

335

tice, I should have plenty to do through the long winter evenings. In the beginning, I'm sure all I'm going to want to do is fall asleep.

Donatelli has forwarded a letter to me from Patterson at Albion. In the January term there they are going to introduce folk music as a genuine, bona fide musical genre, recognize the banjo, fiddle, and the rest of it. He asked me to come back and teach, while finishing my last year as a student there. I have written him that I'm honored, and very glad to know about the courses, which is true, but that I have decided to be a cowboy.

You must know how happy I am with the idea of going back to Secesh, of having a real home at last. I know that if it were not for you and Anne, this would probably have never come about. Price is too stubborn, too proud, and, yes, I may have inherited some of his genes.

What would make it all complete, absolutely perfect, would be to have you there, as my wife. I do understand about your art. Who better? But, please, try to keep an open mind about me, about us.

So now, bonnie Kierstie, we come down to it. I told you the truth on the plane that night. Except for that one incident, of which I am so ashamed, but which I got myself into, there has never been *anyone* but you. I don't see how there could be. If you can't believe me about Susan, would you go and talk with her? There are things you don't know, and that I don't feel free to tell anyone, but maybe she would. Whatever you've heard, except for those weeks at Albion, is lies. Don't you realize how jealous Carol and Michael were? How disappointed and angry with the rest of us? You know, as well as anyone could, how easily Roger lies. Do you remember that one night at Susan's when Carol went out with Roger? I'm no psychologist, and don't want to be one, but I do know that, for whatever reasons, Roger hates me, and would be glad to see anything I try fail. You say he loves me, I know, but if that's true, it's rather like being loved by a boa constrictor. I feel he has a great deal to do with the things, whatever they are, that you've heard.

I would like to think you know me well enough, trust me, so that my word could be sufficient. Obviously, that was not so in June. If it's still the case, when you're back in New York, talk to Rex. There's not much about my life for those three years that he didn't monitor, and he is a wise and incisive person. I even talked to him about my early days once or twice, so that, next to you, he may know me better than anyone does. (I hear that Rex and Ellen Wilsmore are going to be married. When you see them, please give them my best wishes.)

You will be twenty-three in October; I am twenty-four. There are a lot of years yet to come. I *can* wait, if that's the way you want it. I've already been waiting since I was six. I only need to know, for now, that you believe I haven't lied to you, ever. I'd *like* to know you love me. I love you, my bonnie girl, and can't believe there could ever be anyone else. Please forgive me that one shameful trespass on our love. We are both, I suppose, rather old-fashioned about faithfulness and that sort of thing, so I can understand your anger and hurt now. It took a while, because I am also old-fashioned about my word being my bond. This is why I haven't written sooner, why I didn't begin this letter while I was still at Secesh, or on the plane to California. Now, after a little more than a month, I think I can look at things a little more objectively, see your side as well as my own.

I wish you the very best at the art school, and with whatever else you may do. I still have the sketch you made of us at the motel door, with the children and the bus. I wouldn't take anything for it. Please, just don't stop loving me.

I will be in New York early in March to work with Susan on her new album. Would you believe I have the days counted until I can see you again?

This letter is some kind of record for me. Look how long it is! I know that soon you will be involved with haying at the ranch. Then you will be getting settled into a place and a routine in New York. Maybe you will want even more time to think. I earnestly hope not. You could call me here. The phone number and address are on the letterhead. I should be finished with this before the first of October, which is my deadline. Then I go to Nashville to record the bluegrass session. Donatelli can tell you how to reach me there. By the twentieth of October, I should be at Secesh. Surely you will have come to some decision then, about whether or not you can believe me. Please let me hear from you. I promise to be a better correspondent, as soon as I know you still return my love, or will let me try to make up for the rough places our love has had to suffer. I miss you so very much. There are no words I know to tell you how much.

                                        all my love
                                        Nolan

Kiersten read the letter again, in the tiny efficiency apartment she had rented, with the early December dusk falling outside its one grimy window. She thought she must have read it at least once every day since it had come to her at Secesh near the end of July. The pages were worn and frail, cracking in the folds.

Work at the art school had begun immediately after Labor Day. She had determinedly absorbed herself in it. She was also teaching art to small children in the ghetto area where Roger worked. She tried to keep every minute full, so that by midnight she was totally exhausted and could sleep. She tried for the most part to avoid the few people she knew well in New York.

She had gone to see Susan Lister back in September. Susan had moved into a smaller apartment. Her friend, the teacher at the art school, had given Kiersten the address. Susan was bubblingly involved in redecoration, buying right pieces of furniture for the place When Kiersten had called her, Susan insisted on making supper for the two of them.

Afterward, fortified by several drinks, Kiersten had asked her Except to quell her fears of flying, Kiersten had rarely drunk much before this fall. She didn't like liquor and had never felt the need of it. Now, back in New York, desolate, she found herself drinking more and more, in company and alone. She never got drunk with other people, only took enough to make herself feel less self-conscious, less alone. Sometimes, when she actually was alone, she drank enough to make sleep come. There were terrible hangovers the next day, but she felt, in what she knew to be her old-fashioned morality, that she *should* pay some price. It was not like the old Kiersten Savage to try to drown her woes, but perhaps this no longer *was* the old Kiersten Savage.

Susan had said intently, "Kiersten, I swear to you, there was never anything but friendship between me and Chappie. Who's been telling you lies? Is this why you're so pale and thin? My God, you two haven't broken up over . . . Anybody with half an eye and half a mind could see how the two of you belonged together, forever "

"I swear." Nolan had said that and had written it. She resented Susan's calling him Chappie. Well, Susan had backed up his contentions, but she hadn't made any great revelations as he had implied she might do.

So still, Kiersten couldn't answer his letter. Why? Deep down, she thought, I believe him, or is it just that I want to so much. He was a very strong persuasive person. Hadn't she watched and heard him hold so many audiences in thrall with voice, hands, eyes, expressive face?

Rex had found out from Susan where Kiersten was living and he and Ellen had invited her to dinner. She could think of almost nothing to say to them in their neat little apartment until she had had a few drinks. Then they began to sing and play for a long, mostly pleasant evening.

"It's not the same without young Savage, is it?" Rex said wistfully.

Kiersten, who had been thinking that for months, excused herself quickly and went into the tiny bathroom, crying.

"This evening," Ellen said gayly when she came back, determined that Kiersten should not be aware of their awareness of her heartbreak, "is by way of a wedding invitation. We're not having many people at the actual ceremony, it's not going to be that much, but we're having a big bash of a reception at David Harris's place afterward. His place is large enough."

Rex said, "Will you come, Kierstie, please? You're the only one left of that old gang of mine. I think it's God's shame Chap is going to give up just about everything to be a cowboy, but I also know it's what he's always wanted, along with the music. He'll be back here in March, to work with Susan. We'll have another bash then, you can bet."

Kiersten began, "Rex?" and stopped, all too aware of Ellen's presence. She finished rather lamely, "Yes, I'll come. Thanks for asking me."

Ellen and Rex exchanged a compassionate glance she did not see and Ellen said, "Bring a friend if you like."

Rex, deciding the matter might as well be got down to, said gently, "There's trouble between you and Nolan, right?"

"No," she said, "it's just that we're"—she gulped at her drink—"so far apart."

Then she left as soon as she could politely do so.

She asked Roger to come to the wedding reception with her. She knew the party would turn into a jam session long before it was over. Roger didn't care for music. It would make a valid excuse for leaving early.

She and Roger had been seeing quite a lot of each other since the day she had arrived back in New York. He had helped her find the apartment, get the art teaching job. He seemed gentle and understanding now, and they almost never mentioned Nolan. Roger had asked her to go to bed with him on several occasions.

"I can't," she had said bleakly.

"It's all right," he had replied. "You're a for-keeps girl, aren't you? I admire that. Truly I do, but maybe the time will come . . . ."

At the McIver reception, a man had come up to them, someone to whom Kiersten had been barely introduced in the noise, a jazz pianist.

He said, "I hear young Savage has gone back to the wilds. Damn shame. Great musician. The lady fans are going to be a littler harder to come by, off in the boonies, aren't they? It was kind of a shame, all that fooling around, when he had that cute little girl in bed to go home to. Carol something. Wasn't that her name?"

Roger took her home in a cab shortly after that.

"People talk too much," he said, gently taking her hand in the darkness as she fought tears.

And, at her apartment, "May I come in for a drink?"

They sat together on the couch that made into her bed, her oh-so-empty, lonely bed.

Roger said, "Kierstie, of course I know about you and Nolan for those three years, but I'm more than willing to forgive and forget. Are you? Could you forget him as a—a partner? I want to marry you."

It would probably be preferable to have an affair with her, as Nolan had done, being sure to let Chappie know about it, but she was obviously determined to keep what virtue she had, not sleep around. Marriage, in the long run, might be the better choice. She could walk out on an affair, but she was the kind who would hold strongly to marriage vows.

"Oh, Roger," she had begun bleakly

"Please wait. Don't say definite things. It's something to think about. There's time. I only wanted you to know. I've wanted you always. Do you remember the first time we met?"

"Not very well. I was only four."

"We took off our clothes together," he said, smiling, putting his arms around her. "I remember it very well. Can't we do that again? Wouldn't you like someone really near you?"

"No. I mean we can't go to bed."

"You're still in love with—him?"

"I—I don't know."

"Do you write to each other?"

She hesitated. "No."

"Kierstie, I'm sorry, but the word really is around. Any time I've gone to these music things, for the past year-and-a-half now, I've heard it on all sides. Mostly, of course, it's been from people who don't know I'm his brother. The talk was especially rampant at that party after the Carnegie Hall thing, maybe since neither of you was there. People said he screwed his way to fame and popularity with

Susan Lister. I don't like saying this to you, but you really have to be aware of it. Can you still believe he's worthy of your loyalty? You're worth ten of him. Just, please, think about us. We could have a good life. I'm going to go up fast in the academic world. You'll see. I've told you I've already been offered a teaching job at that fine little university out on Long Island while I work on my doctoral dissertation. You could go on with whatever you want to do with art. I'll be able to move to a bigger, more prestigious university in no time. In my field I'm going to do every bit as well as . . . I know what Secesh means to you. It means a great deal to me, too. We could go there summers, if you like, maybe Christmas holidays as well. We could have a good life, children; you want children, don't you?''

She nodded mutely.

"Well, keep thinking about it. . . . Are you sure I can't stay the night?"

Kiersten had been tempted, someone to hold her, a warm body beside her if she woke in those desolate small hours of the morning. But she said no.

They had dated several times since then, dinner, a movie, a show Roger always pressed her, but not too hard. Once he had borrowed a car and they had gone for dinner to a country inn up in Connecticut, enjoying the beautiful fall colors. He had suggested they stay the night. She had refused.

He said a little irritably, "I know you're old-fashioned, not a bed hopper, but if we're going to be married, what difference does it make?"

"Roger, I've never said—"

"But you are thinking about it. I can see it in your face. Your face is an open book. To me, it is. I know you're really considering now."

So, in early December, she read Nolan's letter yet again, a glass of bourbon in her hand. She had forgot the water for the drink, but what did it matter? Scalding tears rolled down her cheeks and fell on the pages. She believed him because she wanted to, and yet . . . She had not been able to answer the letter, with doubts so often gnawing at her, could not make promises for the distant unknown future.

She despised New York, felt hemmed in and too crowded together with strangers, but it was the place to be for an artist, at least until some sort of reputation had been established. Maybe she would want to teach some day. She loved her work with the children now. The work was delightful and rewarding.

Secesh. He would be there now. They were probably feeding with horses and sleds by this time. She thought of the big draft horses, steaming in the cold, the smell of the hay and the cattle. Fool! she

341

flared at herself, don't be such a damned dreamer. See it realistically. It's probably five degrees above zero, with a thirty mile wind, absolutely miserable. But she could see Nolan, standing in the sled, his thin, beautifully muscled body swinging up the bales with the hay hook, breaking them apart for the eagerly following cattle. He had wonderful thin strong hands, which, probably, should never touch anything but musical instruments and her . . . His hands would be hardened now, the straw fair hair perhaps powdered with snow, blowing from the ground or drifting down from the sky. Even in winter, unless it was very cold, he had always eschewed hat or cap

If only she had accepted his word on the plane that night, or answered his letter immediately! Everything might be different. She might be in the house at Secesh this minute, helping with the supper, or driving the horses while he fed out the hay. She looked through her tears at the telephone.

Would marrying Roger be just the least bit like being with Nolan? No, that was totally unfair. They were nothing alike. Roger would be here in less than an hour. He was so different with no Nolan to try to impress, to try to draw what Roger could accept as signs of love and respect, perhaps envy from. . .

The letter had come four-and-a-half months ago. He had said she could have time to think, but he would never have meant this long, without one word. At first, still bitter and hurt, she had hoped there would be other letters from him. Certainly, he could have got her address from Mother. But she knew better than that. The letter she held in her hand was, for him, abject, pleading. He would not do that again, unless she conveyed to him the feeling that it was necessary. She knew how he could harden himself to something he wanted but felt he could not have—like Secesh, before he went back and talked with Price. Suppose she called him this minute and, after all this time without a word from her, he was cold, impersonal, silent? Yes, she knew him. Oh God, but did she? She had trusted him, loved him so deeply, but there had been all the talk and it was still going on   He had said, except for that one thing at Albion   If he'd been willing to admit that, why wouldn't he give the truth to other things? If there had *been* other things? Because there hadn't been, and he would never forgive this long-lived doubt of hers. His word was his bond. She knew, too, how long and hard his unforgivingness could be

In today's mail there had come a letter from Mother. "It's not too early to start making Christmas plans. We assume you'll have a long holiday. Please come home. It's a long time since you've spent Christmas at the ranch. Fern says to tell you we made the fruitcakes last week. Remember how you always used to help with that, from the time you were a tiny girl? Dad says if you need money for the trip, just let us know how much. Reuben says they'll get out the sleigh. Remember how you always loved that, especially when we went for the Christmas tree?"

But no "Nolan says." He had set himself, Kiersten knew. He would not forgive her doubt and questioning and not replying. He should understand . . . No, she should never have questioned. Still, there had been all the talk from all the different people, and she had seen them, Nolan and Susan, in each other's arms, that night after they had heard about Hugh, standing there in each other's arms, Susan sobbing, saying those things . . . But, no, somehow that had been only platonic. Susan could be so emotional . . . This was her doing, but she could never undo it without his cooperation and now, after all these months of silence from her, he would never . . .

She wouldn't go home for Christmas. She couldn't. Not when there had been no further word from him at all. Her volunteer teaching job would cut her holiday time in half. That would be excuse enough. She would not be completely alone for the holidays. There would be Roger. He was having therapy again, changing before her eyes, it seemed, becoming more reasonable, less fixated. Penny and her family would be at Secesh for Christmas. How Nolan's eyes sparkled when he played with those little girls! How they clung to him and romped over him! He needs his own children . . . but they would not be *their* children. He would find a mild, Scandinavian girl for a wife. She would ask nothing more than to cook and clean, care for him and their children. She would not have known him on the road, or at the glorious heights at Carnegie Hall, or . . .

And she? Kiersten? She really had no illusions about herself. She was alone, desperately lonely, but she couldn't go to Nolan, now, after all this time, and ask—what? His forgiveness, his understanding? He had given those things in the letter. She had simply not answered it and now, in December, that was an end of it. She had lost her chance, her opportunity for the future life she really wanted.

Roger *was* different, but maybe that had more to do with Nolan's not being present than with the therapy. Still, he thought almost entirely about himself, talking almost incessantly about his plans, his career, what other people had said about or to him. He did not say something like "I love you." But perhaps they could, in a sense, be together and still go their separate ways, he with his teaching career, she with whatever in hell it was that she was going to be. She wouldn't even expect fidelity from Roger. So why had she so tenaciously insisted on it from Nolan? Because he was different than she . . . If she and Roger were to marry and have children, would one of them look like Chappie? God, she had to stop thoughts like that, and she had to stop drinking before she turned into a real slosh.

If she married Roger, there would be someone to be with in New York, truly *be* with, to break the stranglehold of this aching loneliness, someone *other* that she'd have to think about, to divert her thoughts . . . She was not going to marry him. For one thing, if she did so, it would be for all the wrong reasons. Would both of them do it simply to spite Nolan? But, *if* she married Roger, she'd make him the best wife it was in her to be. She'd truly concentrate on the marriage and that would take the place, to some degree, of never going home again. Of never . . .

She drained the dregs from her glass and stood up, holding the letter. She went into the tiny bathroom, tore it into small bits, and flushed them away, sobbing. What matter, really, she tried to tell herself sternly. Every word had been, long ago, graven on her mind.

"You know, of course," said Roger in the restaurant's barely lit booth, "that I've had other girls. I wouldn't pretend to come to you as a virgin. Besides, it helps me understand how you could sleep with—someone else. Also, I've learned a lot that would make our lovemaking better. We can be frank with each other, can't we? I think you'd believe in complete faithfulness after marriage. I'm not sure I could promise you that, but then, there are things you couldn't promise me, aren't there?"

"Like what?" she said, gulping at a drink.

"Like love."

"We're only talking hypothetically, you said," she reminded him, holding the glass. She'd stop drinking tomorrow. It had to stop and it was time.

"Yes," said Roger comfortably.

"Well, about love, I—I'd work very hard at the marriage."

"I believe that. It's the sort of girl you are. Still hypothetically, we could go back to Secesh, next summer, or even at Christmas. Have the biggest, most glorious wedding ever seen in those parts. Really knock their eyes out. Then come back here, find a bigger apartment than either of us has now—I need a place to work at home. So will you, I suppose, and—"

"No," she said fearfully.

"No, what?"

"I don't want to be married at Secesh."

"Because of Nolan? Be honest with me."

"Yes."

"You wouldn't go through with it if you saw him again?"

"Hypothetically speaking," the words were hard for her this time, "Maybe not."

The waiter came and Roger ordered another drink for her. She made no protest; tomorrow was soon enough. The food on her plate had scarcely been touched.

"Kierstie, he doesn't deserve you. He never deserved even to touch you. What would you want then, for a wedding, just City Hall?"

"Or Maryland," she said, feeling daring, euphoric. "There's no waiting period in Maryland."

Roger was startled, but he thought quickly.

"I could borrow Hal's car again. Tonight. Tomorrow's Friday. We could take the day off, couldn't we? Have a long weekend to spend in the mountains down there?"

He reached across and took her hand eagerly.

"I don't think you're being hypothetical any more. Roger, I have to stop drinking. You know that, don't you? I'm becoming an absolute lush."

"I'll help you. Kierstie, I'll make you love me. You'll see. It won't be as hard as you think."

"I don't have any money for Maryland," she said, almost dreamily now.

"I do. Shall I go and call about the car? Will you promise to try to forget . . . ?"

"Roger, when I marry somebody, it won't be with someone else in mind. All the time, on the road, the others, except Chappie, used to tease me about what a prissy little WASP I was, in spite of the fact . . . Well, I am that. If I married, it would be for keeps."

"For better or worse," he said, savoring the words, smiling in the semi-darkness. "I'll go and call Hal about the car now. We'll pick up a few things at our apartments and—"

"Roger, you really are not being hypothetical any more."

"No, I'm not."

"Suppose we start and, on the way, I decide I can't go through with it? I want to be fair to you."

"I'll understand. I'll try to understand everything. Will you come, Kiersten?"

"Yes," she said, slurring the word into a long sound.

"You stay here and finish your drink," he said, standing. "I'll call Hal."

He made two calls, one to Hal in which he secured the use of the car for the weekend, the other to an elderly man named Philip Grantland.

"I thought I should let you know, Phil, I'm getting married. We'll be away for the weekend."

"Oh, Roger," wailed the other. "I don't like this at all."

"Well, I've told you it would probably happen one day."

He could envision Philip Grantland, sitting in his lush penthouse, eager, lonely, pleading for the only kind of closeness he understood, ready and open with his money.

"I'll still see you a couple of nights a week," Roger said soothingly. "You can count on that."

"I suppose she's some beautiful little cunt," Phil said, whining.

"Her cunt's probably adorable, but she's no beauty. I can make her into a decent proper little wife for a rising professor, a moral professor. This is important to me, for several reasons. If you dislike it too much, then I suppose you and I will have to break things off."

"Oh, no, Roger baby. Never say that."

The bald head, the ruined jowly face, the trembling hand. Roger hated him. He did not, however, hate the penthouse or the money or the sensations, once he got past the old fart's looks.

"Well," said Phil shakily, "when will you be coming back?"

"I'll try to see you Tuesday night."

"I only hope she has half the appreciation of your beauty that I have. There's nothing about you that isn't sheer unadulterated beauty."

"Right, Phil. See you when I can."

"If it was another man instead of a girl," said the other with sudden strength, "I think I might kill you both."

Laughing softly, Roger hung up.

They walked to Hal's place for the car. A few snowflakes were falling in the still, sooty air. He was afraid the walk and the air might sober her too much. Hal gave them a drink along with the car keys.

They went to Roger's place where he packed a few things quickly. He stood before his bathroom mirror, smiling at himself for a moment. Any girl—or guy—who gets this is just plain damned lucky.

Then they went to Kiersten's apartment, where there was a full bottle of bourbon. She packed, then had her own turn, closed in the tiny bathroom, looking at herself in the mirror.

I am not *that* drunk, she thought firmly, and perhaps it was true. I know exactly what I'm doing. Eat your heart out, Nolan Savage! You deserve this. Oh, Chappie . . . No! I'm going to be Roger's wife and a goddamn good one. Tonight, the other is over, finished, forever. I'm going to be Roger's wife and a New York career woman. To hell with Secesh and whatever goes with it! After he had decided to return to the ranch, if he had asked her to stay on . . . No, stop it! These are no reasons for marriage. All right, so there are no reasons . . .

Roger was calling to her through the thin door. "Shall we take this bottle? It's turning a lot colder."

"Why not?" she called back, almost gaily.

Still staring into the mirror, she thought, along with so many other things, Kiersten Savage, promise yourself that that will be the last bottle. You're a strong person. You can handle things far better than you have been doing, and you do not need liquor as a crutch. Yes, I promise, for better or for worse . . .

She slept rather heavily in the car and he touched her now and then, cupping a small firm breast thinking of her nude. She was tall but slender, almost boyish, almost nubile. He could pretend he was taking a virgin, if he didn't know about those three years. Wait till she saw him. Even with all the studying and sitting around, he hadn't neglected his body. It was hard and muscular, beautiful, worthy of his face.

He thought of his mother and all women. They were all whores at heart—well, maybe not Kiersten, so much. She actually might live by that senseless morality she talked about. Still, after he had had his fill of her—which he knew would not take long—it might be fun to watch some other man perform with her. She would be his, after all, to give or take away. He recalled Nolan's saying there was more to women than their female parts. He just remembered Nolan, and the gloating sensual smile on Roger's face broadened. Nolan had had everything he wanted, until now

Again, he thought of his mother All her dressing him up and exhibiting him, like a cute, well-mannered monkey had never been anything more than exhibiting herself. Rogie's looks, Rogie's clothes, Rogie's manners, Rogie's grades. But what she had meant, had wanted, was "Look what *I've* done. Look at me, me, *me!?* God only knew how many men she'd whored with. She'd have gone to bed with him, with Roger, if she'd lived another year or two. It was kind of funny about old Clarence, perverting her darling Rogie, right under her nose. But it wasn't perversion, it felt more right than the other thing.

Women were worthless, all of them. Though maybe he hadn't spent long enough with any one of them to find any more depth than his penis could reach. This courtship of Kiersten had certainly taken long enough. She would see how she couldn't help feeling enticed by it when they were in bed together. And maybe there truly was more to Kiersten than to most others. He'd have to try to give her a chance. Should he make her pregnant right away? Distend the flat little belly he was stroking under her coat? No, not yet a while. The truth was that he wanted no children, though there would be one or two eventually because that would be expected of a rising young professor, and besides, without them, aspersions might be cast upon his manhood. But not now, later, when he could better afford it. Let Kierstie play around with her art for a year or two.

It was raining that morning, in the small Maryland mountain town. Each time Kiersten had roused, Roger had given her another drink from the fifth which had started out full.

"Roger, I have to stop drinking," she had murmured once, compulsively. "This is my last bottle."

"Sure, sweetness, I agree with you. It wouldn't do for a prestigious young professor to have an alcoholic wife. You'll be expected to do a lot of entertaining, formal and otherwise. You will entertain for me, won't you?"

She had made a soft sound that seemed to be acquiescence.

After the brief ceremony, they took a room at an old-fashioned, rather beautiful inn. Kiersten said she did not want breakfast. He carried up their bags, saying, "All right. That's understandable. Neither do I, for the time being."

In the room, her look seemed distant, preoccupied. Was it the booze or . . .

"May as well finish this bottle," he said, taking a sip, offering her the remaining three shots.

"Last one," she said, having emptied it and put it carefully into a waste basket. She was unsteady on her feet. Her face felt numb. Perhaps her whole body would be numb.

"Yes," said Roger firmly. "The last bottle."

He was closing the drapes more tightly, turning on the strong overhead light to go with the two small lamps already burning.

"You take off my clothes, I'll take off yours," he directed, smiling possessively, knowing she had more to look forward to than did he.

What Kiersten wanted to do was sleep, a long long sleep with no dreams. But somehow, they stood together, naked, under the overhead light.

"You're sweet," he murmured, caressing her, "almost like a little girl. Sweet sweet little breasts and those long slender perfect legs. Your hips could be broader, for child-bearing. I won't have a ceasarean scar, not on my wife. Tell me what you see."

"Your body is as—as beautiful as your face," she said thickly, beginning to tremble, timidly touching the dark red-brown hair on his chest.

"Well, don't stop there," he said with a small tolerant laugh as he pulled her hard against him. "Think you can accommodate me? It's been a little—painful for some women, one of the bigger and better organs, I've been told. Tell me, my sweet cunt, are you on the Pill?"

She nodded against his shoulder.

"Still taking them regularly?"

348

"Yes."

"Why?"

"I—I guess it got to be a habit. They—they make for very regular periods and—"

"Yes, I understand. So you've brought them with you?"

Another nod.

"Good girl."

He wanted to ask her things, how much better looking he was than Nolan, how much larger his organ. Well, all that could wait. There would be ample time for finding out.

She sagged slightly against him. Sloshed to the gills. Never mind, he'd make her senses come alive. Some women were better, sexier, less inhibited, when they'd been drinking. He propelled her to the bed, pulled back the covers, and placed her on it to his satisfaction.

Another thing he'd always suspected about his mother and the very exhibitionistic, narcissistic women like her was that they were actually frigid. Just prick teasers. He would not have a frigid wife. He knew that the time would come soon when he would tire of frequent intercourse with her. He was simply too variety-prone. He truly preferred bringing himself off to giving it to a boring woman. But, when he wanted her, she would not be frigid. He'd have her pleading for it, ready to do anything. He knelt on the bed above her Good solid mattress and springs.

He bent and kissed her breasts, touching the nipples lightly with his tongue. Almost no response. It was the liquor. Never mind, he knew how to overcome that. One did away with gentleness. Roger didn't like gentleness anyway. And it had been his experience that women were thrilled by being hurt, a little. Some actually enjoyed quite a lot of hurting, and being frightened.

"Let's pretend you're a virgin, very young," he said, stroking her gloatingly. "I'm the lord of the manor, initiating you to everything. A man, you know, is limited in the number of orgasms he can have, but women, with a man who knows how, can have climaxes without end, sometimes until they faint from the sheer sensualism. Have you read the books? It doesn't matter. Experience is what counts. Tell me, my sweet innocent nubile girl, are you afraid of your lord and master, just the littlest bit?"

Kiersten lay still, wanting the sensations, wanting not to think of that other time, with the little kids and the motel manager and the rest of it. So he had kept that sketch? Nor did she want to think of that other, even earlier time, when she really had been . . .

Before Roger was finished, she was frightened. He hurt her in the most tender places of her body, but he made her respond. He exhausted her with responses before ever he entered her. She lay gasping, tears running down into her hair, when he finally finished his own orgasm.

"You're mine now, aren't you?" he murmured. "I can bring out the very most in you. Say 'I'm Rogie's slave.' Come, say it, or we begin all over again."

"Roger, please," she sobbed forlornly.

"And this next time, my dear little captive, I won't be so gentle and careful of you. If you wanted a cigarette, *where* would you want it?"

"Roger . . ."

"Say it!" He twisted her breast fiercely, and she gave a small cry.

"Do you want some one up here in a minute, knocking on the door to see what the screaming is about?"

But she wouldn't say it, nor scream, no matter what he did. Here was a challenge, maybe something like breaking a spirited horse. She fought him and he was delighted with that. At last, he had her pinned down, spread-eagled beneath him and he was inside her once more.

"It's going to be fun being married to you," he panted. "Fun and games."

At last he left her, went to have a shower. When he came back she was sleeping, huddled small under the disordered covers, her face streaked with tears, and, yes, there were small smears of blood on the sheet. Carelessly, he pulled the covers a little closer around her shoulders. If only she didn't have those damned freckles! Maybe a dermatologist. . . ?

He shaved, trimming his mustache the least bit, dressed carefully, combed his hair into its customary sleek, perfect, chestnut waves, and went downstairs for a large satisfying lunch.

He asked for a great deal of change at the cash register and closed himself in a phone booth. Eleven o'clock there, one o'clock here. Probably, they'd be out feeding. If so, he'd call back.

"Anne, it's Roger."

"Roger! How are you? Is anything wrong?"

"Oh, no, no, nothing at all. Is Nolan there?"

"As a matter of fact, he is. We're having a very open winter so far. They haven't had to do much—"

"I have a surprise for all of you. I'll tell you if you promise to let me be the one to tell Chappie."

"Well . . . yes, all right."

"Kiersten and I have been married. She'll talk to you herself in a day or two, I'm sure. Just now, she's sleeping."

There was a long silence before Anne said almost steadily, "Are you calling from your apartment or a—a room? I'd like to talk with her."

"No, I'm using a pay phone. I wouldn't want to wake her right now. You see, we drove down to Maryland last night, where there's no waiting period. We'll be back in New York on Sunday night."

He waited. She seemed to have nothing more to say.

"May I speak with Nolan then?"

"Yes," she said, obviously shaken. "He and Price are in the office. I'll get him."

As Anne passed rather dazedly through the kitchen, Fern said immediately, "What is it? What's the matter?"

Anne went into the office, saying unsteadily, "Nolan, there's a phone call for you. Maybe you'd like to take it on the extension in our bedroom."

Nolan gave her a quick searching look and Price said, a little impatiently, "Why not on the one here? We're trying to—"

"Because it's personal," she said, leaning on the back of an old armchair, her face pale.

Nolan answered on the bedroom extension, and Anne hung up the hall phone, turning to Price and Fern, crying now.

"It's Roger," he said into the phone. "Did Anne tell you?"

"That it was you? No."

"Nor anything else?"

"No."

"Good, because it was important to me to tell you myself." He waited, letting the silence lengthen.

Finally, "Tell me what?"

"Kiersten and I were married a few hours ago."

There was complete silence. Nolan, beginning to tremble, sat on the edge of the bed, staring at a print of sheep in a meadow, not seeing it.

"Well, don't you have anything to say? Congratulations, maybe?"

And still the silence.

"Chappie, are you there?"

"I want to talk to Kiersten."

"No chance. She's asleep upstairs in this rustic old inn in the Maryland mountains, where we're spending a very satisfying honeymoon. No wonder you stayed with her, more or less, for three years. She's quite a girl in bed. Surprising. I wouldn't think of waking her for a while yet. The poor girl is totally exhausted. We've just had a very long and satisfactory consummation. I brought her off, oh, I should think a dozen times. I doubt you ever did that, did you? One after the other? It tires them out, you know. All that sensation. I mean to go back a little later and—''

Nolan slammed the phone into its cradle. He would have done so moments before, but he hadn't seemed capable of movement. He covered his hot face with cold hands. After a time, he began to shiver, except for a tiny searing spark of anger that was coming up in him.

Damn them! Damn them both to hell! Now, maybe Roger would be satisfied, would leave him alone. . . . But Kiersten, Kierstie, my bonnie girl! Oh God, God in heaven, *why?*

Roger had made her do it somehow. If he, Nolan, took the first plane he could reach for New York . . . Roger was crazy. He had known that more than half his life, and so had she. What had he done to her that this should . . .

Then the anger flared up in him like a raging fire. She had always felt sorry for Roger. ''Be nice to him . . . You call him . . . Your opinion of him matters . . .'' God*damn* her! She was a big girl, quite capable of taking care of herself, making her own decisions, her own . . .

He left the bedroom, climbed the short flights of steps to the door at the top of the house. The wind was damp and bitter, the sky graying with a heavy overcast that reached out from the now invisible mountains to cover and envelop the Park. Nolan was in his shirt sleeves, but he was no longer cold.

Three years had turned out to mean nothing. No reply to his letter, not even care—or daring—enough to tell him herself about the marriage. Doubt and jealousy had won. He had trusted her completely, with everything he was, and she had trusted him not at all. Obviously, the jealousy and doubt on her part had always been there, between them, and he had been too stupid, too much in love, too sure, even to suspect until that night on the plane. He had tried to relieve her mind, to make amends—amends for nothing at all. She had given no sign of being aware of that and now it had come to this. Roger wouldn't want her for long, not now that he had her. She'd come to know that fast enough. All right, she wasn't worthy of his love. Maybe she wasn't even worthy of Roger's—not love—but covetousness? At any rate, she no longer deserved his, Nolan's, concern.

So write it off. Let it go. Jesus Christ! The lessons one had to learn!

23

When Kiersten woke, it was almost evening. Roger had opened the drapes on the drizzly, cold-looking day. Her head was splitting. Her entire body felt bruised and aching and—used. She knew almost immediately where she was, remembered all of it. Roger was sitting in a chair by the window, reading. She lay very still, hoping he might not notice for a time that she was awake, but he looked over almost immediately, and saw something of fear in the blue depths of her eyes.

"Are you going to be all right?" he asked casually.

"Yes," she said quietly.

Aching, she got up, searched in her suitcase for nightgown, underclothing, robe, and aspirin. She went into the bathroom, gulped the aspirin and two more glasses of water. The last bottle; she remembered that, too, stepping under a hot shower.

When she came out, Roger said, "Want to dress and go down for some supper?"

"I'm not hungry," she replied in a still subdued voice. "You go."

"The place doesn't seem to have room service," he said a little irritably. "I'll go down and get us both something on a tray. You haven't eaten since last night, and very little then."

She lay on the bed while he was gone, fighting not to cry. You can't use drunkenness as an excuse, she told herself firmly. You came into this with your eyes at least half-open. You knew what you were doing. Restlessly, nervously, she got up and brushed out her long damp hair.

"My secret, hidden-away girl," said Roger, with that gloating possessive smile, when he came back. "I called Secesh this afternoon. Your mother wants to talk to you when you get around to it. No hurry. I've been thinking, maybe we ought to go back to New York in

353

the morning. There's not much to do here. I suppose it must be nice country, for walking and so on, when it's warm and dry. If we go back, we can get first crack at the apartment ads in the Sunday paper."

"All right," she said listlessly.

When was he going to turn into the sensual, cruel tormenting animal of the morning again? She shuddered, trying to hide it.

He took their tray and placed it outside in the hall, emptying the small table.

"I've got my folding chess set," he said mildly, "or I bought you these magazines downstairs. It seems a strange thing, but I don't know what you like to read. Anyway, there wasn't much choice."

They played two prolonged games of chess, Roger, of course, winning in the long run.

In bed, he scarcely touched her, kissing her once on her bruised mouth, running his hands lightly over her sore body.

"Let's get an early start in the morning," he said and turned over, away from her. "We don't need an alarm clock or a call from downstairs. I usually wake early."

Kiersten was a long time falling asleep. If she began to drowse, Roger's every restless movement made her start violently, wide awake again.

It took them a few weeks to find an apartment. When they did, it was a rundown scruffy place, showing signs of cockroaches and sifting plaster dust, but it had two bedrooms, which seemed almost Roger's only criterion. He would need a place for an office when he began to work on his dissertation in January. There were twin beds in the larger of the bedrooms.

"I got extra furniture stored in the basement," said the landlady. "I can get you a double bed up here, in place of them, or put it in that other room there, where there's just the sofa bed now."

"No, this will do," said Roger without a glance at Kiersten.

He said to her later, "I don't like sleeping the night with anyone else. It makes me restless."

Price and Anne had sent them a substantial wedding gift of money. Kiersten spent her share on linens and other things for the apartment. Roger bought himself a very nice small desk and chair for the room that was to be his office. Kiersten could do her work, he told her, on a small rickety desk which already occupied one dark corner of the living room.

It was a strange marriage. They had little in common and Roger did not really want to share his life with her. He talked of his successes, his future, but rarely of anything else that was going on in the world, not even of the ghetto project in which they were both involved. They had intercourse only rarely. Kiersten could never think of it as 'making love.' Sometimes, on these rare occasions, Roger seemed so preoccupied as to hardly notice what he was doing. Occasionally, he was violent with her, as he had been that day in Maryland, telling her to pretend something, making her cry out in pain and sensuality, demanding things of her which she had never dreamed of doing. But all intercourse fell off quickly to once or twice a month. When he knew she was having a period, he treated her like something unclean, not even wanting their fingers to touch. When he did choose to have sexual relations, they were always in her bed. He had not the slightest interest in her, what she did, what she thought, or felt. If she tried to talk to him, about school, the apartment, anything, he was immediately bored and said she was disturbing his thoughts.

He was away at least two nights a week, sometimes returning in the early morning, but more often not until after his classes on the following day. Kiersten did not question him and he volunteered nothing, only insisted that she keep the apartment spotless and have something prepared when he was ready to eat.

She was afraid of the neighborhood and dared not go out alone at night. Besides, there was nowhere she wanted to go. She was more lonely, more desolate than ever before in her life.

During the holidays, they had given a party for some of Roger's friends. "I wish this place wasn't so damned crummy," he had said, seeming really to notice the apartment for the first time.

He insisted that Kiersten buy new clothes for the party, have her hair styled. He even went along to see that everything was done properly. He chose what would be served and instructed her in the serving of it.

"These people are intellectuals," he said warningly. "You'll be doing me and yourself a favor by keeping quiet, and, for God's sake, try to cover the freckles."

Price had paid a year's tuition for both of them last fall, when the cattle were sold. He directed Anne to write that that would be all, saying that when people were old enough to marry, they were old enough to be on their own. Kiersten still had a little in savings from the last days of The Stewards, and now and then there was a small check for record royalties, but Roger always seemed to have plenty of money. She did not want to know where it came from. He gave her a meticulously estimated household budget and nothing more.

One day when she came home in the late afternoon from classes, he came out of his office to meet her. He had been away all the previous night.

"What am I supposed to do about food?" he demanded. "I'm trying to work. I don't want to have to take the time to go out and eat.

I've been here two hours already. If you can't do better than this, you're going to have to stop your own classes. I expect you to be fully aware that my work is a thousand times more important than yours.''

She couldn't give up school. That and teaching the ghetto children were all that made life worthwhile. She was beginning to think she had found her field, illustrating children's books. An editor she had met through the school had seemed to like some of her drawings very much. "When you've absorbed more, practiced more," she had said tantalizingly.

"I'll make sure there's something in the refrigerator from now on," she told Roger. "So you can at least find a snack when I'm not here."

"When we move out to Long Island, you should probably quit anyway. All the commuting and time will be a waste of money. I don't intend to have you working when I'm an instructor anyway. I can support us very nicely. It wouldn't look good to have you trotting off to some job every day. People would think you *have* to work. If you can find something to play around with at home, I suppose that would be all right. A lot of people have hobbies, and painting seems to be one of the more popular ones. As long as you do your duty by house and meals. Neither of us will be doing any more of the ghetto work after this school year is over. For my part, I've had a bellyful of that. Maybe we can find a decent place to live out there."

Kiersten said nothing more as she went to prepare his dinner. She would not give up the classes. She was going to go on with them, right through the summer, even if it came down to asking Dad for the loan of the necessary money.

She was particularly and most miserably lonely in the first half of March. He had written, "I'll be coming east to work on an album with Susan—before calving begins." She would not see him, of course. She prayed that Roger should not hear a whisper of his being in town. But she thought of him constantly, so very near.

Roger came in at three one morning, to find her still awake and crying. She had not expected him and, at the sound of his key in the lock, she tried desperately to obliterate all signs of tears, and to feign sleep.

"What's wrong," he said impatiently, almost as soon as he had turned on the bedside lamp. "Are you sick or something?"

"No," she said hoarsely. "I—I've been working. Just came to bed."

"Why are your eyes red and swollen?"

"I guess I worked too long."

He came over to her, roughly turning her head.

"Your hair's wet. Don't you think I know when you've been

crying? You're lonely, I suppose. Why don't you take a lover? I'll even choose one for you. I'd enjoy seeing some of the—action.''

"No."

"As long as you're discreet about it, I'd have absolutely no objection. By the way, there's something I've meant to mention to you. I don't see how we can go to Secesh for the whole summer this year. We've got to look for a place to live out—"

"I'm not going to Secesh at all," she said firmly. "I'm going to summer school."

"The hell you are!"

He liked her spirit. He was determined to break it, but her adamance and convictions made the process more interesting. She was, at least, managing to hold a minimum of his interest, for longer than he had imagined possible. She was saying, "I am, Roger. I'm going to finish my degree."

He ranted, bathing her in sarcasm when the summer courses began and she was taking them, but she went on with it doggedly.

They found a house near the university where he was to begin teaching. It had been the guest cottage of a large estate, which was now up for sale.

"I don't think you'll have to worry about having to move soon," the realtor told them. "The heirs to this place are asking a phenomenal price and they all have the money to wait things out and get it."

Kiersten loved the cottage. Roger had found it and taken it without her ever setting eyes on it, but she told him how much she liked it and he seemed pleased with himself. There were three rooms downstairs, one of which would be his office. He arranged to have a few of the pieces of furniture from the cottage stored in the basement of the big house, had his desk moved out from town, along with a sofa for his office, new twin beds, a decent desk for Kiersten. She put her desk in one of the dormer nooks in the large upstairs bedroom. From the window, she could see the ocean, just a glimpse through the trees, but it was there.

Roger still went into the city at least two nights a week, returning on the first morning train. He had wanted to have his dissertation finished that summer, before he began his first semester of teaching, but it was not going at all well, so he nagged at Kiersten, yelled at her, scorned her, and, occasionally, came into her bed like a vicious animal.

They were invited to parties given by other professors and their wives, gave one of their own, a Sunday evening buffet on which Kiersten worked for the entire weekend. Afterward, Roger peevishly criticized everything she had done, her clothes, her conversation, the food. She kept silent, knowing everything had been all right, if not spectacular, refusing to argue about it. This added fuel to his anger, and he kept them both awake all night.

Roger began his first semester of teaching and Kiersten went on with art school. Late in October she actually sold some illustrations for a children's book which had been written by an acquaintance. She was thrilled and even Roger accepted the fact with grudging congratulations. She would have liked to give a party for the author and a few other people she knew slightly, but Roger said, "None of those artsy-tartsies in my house."

One day as Kiersten was leaving her classes, she met Susan Lister on the steps outside the school.

"I've been waiting for you," said Susan, taking her hand warmly. "I've been wanting to see you for ages. You may not know that I went on a concert tour after we cut the album in March and, through the summer I've been on tour in Europe."

"No, I didn't know," said Kiersten uneasily. "Congratulations."

"It all went pretty well, I think, though I did so desperately want Nolan along as my accompanist. Is there a nice quiet restaurant somewhere near by? Could we have supper together?"

"I really ought to be getting home," Kiersten said. It was Tuesday, one of the nights Roger usually spent in town, but she did not want to be with Susan.

"I've heard you married Nolan's brother. In fact, it was Nolan who told me, when he was here in March. I hope you're happy, Kierstie. Roger is certainly the most handsome man I've ever seen. Sharon, our teacher friend, tells me you're living out on Long Island now. Do you have a long commute?"

"About fifty minutes, if all goes well."

"Please call your husband and see if he can get along for a little while without you. I promise not to keep you late."

Kiersten called. There was no answer. When they were settled with food at the secluded table, Susan said, "So Roger's teaching now, not just a teaching assistant?"

"Yes, and working on his doctoral dissertation."

"And what are you doing, besides school and being housewifely, as if that weren't enough?"

Kiersten told her about the recently sold illustrations, and Susan's pleasure and congratulations were real and warm.

A little later, Susan said, "Did you hear that Rex and Ellen McIver have a baby? A little girl, born not more than a week ago."

"I—I don't see the people I used to know. Please give them my best wishes and congratulations."

"Yes, we've noticed you don't see us," said Susan gently, patting her hand.

As they went on to chat about other things, Kiersten was remembering how Roger had complained about having to move her record player, few records, and the old guitar on which she had learned to play reasonably well with The Stewards.

"Why don't you just throw this stuff out?" he had said petulantly. "It represents the past and that's over."

"I want to keep it," she had replied firmly.

"Never play a note of music when I'm in the house," he had snapped peevishly. "I hate it. It's just noise to distract me from my work."

The truth was she had not played the guitar or listened to the records at all since her return to New York. They would have made her loneliness and longing unbearable, but neither could she bear to part with them.

Susan was saying, "I suppose you didn't see Chappie at all when he was in town."

The waiter was pouring coffee, and Kiersten said levelly, "No. Is he—all right?"

"He seems very pleased with his ranch life. I think he's coming in again soon, to do a record with David Harris, or is it John Sage? Well, maybe it's both. . . . Kiersten, he—I always thought it would be the two of you. When he finally told me you were married, he got that—empty look in his eyes. If you're—not happy, then I feel partly responsible. Now that it's too late, maybe, I have to try to ease my own conscience a little. I really didn't know how the talk was flying around, about Nolan, until Rex and Ellen told me, and that was just shortly after you'd married. I didn't know you were married at that time, of course. I tried to find you, but you'd moved. . . . A long time ago, on the first night we met, I told Chappie a secret of mine. I did get it out of him, last March, that he never told you, though I truly didn't mean his promise to be *that* binding. He said he had suggested in a letter that you talk to me, and I remember you did try, over a year ago, when you first came back to New York. I didn't tell you then because I didn't know about all the filthy talk. I was too wrapped up in my own problems really to pay attention to gossip about other people. I also didn't tell you because I've always had—feelings for you. I didn't want to frighten you, or make you detest me. . . . I'm a lesbian, Kiersten, a very quiet and discreet one. I haven't been to bed with a man since before my daughter was born, almost fifteen years ago."

Kiersten just sat there, still, silent, staring into her coffee cup. So it was true, everything he had said was true, and she'd simply been too jealous, too horrible, to believe him. It had been all her own vile, distrustful imagination, watching female fans cluster around him, seeing what was near adulation from people like Susan—but only for his talents, his personality, not . . . Why had Susan had to tell her, *now*, when it was all too late? Oh, God, Chappie, Chappie, it's all my fault and now it's too late. The words crashed through her mind like clanging bells: my fault . . . too late . . . never . . .

Susan was saying, tears in her big brown eyes, "I'm so sorry, Kierstie. Truly I am. I can see that it does matter to you. He wouldn't talk about it—just in bits and pieces—but he was crushed by your marriage. I hope, at least, that you aren't. You don't look well, dear. I'm so sorry. Shall I order you a drink?"

"No," she said shakily, standing up. "I really have to go or I'll miss the last train. Thank you for the supper. And, Susan, your—secret is as safe with me as it's been with—him."

For the weekend of their first anniversary, Roger suggested that they go and stay with friends of his, now living in Connecticut, the same Hal whose car they had borrowed for the wedding.

"Hal tells me he and Gwen have bought an old farmhouse up there and are redoing it. They also have one of those big circular beds and we could spend the weekend being a very sensual foursome. Have you ever done it with another woman, or in groups? No, of course you wouldn't have."

"I won't go," she said with outward calm.

"I can make you go if I choose. I can tie and gag you, put you in the trunk of the car, if you want it to go that far."

"And," she said through clenched teeth, "how do you explain it when it gets around the university what a pervert you are? It *would* get around, Roger. I promise you."

"You filthy little cunt!"

But they did not go for the weekend. He took her out for dinner and gave her a pair of combs to wear in her hair, studded with tiny diamond chips.

"I'll hang diamonds all over you one day. It makes a good press, even with the freckles."

All she had been able to afford for him was a relatively inexpensive desk set and a couple of ties.

Later, in the bedroom, he said distastefully, "When was your last period?"

"It's just ended."

"And the birth control pills? Where are they?"

"In the bathroom. Why?"

He opened the medicine cabinet, took out the half full bottle, and flushed the pills away.

"I want you to start taking your temperature every morning so

360

we'll know when you've ovulated. I certainly don't intend to ball you every night for three weeks running.''

"Oh, Roger, this is no marriage to bring a child into. We—"

"Well, you're going to bring one. I'll certainly finish my dissertation by next fall. Then there will probably be a teaching job for me up in Connecticut, at a bigger, better-known university. I want you with babe in arms, or very prominently pregnant. That's the way the older staff people like it, good-looking young professor, with sweet wife, and budding family. Everything even and normal. It ought to fit right in with your treasured morality.''

"But a baby isn't just something to be *used*, when we—"

"Anybody, anything, is to be used, if it can be. You'll produce I said it's time, cunt.''

How she loathed being called that! It made her feel filthy. She had always tried to hide the feeling, knowing that knowledge of it would make him use the word ten times more often.

"I want to get my degree," she said doggedly.

"When are you going to understand how very secondary that is? Don't you give a damn about doing the least thing toward furthering *my* career? You don't have to answer that. It's obvious. Get out of those clothes before I tear them off. It's our anniversary, isn't it? We're going to do the things we did a year ago today, plus quite a few more.''

He was the one who watched the thermometer, thrusting it roughly into her mouth every morning, reading it with care, charting her temperature. When the temperature change came, they had intercourse regularly for five days. Often, he hardly touched her with more than his penis, performing like a dutiful, but completely bored and passionless stud.

Kiersten had considered renewing the birth control prescription without his knowledge. She had thought that was what she meant to do, but it hadn't happened. She thought about a child. Deep down she wanted one almost painfully, but she knew this was in great part to assuage her own loneliness and desolation, her own sense of failure, bereftness, and worthlessness. It was no responsibility to place on the shoulders of a baby, a child, or anyone else.

When she menstruated again, Roger cursed her violently.

She said wearily, "It almost never happens with the first try Sometimes it takes months . . .''

He glared at her with distaste.

In January there was no period. By the time it should have happened in February, her breasts were very sore and tender, and she was vomiting at odd times.

To her surprise, Roger insisted upon accompanying her to the doctor's office.

"Yes, everything certainly indicates pregnancy," the doctor told them, smiling, in his consulting room after the examination. "Everything looks good, and normal. I'm going to give you some pamphlets to read. The only possible problem I can foresee now is that you're rather small, Mrs. Savage, narrow hips and pelvis. It's possible that a caesarean section might be necessary, but we're a long way from that and—"

"No caesarean," said Roger flatly.

"Beg pardon?"

"Don't women have a joint in their pubic bone, or whatever you call it, that gets loose when they're pregnant, lets their hips expand? If you're going to start talking caesarean this early, she'll see another doctor."

"When do you think the baby will be born?" asked Kiersten, her face hot.

The doctor consulted his calendar. "Before the middle of October, I should think."

The tenth was her birthday, but she didn't mention that.

That night, at home alone, she gave a great deal of consideration to abortion. Roger had no business being a father. Suppose the child inherited his aberrations? But, no, surely those things were not hereditary and she would see to it that he was never, never alone with her child. She could not take its life . . . unless she took her own as well. She badly wanted a drink, something to ease this night a little, but she took nothing. She felt it a lack of courage, the fact that she couldn't face the prospect of suicide. She would never think of this as Roger's baby, only her own. She knew what his attitude would be once it was born. He would find it a nuisance, want it kept well away from him except for brief times of exhibition for the benefit of others. Until it was older . . . Then he might try . . . No, she would see to it that nothing like that was ever allowed to happen.

When she had to begin wearing maternity clothes by the first of May, Roger was delighted. He took her more places than he had since before their marriage, making sure every acquaintance and some complete strangers knew she was pregnant.

One evening, Roger and another couple met Kiersten in the city after classes and they went to dinner. The other couple was dancing. Roger refused even to try these days. Besides being tone deaf he was completely lacking in any sense of rhythm.

"The day after tomorrow is pre-registration for summer semester," Kiersten said lightly. "I can get through that with the baby not due until October."

"You're not going to summer school," he said flatly.

"I don't see why not. I can—"

"We're going to Secesh."

"Oh, Roger—"

"You know I've bogged down with the damned dissertation, with all else I have to do. I've always been able to work well at the ranch. I can get the thing done there, I know I can. We'll come back here by the first of August, to look for a place to live up in Connecticut. You also know I have that job conditionally, with the understanding that the dissertation is finished. We'll leave around the fourth of June. Don't write about it to your mother. I want to surprise them by calling from the Denver airport to be met at Hurleigh."

"You do it then," she said coldly. "I'm going to stay here for summer school and then—"

"You *will* come, Kiersten."

Sometimes, her contentiousness made things interesting, but it had its place and this was not the time for it. He wasn't going to argue much more.

"I tell you I won't," she said hotly.

He leaned close, pressing his fist against her lower abdomen under the tablecloth. "You will do as I say or be hurt—badly. More than that, the kid will get hurt. It's nothing to me if you lose one. We'd just start another."

In Hurleigh, both of them noticed changes. Anne, who had come to meet them at the airport, said, "It's the oil shale business. People are just flooding in here, on prospect, some of them. There aren't nearly enough places for them to live and about all there is for entertainment is bar fights at night. Price will hardly come to town any more. There are four stoplights in town now. When I first came here, there wasn't one. And, did I write you, our road's paved all the way to Mills Crossing?"

She seemed unable to do anything but prattle. This was going to be a tense time for all of them, and Kiersten looked so unwell.

The time at Secesh was a nightmare for Kiersten. Roger asked that they be given separate rooms so that he could work as late into the night as he pleased, but he came into her room at all hours of the night, spying, she knew, thinking he might catch her with Nolan. Nolan was aloof, distant, rarely looking at her. Roger badgered them to sing and play, wanted to have a party for all the Park at which they would perform together. Nolan left the house by sunup and never came in until well after dark. He ate supper with the hands, strongly considered moving to the bunkhouse, but that would be giving too much, showing his desperation to all and sundry too clearly. He and Kiersten exchanged the fewest words possible. One evening in a rare moment of privacy, she cried desperately, "I don't want to be here any more than you want me to be." He gave her a brief cold look and left the living room.

Roger was embarrassingly solicitous of Kiersten in the family's presence, bringing her footstools, cushions for her back, asking if she shouldn't lie down and rest or, if she happened to mention or indicate that the baby was being active, demanding that his hand be placed, sometimes painfully, so that he might feel it move.

The family was worried. Kiersten did not look well and they knew she didn't need this summer's tense situation, sensed that Roger's concern was only for show.

Kiersten's doctor had felt the trip was not a good idea and had insisted she see another doctor several times while she was away. Anne drove her to Hurleigh three times during their stay at Secesh. On the first two occasions Roger made sure to go along, but at the time of the third trip, he was excited about the progress he had begun to make on the dissertation and allowed them to go alone. Gently, Anne tried to elicit information from Kiersten, was she really all right? Was she content enough with her marriage, pleased about the baby? Did things go generally well between her and Roger?

Kiersten answered very little. She seemed to be vague, absent about everything. Her eyes looked red and swollen every morning and she was so thin.

"Kierstie," Anne said gently on that last drive back from Hurleigh, "can you afford to have someone come in and help you for the first week or so after you and the baby come home from the hospital?"

"I don't know, Mother. I think so, but I doubt it will be necessary."

"Would you like me to come? I went to Denver when Penny's girls were born."

"I—yes, of course I'd like it, but I don't think you'd better. I mean, you're needed at Secesh and I—we can manage."

"What if you stayed here with us until after the baby's born?"

Kiersten turned wistful misty eyes to the window. "No, I can't, but thank you. It's a—lovely thought. We'll be going back next week. Then we have to find a place, move again . . ."

"Promise me you'll take it easy."

"Yes, Mother, I'll be fine. Not to worry."

"Kiersten, it's no business of ours, except that we love you very much. But—why did you marry Roger?"

"He—asked me at a time when—well, it just sort of happened."

"Do you—love each other at all?"

"Mother, marriages can be based on a lot of things other than love."

364

"Yes, I suppose so," Anne said dubiously and couldn't restrain a deep sigh of worry and concern.

Roger finished his dissertation and insisted on reading it aloud to all of them as they sat in the living room one evening. Nolan walked out before the reading had begun; Price and Fern nodded with the need for sleep. Anne tried to be polite, say she was sure it was very good, though she really understood little of it. Kiersten said nothing. Roger was infuriated with all of them.

When they returned to the East, they were able to find a house near the university with three bedrooms and a den. The rent seemed phenomenal to Kiersten, but Roger assured her they could afford it

"It's time we had separate bedrooms anyway," he said carelessly "I can always come to you when I choose, can't I?"

"Then we'll make the den into an office and the smaller bedroom can be the nursery."

"No nursery. You keep the kid in with you. I don't ever want to be wakened by squalling. We need the den, the whole lower floor, for the entertaining we'll be doing. I wish there was a wet bar "

When Kiersten saw the new doctor in Connecticut, he said, "You haven't been feeling at all well all these months, have you?"

"Not so very," she admitted, tensing, "but I thought it's just the way pregnancy goes. There's nothing wrong, is there? I mean, the baby . . . ?"

"The baby's fine," he said reassuringly "You must have been told a caesarean could be necessary."

"Only if it's absolutely essential," she said rather grimly, then more intently, "for the baby's sake."

"Yes, of course. I understand. You know, at our hospital here we have a new policy. Fathers are encouraged to be present in the delivery room."

"No," she said quickly, looking, he thought, frightened "He wouldn't want to. Please, don't even talk to my husband about that "

"Perhaps there's someone else you'd like to have, your mother or—"

"No, there—there's no one. I don't want anyone but the necessary medical people."

She went into labor on the seventh of October. The contractions began just as Roger was leaving to teach his early class. They were almost fifteen minutes apart, but violently hard and long-lasting. Good, she thought, that should mean it will be over sooner Soon, I can hold my baby . . . She hoped the pains would be five minutes apart, or less, before Roger came back around three-thirty. She would drive herself to the hospital before he was home. He often bicycled to classes and had left the car this morning. She took a shower, did some light housework, with pauses, packed the rest of her things in the small suitcase, and the coming-home things for the baby.

When Roger came home, he found her lying on the bed soaked in sweat. The pains were still some six minutes apart, but they were so fierce that she was spent, scarcely able to move between them.

"Well, so it's time, is it? Shall we go, little mother?"

She acquiesced weakly. He did not offer help and she was in agony as a contraction came on their way to the car. She had not been afraid of labor but, obviously, she had underestimated it.

A bustling kindly nurse did the necessary preparation, settled Kiersten in a bed in a labor room, while Roger was filling out the necessary papers.

"Have you called Dr. Moore, dear?"

"No," Kiersten panted. "There's still so much time between . . ."

"I'll call and alert him in case he's thinking of going out to dinner or something. Obstetricians rarely get to go out to dinner you know. You have a while to wait. The first baby always takes longer."

Roger came in as the nurse went out. "They say I can go into the delivery room, but you must know I'm not about to witness all that mess. I rather like seeing you here, though, writhing and twisting in pain. Remember, I did this with one little squirt. And, by the way, you're going to breast-feed the kid. I understand mother's milk is an excellent aphrodisiac. If that proves to be true, maybe we'll just keep you pregnant, like a cow."

"Roger, get out!" she gasped.

"Why don't you scream? I understood that the pampered women of this society scream in labor, a great deal."

She twisted a balled-up corner of the sheet against her bared teeth between already dry, cracked lips.

"Let's talk about Nolan," he said, almost gaily. "Did you see how jealous he was? Why didn't you let *him* give you a bellyful? Or wasn't he man enough? I thought he might try to fuck you while we were at the ranch, but I guess he found you as ugly and grotesque as I have these past months, sickly looking and scrawny all over except for the horribly distended belly. Still, he wished it was his. I could see it in his eyes at times. . . . My! that was a strong one! Do you know that seeing you like this makes me want to ball you? I could do it from behind—"

The nurse came in, rustling, saying brightly, "It's time to check you again, Mrs. Savage."

Roger went out, but it seemed only a moment before he was back again.

"You mustn't worry that I'll get lonely, while you're away," he said with mock solicitude. "There's a young man I've had lined up to come and keep me company. Even you must know by now that I'm very much bi-sexual. There's the old goat I see twice a week in New York. When he cashes in, we're going to be rather wealthy. And I'll have earned it, every penny. I prefer them young, though, boys *or* girls. . . . Oh, my dear girl! You really must let go and scream. You've always been stubborn about screaming.

"Have you thought there's the possibility you could die? It's not likely, of course, childbirth is a part of what women were made for, but there's the possibility. Imagine me a young widower with a child to raise . . .

"What *are* you thinking of in this time of travail? Chappie? Do you wish he were here to see you writhe, with your lips drawn back like that? You really look as if you're having orgasms. Is it anything like that at all? . . . Answer me. I think you're playing this pain thing to the hilt, even though you haven't started screaming yet. Women have babies every second. In other societies, many of them deliver themselves and miss hardly a bit of whatever work they're doing. That would make an interesting sociological study, the production of young by females, cunts, in various societies. . . . Do you want me to rub your back or something? Aren't husbands supposed to stand around terrified and addled, waiting for some little thing like that to do? . . . *You* tell me about Nolan, Kiersten. We've hardly talked about him in two years of marriage, almost two years. What was it really like in bed with him? Did he—?"

"Roger, please get out!" she sobbed.

"You know I married you because of him, don't you? If I hadn't been so aware of his wanting you so much, I'd have found a far more beautiful and agreeable woman to marry. Watching him this summer, when he thought he wasn't being watched, made it all almost worthwhile. He's always had everything he's wanted one way and another, but I guess I've finally taught him a lesson, haven't I? With your sweet cooperation, of course."

The nurse came in again and when she had finished her examination, Kiersten gasped, "What time is it?"

"Just after six, dear. You're doing fine."

It didn't seem they had been here over two hours, and yet it seemed forever, as if Roger had been talking forever. She said, "Please, don't let him come in here again."

"Your husband, you mean?"

"Yes." The word was almost a growl as another contraction gripped her fiercely. "He—he upsets me."

"Well, yes, I'll tell him. Doctor's on his way. I'm going to give you a shot now, for the pain. You're dilated enough. Your contractions are very hard. With all this, you know, you don't have to make such an effort to be awfully brave.''

But Roger came back. "It's my wife and child," he told the disgruntled nurse crisply. "I have every right to be here."

Mercifully now, Kiersten couldn't seem to sort out the meaning of his constant flow of words. The contractions were coming very hard and close together. She scarcely seemed to have time to breathe between them. Finally, without her being aware of it for a time, he was gone.

Two nurses came and helped her onto a gurney. She was only half-conscious. The contractions were her whole body, seemingly the entire world, and it would never end. She hardly knew when they lifted her onto the delivery table. But she realized dimly when the doctor came in.

She panted, "Doctor, I have to ask you something."

"All right, Kiersten," he said with a gentle briskness. "What is it?"

Another contraction gripped her, but after a time she gasped, "Isn't there a—a shot or something you can give me, so my—milk won't come?"

"Why, yes, but I thought you wanted to breast-feed."

"No, please!" It was a weak wail.

"All right now, that's all right," he said, patting her shoulder. "The nurse is making a note so we'll be sure to remember the shot as soon as the baby's delivered."

A little later, she dimly heard the words "difficult presentation," and "section."

"My baby," she pleaded. "Don't let anything happen to my baby."

The nurse wiped her face gently with a wet cool cloth, put something on her cracked bleeding lips.

"Now, Kiersten," said the doctor with bright firmness. "We're getting someone in here to give you just a little more anesthetic. Maybe you won't even go completely to sleep, just be drowsy, more comfortable. Don't you agree you've had enough of this? We're going to get this young one born."

She did not really remember the birth. She felt a nurse wiping her face again, heard her saying dimly, "You have a dear little boy." There was a moment of infant cries that seemed very far away and she felt the wet warm weight of her son as he was laid on her abdomen. Later, she wished she might have been more cognizant of that.

She did not remember being taken to a room, placed in a bed.

When she opened her eyes sluggishly, Roger was sitting beside her.

"About time," he said casually, with a little derisive smile. "It's past eleven. Almost two hours since my son was born."

"He's all right?" she murmured, trying to rouse herself, in fear that something might be wrong.

"They say so. Fine. Ugly little bastard, but so are all the others in the nursery. He's got my hair. That's about as much as I can tell so far. They've got a thing strapped on his wrist that says 'baby Savage.' Sounds dangerous, doesn't it? They were asking about a name. We never really discussed it, but it's going to be Roger, of course. I never have cared much for Paul, my middle name. Had you thought of anything?"

"Price, for Dad," she said drowsily.

He laughed, "Oh, no, that's Chappie's name, too. Did you really think I'd forget? What about your own poor, long-dead father? Your real one? What was his name?"

"It was—Tim."

"I don't like that. His last name was Owen, wasn't it? That might do. Roger Owen Savage. Yes, I'll tell them that. The doctor said you had a bad time. People always say women birthing have had a bad time. He wanted to give me a full explanation, but I'm afraid I'm not very interested in that sort of thing. You're okay now, right?"

"Yes," she said, but when she moved a little, she felt torn to pieces inside, and she could feel that she was bleeding rather a lot.

"I've called them at Secesh," he was saying, "told them everything's fine. Your mother suggested she could come when you get out of the hospital, but I don't want her here. I told her you'd be able to manage." He did not say that he had promised Anne Kiersten would call as soon as she was fully awake.

Roger stood up. "Well, you came through with a son after all, didn't you?" He kissed her forehead. "Think what a normal happy little family we'll be with the little stranger come among us. I'm going home to bed now. I'm worn out. By the way, you told them you're going to breast-feed, right?"

When a nurse came in almost immediately to check her vital signs, Kiersten made sure the shot had been given her to dry up the milk.

They brought her the baby a little later and she looked at him in wonder. "Who are you, little boy? What will you grow up to be? What sort of person? A safe one," she said, holding him close, a fierce protectiveness rising up in her. "Safe and sound and whole. I promise you, I'll never let him—"

The nurse came back, saying gently, "I have to take him now, dear. Doctor said only for a minute. You still have some excess bleeding and you must lie very still. Miss Fraily is coming with a shot for you.''

Kiersten dozed and dreamed the birth over again, dreamed it had been Nolan who was with her. She woke groggily, tears streaming down her face, a nurse patting her hand.

"There, there, everything's all right now. You're doing nicely and you have that beautiful, healthy little baby boy. I thought you were calling for someone. Do you want your husband? You have this private room, and if you really feel you want him here, we could—''

"No," said Kiersten, gulping, trying to stop the tears. "I don't think I was calling for anyone. I don't need anyone here. Tomorrow, I want to be moved into a room with another mother.''

24

"There's going to be a houseful," said Fern happily at breakfast one early June morning. "Kiersten and Roger and the little boy here for almost the whole summer. What is little Owen now, four?"

"He'll be four in October," said Anne, a shadow crossing her face.

How she had longed to see this grandchild! Kiersten and Roger had not been at Secesh since the summer before the baby was born. Roger had taught summer classes sometimes; other summers they had gone to places where friends of his spent their holidays. There had been a time, two years ago, when Anne felt she could not bear waiting any longer. On top of her yearning was a deep concern about Kiersten and the child. Kiersten's letters were very much as they had always been, light, chatty and full of small bits of information about the baby, but Anne had known there were serious things wrong with the marriage from the first. Price refused to go east, but she made up her mind to pay them a visit. However, she had called Kiersten first.

"Mother, I wish you could," Kiersten had said carefully, after a silence, "but I'm really afraid it would be better if you didn't come. Roger—doesn't like people in the house, unless he invites them. You know, he's trying to work on a book now, when he has time. He . . ,"

The tears spilled over from Anne's eyes, but she had said levelly, "All right, Kierstie. I think I understand, but you are all right? You and the baby?"

"We are, Mother, as long as home life goes smoothly. We're fine."

"You'll keep writing, or you'll call if . . . ?"

"Of course I'll keep writing. Don't you know I'm too much of a chatterbox not to write letters?"

Fern was going on now happily to say, "Penny and the girls here for August, Chris for some of that time, and those friends of yours,

Nolan, what's their name? McIver?, some time in August. Isn't it two children they have?''

"Yes, two," he said.

"Well, it's none too early to think about airing the quilts and extra mattresses from the attic. We're going to need a lot of pallet beds and things."

"Sounds like a lot of young 'uns under foot to me," complained Reuben. "Mostly right in the middle of hayin'. Couldn' a picked a worst time."

"They won't be sleeping in the bunkhouse," Anne reminded him pacifically. "It'll be fun."

"Them of Butch's don't sleep in the bunkhouse neither," said Reuben unpacifically, "but they're always under foot. Somebody ought to tell him an' Yola there's ways *not* to have kids, for Chrissake We've already built one extra room on down there."

"Like what?" Nolan asked him, grinning.

"Huh?"

"What ways to stop having kids?"

"Ah, towhead, you ought to know more about that than I do. What do you do, them Saturday nights you go to Hurleigh?"

"See movies," Nolan said blandly. "Eat. Dance."

Fern had got up to get more biscuits. She set the plate on the table and stood beside Nolan. First, she pushed the hair off his forehead, then stood there with her hands on her hips.

"And when are you going to marry, young man? Bring some children into this house to stay? You've got to do it before us old ones get too cranky to put up with them."

"There's no one to marry," he said, placidly taking a hot biscuit to butter.

"Why, there's that pretty school teacher, Martha Paisley, just waiting for you to ask her."

"No, she's not," he said, adding jam to his buttered bread "She's gone back home for the summer."

"But she'll be back," Anne prodded gently.

"She's a pretty girl," Fern said stoutly. "Been teaching here three years and I can't believe that's all she wants her life to be."

"Watches him with calf's eyes," said Reuben, grinning toothlessly He had finally got a set of false teeth, but kept them locked in a trunk in the bunkhouse. His gums were now hard, and strong enough to handle anything.

Price said soberly, "If Secesh had a bad year, a teacher could always go back to work."

Fern said fervently, "I want you to give her a lot of consideration over the summer, Chappie. She likes you—a lot. You don't want to turn into a dried-up old bachelor like Reuben."

Reuben snorted. "I got more juice left than you'd imagine, *Miz* Marvle."

This served to turn Fern's attention, and Nolan was relieved when she sat down in her own place again.

That morning, Price and Nolan took a herd of first-calf heifers, with their young, up to the high pastures along Cranky Creek. This lot of calves had been branded and vaccinated.

Nolan rode in front of the cattle, opening and closing gates. Price rode behind, with two of his cattle dogs working the sides of the herd. Nolan could handle the dogs well now, but not with Price in evidence. When they could see him, they heeded signals from no one else.

Nolan had a puppy, only a few months old, whom Price had decreed should be the next Matey. Nolan kept the young dog always with him around the buildings and brought him into the house to sleep, somewhat to Price's consternation. This dog was going to be his, heed only him when the training and working time had come. Young Matey was not strong enough yet to bring on a drive like this; he would only get in the way and become exhausted.

The spring had come early this year. The country was beautiful, meadows starred with dandelion, wild iris, and other flowers. Today there was only a mild breeze, warm, but smelling of the snow pack that still lay heavily in the high mountains. Nolan never saw change in the country without thinking of Kiersten: how she would love a day like this.

He opened a wire gate with some difficulty, waited for the bawling cattle to pass, secured it, and rode back to the head of the herd, wondering just how to classify his status at Secesh. In the fall, he would have been back for the better part of six years. He had no ideas on a grand scale, as Hugh had had, but, very often, when he suggested something, all the hands except Butch waited to see that it would check out with Price. Well, that was all right, normal, he supposed, but he was thirty years old; threads of gray were appearing in his hair, though they were scarcely noticeable because of the hair's fairness and streaking from the sun. He ought to be considered foreman instead of Reuben, but that would certainly not happen until the old man could no longer hobble, and he certainly wished him no ill, nor Price either, who didn't seem to be slowing down at all.

During this time of the return to the ranch, Nolan had participated in the cutting of seven record albums and had written music for two television commercials. He had been asked to do the music for another movie, but had turned that down. With these times away, it was natural that the hands, the new ones, did not look to him for much on the ranch. He was not there all the time, and often, on his return, there was practically a whole new crew. What really bothered him was his own restlessness and small gnawing dissatisfaction. He couldn't say why these things existed. There was nothing better he could wish for, on this cool-warm June morning, than to be riding easy across the meadows.

Well, there was one thing. He could wish that Kiersten and Roger were not coming for the summer. They hadn't been here since before the little boy was born. Nolan's life was made bearable by not seeing them together.

Fern had come to Nolan's room one night in the winter after Roger had announced the wedding. It had been spring, actually, early April, though the country was still in the grip of deep winter. Nolan had just come in from a stint in the calving barn. He had been very tired, sure sleep must come immediately but, as usual for the past four months, it had not. He had turned his lamp on again and tried to read. It was hard to concentrate on the book, or on anything. The hurt was still like a huge knotted fist inside his chest then.

Fern had said gently, "Don't get up. There's nothing wrong that needs you. I just want to talk for a minute."

She had sat on the side of his bed, pushing back his hair.

"Chappie, hon, you've grieved long enough. It's four months now since they were married. What's done is done. Your hurt won't change it. It's a little like there's been a death in the family for all of us. We're bothered by that marriage, but there's no way to undo it. We haven't seen you smile in a coon's age."

"I hadn't meant to make it worse," he had replied huskily, turning his face away from her kind concerned eyes.

"Well, hard things happen, but you—a person—has to go on living. None of us can quite imagine why Kiersten's done this, but she's a grown girl and there's no changing it. Try to let your mind be a little easier. It's plain to us that you're not sleeping well. You don't relish your food. You never play music any more. I guess what I'm asking, really, is for you to try to make it a little easier on the rest of us. Maybe that's not fair, but it's something you can do with your mind besides grieve."

He had tried and it had worked to a degree, but it had all come back, worse than ever, that summer they had been here, with Roger exhibiting Kiersten and her pregnancy, that gloating, possessive look on his smooth handsome face . . .

After they had gone Nolan had begun all over, pretending it didn't matter, that he didn't care. Still, he thought, this really was the heart of his restlessness and vague dissatisfaction with everything he did, the fact that Kiersten was with Roger, always, that they . . .

Maybe marriage was the answer for him. He didn't see how he could ever possibly love anyone as he had loved Kierstie, but he knew there were different kinds of love, all manner and gradations. He did sorely want his own children. His wife, their children, would ease the seemingly everlasting hurt and anger in him, maybe eventually obliterate the pain and bitterness. But were these things justification for a marriage? Would this be fair to a wife? No, he'd have to tell her, a part of it at least. Would anyone then accept him, suspecting he still harbored a strange painful love for someone else? Well, he wouldn't have to put it that baldly. And with time, working at a marriage, perhaps he could stop loving Kierstie. If only the anger would overcome the pain, dispel it, wash it away, then he could try to overcome the anger . . .

Maybe he would move into the bunkhouse with all these people coming, have most of his meals with the hands, at Yola's table. That way he wouldn't be so conscious of them, right across the hall, or in the room next to his, wouldn't have to look at Roger's placid gloating face in the morning, see Kiersten avert her eyes from his, looking as if she, too, were covering a wound. . . . But why had she done it? No, not that again. There had been years of trying to reconcile that and it was time he drove the questions—and Kiersten—out of his mind.

Another of his difficulties was with Price. There was still something between them that neither seemed capable of overcoming. Nolan couldn't understand it; perhaps Price couldn't either, if he ever really thought about it. Price was often critical, or simply seemed to withhold judgment, indifferent, aloof, maintaining a little distance between them. Nolan was aware that he did the same thing. Perhaps they could never be close, good comfortable friends, but he would like to feel, just now and then, that he had Price's wholehearted approval, his open caring. Perhaps, he thought, the idea was always there, in the back of Price's mind that he might decide to leave again. Perhaps it was simply that his father really was still disappointed in him, let down, unhappy. Nolan had done all he could to show his love for and pride in Secesh, to prove he would never go away again for any lengthy period of time, but the coolness between them, the reticence persisted. He knew it was not entirely one-sided. He had streaks of the same things in himself. If Price ever gave him an opening, though . . . what? That would be when his own reticence would surface, in the form of indifference or silence or . . .

When they had brought the cattle through the final gate, they sat down on the bank of Cranky Creek to eat the lunch which had been packed for them, and to watch the young animals get themselves sorted out, the right calf with the right heifer, all of them milling about, calling and bawling loudly. The horses, ground tied, moved about a little to munch at the short thick fresh grass. The dogs, panting heavily, lapped a little water from the creek and lay down tiredly in a shade of their own.

"It looks like a good year," Nolan said, after they had eaten in silence for a time.

"Maybe," Price said. "I want to set the irrigation gates up here today, and ride the fence line between here and Nelson's. That whole fence ought to be replaced. So many posts have been frost-heaved out of the ground. You go up there and see just how much damage there is. We ought to rebuild it, but unless he'll send some hands to help, I don't know that we'll get it done this year."

There was another silence. Nolan poured them each another cup of coffee from the big thermos.

Price said, "That government man was around again yesterday." Nolan nodded.

"They want to buy that piece of land we've got that runs up into Kilrayne Canyon, add it to the wilderness area they're proposing."

"And you told him . . . ?"

Price's look was fierce. "At the last, he said they might be able to condemn it, buy it whether we wanted to sell or not. I told him no. There's never been an acre of this place sold off, and there won't be, so long as I'm alive. We don't do much with that land, except use it for a wood lot, but it's part of Secesh. I'm half-minded to start carrying a gun anyway, all these people coming in when every bit of the land is posted."

"Have you talked with Walters about the forest grazing?"

"I have. The per unit price is up again, but we need to use it. We'll get the water started up here, the next few days, and then get all the stock off the meadows down below."

They finished their lunch in silence. Nolan poured the rest of the coffee and lit a cigarette. Price filled his pipe and lit it, leaning back more comfortably against a tree.

"It's beautiful up here," Nolan said softly, almost to himself.

"Yes, but I always favored Picketpin Creek myself."

Nolan smoked the cigarette down, put it out carefully and stood up.

"I'll go have a look at the fence then."

He had reached his horse, brought the reins over its head, and put a foot in the stirrup when Price said, "Nolan, it wouldn't be a bad idea."

"What's that?" he asked, looking back.

"What Fern was talking about at breakfast. There ought to be young ones on the place, young Savages."

A few nights later, on a Saturday, Nolan went down to The Reserve, the bar and cafe at Mills Crossing. He was very tired, but the restlessness was on him, so after he'd had his shower, he told Anne he wouldn't be home for supper.

Often there was a dance at The Reserve on Saturday night; usually Butch and Nolan played for it. Tonight there was no dance, but the place was full, ranchers and hands, saw mill people—all of them Nolan knew, at least by sight—some fishermen, and a few dudes from the Shadow River Guest Ranch.

Nolan liked Saturday nights at The Reserve because they served Mexican food. He was standing near the door, acknowledging greetings from all sides, when a louder voice called his name. It was Terry Ellenbogen, sitting at a corner table with his new wife.

"Barbara, this is Nolan Savage. I'm showing her the night life of Dunraven Park."

"It must not seem like much," said Nolan, shaking the proffered slim hand and sitting down in the chair Terry was indicating.

"I'm so pleased places like this still exist," she said warmly. "I think I'd be willing to stay here all our lives, if Terry would."

"Have you got your office set up yet?" Nolan asked.

"Well, no, I've decided to stay on staff at the University Hospital, for a while at least. I'm doing some teaching and there's some research I'm working on. We sure won't get rich, but Barbara's a nurse, so we'll get by."

"If he does decide to set up private practice some day," said Barbara, "I hope it will be in a small town. We wouldn't get rich there, either, but I'm originally from Chicago and I love the country here so much."

Grace Anderson, the waitress, came and rested her hand on Nolan's shoulder. "I guess you want the number three combination with extra green chile and a pot of coffee."

"Right," said Nolan. "Grace, you are a true beauty and a joy forever."

Grace was well into her fifties, but her face, flushed from the work, grew a little redder and she giggled like a girl.

They talked about ranching, about the Park, about Denver, and some of Terry's and Barbara's work there. The Ellenbogens finished their supper as Grace was bringing Nolan's.

"You're doing quite a business tonight," Terry said to her.

"If every night was Saturday," said Grace, "we might break even. The bar is the only thing we make money from." Then, soberly,

"See that girl over there, little thing with long black hair? She's staying at the dude ranch, been in here two or three times before. There's not an extra table. Can I bring her over here? She always looks sort of lost and lonesome."

"Sure," said Terry. "We can't stay much longer anyway. No reason why Nolan should eat alone."

She introduced herself to Grace as Marny Everett and Grace introduced her to the others at the table. She was a small girl, hardly five feet tall, and very thin, but with a perfect little figure under the obviously new jeans and western shirt. Her hair was black and fell below her waist, tied back with a red ribbon. Her face was small and perfect, heart-shaped, dominated by large dark eyes.

"I'm staying at the Shadow River Ranch," she told them, a little shyly. "They said there might be a dance here tonight."

"This is one of the regular musicians," said Terry, indicating Nolan, "and I haven't seen him tuning up anything."

"They'll be dancing in the bar any time now," Nolan said, "but just to the jukebox tonight."

Her beautiful sad eyes kept flicking to his face and away.

Grace came to take her order. Marny asked only for a sandwich, but she also wanted a drink.

"Never mind, Grace," said Nolan. "I'll bring the drink."

Terry and Barbara stood up to say their goodbyes. When he came back, carrying the scotch and soda, Nolan thought how alone she looked at the table, small and vulnerable.

"Are you at Shadow River for long?" he asked.

"I'm afraid so," she said ruefully. "You see, I'm an actress. That is, I have been. I've played summer stock since I was sixteen, then I went to an acting school and I've been in repertory theater. It's what I've always wanted, to be an actress, and just when I'm really getting started, ingenue parts and all that, I had a sort of breakdown . . . too much into drugs and things, I guess—too excited with what I was doing. Too much tension all the time. The doctor said I shouldn't play the summer stock I'd been counting on this year, that I should have a complete rest and change for several months. I've been to Europe and all that bit, lived there, didn't really care for it. I went to school, years ago, with the daughter of the people who own Shadow River, and we've kept in touch—sort of. So I thought I'd come west. I've never been in this part of the country before, if you don't count flying over in planes. I drove out. It was an awful bore, though the mountains are truly beautiful, once you finally get to them. I've been here about ten days—since they opened up the guest ranch—and already I'm getting a little—wild. What in the world do you *do* here?"

"Well, *I* work," he said, smiling.

378

His smile was beautiful. All of him was very handsome, the face of planes and angles, the abundant curly hair, the intense gray eyes, and the voice made chills run along her spine. She said, "You own a ranch?"

"No, it's my dad's place, Secesh, just at the opposite end of the Park from Shadow River."

"Yes, I think I've heard the name. Well, *I* can't find anything to do. I mean, how much can you sleep? I brought about half a ton of books, but I'm not really that fond of reading. I had riding lessons years ago, but I'm still afraid of horses. I've had some long walks, and that was nice, but how much of *that* can you do? Look, I don't mean to sound forward and facetious, but don't I know you from somewhere? You have a face that people would remember and there's definitely something about your voice. I keep trying to connect you with a record album cover."

"I've done some records," he said. "Several with Susan Lister and I used to belong to a group called The Stewards."

"Yes!" she cried. "You tell those fabulous stories and do that wonderful music for lots of people as well as for yourself. It's your voice I remember, as well as your face. My God! and you *work* here? *Stay* here?"

"That's right."

"I'd give a lot to meet Susan Lister, David Harris, John Sage, all those super people. Weren't you with Susan at Carnegie Hall once? And I do remember The Stewards. What happened to them? It was really a good group."

"We broke up, a long time ago. Will you mind if I smoke?"

"No, go ahead. I'm supposed to be off cigarettes, too, but—"

"Then I won't."

"No, please do. Don't make me feel like a louse. It's the pills I miss, the uppers, especially. But I *can* get a little high, just looking at this country. I've been popping lots of pills for years, just to keep me going, but I'm not to take anything more than aspirin this summer, and I'm to gain at least ten pounds. I've gone on their float trip, down through Spanish Canyon to the lake. That was fun, and really beautiful, but how many times can you do it? And I loathe fishing."

"But you like folk music, do you?"

"I love it. I wish it weren't so hard to find records any more."

"There's a place in Denver where you can find all that are available these days."

"Yes, I've been thinking of Denver. God, you have to drive seventy miles here, just a see a movie, and I've already seen what's been showing."

"Probably, you shouldn't go to Denver if you're to rest and—"

"Well, what *am* I going to do? The other guests at the ranch are a lot of old bores, fat bald men who puff over anything, their wives who are gushy and more afraid than I am, couples in their thirties with bunches of children. I've thought a couple of the people who work there might be interesting, but they're always busy, of course. What do you do on a real ranch? Ride around with a guitar, singing to the cows?"

"Not bloody likely," he said, smiling again. "Right now, we're branding and vaccinating calves, moving cattle to our high pastures, fertilizing the hay fields, getting the irrigation water going, mending fences. You have a car. Would you like to come and watch some day?"

"Well—maybe, but I couldn't be any help. How many people work there? Now I remember what I've heard about Secesh, that it's the biggest ranch around here."

"There are only five of us working now, though we'll need more for the haying."

"Secesh is an odd name, isn't it?"

He explained briefly about his great-grandparents.

"I like it," she said happily, "the idea of seceding from everything, just on general principles."

He said, "Would you like to dance?"

No wonder they had told her to gain weight, he thought, holding her. It was rather like holding a small bird, tension, fast heartbeat, and all.

Soon they went back into the restaurant half of the building, where it was quieter. There were plenty of empty tables now. This time, Nolan brought drinks for both of them.

"Do you have fights here?" she asked, her dark eyes a little feverish with interest and anticipated excitement, "like in the movies?"

"Sometimes," he said, feeling a little impatient. "You know, westerners aren't that much different from easterners. There are just fewer of us."

"I suppose so," she said, a little deflated and apologetic. "But, do you know, I actually expected Indian encampments, things like that?"

"I'm not surprised," he said dryly. "That's always how we seem to be presented east of the Mississippi, particularly east of the Hudson. There is more here than just empty country to fly over, going from coast to coast."

"Of course," said Marny soberly. "I'm twenty-four years old. I should have been able to figure some of that out on my own, if I'd ever just thought about it."

"Have you mostly lived in New York?"

"Oh no, but not so very far from there, most of the time. I've spent my life in boarding schools and summer camps. You see, Daisy, my mother—she likes to be called by another cutesy name, but *I* won't use it—Daisy's vocation is marrying people. Two of her husbands have died; one was my father, but that was years after they had divorced. Each time she's married it's been a higher step up the social ladder, and more money, too, of course. I think it's her sixth she's working on now. Anyway, a kid got in the way, so I went to all these schools and camps and things. She introduces me, when she has to, as her niece, her ward. Most of the husbands haven't known I was hers. God, if I ever have kids, I'll know what *not* to do. At least there's that. I want kids some day, I really do, all nice and legit and cozy, with a very special father. My father died when I was five. I don't remember very much about him, except that he was nice. They had to get married, but Daisy was about six months along before she'd do it. Abortion then wasn't what it is today, and she was afraid she'd ruin her health or something. My dad really loved her, I think, but all he owned at that time was one medium-sized department store. As soon as I was born and her episiotomy had healed, she was off to Nevada for a divorce. My father loved me, too, kept me with him, with a housekeeper, until he died."

The big dark eyes were bleak and misty. She tried to smile, to alter her mood.

"God, I do go on! You're a very good listener. Has anyone ever told you that? And very handsome, too."

"Would you like to dance again?"

"I'm afraid I'm not very good with cow music," she said with a forlorn smile. "Could you just get us another drink, maybe?"

"Are you sure you're not supposed to be off alcohol as well?"

She scowled. She was even pretty frowning.

"Oh, please don't do that. I didn't come all this way to find another damned doctor."

He brought another drink for each of them. Setting her glass before her, he said firmly, "Okay, this is the last one. They're running out of scotch."

She laughed a little, but her eyes were still sad. She said, "You're kidding, aren't you?"

"No. Remember this is the backwoods, the other side of nowhere."

Now the smile was gone. She stared at her glass sorrowfully.

He said, "If you remember the picture on Susan Lister's Carnegie Hall album, maybe you remember that there were three of us in the background."

"Yes," she said with an abrupt change of mood, eagerly, "you and a girl and a big black man."

"Well, we're all going to be together again. It'll be later in the summer, the middle of haying, but I should think there'll be some playing and singing done somehow. You might want to come for that?"

"Oh, could I? It sounds awfully far away, though."

"Do you play anything? Sing?"

"I've had to have piano lessons all my life, though I still can't do much by ear. I *can* carry a tune. When I was at school in Switzerland, my finishing-off school, they gave lessons in playing the lute. I've brought my lute with me."

"Grand," he said. "Then you can really join us."

"Well, I'll have to do a lot of practicing and I really hate doing almost anything alone."

They sat on. She nursed her drink, making it last, talking while he listened.

"Two o'clock!" said Marny incredulously as there began to be signs of closing. "This is the best evening I've had since I came here. But"—with a little pout—"no fights."

"We should have danced more," Nolan said. "Then there might have been a fight over you."

"Would you have fought?"

"I'd have done my damnedest not to."

"Not even over me?"

"Well . . ."

She leaned toward him. "Will you come home with me? I have one of their little rustic cabins, not a room in the lodge, so there's privacy. I—I'm afraid of the dark and I—hear things. Please? Just for a while?"

So they drove down to Shadow River Ranch in their separate cars.

"Like, what was that?" she said a little tremulously when they had shut off motors and lights and stood together on the graveled drive.

"Only coyotes," he said, taking the key she held out.

"Yes, I thought so. They're spooky. I don't like them. Even the wind makes scary noises here. God, I hate being alone!"

When they were in the cabin, she turned on all the lights there were.

"I've brought a little really good hash," she confided. "Want to smoke some before we—go on to other things?"

"No, let's not do that," he said gently.

She gestured to an armchair. He sat down and she sat on his lap, curled up like a kitten and, he thought, scarcely heavier.

"I want to tell you something," she said in a small voice. "You'll believe me, won't you?"

"Yes."

"I haven't done much sleeping around, though it's expected of someone like me and I did get into it pretty heavily there for a little while before I—had the breakdown or whatever it was. Lovemaking is important to me. I wouldn't have asked just any cowboy to come back here."

"We don't have to make love," he said softly, and she shivered, drawing close to him, feeling the slight tremor through his body. "I can just stay here for a while and then—"

"I want to make love with you," she said urgently. "Just your voice could seduce anybody. But, you have to understand, even if we did it all summer, there'd have to be nothing *to* it. I mean, I can see and hear in all you say that you'd never go away from here to live and even if we should—fall in love—which I think I could do with you, without half-trying—I'd never stay here."

He caressed her small body with his thin strong calloused hands, saying nothing.

"You have magic hands," she murmured, luxuriating in his touch. "Will you do two things for me?"

"If I can."

"While we're making love, will you say 'I love you, Marny?' Not for real, you know. It's just that I like to hear the words." Her breath came faster as he deftly unsnapped her shirt. "And—and will you stay here until I'm asleep?"

It had been so long for Nolan. His trembling increased, holding her.

A long time afterward, she said dreamily, "You're a fantastic lover. Lots of people must have told you that." Then, a little more sharply, "Are you in love, for real, with someone?"

"No.'

"It's just a feeling I have. It's all right, you know, with me, only I wouldn't want her to mind, and she surely would. You do make beautiful love."

"You make it beautiful," he said tenderly. "Go to sleep now. Shall I turn off the lights?"

"Leave the little lamp on the dresser burning. I told you, I'm afraid of the dark." She snuggled against him. "Thank you for coming home with me, Mr. Savage, and for—everything."

"You know my name is Nolan."

"Yes, of course I know, but I love the sound of Savage. Maybe that's what I came west to find. Could you—do something for me next Saturday? I'll really have to go to Hurleigh by then, to get my birth control prescription renewed. Maybe there'd be a bit more of a variety of restaurants to choose from, a movie I haven't . . ."

Her voice drifted to silence, her breathing at last becoming calm and slow. She was hugging his arm and it was a long time before he dared try to extricate it. He was going to have no sleep at all this night, but it didn't matter. Having this perfect little body respond to his desperate eagerness was the best thing that had happened to him in years. His gratitude was immeasurable. He felt that he could fall in love with her, though he didn't mean to, and he was grateful, too, for discovering that it was a possibility. It had come at just the right time, with Kiersten and Roger due to arrive next week. Perhaps he truly was free at last, and he would stay free with Marny, too, as she had said She *had* given him fair warning . . .

He eased out of bed finally, dressed, found pencil and paper on the small desk.

"Dear Marny, Thank you for coming west this summer, even if there are very few gun fights these days. I'll be happy to go to Hurleigh with you next Saturday. I'll call one day soon about it. If you're ever bored enough to want to find out what ranching is really like, come to Secesh, any time."

25

The following week Anne drove down to meet Kiersten, Owen, and Roger at Hurleigh's airport. She found her heart beating fast and her throat dry with excitement as she waited for sight of the twin-engine plane which would bring them. She parked carefully, though there was plenty of room. She had brought a trailer down and stocked it with groceries before the flight was due. She sat in the car to wait for the plane.

Kiersten had always been good and thoughtful about writing letters. Some of them over these past years had sounded almost happy, though there was the undertone of working hard at it, and the best ones had come when Roger was away from home. She had sold illustrations for almost a dozen children's books now and recently she had done the artwork for the jackets of two adult books. They had a new house. Someone Roger had known in New York had died, leaving him a very sizable legacy. The house, Kiersten had written, was perfect for their needs. Roger had his office and bedroom in an almost detached wing on the first floor. The second story contained Kiersten's room, Owen's, and a guest room and, above all, there was an attic, which doubled as Kiersten's studio and Owen's playroom. A woman came to clean twice weekly.

Anne was still deeply disturbed by Kiersten's asking her not to come two years ago, when Anne had felt she could wait no longer to see her grandson, and that she must try to see for herself if Kiersten was all right, reasonably safe and happy. Anne did not trust Roger, feared him a little for her daughter's sake. How good it would be to see them at last, Kiersten and Owen, to talk, to be able really to use her own judgment. She remembered the summer of Kiersten's pregnancy with worry and concern.

Kiersten had sent many pictures of Owen, some of them her own drawings. Often an entire letter was concerned with him, things he had done and said, his weight, height, and so on. They agreed at Secesh that he was a handsome little boy. He had dark wavy chestnut hair like Roger's, eyes of a darker blue than anyone's in the family, and the Savage face. It made for a happy mixture and Anne, as Fern said, "Couldn't wait to get her hands on the little monkey."

She knew, too, that Roger was working on a book, that the university where he taught insisted that its professors publish something now and then, and that he had not yet done so. He said he had always done his best work at Secesh and that was why they were coming, at last. She wasn't sure it was going to be such a fortuitous place for him this year. Penny had called to say that she and the girls were coming earlier than planned, and there was a black couple, with two children, who were taking a month off to look at the West, and whom Nolan had invited for a visit the last time he was in New York. There would be a houseful of children at times. Anne looked forward to this, but it did not bode well for someone who was trying to write a book. She had felt it only fair that Roger be warned, so she had written about the various visitors, but they were, thank God, still coming. Very soon now she would see her daughter for the first time in four years and her grandson for the first time ever.

Kiersten, in a window seat with Owen on her lap, answered the little boy's questions rather absently. She was so eager for Hurleigh, Fairweather, and at last Dunraven Park and Secesh that it made a physical pain in her chest. Surely it would be her mother who met them. Anne did almost all of those sorts of errands. Kiersten could see her in her mind and she longed to throw her arms about Anne and cry and cry, for all the years and for the sheer joy of coming home. Her loneliness and fear would be assuaged for an entire summer.

A stranger sat in the seat beside her. She thought he must be a salesman. Roger was across the aisle, reading some of his research material. Owen's chatter drove him to distraction. Almost everything about Owen and Kiersten irritated Roger, at the least, but he refused violently to see an end to the marriage. He took his meals alone, kept to his own private wing of the house when he was at home, except when there was entertaining to be done. Then he wanted Owen, scrubbed and shining, trotted out for inspection, then put away and forgotten, like some slightly unusual toy. Then, during a party, when he had several drinks, he became almost the maudlin husband, touching Kiersten possessively, watching her every move, trying to listen to her conversations. These last, of course, were for later criticism.

They had reached an understanding, or perhaps impasse was the better word, soon after Owen's birth. When the baby was a few weeks old, Kiersten had become so depressed that she thought again of suicide. It was impossible, of course; there was the baby and she loved him fiercely. One night when Roger was out, she decided she must leave him. She could bear the situation no longer. She had begun to pack her things and the baby's when Roger walked into the room, taking her completely by surprise. His face was frightening, bloated, and flushed with anger. He had been drinking. He had begun to fling about the things she had laid out on her bed, ripping clothing, throwing a suitcase against the wall, shouting, waking the sleeping Owen.

"You'll never leave me, do you hear!" he had cried, "unless *I* tell you to go. Just where did you think you were going to get away from me? Secesh?" He had laughed horribly.

Then he had gone to the crying baby, twisting a tiny arm until the infant screamed in pain. Kiersten had fought to thrust herself between them, receiving a bad bruise on her cheek and a bloody mouth.

"If you went to Secesh, I'd be there the next day. If you went somewhere else, anywhere, I'd find you and I'd kill the kid. Do you believe that? You'd better believe it because it's true if truth was ever told. We'll live separate lives, so long as you do your duty by the marriage, but we'll stay together. Do you understand? Keep that understanding because it's going to be this way forever, unless *I* say differently."

She was terribly afraid of him then and for several weeks she would run to silence the baby at every little noise he made. Then one day she decided this wasn't going to do. Roger's great fear, his great anger was the thought of her leaving him. Well, then, he'd just have to get a little accustomed to having a baby in the house. She fed and changed the baby, put him into his crib, showed him his toys there, and went downstairs. She would make certain that Roger never touched him again like that. He would have to kill her first. Owen was still crying fifteen minutes later when Roger came in, a little early from his last class. They were still living in the rented house then, with Roger's office in an upstairs bedroom.

"What in hell's the matter with that kid?" he had demanded petulantly.

"Nothing," she said calmly, "except that he's being spoiled by being picked up every time he opens his mouth. He's just going to have to cry it out a few times."

"Not while I'm around. I've got those little bastards' papers to work on."

"I thought you'd want to eat soon," she said easily. "It's going to have to go on this time because it's already started. He'll be quiet soon."

Roger had a quick drink, then a second one. Kiersten was making a salad.

Finally, he said fiercely, "Well, I'm going up there and give him something to cry about."

Kiersten reached the foot of the stairs before he did, and she had the paring knife in her hand.

She said coldly, "You will never touch that child in anything but love, or simulated love, which is all you can feel."

He cursed her violently, but her eyes, her whole stance, made him wary, and after a time he had slammed out of the house, taking his briefcase with him.

That confrontation gave Kiersten courage. She was no longer afraid of Roger, except where leaving him was concerned. He could rant and rave, curse and threaten, but so long as she knew Owen was safe she could almost shut it out.

She never took the chance of Roger's being alone with Owen. When the new house—about which she was not consulted—had been finished, she and Owen had a fine retreat in the attic. She didn't mind the noise and chatter while she worked, and he was very good about entertaining himself. On the occasions when she had to go into New York for consultations, Owen went with her. There was not a maid or baby-sitter in the world whom Kiersten could trust should Roger come home. Owen was a good, quiet, shy child and, even as a baby, rarely interrupted her conferences. As he grew older, he loved staying overnight at a New York hotel and Kiersten always gave him a treat, a visit to the zoo, a new toy.

The shore was only two blocks from the new house. She took him there often, hoping he would make friends with one or more other children, but he played alone, contentedly. This past year, he had attended nursery school, which had done a good deal toward overcoming his shyness with other children.

Owen's and Kiersten's new bedrooms were joined by a bath and she had had heavy locks installed on their doors to the hall. She kept them locked at night. Once Roger, drunk, as he more and more often was, had come pounding at her door, waking Owen, who began to cry quietly in fear.

"Open this goddamn door, Kiersten! I know my rights!"

Kiersten went close to the door and said quietly and firmly, "If you don't go away and be quiet, I'm calling the police. What would the neighbors, and the university, think of that?"

And, to her relieved surprise, he had gone. They had not had sex since long before Owen was born. She refused any longer to be something used, hurt, then disdained.

Roger brought people to his private wing, men and women, though he was very discreet about it. One morning he had ordered Kiersten to cook breakfast for a Grecian sort of youth. She had refused.

He slapped her so hard she almost lost her balance, but still she refused and he let it go, with curses.

Two years ago, when Roger's department head had begun to put pressure on him to work on something for publication he had become desperate. His mind was a blank when he tried to think of research subjects. He drank more and was all but impossible at home. That had been the summer when Kiersten had had, with tears, to ask her mother not to come for a visit. Roger had begun seeing a psychiatrist again, to break his mental block, he said. He went into New York every Friday when his last class was finished, and spent the night, always, though Philip Grantland was dead.

Last summer with the writing project still hanging over him, hardly begun, Kiersten had suggested they go to Secesh. Because it was her suggestion, she thought, he had refused.

"You've always said you could do your best work there," she had reminded him.

"Not this time," he said sullenly. "I think I may be getting somewhere with my therapy. Besides, you know I've been asked to teach this summer term."

"Then Owen and I could go, leave you the house entirely to yourself. Mrs. Beatty would come in to cook and clean and, while you don't have classes, you could—"

"Oh, you'd love that, wouldn't you," he broke in, smiling sardonically. "All of them making over you and the kid, and a room right next to Nolan's."

Kiersten had decided by then that she and Nolan would be all right. It would have been three years since they had seen each other. Maybe he had already fallen in love with someone else. She hoped so, though the pain of the thought made her almost physically ill. If only they could look at each other with something other than hurt and anger, that would be enough. Well, wouldn't it?

"No," Roger had said knowingly, pouring himself another drink. "You're not going. You still think you can leave me, but you and that kid are mine, like these pieces of furniture. You stay as long as *I* say Nobody leaves *me* "

"Roger, if you can't try to do something about your drinking—doesn't the therapist—"

"And don't nag or I'll turn your head around backward. When is dinner?"

"In about twenty minutes."

"Have you fed the brat?"

"Yes, Owen has eaten and he's in bed."

"Let me tell you this," he said, coming close to her and holding her upper arms so that his fingers left large painful bruises. "If you ever so much as think of leaving me again, I *will* kill your precious kid, or hurt him so bad you'll wish he was dead. I've told you that before and you goddamn well better keep it in mind. You're *not* going to Secesh!''

Kiersten did believe, she had believed since that first time. She felt that she was, in a way, holding her own against him now, but no matter what she did, how careful she might be, crafty Roger would, if he wanted to badly enough, find a time when Owen was unguarded.

So the marriage was a standoff. It was no marriage at all, but a life more or less spent in the same house. If Roger made things too difficult for her, there was the tacit threat that she'd let word get around of his immoral behavior, his drinking, to his department head at the university and others. And there were his threats to Owen with which he held her.

That summer, a year ago, Kiersten had begun giving lessons at a nearby riding academy just to have something to do with horses again and because she loved children and being outdoors. Roger told people she was doing volunteer work. So long as it was called that, so long as she did her illustrations mostly at home, he did not mind her working, provided meals were ready on schedule, house cleaned, laundry done, and provided she was there to give or go with him to the round of academic parties. He laughed nastily and told her to use her own money if she mentioned anything the house lacked. Kiersten took Owen with her to the riding academy, of course, and he played happily in an empty stall while she gave her lessons. Almost every day they were there, she managed to give him a ride on an old, fat, good-natured pony called Trix.

Also during this past year, she had unpacked her records and guitar. She had always shown Owen pictures of the family at Secesh, talked about them since he was old enough to understand. Now she played the records, saying "That's Uncle Nolan playing," or "That's Mommy and Uncle Nolan singing." She began to play her guitar again up in the attic, recalling songs The Stewards had done for children's concerts: "I Knew an Old Lady Who Swallowed a Fly," "When I First Came to This Land," "Let's Go Riding in the Car," "We're Going to the Zoo," and on and on. Owen loved it, learning quickly, and coming very near to carrying the tunes.

So Kiersten kept herself busy through the days and sometimes, with Owen, knew moments of almost unadulterated joy. The nights were another matter entirely. There were even rare times when she was tempted to go down to Roger's room, when she knew no one else was there, but the prospect always turned her sick and she never succumbed. Her only outlet was in the orgasms of dreams. She was glad of the brief release they brought, but then it was worse because there was no real person to hold her afterward, no one to snuggle against for a time of long sweet sleep.

On Roger's last birthday, after Kiersten had given what seemed to her a rather nice surprise party, he had paced the living room, glass in hand, drinking freely now that the other people were gone.

"You *had* to point up the fact that I'm thirty, didn't you?" He stormed, then, "Goddamn it, I don't *have* to write a book. I don't *have* to teach. There's enough income from dear old Phil's stocks and bonds that I don't *have* to do anything at all."

Kiersten had feared this since the death of Philip Grantland. How could she possibly have him in the house all the time, or coming in and out at odd times, unexpectedly? Of course, he might travel as he had done just after Grantland's death, going to Europe for two months in that first summer after Owen was born. But with the threat of his constant presence always hanging over her . . . She kept quiet, putting glasses and plates onto a tray. Anything she said, one way or another, would compound the problem.

"No, by God," he said angrily, "I'll show them first, then retire. Morse has done that piddling little book they all boast about, and it's not worth the paper it's printed on. My research is practically all done. I have the first few chapters outlined. It's going to be excellent work, better by half than anything that's come out of this stinking school so far. I'll get it done, throw it in their faces, and then quit. Morse, our fair-haired boy, is only twenty-eight, and I'm thirty today. You had to throw that in my face, didn't you? Why couldn't you just let it pass? Goddamn it, who asked you for a party?"

And he looked thirty-five, or more, Kiersten thought as she loaded the dishwasher. His dissipations were beginning to catch up with him. He no longer cared for his body as he once had and he was getting more than a bit paunchy. There was a kind of slackness about his beautiful face, his nose was showing red blood vessels from the drinking, and gray showed in his dark wavy hair when he forgot to use the tint. A little bald spot had appeared in the center of his thick hair and he had shaved off the moustache because he couldn't keep the gray from showing there. He had followed her into the kitchen.

"You can't even listen to me." There was something of a whine in his voice.

"I was listening, Roger. It's just some kind of block with the writing. One day it'll go away. The same sort of thing happens to me sometimes, with ideas for illustrations and then—"

"Who gives a fuck about your illustrations?" he shrieked. "I'm trying to talk about something important. I think we'll go to Secesh this summer."

The plane touched down, rolled to a stop, and Anne was there, even before the steps were rolled into place.

"There's Grandma," Kiersten said to Owen, fighting tears. "See her? Remember in the pictures?"

They had given Roger his old room at the top of the house, across from Nolan's.

"But you'd better work fast," Fern warned teasingly, "because you'll have to share when all those other people get here."

Penny and the girls came soon and they shared one room, as did Kiersten and Owen, so Roger still had his room to himself, sometimes not working at all, sometimes typing far into the night. They scarcely saw him. Often, he did not emerge for meals, but told Kiersten to bring him something on a tray. She never saw the room without a bottle in evidence. The first time he demanded to have a meal brought to him, she asked brightly, "How's it going?"

"Just shut up and get out," he answered viciously. "A lot you care. Don't have too much fun. I'm very well aware of what could go on and I won't forget."

Kiersten was as near to happiness as she had been in years. She and Penny both fell relatively easily back into the routine of outdoor ranch work, though they had sore muscles and blisters to show for it. Kiersten made sure her mother and Fern knew, in a delicate, round-about way, that Owen must not bother Roger, that they must not be alone together. But there was little fear of that because whenever he could, Owen trailed Nolan like a shadow. When Nolan was going away from the home ranch for only a little while, Owen was riding before him on a saddle or tractor, beside him in jeep or pickup. It was difficult to get Owen to take his nap, though he was always thoroughly exhausted by lunch time. He did not make friends with Butch's younger children because they were jealous, and Owen didn't care anyway. He clung to Nolan as he might have done to the father Roger had never been to him. Roger noticed this eventually and was furious.

"He's not to be outdoors any more," he ordered Kiersten curtly. "Can't you see he's chapped and sunburned? Don't you give a damn about your own brat's health?"

Owen's fair unblemished skin was tanning beautifully and he had never looked healthier. Kiersten said nothing and things went on as they had been, once Roger had withdrawn into his room. He might not notice again for weeks. Though Roger did not always eat with the family himself, he insisted that Owen be fed his supper and put to bed before the others ate. He couldn't stand the sloppiness of the eating of a child, Roger maintained.

As for Kiersten and Nolan, they were reasonably easy together, talking about the ranch, working. He was seeing a good deal of a pretty little girl named Marny Everett who was staying at Shadow River Ranch. As more of the summer passed, Marny was more and more often in evidence at Secesh, watching the work, visiting with the women in the house. Nolan was sometimes out very late. Kiersten hated herself for it, but she often lay awake on those nights, until she heard the muted sound of his car in the drive, the quiet opening and closing of the door at the top of the house, then the door to his room. She ached with loneliness on those nights, unable not to think of what must be going on. It seemed that there was an understanding between Nolan and Marny that this was only to be a summer thing. Marny would return to her acting career.

Marny loved the people at Secesh, a real family, except for that strange Roger. She had always wanted a family and being here, even with Nolan working, as he always did, was far less boring than trying to find something to do at Shadow River. She felt less like a stranger every time she came and there was always someone to talk with. She was too fastidious to try any of the outside work, and almost lost in the kitchen. Fern began by showing her how to load the dishwasher, then went on to initiate her into some things about cooking.

"If you're going to be here, which you are, and welcome, you may as well do a little work. It'll help you sleep better at night if you get a little tired in the daytime."

Marny seemed to seek Kiersten out, always for talk about Nolan.

"I know you all grew up together," she said one day, "you and Nolan and your husband. Do you think there's *any* way I could persuade him to come back and live in New York? I know he could have a fine career in music and I could go on with mine. I'm afraid I love him—a lot, but there's no possible way I could stay here."

"I'm afraid Chappie would never stay anywhere else," Kiersten said with a sympathy that was almost real.

"Chappie?"

"Oh, it's just—just a name his Nolan grandfather gave him, and we all got to using it."

Kiersten wished they could settle their differences about where to live and would marry. Marny could probably make him a good wife and what Kiersten wished most for him was children. He loved them so, always was surrounded by a cluster of them when he was working down around the buildings, never seemed to let them bother him in his work, just waded through them, absently answering their questions, going on with whatever he was doing. He and Marny should have beautiful children together. So here she was, Kiersten thought, considering bloodlines, thinking about them almost as if they were a pair of animals she'd like to see mated, but it was better than the old scalding jealousy. Surely that had all been burned out of her long ago, by her own . . . what was it? getting back at him? her own   Well, she was trying to be objective now, wasn't she?

Haying time came. The grass was thick and lush, the weather fine, but they didn't really have a proper hay crew. There was only one hand in the bunkhouse with Reuben, a boy of eighteen called Buddy. They needed eight hands, and had them if they counted Kiersten, Penny, and Butch's oldest boy Aaron, who could handle a tractor well. Penny's girls, though older than Aaron, had not grown up driving tractors, and Price had decreed that Anne was to stay out of the fields this year. She hadn't been feeling well, "Menopausal," she said to Kiersten with a grimace. There were always breakdowns during haying and they pulled Butch away from whatever else he might be doing. Sometimes the entire operation had to be held up. Buddy, who didn't know the land or much of anything else, seemed eternally stuck in boggy places with whatever piece of machinery he might be handling.

Marny came often to help in the kitchen, along with Penny's girls, Fern and Anne. If she were going to see Nolan during this time, this was the only way to accomplish it. What the women would have liked would be to set up one long trestle table outside, for the noon meal, but the mosquitoes were too bad even to use the screened part of the porch. Instead, they used the big house's kitchen and dining room and pooled all their resources of work.

Kiersten had forgot about the mosquitoes. In her dreams of home, she now realized, she had left a lot out. She had also forgot the flies, the dust, the chaff, the wind . . . The first time someone went to Hurleigh after her arrival, she had sent for the best mosquito repellent to be had, but it was all but ineffectual. The men were used to the insects and rarely said anything, but they drove Kiersten and Penny to distraction. Owen, who was always riding some tractor or truck, was beginning to look like one solid mosquito bite, though he said manfully that they didn't bother him.

They were about ten days into haying, things going reasonably well, when Rex and Ellen and their two small children arrived. They called from Hurleigh, two hours before suppertime on a Friday and Anne told them certainly to come right out, and how to find Secesh.

"I'm here to help," Rex said rather condescendingly at the supper table. "I was raised on a farm and we didn't have any three-acre parking lot full of machinery either. I remember my daddy cutting hay with a scythe."

"I guess he didn't have a thousand cattle to feed through a long cold winter either," said Ellen dryly.

Nolan looked round at the others, winked at Kiersten.

"We'll be working fairly near the house tomorrow," he told

Rex, "so you can come home if you get tired. Since you're not used to machinery, how about a simple pitchfork. We'll be stacking tomorrow while Price and some of the others are baling in the lower fields. We'll put you in the stack pen."

"Get tired! Why, man—"

Ellen, sensing something, interrupted warningly, "You better hush your mouth, token basketball player, before you bite off more than you can chew."

Nolan gave his room to the McIvers and slept in the bunkhouse. He didn't want Kiersten and Owen with Roger any more than the three of them wanted it.

They sat up talking for a while that first night, Kiersten, Nolan, Rex, Ellen, and Marny. The McIvers were very much impressed with what they'd seen of the western country, talked about it, asked questions. Marny switched the subject to their home in New York at almost every opportunity.

"Well," said Ellen finally, yawning, "we'd better let these working people get to bed. Thanks again for your room, Chappie. We've had a pretty long tiring drive ourselves today."

Rex said urgently, "Remember what Butch said about playing music. We just have to get some of that done since we're here."

Marny got up and said goodnight, walking out to her little red sports car, Nolan accompanying her.

"Anything there?" Rex asked Kiersten as soon as they were out of hearing.

"There could be, I think, if they agreed on where to live."

"She sure is a pretty little thing," said Ellen.

They were at work next morning as soon as a very light dew had dried off the grass. Buddy and Rex were in the stack pen, looking rather like Mutt and Jeff. Rex, standing on the empty ground, leaned on his pitchfork and grinned benignly.

Kiersten was running the sweep, which brought the windrowed hay to the ramp leading up to the stack pen. Nolan was operating the pusher, attached to an old pickup truck. Owen, grinning broadly, was in the cab with him.

"When are we going to get some hay in here?" yelled Rex, spitting on his hands and rubbing them together.

"The man wants hay," Nolan yelled to Kiersten over the noise, gesturing.

She nodded, smiling, and gave a thumbs-up signal.

Rex got his hay. He was virtually inundated with it. He did know how to use a pitchfork—Buddy didn't—but they were bringing it as fast as they possibly could and Nolan obviously didn't even look when he shoved the next great pile up the ramp and into the pen.

After a short, wild, frustrating time, Rex yelled at Buddy, "Get out of here. You're nothing but in the way"

Buddy was more than happy to go.

Puffing, trembling in the legs, Rex finally finished one good stack, thinking it must surely be noon, but it wasn't, not nearly There was a lot of wind, which dried perspiration quickly, making one feel not so hot, but it didn't take away much of the dust and chaff that stuck where the perspiration had dried. Rex looked at the sky, resting briefly beside his fine stack. No clouds. The wind and sky had a white, hot look and feel. Ruefully, he studied his huge blistered hands, then gingerly moved to the bottom of the ramp, just in case Nolan might be considering another bombardment

Nolan was making gestures to Kiersten who stopped the sweep and ran easily across the field to bring another nearby truck

"Nice stack," said Nolan judiciously, straight-faced "Buddy in there somewhere, is he?"

"What do you do with it now?" asked Rex, still not breathing quite right.

"Move the pen, leave it till we get the stack mover and put it in a stack yard. We'll make the next one over there by that big rock You need a drink of water, maybe?"

"You son of a sawhorse."

"I've never seen a faster stacker, Rex, besides me, and that's God's truth. What I really like is the mowing, but the big guys always get to do that. The girls can't stack. It would be too hard for them, so I usually get left with it. But I've never done better than that, or faster"

"What would you do if some bastard was deliberately trying to bury you in the stuff?"

Nolan finally grinned. "I'd stack, man, stack. Come on, help me take the pen apart. Be a sport."

"Sport, my ass," Rex muttered, but then they were both laughing

"Damned mosquitoes," complained Rex when he had had a long drink from the canteen.

"You'd better hope this wind keeps up. They're not bad by half today. Ah, there you are, Buddy. Give me a hand and let's get this pen apart, will you? Mr. McIver needs a little rest. By the way, where's your pitchfork?"

"It's—uh—in there somewhere. He told me to leave and I guess I forgot it."

Nolan frowned. "I ought to make you dig it out," he said sternly, "but it's such a fine, perfect stack—"

"I'm fixin' to lay one right up-side your head," said Rex, falling back into pure Alabama.

Kiersten was laughing merrily as she drove up with the truck. "Ole farm boy, right, Rex?"

"Some hospitality," he said, "and I'm not even used to the damned altitude yet. On a ranch, I thought you punched cows around all the time."

"We work to feed them," she said blithely. "I've hardly seen a cow all summer."

"Well, back down where I came from there was a saying, when a guy was courting a girl, you'd say he was buildin' a stack to her. If it took that much to court a girl . . .'"

"You had another saying that I remember," Kiersten said when they had finished laughing. "When you were in a hurry, you'd say 'I've got to light a shuck out of here.' If that's what you want to do now, you can have this truck as soon as these things are moved. You look a little tired."

"Or trade places with Kierstie," offered Nolan, heaving a part of the pen farther onto the truck.

"You didn't do that," said Rex, rubbing dusty eyes with dusty fists which made them itch and water more. "You're not strong enough to move a thing like that."

"I didn't see or feel anyone helping me," Nolan said. "This kind of work builds strong muscles."

"You're still nothing but a skinny kid," said Rex and punched him on the arm. "Like a rock, by God."

"His head, too," said Kiersten.

"That, I know, and do you mean you'd put a girl to this kind of work?" he gestured at his stack.

"No, you'd be doing it, because you wouldn't leave it to a girl. I said do *you* want—"

"Oh, just shut up. I can do one more, at least that."

"I tell you what," said Nolan relenting, "I'll stack—though it's my least favorite job and I always get stuck with it—and you run the pusher. Owen here can show you how. He knows all about it by this time. Come on, Buddy, you're going to be a boss stacker before you leave Secesh."

"If I ever do," said Buddy sorrowfully.

Then Kiersten and Rex tried to drown Nolan in hay.

At dinner time Price said, "I see you got some stacks up."

Rex was showing Ellen his blistered hands. "And I itch all over," he said, pleading for sympathy from some quarter. "I mean *everywhere*."

"Poor baby," said Ellen, but without a great deal of concern. "It's a long time, isn't it, since you were an Alabama dirt farmer?"

"Look at those thunderheads," said Anne in consternation.

Price frowned, looking out the window. "We've got to get the baling done down in the river fields."

"But maybe it's going to rain," said Rex with hopeful ingenuousness.

Fern had just set two pies on the table. She grasped Rex's shoulder hard with her old worn hand.

"Black boy, you'll have your mouth washed out with soap if you mention rain in haying season one more time."

It did rain, by mid-afternoon. First there was a crashing thunderstorm that woke the little children from their naps, then the whole sky clouded over and a light rain fell, promising to last for at least several hours.

"Thank you, Jesus!" murmured Rex, holding his face up to the first downpour to have the dust washed off. He looked around, making sure no one but Kiersten would see and hear, and she laughed.

Reuben said at the barns, "Do you reckon somebody could just bring sandwiches for supper? I'd like to just go to bed."

"Me, too," said Buddy wearily.

"I don't know why," snapped the old man, "young kid like you. I tell you this: it couldn' pick a worst time to rain."

"Buddy's been stacking today, Reuben," said Nolan. "I mean really stacking."

"I've got to look into that green pickup a little," said Butch. "It won't idle, just dies. But this will be the night we play music, right? The night I get to play with the big kids?"

After supper, it was still raining. Price said dismally, "No work in the fields tomorrow, looks like. We can work on the upper ditches if the ground doesn't get too soaked."

Rex and Nolan, Kiersten, and Butch were tuning instruments, Rex worrying pathetically about his hands. Rex had brought his fiddle and banjo, Butch had his bass, and Nolan brought Kiersten his classical guitar. Ellen sat at the piano. Marny had her lute, but was very shy about playing it and mostly did not participate in the music, except for singing the songs she knew.

Roger had been at supper, seemingly preoccupied, and he went back to his room when instruments were brought out.

All the children were there, the four Morenos and the five from the big house. They began immediately to clamor for various songs from records, for Nolan to tell them a story. When Yola, Ellen, and Kiersten agreed it was time for the little ones to go to bed, Nolan said that, first, he would tell the story of the wee ghostie of Bessie McGee and the whole room sat spellbound.

Kiersten couldn't help watching Marny watch Nolan. The girl was all but hypnotized by his expressive face and his deep gentle voice. Have some sense; Kiersten tried to send out the thought to Marny. You'll never do better . . . . Oh God, I still love him so!

They put the children to bed, then did a long jazz series with Ellen Then they began on Stewards songs, mostly the unrecorded ones

Gradually, listeners drifted away, first Price and Yola, then the older children. Reluctantly, Anne and Fern got up.

"We're privileged people," said Anne warmly, and gave each musician a kiss on the cheek.

"We'd better stop," said Ellen without conviction. "It's past one o'clock. We don't want to keep everyone awake."

"This old house is well insulated," said Fern. "You're not going to bother a soul."

"Yes," urged Anne. "Play all night. It's still raining. There'll be no heavy work tomorrow."

Roger was standing in the doorway, nodding. "I haven't heard a bit of the music in my room and I've finished another chapter. How will you feel, twin brother, not to be the only one in the family with something published or recorded? If I stick with my outline, I should have only five or six more chapters. I'm hungry."

"I'll make you a sandwich," said Kiersten, getting up quickly. "Anyone else?"

They found they were all hungry and trooped into the kitchen.

Anne said, "Marny, if they're going to play some more, you'll want to hear it. Why don't you just stay for whatever's left of the night? That big old brown couch makes a comfortable enough bed."

"Or you could share my room," offered Fern.

"Thank you," she said. "The couch would be fine."

"I'll bring you some bedclothes then," said Fern.

"And you're no bigger than Mary," Penny said. "I think she has an extra nightgown. I'll get it for you. I'm afraid I have to go to bed, too, though I hate to miss any of this."

They went back into the living room after they had eaten. Sometimes Ellen played along on the piano, sometimes she just turned and watched the three old Stewards with shining eyes of appreciation Butch could follow along with his bass, but sometimes he didn't, he just stopped to watch and listen.

Nolan and Kiersten sat on a small sofa together, Rex in a chair opposite them. Roger and Marny sat a little apart, Marny watching the musicians, listening, absorbed. Roger watched, too, but with no interest in the music.

The three old troupers watched each other's lips, hands, and eyes for signals, as they had practiced doing for so long, and the old magic was back, the near-perfection.

When there was the briefest of pauses, Marny said eagerly, "Nolan, would you and Kiersten do that one from your first record, the one about the web of birdsong? You did it at Carnegie Hall, too. I love it."

They exchanged glances, neither of them wanting to sing the song.

"I don't think I remember the words," said Nolan.

Rex immediately began on another song and they joined him.

"Did you know they lived together, all those three years on the road?" asked Roger softly. "Nolan and Kiersten, I mean."

"What? Who?" asked Marny, preoccupied with what she was listening to.

He made a careless gesture. "I thought you should know, in case you're considering anything serious. My wife and my brother is who And that's not the half of it, of course. He has had a very checkered past, my twin."

After a moment, Marny got up and moved to a chair near Ellen Shortly after that, Roger said goodnight.

It was after four when Ellen helped Marny spread covers on the old brown couch.

"I sure hate to quit," said Rex wistfully, "but this stacker's mighty tired."

Butch said, "Don't let Price know I said it, but maybe we'll have more rain before you leave."

In her room, lying beside the warm sleeping little boy, the song ran through Kiersten's mind. It was like a record. She could hear their voices harmonizing, feel him stand beside her. On the first verse, she had the melody.

If you will weave me a web of birdsong from the thrush or the linnet,
Then I will give you my heart and hand and all the love that's in it.
If you will weave me a scallop shell, as purple as violets in May,
I'll belong to you and only you and never go away.

Then his verse, with her harmony:

If you will weave me a green grass basket to carry our hearts' love in,
Then you shall have my heart and hand to lock with a silver pin

If you will weave me a cloak of kisses, for cover on a rainy day,
I'll belong to you and only you and never go away.

And hers again, with his harmony:

If you will build me a bonnie boat to sail the waters so wide,
We shall sail the seas of love and you shall ride inside.
If you will build me a house of moonbeams that lasts into the day,
I'll belong to you and only you and never go away.

And his verse:

If you will love me more than fully and longer than forever,
We two shall soon married be, by a knot that none can sever
If you will love me in the night, and love me in the day,
I'll belong to you and only you and never go away.

And at last, her final verse:

If you will give me the child of our dreams, raise him to be a
    man,
Then I shall love you more than fully, and much more than I can
If you will weave me a cobweb child that lasts into the day,
I'll belong to you and only you and never go away.

Nolan really might not remember the words, but she did, every one. She hugged Owen, the tears starting to come. The sturdy little body moved, he murmured something in his sleep. Kiersten turned away from him and pulled the covers about her face. The only sound she made was the whispered pleading word, "Chappie!" It had been a mistake to come here, to sing the old songs, to believe that she could handle her feelings.

After what seemed a long time, she stopped crying abruptly and strained to listen. She thought she had heard the creaky stair near her door. There was no sound now, the rain had stopped, there was only Owen's quiet breathing. So what? Someone was going to the bathroom. But there were no sounds of flushing, or returning footsteps. It had been just the old house settling then.

She got up and found a handkerchief, blowing her nose as quietly as possible. The pillow, the corner of the sheet, her hair, were wet with tears, and she couldn't stop the song in her mind. "I'll belong to you and only you . . . and never go away." Well, she would have to have at least a little sleep. It seemed there was a grayness coming around the edges of the drapes at her window already.

In the big dark empty living room, Marny was wakened from first sleep by the beam of a flashlight. A man's hand grasped her arm and the light went out.

"Nolan?" she whispered incredulously, but then she knew that the hand was not Nolan's.

"You're not—" she began in less than a whisper and the hand moved to her mouth.

"You cooperate, cunt, and you won't get hurt. You'll enjoy it. Don't cooperate or go blabbing this to anybody—anybody, do you understand?—and I'll hurt you, here and here and here, where a broad can really be hurt. Get that kid's nightgown off before you have to explain how it got torn to shreds."

"I'll scream," she said, shaking.

"And I'll kill you," he said gutturally "Just pretend it's good old Nolan."

Marny drew in a breath. Immediately something hard and cold and sharp touched her throat.

"I wouldn't scream if I were you," he said with a little gloating laugh. "This is a knife you're feeling."

She believed him.

When he had gone, what seemed hours later, Marny got up, crying in humiliation and pain and anger. She fumbled about until she had found a lamp, turned it on and dressed as quickly as she could.

Outside, the light was coming under a cloud-scudded sky. There was a big light patch where the sun would be coming up in a few moments over the Fairweather escarpment How could she ever face any of these good people again? How could she see *him* and say nothing? Particularly, she felt, it would be difficult seeing Nolan, whom, she was now sure, she loved. Right now, when she needed him most, she mustn't see him. She knew that if she did, she would tell him all of it, start crying and telling him, and then   Then what? Some terrible thing would happen, to him, to her   this lovely family, except for that viper, would never be the same She even had room for sympathy for Kiersten. She ought to start east right now But, no, the doctor had said four months or her career might be over forever.

Just now, she actually *wanted* to be alone in her rustic little cabin, to shower, scrub her body viciously, cry with the door locked, where no one could possibly know. Why, she wondered disconnectedly, inanely, had he never told her he was called Chappie, when the others, particularly Kiersten, almost always called him that?

In the bunkhouse, Nolan lay wakeful, wishing Reuben would bathe more often, that Reuben and Buddy snored in the same key, wishing Kierstie . . . Kierstie . . . "A cobweb child that lasts into the day . . ." my bonnie, bonnie girl . . .

26

The summer visitors left gradually, first the McIvers, then Kiersten, Roger, and Owen—Roger with his book still unfinished—and, on the Labor Day weekend, Chris Bergen came to take his family home. The hay was in. Fern would be leaving soon for a visit in California, where her eldest granddaughter was to be married.

On a warm windy day in mid-September, Butch and Nolan were working on new corral fencing, with Reuben supervising. Price and Buddy, with the dogs, had gone up to bring down the first of the cattle from the high pastures. They had cut the corral poles gradually, through the summer, whenever there had been a few idle hours. Now, Nolan was cutting them to length with a chain saw, while Butch worked at fitting them into place. They would have a relatively relaxed few weeks now in which to bring in the huge supply of wood, needed through the winter, sort the cattle, pregnancy test the cows, vaccinate and prepare some for shipping. The Ellenbogens operated a small truck line and did virtually all the stock hauling out of Dunraven Park. This corral they were building was a new one, and it would have a chute for testing, vaccinating.

The afternoon was drawing on. It was almost five when Anne came down to where they were working on the fence.

"Nolan," she said, looking concerned, "there was a call for you. Someone named Mavis Butler from Shadow River Ranch."

"You ain't fixin' to go off now?" demanded Reuben. "I wanted this here done by dark, except the chute. We'll git that up some other time when somebody ain't got nothin' to do."

Nolan had seen very little of Marny since that night they had played music until after four in the morning. She had been gone when the rest of them got up at their usual early hour. Since that day had been too wet for haying, he had driven down later, taking Owen with him, to ask if anything was the matter.

"I just wasn't—feeling well," she had said, averting her eyes. "I thought I might as well come back here to get some more sleep. I'm sorry. I should have left a note or something."

It was clear that she had not got more sleep. Her small face was pinched and white. There were large shadows around her eyes and the eyes themselves kept avoiding his.

"Want to go into Hurleigh the next time it rains?" he asked, pretending with her that she was not hiding something.

"Yes," she said with a faint note of desperation. "I don't see how I'm going to stay here another month and a half."

She had made excuses not to come back to Secesh until all the visitors had gone and since that time had come only once, as if it were a courtesy call she had to make. Both Anne and Fern had commented on her thinness, the haunted frightened look in her big dark eyes. Each time they had made love—and the times had been few since she had left the ranch at daylight that morning—she had clung to Nolan and cried.

"Tell me what's wrong," he had pleaded. "Tell me all of it. If you don't want to see me again, I won't—"

"Oh no!" it was a small cry and she had pressed even closer to him. "It's just that you're so—thoughtful, so gentle, so kind. I can't wait to get out of here, but I won't like leaving you. Come back to New York with me," she said in a small wistful voice. "Rex said there were all kinds of jobs you could get."

"I'll be going back in October, to work on a record with David Harris, but I can't stay, Marny. You should be able to understand that. I feel about New York something like the way you feel about the Park, only the opposite, I guess. Sometimes, I think I'm going to choke for air in the crowds. The traffic drives me wild, and the city, the buildings and people and cars, stretch on and on. I—"

"Yes, I suppose I understand," she had said forlornly, "but promise not to leave me tonight until I'm asleep."

It had been more than a week now since he'd seen her. He gave the chain saw to Butch, Reuben spitting tobacco juice and muttering vituperations, and ran up to the house. He used the extension phone in the small cluttered office.

"Mavis Butler, please."

"This is Mavis," said a high strained voice.

"I'm Nolan Savage. You asked me to call?"

"It's about Miss Everett," she said and stopped.

"Yes?"

"I was passing her cabin a little while ago and there were these funny—noises."

"What sort of noises?"

"Like—like little screams and crying. She didn't answer when I knocked and the door was locked. I know you've been seeing quite a lot of her this summer and I thought—well, maybe she needs help, or something."

"There's another key for her room?"

"Yes, but I didn't really feel I ought to—"

"Make sure it's at the desk when I come. I'll be there in twenty minutes."

"Is it Marny?" asked Anne as he changed from his outer, saw-dusty clothes in the bootroom. "Has something happened?"

"I don't know what's happened, or when I'll be back. Tell Price I'm sorry not to have finished the day's work."

She followed him out the back door. "Nolan, will you call if we can help, or   Bring her here if she's sick. The poor child doesn't have anybody   "

Marny was on the floor, her head and shoulders propped awkwardly against the bed. Nolan stopped Mavis Butler from coming in, blocked the inside of the cabin from her avid view. Marny's eyes were unfocused, her small face utterly white, the wandering eyes burning in it like horror-filled flames. She was breathing as if she had been running hard. He sat down on the floor, tried to take her in his arms, ease her uncomfortable position.

"Don't touch me!" she all but screamed. "Are you real? If you're real, get out of here."

Her eyes and face filled with fresh horror. She whimpered, tears running down her white cheeks. Her long black hair, always so neat, was disarranged and tangled now, as if she had been pulling at it. Her hands groped in front of her, as if she were trying to ward off something absolutely terrifying.

"Marny, it's Nolan. Can you tell me what happened?"

She made no answer except a strange guttural growl. Then she turned on him, trying to claw at his face, his eyes. He held her hands away easily. Finally, he got up, completely uncertain of what to do. He brought a cold wet cloth and wiped her sweating face gently. Her hands were cold and clammy, but the rest of her was pouring perspiration. She went on, looking with horror at things he could not see. He sat down again, was able to ease her almost catatonic position a little. He began talking to her quietly, the only other thing he could think of to do

"You're going to be all right. I'll stay with you. Everything's going to be all right."

He wasn't at all sure she would be all right, but felt it didn't matter at all what he said. Maybe the sound of a voice, someone she knew, would help.

After a time, she whimpered his name and let him put his arms around her.

They sat like that on the floor for a long time. Now and then she would writhe in fresh terror, crying out words that were disjointed, virtually meaningless to him, then the worst would seem to pass and she would hold on to him with a surprising strength and be relatively quiet for a time, sobbing, "It's so ghastly, what I'm seeing, hearing, feeling! Oh, I can't! I can't—" Then she would be wild again, tearing at her hair, scratching at her eyes and his.

"Acid," she gasped in one of her more lucid moments. "A friend sent it to me more than a week ago. I intended not to drop it, but I was so lonely today. Oh God, it's never been like this. It's always been beautiful and—"

Then she was screaming again, not loud screams, but cries stifled by sheer terror.

Nolan was at a loss, deeply frightened, knowing no more to do than stay with her. In one of her quieter moments, he said, "Will you come with me to a doctor?"

"No!" she sobbed. "No, please! Just stay with me!"

"Do you know what time you took it?"

"About—about two, I think. Oh God! Oh my God! Stay here, hold onto me! Talk—talk to me!"

"It has to pass soon," he said, with more assurance than he felt. "You'll be all right soon. You will, Marny. It's going to be over."

He wiped her cold, sweating, tear-streaked face again, gently disengaged her hands from her hair. If he kept talking, the quieter periods seemed to last longer. Now he was sure it didn't matter much what he said; she wanted only the sound of a familiar voice. At last, he was able to pick her up, sit in the armchair, holding her on his lap, stroking her back, arms, shoulders, face, hair, with his rough strong gentle hands. She was a small crumpled thing, holding on to him, the bad times getting farther apart now. When it had been a half hour since the last attack of terror, he said softly, "Let me help you get into bed, then maybe I could go up to the lodge and get them to find something to eat. If you ate something, that ought to help dissipate the—"

"Don't!" She clung to him. "Don't leave me. It's getting better now, but if you leave me, unless I'm wrapped up in your arms—" She had started to tremble again, violently.

"All right. It's all right. I won't go."

She was breathing more normally, though still as tense as a spring stretched to its breaking point. After a time, he drew away one of his arms, reached for the brush on the dresser and began to straighten her tangled hair.

She drew a deep shuddering sigh. "Oh, Chappie, if you hadn't come, I think I might have—killed myself, just to—get away from it '

"You have some fine friends," he said angrily.

"But I've done it lots of times before and it was always good—always . . ."

"How about getting into bed now?"

"I have to have a shower first. I feel so—filthy. Stay with me, please?"

"I'm here. I will."

Her fingers were stiff with tension. He helped her get her clothes off, took off his own, and washed her gently. There was a brief return of the terror and she screamed at him to turn off the water, that she would drown in the black dark water.

He dried her, carried her light stiff body to the bed.

"Oh, I can't bear it if it happens again," she said hopelessly. "Will you do something else for me?"

"Whatever I can."

"Make me a cigarette? The hash and papers are in the top drawer. I've tried to be good. I've hardly used any of it. It will relax me, I know it will, and if something doesn't do that soon, I'm going to break, just fly into millions of pieces."

Nolan complied reluctantly.

"You smoke, too," she pleaded guiltily.

"No, I'll just have a regular cigarette."

He hadn't realized until now how tense his own body had become. He was exhausted. Surely, she couldn't have stood much more of what she had been going through. It was a little past midnight.

She took deep drags of her cigarette, holding her breath as long as she could before exhaling slowly.

"Why didn't you ever tell me," she said in a small wistful voice, "the first time we met, or the second or the third, that all your friends and family call you Chappie?"

"I don't know," he said. "I guess I just didn't think of it. Maybe I'm too old to be called Chappie."

"Can't I be your friend? You're my best friend in the whole world, especially after tonight. Thank God you came."

"Of course, we're friends," he said, kissing her smooth wan cheek into which a little color was beginning to return. "Now why don't you try to sleep?"

"One more joint?" she asked tentatively, pleadingly.

Something was easing the tension from her; perhaps it was the hash, so again he clumsily made a cigarette for her.

"If you're hungry, I have some candy bars and things in the bottom drawer."

"Will you eat something?"

"No, I can't now. In the morning I will. Could you stay with me? I don't think I could ever sleep alone tonight."

He ate a candy bar, drank water, brought her some. She insisted that the small lamp on the dresser be left burning.

"Make love to me," she whispered when they had been lying close and silent for a long time, when she was beginning to feel safe, to believe the black terrible times were over.

"Marny, you're so tired. You should just sleep."

"I want you more than I've ever wanted anything. It won't make me more tired. Afterward, I'll be even more relaxed."

So they made love, gently, lingeringly.

Later, when he thought she was asleep and was himself beginning to doze, she snuggled her face against his neck and whispered softly,

"I love you, Chappie Savage. I'm twenty-four and I've never truly loved anyone before, except, I think, my father. I know you don't love me, but maybe you could some day. I'd try my damnedest to make it happen, if only we could agree on where."

"I'm sorry, Marny. There's nothing I'd like better than being with you, but I can't live in New York."

"Better than *anything?*" she asked wistfully.

"Anything." He turned slightly to hold her more closely.

"Yes, I guess I understand how you feel about New York and such places. Maybe I'd feel the same if I'd been raised here, with all those lovely people to love me. But would you do one more thing? Another favor?"

"Yes."

"Please don't leave me in the night this time. I want to know I can wake up in the morning and find you here. Trips can recur, especially bad ones, it seems, and I'm afraid . . ."

"I'll be here in the morning. Why don't you pack some things then come stay at Secesh for a few days? Or, come to that, you could just move out of here, stay with us until time for you to leave. You said you were going to make reservations. Have you done that?"

"Yes, for the first of October. Maybe I will come to the ranch for a few days, if it wouldn't be too much trouble for them. I *can* be some help, after Fern's and Anne's teaching me all summer. But I want to keep the cabin, so we'll have a place to make love. It wouldn't be right, under their roof, knowing how they feel. Anyway, I'd move back here after a little while and . . ."

Suddenly, she was shuddering and he held her closer, fearing another bad time, both of them, but it passed quickly and, at last, she slept.

On the last day of September they were finishing with sorting the cattle at Secesh. An Ellenbogen truck was to arrive at noon, to take away some of the stock they were shipping.

Marny drove up from Shadow River and watched the work. To Nolan, her face looked troubled and weary. She went in with them to a late lunch when the truck was loaded and whining down the ranch drive. She barely joined in the conversation and scarcely touched her food. Afterward, she asked Nolan privately if they could go for a ride.

"You mean on horses?" he asked in surprise.

"Yes, just a short ride. I have to talk to you."

They rode down by the river, Nolan's young Matey following. The mosquitoes were still bad along the Shadow, though there had been several nights of frost. They were a torment to Marny.

"I'm sorry," he said contritely. "I guess I just wasn't thinking. Shall we go somewhere else?"

"No," she said absently. "This will be all right."

"Are you about packed and ready for going back to the city?"

He tied the horses to willows and they sat down on a grassy bank, the dog lying nearby, head on paws, but watching Nolan. Marny's face did not have the glow it had used to take on when she thought or talked of going east. She was, in fact, quite ill-looking.

"I—I think I have to change my plans," she said, looking away from him at the quietly rippling Shadow, slapping desultorily at a mosquito on her bare arm. "I know I shouldn't have waited until the last possible minute like this, but—I was in Hurleigh yesterday. I saw the man who was going to buy my car, told him I'd be keeping it a little longer at least."

She plucked a long blade of grass and began folding it, accordion-fashion, with nervous fingers. Nolan sat very still, watching her face.

"It's my fault," she said shakily. "I suppose Freud could have made a lot of it. You see, I ran out of birth control pills about the middle of July. I hate that long drive to Hurleigh alone, and you and everyone were so busy. Like so many idiots, I thought, it won't happen to me. *I*'ll be safe . . . But it has happened, Nolan. I had no period toward the end of August, when it should have come, and there's been none this month. I saw a doctor yesterday. The urine test and everything else says I'm pregnant. I won't have an abortion. I want my baby."

"Yes. Of course you do."

"I was never wanted, except by my father, and he died so early. I've always promised myself that if and when I got pregnant mine would be the most wanted baby in the world. It's my promise to this baby. I—I want to ask you to give it legitimacy, but there are so many things involved. There's no one whose child I'd rather have. I'd stay here until it's born—early May, the doctor says—but I don't think I could go on staying. You know how I feel about that.''

"And you'd take the baby," he said, suddenly feeling very tired.

"I could just not ever come back here after the hospital. You could not see it, if that would make things easier for you. I realize I'm taking a lot for granted, making plans for leaving the hospital when you haven't said . . . I know how much you love children, want them, of your own. God, I'd hate doing that to you! But I've told you that I was all but illegitimate. I don't want that for my child. I can't face the thought of running around New York, asking all the available men if they'll be the legal father of my baby.''

He said nothing and her eyes filled with tears.

"I know I'm asking a God-awful lot of you, Chappie. You don't love me and that makes it just a little possible. You might never love me, if we stayed together fifty years, but you'd love a baby, and I'm asking you to give it your name, when I mean to take it away from you as soon as it's born. Maybe, if you *would* marry me, I should just go ahead and go back to New York, as soon as that's done. I have to be there by the first of November anyway because that's when the sub-lease on my apartment is up and there are other things I have to put in order.''

"Who would look after you?''

"I have friends—''

"Who send you acid.''

"They're not all like that.''

"Your mother?''

"Oh Christ, no! The last I knew, she was in Bavaria for the summer. We hardly write to each other and I'd be glad if I never saw her again. I get a respectable check from a trust fund each month. That's to ease her conscience or keep me away from her or whatever Sometimes she sends a picture postcard, dropping names of people or places, but that's almost the only contact I've had with her for years. It's her, the way she is, the way I was born, that makes me such a nut on the legitimacy thing. A lot of girls—women—are having kids on their own, no husband these days, but I just can't seem to make up my mind to do that, not after having no parent at all since the age of five. Anyway, I don't need to be looked after. I'm a big girl now and—''

"Yes, you do," he said a little desperately. "I don't want you dropping acid or trying to work or—''

She said humbly, "I did the acid that time, a couple of weeks ago, because I was already convinced I was pregnant, and I just

410

couldn't handle it, face up to it, at first. But I could certainly work for a while, as a dresser or something in the theater." She tried to smile "Or maybe there's a pregnant lady part just waiting for me somewhere."

He said gravely, "I think you'd better stay on at Secesh. Surely, you could bear it that long, with Anne and Fern to look after you and talk to."

"And with you, Chappie," she said timidly. "Oh, I do so love you!"

"There's always the possibility that you might come to—want to stay on—longer."

"It's a possibility, I suppose, my darling, but it seems such a very remote one. For one thing, I know how you love Kiersten, and I think you're a one-love man."

"What makes you say that?" he asked and his eyes looked empty.

"Because I've seen it, in your face and hers. I know you lived together when you were on the road with The Stewards. I don't know how things came to be such a tangled mess, with her married to Roger and—"

He turned back to face her, his eyes open and candid now. "I do—care for you, Marny, very much. I'd be proud to have you as my wife and maybe, with time, you'd decide you could bear the staying."

"I wouldn't want you to count on that. It would be terribly unfair of me to lead you to believe I'd even consider it right now. Stranger things have happened, I suppose, but Marny Everett, ranch wife? I just can't see it."

There was a long silence. Marny watched some cattle come down to drink on the other side of the river. Nolan was following the flight of a red-tailed hawk on the light west wind.

"Nolan?" she said hesitantly, waiting until he looked at her, then turning her own eyes away. "There—there's more."

He waited, with that concentrated look of attention she had always appreciated so much in the past.

"That night," her voice barely audible, "when all those people were here at the ranch, when you played music and I slept on the couch in the living room, I was . . . Roger . . ."

She saw him raise a hand to cover his right eye, the left one still watching her relentlessly.

"He came and he had a knife. He said it was a knife and it felt like one. He said if I made any noise or didn't—didn't cooperate . . ."

He sprang to his feet, fists clenching and unclenching. "God in heaven! I'll never be free of him. I should have killed him twenty years ago."

411

He strode away from her, a long way, almost out of sight among the willows. She sat there tensely, a little frightened of the look that had been on his face. When he came back, finally, his expression was calm and there was that blanked-out look about his eyes. He sat down and put an arm about her.

"I'm sorry. I should have thought first about how it must have been for you. You should have told me at the time."

"I was afraid of some—awful trouble. It's such a wonderful family, the Savages, except for—him. I didn't want to be the cause of—of open trouble between you."

A long silence and she said pathetically, "So it *could* be Roger's baby. I don't believe it is. I want it to be yours, but it seems only fair to tell you . . ."

"Can I have time to think about it, Marny, all of it? A day?"

"Of course. Who am I to set any limitations?"

"But if we *are* married, you'll stay here at Secesh, at least until time for the baby to be born?"

"If you're kind and—and generous enough to marry me after this, I'll do anything you ask until that time."

"Don't be humble. You don't have to—"

"It's not humility, not really. It's—it's love, Chappie. I'd give almost anything to see you truly happy."

"Anything," he said with more than a touch of bitterness, "besides staying here with the baby."

Marny managed not to cry until she was back in her cabin, with the freshening wind whining and moaning about its corners.

It was a very quiet wedding in the ranch house living room. Anne had driven to Hurleigh especially to buy fresh flowers. The room looked clean, comfortable, and beautiful, with a fire snapping on the hearth and the season's first snow falling outside the large windows. Butch and Yola were there, Buddy and Reuben—Reuben had taken a shower for the occasion and was wearing his false teeth with some awkwardness—Anne and Price—Fern had left for California. The minister had come down from Fairweather. The two chief participants were sober, almost glum, with Marny just managing to fight back tears through the ceremony, until she escaped and locked herself in a bathroom for a time. If only he could love me, she thought, gasping with almost silent sobs. If he truly loved me, I'd do anything, anything . . .

Before leaving, Fern had insisted on moving out of the room that had been hers for years, one of the two with a private bath. "Young folks need their own place, their own privacy," had been her last word on the subject and she would discuss the matter no further

On the wedding night, Anne sobbed miserably in Price's arms. "Oh dear God, is nothing ever to go right for any of them?"

Nolan and Marny went to New York near the end of October. The couple sub-letting Marny's apartment were moving, but she had no trouble finding new tenants to take it for six months, the remainder of her lease. For a few days it was theirs and Marny said wistfully that this was the real honeymoon.

Nolan worked long sessions with David Harris, preparing for the new album. There was a party every night at the apartment. Marny seemed to know at least half the people in New York.

"Tomorrow, let's invite Rex and Ellen," she said. "Do you think David Harris would come? I'd love to meet him."

"I think he would. What about Susan Lister? He tells me she's in town for a while."

"Oh, Chappie!" she cried like a delighted grateful little girl. "*Would* you ask her? Do you think she'd come?"

"It could deteriorate into a jam session," he warned, smiling faintly.

"I'd like nothing better," she said excitedly and kissed him. Then soberly, "How far is it to—to where Roger and Kiersten live?"

"A good fifty miles. God, you're not thinking of—"

"No," she said quickly. "I've just been—afraid they'd find out we were here and—oh, I don't know. Do ask David and Susan. I'll call the McIvers and some others."

Nolan, David, Susan, and Marny went out for supper before the party, which had been scheduled for nine. When they returned to the building, friends of Marny's were already waiting downstairs. The little apartment was soon jammed. Marny wanted Susan and David and the McIvers to stand in a sort of receiving line so that everyone would be sure of meeting them. Nolan had already met most of these people, though he could remember only a few names, and doubted that he'd recognize any faces on the street. After a brief time, he edged through the crush and went into the relatively uncrowded bedroom. Susan was sitting on the bed, signing autographs for a starry-eyed boy and girl who hardly looked to be out of their teens.

"Folk music may be dead, Miss Lister," the boy was saying earnestly, "but people like you and David Harris and Nolan Savage will go on forever, because of your beautiful styles and voices and—even in the middle of a hard rock party, we can put on one of your records and everybody just shuts up and listens."

"That's awfully nice to hear," said Susan. "You really have Mr. Savage to thank. He does my arrangements and those absolutely brilliant accompaniments."

"Is he here tonight, too?" gasped the girl, wide-eyed.

"He's standing right behind you," said Susan carelessly, with a mischievous smile.

They turned and stared at Nolan.

"I sometimes live here," he said mildly.

"*That* Savage!" cried the girl. "*You're* the one Marny married? My God, we hadn't realized . . ."

They held out their autograph books in a kind of worshipful silence, then hurried off to set anyone else straight who mightn't have realized.

Nolan pushed the bedroom door open to its widest and sat down beside Susan.

"It's getting to you, isn't it?" she said solicitously. "When did you say you leave?"

"Friday, if I can last that long."

"You could go out on the fire escape now, but it's pretty cold."

"Someone would follow me and I'd jump. Do you want a drink or something?"

"I don't, but if I did, I wouldn't ask you to go back in there for it. Tell me, how are you, aside from claustrophobic?"

"I'm all right."

"Things going well at the ranch?"

"Reasonably."

"It's still Kiersten, isn't it, Chappie?"

"I don't . . . Yes."

"I never understood why she married Roger."

"Nor did I." But a thought struck him. Roger had raped Marny, held a knife at her throat. Maybe with Kiersten . . . And she had lived through just about six years with Roger now. He ought to go up there, to Connecticut, that place where they lived, and stop whatever he was doing to her and, no doubt, to Owen. He ought . . .

"I'm sorry," he said, looking back at Susan. "I didn't hear what you said."

"I said, try to give this little girl a chance. She's lovely, she's sweet, she adores you. She's pregnant, isn't she?"

"Did she tell you?"

"No, there's a certain look some women get when they're pregnant, an inner look. She has it. She's almost showing, anyway, small as she is. I predict she'll be an excellent mother, and an excellent wife, if given a real chance."

"But she hates the ranch. My grandmother hated it. It drove her a little mad. My mother hated it, couldn't get away fast enough. She took us away, Roger and me, until she was so fed up with kids she'd let us spend some summers there. I—guess I can't bring myself to try

414

too hard with a third-generation ranch hater. History does repeat itself, doesn't it? Marny plans to leave as soon as the baby's born, if not before. She only wants legitimacy for the baby."

"Oh, Nolan," she sighed compassionately, "the messes we *do* make of our lives. That's *not* all she wants. I think, if she could believe you truly loved her . . Let yourself go with her. It's too late for you and Kierstie. Let this sweet little Marny be happy and you might have everything. It might be a different kind of everything from what you've thought you wanted, but one thing you have always wanted is children. You've wanted—" she smiled a little uneasily "Oh, sure, if you want to know how to straighten out your life, bring it to good old Auntie Susan. She knows just exactly how to fix up everybody but herself "

"Have things—changed any for you?"

"Nope. I've spent a fortune on psychotherapy and I still feel as I feel. I'm almost forty-four and it just seems high time I accepted myself for what I am, make the best of what there is."

He leaned to light her cigarette, lit one for himself

Susan smiled a little tremulously "All that filthy talk that was going around years ago, about you, and me, among others, I really wish some of it could have been true, for my sake, at least. If I ever again went to bed with a man, you're the one I'd want to choose. So, if I ever get the urge, can I come to your home on the range and be—accommodated? Don't answer that, you idiot . . . . Rex says you damned near killed him with work during his vacation last summer "

The doorbell rang. Nolan wasn't sure it could be heard amid the hubbub of living room and kitchen, but then he saw Marny wending her way toward the door. He had a clear view when it was opened.

"My God, it's Deedee Gorman," he groaned incredulously.

"What? Who?" asked Susan avidly, seeing the fiery blush rise up from his collar. "You must be blushing all over, Chappie."

"Don't say that. Don't ever say that," he said between his teeth "Well, who is it?"

"Marny, *darling!*" cried the fur-wrapped woman, her voice carrying well above the stilling crowd. "I just heard today from Wilma Felberger that you were in town and that you've been *married!* Weren't you even going to let me know? You naughty girl! Where's the happy bridegroom? I've come to look him over. As your guardian for all those years, don't you think I *should?*"

Marny was looking around helplessly, like a frightened little animal about to be trapped. She saw Nolan through the open bedroom door, sent him a plea: Help me! Get her out of here!

He got up unwillingly, made his way through the interested crowd to stand beside his wife. Deedee stared, her mouth dropping open a little. The years had not been kind to her. Even expertly applied makeup could not conceal that. What was it? Nine years?

Marny said, "Nolan, this is Daisy. I've forgotten the latest last name."

"Deedee Carrington," said the loud commanding voice. "And I do believe, Marny dear, that we've met before, haven't we, Mr. Savage?"

"A very long time ago," he said casually, but still feeling the heat in his face.

"Well, aren't I to be invited in, even for one drink? I'd bet Mr. Savage even remembers my choice."

"No," he said, "I don't. What would you like?"

"A Manhattan, dear boy. Please hurry. Now, Marny, you must tell me how all this came about. Will you be living here?"

Nolan went to make the drink, and Susan interposed herself between Deedee and a grateful Marny. Everyone was glad she didn't stay long, but as she was leaving she drew Marny and Nolan into the corridor, firmly closing the apartment door behind them.

"I had made out a check as a wedding present, Marny, but I've torn it up and doubled the figure, remembering that *both* you and your husband have expensive tastes. You'll continue to receive the trust fund income, of course, so that when you get the stars out of your eyes, or have the baby, or whatever it is, you can come back to live in civilization. Unless you're an even bigger fool than I think, this won't last long. Contracts are made to be broken, aren't they? Especially marriage ones."

She stabbed the elevator button with a red-nailed finger, held the door open when it came, thrusting the check into Marny's hand.

"You haven't been grateful to me for much I've done for you, young woman, but if he's a good lover, you *do* have me to thank."

They stood silent in the hall, not looking at each other.

"You see what I mean about not wanting anything to do with my dear mother," Marny said brokenly.

"Yes," he said with fervor.

"Chappie, just what was she talking about?"

"Years and years ago, when I was in school at Albion," Nolan began, and he told her as quickly as possible, the humiliation not having lessened in the least in all this time.

"Oh Christ, that's just like her!" Marny said bitterly. There were tears of anger in her eyes, anger toward her mother, not him. "To use people, take advantage when they're starving or—"

"I could have managed, Marny," he said, shamed further by her championing. "I was old enough to know exactly what I was doing. It

416

wasn't all her fault. It's the thing in my life that most embarrasses me. I wish you'd never have had to find out—"

"And to come here and humiliate both of us," she was going on fiercely. "That's just her dish of tea. It'll make her entire week. If God is good, neither of us will ever see that—that woman again."

He took her in his arms and kissed her gently on the mouth "Thank you."

"You've got the hours counted until flight time on Friday, haven't you?" she said, putting back his hair.

"Just about."

"Well, knowing *she*'s going to be in town for the winter, after *that*, I may just start counting with you. Meantime, we'd better get back to the party. Everyone wants all you real music people to play for us. Do you think they all would? Please?"

27

Marny tried hard at Secesh, she tried very hard. She was unwell most of the time, but didn't like it mentioned, in a cautionary manner or otherwise. Right from the beginning, Dr. Jackson in Hurleigh had asked her to come in every two weeks, rather than monthly. She drove herself into town, usually, in what Nolan thought of as "the crazy little red sports car," until the roads became permanently snow-packed. Then Anne always went in with her in Nolan's little station wagon, which was the best car at the ranch for holding to snowy roads. There were always errands for Anne to do, and Marny couldn't drive Nolan's car anyway because it had a standard transmission.

Marny learned to knit and sew. Between them, she and Anne and Fern made enough clothes, afghans, and quilts for three babies. Marny helped in the kitchen and with the housework, read many books, did anything to keep her mind off the isolation and the constant wind. It was a hard fierce winter and the wind never seemed to stop. It was a searching whining breeze, or a shrieking whooping gale, or anything between, always fingering or tearing at the house.

The men were out by eight in the morning to begin the feeding. Buddy had, to everyone's surprise, including his own, stayed on, and they had a new man, Lem Collins, a quiet man, well into his forties, a born ranch hand, who seemed as if he might stay. Often Reuben, now seventy-eight, would admit to his aches and pains and stiffnesses and not go out to feed, staying in and around the bunkhouse, finding little chores around the buildings or sitting in Fern's or Yola's kitchen. Technically, they had two feeding teams, a driver and a feeder, and one man to load the sleds at the yards of stacks or bales. Often though, Price and Nolan worked alone, using the two oldest and most dependable work teams, who could be trusted most of the time to stand still for gates and while the hay was being fed out to the eager cattle. They had stack yards, both baled and loose hay, strategically placed around the lower part of the ranch and Butch was there with a loader to keep the sleds supplied. If they worked three teams, they could finish in the river pastures by noon and be at the house for lunch. Then they would work west of the home pastures, almost until the early darkness drew on.

By December, the temperature was falling to thirty below or more every night and the cattle needed tons of hay to keep warmth and life in them. The wind sculpted the snow into a new landscape of drifts every day and the big Percheron horses had a job of it, fighting their way through with the heavily loaded sleds. No trail lasted more than a day or two. The time came when they had to use a four-horse hitch for each sled.

The men usually finished by around four and they were exhausted. Reuben was usually there to take care of the horses as they came in, helped by Butch's boy Aaron. Even Nolan wore a cap now, with earflaps. They all dressed in several layers of heavy clothing, wool socks, which Fern or Anne knitted, heavy gloves, boots, sheepskin coats, but they came in worn out and half-frozen from struggling with hay, gates, and wind. Price would have a hot shower and go to bed until suppertime. Nolan would peel off the outside layers of his clothing, try to talk with Marny or read a book by the fire, but he almost always fell asleep for a few minutes at the least, lulled and half stupefied by the enwrapping warmth of the house.

After supper, he would light a fire in his and Marny's bedroom, knowing how she liked to fall asleep watching the embers. Sometimes he played his guitar or they would all join in some card game or watch something on television, but it was very rare for anyone to be up past ten-thirty. They were captives of the weather and the work.

Marny rarely felt thoroughly warm. They used the propane forced-air furnace—closing off unused rooms—and the fireplaces where people were gathered together, but the old house was drafty, and the mere sound of the wind, or the sight of snow, driven by it, could set her shivering. Her only time of real comfort and near security came when she and Nolan were in bed together, under an electric blanket, which he didn't care for, with the fire burning low before her eyes, while the wind roared derisively in the chimney.

Nolan often made gentle tender love to her and struggled to keep awake for talk. When he gave up the fight and slept, she joyed in snuggling against his warm back. He slept in nothing but jockey shorts, though she was in heavy flannel pajamas. She could, ever so gently, caress the warm smooth skin of his slender back, thrilling at the feel of the heavy musculature beneath the skin.

Sometimes she cried in the night, tears of fear and sadness, fear at what she felt was their dangerous threatening isolation, sadness because she meant to take the child from him. If only he loved her! Could she bear it here forever, even then? She might be willing to try. They rarely mentioned the baby. It only brought pain to Nolan's eyes before he could think and blank them out.

Christmas was a lovely time. Marny had never had a real family with whom to spend the holidays. Penny and her family were there. Mary and Emmy were not little girls any more, but their Christmas excitement was still a fresh and happy thing. Anne, Fern, and Marny had done a great deal of extra baking and on Christmas day Marny was initiated into the proper making and cooking of stuffing and turkey.

They had a party on Christmas Eve, with the three men from the bunkhouse, Butch and Yola and their family in attendance. Marny played Christmas songs and carols on the piano and everyone sang. Nolan put together a story he had never told, "The Christmas of Teddy O'Reilly and the Wee Folk." The big tree sparkled with lights and the room was lit only by them and by candles. But the wind still snarled ferociously outside, the temperature was fifteen below on Christmas morning when the men began the feeding, and the Christmas dinner was held off until six in the evening.

"We don't usually have wind unceasing," they kept telling Marny, "nor so much snow."

Reuben went around, outside and in, with a stocking cap on his bald wrinkled head, pulled down over his ears, and his worn, faded, spotted old hat atop that.

It was hard to keep the ranch roads open, or any road, for that matter. As the plows struggled through, and this was something which must be attempted almost every day so that the Moreno children could go to school, the wind quickly drifted the roads shut behind them.

The hardest winter in years, everyone kept saying. The phones were out half the time and the electric power was often off. Cattle began to die from the sheer effort of trying to stay alive and the men grew hollow-eyed and vague with their own exhaustion. March came and there was no noticeable let-up in wind and snow, though the temperature did not fall quite so low at night.

At the first of the month, when Marny and Anne struggled out to see Dr. Jackson and restock on groceries, the doctor said, "In another month or so, you should get yourself nearer a hospital, in case there's a bad storm on the big day. Oh yes, we can still have them in May, the worst kind, warmer temperatures, so the snow is heavy and wet and plasters everything."

"We know people here in Hurleigh you could stay with," Anne suggested, but they were strangers to Marny.

She said, "Do you think Chris and Penny would have me?" wanting to ask "Can't Nolan be spared to stay with me there?"

knowing it was a useless question. Still, she couldn't help the faint wistful hope that he might insist on it.

"I'm sure they'd be delighted," Anne said.

"All right," said the doctor. "At least two weeks before you're due, you ought to go over there. You know Terry Ellenbogen, don't you? He's a fine OB/GYN man, unless you'd rather choose someone else. When you go over, you ought to fly. If the roads are bad, that makes a very long trip in a car, for a pregnant lady."

Marny went into the bathroom and the doctor said worriedly to Anne, "I'm concerned about her. There's something just—not quite right about this pregnancy. I should have sent her to a specialist long ago, but she's seemed so uneasy and frightened, I didn't want to make it worse."

"I'm afraid she's been pretty unhappy," Anne said with concern.

"Well, yes, it might be that. I guess I've just been a country GP for too long and haven't really kept up with everything as I should have. Tell Nolan he ought to be with her. Wouldn't that make her a lot happier? She's a little thing. They may decide on a C-section."

In late March, calving began. They had, with difficulty among the drifts, sorted out the breed cows, putting the older ones into one home paddock, the heifers due to bear their first-born into another. They were still having trouble keeping waterholes open in the ice of creek or river. The heifers had to be watched carefully, Anne and Yola keeping an eye on them while the men were feeding. When a heifer was in labor, or seemed about to be, they put her, often with difficulty, into the big calving barn, where she and her calf would be kept for a day or two out of the wind. The older cows calved outside, no matter what the weather, and there were remarkably few losses among them. A cow was not kept at Secesh who was not a good natural mother. One didn't count poor motherhood against the first-calf heifers. They always seemed surprised, sometimes appalled at having produced a calf and often wanted nothing to do with it until it could be helped to begin nursing.

And now the men's work was almost doubled. They took shifts during the night, sitting in the battered old armchair, or lying on a cot, the small space heater the only heat in the barn, while they looked out for the heifers.

On a Sunday night when it was Nolan's turn in the calving barn and the rest of the household was sleeping, Marny became suddenly, inexorably desperate. She had been heaping wood on the bedroom fire, sitting close to it, trying to read. Abruptly, she knew she could bear it no longer. It was the first of April and the winter showed no indication of loosing its hold on the country. Granted, the temperature was not falling as low as it had done during January, but, as Reuben said, "The only reason it warms up is so it can snow more."

The wind was roaring around the house and as she peered from the window, it was what they called a white-out, with no distinction between snow from ground and sky.

Marny was so tense she felt stiff, trying to move around. She yearned to scream with the wind or at it. She took suitcases from the closet and began feverishly to pack her things and the baby's. She had been in pajamas, robe, and slippers, but she dressed hurriedly in the warmest maternity clothes she had, pulling on an extra cardigan which Fern had given her for Christmas. Then she went to the bootroom, found some old boots, Penny's or Kiersten's, and pulled them on over woolen socks, also a gift from Fern. She wanted to cry over these gifts, over the goodness of the family to her, but she couldn't let tears start now. That would be too dangerous. She took down Price's sheepskin coat which all but swallowed her, found gloves and cap. She picked up a big electric lantern.

Getting out of the back door was a struggle, with the wind against her. It seemed miles to the calving barn.

Nolan had a heifer tied with a halter, chain, and ropes to keep her on her feet. She had had a long hard labor and he had almost given up on trying to save the calf, when he had finally been able to turn it, and now it was coming.

"Marny, for God's sake! what are you doing out in this?" he cried, but with barely time to turn his head at the heavy draft from the door as she came in. Her face was white, her hand, holding the lantern, shook badly. "Sit down over there by the heater," he said curtly and went back to the heifer, who was trembling and swaying on her feet with exhaustion.

Marny moved the book, lying face down on the chair, to the cot, and sat down gratefully, edging closer to the heater.

Nolan put a rope around the calf's front legs and, with every fast-coming contraction from the mother, pulled strongly. The calf was born quickly then. Its movements were weak and listless. He took the restraints off the heifer. She almost collapsed, but finally managed to turn and look at what she had done. Tentatively, she began to lick the calf and its weak movements became less aimless. It was trying to get on its feet. Nolan waited for the afterbirth. It came quickly, the heifer turning to sniff it and going back to the calf.

He dropped the placenta into a large bucket, scrubbed his gory arms and hands and replaced shirt and coat.

"So that's what it's like," said Marny tensely.

"No, it's not," he said, looking at her severely. "This is the third one that's calved since I've been down here and I didn't lift a finger with the other two. And of course it's nothing like that for people."

He came and stood beside her, a hand on her shoulder, still being censorious because he was worried about her.

"Tell me why you came down here, plowing through this snow and wind. Don't you know it could be bad for you? You might have fallen or—"

"Nolan, I can't stand it any more, I just can't!" There was more than a faint hint of hysteria in her voice. "I have to get away from here, now. Tonight. I've got most of my things packed, and the baby's. I'm going to Denver."

"You can't leave in a storm like this. Marny, it's going to get better, the weather, it has to, some time soon."

"I'm sorry. I just can't wait any longer. I won't stay another minute longer than it takes me to get things together in the car. I can't, don't you see?" Her voice was rising desperately.

"You're not thinking of driving?"

"How else could I go?" she cried harshly. "If I don't get out, I'm going to start screaming and never stop. I tell you, I—can't—stand—it!"

Her pallor and trembling frightened him. He would try to seem to acquiesce, though he knew the prospects were almost hopeless. If she saw that he was trying, and helpless, as she obviously felt herself to be, would that ease things or make them ten times worse?

"The roads aren't cleared. We'd have to—"

"I don't care!" she shrieked. "I don't care, I don't care, I don't—"

His arms around her made it possible for her to stop this time.

"All right," he said tensely. "You stay here by the heater and I'll go and wake Lem to watch the heifers. There's another in labor over there. We'll take my car, try to get through."

"No, my car," she said, close to screaming again. "I want everything I have in Denver because I can never come back here again."

"Marny, what we ought to take, if we're going to try, is one of the four-wheel-drives, the jeep or a pickup, but that would make too rough a trip. We might make it in my car. I could bring your car over later."

"No!"

"I hate that silly car of yours even on good roads. The heater isn't much good, it has practically no traction—"

"There are chains, for all four tires."

"Oh, Christ! All right, we'll try it. Are you feeling all right? I mean, you don't think the baby's coming or—"

"No, it's not that. It's this place. So far from everything. The damned everlasting wind and snow and I think the electricity is going to go out again. Look how the lights are flickering."

"I'll get Lem," he said wearily and took up his own lantern.

He was tired, so tired it seemed he could hardly fight his way to the bunkhouse. How was he going to drive that damned little sports car for at least eight hours on bad roads? But he had to try. The look of her frightened him. She seemed almost as tense as when she had taken the LSD last summer.

"Did you take any of the tranquilizers the doctor gave you?" he asked as they struggled back to the house.

"Yes," she cried defiantly against the wind. "They don't help. Nothing will help but to be away from here."

"There's snow and wind in Denver, too," he said, but she did not hear.

In the house, they found Anne awake and up.

"Nolan, you can't possibly mean to go out in this when there's no need, no real need . . . ?"

She followed his glance to Marny's face, saw the tight desperation there.

"Marny, honey, just try going to bed, won't you please? There are those sleeping pills the doctor said you could take if one was absolutely necessary—"

"I've been taking them, and I don't sleep," Marny said sullenly, with, again, the faint rising note of hysteria.

Anne said urgently, "I'll stay with you until you fall asleep if Nolan's too tired, and I can see he is. This winter has been the hardest, most wearing on the nerves since I've been here, and that's almost twenty-five years, but it won't look quite so bad in the morning if you just get some sleep. Then, in a few days, as soon as we can go out safely and the planes are flying again, I'll go with you to Penny's, or Nolan—"

Marny ran away from them, into her bedroom, closing the door No matter what Anne said, or anyone else said, he had to try. He had promised, or as good as.

"I think I'll have to try," said Nolan.

Anne sighed. "Yes, I suppose you will. Shall I come with you, in case she . . ."

"She thinks we have to take her car."

"Oh God, Nolan! In this weather?"

"I'm going out to see if it will start. If we're lucky, it won't. If it does, I can get it warmed up for her, put the chains on."

Anne looked at him for a worried moment and then said resignedly, "Well, I can at least make some coffee for you to take along."

Nolan packed a few things for himself, put blankets and other things into the sports car, along with the suitcases, in case they should be stranded.

Anne kissed Marny. "I wish it could have been less trying for you. We've come to love you very much."

Marny almost lost control then, began to cry. If she did that, they would persuade her somehow not to go tonight and in the morning she'd be insane. She clung to Anne briefly and said in a choked voice, "You're the kindest, loveliest people I know. I wish I weren't such a baby, but I just can't . . . I have to . . ."

"Yes, I think I know," Anne said. "Just keep warm. Nolan's always been a very good driver."

Nolan began cursing the sports car under his breath almost before he had put it into gear. He drove because he knew, more or less, where the roads were supposed to be. He had ploughed them out often enough. He had to learn the hard way to remember about the damned power steering, the automatic transmission, and the too powerful engine. He had brought a shovel and had to dig the car out twice on the ranch drive and once again before they reached Mills Crossing. The fact that the road was paved from Mills Crossing didn't help much. The plows had not been out tonight or, if they had, their work had been destroyed. On the Fairweather Grade there were deep drifts, alternating with almost bare spots. Up on the plateau, the falling snow seemed to lessen, but the wind was worse.

Marny had started to cry before they reached Mills Crossing. It was not hysteria, but a hopeless pathetic crying. She clung to her seat or twisted her hands together in her lap in fear of the roads and desperation against the wind.

Nolan had to concentrate too hard on driving to be able to offer anything by way of comfort or reassurance. He had to dig the car out once again near the little town of Fairweather.

Getting back into the car, he said curtly, "Why haven't you got your seat belt on?"

Marny's tears were slowing. She said hoarsely, "I don't want to use it. If we had an accident, it might hurt the baby."

"Not as much as your being thrown around or through the windshield," he said.

But she did not put it on; instead she said in a small voice, "Nolan, I wish you weren't angry. I'm sorry."

"It's this damned car. I suppose I'm not angry with you. I just don't like the feeling of riding six inches above the road with my legs practically stretched straight out in front of me, and of having more power than anyone would know what to do with in this little tin can."

They had left Secesh shortly after ten. It was one-thirty when they

426

reached a dark, closed Hurleigh. Even the all-night service station where Nolan had used to work was closed on this night. They turned onto the state highway where there was more visible evidence that plows and sanders had been at work.

"Could you pour me a cup of coffee?" asked Nolan, lighting a cigarette and feeling a little contrite.

She gave the steaming cup to him quickly.

"Chappie, I'm ashamed of myself, but it just seems . . . I know you're worn out but . . ."

"It's easier driving now," he said. "We'll be all right. How do you feel?"

She touched his hand on the wheel tentatively. "Besides feeling ashamed, I feel relieved and very much—cared for. I love you, Nolan, and I—thank you."

"Could you try to sleep some now?" he asked. "There's that little pillow for your neck just behind you "

It was a long time before she could relax. The road was snowpacked all the way. He stopped for gas when they finally came upon an all-night service station there chiefly for the benefit of truckers. They looked at each other in the lights, each seeing great weariness, hollow-cheeked and shadow-eyed. Nolan was relieved, however, to see that some color had come back into her face, that some of the tenseness was gone.

Marny got out, went to the rest room, walked around a little, carefully on the vehicle-packed, slippery snow.

Scarcely any snow was falling from the sky now, and the wind was just a bitter breeze, compared to what it had been at Secesh.

Nolan thought of taking off the chains. Their presence made the ride of the stupid little car rougher and more uncomfortable They were also going to wear out, but there was still one high mountain pass to cross, and the tires were just not that good.

Marny's ankles and feet had been swelling badly of late. She had taken a look in the rest room. They were badly swollen now. Maybe, with the passage of another two weeks, the doctor might have said she couldn't make the trip at all.

She said, "I can drive for a while. You look positively awful."

"You will not drive," he said curtly and opened the passenger door for her. "Please fasten your safety belt."

"Nolan," she said a little later, having forgotten his request, "I—I really did try."

"I know you did, Marny."

She desperately wanted to ask him to be there when the baby was born. She was frightened of the process of birth and his presence would bring reassurance. They were letting fathers into more and more delivery rooms these days. But that would be so very unfair. Once the baby was born, as soon as they were both strong enough, they would go back to New York. She had enough money to find an apartment, hire a live-in woman to look after it and the baby. She had wanted to contribute her monthly income to the ranch coffers, but everyone had refused. So now she had enough saved to try to make a new start. God, it would be hard to get back into acting! After all this time, people would have forgotten her name and face. But she could do it. It was what she really wanted, the theater. She might never be famous, but if she could just keep on working . . .

She had always wanted so much, been so strongly convinced that the baby would be a boy. She meant to name him Nolan. And if it were a girl, she would be called Anne. She had not told them this because some day Nolan might have another wife, other children, and want to use the names himself. She would stay with Penny, with deep gratitude until the onset of her labor, but once they were ready to leave the hospital, they would go to a hotel for a week or two. That was the best way, a clean break with everyone connected with Secesh. She thought of the only times she had felt truly warm all winter, snuggling against Nolan's back while he slept, watching embers. Even the wind, whatever it might be doing at the time, did not frighten her or make her so nervous then. It was going to be hell now, sleeping alone. . . . If he loved her, could she go back? Honestly, now? No, probably not, but she would never love anyone else as she loved him.

She touched his hand on the steering wheel. He turned his hand and held hers briefly, her hand trying to memorize the hard thin strength of him, his warmth, his interested incisive eyes. In her mind, she would always hear the sound of his voice, feel its quiet depth and warmth.

He said chidingly, "You're still not sleeping."

And after a time, she was.

Nolan's throat was sore from chain-smoking, but that and the coffee were what kept him going, thinking, reacting with a reasonable amount of rationality. Even so he sometimes felt dizzy, unreal, and his vision seemed to blur slightly. He turned on the radio, but whatever station he found, music, all-news, nighttime talk shows, only seemed to serve to lull him. Finally, he stopped, got a blanket to put around Marny, and drove with his window open.

It was clearing this far east. A few stars showed amid scudding clouds. Soon it would be dawn. A few snowflakes still fell from time to time. He thought they had just outrun a slow-moving storm, that it would be coming into Denver later in the day.

He tried not to think about how Marny was taking all her things, and the baby's. He would get some sleep at Penny's, then take a bus or plane, whatever might be moving, back to Hurleigh. They needed him badly at Secesh . . . . He did love Marny, in a way, she was dear and sweet, sometimes funny when she was feeling relatively happy. She was a joy to make love with. So why hadn't he told her these things, in addition to saying the automatic "I love you" that she always wanted with sex? Because his love was not of a kind to keep her at the ranch, as, evidently, hers for him was not that kind . . . . He didn't want to hear anything about the baby, what sex it was, what it looked like, only that it and Marny were safe and well after the delivery. After all, he kept reminding himself bitterly and protectively, it could just as well be Roger's child. Still, in the depths of himself, he wanted the baby, and Marny, and he struggled against the loneliness, the feeling of a loss that had not quite yet happened.

He lit another cigarette, the last in this pack. They were on the final part of the journey now, the interstate, sweeping down out of the high Front Range. It was daylight. The rising sun blazed into his aching eyes from time to time, out of thickening clouds. There was a truck in front of him, in the right lane, a highway patrol car behind. He pulled out to pass the truck, moving very cautiously on the steep downgrade, when he saw a west-bound car, a big white sedan with its lights still on, come at him across the median strip at what seemed a terrific rate of speed. He braked the little car as much as he dared on the snowpack, saw the police car slow and the truck speed up, to give him maneuvering room in the right lane, but it was too late. He was losing control of the damned crazy little car. Then the sedan struck it a mighty blow at the left front fender. The little car spun so that it was at a right angle to the road and hurtling down the embankment. To Nolan, it all seemed to happen in an insane slow motion, to take long minutes.

First, the red car leaned very sharply to the right. He grabbed for Marny, but her door sprang open and she was gone from beneath his grasping hands. Then, following the contour of the embankment, the car ran on, leaning so sharply to the left that it rolled, once and then again, coming to rest in an iced streambed.

Nolan was unconscious for a brief time. It seemed a long while, but it must have been only minutes, for he was rousing dazedly by the time two men, the patrolman and the truck driver, scrambled down to him.

"You all right, buddy?" came the concerned voice of the truck driver.

"Yes," he said, hearing his own voice only faintly.

"You sure?" asked the policeman. "Can you get out through the window? These doors will never open again except with torches "

Groggily, Nolan fumbled at his seat belt fastener. If Marny had been wearing hers—Marny!

"Marny," he said fuzzily. "My wife . . ."

"She was thrown clear," the policeman said reassuringly. "It happened that there were a doctor and a nurse in the car right behind mine. They're looking after her. She'll be fine."

"But she's eight months pregnant. She . . ."

"We've got an ambulance on its way."

The truck driver had found a good-sized rock and was smashing away the glass and plastic sandwich of the driver's window. Nolan released himself from the safety belt, other loose parts of the car and luggage, and managed to crawl out. He was sick and dizzy when he stood up at last.

"All right you said," chided the big burly truck driver. "Looks to me like you're bleedin' in about a dozen places an' somethin' pretty serious has happened to your right arm or shoulder."

At the words Nolan's shoulder began to hurt fiercely, and there was the large cut on his scalp above his forehead bleeding down into the thatch of hair that always fell over his brow, making it wet and warm and sticky, saturating it so that now blood began to seep into his eyes. He felt as though he were sticky all over, with blood and dirt, and the sweetish rusty smell of it made him retch.

After a moment, he turned and began trying to climb up the embankment. The big truck driver took him by his left arm and was a strong bulwark. They struggled up, holding onto rocks and shrubs that protruded from the snow.

Nolan was in such a dazed state that he felt no surprise, no sense of coincidence on seeing that the doctor and nurse kneeling by Marny were Terry and Barbara Ellenbogen.

Terry said to the truck driver, "Could you get those blankets you mentioned now?"

The big man hurried off purposefully.

Marny lay on her side. Barbara knelt, holding pressure on an artery in her fractured right thigh. The right side of her beautiful little face lay against a rock, blood seeping into the light snow cover beneath it. Nolan dropped to his knees beside her. She was breathing, but unconscious.

"Let's have a look at you," said Terry, putting a hand on his shoulder. Then, "Nolan, my God! I didn't even realize it was you, didn't recognize Marny."

"How bad is she?" he asked, not looking up, beginning to tremble.

"Can you stand up?" Terry urged. "You're bleeding quite a lot."

"I want to know about Marny."

"Stand up and I'll tell you what I can."

The truck driver came back then, with several blankets from his sleeper over his arm. They doubled two and laid them on top of one another, on the ground beside Marny, then, with Barbara still holding the pressure point, the policeman and Terry lifted her onto them and covered her with the others. Nolan had moved out of the way, standing again, dizzily. The truck driver held his uninjured arm in a firm grip. His touch was kindly, the only reassurance Nolan could find just now.

Terry came to him then, looking first at the scalp wound, then running practiced hands over his body.

"You're going to have to have stitches in your head and you've done something a little drastic to your right shoulder. Are you in much pain?"

"No. Marny—?"

"She's got a compound fracture of the right thigh and the right side of her face is—pretty well smashed up."

"The baby?"

"She shows no signs of going into labor yet and we're getting a fetal heartbeat. I should think there'll be an emergency C-section at the hospital. Best for both of them."

Still the truck driver held his arm and Nolan was vastly grateful, comforted, by the gentle pressure of those big gloved hands.

"You come set in my truck cab where it's good an' warm till the ambulance comes," rumbled the big man "You're shakin' like a leaf."

"No," he said. "Thank you."

"But, son, you're—"

"I'm all right."

"Well, here, take this here handkerchief to keep the blood out a your eyes."

Terry bandaged the scalp wound, rigged a makeshift sling for Nolan's right arm, which helped the pain a little. They stood looking down at Marny, so small, so vulnerable, with Barbara crouching beside her.

Other cars kept slowing, stopping, the patrolman gesturing them on.

Nolan said suddenly, "That bastard in the white sedan . . . ?"

"He's over yonder," said the truck driver, spitting in disgust "Hit your car, then went back into the median and turned his on its side. There was a smokey, comin' up from the other direction got 'im. Don't seem to have a scratch on 'im. The sonofabitch is drunk as a hoot owl an' it not nine o'clock in the mornin'."

Terry said to Barbara, "Let me do that for a while." And to Nolan, "I'd feel a lot better, so would you, if you'd go sit in the truck or the patrol car for a while."

"No," he said.

Snow had begun to fall rather heavily.

"Son, you can't do 'er no good standin' out in this."

Nolan's utter helplessness swept over him and he retched again, tears mixing with the blood that dripped into his eyes. Terry searched in his bag, gave him some kind of shot, explaining it, but Nolan didn't listen. After what seemed an eternity, the ambulance came.

"I'll go down with her," said Terry. "You ride with Barbara. We're taking her to University, all right?"

Barbara tried to make talk in the car. "We'd been up skiing for the weekend. That must have been some storm you drove through, according to what we've heard on the radio."

As they came into town, reached stoplights, she watched him warily. He was already in shock. Was it going to get worse before she could reach the hospital?

Nolan made no answer to her small talk. It seemed hundreds of miles down, then across the city to the hospital. They had lost the ambulance right away. The pain in his head and shoulder grew worse. Several times, dizziness and nausea all but overcame him. He tried to light a cigarette but was shaking too much. Barbara took it, lighted it with the car lighter. He couldn't smoke much. His hands were not just shaking, they were jerking, and his teeth chattered. When he did manage to inhale some smoke, it only made him feel sicker. He got the window down a little and threw out the cigarette.

When they reached the emergency room, Terry was waiting for them. They had already taken Marny somewhere else.

"They're preparing her for surgery," he told Nolan. "You'll have to sign the consent forms."

"What—what are they going to do?"

"There'll be an orthopedics man working on her thigh and face, just preliminary work. We'll do the C-section."

"You—you're an—OB/GYN man."

"Yes, I mean to scrub, but we have to have your consent."

"How long will it take?" He could scarcely keep his hand steady enough to scrawl left-handed at the papers thrust before him. Terry and Barbara exchanged concerned glances.

"How—long will it take?"

"I don't know, Chappie. Maybe long enough for you to get fixed up. Come in here and lie down on this table. This is Dr. Willis Cooper, emergency resident of the day. He's probably going to sew up your head and do some X-rays. You're going to need blood. They're getting ready for you upstairs."

"No bed," he said doggedly.

"We'll see," said Dr. Cooper, who looked at Terry, their lips forming the word "shock" at the same instant. They nodded at each other.

When Nolan woke, Penny and Chris were sitting by his bed. An IV dripped blood into his arm and there was some sort of brace and harness around his neck and shoulders. His head hurt viciously and he touched the bandages gingerly with his free hand. This was a two-bed room. The man in the other bed seemed to be coming out of some anesthetic, snoring and making garbled noises, attended by two worried-looking visitors.

"How are you?" asked Penny, kissing his cheek.

Except for the pain, he felt light and free, almost as if he would float from the bed and through the window to where snow was now falling heavily.

"What time is it?" he asked groggily.

"Just a few minutes after noon."

"Marny?"

"She's not out of surgery yet."

"The baby?"

"The last we heard, they said there was a strong heartbeat. Just try to relax, Chappie. You've got a concussion, a hurt shoulder, and bruises all over the place. You've been in shock and need this blood. Barbara called us right away, but it took some time, getting across town in the traffic and snow. I called Aunt Anne. She said they'd get here as soon as they could, whatever way they could. She said the snow had stopped out there, but now we seem to be in for it. Is there anything we can get you? Do for you?"

"No. Yes. Make them take the needle out of my arm. I need to be there when Marny—"

Terry Ellenbogen stood in the doorway, his face tired and drawn.

"Would you let me talk to Nolan alone?" he said to Penny and Chris and to the two people hovering near the other bed. "Would you give us just a few minutes alone? The nurses tell me Mr. Sykes is doing beautifully."

They all left, with various measures of reluctance. Terry sank into a chair.

"Want a cigarette?"

He lit one for each of them.

"What is it?" Nolan asked, his hand shaking, his eyelid beginning to twitch.

Terry cleared his throat. "Well, first of all, Marny is doing well. Don't look at me like that. All things considered, she really is. The orthopedist, Dr. Trask, is still working on her. He'll be in to talk to you later."

"And the baby?"

"Chappie, the baby's—alive, but it's one of those—things that rarely happens. A—a mistake, some time in the very earliest cell division. It's a—freak, a—oh God, I'm so sorry."

"I have to get up," Nolan said urgently. "I have to see—"

"No, I don't want you to yet."

"Is it—?"

"It's extremely malformed," Terry said, feeling the sickness all over again. He was a doctor, supposed to be objective in such matters, but he had never come up against this before, and with a friend's child into the bargain. He said, "It hardly resembles a human being."

"Take the needle out or I'll do it myself."

"That would be against medical advice."

"I don't give a damn, Terry. I've got to know what Marny can be told."

"Yes, I can understand that but—"

Nolan had struggled to a sitting position.

"All right, let me check with the doctor who's in charge here, get a nurse with a Band-aid and some kind of robe and slippers."

They went up two floors in an elevator, Nolan clutching the rail, swaying, his vision blurring. Terry led him to a cubicle set apart, hidden away behind the main nursery. He tapped at a small window and a nurse drew back a curtain. They looked through the glass, Terry holding Nolan's arm.

Both Nolan's fists went up against his mouth. "God, oh my God!" he breathed in an almost silent scream.

He began to retch. Terry guided him quickly to a basin in a household supply closet, where he stood for a long time, grasping the cold porcelain, heaving, half-conscious. Then, gently, Terry guided him into an empty room.

"Lie down," he said and Nolan lay there, shivering.

At last, he said, choking, "There's no—nothing that can be done."

Terry shook his head compassionately. "There would be no way on God's earth, Chappie, to make it a—child. Our EEG's show only the lowest primal brain function."

"Can't you just—let it die?"

"It's not on any life-support systems. It can take food, sleep, eliminate, and that's about it. There's nothing we can do."

"The accident this morning . . ."

434

"Now, look, don't be a fool. I've told you this is something that happens during the very earliest days of pregnancy. Often before a mother even realizes she's pregnant. There are a lot of reasons why it *might* happen, a defect in the egg or sperm cell, the ingesting of certain drugs by the mother. We haven't come close to knowing the possibilities, let alone finding anything to do about them. When you think of it, about a million miracles are involved every time a very nearly perfect baby is born. There are so many possibilities of something going wrong in that relatively short period of fantastic development in the womb. A—a case like this usually culminates in a natural abortion. A miscarriage. Very very rarely is the fetus carried to term."

"Marny was counting so much on the baby."

"And so were you," said Terry, turning away briefly to hide his misting eyes.

Nolan closed his eyes for long moments. It seemed difficult to breathe, to draw in enough air in each breath. He said stonily, "She has to be told it was still-born."

Terry nodded. "I thought that's what you'd want. It seems best to us."

"Everybody has to believe that, the family and . . . will the hospital people keep quiet?"

"Yes. When she comes out of recovery, we're going to put her down in orthopedics. She doesn't need to be on the floor with mothers and babies. That's the last thing she'll need. Everyone in orthopedics will be told the child was still-born. That little room I showed you is off-limits to almost everyone. There's no reason Marny should come in contact with any of the nurses, or anyone from up here, except me. Look, I know I'm laying an awful lot on you, but I think you ought to consider having the—child moved from the hospital in a few days. There's a care center for such—cases, not far from here. It's expensive, but not as expensive as the hospital and . . ."

"How long can it live?" His eyes were still tightly closed.

"They've been known to live up to three years. I can call the place for you, find out costs and the like."

"Yes. There'd have to be some kind of—funeral, too."

"A mausoleum crypt," said Terry quietly. "I know a mortician who'll sell you a baby's coffin, take care of everything. It's not exactly legal, but under the circumstances . . ."

"Marny mustn't ever know, or even suspect. She'd want to try to—care for it herself."

"That would be impossible, nothing but heartbreak."

"Yes, but she—"

"I understand."

A long silence, waves of horror washing through Nolan.

"How much longer will she be in surgery? When will she begin to wake up?"

"I'm not sure. They've done about all that can be done, orthopedically, in her condition, but it will be several hours before she's out of recovery. Can you come down now? Finish the transfusion?"

"I have to be the one to tell her. God knows I don't want to, but . . ."

"Yes, I understand that, too. But you're not in the best of shape yourself. I promise you'll know when she starts to come round. Barbara and I took the weekend off, so I'll be right here until late tonight."

"And how bad are her injuries?"

"Pretty serious, I'm afraid. They're patching the thigh bone together. Dr. Trask is one of the best. She'll be in a cast, a partial body cast, when the caesarean wound heals. She may still come out of it with a slight limp. Her face—they're wiring and pinning bones. She's lost most of her teeth on the right side, along with having the broken bones, and there's going to have to be a lot of plastic surgery."

"She's—she's always been so beautiful . . . . If only I could have held that goddamned bloody car on the road . . ."

Terry put a hand firmly over his, which was cold and still trembling. "We saw that accident, remember? There was no way, no way in the world, with the impact that fool gave you. He must have still been doing sixty when he got across the median. You ought to get a lawyer as soon as you feel up to it, sue holy hell out of him. Can you get downstairs now? Back into your own bed?"

Penny and Chris met them at the elevators, looking puzzled and very worried.

Nolan gulped and said almost steadily, "The—the baby was still-born."

"Oh, Chappie!" cried Penny softly and put her arms around him. Chris took his hand in wordless empathy. Terry went to the nursing station, and they moved slowly back to the room.

"I've cleared this with Dr. Clarridge," Terry said to the charge nurse. "Did he tell you? All right, I want him to sleep very deeply and for a good long while. Where's his chart, please? Start the IV again and I'll write up the other orders."

28

On the same Sunday when Marny could no longer bear Secesh, Kiersten and Owen were in New York. They came in the early morning and spent a long time at the zoo. At one o'clock, Kiersten had a luncheon with an editor friend for whom she had done a good deal of work. She came away with a briefcase full of manuscripts for which illustrations were wanted, and a very tired and sleepy little four-year-old.

It was spring now, even in the city. She was always a little surprised at how the smells, sounds, even the very feeling of spring could make itself known in the midst of all the buildings, people, and traffic. The air had a soft freshness to it. Sparrows quarreled wherever they could find room. Plants bloomed in window boxes. People left off heavy coats and hats so that there seemed to be more room on the sidewalks.

Kiersten thought wistfully of going to visit with Ellen McIver and her children. Rex should be home, too, today. She had meant to see them for months now, but there was only time to get home and finish the dinner preparations she had begun in the morning. Roger had planned a morning of golf, lunch at the club and he had said most of his afternoon would be occupied, though she didn't know or care with what.

Tomorrow, Roger was going to a three-day seminar in Boston. Maybe she'd call Ellen. She and Owen could come back to the city, stay overnight somewhere.

Roger had still been unable to finish his book, though he sometimes said there were only four chapters to be done. The university people were beginning to put more and more pressure on him about it. He was very difficult to live with. Kiersten was glad and grateful that the spring was coming. Now she and Owen could spend more time out of the house when Roger was home. She got her best ideas for children's illustrations by taking along a sketch pad when she watched Owen and others at the park, the shore, the tiny zoo their town had, the riding academy. She was afraid Roger was going to announce at any moment his resignation from the university. He still came into the city for every Friday evening and night, but she had no idea if he was still in therapy. His drinking was getting worse. She was afraid of him now—again—when he was drinking heavily.

Owen slept, leaning against her on the train ride home, and she thought about what a good, self-sufficient little boy he was, sturdy and healthy, growing up almost normally, with as little contact with his father as she could manage. He still talked often of Secesh, particularly of "Uncle Nolan and Grandma and Grandpa," and said he was going to be a rancher when he grew up, wanting to know if they would go back there when it was summer again. Kiersten had bought him, among other things at Christmas, a sizable herd of tiny cattle, with men on horses, a barn, and fencing. He played with them by the hour on the floor of his room, or in the attic while she worked. But he wanted tractors and haying machinery. "We have to *feed* the stock when it's winter," he reminded her soberly.

Kiersten thought sadly about Nolan and Marny. What a sweet lovely girl Marny was. Their baby should be beautiful. Anne's letters had hinted strongly that, once the baby was born, Marny meant to bring it back to New York, take up her acting career again. Don't do that to him. It was almost a prayer in Kiersten's mind. She had seen love for Nolan in Marny's big dark eyes. If he doesn't truly love you yet, he will if you bring his baby home to Secesh. Don't leave him.

She was finishing up supper preparations when Roger came in. Whatever he had been doing, at least a few drinks had been involved. He went straight to the bar in the den to make himself a gin and tonic. Owen was upstairs, playing, but he would have to eat with them. There hadn't been time to finish up things and let him eat alone. On what had seemed to be Roger's better days, she had been insisting lately that Owen have his meals with them. He was, after all, four-and-a-half. There was nothing very wrong with his table manners. She told this to Roger again. His mood, for the moment, seemed good, almost mellow.

"Why don't you have a drink with me?" he asked, trailing a hand across her breast. "In fact, why don't we ball after dinner? I haven't ever minded not sleeping with you all these years, but it's a long time since I've brought a guest home to my room. I'm horny as hell. It's been several *years* since I balled you. You say the kid's four-and-a-half? You ought to be pregnant again. Should have happened a year or two ago. Nolan's little wife is, isn't she? I hate to think of that pretty little piece trapped at the ranch."

Kiersten went on with dinner preparations.

Roger said slyly, "And she's a honey in bed, for a girl."

She turned to stare at him.

"Oh yes," he smiled gloatingly. "We had a little romp. Remember that night when all that damned music was going on and she slept in the living room? Well, what possible difference could it make? Nolan had been fucking her, I know that. She'll just have kids, one after the other. You wait and see. I like it when you're pregnant. It makes me proud to have people see you. Maybe *I'm* the one who should be feeling proud that *she's* pregnant. It only takes once, you know. I haven't minded, all this time, not sleeping with you. Haven't missed you or pined a bit. It's why I had the house built as it is, so I could lead my own life. I really do prefer boys. But you and I had some good times in bed, didn't we? Remember how we started out the honeymoon? If you think those locks you had put on upstairs matter worth a damn, you're crazy. I'll have you if and when I choose. You're *my* wife. Are you still taking birth control pills, after all this time?"

She said she was, but it wasn't true. She thought that if she were pregnant again, she would have an abortion. She loved Owen fiercely and she'd love another child just as much, but it mustn't be Roger's.

He was saying, "That's a waste of money, Kiersten, and those pills can be dangerous. Or is it that you've found a lover, or keep hoping to find one? I've told you, I wouldn't mind in the least, so long as you were discreet, as I am. I would enjoy watching some of the action. But those pills really *can* be dangerous over the long term. What do you suppose would happen to your precious kid, if something happened to you?"

He went back for another drink, brought her one, ordered her to drink it.

"What do you do with all that sexiness you used to have? Masturbate? Have you bought yourself some tools of the trade? I'm going to fix it all up tonight, relieve all your tensions and deprivations. Isn't that what any good, loving, moral professor, husband, and father would do when he's about to be away from his loving little wifey for three days?

"Do you know what Hornsby said to me on Friday?" Hornsby was his department head. "He as much as said shit or get off the pot. That lousy book! I'm resigning at the end of this semester. Other schools would like to have me, book or no book. I've had offers."

Now he was getting an ugly morose look to his handsome dissipated face. Kiersten hurried, putting things on the table. It was important to get the meal over with as quickly as possible, particularly since Owen would be present.

Roger said, "I don't have to work at *any* shitty school. They don't know how lucky they are to have me. I want to go back to Europe. You'll come with me. You can find somebody to look after the brat. You haven't finished your drink yet, for Chrissake?"

"Will you want wine with dinner?" she asked, thinking that wine would be better than the almost straight gin he was drinking.

"No, I don't want wine with dinner," he mimicked. "And don't start bitching and nagging about what I drink."

She called Owen and when the child did not appear instantly, Roger bellowed up the stairs.

It was a mostly silent meal, as theirs usually were, Kiersten and Owen both apprehensive, Roger glum and angry. Then Roger seemed to pull himself together a little, remember his father role for a few moments.

"What are you doing in pre-school, Owen?"

The child's dark blue eyes flicked to his mother before he answered, almost in a whisper, "We're learning our letters and numbers. Yesterday, I drew a picture of—"

"Speak up, for God's sake. Try to at least pretend you're human. What do you want to be when you grow up?"

Owen, with Kiersten and other people he knew well, was usually fairly loquacious, but with Roger, he hardly dared open his mouth. Now he said, too loudly, "A—a cowboy, a rancher."

"Don't yell at me, you little bastard," shouted Roger and, to Kiersten, "Jesus Christ! You're putting those ideas into his head, aren't you? There'll be no more trips to Secesh."

Owen looked as if he would cry. He said in a very small voice, "M—m—may I be excused?"

"You may not," snapped Roger. "And if I ever hear you stammer like that again, I'll knock your teeth out. No, you're going to sit here and eat every scrap of food on your plate. If your dear mother insists on having you at the table, then you're going to learn proper behavior. Eat your salad. You haven't touched that."

Owen reached for his salad bowl and knocked over his milk glass.

Roger shrieked at him, hoarsely, wordlessly, and hit him, so hard that the child fell and his chair fell, partially on top of him. Kiersten sprang to her feet, knocking her own chair backward.

"Don't touch him!" Roger bawled at her. "He did that on purpose, clearly on purpose."

She lifted the chair and then the child, her hands trembling. There was blood on Owen's face, she thought from his nose.

"Run upstairs," she whispered. "I'll come as soon as I can."

He went, scuttling like a small terrified wild thing. Tears came to Kiersten's eyes, seeing him like that. There must be no more of this sort of treatment.

Roger was up now. He took her by the hair and began slapping her viciously.

"*I* am master of this house. Understand that, once and for all. You and that kid do as I say. Now get him back down here to finish his food."

"Roger, please . . ."

The gloating sensual smile came to his lips. "Roger, please," he mimicked. "I like to hear you say that. Say it again."

His fist struck hard at her mouth. "Now get the brat back down here. Maybe none of us wants the rest of our supper. We'll initiate him into the birds and the bees syndrome instead."

"Please, Roger, I'll do anything, but not—"

He still held her hair painfully as she cowered away from him.

"Damn right you'll do anything and there are no buts. *I*'ll draw lines, if any are to be drawn."

He was getting very excited through the drunken haze. Hurting her had always excited him. Suddenly, he forgot about Owen, ripping savagely at her clothes.

A long time later as they lay on the floor of the den, he panting, she whimpering, her body bleeding in some places, he said thoughtfully, "I've always wanted the experience of fucking someone who's dying. I understand it's most stimulating."

He put his hands with a false gentleness around her neck.

"Good," he said triumphantly. "I like you scared. You haven't looked at me like that since you were in labor with the kid."

The pressure on her throat increased suddenly, violently. She could not breathe. She fought him, but she was already weakened from what had gone before. He went into her, laughing.

When Kiersten regained consciousness, Roger was sitting in a chair, watching her speculatively.

"Get up, cunt, and pack for me. I'm leaving tonight. I'll take the car, leave you barefoot and maybe pregnant. Oh, no, no clothes. I may want another little session before I go. Besides, those clothes are pretty well shot. Tonight you've become very sexually attractive to me, almost as I felt before we were married when you were still—I said get up. Before you start packing, make me a drink, and be quick about it or I may go upstairs and do interesting things to that pampered kid. I can't stand pampered kids, but, like females, they do have their interesting parts."

Trembling, shivering, her throat and other parts of her body aching, Kiersten did as she was told, in everything. He followed her into his bedroom and began dressing, drink in hand, while he told her what to pack.

"It's been fun tonight." He smiled. "But suddenly I'm in a hurry to get out of this house."

He took hold of her with rough cruel hands and she could no longer hold back the tears of pain and terror.

"Yes, cry," he said. "I like that. We'll just have one more little quicky before I go. I'll bet you didn't think I could get it up so many times in so short a while."

He flung her across his bed, her head hanging down and began again, brutally. "It seems I've rediscovered my wife."

Not until she heard the car leave the drive did Kiersten dare move to go upstairs. I hope you kill yourself, she thought, teeth clenching. Driving drunk as you are, maybe there's a good chance of that.

She went silently up the stairs, still naked. Her clothes, scattered about the lower floor of the house were too torn to cover her. She went into her room and put on a long robe, which covered the worst of the bruises and scratches. She didn't want Owen to see her face in its present condition, but she had to check on him.

He was in his bed, his head under the pillow and the covers drawn up on top of that.

"Owen?"

She saw the covers tremble. Cautiously, he looked out at her with one eye.

"I thought he was going to kill you—and me, too."

"No, he's gone now." Still, she had carefully locked their doors into the hall.

There was blood on Owen's sheet and pillow.

"My nose was bleeding," he said, still almost whispering. "I didn't know how to make it stop, but it stopped all by itself."

"Do you hurt anywhere?"

"I have a heggit," his word for headache, and he showed her a largish lump behind his ear. That must be where the chair had struck him. The marks of Roger's hand were redly visible on his nose and cheek.

Suppose his skull had been fractured by the chair. No, that was unlikely, she prayed, wasn't it? With him behaving so normally, under the circumstances? But there might be concussion. She ought to take him to the hospital, but there was no car.

"He hit you and hit you," said Owen somberly. "I could hear him yelling and yelling, even with my head covered up. I thought he was going to come up here. But, Mommy, I didn't cry."

No child, no adult, should have to live like this, she thought,

442

unconsciously touching her badly bruised mouth, which still bled inside.

"You're very brave," she whispered, hugging him. "Now come into the bathroom," she went on as calmly as she could, "and let me bathe the blood off your face. It's going to be all right, Owen. He's gone now and before he comes back, we'll be gone."

He had got into bed without taking off anything more than his shoes.

She said, when the blood was washed away, "Get into some pajamas now. I'll help you and change your bed."

"Where will we go?" he asked with growing interest. "Can we go to Secesh? If we were at Secesh and he tried to beat us up, Uncle Nolan and Grandpa and the rest of them wouldn't let him. Maybe they'd make him dead forever."

Kiersten said abstractedly, "I don't know yet where we'll go. Now get into bed and sleep. I'm going to have a shower, then I'll be packing some things, so don't worry if you hear noises."

She held him, kissing his unmarked cheek. "Oh, Owen, I do love you so much, and everything will be all right, my dear little boy."

She had her shower, then went downstairs and put her tattered clothes out with the trash, which would be picked up tomorrow. Compulsively, hardly knowing what she was doing, she cleared away the supper, put dishes and pots into the dishwasher, took the milk-stained tablecloth to add to some laundry she had to do for Owen and herself.

From the basement she brought up boxes. She would pack all of Owen's things, most of her own personal things, put them into storage until she knew what they were going to do.

Her first thought had been, of course, yearningly of the haven of Secesh. That had not really been far from the surface of her mind for more than six years. She was going to divorce Roger, somehow hide herself and Owen from him the rest of their lives, but it wouldn't be easy. He considered them a part of his property, chattels, and he was going to be embarrassed and furious at the possibility of losing them. She was reluctant to involve the family at Secesh, while she cried for what seemed the safest haven in the world. They could go to another large city, use other names, but she would have to work and some-how, he would find them, through the publishers for whom she worked, or simply by his own devilishly clever cunning and cruelty.

She glanced at a calendar in passing, then stopped and looked at it more carefully. There couldn't have been a less safe time of the month for her to have had intercourse. Suppose she were pregnant . . . ? Oh God, there just wasn't time and energy to think about everything now. She'd just have to wait out the time, then think what to do, *if* anything were necessary. Had Roger been lying about sleeping with Marny? If not, had Marny told Nolan? She almost laughed, at the sharp edge of hysteria. Tune in tomorrow . . .

She did not go to bed that night. She packed and watched Owen carefully. He seemed to be all right, sleeping normally.

She was on her second pot of coffee by the time the moving company office opened. At first, they said they couldn't possibly pick up her things until the day after tomorrow. That was not soon enough. Roger might get bored with the seminar, decide to come back at any moment. Kiersten browbeat and harried various people in the office until they said the things could be picked up late that day, if she were willing to pay the overtime costs.

There was not much else left to do, a note for the milkman, calls to the cleaning woman and newspaper. Let Roger arrange his own deliveries and house care. It would be a new experience for him. Kiersten was wildly nervous, Owen quiet and tense. He asked to go down to the shore, but she was afraid of meeting people they knew, literally of showing her face. She did dress, put on a hat with a veil, one of the two hats she owned and, Owen with her, went to the small neighborhood bank to write a check on her New York account.

It was past six when the moving men came. It took them only a few minutes to carry out their things. Then they said they'd have to be paid in cash. No one had warned her of that and she had forgotten since their last move. She didn't have enough money, not for them, taxis and trains and a hotel room for the night. Her own private bank account, which Roger had never discovered, was in New York. She had planned to withdraw most of it tomorrow. The two men said sullenly that they'd have to bring their things back into the house. Kiersten thought seriously of a tantrum, banging her head on the floor and screaming was just about what she was ready for now. But suddenly she remembered Rex and Ellen. Surely, it would be safe to stay with them for one night. If they would lend her money for New York taxi fare, she'd have just about enough. Of course they would do that.

She paid the moving men, got them out of the house, and called the McIvers. Ellen sounded warm, eager to see them. Of course they would advance taxi fare, she said, and asked no questions.

All of Kiersten's and Owen's things they would be taking with them, clothes, a few toys, Kiersten's manuscript case, were packed and waiting in the hall. There would be a train at seven forty-five. If they left now, it would mean a wait at the station, but they could eat nearby, and waiting anywhere would be better than staying in this house a moment longer. She put on the hat again, the veil covering most of her face. She had been wearing a turtleneck sweater all day to hide the marks on her throat. She had checked their baggage in the hall again and was reaching for the kitchen phone to call a taxi, when it rang. She started so violently that she hurt all over. Maybe she shouldn't answer. Maybe it was Roger. Maybe . . .

"Mommy?" said Owen curiously.

She picked up the phone. From the slight crackling noise before she said a word, she knew the call was long distance. Roger—

"Kierstie, it's Mother."

The voice, the words, brought a huge lump into her throat. She was twenty-eight years old and what she wanted just at this moment was to run crying into her mother's—or daddy's—arms.

"Oh, Mother, I thought . . . We were just about to . . . How are you? Has something happened?"

"Yes, I'm afraid it has and I thought you'd want to know, but you don't sound well, honey."

"No, I'm all right. What is it that's wrong?"

"Last night," said Anne, "Marny got a little—well, hysterical about staying on at Secesh. She wanted to come and stay with Penny until the baby was born. Nolan was driving her over. They had an accident. Someone hit them and Marny was thrown out of the car. She has some very serious injuries. They did an emergency caesarean and the baby was still-born. We just got here, Dad and I, to the hospital—"

"Nolan?" Kiersten was trembling.

"He has a bad scalp laceration, concussion, and a dislocated shoulder. He's sleeping now. They've given him something. Marny's still in the recovery room. A highway patrolman, a truck driver, and Terry and Barbara Ellenbogen, of all people, saw the accident. The man in the other car didn't have a scratch on him and he was so drunk he could hardly stand. If Terry and Barbara hadn't been there, or some nurse and doctor, Marny would probably not have lived."

"What are her injuries?" asked Kiersten shakily.

"She has a compound fracture of the right thigh and her poor pretty little face is just smashed, where she fell on rock. It's all bandages and the doctors say she'll need several operations, rebuilding bone structure, plastic surgery. They're going to keep her pretty well sedated, I think, so maybe she won't have to know about the baby or her face for a little while yet. She wanted that baby so badly, Kierstie."

Kiersten thought of what Roger had said last night. Was he always to rob Nolan of everything? She wanted to blame him for the baby's death, but she said, as normally as she could, "The baby, did it—was it because of the accident that it didn't live?" That would kill Nolan, even thinking it might be Roger's baby, if he had been driving and . . .

"No, Terry told us there was some serious birth defect that began to happen months ago. It couldn't have lived anyway."

"God!" groaned Kiersten, but half gratefully.

"Barbara called Penny as soon as they got them to the hospital, and Penny called us. It seemed to take us a long time getting here, though Price drove faster than he should have done. The weather on our side of the mountains has been just terrible this year—I've written you all that. There was a terrible storm last night, though it had cleared by the time we got up, and the wind had gone down. The plows were out and working, so it wasn't nearly so bad for us as it must have been for them last night, though it's snowing here now."

"Mother, I'm coming, Owen and I are."

She knew it was mostly just an excuse to do what she had most wanted all along, to be surrounded by her family, people she loved, and who loved her. What possible help could her presence be to Marny or Nolan? Well, she could go to Secesh, take Nolan's place, in part at least, in the work. She had to go.

"We'll have to take a morning plane, something after the banks open. I'll call Penny's house a little later, when we've got a reservation."

"Will Roger—" Anne began and broke off.

"Roger's in Boston, attending a seminar. He left last night. Owen and I were just about to leave now to spend the night with Rex and Ellen McIver. That's where we'll be, if—if anything more goes wrong." She gave Anne the McIvers' phone number. "With the time difference, we might be able to get to Denver by noon."

"All right," Anne said, still sounding a little taken aback. "We'll be glad to see you both. Give Owen a big kiss from Grandma and Grandpa. Let us know when you're coming so someone can be sure to meet you."

It was dark outside, probably about eight o'clock. Nolan sat beside Marny's bed. He was dressed. Dear, foresighted, practical Anne had brought him some clothes. They had retrieved what they could from Marny's car, but the things were in pretty bad shape. The only suitcase that had failed to spring open was the large one, containing the things for the baby.

Marny was white. They had washed her black hair, braided it, wrapped it around her head. It accentuated her pallor and made her look even more like a little girl, if you looked at the perfect left side of her face. The right side was swathed in bandages. Her right eye was not covered, but it was badly bruised and swollen, the lid scratched. Her right leg, in its temporary cast, was in traction and would have to remain that way until the proper healing of the caesarean wound allowed them to complete the cast by bringing it up around her waist.

She moved listlessly now and then. Her left eyelid fluttered. They were giving her intravenous fluids in both arms, the arms from the elbows down strapped to padded arm boards. Nolan felt a great overpowering tenderness for her, more concern than he had ever known for anyone. No matter what they said, if he had been driving his own car, if he had been quicker at handling the sports car, she might not be here, like this . . .

He had checked himself out of the hospital after several hours of drugged sleep and the completion of the blood transfusion. Dr. Clarridge refused to sign him out, saying that he should have at least two days of complete bed rest, but he meant to be with Marny. Why pay for a bed that was not to be used?

His head and shoulder hurt badly. They had given him a shot for pain as soon as he woke and Dr. Clarridge had grudgingly given him a prescription for pain, but it had not yet been filled. Every inch of his body seemed sore and bruised from being flung about by the impact, then the rolling of the car.

What would Marny feel when she regained consciousness? The orthopedist, Dr. Trask, had told him that, after their initial wiring and pinning job on her face, she would be able to open her teeth only enough to accommodate a drinking straw, wouldn't really be able to talk for a few weeks. He said a plastic surgeon had been asked to come in during the operations. This doctor felt, with several operations, over a period of time, he would be able to restore her face to a fair degree, but there would always be scars.

Anne tiptoed in to whisper that she had forgot to tell him she had called Kiersten while he was sleeping, that Kiersten and Owen would be arriving tomorrow. He made a slight shrugging movement which hurt his shoulder badly. What did it matter that Kiersten was coming now? There was only Marny to think of, but he did wonder, very fleetingly, if she might be leaving Roger. It wouldn't be very like Roger to let her come here alone, with the little boy, unless . . .

Anne was saying urgently, in a very low voice, "Don't you think we ought to try to reach Marny's mother? I know they don't get along, but at a time like this . . ."

"No," he said definitely. "She wouldn't want it."

Marny roused after a few minutes. She could not open her swollen right eye, but the left one focused on him waveringly. The most he seemed able to do was lay his hand over hers on one of the arm boards, kiss her forehead. In a moment, vaguely seeing the IV's, the traction apparatus, she began to look frightened.

"It's all right," he said softly. "We were in an accident, but everything's all right now."

They had said to him, Terry and the other doctors, that he should

447

try to avoid telling her anything for the time being. Maybe it could be put off, about the baby and her face, until tomorrow, when, please God, she might be a little stronger.

Nolan had rung for the nurse, as instructed, as soon as Marny began to rouse. The nurse had looked in and gone to summon a doctor.

Marny tried to say something, realized she couldn't open her mouth, and looked terrified.

"You've got a broken jaw," Nolan said quickly. "They've got it wired for a week or two. It's all right."

But when Terry hurried in, her fear had her fighting to get free of the arm boards and traction, struggling to open her mouth, gasping for breath.

"Hey, now!" he said with light quiet reasonableness. "You've got to take it easy, young lady. We've got you pretty well trussed up here, but most of it won't last long. Just relax now, okay? Mrs. Stephens is going to give you a shot and you can go back to sleep. Do you have much pain?"

She nodded, still with that look of terror in her eye.

"Look, I'll tell you what. We'll take these straps and boards off your arms, if you promise to lie still. We don't want the needles coming out. You need that stuff you're getting through them. I want you to show me where it hurts most, okay?"

She indicated her face, feeling the bandages in dazed surprise Then her abdomen. Suddenly she was staring, again in terror, from one to another of them.

"Baby?" Her lips formed the word, and she held up her arms, so weak they trembled, as if to take a child.

Terry looked at Nolan.

"I can't lie," Nolan said soundlessly, "give her false hope . . "

Terry nodded wearily and sat in the chair at the other side of the bed.

"Marny," Nolan said slowly, and the full attention of the big dark eye was turned upon him. "There was an accident, and when they brought you into the hospital, they did an emergency caesarean section. It was the only way but . . . the baby didn't live. Darling girl, I'm so sorry."

She seemed to grow smaller before their eyes. Her own eye closed and tears seeped out from both of them. Nolan took a small box of tissue from the table and began blotting the tears which fell on her left cheek. Those from the other eye soaked into the bandages.

"Marny," Terry said rather strongly, "Marny, are you listening to me?"

She gave a barely perceptible nod. Then suddenly, the eye opened and focused on Nolan in pure hatred.

"You," she mumbled. "The car . . ."

He drew back as if she had struck him.

"Marny," Terry said, sternly now, "look at me."

But her hostility went on boring into Nolan's face until he had to turn away.

He said hoarsely, "It wasn't the accident . . ."

Terry said, "There was a birth defect, Marny, something that happened, went wrong in cell division a long time ago. The accident had nothing to do with it. There's no fault or blame on anyone's part. It's a hard thing to bear, I know, dear girl, but what happened is really for the best. The baby wouldn't have—survived."

Still, she stared at Nolan's averted face. "Get out!" Her lips formed the words and her tears came faster.

Terry said matter-of-factly, "Dr. Trask should be in to see you in a little while. He's looking after your face and your leg. He won't mind if you're asleep."

Then, aside to the nurse, he said crisply, "Strap the arm boards back on and stay with her till she's asleep, can you?"

He walked around the bed and took Nolan firmly by his good arm. They walked down the hall, toward where Price and Anne sat in a small waiting room.

Terry said to Nolan, "You know she probably won't remember this in the morning. Try not to be too upset. I know that in a way you have more to carry than she does, but hers is not an unusual reaction. Again, I'm sorry to bring up the hard things, but I called the place I told you about. Their charge would be about twelve hundred a month."

Nolan stiffened further under his grasp.

"It's about the best you can do, I think," Terry said compassionately. "Here, or at any other hospital, the charges would be a lot more."

As they reached the door of the waiting room, Terry was saying, "Don't stay with her yourself, when she's having this sort of reaction. I think you might consider a private nurse, just for tonight, at least."

"We'll stay," Anne said quickly as she stood up. Price was already standing at the window and he turned. Anne said, "Penny's gone home now, for a little while, but she and I will take turns during the night. We can get some sleep on this couch. It's better than having her looked after by complete strangers."

Terry wasn't altogether certain in that, but he let it go. "I'll go back and check the dressings and the caesarean wound when she's asleep."

"How is she, really?" asked Anne worriedly. "She was awake?"

"Yes, just for a few minutes and she wasn't really conscious then. She's doing well, all things considered. I think it's the emotional things we have to be concerned about. As soon as she's able, I think you might consider some psychotherapy."

He turned to Nolan and said disapprovingly, "They tell me up on six that you've released yourself from the hospital. I know you've already got a prescription for pain. I'm going to give you one for sleep. Get the prescriptions filled. Take the one for pain immediately. Let Price drive you to Penny's, try to eat something, and go to bed. Take a couple of these strong sleeping pills. Don't mess around with that stuff on your shoulders, it's—"

"I'm going to stay here."

"No, you're not. If you hadn't checked yourself out, you'd have a bed very nearby. Will you re-enter as a patient?"

"No."

"Then you'll do as you're told. We're going to keep Marny pretty well out of it for the night. Chappie, this isn't the time for you to be with her. You could see that. She's going to need you later on, a hell of a lot. You can't do her any good by making yourself sicker."

"Like she needed me tonight," he said painfully.

Terry put a compassionate hand on his arm. "I tell you that's a natural reaction. Can't you see that, no matter how hard it is to take? She very likely won't even remember it. Now, will you, for once in your life, go along and do as you're told?"

"He will," Price said sternly.

When they had helped him into the coat they had brought for him, Anne put the back of her hand against Nolan's cheek.

"You feel feverish," she said in consternation. "Please take care of yourself."

She pushed gently at the hair over his forehead, but the bandage behind it held it in place. She tried to smile.

"Terry says they shaved a strip across your head to clean and sew up the cut. You're going to be an odd sort of looking Savage when the bandage is off."

She put her arms around him then, her eyes filling with tears. "Sleep the night through, son. The worst of this will pass, with a little time."

Nolan tried to eat at Penny's, but food and drink seemed to stick in his throat. Chris wanted to give him a stiff drink, but Price reminded them that both the pain medicine and sleeping pills were said to be strong stuff, and probably should not be mixed with alcohol.

Price and Nolan went down to the basement guest room, where

Penny had turned back the twin beds' covers invitingly. It was almost eleven o'clock.

Price said, "I think I forgot to say I hope you don't mind our using your car to come over in today. You must have had a hell of a lot to go through with, with the roads last night, by the looks of what the plows had managed to do by this morning. That little foreign thing of yours handles so well, I'm thinking of getting one myself."

"I wish I'd had it last night," Nolan said glumly. "We'd have been in Denver before that idiot crossed over the median."

"You can't go on thinking like that. It's happened."

But he could go on thinking, and he kept seeing the freakish thing that they had hoped would be a strong healthy child. He wanted to wash his eyes out with soap, to try to stop the flashing, recurrent visions of it. Had it been his genes, Roger's, Marny's, the acid she had dropped when she had first begun to fear pregnancy? Or was it, as Terry kept insisting, a one-in-a-million going-wrong of nature, with no one or no thing to find as cause? All he could be certain of was that he never again wanted to believe himself the father of another child. If it happened again . . .

Almost as soon as they were lying in the beds, Penny tapped at the door with hot milk for both of them.

"It's like chicken soup," she said, trying to smile. "What harm? I'm going to the hospital now to relieve Aunt Anne for a while. I think it's good that Kierstie's coming. Marny seemed to like her a lot last summer. She'll be good for her and Mary and Emmy will be tickled to pieces to look after Owen. Did you take the sleeping pills, Chappie?"

"I think I can sleep."

"Well, *I* think you ought to take them, but then I know how you are. Goodnight, both of you. Love."

Price was exhausted and slept quickly. Nolan, also exhausted and in pain, lay tensely awake. He didn't like sleeping in basements. It aggravated his claustrophobia. He heard cars moving cautiously on the snowy, slushy streets outside, a siren at some little distance, the nearer barking of two dogs.

How could he come up with twelve hundred dollars a month, possibly for as long as three years? He did not draw wages at Secesh, but a percentage of the profit when the cattle were sold each year. He might pay for the care out of that, but there would be nothing left. Marny had her trust fund income, but they would need that for clothes, essentials, some of the hospital bills. Besides, she must never suspect that money was going to that quarter. He carried reasonably good insurance, but it wouldn't be much for catastrophic illness. He felt Marny's plastic surgery might fall into that category, as he was sure

451

would the care of the—baby. Accident insurance. They surely had a right to collect from the man in the white sedan, but, even if it would cover, Marny must be protected at all costs from knowing what the money went for.

He shuddered, seeing the white car rushing at him again in the spotty dazzling morning light, then seeing the—child again. He wanted to have the lamp burning, on the table between the beds, remembered how frightened of the dark Marny could be, prayed there would be light enough for her if she woke. He fumbled on the table, found the bottle of pain pills, swallowed two more, along with the last of his milk, now cold.

He slept finally, but he dreamed some dream of nature's error that had been delivered from Marny's body. That it was at Secesh, in the living room, in a beautiful hand-carved cradle, the quilts and afghans they had made about it. Fern, Anne, and Marny were trying to dress the unformed thing in the clothes they had so lovingly made. They kept casting questioning glances at each other, quizzical, not seeming to understand the horror of what they were trying to do. He kept screaming at them, though no one heard, "It's not a baby. It's not even human! Can't you see . . . ?"

He woke himself, crying out, soaked in sweat, shaking, with chattering teeth.

"What is it?" Price was standing over him, then he turned on the light, appalled by the look of the boy. "Did you take the sleeping pills?"

"No," gasped Nolan.

Price went into the bathroom for water, padding barefoot, his body, big and solid as it had always been, casting huge shadows with only the small lamp burning. He brought water, opened the other bottle, with some muttering and cursing of child-proof caps. He held out two sleeping pills. Nolan took them, drained the water glass.

"More water?"

"No. Thanks."

Then Price sat on the side of his own bed and said gruffly, "Now while those are taking effect, I want you to tell me the whole truth of this. You haven't, have you? I can see in your face, and in Terry Ellenbogen's, that there's more than the rest of us know."

Nolan, still shaking, sat up and found his cigarettes and lighter. He inhaled the smoke tremulously.

He said, almost levelly, "I'm afraid I have to tell you, because I think I'm going to need some money . . . . The—the baby isn't dead. It's a—a freak, a terrible . . . You have to promise not to tell anyone. I can't take the chance of Marny's finding out. She'd feel she'd have to take care of it and it's not even—human."

There was silence for a moment and Price said, "I'll promise, but the promise includes Annie. There's not much we've kept from each other in twenty-five years. I think you know you can trust her. I do. And I won't tell her right away."

Nolan said doggedly, "Terry has told everyone there was a birth defect, that it was better for the baby not to live. He's said it's something that happened right at the beginning of pregnancy, and that's true. He says such infants are usually aborted naturally, but somehow this one . . . Marny will be told those things. The only thing we're not telling anyone is that it's still alive. She must never guess that. It breathes on its own, eats, sleeps, in a way, eliminates, but it's not . . . Their EEG's show nothing but minimal brain function. There's absolutely nothing to be done. Terry knew about a place where such—infants are cared for, and he called them. It's going to cost twelve hundred a month and such—babies, have lived as long as three years."

"Christ!" murmured Price in deep gruff empathy, feeling his eyelids sting.

"I was thinking," he went on tonelessly, "of various insurance policies, and I'm not even sure we have anything that will cover Marny's plastic surgery, not to mention the—the care. Marny's mother has a lot of money, but I can't ask her for that kind without having her coming here, driving Marny up the wall, and if she found out the baby is alive, she'd let Marny know somehow I just can't . . ."

"All right," said Price quietly. "We'll look into insurance policies first. It seems to me you've got a good bit coming from the man who hit you. We can talk with Chris about that. If we find there's not going to be coverage, we can see what else is to be done. I won't talk to Judd Ferris, our agent, about it. He'd have the word out from Hurleigh to Dunraven before the sun went down. Maybe Chris can talk with an agent of the same company here. There's no reason they have to know about the child. It seems to me some lump settlement could be made, eventually. Meanwhile, we'll do what we have to. We will have a talk with Chris before I go back; maybe it will ease your mind a little. You know I'm going to have to *go* back, maybe tomorrow. I don't like it, but you know the situation at Secesh."

"Yes," said Nolan, stubbing out his cigarette. "I know."

Price turned off the lamp. "Now try to relax. You need rest."

After a few moments in darkness, he said, "That government man that keeps coming around, wanting to add some of our land to their wilderness area . . ."

"I couldn't let you do that," Nolan said hoarsely, after a moment of silence. "Selling off part of Secesh, I don't want that any more than you do."

"We do what we have to do," Price said quietly. "I'd rather

think of that land as part of a wilderness area, a hundred years from now, when you and I are both gone and the population has exploded to where Dunraven Park is one big housing development.''

"I'm sorry," Nolan said shakily. "I don't want it sold."

"Nor do I, but we'll see."

Another silence. Nolan felt gratefully that he was beginning to relax a little.

"Chappie?" very softly.

"Yes?"

"Where are they keeping the baby?"

"In a little cubicle behind the real nursery, where no one—why?"

"Because tomorrow, Terry's going to show it to me."

Tears began slipping from Nolan's eyes. "Why? It's. . . you don't want to do that, it's . . . why?"

"No, I don't want to do that, but you shouldn't have to bear all of it—alone."

Price was out of bed, kneeling beside Nolan, his arms awkwardly around his shoulders, hurting the dislocation badly, but it was the most cleansing pain Nolan had ever known. He sobbed aloud, like a child, and with almost no shame. Price cried with him, more or less silently. "Son, son," he kept saying raggedly, compassionately "Son, son," over and over.

When Nolan woke it was almost midmorning. He started, hurting his shoulder, when he saw the clock. The other bed was empty, of course. He got up, dressed as quickly as he could. With the shoulder braces and harness, he couldn't manage his own shirt. He combed his hair as best he could, glaring at the unshaven, bruised face in the mirror, and went upstairs, carrying the shirt.

Price was alone in the breakfast nook, looking through a paper, drinking coffee. He got up casually and awkwardly helped with the shirt.

"How was your sleep?"

"I feel dopey. I need coffee, a lot of coffee."

He took a cup from the rack, turned to the pot. With his right arm virtually immobilized, everything seemed difficult, but Price did not offer help. Both of them knew too much fussing would make them uneasy.

"Chris said to help yourself to his shaver, anything else you need."

"What about Marny?"

"Well, I went in about four this morning. Couldn't seem to sleep much. Sent Anne and Penny home. All they wanted, really, was someone to watch Marny, in case she waked up, then you'd call a nurse. But she didn't wake up while I was there. It seemed to me she was getting a little color back, though. Penny's at the hospital now. She rode in when Chris went to work. . . . You can see it's cleared up. Clear on the western slope, too, according to the weather people. . . . Kiersten and Owen are due at the airport about twelve-thirty. I'll go out and meet them, turn your car over to her and take the one-fifteen plane for Hurleigh. . . . Anne's asleep in Penny's and Chris's room. . . . I'll take you by the hospital when you've had something to eat. That will leave Anne Penny's car to use when she wakes up. She said to tell Kiersten to bring Owen here and I suppose I'll do that, since I generally do as she says. The girls fixed breakfast for me, Mary and Emmy. You want some eggs? Toast?"

Nolan shook his head, looking out at small birds scratching in the melting snow of the back yard. He couldn't recall his father's ever talking so long to him before, unless Price was setting him straight on how something should be done, or should have *been* done. He felt like crying again, with this and the memory of last night.

Price said very softly, "Terry took me to the nursery, Chappie. There's no more need to talk about it, is there?"

Shaking his head, giving him a grateful look, Nolan lit a cigarette and said, "No, I—I don't . . ."

Price coughed, fiddled with his pipe, and went on more strongly.

"I had time for a little talk with Chris this morning. He's been checking around already. The man driving the other car is named Weldon Thomas. Does that mean anything to you?"

"No."

"It didn't to me either, but it seems he's a state legislator from one of the suburban counties, into real estate and the like, quite a well-known, wealthy man. He was going home from a party at that hour of the morning, drunk as a lord. Chris says you can sue him and he and his insurance company would probably settle out of court, to keep Thomas's name out of the papers, and for the sake of his private life. Chris said to tell you not to talk to anyone who even seems like an insurance person and, above all, sign nothing. He said he'll talk with you when he has the chance. I thought there might come a time when it would be handy to have a lawyer in the family. I didn't say anything to him, about the—other. He's talking about a very large lump-sum settlement, plus payment of all hospital bills, so you could take the money for—out of that. Chris said he'd start the paperwork any time you're ready, that if anyone tries to talk to you, you should refer them to him. I believe we could get by with what's needed for a few months, if you want to see about this. Then, if it dragged on, we'd be shipping cattle in the fall."

"I don't like the idea of lawsuits," Nolan said soberly.

455

'Nor do I.''

'And what if Marny found out somehow that the money . . .''

''I don't see why she should, with no one knowing.''

''Well, it would beat hell out of selling off pieces of Secesh, and sonofabitch ought to have to pay something for what Marny's going to have to go through for the rest of her life. Dr. Feldman, the plastic surgery man, says she'll always have scars.''

''And not all scars show,'' Price said gently. ''I want to remind you of one thing. When that doctor was refusing to sign you out of the hospital, he said you're not to drive. See you don't do it.''

Anne came out of the bedroom yawning. She put her hand on Nolan's head.

''I do believe you look a little better this morning, though it could be just the whiskers. No, you sit right there and have some more coffee if you want it. I'm going to make flapjacks and bacon and you're going to get something into you in the way of food. I'll bet my flapjacks are just as good as Fern's, maybe better.''

Price said, almost smiling, a merry twinkle in his dark eyes, ''Well, you couldn' a picked a worse time to make 'em then, for I think I may be hungry again.''

29

Marny was in the hospital for two months that first time. They finished out her cast with a broad band of plaster around her waist and coming down over the right hip to join the part which already encased her entire leg. More surgery was done, rebuilding the bone structure of her face. She had physical therapy, learning to walk with crutches, to exercise her body, wasted by such a long time in bed, and she had intensive psychotherapy.

In the beginning, tears spilled from her eyes almost constantly. She indicated she did not believe them about the baby, that the accident had been the cause of its death. After all, Terry and Nolan were life-long friends; they could make up the lie and get other people in the hospital to go along with it. Still, she wanted Nolan close to her, and he stayed, almost night and day.

He could not have done much work on the ranch, yet the confinements of the hospital and Penny's house, the need to be driven everywhere because of the injury to his shoulder, Marny's accusing eyes, drove him to distraction. He brought her flowers and books, reading to her by the hour, though a good deal of the time he knew she was not listening.

One day early in this period, a small oily man from Thomas's insurance company waylaid him in the hospital corridor, papers in hand. All Nolan need do, he indicated, was sign the papers and the company would pay all his and Marny's hospital bills, plus make an additional settlement of fifty thousand dollars. This was eminently fair, pointed out the attorney, because Nolan might have avoided the accident; furthermore, he had checked himself out of the hospital in the very beginning against medical advice. Chris had told Nolan to expect this and sign nothing. Chris was already setting in motion the filing of a suit against Thomas and his insurance company for a great deal more money. Nolan, had he had the use of both arms, would have been tempted to throw the insinuating, slimy-seeming little man out of the hospital.

Kiersten, Owen, and Anne had gone back to Secesh after a week in the city. There was really nothing they could do; it was Nolan Marny wanted with her.

Roger had called Penny's house on the second night Kiersten and Owen were there.

"I tried to find you at the ranch, but that old witch Fern claimed not to know anything about where you were. She said there's been an accident of some kind."

"Marny's been very badly hurt," Kiersten said as calmly as she could. "She lost her baby."

"So you went running to comfort Nolan, isn't that it? You get yourself and the kid back here on the next plane. *I'll* tell you when you can leave this house, this state, with *my* kid."

"I don't know just when we'll be coming back, Roger," she said, trying to postpone the storm.

He loosed a stream of obscenity and invective on which she hung up. He kept calling, almost daily, after they were back at Secesh.

One night, he called Nolan at Penny's, obviously drunk, making every kind of accusation.

"I'm sorry," said Nolan to Chris who had answered the phone after it had rung long enough to wake everyone in the house. He was still shaken, having feared the call had something to do with Marny.

Chris put a hand on his shoulder. "He's not going to make it easy," he said, referring to Roger. "Kiersten better file suit for divorce as soon as she's established residency. I've told her so. Look, you've known him longer than anyone else. Do you think he's likely to be dangerous, physically dangerous?"

"I don't know him. Yes . . . maybe."

"Kierstie ought to see about a restraining order to keep him off the ranch. It seems pretty obvious to me that he's going to be out here sooner or later."

"Doesn't she have to have proof that restraint is needed before she can get an order of restraint? And what good would a piece of legal paper do if he—"

"You do think he's dangerous then?"

"Chris, I've hardly seen him, talked to him, in years and years. I know Kiersten's afraid of him. It's in her face. That ought to be enough."

"Yes, I'd say she's been through quite a lot. When they first got here, her face was a mass of bruises. She didn't say anything, and none of us questioned her, but there had obviously been physical damage at that time, not to mention the mental condition that would have put her in, and Owen."

Nolan said, "But I didn't mean just to apologize for Roger's calls. We've disrupted your whole household with my being around so much, Penny having to drive me everywhere—"

Chris took his hand warmly. "Chappie, we're all family, and friends, I hope. What else are that kind of people for at a time like this?"

When Marny could leave the hospital, school was over for the summer. Penny and the girls were ready to leave for the ranch. They made a bed for Marny in the back of the Bergens' large station wagon. Kiersten, with Owen, drove over to give additional car space. Marny, now moving cautiously about on her crutches, was reluctant to go. She was afraid of riding in a car again, and the hospital had been her relatively safe haven for two months. There were prescriptions for pain and sleep, there were tranquilizers and anti-depressants. The young woman psychiatrist who had been visiting Marny almost every day, advised Nolan that the pills should be put away in a safe place with Marny not knowing where they were.

"She's still very depressed and she doesn't want to go back to the ranch. It isn't home, she says. She says she's never had a real home."

"What can we—I do?"

"Try to make her feel loved. It's going to be very trying at times. Her whole plan of life has to be changed because of the facial disfigurement, and she was counting very much on the baby on making up to it—herself, really—for the home life she never had."

"She still—blames me, doesn't she?"

"Deep down, I think not. You see, these world-shaking things have happened to her, and she very badly needs something concrete to hold onto as cause. It's much easier to believe that someone, some thing, was at fault, rather than that they were just things that happened, unavoidable, over, and one must go on with a changed life. I think she's convinced, underneath, that the accident didn't kill the baby, but about her face, well, it's going to be a physical and psychological deformity for a long time. I wish there were a therapist somewhere near your place, someone she could talk with once a week or so. I realize that's not possible. You have my phone number, so does she, if I can ever help at all in that way. Be patient and as loving as you can. She still has, literally, to face reality. It's a great deal of responsibility for you and the family, but especially for you. She still very much needs you to lean on, whatever she feels, or thinks she feels about the accident. I've brought you a couple of books. I don't much condone amateur psychology, but it would be a good idea for you, and possibly other members of the family, to read them, without Marny's knowledge, of course.''

Marny was to come back in four months, to have the cast removed, and for further facial surgery. Meanwhile, she was to go at least twice to a doctor in Hurleigh, who would take X-rays to send to her Denver doctors.

She huddled small in the station wagon bed, the hulking cast by far the largest thing about her. She cried, trying not to let Chris or Penny or Nolan see. The trip exhausted her. She was in a dazed state when they finally reached Secesh.

Anne, Fern, and Price greeted her with warmth. Nolan had arranged to have a portable television set, with remote control, installed in her room. He had also bought a new reclining chair for her to use in the living room. He had to stop for a moment after getting out of the car to hug his ecstatic Matey, who followed him like a shadow from that time on.

Marny struggled out of the station wagon, with Nolan's arms, now strong again, to help her.

''Just carry the crutches for now, will you?'' he said to Chris

He picked Marny up and carried her into the house, Kiersten carefully guiding the unwieldly cast through doorways.

''We've moved in a twin bed,'' said Anne brightly, when most of them had trooped into the bedroom. ''Nolan will be working hard all day, so Fern or Kierstie or Penny or I will sleep in here, in case you want something at night, or need some help. Isn't it a good thing these old rooms are so big?''

They had laid a fire for her, though it was a warmish June day, and Price lit it.

''Now everybody clear out of here,'' said Fern crisply. ''There's plenty of time for a good long nap before supper. You'll be wanting some rest, Marny. I'll help you get into a fresh nightgown.''

But she was looking pleadingly at Nolan.

''Fern's cooking all your favorite things,'' said Anne. ''We thought we might all have supper in the living room tonight, so you can sit in your new chair.''

''I don't want them to sleep in here,'' she said to Nolan, almost whispering, when the others had gone, feeling that they were letting her down somehow. Marny's ubiquitous tears were beginning. ''And I don't want to have supper in the living room. You can bring the new chair in here, can't you? Have something on a tray with me?''

''All right, Marny,'' he said, helping her with her clothing. ''I'll sleep in the other bed. That's no problem. I wanted to do it anyway And we can bring the new chair in here for a while, a few days, but you can't just hide, stay in here alone. I *am* going to have to go to work. They need me."

"*I* need you," she sobbed reproachfully. "I don't want to go out there, looking like a half-mummy. I don't want to be with people."

"Well, you're not a half-mummy and they want to help. Just having people around, someone to talk to will be helpful, if you can let it be."

"You're going to leave me . . ."

"I'm going to help you to the bathroom, and then into bed. I'll stay with you until you're asleep. That drive must have been exhausting for you."

"Nolan?" she said in a small pathetic voice when she lay in the big bed. "Remember the time you came and stayed with me when I dropped the acid and . . ."

"I remember."

"Do you think that's when things—went wrong, with the baby?"

"I don't think so, Marny. That sort of thing just—happens sometimes. It's inexplicable. But it did happen. There's nothing we can do or undo to make it not true."

"Maybe it was my punishment for planning to take the baby away from you."

"It was nothing like that at all. Now relax and try to sleep. Do you need something more for pain, a tranquilizer?"

"I never had a family, a home."

"You've had one since we were married last year."

"But I'll only be a burden, an ugly—"

"Stop it," he said, gently putting his fingers on her lips. "It's not true. You're just very tired. Please try to sleep."

When he left her, Nolan went almost immediately down among the buildings where Price was shoeing horses.

"I'm getting too old for this," Price admitted rather sheepishly, straightening to ease his back for a moment.

"Shall I have a go?"

"No, I've begun, I'll finish. We've started replacing the fence between us and Nelson's. Lem and Buddy are up there now. Old Gunnar sometimes sends one hand. We've creosoted most of the posts, cut practically all of them. Butch is working in the shop and Reuben's out spreading fertilizer. The old man oughtn't be doing anything, but I guess I know how he feels."

"What about Roger?"

"Wait till I ask about your shoulder."

"I'm in good shape."

"Well, tomorrow you can go up and get the weir gates in shape. We're bloody late with the water. Fortunately, it's been a fairly wet spring. We've got nearly all the cattle moved . . . . About Roger . . . well, he's waked us up, many's the night, with phone calls. He's been up here three times. He's living in Hurleigh.''

"He is?"

"Yes. Kiersten filed her suit about a month ago. The first hearing's to come in July some time. Roger resigned at the school where he'd been teaching and came out here the middle of May. We didn't want to say anything about it to you until you were home again. We've taken to locking the house at night, a thing that's never been done on this place. Owen has got to be within someone's sight at all times.''

"It's that bad?"

"Yes, I think it is. He's been civil enough to us most of the time, but he gets Kiersten alone and she comes out of it looking like hell. I've told him if he comes again or keeps calling the way he has been, I'm going to get a restraining order. Some nights he calls and just breathes into the phone. We don't tell Kierstie about the calls. We've got that extension in our bedroom and sometimes she doesn't hear the phone in the hall. She's that worried about making trouble for *us*. You might take her and the boy up to the canyons tomorrow. It would do her good, maybe, to get completely away from the house for a while, and still know exactly where Owen is, and that he's safe.''

Marny did not want Nolan to leave her the next morning. She never wanted him to go. She had had a bad night, able to get only bits of sleep, and he had been awake, reading to her.

"I've always loved the sound of your voice," she had said at one point, half apologetically.

Nolan and Kiersten worked at the ditches all day. They ate a packed lunch and Owen, who had been dashing around in pleasure all morning, had a short nap on the truck seat. When she was sure the little boy was asleep, Kiersten came to Nolan where he was clearing out a beaver dam with the bulldozer.

"Can we talk for a few minutes?"

He left the machine and they sat down in the shade, Matey flopping down beside Nolan, tongue lolling as though he, too, had been working hard.

"You know I shouldn't have come back here," Kiersten began somberly. "We should have gone just—away, where Roger wouldn't have had any idea of looking. I didn't have the money, for one thing. All that legacy he got, I've never known how much it was, or is. He only ever gave me household money out of his salary. I'd saved some money from my artwork, and I can still go on doing the work, some of it, at this distance. But I wouldn't have had enough to live *and* pay a lawyer. I'd have had to find other work and there isn't anybody in the

462

world I could trust with Owen if Roger found us and was determined to get him away. I've said this to them at home, and I wanted you to know, too.''

"You've got every right to come home," he said quietly.

"That's what they say too, Dad and Mother, but he's never going to leave us alone, no matter what I do. He says he's going to file a counter-suit for the final hearing, in six months or so, to try to take Owen away from me.''

Tears began to roll down her cheeks and her mouth trembled, but there was no sound. She wiped impatiently at her face with a man's large handkerchief.

"He doesn't have a snowball's chance in hell of doing that, does he?''

"He's going to claim, he says, that you and I are—living together. I haven't told them any of *this* at the house. He says I left him the instant I heard about Marny's being hurt so badly for that very reason. My lawyer doesn't think the judge will pay any attention to such a claim, unless Roger can come up with witnesses, something concrete, but I suppose a time like this now would be almost proof enough for some people. And it will be all over the county, Roger will see to that. It will hurt Mother and Dad—Marny, if she should find out.''

Both of them wanted his arms around her, but neither moved.

"It's been bad," he said softly, "hasn't it?''

"Oh, Chappie, it's been absolute—" she struggled to get herself under control. "I—I finally left because he started knocking Owen around. I couldn't let that happen.''

"No." He put out his cigarette carefully.

"He tried to kill me that last night." The words burst from her while she tried to hold them back. "Don't let them know that at home. I'm so frightened of him, for Owen and me, and for anybody else if he gets drunk enough, and insane enough.''

"My God, Kiersten, why did you stay so long?''

'I've always been afraid of him. From when we were first married. I didn't know it was going to be like that. I did know that he wouldn't pay me much attention once we were married, or be interested in Owen once we had him. Most of the time, we've just gone our separate ways. He had—company, often, in his bedroom and he left me alone. I was afraid of him, but he was also afraid of me. threatened once or twice to let word get around the university about his—companions and, later, his drinking, which has got very bad. He threatened to kill me or Owen, or both of us if I ever left him, so we were at a sort of standoff. But then, he started with Owen and I couldn't . . .''

"I—we'll all help, Kierstie.''

"I know," she said tremulously.

"Try not to worry. You are exactly where you belong," he said soberly and went back to his work.

It took time, but Marny was ultimately persuaded to move around the house on her crutches, the right side of her face heavily swathed. When guests came to the house, she remained adamantly in her bedroom, door closed. She had her recliner moved, not back into the living room, but into the kitchen. There was rarely any action in the living room. She was not fond of reading or of television, so she sat in the kitchen while the big meals were prepared, one after the other.

Kiersten and Penny were out, working with the men. Sometimes one of Penny's girls would try a turn with tractor or horse.

"You should see the looks on the faces of my bridge club," Penny said once, laughing, "when they see my hands after I've been out here for a summer. They say what a lovely tan I've got, or something like that, but they positively stare."

Fern and Anne encouraged Marny to take up knitting again, now that she had learned.

"Make a sweater for Nolan or yourself. Or it's never too early to start on the winter sock supply."

But she did almost nothing, sitting there, staring into space, hardly aware of what went on around her. Sometimes they brought her apples or potatoes to peel, beans to snap, and she would do the work dutifully, absently, but mostly, she just sat, trying inwardly to adjust her thoughts to her new life, her new self.

She had kept up communication with only one friend in New York. This girl wrote often, long letters, while Marny answered with brief notes.

"You remember Mimi Brownell?" she said to Nolan once. "A really cute little blonde. She had a bit part in something off Broadway when we were in New York and always came late to our parties."

He nodded absently, thinking about a hay crew. He really did not remember the girl.

"Mimi's married a Texas oil man, of all things," said Marny, trying to impart the news eagerly, but, dismally, seeing that he did not remember or care.

She slept poorly at night and Nolan, who had always been a deep, sound sleeper, learned to attune himself to her difficulties. He would often wake to find her crying.

"Oh, hold me!" she would plead piteously. "There's nothing here but the wind and coyotes. What am I going to do when it's winter again? If I had the baby, I could stand it, but . . ."

And he would lie down behind her, avoiding the great bulk of the cast, holding her tenderly, trying to find things about which to talk.

Or he would lie with her and read aloud from the light romantic novels, which were the only reading matter she seemed to want. They had used to discuss world affairs before the accident, Hurleigh County affairs, the constant skirmishing between ranchers and the Forest Service or BLM people, the wish of the loggers to have the national forests turned into tree farms for their exclusive use. Price had once all but forced Nolan to go with him to a stockman's meeting, but there had been only the one time. He had told Marny about it in detail and they had shared feelings and thoughts about the western country's future.

Marny tried now, sometimes, but all her concentration was so markedly inward. Nolan wished fervently that there was a way she could continue therapy. What *would* she do when winter came?

One night when he was reading to her, he broke off in mid-sentence as Matey stood up and growled softly. "What is it?" she gasped, unreasonably frightened.

"I thought I heard a car," he said. "Far away, down the ranch drive. Probably some damned fishermen trying to move in."

He heard no more sound and finally spoke to the dog, telling him to lie down, and went on with the reading.

Most of the nights were bad. The prescribed sleeping pills had no effect at all after a time. Often, Marny did not sleep before three or four in the morning. Nolan was worn and pale, deep shadows around his red-rimmed eyes, when he dragged himself out of bed by six. There was scarcely time for his own horror dreams, which came nonetheless.

One night he came to her, dazed for sleep, as she sobbed helplessly.

"Marny, Marny," he said softly, brushing the tendrils of wet hair from her cheek.

"All of you lied to me," she wept, her voice more than a little hysterical. "My baby died because of that accident."

"No," he said quietly. This came up every week or two, and he was so tired.

"Why didn't they at least show him to me?"

"You were so ill . . . ."

"What was the defect?" she demanded, pushing away his stroking hands.

"Terry and Dr. Leonard both explained that to you, several times. It never could have breathed on its own. It was—"

"Don't call him it. They said a boy. Why do you always . . . He was almost a person. He moved inside me. He was almost alive on his own. You have no right to call him it."

He couldn't suppress a shudder but she didn't notice. "Yes. I'm sorry."

"I want another baby, Nolan, right away. If I have to stay in this Godforsaken place, hiding my face all my life . . . You can make love to me. Do it from behind. I want—"

"Marny, I love you, but we—"

She stopped her listless tossing on the bed. Almost, the flow of tears stopped.

"You've never said that to me before," she cried angrily. "Except when we were having sex and I asked you to. Do you know that? And you don't mean it now. You pity me, that's what you mean. Oh, go away. Leave me alone."

He got up. "Shall I bring you a couple of tranquilizers? Maybe they'd help."

"Why do you hide the pills? You think I'm going to kill myself, don't you? There are other ways besides pills, you know. And I *want* to do it, sometimes more than anything, but I want you to suffer, too, something of what I'm feeling. *You* were driving when it happened. There was *something* you could have done."

He brought her the pills and water in silence and got back into his own bed.

After a while she said in a small tight voice, "Chappie, I know it wasn't your fault. What happened to the baby would have happened anyway. If I'd been wearing my safety belt—and you asked me to—this wouldn't have happened to my face. When I'm sane, I know those things, but so often I'm—not sane. I can never act again. You don't want another baby." Then she was almost screaming again, "What am I going to do with my life? The years and years and years and—"

He was beside her again, stroking her hair, the callouses on his hands snagging the fine strands of it.

"I want to go away," she sobbed like an exhausted child. "After my next surgery. Please, please say you'll come with me. I can't do it on my own. I used to be so self-sufficient. I used to be so many things."

"Your face is going to be pretty again," he said gently. "There'll be scars, but they've told us they'll almost disappear in time."

"Time!" she cried. "How *much* time? You don't break back into acting at the age of thirty. What kind of time? Five years? Ten? I have to go away from here when I'm strong enough, have this cast off. If you do love me, you'll understand and come with me. *You* went away when you wanted to. You were away six years and the damned ranch kept going. A thousand people would snap you up for your music. Even if I'm ugly I still want to eat at nice restaurants, go to plays, and concerts and . . . If you won't do it, then I may as well be dead. There's your razor in the bathroom, a piece of broken glass.

If you cared, you'd know what I have to do and help me do it. All of what's happened is your fault, and you're not really thinking of Secesh, you're thinking of Kiersten."

And so it went, night after weary night. He stayed with her now until he was sure she was soundly asleep, then he hid the razor and lay down again. It was quarter past four.

Marny would sleep, often until noon, with Fern or Anne looking in on her quietly from time to time. She said she couldn't bear the place in darkness, that sleep came more easily and deeply after daylight.

One day when lunch was over and Marny was sitting in the kitchen, listlessly watching the clean-up, Anne said gently, "Marny, let me or Fern sleep in your room. I know the nights are the worst times, but Nolan—"

"Has he been complaining?" she snapped petulantly.

Fern said angrily, "He doesn't know the meaning of complaint. He'd do anything for you, hon. You're driving him crazy is all. He never looks like he's had a bit of sleep is all, while you can sleep the whole day away if you feel like it. That's partly why you don't sleep at night. Now, Anne, don't look at me like that. She needs to hear some good solid facts. She's a big girl. Terrible, sad things have happened, but they *happened*. They're over, except, Marny, that you're going to have a lot of years to wait until your face is through healing. That's a fact, too, and Nolan can't help it, any more than you can. You torture him with these things all night, then sleep half the day so you can do it again. *I* won't stand for it any longer. You don't even *need* anybody with you. You can handle those crutches just fine now. Oh, I hear you, crying and screaming at him, all through the night. And some day, because he's so tired he doesn't know what he's doing, he's going to turn over a tractor or be thrown from a horse and killed. Will that satisfy you? If he's dead? Will it make one other thing that's happened not a fact?"

Marny had struggled to her feet and she left the room, sobbing.

"Oh, Fern, I wish you hadn't," began Anne.

"I can't stand any more misery in this house," Fern flashed. "Kiersten scared to death of Roger, Marny getting worse in her mind instead of better, Nolan coming to the breakfast table looking like he's been through hell in the night. I just can't stand any more. I guess I'm getting old, Anne, but I'd give anything for a little bit of joy from even one of those three young people."

Chris came for a long weekend, telling Nolan that Weldon Thomas and his insurance company were coming closer to his, Chris's, settlement figure.

"The date for the court hearing is October, but—"

"I don't want Marny to have to go to court, not under any circumstances."

"I understand that. I was just going to say that I think they'll settle out of court, but it may not be until the day before the hearing, or the very day itself. That's how these things go."

Price sold off some promising breeding yearlings to keep up the monthly payments for the child care.

"I'll make it up somehow," Nolan told him miserably.

"Look at this," said Price, with a wide gesture all around them. "We've always been land poor. But my grandad always said 'Hold onto the land. It'll never let you down.' So we sold the yearlings. We'll have more good ones next year. There's a bull sale over at Wallace. Do you think you could go? We need two more bulls badly."

"Bought with what?"

"A bank loan. They'd just love to lend me money at Ute Valley Bank in Hurleigh. I haven't borrowed anything in almost thirty years. Why don't you go down and pick out a couple, if they're worth the money? Sam Wyman has good stock. I know that. I could arrange the loan on the phone. You could have a couple of days off, get rested a little."

"Thanks for trusting my judgment, but I can't do it. Marny . . ."

"Maybe you could figure a way to take her along. Borrow Penny's station wagon, find a nice motel. It might do you both good."

"A bull sale?" Nolan smiled tiredly. "That's not exactly most people's idea of a vacation."

"It couldn't hurt," maintained Price, but he ended by going himself, taking Anne along, and returning without any bulls.

Kiersten's initial divorce hearing came. Anne went down to court with her and Kiersten cried most of the way back to Secesh. Roger's counter-charges had been so horrible, so patently unfounded that the judge had given her sole custody of Owen for the time being. She had hoped against hope that the procedure might be a simple matter of incompatibility, but Roger, with his attorney's sanction, had been intent on embarrassing and humiliating her to the fullest. Roger would have been resident long enough to file his counter-suit soon and the second and final hearing would be far worse.

A long spate of tears was so out of character for Kiersten that Anne was deeply concerned. God knew the child had reason to cry, but of course those claims of Roger's were without foundation. It was all these months of tension, added to the day in court.

"Can you try to talk about it?" Anne asked gently. "Sometimes that really does help."

Kiersten just sat there for a time, the silent tears rolling down her pale cheeks. It was a hot day but she shivered, her hands cold and clammy as they twisted together nervously.

"Oh, Mother, it's just everything," she got out finally. "Don't pay me too much attention. I'm sorry. It's almost seven wasted years. If I could believe the divorce, no matter how nasty, could be the end of it with Roger . . . And you're all so good to Owen and me. We should be somewhere else so that all the family, all the county, doesn't have to be involved in the bloody mess . . ."

"Kierstie, if you were somewhere else, we'd all be worried sick, not knowing, or thinking we didn't know. Think of Owen, how happy he is at Secesh, how we all enjoy him. When you first came home in April, he seemed such a shy, frightened little thing. Now, he's positively blooming."

"Yes. Thank God he doesn't have to know how close Roger is. Thank God Roger can't see him following Nolan around, adoring him. Thank you all for—for . . ."

"Kierstie, don't answer this if you don't want to, but I can't help asking. Is it still Nolan, with you? Is that a part of the problem? Why you're crying like this now?"

She nodded and Anne caught the movement out of the corner of her eye.

"I've never loved anyone else," Kiersten said, almost inaudibly.

"Oh, my dear, then why?—well, never mind that now."

"He'll never love me again," Kiersten said, sobbing now. "He feels he owes himself to Marny, and even if she weren't around, he can shut things, people, out so successfully. I—I betrayed his love when I married Roger. I believed some things about him that were completely untrue and he started to stop loving me. I can't blame him for that, but, oh, Mother, we had such happy years together, even with all my petty jealousies and . . . I want to stay at Secesh. I want Owen to grow up there, because it was so wonderful for me as I was growing there, but I don't know if I can do it, manage to stay, with Nolan . . . Oh, we're civil to each other, sometimes he's kind, but I don't want kindness and civility from him. I'd rather be fighting with him, the way it was so often when we were kids, than to be treated like a—a guest, a stranger."

"He's going through a very bad time," Anne said, feeling silly as the words were spoken, silly and helpless.

"God, I know that! Marny needs him, but I—need him too."

With sudden decision and before she could take time to think it through properly, Anne told her then, about the baby who hadn't died. Price had told Anne as soon as she had come back to Secesh in the spring after the accident. "You'd see it in the books anyway," he had said sternly, "when I turn over the money to Nolan, but you're

469

not to mention it to anyone, ever." And Anne had sensed a change in Price's feelings toward his son. They were closer than even she had hoped for, with sharing this terrible secret. She told Kiersten, thinking it might account to her for some of Nolan's abstraction, pain, aloofness. It wasn't fair to poor Marny, hoping Nolan and Kiersten might reach a livable understanding in time, but Kiersten was her daughter and Nolan the same as a son. She couldn't help hoping for happiness for both of them some day.

"Don't ever tell anyone," she finished, feeling a compassion for the three of them that was a physical pain. "Not even a whisper of a possibility must ever get to Marny. I've told you because maybe this extra—burden he's carrying has to do with Nolan's—aloofness. He can't talk about it and, when she's at her worst, she still blames him for killing the baby and for her own injuries."

"My God!" Kiersten whispered. "Oh, poor, poor Chappie."

One afternoon when Kiersten had taken the day off from ranch work to work on her illustrations, Marny wandered in at the open door of the room Kiersten shared with Owen.

"You have a fan," Marny noticed, "and the windows closed."

"It's—it's better this way. I don't have to worry about gusts of wind blowing my things around, or about dust."

"It's a good idea," said Marny. "Maybe you wouldn't even notice the damned wind so much."

She looked over Kiersten's shoulder at an almost finished picture of little Mrs. Brown Mouse, coming out of her house, wearing a ridiculously fancy hat and carrying a shopping bag.

"Nice," said Marny, even smiling a little. "Cute. I don't see how you do it."

"Marny, last summer you showed me three poems, remember? I liked them all. Why don't you think about writing, seriously. To me, the poems showed a lot of feeling—understanding of people. If you ever wanted to try a book, I know some literary agents and editors in New York who might—"

"I don't think I have much feeling and understanding left, Kiersten. I've turned into a horrible person."

"Even if you didn't care about trying to sell something, writing could take so much time, make time pass faster for you, until—"

"Something I could do behind closed doors, right?" said Marny bitterly.

"I didn't mean that. I just—"

"You want me to leave here, don't you? Everyone does, so they won't have to put up with my gloom, and I don't blame any of you for that, but you also want me gone so you and Nolan can get together. Well, I want to go. I want him to come with me, but maybe he never will. When I do leave, one way or another, I hope you'll be happy together." There was no wish for happiness in her voice or expression; rather, it was threatening.

"You can't talk about just—handing around some person, like when you're through with him, I can—"

"He still loves you," Marny said dully. "One night he actually said he loved me, but that was just pity. And it was guilt. I don't want that kind of love, even from him, though I'd give almost anything—I *have* given almost everything—to have his real love. It's you. It's always been you, and I hate you for that, for that and for having a living child who loves Nolan and whom Nolan loves. If he had asked me with real love to stay on here with him and *our* child I might have agreed. Then there wouldn't have been the accident and . . . ."

"And you're going to see that he pays for the accident, and for everything else with the rest of his life," Kiersten cried fiercely.

Marny hobbled away, weeping.

At the beginning of August, Price went to see about rounding up a hay crew. Anne was with him. Penny and the girls had gone for a brief visit with Chris's people in Hurleigh. On a particular night, after Fern and Owen had gone to bed, Nolan, Marny, and Kiersten were sitting on the screened part of the porch, playing a three-handed card game, Marny's cast resting on the old glider.

Kiersten said suddenly, tensely, "Someone's coming," and they all heard the car on the ranch drive.

Kiersten knew it was Roger. He hadn't been at Secesh openly for more than two months, had almost stopped the phone calls.

He stopped the car before the lighted part of the porch and came up the steps, swaying only a little.

"Well, this is an interesting cozy threesome," he said maliciously. "You take care of them both, do you, Chappie?"

"Leave, Roger," said Kiersten, her voice hard, "or I'll call the sheriff."

"Do you know how long it would take that hick sheriff to get here, cunt? Everybody in this house could be dead—or something."

Nolan said, "We don't need the sheriff. Go."

"I've come to talk to *my* wife, twin brother, and she *is* still mine. Nothing's final yet. I'd appreciate it if you and Marny would go in and give us some privacy."

"Do you want to go in, Marny? I'll help you and then—"

"On second thought, stay," said Roger affably.

He went toward a chair and, passing Kiersten, touched her roughly, possessively. Her face flamed and she fought tears.

Nolan was still standing, fists clenched.

"Got anything to drink around here? Kiersten, go bring me some

471

whisky, and bring my son, too. I haven't seen the kid for months."

"No," she said, "to both things, no."

"That *is* my son," he said nastily. "*I* know. You never would have been sure, would you, Chappie, if Marny's kid had lived?"

He chuckled, watching Kiersten's face. "Good old Kierstie is always the last to know—about everything. Well, wife, Marny and I had a little romp on the living room sofa in there one night, didn't we, Marny. And I'll tell you this, I, or anyone else, would choose you over Kiersten, if you still had your looks."

Kiersten was staring at him helplessly. Had he forgotten he had told her about himself and Marny? And again, as she tried to pull her eyes away, she thought of the simile of a snake.

Roger was saying brutally to Marny, "I understand your face is quite—"

"Roger," Nolan said coldly, "somebody ought to kill you."

Roger was pleased. Here was, at least, a show of anger from Nolan.

He said, leering, "But you haven't got the guts, have you, twin brother?"

"I think your blood would run green slime."

"I really only came to tell Kiersten, while I can see her face, in somewhat graphic detail, what I'm going to do to her brat when I win custody in December. Or is it really better left to your imagination, my dear wife? You do remember our last little love-in, don't you? I'm going to take the kid and—"

Nolan had him by his collar, twisting. "Get up."

Roger, choking, was dragged to his feet. Then Nolan hooked his other hand through Roger's belt and dragged him to the screen door, which he opened and allowed his brother to fall down the steps, latching the door behind him.

"You broke my nose once, you bastard," Roger shrieked.

Nolan stood silently watching him. Roger struggled unsteadily to his feet, brushing himself off, his face flaming in angry humiliation.

"It's this whole bloody lot of goddamned bastards," Roger cried, almost incoherently. "If Kiersten didn't have this place to run to, she and the kid would be with me, where they belong. You're all going to pay for this. You, especially, Nolan. I know how the two of you carried on in those haystacks last summer, while I was working to finish a book that she should have been helping with. If she'd tried to help me with my life . . . But she *does* tell me everything when I beat hell out of her. Did you know about that, Marny? The haystacks? Or what they're doing right here, now, under your poor disfigured nose? Where do you think he goes when you're asleep? I'll settle with all of you."

He was in his car now, turning around crazily, knocking down one of Anne's cherished peony bushes, flashing away in a spurt of gravel and dust.

Fern was at the door in robe and bare feet. Kiersten darted past her.

"Was that Roger?"

"Stay with Marny for just a minute, please," Nolan said hurriedly to Fern, and went into the house.

Kiersten had run to the bedroom she shared with Owen. The door was open just a bit and she was peering in at the peacefully sleeping child by the dim light of a hall lamp. She closed the door as Nolan came up beside her, sighing shakily, leaning against the wall for support. Nolan dared not touch her, dared not endanger his resolutions, his obligations to Marny.

"Oh God! I'm so afraid of him!" she was sobbing, trying to keep her voice down.

Then he did take her in his arms, remaking his vows to Marny, and she almost collapsed.

"He's crazy, Kierstie. I think we could have him committed."

"Yes, he's crazy," she said, shivering in his arms. "But he's clever. He wouldn't be in a hospital more than a month. You don't know how clever he is—and sadistic."

"How about a couple of Marny's tranquilizers?"

"Yes, please, and I can't play cards any more. I have to be—just locked away with Owen. I can never quite believe he's going to be all right."

He brought the pills and, concerned eyes searching her face, asked gently, "Will you be all right here?"

"Yes," she said shakily and gulped the water, her hand trembling. If only she could be certain of the haven of his arms, would any of this be so horrible, so very frightening? "I could never have dreamed," she said almost inaudibly, "when I was growing up here, of standing in this hall in absolute, pure terror."

"He won't hurt you, or Owen, ever again—nor the rest of us."

"He's been coming, Chappie, at nights, once or twice a month He's outside our window and he whispers things, filthy names, threats. Now you're looking at me as if you think *I'm* crazy. Well, it's true. It's why I keep the windows closed and locked now. It's why I use a fan in there for ventilation. It's why I've taken Dad's old pistol from the office. I keep it on a high shelf in the closet, out of Owen's reach, and he doesn't know about it, but I feel I have to have it. Since I've been keeping the windows closed he's come once, and just stood out there, scratching on the screen. I haven't wanted to upset the others but—"

"We'll see about having the injunction tomorrow."

"What good is that going to do," she said hopelessly. "He's right about the sheriff being very far away."

"If he comes again, will you come and tell me right at the first? I thought I heard a car one night and Matey was upset."

"I don't want the whole house upset. What good is that—"

"I'll see to that. Will you tell me?"

"Yes," she said with drooping head. Again, both of them wanted his arms around her, but he only touched her hair fleetingly.

"Goodnight," she said and slipped into the bedroom.

Nolan went back to the porch to help Marny inside. She was bitter and hurt at his leaving her to follow Kiersten. Roger's insinuations had after all been as damaging, as humiliating to her as to any of them. As he helped her make ready for bed, himself longing for a night of deep dreamless, uninterrupted sleep, she said petulantly, "Is it true?"

"Is what true?"

"You and Kiersten, last summer, now . . ."

"No."

"Everyone knows you lived together for those three years and maybe—"

"God, Marny, that was two lifetimes ago. Now, please, try to sleep."

30

The spring was a long slow time in giving way to summer. The hay crop was good, but had to be left to grow as long as possible because of its late start. They had two college boys working at Secesh, but they had to leave at the Labor Day weekend, as did Penny and the girls. A day came toward the middle of September when all the men were working in the upper fields and something went awry with the baler. Slowly, work ground to a halt. Butch was buried head and shoulders in the machine, cursing it quietly and without much vituperation.

Price said to Nolan, "I'll take the pickup down and get the things Butch thinks he needs. Why don't you take the saddle mare there and go try to find that sick heifer the boys were telling us about? She ought to be somewhere near Nelson's fence line, not too far above here Take the rifle out of the truck and finish her if she still can't get up I don't like to think of an animal suffering."

There was little that could have pleased Nolan more. He disliked finding and dealing with sick animals, but to ride up among the trees, away from the dust and chaff of the fields on this pristine autumnal day was a great relief. He was tired to the point of dropping and felt he might fall asleep in the saddle of the easy-gaited mare.

He found the heifer. She was bone-thin, but up on her feet, cropping listlessly at bits of grass, so uncertain in her stance that she looked as if she might fall each time she lowered her head. The calf nuzzled round her, looking hurt and quizzical. Nolan smiled at the expression on the little animal's face. This was a calf he had helped to deliver—runty and knot-headed—and both mother and calf had been in precarious health all summer. If they were well enough for health certification in another month, both should be sold.

He didn't understand people who found it strange that a rancher could find and identify individual animals. If Price sat a horse at an open gate while a herd streamed through, he could tell, without really counting, how many animals were missing, and, usually, what they looked like. Nolan wasn't that good yet, but he meant to be.

He was about to ride back to the hayfield when he heard voices. Some of Nelson's people? He ought to check. This was sage grouse hunting season. Hunters wouldn't be too bright to look for the big stupid birds up here in the woods, but maybe they meant to work down from here, past all the posted signs.

There were three of them, an older man and two young ones. By the looks of things they had just come through Nelson's fence. He could see a fancy crew-cab pickup parked over there in the trees. Nelson's land was leased to a sportsmen's club, but if they had entered Secesh here, they had done so within twenty feet of a no trespassing sign.

"Morning," said the older man with a kind of cheerful uneasiness.

Nolan hadn't had time to shave for three days and he looked strange with the band of hair, shaved to clean and stitch his scalp wound, still shorter than the rest of his hair. His tired eyes were bloodshot and a little vacant-looking.

"You're on private land," he said quietly.

"We're from the sportsmen's association," said one of the younger men, starting to bluster. All three were carrying shiny shotguns.

"You've just crossed a fence line. It's that thing behind you, with the barbed wire strung on posts. (Thank God, they hadn't cut it.) And that sign there. You do read?"

"Now look here," began one of them, but Nolan was slowly raising the rifle he had been carrying across his saddle.

"Drop the shotguns," he said calmly, "over the fence, please. We'll go down and see the boss. It's not far."

The men grumbled and muttered to each other, but this was a wild-looking fellow, holding the rifle.

"You know," he told them conversationally as he walked the mare behind them, "sage chickens don't stay much in the woods. That is what you were after? You want brushy grassland for sage chickens, and they're not fit to eat even if you get some."

By the time they reached the gate into the field, the men were sweating profusely and Nolan's whiskered, chaff-encrusted face was smiling.

"You can leave the gate open for now," he said to one of the young men, who was having trouble with it. "It's what you'd have done anyway."

Grinning wickedly, he called across the field to Price, "I got us a new hay crew."

Price stared for an instant, then his face became serious and hard.

"Well," he said as the men neared him, "weren't trespassing, were you?"

The older man, now somewhat shaken, said, "If we were, we sure didn't know it, mister."

"We didn't see any fence or signs," said another defensively.

"They might make stackers," mused Nolan, lighting a cigarette.

Now all the Secesh men had gathered round and were hiding grins.

"Where are their guns?" Price asked.

"We didn't have any guns. Honest, we were just—"

"On Nelson's side of the fence, along with their bright shiny new pickup."

"This is private land," said Price severely. "You may not believe it, but God didn't make all ranches out here just for the benefit of all you city flatlanders. I could call the sheriff and have you arrested for trespassing. That would make a good story when you get back to the office."

"Naw," said Reuben, straightening as best he could to his full diminutive height. "We need hands. Le's let 'em work it out for, say a week."

Price considered, the three strangers looking at one another with deepening concern.

"No," Price said finally. "Look at them. It would take a week just to get them broken in. Personally, I don't think they'd be worth the trouble." And, to the strangers, "Anyway, if you're after sage grouse—"

"I already told them," said Nolan, glowering at them fiercely.

"Well, let's let Lem go back with them to where they came through the fence. I need you down here; besides, I don't trust you that long with a rifle."

Lem went off on the mare, holding the rifle, herding the men ahead of him jauntily, grinning.

All through lunch, which Yola brought up to them, the men chuckled and guffawed about the hunters, the looks on their faces, the way they had hurried, puffing for breath, in front of Lem and the mare. Nolan only smiled a little, occasionally, for he had begun to wonder. Suppose one of them had pointed a shotgun at him? Would he have fired the rifle? The idea was frightening because it seemed so possible. He was so tired of gates left open, shot up locks, and posted signs. He was just so tired . . .

Two weeks later, Nolan took Marny back to Denver to have her cast removed and for further facial surgery. Owen cried because he was not allowed to go with his uncle. They made a bed in Anne's big ranch wagon and Nolan drove alone. It was what the dudes called "round-up time" at Secesh, the time when the cattle were mustered, sorted, preg-tested, vaccinated, when the shipping began. He was badly needed. He chafed at having to be away for at least two weeks at such a time, and felt ashamed of himself, for Marny's sake, at the chafing.

Marny cried in her station wagon bed as they climbed up on to Fairweather. He asked her why, as gently as he could, but she said it was nothing. He knew she sensed his growing hostility, his interminable weariness, and he was ashamed of those things, too, but there seemed no way of negating them.

He drove her straight to the hospital, since getting in and out of the car was difficult for her. Before the nurses had her properly settled in bed, Dr. Feldman, the plastic surgeon, Dr. Trask, the orthopedist, and Terry and Barbara Ellenbogen had all been in to see her. They would remove the cast right away, if the X-rays were favorable, give her a day or two to become reoriented on two legs, then do the next step in her plastic surgery. There would probably be two more operations after this one.

Nolan was there to hold her arm when she stood swaying, on two legs once more. As she tentatively tried a step, Marny gave a little joyous laugh, the best thing Nolan had heard in months.

"You're not quite ready to give up those crutches yet, young lady," warned Dr. Trask, smiling. "You have quite a program of physical therapy to go through. For now, sit in the wheelchair and let your husband take you back to your room."

"I can bend," she said exultantly as they helped her to sit. "God, I feel like somebody else."

She was still smiling as Nolan and a nurse helped her to get comfortable in bed.

When the nurse had gone, Marny sobered, taking Nolan's hand. "Chappie, go to Penny's and get some rest, a lot of rest. You look just awful."

He met Terry in the hospital cafeteria for coffee.

"They say she's looking fine," Terry reported, "but you're not."

"I'm going to get some sleep, leaving in about five minutes."

"The emotional part of this has been pretty rough, I guess. I just ran into Kathy Wilder, the psychiatrist. She said she'd see Marny right away."

"I think that will be good. Marny likes her."

They talked about the summer in Dunraven Park for a few minutes and when they stood up, Nolan said, "Terry, it's still . . . ?"

"Still alive," Terry said, putting a compassionate hand on his shoulder. "They'd let us know, right away, if there was—any change."

In Penny's guest room, basement or no, Nolan slept for almost sixteen hours. Vaguely, he remembered rousing, staggering once to the little bathroom. When he finally woke, it was almost dinnertime and Penny was getting a roast ready.

"We were going to come in there and dig you out," she said, "if you hadn't waked up within the next half hour."

"How's Marny?"

"She's almost a different person with that cast off. I was at the hospital for a while this afternoon. They've scheduled her surgery for tomorrow. She's apprehensive, but she's also seeing a lot of Dr Wilder, which seems to help."

Five days after Marny's surgery, Weldon Thomas and his insurance company settled, just before the court hearing was to start. Nolan sat by Marny's bed while she napped and thought about the money There would be taxes, Chris's fees, the money he already owed Price money needed for continuing care of the child. Still, there would be a sizable sum left. He meant Marny to have it. Nothing could ever be enough to pay for her beautiful face, for the emotional damage done to her . . .

"What is it?" she asked softly, startling him.

"The insurance people settled today."

Tears sprang to her eyes. "I'm sorry. Almost everything still seems to make me cry, but do you know what day it is?"

He thought of the date and suddenly knew what she meant.

"Our baby would have been six months old today," she said, trying to stop the tears. "I hope they took everything that man had."

Nolan didn't say that all that had happened to Thomas was a large fine for drunk driving, the loss of his driver's license, cancellation of his insurance, and some unwanted publicity.

He said instead, "I've been talking with your doctors. You have permission, if you'd like to do it, to come out with me for dinner at a Chinese restaurant. Will you do that? It's only a few blocks from here."

"Is it—dark inside?" Self-consciously, she touched her bandaged cheek.

"It looks to be."

He helped her to dress and the nurses made cheery comments as they made a slow progress along the hall.

Marny had always loved Chinese food, but she ordered little and ate less.

"Nolan, there's something we have to talk about—several things."

"All right," he said, trying to read her expression in the dimness.

"You know my friend Mimi Brownell, the girl from New York, the one who's kept writing me, the one I told you married the Texas oil man? Her name is Staley now."

"Yes," he said, though he might not have remembered if Mimi's fat chatty letters hadn't drawn looks of momentary interest and enthusiasm from Marny through the summer.

"She lives near San Antonio, a big house in the country, with all manner of landscaping, servants, and parties. It's a Cinderella story— girl from the chorus line makes it big.

"I didn't write her for a long time about—about my face; just the baby and my leg. She kept inviting me to come for a visit when the cast was off. She misses the old crowd and I'm the only one who's not—well, *doing* something.

"Finally, a few weeks ago, I got the nerve to write her— everything. She wrote right back, the same day she got my letter. There's this center in San Antonio—it's mostly for burn victims, but they do everything, skin grafts, bone restructuring—Dr. Feldman mentioned it to us last spring. Remember, he said he didn't think it would be necessary for me to go there, that they could do my work here? I've talked to him about it again, and to Kathy Wilder. It's a—a way of—getting away. I can't *be* at Secesh for another winter. Dear as everyone is, I just can't bear the thought of it. I'm afraid I *might* overdose. I *know* I'd make things more miserable for you than I already have."

"You want to go to Texas," he said quietly, taking one of her restless hands in both of his.

"I love your voice," she said, brushing at tears. "I don't know how many nights the sound of it, reading those silly books, has just—saved me. . . . Yes, I want to go, and now that we have that money, it would be possible, wouldn't it?"

"Most of what's left, after taxes and—fees, is yours, Marny. I never intended anything else."

"Mimi says that they wouldn't even know I was in their big house unless I wanted them to. She says maybe I'd want to get a job, later on, with her husband's company. I think I can still type fairly well, and I could learn filing, shorthand, whatever, and work in some little back office, out of sight of clients."

"I wish you wouldn't talk like that, think like that—"

"I wouldn't want to stay on with Mimi, of course, only until I could get my bearings, find some little place of my own."

"I don't like the idea of your being alone."

She gripped his hand more tightly in gratitude. "Kathy Wilder thinks I could handle it. So do I. I'd begin right away, with a therapist down there. I know I need that. And maybe I would take a job with the oil company, for a while, you know, until I could feel—all right about being seen in public.

"Some day, years away, maybe, I think I'd still want to go back to New York, have some part in the theater. Kathy has suggested I might take classes, in costuming, or stage design, for instance."

There was a little silence. She took a gulp of cold tea, feeling the intensity, the caring of his look.

"When we were driving away from Secesh and I was crying, this is the reason why. I've never known a family like yours, or anyone like you. With all my crying and self-pity, all the things I've said to you about—about killing our baby and the rest of it, you've never once showed me bitterness, hardly even any impatience. Probably, the acid I dropped when I first began to think I might be pregnant is what caused the defect in the baby. As for my face—"

"Marny—"

"Please, I have to say it so that I can begin feeling like a clean human being again. This may just sound like a poor excuse, but I really don't remember all the things I said to you on all those nights. I know most of them were cruel, but I've realized this for a long time . . . If I'd been wearing my safety belt, as you asked me to do, it—it couldn't have been so bad, my face."

She sipped the tea again and said shakily, "The damned stuff's cold."

Nolan signaled the waiter for a fresh pot.

"You like fortune cookies?" asked the smiling young man.

"No," said Marny, shivering. "No."

She held her hot cup in both hands, and still it trembled.

"I want us to be divorced," she said after a time, barely audibly. "If Texas will do it on grounds of incompatibility or something uncomplicated like that, then I'll file as soon as I can. If they won't, then you sue me. . . . Chappie, I'll never love anyone else the way I loved you—not this past six months, the self-pitying, cruel, dependent kind of love, but—last year, the way it was before . . . Oh God, I'm such a coward!"

"I think you're one of the bravest people I've ever known. Are you sure you want to say final things now about divorce? In a year or two, maybe you'd—"

"No, it may as well all be taken care of right away. I'll never come back here, back to Secesh, and I know you can't live anywhere else. Besides, how could you want to stay married to me, after the hell I've put you through? Don't say anything. That's a rhetorical question."

She sipped her tea, drew a long shuddering breath as he lit a cigarette with hands that were none too steady.

"Some day I may want to marry again," she said, trying a shaky smile. "Maybe one of Mimi's husband's oil buddies, and I—I hope you and Kiersten will get together. Do you think that can happen?"

"Your marrying again, yes," he said, meeting her big dark sad eyes. "The other—I just don't know."

"I've resented Kiersten—bitterly—for a lot of reasons, her having Owen, the way I'm certain she still feels about you, the way, I think, deep down, you still feel about her, but she's paid her price, Chappie, whatever her reasons were for doing it in the first place, by living with that—that man for all these years. I hope you'll marry her and have children and Secesh together. I believe it's what you both really want.

"The others, Anne and Fern and the rest, I'll try to write, some day soon, try to thank them . . ."

She reached out, took his cigarette, drew on it deeply, and handed it back.

"They say I'll have to spend about a week more in the hospital. I—I want you to go home. Please ask Penny not to come see me. Goodbyes are so—hard . . . Kathy has said she'll drive me to the airport. I'll write you when I find out about divorce proceedings in Texas."

"Marny, it's all too sudden. It may turn out that you'll change your mind—about some of it . . ."

"There are always telephones," she said with that tremulous smile, or half-smile that seemed to tear at his heart. Tears would have been easier to bear. He was so accustomed to tears.

She finished her tea and they went back to the hospital in silence. Again, the nurses had cheery questions, things to say. The unbandaged side of Marny's face looked rigid but she tried to give back some of their repartee. Nolan remained silent and grave.

In her room, she came into his arms, trembling and clinging to him. They stood that way for long moments until she began, slowly, to draw away.

"I don't need help undressing any more," she told him softly. 'At least I'm really past that."

He stood uncertainly, concentratedly watching her face.

"It's all true, Chappie. It's the way I want to—have to—do things. I'll be all right. Truly I will. Thank you for—for caring. I'll always love you, for the way it was in the beginning, and for all the—caring since." She pulled her eyes away from his. "Please go home to Secesh. They need you badly right now. Let's not say any more."

He kissed her unblemished cheek. "You're kind, and brave, and I love you, in my own—garbled way. You *will* call if you . . ."

Once more, she put her arms around him, tiptoeing to kiss him on the mouth.

"Yes, I will. Goodnight, Chappie. Thank you for—a lovely dinner."

At a pay phone in the hospital lobby, Nolan searched through slips of paper for the home phone number of Dr. Katherine Wilder, which she had given him months ago. She answered on the second ring.

"Dr. Wilder, it's Nolan Savage. Marny has just told me—a lot of things."

"Yes," she said, making it easy for him. "She said she meant to tell you this evening."

"I'm worried—concerned. These seem to be very big steps she wants to take. She's asked me to go back to the ranch now, says she doesn't want to see any of the family again. I don't know what to do."

"She's been through a hellish six months, Nolan. I'm sure you have, too. But Marny's beginning to come out the other side. This Texas thing isn't as sudden as you may think. It's something she's been thinking of, openly to herself, for weeks and maybe, subliminally for months. I think it's truly what she wants. They have some absolutely marvelous plastic surgeons at the center in San Antonio, and there's a therapist, someone I was in school with, whom she's promised she'll contact immediately. She's had a rough life up to now. I'm not talking about you. I mean her childhood, losing the baby, the terrible marring of the face on which she counted so heavily. She has emotional scars that may never be fully healed. I think it's a very good sign that she wants to look now for a fresh start. She knows it won't be a *new* start, because the old Marny will always be with her, but she's looking for changes, ways of taking control of her life again. My advice would be to do it all her way. Let her try. From what I've seen this past week, I'd say that the chances are more than even she'll make it, succeed. Things may not turn out at all the way she's thinking of, but I believe she will, more or less, manage all this. She can always get in touch with you if things go wrong?"

"Yes, I've said that."

"Good, and she can always reach me."

"If there are any serious problems that you hear about and I don't, will you let me know?"

"I will if it seems the best thing for Marny. I promise you that. For now, let her have things as she wants them—needs them—to be. She knows her mind, I think, but she's shaky. She doesn't need anyone else's uncertainties. She doesn't need to feel she must keep reassuring someone else, making you, or anyone, feel all right about all of this. I'll be seeing her every day while she's still here, and I've told her we'll go to the airport together, if that's what she really wants. Suppose I call you at the ranch and tell you how she seems to me when she leaves?"

"Would you do that? I'd appreciate it, but I'm still not sure that I ought to—"

She said kindly, "Let her go, Nolan. She's trying very hard."

He went back to the Bergens, told a part of the story to an amazed Chris and Penny, packed his things, and left for Secesh.

He had always liked driving at night, but this night he noticed little about the driving. He was feeling a strange, almost crushing sense of loss, plus guilt. All he had tried to do for Marny had not been enough. She still wanted free of him and of the ranch. But he was also feeling an inchoate sense of relief which, at this point, did little more than deepen the guilt.

Christmas was a lovely time that year, new-fallen snow, very little wind, and, best of all, Owen's boundless excitement. Before, living with Roger, he had been virtually confined to two or three rooms of the Connecticut house. Now, he romped through the rooms of the old ranch house, discussing Santa's busyness, humming Christmas music, decorating the big tree in the living room with anything he thought suitable.

There was tension in the household, but Owen was oblivious to it. Kiersten might be found at any hour of the night checking locks. Roger's phone calls had begun again. The date for her final divorce hearing had been changed from December to early January.

Feeding with the work horses had not had to be begun until after Thanksgiving; they were able to work with tractors and hayracks up until then, once the fresh grass was gone. Now the cold was hard and unrelenting but there was relatively little wind. Kiersten was an almost daily driver of one of the big teams. Sometimes she took Owen with her or, better to his liking, allowed him to go with Nolan. Nolan and Kiersten rarely made up a feeding team. As in the house, they were civil, even friendly with the outside work, but there was tension, wariness between them. They did not know where they stood with each other and were chary of finding out. Almost three months had passed since Marny's leaving and Nolan had made no move toward Kiersten whatever. Sometimes Kiersten cried about this secretly, sometimes she felt impatient; at other times she was so angry that if he had spoken to her at that moment, she would have ruined any future he might have been ready to mention.

A letter had come from Marny, two weeks after she reached San Antonio. It was for all the family, pouring out love and appreciation. On a separate page, she wrote Nolan that the plastic surgeons there

484

gave her hope for a more fully restored face, that she was looking for a small apartment of her own, considering night classes, and a job, seeing a therapist she liked and respected. She also asked him to file suit for divorce. He complied, with reluctance and embarrassment.

Nolan had moved back to his old room, the top one at the southwest corner of the house, the room he had used as a boy while visiting the ranch, the one Price had grown up in. Often he lay awake, thinking of Kiersten and himself. Forgiveness came hard; forgetfulness was almost impossible. He pitied what must have been her situation with Roger, but was there still love? Love could change its conformation. They were no longer kids, on the road with a folk group. Could they live here for the rest of their lives, two divorced people, working together, sharing evenings in the big living room with the rest of the family—and no more? And what about Owen? Suppose she married someone else eventually, and took Owen away? Still, Owen was Roger's son. There seemed to be no way of getting past that.

Sometimes, if Owen woke in the night, he would get up, go up the hall and crawl into Nolan's bed. "You're warmer than Mommy," he would murmur sleepily. Nolan would hug him close, something inside him aching wistfully. Then, when Owen was soundly asleep, he would go and tell Kiersten the boy was with him, knowing what her terror would be if she woke to find him gone.

Kiersten, too, lay awake, or wakened in the night, to wonder about her situation with Nolan. She recalled those shabby thin-walled motel rooms when The Stewards had first started out, his arms warm around her, their talk of marriage, which had come to nothing because *she* wasn't ready. She would be asking him to forgive her for a great deal, if she ever could ask. And the move would have to come from her. He'd never make it on his own. But then, why should he? She was the one . . .

One day in the kitchen, Fern, at the end of her patience, said to Anne, "It's past time somebody had a talk with those two. You can see how they feel when one looks at the other and thinks nobody else is looking. Kiersten breaks my heart. Nolan makes me mad. Why don't you get Price to talk to him? Price and Nolan seem to have their problems settled between one another and maybe, just maybe, Nolan would listen to his daddy."

"I don't think anyone else can do anything," Anne said sadly. "I'm afraid they're better just left on their own."

"Well, what are they going to *do?*" demanded Fern, bony hands on bony hips. "Live here the rest of their lives, a bachelor and a maiden lady? Don't you see this family's dwindling away, hon? Out of the five that we started with—Stanley's two, Price's boys, and

Kiersten—there are only three now, Penny's girls and Owen. This place needs more young ones.''

Anne smiled wanly. ''You've been saying that ever since I've known you.''

''Well, I'll soon be sixty-five and I won't live forever. I want to see more promise for Secesh going on.''

''It will, Fern, somehow. Owen is certainly hooked.''

That night in bed Anne said to Price, ''Is it ever going to be all right between them? Kierstie and Nolan?''

''I don't know,'' he answered with a hint of impatience. ''There are a lot of years for both of them to get over. Maybe some day . . . I know you and Fern have been talking, wanting it made up like magic, with pink ribbons and roses and sunshine, but I can't see that happening, especially if Roger stays around the county.''

They heard endless rumors of Roger, where he was staying, how much he was drinking, how he picked up anyone, male or female, off the streets, in bars.

The time came for the final divorce hearing. Kiersten's lawyer wanted Anne and Price as witnesses, along with a more disinterested party, Yola Moreno. He also called the owner of the motel where Roger had been staying, to testify to the company he kept, his drinking, generally to prove him an unfit father.

Roger's lawyer, known to be the biggest shyster in the county, found a disgruntled ranch hand who had worked briefly at Secesh, and held a grudge against everyone there because he had been expected to work for his pay. This man testified that he knew for a fact that Nolan and Kiersten slept together, even while Nolan's poor disfigured wife had still been present on the ranch, that Owen did not receive decent care and consideration because his mother was too busy satisfying her lusts.

Kiersten's lawyer tore the man's testimony to pieces, but nothing could unsay it, nothing could take away the baleful gloating stare Roger kept turning on Kiersten through the hearing.

Everyone in the county knew Roger's reputation by now and the judge gave Kiersten sole custody of Owen. She had asked for nothing, alimony or child support. She was still doing a good deal of illustrating at long distance, and she was a full-fledged ranch hand again. All she wanted from Roger was the peace of knowing she'd never see him again, but she knew dully that this would never be. The rest of her life, and Owen's, would be haunted by his existence, by fear.

They rode back to the ranch mostly in unhappy silence. Kiersten's had been a pyrrhic victory. Owen, Fern said, was out feeding with Nolan.

"Why don't you get into bed?" Anne said gently. "Get all warm and cozy and try to sleep for a while. It all won't seem so—raw when you've had some sleep."

Kiersten went into her room, but she was far too tense and nervous to get into bed. A deadline for some artwork was fast approaching. She tried to draw, but everything she began, for a book about a poor scraggly little bear, seemed to have dirty overtones as the words of Roger and the ranch hand kept going round in her mind. Her parents had had to hear all that. Many other people had heard; it would be all over the county by the end of the day. Never mind that it was all lies. People enjoyed such talk with a great unquenchable salaciousness.

Nolan came to her room to tell her Owen was back, having a snack in the kitchen. It was obvious that she had been crying.

"I knew you couldn't lose," he said quietly.

"But I did," she cried miserably. "No one will ever forget the things they said, implied. I'm—marked, despite the judge's decision. I'm so shamed . . ."

"Kierstie," he began, taking both her hands in his. Then he stopped, waiting until she would meet his eyes. "To the people who matter, you're not marked. You're home. We'll all see to it that you and Owen are safe. Try to relax. I've promised Owen we'll make a snowman. Do you want to help?"

A few days later, Fern went off to visit her own children and grandchildren for six weeks or so. The house always seemed strange and empty without her.

Butch, who had driven Fern to Hurleigh, reported that Roger was gone. He had checked out of the motel where he had been staying for months, and the rumor was that he had said he was going to Europe.

Kiersten slept better than she had done in years, though the nightmares still came: Roger cutting screens and smashing windows to force Owen from her arms; Roger, coming upon the little boy at play, while, just for a moment, no one was watching him. Perhaps he had just *said* he was going to Europe, a ploy. Still, with the hard outside work and the icy fresh air, her sleep was less fearful, often deep and untroubled.

On a day in mid-February, when Nolan, Kiersten, and Price came in from the feeding in the early dusk, Anne gave Nolan a slip of paper.

"Terry Ellenbogen called," she told him. "He said you could reach him at one of these numbers."

Nolan knew why. They all did, though they pretended not to.

When he had made the call from the office phone, Nolan came to

487

Price, alone in the living room, his cold woolen-socked feet near the fire, reading a stockman's journal. Price looked up at him, closing the magazine.

"It—the baby died this morning."

Price nodded. "I thought that must be it."

"There are—things I have to do in Denver. I'll leave tonight after supper and try to be back some time tomorrow night."

He nodded again and there was a silence while Nolan moved restlessly about the room.

"It's strange," he said abstractedly. "All these months, I thought I'd feel just—relieved, but I feel there's been a loss . . ."

"That doesn't seem so strange," Price said quietly. "Do you want me to come with you?"

Nolan shook his head. "There's no need for that . . . Thank you."

The calving went well that year. Owen kept wanting to help, to see calves born. Finally, in mid-May, when one of the gentle little Jersey milk cows began her labor, Nolan asked Kiersten if Owen might be with him in the barn.

The cow was huge with her pregnancy. Nolan became concerned that there was going to be trouble and wondered if he had made a mistake in bringing the boy. They had no Jersey bull, so they had artificially inseminated Iris, but perhaps one of the big Hereford beef bulls had got to her first somehow.

Owen had a thousand questions and comments. "How does the calf get out? Does it crawl out? Babies crawl before they can walk, don't they?"

Nolan was tired of trying to make simple replies. He said, "The cow has uterine contractions that extrude the calf into the birth canal, and so into the world."

"Oh," nodded Owen knowingly.

The front hoofs were accessible and a nose protruded from the cervix. Nolan got the calving rope. Evidently, there was going to be no problem after all, but it couldn't hurt to give Iris some help. For the last few pulls, he let Owen hold the rope with him.

"Do babies get pulled out like this?"

"Well, sometimes they need some help, but it isn't like this."

"Like what, then?"

"Well, not with a rope and—come on, one more pull and we'll have it."

The calf was surprisingly small, though active enough. Iris, who had always been a good mother, paid it little heed. It was soon obvious why. Another pair of front hoofs were entering the birth canal.

"Owen, she's got twins," Nolan said exuberantly.

"Twins like you and my real dad are twins?"

Nolan nodded, deflated, not knowing any answer to make.

When they had washed up, supper was ready. Owen said, to the table in general, "It's two girl calves, heifers, and I have to help teach them to start drinking out of buckets in a few days, so they won't use up all the milk from Iris. Uncle Nolan told me just how calves get born, and I saw them. The cow has contraptions and they protrude the calf right out."

After supper, Nolan went up to his room, but couldn't seem to settle to anything. He took his guitar from its case, something he had scarcely done in a year. Then he laid it on his bed and got a light jacket from the closet. Matey following, he carried the guitar out of the door at the top of the house and sat there on the stone steps still slightly warm from a day of sun. There was still some light in the western sky, turning a few little puffy clouds orange and pink. It was unusually warm for the time of year and the wind was strangely calm.

He tuned the guitar softly. It needed new strings but he had none. After sniffing about carefully, Matey came to him, climbed to the step above where he sat and leaned companionably against his back.

Nolan tried to play the evening, first the little boy and himself, watching the wonder of birth, then the frogs and not-too-far-away coyotes, the weird-sounding nighthawks peculiar to Dunraven Park, the warmth left by the sun on the smooth stone steps, the moon, coming up over the eastern ridge, full and voluptuous, a cow bawling somewhere far away.

He wasn't satisfied with the playing. It didn't go well at all, in fact, but he kept trying. Matey lay down, not leaning against him anymore, panting very softly

At some point, when there was only moonlight left in the sky, the door behind him opened and Kiersten, wearing a cardigan, came out diffidently.

"Will you mind?" she asked timidly, indicating a place on the step beside him.

He shook his head.

"I see you already have an audience," she murmured.

"Matey will put up with anything," he said rather absently "Owen asleep?"

When she had answered that he was, Nolan went on playing.

After a while, Kiersten spoke, just above the music. "Chappie, it was jealousy and stubbornness and stupidity and loneliness. Will you ever be able to forgive me?"

"It's hard for me, Kierstie," he said after a moment, "to change how I think and feel, reverse things—again. It took months, years, to accept, get used to the other—situation. You've been home over a year now, but there have been other things, Marny, the baby . . ."

"I loved you so much," she said, swallowing with difficulty. "And I think you loved me—then. I was so jealous. It started when you went off to Albion. No, it was even before that. When you and Roger came here to live, when you were here in high school, I'd get so angry at the girls who talked about you, wanted to date you. Then, when you went away, I—imagined you with other girls—the way you and I had been together. When Roger and I came to Albion and I saw how so many of the girls looked at you, watched you, acted differently when you were close to them . . . Then, when we were on the road, the female fans would simply flock around you . . . And then there was that night with Susan Lister, when you didn't come back to the motel until daylight and she seemed so—possessive of you. I think now that if I'd talked with you about those feelings, they might have got better, but I was ashamed. I knew, deep down, that I was the one who was being unfair, only that just seemed to make everything worse.

"Susan told me about herself. I'm sure you know that, but it was too late to undo—what I'd done. I've had some lessons in real jealousy, possessiveness, these past years. I think they've burned those feelings out of me. I've been treated like a piece of furniture, a thing to show off and then put away, with no feelings of its own, no mind. I hope the idiotic jealousy has been burned out of me. I think it has been. But, at the time, I just couldn't seem to help myself. I—I guess I wasn't that different from Roger, in a way. There was all that talk about you and Susan and the other women. I think I knew you were telling me the truth on the plane that night, but some—perversity wouldn't let me believe. I was even jealous, or envious, when you decided to stay at Secesh. It was what I'd hoped you'd be able to do, but I wanted to stay here with you. I'd talked so much about getting my art degree and I couldn't just throw it up without—losing face. If you'd asked me . . . I think I was determined to go on with it because you'd stayed at Albion those three years and I'd missed you so. Yes, I was even jealous of the music, the way you'd stay up all night working on arrangements, go flying off to work with other people, though I was terrifically proud, too."

Nolan lit a cigarette and went on softly fingering random chords.

"I started drinking a lot when I went back to New York. That's not an excuse, just a fact. You sent me that letter from California while I was still here, and not a day passed that I didn't read it at least once. I wanted to answer it. I can't tell you how many times I started to, or to pick up the phone. But I wanted something more from you, I suppose, the knight on the white charger or something like that. I think I wanted you to come here, or to New York and no matter what I said or did, to bear me off to California with you. I was so lonely and miserable and Roger . . .

"I was almost falling-down drunk when we were married, but I knew what I was doing. I knew it would hurt you. I knew it wouldn't do Roger any good. Mostly, in retrospect, I wonder if it wasn't some kind of masochistic punishment for myself because I couldn't go all the way, believe you fully, drop the suspicions once and for all.

"Well, it was a punishment. I existed in Roger's world only when he wanted me to. I was a *thing*. Until Owen was born, there was such loneliness, such confusion, such cruelty as I'd never dreamed of. After Owen came, I pretty much stopped being afraid of Roger, for more than four years. I wasn't any fun any more, no novelty. I was just there and that's all he insisted on. We lived very separate lives, except that I saw to meals, laundry, the house. He prefers boys anyway. Actually, I think he hates all women, feels nothing but contempt for them.

"Then there came that night when he knocked Owen off his chair at the table and the chair fell on top of him, when he choked me until I was unconscious and did other . . . I was afraid of him again then, terrified. I knew I couldn't—lie in the bed I'd made any longer It *was* that, you know, stubbornness. I'd married him and I was going to by God stick it out. More masochism? Probably. I don't know. I thought I'd made up my mind not to run home, involve everyone else in the mess, when Mother called about your accident. It gave the excuse I needed, and—we're here. Chappie, are we, you and I, going to go on being just—distant friends?"

He spoke as softly as she. "You said 'loved.' I *loved* you so much."

"That was because I was talking about then. You must know I love you. I always have and I always will. I don't think I could ever possibly love anyone else in this way."

"Yet you—and Roger . . ."

"Please stop punishing me," she said, choking a little over the words. "I don't know any more ways to say I was wrong. We can't have back those years, though God knows, I'd be almost willing to give my life if we could. And please remember that there *was* you and Marny. I know the circumstances were different, but I think you came a lot closer to loving Marny than I ever could with Roger. . . ." Now her voice was almost inaudible, broken. "Chappie, can't we love each other again?"

After a little, he said almost tonelessly, "I don't know, Kiersten There are—other things now."

491

Haltingly, he told her about the freakish deformity of Marny's child, and that it had lived, up to three months ago. She thought it surely would have been easier for him if she had simply said "I know," but then he would have been hurt and angry with Price for telling Anne, and with Anne for telling her.

He finished haltingly, "Maybe it was the LSD Marny took when she was first pregnant. Maybe it was something in her genetic make-up, or Roger's, or mine. Maybe it was none of the above, but, Kierstie, I'm afraid of fathering other children."

"Oh, my darling—"

"If you'd seen it," he broke in, beginning to shiver.

There was a long silence before he said more calmly, "Secesh needs kids. Suppose Owen and Penny's girls don't want it?"

"I'd love nothing better," she said, tentatively touching his hand, "than to bear your children. And they'd be strong and healthy and normal. Please love me again. All my good dreams, over all the years, have been of you—of us."

She was shivering, too. He put the guitar down carefully on the steps and put his arms around her.

"Bonnie Kierstie," he breathed, "there was never a time when I didn't love you, but things have got so complicated . . ."

"We could make them simple again," she pleaded. "Our making love could always straighten out just about everything."

Still, he hesitated, simply holding her gently, until, finally, she drew away.

"Is it all really spoiled forever? You can never forgive me?"

"I want you. I love you, but I—don't know . . ."

"Will you think about it?"

"I've been thinking about it since you came home. No, since long before that."

"Then maybe you think too much," she said, deeply hurt, drawing completely away from him, standing up. "I can be as stubborn and as hard as you are," she said angrily, struggling with tears. "I won't try to explain, apologize, plead any more. Goodnight."

After a few moments, Nolan went in to put the guitar away, then he came out again and walked up along Cranky Creek, the dog going with him. This was where he had walked after that phone call from Roger, announcing his marriage, where he had told himself, write it off, forget it. But he'd never done that, not really. And now, he loved her, she loved him, so why was he here alone? Aching with the loneliness. Because she had been Roger's, he thought, clenching his teeth. She had lived more than six years with Roger. Suppose it had been someone else, a stranger to him, that she had married. Would things be easier now? He thought they would.

And then there was the thing of children. Could he forget Roger and go to her, without wanting her to have his child? "If you will weave me a cobweb child that lasts into the day, I'll belong to you and only you and never . . ." No.

31

At the end of May they heard Roger had returned to Hurleigh. Price saw him once in town, said he seemed relatively normal. Roger did not call or try to see Owen or Kiersten.

Owen could sit and handle a gentle horse well now and he solemnly but happily rode with them as they shifted the cattle to summer pasture. He went with the men while they cleared ditches and set weir gates. Better to have him up in the canyons, Kiersten thought, with two or three men around him than at the house with only women. She became sleepless and strained again. Was this to be her life? What about the fall, when Owen would have to begin school? She sent away for information about teaching children at home, making them accreditable for the school systems. She felt that Owen badly needed the company of other children. He was taking ranch work far too seriously for a five-year-old. Yet, how could she dare trust the school not to let Roger take him some unexpected day? There was the injunction that he was to stay away from them, but a sudden whim on his part, grabbing Owen, could not be adjudicated by the courts until it was too late and the damage had been done. The damage . . .

During June Price heard of another rancher named Helmut down near Wallace, who was selling off some fine Hereford breeding stock. He asked Nolan to go down and look at it. It was an almost three hundred mile round trip, but their good breeding stock was somewhat depleted by the yearlings they had sold off last summer. Owen begged to go and Kiersten agreed.

Nolan had a heavy cold and the trip and cattle inspection were, according to Price and Reuben, a rest for him.

They left early, right after breakfast, under a clear and pristine sky. Mrs. Helmut gave them lunch. It was nearly five o'clock by the time they had ridden around, looking over the stock, and Nolan had committed Secesh to forty cows and two bulls.

Starting back, Owen fell almost immediately asleep on the back seat of Nolan's car. The sky was curdled with great heavy thunderheads, as it often was on a late afternoon in summer. The storm began, sheet after sheet of great heavy raindrops, almost hail, assaulting the car. Abruptly the car's steering felt strange and through the roaring sound of rain and thunder, there was the mushy clumping noise of a flat tire.

Nolan put on the light jacket he always kept in the car and got out with some trepidation to look at the spare. He hadn't checked it for a long time, but it was, fortunately, in good shape. He changed the tire in the downpour, wind rocking the small car. He was thoroughly soaked, his chest and throat aching badly. He kept coughing, sneezing, and sniffling. Owen slept through the whole thing.

When he got back into the car, Nolan took off the jacket and tried to use it as a towel, mopping his face, trying to stop the trickles of water down his neck from his more than saturated hair. This was a very cold rain, the kind most such storms produced. The jacket was no help, really, it was already too soaked. There were good things to be said, he reflected miserably, about wearing hats.

He stopped at a service station on the highway, out on the edge of Hurleigh, the one that kept open all night, the one where he had once worked. The ownership had changed long since, and the area had built up. There was a liquor store on one side of the station, a motel, and diner on the other. It was still raining, but lightly now, and the wind had died.

Owen woke up and they went to the diner while the tire was being repaired. The little boy was ravenous and he loved to eat out. He kept up an almost continuous stream of talk, Nolan answering absently and mostly in monosyllables. Nolan ate because he thought he ought to. He felt no hunger, only ached all over and knew he was feverish.

When the repaired tire was replaced and paid for, he decided he should call the ranch, let them know there had been a delay. He left Owen in the car and went to use a pay phone.

When he came back to the car, Owen was in back and Roger sat smiling in the front passenger seat. Nolan stood there, with the driver's door open, staring at his brother. It had grown dark early, with the clouds. Scattered drops of rain still fell, but under the service station lights, he could see that there was something odd about Roger's expression and the tense position of his body. Behind the smile, there was something a little frantic about his expression and, was it fear, in the depths of his hazel eyes?

"Nice coincidence," said Roger. "I've been watching the car

ever since you came here. Thought you'd never get through fooling around. You'd do well to buy a new car now and then, so you wouldn't be so visible. Well, get in. I want to go somewhere."

Nolan hesitated. Roger was holding a paper bag from the liquor store and, under it, he surreptitiously showed Nolan a pistol.

Slowly, Nolan got into the car. He was feeling dizzy floating sensations, disembodied, as if he were only watching this tableau.

"Where do you want to go?" His voice was growing hoarse and his clothes, still damp, clung to him with an unpleasant sensation. He shivered.

"Wyoming," said Roger immediately. "It's the quickest way out of the state."

"Uncle Nolan, Mommy will—" began Owen.

Roger broke in harshly, "You shut up. Lie down back there and go to sleep, unless you want to get hurt."

Nolan had pulled the car onto the highway. All he could think for the moment was, poor Kierstie. She's known something like this would happen, and I'm *letting* it happen. He said to Owen, "Get the blanket from the back again. Can you reach it?"

"Yes, but—"

"Just be quiet, Owen. Try to sleep some more. We won't be going home just yet, but it's all right."

"I see he's been spoiled rotten," Roger said sullenly. "Just as I'd expected. He never used to talk back. You can bank on that."

They drove a long time in silence, broken only by Nolan's sporadic coughing.

"Sounds like you've got it bad, twin brother. Here, take a little gin. It'll warm you up. Are you shivering from cold or fear?"

Roger opened the bottle, keeping the gun well out of Nolan's reach. Nolan drank a little, handed it back, and Roger had a long drink.

"Remember when we were kids?" Roger asked, almost companionably. "I got pneumonia once. I was in the hospital for a few days and when I came out Grandpa took such good care of me. I really hated going back to school after spending those days with him. I almost thought he loved me."

"He did love you."

"*If* he did, it was only because I looked like his precious Darlene."

Another long drink from the bottle and he said, "It's cold tonight. You forget how fucking cold it can get in this country in the middle of summer."

He turned up the heater and asked avidly, "Are you afraid of me?"

497

Nolan weighed the question, feeling his eyelid begin to twitch. He thought, thank God it wasn't Kiersten's car he got into. At last he said, "I have a healthy respect for guns."

Roger wanted him afraid. "But I said of *me?* Nobody ever considers *me,* just the trappings. Are you?"

"Yes." Kierstie, bonnie girl, I won't let anything happen to Owen, or to me, if there's any way I can prevent it. I *do* want to be with you. I *do* love you, I always have. God forgive me for these past lost months.

Roger sighed, drank again. "That's good. I want you afraid. I've tried to get your attention, one way and another, all my life. Want another slug of this?"

"No."

"Suppose I make you drink it? Hold the pistol against your head, or the kid's?"

"Then I suppose I'd drink, but I wouldn't be able to drive very well. We might be stopped."

Another long silence before Roger said petulantly, "Grandpa loved you for yourself, not because you looked like that fucking cunt. I always hated the way you two were such palsies and shut me out."

"I don't think either of us meant to do that."

"It was the crappy music you were always fooling around with. I couldn't tell one note from another and, do you know, I used to be ashamed of that, like it was some great lack in me? You had the talent. I had the looks and intelligence, but it was always you people gravitated to. You had all the luck, always got exactly what you wanted. You went to your music school, had your musicians' group, made records, and, ultimately, came back to Secesh, where they'd been waiting for you with open arms, and which was just what you'd always meant to do."

"You often came back to Secesh."

"But not the way you did. Not as the prodigal, with people loving me. They liked my looks, admired my various report cards, Anne and Fern did, at any rate. To Price and you, I've always been just a—nothing. My own father never cared enough even to talk to me about anything. You ignored me like a pile of cow shit you'd step over."

"You got the degrees you went after. You're a wealthy man who doesn't even have to work now."

"I never did finish that damned book. I wanted that, just to show everyone I could do it. But I did have Kiersten, for a while, and she had my kid."

He then went into long rambling descriptions of the things he had done to and with Kiersten. Nolan tried not to listen. It wasn't too difficult because he was feeling so weak and fuzzy. Driving demanded practically all his attention.

Roger was saying, "It was your idea that she leave me, wasn't it? You promised her safety and God knows what other crap. You two always kept in touch, didn't you?"

"No." He coughed so hard he had to slow the car. He reached for a cigarette and Roger almost shrieked at him.

"No smoking! I can't stand cigarettes. Besides, they certainly won't help your damned cough." Then he returned to former thoughts. "And you had Marny, the prettiest little piece I ever saw. Oh, I got one crack at her, but she loved you. *Love!* The very word makes me sick. Love is a nothing, just like everything else. Everybody *loves* good old Chappie." He made the word a mockery, something worthy only of derision. "I hear she's left you, that you're being divorced."

"Yes."

"Then you'll marry Kiersten, I suppose."

"I don't know," he said and sneezed. But he did know. Somehow, this night had, or was, squaring things away in his mind. He would marry her, if only . . .

Roger smiled broadly, Nolan could hear it in his voice. "You don't mean I've succeeded in spoiling that piece of merchandise for you? That's really a hell of a shame, Chappie." He laughed softly, but then said harshly, "Still, you've got her, and my kid, up there at Secesh."

Another drink from the bottle, another silence before Roger said almost challengingly, "That baby of Marny's wasn't mine. I thought it was going to be, but I wouldn't produce anything defective. It's a wonder she didn't kill herself, or you, or both of you, after you smashed up her face that way. They say she's going to be a scarred-up freak for life."

Another silence, another drink and he said thoughtfully, "They hated you at home when we were kids. I used to feel guilty about that—and jealous. They didn't love me either, though it came out in different ways. You got a lot more attention than I did, with that buddy-buddy bit with Grandpa. I was just something for Darlene to trot out to show herself off with. Clarence hated me. He'd have knocked me around the same as you if he hadn't been so afraid of her. I guess he thought if he crossed her, he might lose her. Can you imagine any man, even Clarence, being afraid of a woman, any *real* man? He did turn me onto a couple of good sex things, the stupid old bastard. There is *that* to say for him, at least. He did it out of frustration, you know, to get even with Darlene for the way she pretended to feel about me, or maybe just because she just wasn't giving him enough."

Another long pull at the bottle.

"I'll tell you this: I was the—loneliest kid who ever lived. I wanted to be friends with you, but you never had the time or the interest. You've always seemed to want to forget I'm alive. People, even books, say twins are close, even fraternal ones, that they share almost everything. You started out by having a different birthday and just went on from there. Whatever I've wanted, and had, has turned into dust as soon as I've got it. You've had everything."

They crossed the Wyoming border at almost eleven o'clock. Roger was getting thoroughly drunk. Nolan thought he could try to take the gun at any time, but was afraid it might go off if there was any struggle in these close quarters. He dared not try yet.

"All right," he said into a long silence, "we're in Wyoming. Where do you want to go?"

"I don't know. Just keep driving. Casper, maybe. There's a good-sized airport there, isn't there? I'm leaving the country. Not a month ago, I came back from Europe and now I'm going to leave again."

Another silence as miles passed beneath the wheels. Nolan tried to refuse to acknowledge his symptoms. Breathing was beginning to be very painful and everything about his body hurt, even his hair, it seemed. But there was Owen who must be thought of. In Roger's present state, there was no telling what he might do, or try.

Roger said peevishly, "Aren't you even interested in why I'm leaving the county, the state, the country?"

"Why?"

"You see, that's the way you've always talked to me, as few words as possible. Maybe I'll have to do something to really get your attention. I *will* have your attention, if it's only because of fear. You're going to pay for the years you've ignored me, made me feel unwanted. You'll pay, Price will pay when he loses his fair-haired boy and only grandson, and Kiersten will pay, damn her to hell!"

Another drink, then in quieter tones, "I'm going because I killed someone a few hours ago, at that motel by the service station. No one will find him until they come to clean in the morning."

Something in his voice, a scary tremor, made Nolan believe this at once.

"Who did you kill?" he asked carefully.

"Billy something. I picked him up off the streets a few days ago. A good-looking kid, sort of Indian, American Indian. He was hitchhiking from St. Louis to California. At first he told me he was eighteen, but then it developed he was only fifteen. Remember how you used to lie about your age, for jobs and things? This Billy had no money left, not a cent. I bought him some good meals, a few clothes, and then we shacked up in my room. Late this afternoon, I was—I believe the correct word is sodomizing—I was sodomizing him again, and I got this irresistible urge to choke him meanwhile, so I did it. It was very exciting. I get horny again every time I think of it. Quite an experience, but you can see why I have to leave."

Nolan coughed hard. "I'm not sure I can drive all the way, Roger. Casper is a long way and I'm—"

Roger held the cold gun barrel mouth against his temple.

"Does this make you feel any surer? If not, I can shoot you and the kid now, dump you, and drive myself, though I rather like being chauffeured. I'd think you'd want to live as long as possible. Most people try for that; Billy did. And you owe me, Nolan. You owe me a lot."

"For what?"

"For all the times I wanted to be with you, talk with you, share things. For the restlessness I've seen in your face when we're together, the boredom, the downright contempt and disrespect. For the way you've shut me out with your eyes, making them go all blank and empty when I needed your attention, your brotherly care. Are you afraid of this gun?"

"Yes, I am."

"More important, are you afraid of me now?"

"Yes," he said, though he was too dazed with fever really to feel fear. But there was Owen to think about.

Roger took the gun away.

"At least I do have your attention. I'll have to kill you both eventually, of course. I've admitted my crime to you. Most people want life, no matter how miserable it is. I've thought of suicide many times myself, but it always came round to the fact that I had the *right* to live, no matter how screwed up other people were. I'm going to see you beg for life. Maybe I'll shoot both you and the kid a number of times, let you truly know what it is to die."

"But they'll know, Roger, about the boy. He's in your room."

"I could have said I wasn't there, but now you're the same as a witness and you *would* talk. You'd love to see me put away. I'm not about to make things that easy for you and Kiersten."

"Maybe he wasn't dead. Maybe he was just—"

"He was dead, no breathing, no heart beat. You think I'm crazy, don't you? You've thought that for years. So have the rest of them. Well, it's true—sometimes. *I* know that. Once I got a look at my shrink's notes on me. They said things like narcissism, personality deficiency. That's when I stopped therapy in New York, years ago. But I could make a plea of insanity that would stand in any court. I've got money enough for the best lawyers. If I didn't have, Price would

501

pay, wouldn't he? I'm his son, too, though he never likes recalling that. But I don't want to be shut up some place, even some classy sanitarium, so I'm going to be a long way from Hurleigh by clean-up time in the morning, with no witnesses left behind."

He drank. There was another long silence and he drank again.

"I know what you're thinking, that I'll pass out. Well, I won't. I can hold my liquor. Here, have some more yourself. Your damned coughing is getting on my nerves. I don't think you want me nervous."

Nolan drank, returned the bottle, and there was another long silence.

"I saw Clarence," Roger said abruptly. "I found out he went to stay with another cousin down near Wallace and I went to see him last week. Just for the hell of it. He's a shrivelled-up old man. What would he be now? In his sixties or more? He's got at least three pictures of Darlene in his room. He hasn't worked since she died, just keeps a little drinking money and turns the rest of his pension check over to the cousin's wife for room and board. Now *there's* a nut for you. I bought him a bottle of whiskey and all he'd do was talk about her—even cried, still threatens Davis King for killing her. . . . Do you remember the time he broke your arm? I don't know why I went there, just to see if I still hated him as much, I guess. . . . Maybe I went there, just to prove to him that we were, both of us, too big for him to knock around any more. He did mistreat me, too, though in different ways. Way back then, I hated both of them so much. I promised myself that no woman would ever have any hold over *me*. I could have made records with that Lister broad, but not for the stereo. . . . I loved you so much while I was hating them. I suppose you hated them, too. They certainly hated you. People have always had such definite feelings about you, love or hate, while they've just pushed me aside. And all you've ever done is be—yourself. You were always so damned selfish about just being yourself."

Something about the tremulous vehemence in his voice made Nolan feel real fright—and sorrow for him. His scalp crawled with fear, his hands turned clammy, and his eyelid twitched constantly. There was something so eerie about Roger's half-controlled violence.

"Price is going to leave all of Secesh to you," Roger said matter-of-factly, gulping at the gin which was now very low in the bottle. "He won't parcel it out, the way he would if Hugh had lived, or if I had ever come in for anything in his mind. Kiersten comes with the place. Roger gets nothing, Roger *is* nothing, as far as most people have ever been concerned. Kiersten has shown proper respect for me at times, but only because she's been scared silly. My kid could have

502

been something special. . . . I'm going to Canada, maybe Australia, start a new life. Good teacher, fine references, just got a mental block and couldn't finish the one lousy book. The book might have worked out if anybody had ever loved me, if I ever loved anyone, besides my twin brother, who always treated me like shit. I loved you, in all ways. Sometime, I started to hate you because of that love. Love turned to hate is the worst, or best kind of hating.'' Now the pathos was gone from his voice and there was only the vehement fury. ''People who call themselves normal think only men and women should love in certain ways, but I loved my twin brother in all ways. You once broke my nose for just trying . . .''

The voice went on, falling now to a dull monotonous mumble.

Nolan could see the night lights of a town far in the distance. He'd have to do something while he was still able. His feverish mind was getting duller by the moment, but now, for perhaps the first time in their lives, he was truly taking his twin seriously. Roger was silent now, slumped in the seat, head back, not moving.

As they came into the little town, Nolan easily took the pistol from lax fingers, dropped it down between the door and his own seat. When he stopped in front of the sheriff's office, Roger began to mumble again, but did not open his eyes or seem to miss the pistol.

Nolan got out fast, taking the gun with him. He left his door open to keep things quiet, likewise the back door, after he had opened it to grab Owen, blanket and all.

He went into the office, carrying the boy, staggering.

''Can I—'' began the man at the desk, then he rushed around to take the child. ''Sit down, friend, you look to me like passing out.''

The pistol had been concealed in his hand beneath Owen. He laid it on the desk and sank into a straight chair. After a fit of harsh coughing, the words seeming to choke him, he said, ''There's a man outside in my car. Drunk. He says he killed someone down in Colorado, at Hurleigh, tonight.''

''What happened? He kidnap you and the kid? This his gun?''

The deputy had laid Owen on the couch and was fingering his gun, watching Nolan avidly.

''He's my brother,'' Nolan whispered, ''my—twin brother.''

The words brought pain, pain unrelated to the pneumonia that was sapping his strength, even his mental abilities, and making him feel strangely like a mere bystander in all this.

Another deputy had come from somewhere in the back of the building. The two men went out warily. Nolan sat on the chair, swaying a little, staring at nothing, thinking of nothing, until two heavy pistol shots roused him to a degree. He stood up unsteadily and looked from a grimy window. There was not light enough to see clearly, but the right front door of his car was open and someone lay on the sidewalk.

"Uncle Nolan!" cried Owen, suddenly roused and frightened.

He knelt by the boy, putting his arms around him in the rumpled blanket.

"It's all right, Owen. Everything's all right."

"But where *is* this place? I want to go home. I want my mommy."

The little boy began to sob and it was the last thing Nolan remembered for what seemed weeks.

When he woke, it was to a hospital room and he began automatically to struggle against it. He had come to fear and hate hospitals after Marny's child was born.

"Just lie easy now," said Price, turning from the window. His voice sounded unsteady and his face looked strained.

"Owen—Roger—I don't know . . ."

"You've been out of it for two days. Owen's home at Secesh with his mother and the rest. Your fever's broken. They'll want you to rest here two or three days but you're going to be all right now."

"Roger—had a pistol, but I took it. He said he'd . . ."

"Roger's dead, Chappie. When they went out to get him out of your car, he came to enough to grab one of the deputies' guns and get off a shot. So the other one shot him in the chest. He died right there."

"My God," he whispered, feeling that pain again, not of the body.

There was a silence before he could bring himself to ask, "That boy back at the motel in Hurleigh . . . ?"

"Let's not talk any more. You need to take it easy for a bit, get rested up."

"I want to know."

"What did he tell you?"

"That he'd picked up a kid—fifteen, I think—and that while . . . that he'd strangled him to death."

Price was silent and Nolan's eyes fastened on his face.

"They found him . . . ?"

Slowly, reluctantly, Price shook his head.

"The people at the motel said he'd had a kid staying with him, but several people, the motel manager, someone working at the service station next door, saw the kid leave, late in the afternoon that day, saw him go out to the highway and start thumbing. A car going west stopped for him. Roger went over to the liquor store soon after that, and he'd been again, I guess, when he saw your car. At any rate, they found a nearly empty gin bottle in the car."

504

"But he *told* me . . . Jesus Christ, I know—knew—how he lied. It came easier for him than the truth. Why didn't I think—realize . . . ?"

"He had the gun, didn't he? He'd threatened you and Owen?"

"Yes, but I took the gun. He was so drunk, I don't see how he could have stood, or . . ."

"Well, he did, son. Try not to be too upset."

"He was my brother," Nolan said unevenly.

"And he was my son," Price said quietly. "Maybe both of us could have done better somewhere along the line. But this has happened, it's over."

A nurse bustled in. "Well! You're awake. That's good to see." She thrust a thermometer into his mouth and went out.

Nolan removed the thermometer. "What happened to Owen, all that time before they could let you know?"

"Keep that in your mouth. Don't talk. The sheriff's wife came and got him. It was about noon the next day before we got here, but she had a couple of kids around his age. He was scared and bewildered. They couldn't give him a real explanation, but as soon as he saw Kiersten, he seemed ready for anything."

Eventually, the nurse came back, finding the temperature almost down to normal. "I have an injection for you," she said, as if announcing something marvelous on a silver salver. "And we want you to eat something light and go to sleep again." She studied Nolan's face with concern. "You told him," she said accusingly to Price.

He nodded and she whisked from the room disapprovingly.

Nolan got up to walk the few steps to the bathroom. He was appalled and irritated at his weakness.

"There'll be a—hearing or something, I suppose," he said wearily when he was back in bed.

"Yes. They'll need your testimony to justify the deputies' going after him, but that won't come until you're stronger."

Another nurse came, bearing a tray with broth and some nondescript pudding. Nolan frowned at it, but began trying to eat. Sudden hunger surprised him.

When the tray had been removed and yet another injection administered, Price was moving restlessly about the room. He said reluctantly, "Did you buy any of those cattle of Helmut's?"

Nolan frowned trying to remember. Everything about that day seemed to have gone blurry, unreal.

"Yes," he said finally, "I contracted for—forty cows, I think it was, and two bulls. They're fine breeding stock."

"Yes, next to ours, they're about the best around. I'll see about getting a truck from Ellenbogens' to pick them up. . . . Nolan, I have to get back to Secesh. You know how it might be, with both of us away. We'll keep in touch with them here so we'll know when you're ready for release."

"I'm ready now," he said challengingly, sitting up and swinging his feet over the side of the bed once more.

The nurses summoned a doctor from his clinic office, but nothing anyone could say, even Price, could stop him. Once again, he signed himself out of a hospital against medical advice.

When they reached the car, the world was spinning around him and he breathed with a painful heaviness, trying to hide it all. Price said nothing. He was angry and worried. Nolan sprawled on the seat, his head back against the headrest. This was where Roger had sat, in almost this same limp position, when Nolan had taken the gun from his unfeeling fingers. Why had he drunk so much if he meant to do them harm? Why had he said he was leaving the country? Why had he lied about the boy in the motel? Most important, why had he, Nolan, not been able to pick through the tissue of lies for bits of truth? Roger might be alive now if . . . The way he had talked . . . Mental care was what he obviously needed, had needed for a long time. Why hadn't any of them done anything about that? Roger was right in saying that Nolan preferred to ignore him. It had always been that way, and it was wrong. . . . What had he really intended, if he had any concrete plans, for the end of that ride?

Nolan slept exhaustedly and did not awaken until they were on the road between Fairweather and Dunraven Park.

"Are you all right?" Price demanded curtly, seeing his eyes open.

"Yes, I feel better, stronger now."

There was a long silence before Price cleared his throat with a little difficulty.

"I don't know how things stand between you and Kiersten."

He seemed to wait for an answer but none was forthcoming.

"She told her mother—you must know that Annie and I talk over most things—she told her that she doesn't know if you still love her or not. She thinks not. She said you talked about being—afraid to father a child, after what happened with Marny."

Still no response.

"I'm going to tell you something about myself," he said, sounding angry. "Everyone's wondered why Annie and I never had children of our own, together. We wanted them. They were a big part of our life plans, but we found out, before we'd been married very long, that we'd never have them.

"After Darlene took you boys away from Secesh that first time, when you were four, I had some kind of illness, with a high fever for over a week. They never quite knew what it was, but the doctors think that's what may—have caused it. I'm sterile, Nolan.''

Still no words, but Nolan was watching his face with gentle grave eyes, and Price could feel himself flushing hotly.

"I saw that—child of Marny's," he went on painfully, "but it was just a—"

"And there's Roger," Nolan broke in abruptly. "He had mental problems all his life. Maybe Darlene did, too, though I think she was just shallow and stupid.''

"Who's to say Roger's problems weren't environment. Owen certainly shows no—damage.''

"But the possibility—"

"All right, damn it, pass up children, though I can almost guarantee you there'll come a day you'll regret that. Don't produce any kids, but if you love Kierstie, for God's sake, give over. She's had punishment and to spare. Let things be easy and—congenial at Secesh again. But you'll have to do as you see fit, of course, and this will be my last word on it.''

The women, surprised and concerned by Nolan's return, bustled about getting his room ready. Fern even made him put on pajamas. It was cool for the time of year, she insisted immovably, and he mustn't take any chance of getting a chill. They bundled him into bed, brought food and drink.

Kiersten was up working on fences in the high pastures and had taken Owen with her. Price changed his clothes, ate a bit, and went out to work.

Nolan slept through what was left of that afternoon and through the night. When he woke, it was past nine. He got up and went to the bathroom, feeling little of yesterday's dizziness and weakness. When he returned to his room, Kiersten was standing by the bed with a steaming cup of coffee.

"Yes," he said, his voice sounding weaker than it should. "That's what I need.''

"Get into bed first," she said.

He obeyed. "Anything for a cup of good coffee.''

"You're very foolish," she said, sitting down on a chair near the bed, "to keep checking yourself out of hospitals. Mother and Fern and I say you don't even attempt any work for a week, and when we three agree, it's a very forceful agreement. Now, how do you feel?''

"Only a little weak and shaky. Much better than yesterday. I'm fine.''

They were silent for a little until he said hesitantly, "I don't

507

really understand any of it. I guess I never did really try to understand him. Maybe if I—"

"I don't understand either," she said, looking miserable, "but I do know that, with the way things turned out, the very least he would wish for would be our feeling guilty, especially you."

"After he was really drunk, he talked so much about love . . . and hate."

"I think I told you a long time ago that it seemed to me he wanted to absorb you, *be* you, and himself, make up only one person."

"I don't see why I didn't know that thing about killing the boy could be a lie. He's lied all his life—all our lives . . ."

"Yes, and I think he was past knowing the difference himself, between true and false, especially when he'd been drinking."

"But if I'd realized he was lying, he probably wouldn't be dead There would have been something I could have . . ."

"Don't you see, this is exactly how he'd want you to be feeling?"

"Did he get into my car that night with the idea that, one way or another, he was going to be killed? Did he mean me to do it?"

"Maybe," she said slowly. "I've thought he had suicide in mind more than once, but I thought he wasn't the kind. He is—was—a survivor, it seemed to me. Maybe he meant to make you do it for him, but I think it's more likely he really meant to kill you and Owen, when he started out. He would have stretched it out as long as possible, but finally he might have killed you. Then, he let himself drink too much. The gun gave him power. It got your—respect, through fear. He always felt you had no—feeling for him. That's why he was so determined to ruin things for you, why he thought about you so much He had to have your—attention, no matter what."

"If he meant to kill us, why did he—"

"Oh, Chappie, I don't know," she said, sighing, her eyes misting. "He was—deranged. He'd been sick for a very, very long time. I was afraid of him. Often I hated him, but now I just feel sorrow, and relief—relief, and I feel guilty about the relief. No one should be *glad* anyone else is dead."

There was another silence. Nolan sat up on the side of the bed in the pajamas Fern had made him put on and lit a cigarette.

"I'm free," Kiersten said brokenly. "I'd got so used to the idea that I'd have to be afraid for Owen and me—and for you and the rest of the family—all my life, and now I can breathe easy. That is, if it ever really sinks in."

She had covered her face with her hands and tears squeezed between her fingers.

Nolan took the few steps to the chair, took her arm gently and brought her to sit on the bed beside him, his arm warmly around her. She leaned against him and cried.

"I was afraid of him some of the time," he said softly at length, "afraid for Owen and for me, but there was time to think, about a lot of things. What I mostly thought was that if I died, all the chances to see you, to love you, would be gone. Bonnie bonnie Kierstie, I've never *not* loved you. It's time for me to give over, as Price puts it, but I want to. I want to spend my life with you, really *with* you. Do you think we could still do that? Will you forgive me for being so hard and stubborn?"

"I already did that," she sobbed. "I'm the one who—"

"Let's not keep hashing it over. Let's try to think about the future—our future."

"Yes," she said, putting her arms around him, resting her head on his shoulder as he put his cheek down against her hair.

"As for children," he said huskily, "there's time. I—we—have to think it all over very carefully, take a lot of things into consideration . . ."

"I'd love to bear your children," she murmured, "and I'm sure they'd be healthy and normal, but you're the one I want. I don't love you as the potential father of my children. I just love you. I always have."

He was caressing her gently and she said in a very small voice, "There's no one in the house. Mother and Fern went to Hurleigh. Owen's with them."

"Come to bed with me then."

"You really shouldn't. You're still not—"

"Oh, Kierstie, I should! I have to. It's been so long and I can't tell you how many times I've dreamed . . ."

"Me, too," she whispered, beginning to unbutton her shirt, letting all her clothes fall to the floor.

"Damn pajamas!" he muttered frustratedly, having trouble with the drawstring at the waist. She smiled tremulously and helped him.

It was a slow voluptuous love-making. Both of them were wildly excited, starved for each other, but both wanted to draw this time out as long as possible, until they were all but mad for the final satiation. After it came, they lay still and silent, side by side, her head on his shoulder, for a long time.

Finally, she said softly, "What are you thinking of?"

He had been frowning and the frown deepened. "The truth is, I was thinking of Roger. I'm sorry."

"So was I," she said bleakly. "He'd want that, to come between us when we're—at our most intimate times."

"It'll happen less and less often," he said with conviction. "I love you, bonnie Kierstie."

"Oh God, Chappie, I love you so much it hurts. But it's a good hurt now, a clean, exciting thing, since we're finally really together. And you're right. Other—things will intrude less and less."

Still in his arms, she sang softly, tears filling her eyes, "I'll belong to you and only you and never go away."

"Yes," he said, holding her with all his debilitated strength.